READER'S DIGEST

CONDENSED BOOKS

FIRST EDITION

THE READER'S DIGEST ASSOCIATION LIMITED
25 Berkeley Square, London W1X 6AB

**THE READER'S DIGEST ASSOCIATION
SOUTH AFRICA (PTY) LTD**
Nedbank Centre, Strand Street, Cape Town

Printed in Great Britain by Petty & Sons Ltd, Leeds

Original cover design by Jeffery Matthews M.S.I.A.

ISBN 0 340 23661 2

Reader's Digest
CONDENSED BOOKS

COLLECTOR'S LIBRARY
EDITION

In this volume

THUNDER AT DAWN
by Alan Evans (p.9)

"Wars are better won than lost, better avoided than won. They are not an excuse for stupidity and carelessness."

These were words that Commander David Cochrane Smith had attempted to live by throughout his chequered career as a naval officer. And was prepared to die by also when, one misty morning in March 1917, he led HMS *Thunder* quietly out of harbour, to a confrontation he could clearly neither avoid nor seriously hope to win.

TISHA
by Anne Hobbs
with Robert Specht (p.133)

In this exciting book the author looks back on her career as a schoolteacher in the Alaskan wilderness. To the children in her little one-room schoolhouse she quickly became their beloved "Tisha". But the grown-ups in the tiny settlement were slower to make friends, and the young teacher's treatment of the Indians soon caused trouble. Then there was the cold to contend with, so sharp that you could hear the nails snapping in the woodwork of your house as they contracted. . . .

In the end Tisha proved more than equal to the challenge. And the story of her life in the North makes thrilling, and romantic, reading.

THE LONG LONG DANCES
by Eric Malpass (p.257)

A little girl dancing in a water meadow; a spotty youth with a motor bike; a peevish old gentleman carrying a shotgun; and of course, in the background, the entire wildly eccentric Pentecost family—father, mother, young Gaylord their son, and several aunties (was it really only two? It felt like six at least!) —not to mention the obnoxious Miss Mackintosh. . . .

These, then, are the ingredients of the latest richly comic and heartwarming book by Eric Malpass. But there is, inevitably, danger also, and pain. For the sun cannot always shine, not even on the Pentecosts. And life does sometimes have its more cruel, unpredictable moments.

THE R DOCUMENT
by Irving Wallace
(p.355)

Terrorism, civil disturbance, violent crime . . . governments argue and dither, and still the chilling statistics of death and destruction mount.

The hero of Irving Wallace's new novel, US Attorney General Collins, believes in tough measures. He supports with all his strength a bill giving his government far-reaching emergency powers. But there are others, less scrupulous than he, who support it also. So that finally only Collins himself, and the damning existence of the R Document, stand between them and the satisfaction of their lust for power.

THUNDER AT DAWN

a condensation of the book by

Alan Evans

Illustrated by Jack McCarthy
Published by Hodder & Stoughton

Under international law a warring battleship might take refuge in a neutral port for twenty-four hours before being interned. HMS *Thunder's* time was almost up. She must leave the South American harbour at dawn. And the Germans were outside, waiting for her.

Captain David Cochrane Smith had been warned of the Germans' approach, and he knew of their ships' superiority. But he knew his duty also—even though the uncompromising Sarah Benson believed it would be suicide.

In this book Alan Evans tells an epic tale, firmly in the magnificent tradition of British sea stories. It shows men—and women—at their very best, humorous, compassionate, brave, infinitely resourceful.

MARCH 1917

The night was dark under an overcast sky. HMS *Thunder*, a darkened ship, was a black speck on the black immensity of the Pacific. Her crew were tensed at their action stations and Commander David Cochrane Smith stood on her bridge. He was thin-faced and sharp-featured, a very young man for that rank. His hands clenched tight on the rail as look-outs strained their eyes against the darkness. Somewhere to the east lay the coast of Peru but the "enemy" was close.

A look-out shouted, "Ship bearing green four-oh." There was a rumble as the guns trained around and the searchlights on the wings of the bridge and up in the tops stabbed out across the dark sea to light up the target. They lit up *Thunder*'s forty-foot steam pinnace with its stubby funnel, young Midshipman Somers at the wheel. Buckley, Somers's leading hand, waved, the pinnace spun away, the searchlights snapped out. The exercise went on.

Smith had started the exercises as soon as he joined *Thunder*, so they called them "Smith's game". They groused about the exercises as a matter of principle but secretly found the game a break in the routine of work and drills. They had become expert.

Smith stood aloof on the bridge, his face grim. He had reason. He had come to *Thunder* certain that he was banished, his career virtually at an end. He joined her as second-in-command at Esquimalt in British Columbia where she had just had a refit. In the first hour, through a chance-heard conversation, he learned his reputation had preceded him: he was a pacifist, his nerve gone. He knew the crew were wary of him and pride would not let him explain.

He could have told them that a drunken armchair-tactician at some Whitehall party had been critical of the Navy's inability to destroy an enemy who refused to come out to be destroyed. Smith had boiled over and replied that he had seen enough men killed at Jutland, and *that if the rest of the country were like the drunk* the Navy would do well to stay at home. The story had been repeated but not the words in italics.

Now he paced restlessly out to the wing of the bridge. He had found the ship run by Garrick, the first lieutenant, because the captain, embittered at his backwater command, kept to his cabin and his gin. *Thunder* was a four-funnelled armoured cruiser of twelve thousand tons. She had served on the Pacific seaboard, based at Esquimalt cruising off the coast of South America, for the two-and-a-half years since the outbreak of war in 1914, the sole representative of a navy stretched thin by the concentration in European waters.

She was too old. Laid down when Victoria reigned, even her designed speed had been lower than that of later, more modern, cruisers and it was doubtful if she could attain that speed now, let alone maintain it for any length of time. Davies, her chief engineer, lieutenant-commander RNR and recalled from the Merchant Service, swore that she could. But he always evaded putting it to the test and nobody believed him. She was slow. So on the mess-decks they said, "Had to call her *Thunder* 'cause it's a bleeding certainty you couldn't call her *Lightning!*"

Joke. Plenty of jokes. In the wardroom that first night Aitkyne, the navigator, tall and elegant, said, "We wondered if you'd arrive in time for resurrection day, sir."

Smith, stomach rebelling on what was also the first night at sea, clutching a glass of sherry he wanted like the plague, asked blankly, "Resurrection day?"

"Bringing the old girl back to life again, sir. Taking her to sea." Laughter. Then Aitkyne added, "If she was a house, you'd expect to find bats and ghosts."

Smith replied, "One carries one's own ghosts around." And told himself he had still to learn to keep his mouth shut. He had spoiled the joke and they looked at him oddly, wary of him. And that was a pity because he liked the look of them.

And *Thunder*'s wardroom was comfortable, with a long table at which the officers ate, two sideboards, easy chairs, carpet on the deck and even a piano and a gramophone, though the last belonged to young Wakely, one of the midshipmen, and had been borrowed from the gunroom for the occasion.

On the surface they made Smith welcome. A new face aboard *Thunder* was an event. Most of her crew had served in her since the war started. The midshipmen had joined not long ago as fifteen-year-old cadets to fill the gaps created by ageing officers invalided out. A score of young seamen and reservists had accompanied the cadets: *Thunder*'s first and only draft.

The crew of the fore-turret was a fair sample of her crew. Farmer Bates was a grandfather, one of seven aboard. Rattray and Chalky White were youngsters but Gibb, at seventeen, was far and away the youngest in the turret. *Thunder*'s slowness and her old guns did not worry him. She was his first ship.

She carried a 9.2-inch gun in a turret forward and another aft. Of her twelve six-inch guns four were on the upper deck, the other eight on the main deck below, four to a side. The guns were elderly and it was a notorious fact that in her class of ship the eight guns on the main deck could not be fired in bad weather because opening their ports would let in the sea. That did not matter in the case of *Thunder* because she sailed with a reduced complement. That is to say that, as she was not expected to fight in a Fleet action, she was not manned for the purpose. She was due anyway to return to home waters in six months' time, at the end of her commission. Half her crew of six hundred were engineers or stokers because at her most economical speed she burned one hundred tons of coal a day, every piece of which had to be shovelled from bunkers to fires. Garrick, as gunnery officer, had trained his men for two-and-a-half years, but there were barely enough just for the two turrets and the four upper deck six-inch guns.

Smith shrugged; these things did not matter. *Thunder* would

11

drag out her last days beating up and down this coast, then return to home waters to become a depot-ship—back to the dockyard wall. What mattered was that he had his duty and he would do it. He heard a scrape of a boot on the ladder and stepped forward as the captain stumbled unsteadily onto the bridge and fetched up against the rail. Before Smith could speak he growled, "Get on with it!"

"Aye, aye, sir."

Now instead of tension there was unease on the bridge. A lookout yelled, the guns trained, the lights blazed out at the pinnace then died and the darkness returned.

The captain turned slowly on Smith and said thickly, "Waste of time." And added an obscenity. Smith did not answer. The captain pushed past him to the head of the ladder, and fell head first to the deck below.

It sounded like a sack of coal hitting the deck.

Smith shouted, "The captain's fallen!" He dropped down the ladder and knelt by the captain. Aitkyne leaned over him. "I shouldn't touch him, sir. Doctor's on his way."

ALBRECHT THE SURGEON came. His examination was swift. When he carefully lifted the captain's head, they all saw the terrible wound at the back of the skull. A party carried the captain down to the sick-bay and Smith waited there until Albrecht made his report. "Massive concussion. God knows what damage may have been done to the brain."

"He has a chance of recovery?"

"I wouldn't have been surprised if an injury like that had killed him instantly. Add to that the effects of shock and. . . ." He did not need to finish; the gin reeked.

Smith went to his cabin. He managed to sleep, only to jerk awake, running with sweat. It was an old dream again: two great ships growing huge out of the dark to hurl the fires of hell at him. He made his way forward through the sleeping ship to the sick-bay, and found Albrecht alone. Smith raised his eyebrows in inquiry and the doctor shook his head. "No change."

They stood in silence watching the captain, until Smith murmured, "An unusual name, Albrecht."

Albrecht smiled sardonically. "In this navy, yes. My grandfather came over from Germany in 'forty-eight. He became British. I was born British . . . But the lower deck still call me the 'orrible 'un." His smile faded. "And I do think the war is stupid and ought to be stopped."

Smith said, "That's a view that takes some courage with a name like Albrecht."

The doctor shrugged. "When you're a ministering angel it's different. If I was a sea officer—" He broke off, now embarrassed for Smith.

Who said deliberately, "I think wars are better won than lost, better avoided than won. They're not an excuse for stupidity."

Albrecht stared at him. "You are not a pacifist?"

"If you see a risk that has to be taken, Doctor, you take it. You cut away. And so do I."

Albrecht grinned. "But my patients don't cut back."

Mention of patients sent his gaze back to the captain. His feeble hold on life was slipping away with the night.

He died at daybreak.

THEY BURIED HIM at sea. Afterwards Smith confirmed the course he had ordered the previous night after the captain fell. Then it had been an attempt to get the captain to the hospital in Castillo but now it was to reach the telegraph office there and inform the British Consul in Chile. *Thunder* had radio but the Navy's signalling stations did not cover South American waters. Admiralty kept in touch with her by cables and she entered ports at intervals to collect them. The consul had to be informed of the captain's death and that Smith had assumed command; he would advise Admiralty.

The weather was breaking and the wind rising. When they raised the coast of Chile in the early evening a bright sun still shone but astern the clouds were breeding black.

The sun had no warmth in it. Smith shivered. The captain's death was a bad start to a command and Smith was still not accepted, nor likely to be, he was certain. . . .

The signal yeoman shattered his mood of introspection. "Signal from shore, sir! SOS! Bearing red three-oh!"

13

Smith swung around and raised his glasses.

"T-H-D-R." The yeoman spelt out the slow flashes. "Think they mean *us*, sir. SOS again, sir. An' it's a light from a motor car. Front light."

"Hard to see but I think it's a 24/30 Buick tourer." Midshipman Somers was on the bridge and had a telescope clapped to his eye. He was a tall, handsome boy, a fine athlete with a good brain. In spite of all these reasons for envy he was well-liked.

Smith ordered, "Port ten." *Thunder* began to close the shore. "Ask nature of emergency."

Thunder's signal-lamp clattered out but there was no answer.

The yeoman grumbled, "Stopped now, sir. Can't see much of anything. Thought I saw a flash, though."

Garrick had pounded up onto the bridge. He panted, "Damn funny business. SOS from the *shore!* And *naming* us?"

Smith said laconically, "Yes." He tried to hide his own curiosity. "Fires lit in the pinnace?"

"Yes, sir." Somers answered for the first lieutenant. "And steam up."

"Bit early, weren't you?"

Somers replied straight-faced, "Mr. Knight said we had to be ready, sir."

Knight was the signals officer and also drew an interpreter's pay for his labouring Spanish so he went ashore to send and collect telegrams. He was stout, and when the ship held a concert he did a knock-about turn, vulgar and very funny. He was also very eager.

Smith grunted, "Then we'll go and see what it's all about." And to Garrick: "I'll go myself. Tell the doctor to come along ready to do his stuff."

Thunder hove to, the winch hammered and the derrick swung the pinnace over the side and down to the water, Smith, Albrecht and her crew aboard. Smoke belched from her stubby funnel and they could hear the rapid scrape and clang as the stoker below hurled coal on the fire. They ran in to the shore, Somers at the wheel steering for a stretch of beach. The engines stopped, and they ran in to the shallows.

The shore was quiet, peaceful, empty. Smith wondered uneasily

14

if he was the victim of some practical joke. He snapped, "Come on, Doctor. You too, Buckley." He jumped over the bow and up to his waist in water and waded ashore, followed by Albrecht and the burly leading hand of the picket-boat. Beyond the beach the ground rose steeply. They could not see the motor car nor any sign of life.

They climbed up from the beach and over the crest, crossed a little plateau and looked into a shallow depression that twisted away inland. Now they could see the big Buick tourer, a dull gleam of metal in the dusk, a score of yards to their right. They halted, peering. There was a body at the front of the car, lying crumpled under the dead carbide lamps, one arm thrown out. Albrecht took a pace forward and a shot cracked out to their left, from farther inland up the depression. Immediately it was answered by a shot from the car. In the flash Smith saw a head lifted briefly from behind the car, then the darkness closed in. "Get down!" He shoved Albrecht down. "Buckley! Back to the pinnace and bring back two men, rifles for all of you!"

"Aye, aye, sir!" Buckley plunged away. This coast was neutral, Smith and his men were belligerents, but they had to be ready to defend themselves.

Pistol shots came again, from left, from right. A slug clanged against the motor car and howled off into the night.

Albrecht whispered, "Somebody's going to get hurt if this goes on, besides that chap lying there already."

Smith ground out, "Keep still." He rose to his feet. He was a score of yards at least from either of those firing, and he knew it was very long odds against anyone hitting him with a pistol at that range in this light. He swallowed just the same before he shouted: "Cease firing! I am a naval officer!" He spoke in English as he had no Spanish. "Show yourselves and put up your hands!"

It worked. A moment of silence, then a man rose from behind a rock to the left, his hands lifted above his shoulders. He started to walk towards Smith. As he approached, he spoke. "Ah, sir. I'm very glad to see you—"

But Smith's eyes were on the girl. A *girl!* He stared dumbfounded as she stepped around the motor car and walked towards him, holding herself stiffly, hands at her sides in the folds of her

15

skirt which ended just above her buttoned boots. He saw her face, pale under a mass of dark hair, and the lips were a tight line and the eyes glared past Smith.

They were close now, the man's hands coming down, one sliding inside his jacket. "I have my papers which will—"

The girl lifted her arm straight, the barrel of the pistol like a pointing finger. She shot him.

The flame seemed to burn past Smith's face as he started forward. He was momentarily blinded but his outstretched hand clamped on hers and tore the pistol from her. The shot at point-blank range had kicked the man onto his back. He lay spread-eagled, eyes wide, a huge stain across his chest. Albrecht came running and dropped to his knees. When he arose he shook his head and started towards the man who lay by the motor car.

The girl said, "Luis is dead!" Her voice was flat, without emotion, and Smith wondered if this was really a *woman*.

Light glowed inland along the depression and they heard the sound of an engine. Albrecht came back to Smith. He said softly, "He's dead too, sir."

Another motor car lurched around a bend in the depression and its lights wavered across the little group as it halted. The girl tried to run but Albrecht grabbed her. She fought him. "It's the rest of them!"

Before the words could sink in the firing started. One shot, then a fusillade and Smith heard the air whisper around his head. He thrust Albrecht towards the beach. "Run for it!" Albrecht ran, the girl ahead of him, Smith dropped to one knee and fired twice towards the lights, aiming high. He heard a yell and the firing stopped for a few seconds. It gave him time to run up and across the plateau. As the firing started again he knelt and fired again, just one shot, then the pistol was empty. He started towards the beach, skidding down the slope in a shower of sand and pebbles.

Halfway down he met Buckley and two seamen, all three of them with rifles at the high port. Smith panted, "We're being fired on and they may be following. Return the fire to keep their heads down but *aim high!* I don't know who they are." It was certain they had more right on this coast than he. Suppose they were police or troops? What a *bloody* mess!

They fell back towards the beach. A shadow lifted above the crest and spurted flame, and sand kicked up a yard away. But Buckley and the seamen fired a volley and the shadow ducked from sight.

They retired to the beach in good order, waded out to the pinnace and scrambled aboard. Smith gasped, "Return to the ship."

"Aye, aye, sir." The pinnace headed out to sea. Smith watched the shore but he saw no one, there was no firing. It was still and silent, empty as they had found it, as if nothing had happened.

The clouds humped black overhead now. Lightning flickered and thunder rumbled distantly. A flurry of rain blew in their faces. The sea was getting up and the pinnace pitched through it.

Smith asked, "Where's the doctor and—and—"

Somers answered, "He took the young lady into the cabin, sir."

Smith could feel Somers's curiosity and knew the seamen were watching him, too. They weren't the only ones who were curious. Just then the girl blundered from the cabin, staggered to the side and hung over it, very sick. Smith stood beside her. When she raised her head he said, "I would like an explanation." He said it formally, because this was a formal business; a man had been killed in front of him.

The girl said, "I'll tell the captain." There was a trace of cockney in the accent.

"The captain is dead. I am in command."

Her face turned up to him, eyes searching. The lips trembled but the voice was tightly controlled. "What's your name?"

"Smith. Commander David Smith."

"You're new."

"I came aboard two weeks ago." Then, realizing: "But how do you know—"

"I know most of the names—Garrick, Aitkyne, Kennedy—" She shook her head as if to clear it. "My name is Sarah Benson. I suppose you could call me a spy." Her lips twitched in bitter amusement. "Mr. Cherry, the consul at Guaya, got me into this business. You can ask him or any of the consuls, they'll vouch for me."

She paused but when Smith only nodded guardedly she went on. "German intelligence agents are thick as fleas on a dog's back all up and down this coast. The last three months I've dug up a little bit 'ere and a little bit there and maybe I dug too much because yesterday some fellers came looking for me. We had to run for it, me and Luis, the chap with me, sort of chauffeur and 'andy-man. We were trying to reach Castillo so I could send a telegram to Cherry but they got ahead of us somehow and 'eaded us off. They drove us down the coast, trapped us. Then I saw the ship. I knew 'er. I've seen the old *Thunder* many a time since 1914. Luis used 'is jacket across one of the lamps to flash a message but then they shot him. Killed 'im. Poor Luis."

Was there a catch in the voice then?

But she went on steadily. "The point is this: in this business you don't go round stealing the plans and all that nonsense. You can sometimes find out what they know, but more often what you find out is what they *want* to know and that's very important. I've been all up and down this coast the last three months. And everywhere it's the same. They want to know about *Thunder*. Where and when she made port. Where she 'eaded. If any ship at sea reports sighting you, the information goes to them. They have contacts of one sort or another in the telegraph offices and the shore wireless stations who pass them the information." She paused. "That's all. What it was all about. They're tracking you."

Smith was aware again of the pinnace plunging and soaring, that they were close to the great black loom of the ship. Smoke from the four funnels rolled down to them on the wind. He believed her. More than that, he felt the excitement building inside him as always before impending action. But action? Here? He asked, "Why?"

"I don't know. I don't *know* for God's sake!"

Lightning flashed again, close now, and Smith saw the girl's face, drawn, bitter. But he remembered her face as she shot the man who stood before her empty-handed, remembered the flash, the slam of the shot.

And she saw his reaction and turned from him. She had told him all he needed to know, she thought. She had not told him about being huddled behind the car while Luis showed himself to send the signal, risked his life until they tore it from him. Of crouching and firing and sobbing with fear as the bullets smashed into the car. She had done enough; she was finished. She had been through a very bad time and she craved comforting, but Smith stood remote and stiff-faced.

Memory stirred. She said, "Smith. David—David C. Smith?"

Smith blinked. "That's right. How—"

But then she crumpled and he caught her.

The boat derrick swung out, and the pinnace was whipped up from the sea and swayed inboard. Sarah Benson, covered in blankets, was hurried aft to the captain's cabin in the stern. There were already two men in the sick-bay and Smith himself had not yet moved into the captain's cabin.

He paced the bridge restlessly as he went over the girl's story. It boiled down to that one phrase: they're tracking you.

Why? *Why?*

It was important. Smith knew it and was uneasy.

Off the port they hove to again and sent the pinnace in to send the telegram advising Admiralty of the captain's death. Knight came to him. "Any further orders, sir?"

Smith shook his head. Behind him Garrick glanced at Aitkyne, concerned. The story was all over the ship that there had been shooting ashore and men killed. So Smith should make a report to the authorities here.

He knew it. But there was the girl and her story. He was fishing in strange waters. He would take her back to her master— Cherry. That was it—at Guaya. After he'd talked to Cherry he would decide on his report and to whom to make it.

The pinnace crashed back out of the night in bursting spray and Knight reported to the bridge. "Telegram sent, sir. An' there was one for us, in code."

Smith nodded. "Get on with it." Knight went off to decode the telegram and Smith ordered a southerly course for Guaya and went to his sea cabin below the bridge. *Thunder* had a rendezvous with a collier to the north but that was two days hence and she held coal now for eight days' cruising.

SARAH BENSON lay awake. Exhaustion claimed her but memory hinted then eluded her. Purkiss, the sick-berth attendant, brought her a cup of tea. He was twenty years old, nearly three years out from home. He looked at her and was smitten. So she pumped him. He talked to her about Albrecht the doctor, Garrick and the others. And Smith. "Real mystery man. They shipped him out in a hurry—practically shanghaied him—"

Albrecht came then, but it was enough. Memory clicked into place. Her sister, Alice, was a governess in London and wrote her long weekly letters about The War and The Town. Sarah read them, fascinated by an alien world. And one small item concerned a Commander David C. Smith, "They're telling his tale all around town. 'Enough men killed—the Navy ought to stay at home. . . .'"

Sarah had looked to find a *man* in command of this ship because she felt *Thunder* might soon need a man. Instead there was this defeatist who had stared at her with horror as she shot the German agent. She had never before fired a shot in anger and the memory would haunt her the rest of her days. Oh, she knew the man and knew that he carried a pistol in a shoulder holster and knew that his empty hands meant nothing. But she would not explain to Smith. He could think what he liked.

Curled small in the bed, she cried herself to sleep.

KNIGHT BROUGHT the decoded telegram to Smith. It came from the consul in Guaya, Chile: "Request urgently your presence this port. Extreme importance." Cherry would know *Thunder*'s whereabouts. This telegram would be one of several sent to ports along the coast where she might call for news or orders.

Smith handed it back to Knight without comment. Cherry's telegram came on the heels of the girl's message and each carried its own warning. Of the same danger? What danger? The girl knew of no danger. Cherry spoke of none. But Smith was certain that danger was there.

2

In the morning Horsfall woke Smith with a cup of coffee. Tall and thin and lantern-jawed, he was usually called Daddy. Smith had inherited him. He shuffled about in an old pair of plimsolls by express permission of the doctor because his feet troubled him. They also served him and a lot of the crew as a barometer because he claimed he could predict the weather by the feel of them.

"Lovely morning, sir. Sky's cleared beautiful but I reckon it won't last. I can tell. Me feet, you know, sir."

"Yes, I know." Smith sipped at the coffee and thought about Sarah Benson and Cherry.

"Gabriel, that's the doctor's mate, sir, he says the young lady woke up and ate a breakfast fit for a horse and turned over again."

"Good." He would be rid of her soon.

"Funny her coming aboard like that, sir."

There was nothing funny about it. Two dead men. Smith might have been another.

"All the lads are wondering about her, sir, keep asking me they do, what about that young lady? Course I can't tell them anything."

"Of course not." Smith paused, thinking. "Well, when they ask you again you can tell them—"

"Yes, sir?"

"You can tell them I've sworn you to secrecy."

Daddy looked at him blankly and Smith went on, "Well, it's better to be sworn *to* than *at*."

Daddy took the point and the empty cup philosophically. "Aye, aye, sir."

Smith grinned wryly at his departing back.

THEY RAISED GUAYA at noon. The coast was hills dropping green forest down steeply to the sea and the river. The port itself lay two miles up-river on a big basin. The river ran down wide from the basin for a mile, then on approaching the sea split into channels that threaded through a tangle of tree-clothed islets, most of the channels so shallow as to be swamp. *Thunder* steamed up the most direct channel, kept clear by dredging.

They passed the signalling station to port where it stood on a low hill, Punta Negro. Past it another channel wound away between forest walls. There was no road between the signalling station and the harbour, only a telephone line to the mainland looped across that channel. To starboard a cove was bitten out of the forest: Stillwater Cove.

Smith thought that Cherry would have known of *Thunder*'s arrival since the station saw her lift over the horizon. So he could expect explanations soon. He shifted restlessly on the bridge.

Thunder steamed slowly up-river. A bend lay ahead. They rounded it and opened up the basin and Guaya. Smith took in the town, white buildings against the green of the hills behind. He also took in the ships in the basin and one of them in particular. As *Thunder*'s three-pounder saluting gun began its metronomic popping, saluting the port, Smith stared at the ship.

His first officer, Garrick, telescope to his eye, said quickly, "USS *Kansas*, sir. She was reported in these waters. Brand new, her first cruise. Rear-Admiral Donoghue."

America was still neutral.

Smith grunted. "He rates a salute. See to it."

Aitkyne said softly, "By God, what a ship. Twenty-one knots and thirty-odd thousand tons." (*Thunder* was twelve thousand.) "Twelve fourteen-inch guns and twenty-two five-inch."

"And one of those fourteen-inch shells weighs half-a-ton." Smith grinned at him. "So if they look our way, smile."

The salutes rolled flatly across the basin, *Thunder* rode to her anchor, the port medical officer came and went and Cherry, short and dapper, came aboard.

He held out his hand. "Cherry. Delighted to meet you, Commander. Only wish your captain. . . ." He shook his head then took an envelope from his pocket. "Telegram for you, coded." And as Smith passed it to his signals officer: "Can we talk?"

Smith led the way to his cabin, but not before he had growled an aside to the plump and gramophone-owning Midshipman Wakely. "Ask Miss Benson if she'll be good enough to join us in my cabin."

"Aye, aye, sir!" Wakely shot away.

Cherry asked, "Did you say Benson? Would that be Sarah Benson?"

"It would." Smith's tone was neutral. Once in his cabin he told Cherry how he had brought the girl aboard. "You understand, I must make a report. I should have reported to the authorities ashore immediately after the incident but in view of Miss Benson's position—I thought it best to see you first."

22

Cherry nodded. "I've been worried about that girl. Had no word from her for a week. She's the best agent I have. But I've known her a long time and I feel a special responsibility for her. Her father came out to South America from Wapping ten years ago. He works on building harbours, a foreman. He started in Argentina and later moved over to this coast. So Sarah speaks Spanish and Portuguese like a native and she learned German from a ganger who boarded with the family for two years. On top of that she's clever and brave, sometimes too brave for her own good and my peace of mind."

He thought for a moment then shook his head. "Say nothing. Report to the Admiralty, of course. I will do the same in confirmation. But say nothing to the Chileans about the murders and I'll lay the Germans will keep their mouths shut. They can't make things awkward for us without exposing their own involvement. . . . But they have lodged a complaint about Sarah with the Chileans and now the local authorities want to ask her about her activities. We can't have that, so she can't go ashore."

Smith protested, "But this is a warship, not a liner! If she can't go ashore then she must be put aboard a British merchantman."

Cherry said apologetically, "That would be a good idea. Unfortunately, for once there isn't a British ship in this port." He scribbled a note. "She'll need clothes. If this could be given to my boatman, urgently, for my wife."

Smith glared at him. This coast swarmed with British shipping but it was his bad luck to find a port without a British vessel. There was a rap at the door and Sarah Benson entered. He scowled past her: "Here, Mr. Wakely." He passed him Cherry's note. "For Mrs. Cherry and it's urgent."

Sarah Benson said an emphatic damn as Cherry explained why she could not go ashore.

Smith said stiffly, "A warship is no place for a lady but we'll try to make your stay as pleasant as circumstances permit."

Sarah laid the cockney on thick. Clearly he did not understand the life she'd been leading. "Well, it ain't my fault I'm a woman. What do you want me to do? Swim ashore and give meself up?"

"Sarah! Please!" Cherry was embarrassed. He had sensed the atmosphere of hostility and was baffled. "The captain is right. He

23

should not have to accept responsibility for you in this ship. And I'm certain you were glad enough to come aboard her."

Sarah was silent a moment, then: "That I was." It came quietly. She looked up at Smith. "I'm sorry. I'll try not to be a nuisance."

Smith inclined his head. Then he looked at Cherry. They had wasted enough time. "You sent me a telegram."

Cherry got down to business. "I believe we have a contraband runner in this port. When Miss Benson passed through on her way north she remarked on a ship that had just arrived. She was Argentinian—the *Gerda*, carrying Welsh steam coal—a seemingly ordinary tramp of three thousand tons *but fitted with modern wireless.*" Smith's eyebrows rose. Fitting wireless was expensive, and unusual in that class of ship.

Cherry went on, "I asked our people in Argentina about her. She was one of a pair bought by an Argentinian firm only three months ago and fitted with wireless. This is their first cruise. Their skippers and crews are all of German extraction and the money for the ships came from German funds in the Argentine. That last can't be proved but it's known."

He paused for breath and Sarah Benson beat Smith to the question. "You said a pair?"

Cherry nodded. "The other is the *Maria*. I made inquiries and found she was at Malaguay." A port a hundred and fifty miles to the south of Guaya. "The *Gerda* has lain here for nine days. She hasn't discharged her coal and she claims to have engine trouble which her own engineers are working on. I asked Thackeray, the consul in Malaguay, and he confirmed that the *Maria* is telling the same story."

"Thackeray?" Sarah Benson said caustically. "He'd do nothing on his own. He doesn't want anybody stirring up the water in his little pool."

Cherry said, "It's my belief they're just waiting while a cargo of nitrates is arranged for each of them. Then they'll discharge and mend their engines quickly enough."

It could well be. Smith thought. Munitions needed nitrates and Germany needed munitions.

Cherry said, "I've protested to the Chileans, of course, but

24

there is a large German element in the population and they have a deal of influence. The Chileans say that I have no evidence that the ships are really German, so they will do nothing. That's why we need you outside here or Malaguay when they sail, to stop and search them. They're certain to have *some* evidence aboard."

Smith shifted impatiently. "I want to see her."

They walked forward of the bridge. The collier, *Gerda*, lay at anchor near the northern shore which was almost deserted, the buildings of the town being spread in a half-moon around the eastern and southern shores of the pool. A thread of smoke twisted from her funnel, and the wireless aerials strung from her masts were easily seen.

Smith said, "Engine trouble or no, she has fires." He stood lost in thought, chewing it over. Two ships. German crews, German money. Wireless. Nitrates. He was ready to accept Cherry's reasoning, to act on it, only. . . .

He was aware of Cherry telling Sarah, "I sent a note ashore to Mrs. Cherry asking for that suitcase of yours."

Smith said absently, "Fortunate that you have some clothes at the consulate, Miss Benson."

"I have suitcases spread over a couple of thousand miles. I travel a lot and I often have to travel light."

Smith nodded, then stared again at the *Gerda*. Sarah went on slowly, "I don't know. There's something—not *right* about it. It all fits but—" She shook her head.

He turned to her. It all fitted but—she was right, there was a piece missing. He caught Aitkyne's eye, and the navigator quickly crossed the deck. "Ah, Mr. Aitkyne. I'm sure Mr. Cherry and Miss Benson would like to meet some of the officers. I wonder if the hospitality of the wardroom . . .?"

"A pleasure, sir." Aitkyne, handsome, tall, escorted them below, leaving Smith to prowl the deck, eyes on the *Gerda*, ill at ease.

ARNOLD PHIZACKERLY had woken early, perforce. It was not long past noon when a hand shook his shoulder and he peered out through gummy lids at Perez and asked huskily, "Wassamarrer?"

Perez was a clerk in the port office but also on a retainer from Phizackerly. He whispered, "The British warship, *Thunder*, she is headed for the river. The signalling station has telephoned." Then, apologetically, "You said whenever she came I was to tell you."

"Ah, God!" Phizackerly covered his eyes for a moment. But he was not a man to shirk his duty. He crawled slowly out from under the single sheet to stand in long-sleeved singlet and long cotton drawers that hung loose around his bony rump. "You're a good lad. Come round tonight and I'll fix you up with somebody special."

He leered gummily, his teeth still in the cup on the dresser. Then he made his way down to Olsen the Swede, in the bar, who got him coffee with a stiff tot of rum in it and shaved him.

The rest of the house was silent; none of the girls would stir until the cool of the early evening. Back in his room Phizackerly opened the wardrobe. Next to his suit hung his old river pilot's uniform, designed by himself. He touched it with ritualistic pride, in the old days he had been a pilot, *the* pilot.

He dressed in the suit: striped trousers, dark morning-coat, patent leather boots and spats. He did not bother with socks; it was a warm day. A jewelled pin went in the tie; cologne on his face and oil on his hair. He combed the scanty locks down on either side from a centre parting with twin little quiffs at the front. He picked up the topper, fished his teeth out of the cup, surveyed himself in the mirror and decided he looked what he was: a man of substance in this town.

He strolled down to the waterfront. *Thunder* lay out in the basin and a small crowd on the quay stared and pointed at her. Phizackerly regarded her, his gaze pensive, calculating. He knew the size of *Thunder*'s complement almost to a man and the value of each man in terms of spending power. The unknown factors were whether any of them would be allowed ashore and if they were, where they would be allowed to spend their leave and their money. The latter factor was the reason for his being on the quay.

Perez, his contact in the port office, had already told him of the captain's death. A new captain could mean a new start. At any rate, Phizackerly would give it a good try.

He came to where Vargas's motor-launch bobbed at the foot of a ladder. Vargas slept under the awning he had rigged aft over the well. His bread and butter trade consisted of taking patrons

26

of Phizackerly's and similar establishments back to their ships. At this time of day however, business was non-existent.

Phizackerly climbed down the ladder and nudged Vargas awake with his toe. Vargas rubbed at his face and said politely, "It is good to see you, Fizzy."

"You're a lazy bastard." Phizackerly sat in the stern. "Let's 'ave a run around the pool. 'Ave a scout round the old *Thunder*."

"We can't go close unless you keep under the awning. That captain, he said he'd sink us if you went alongside again."

Phizackerly said seriously, "I have some sad news. He's dead."

"Dead? Ah. That is very sad." Vargas cheered up a little but then said, "There is still that first lieutenant, Mr. Garrick."

"He isn't captain. The new captain is *new*."

"Ah-ah!"

So they cruised slowly around *Thunder* where she lay at anchor. Phizackerly saw that Garrick was on the bridge, and the consul's boat lay alongside, at the foot of the accommodation ladder. So he pointed and Vargas swung the launch around *Thunder*'s stern and tucked her in beside Cherry's boat. Phizackerly nipped across it and up the ladder with a facility born of years of practice.

Smith stood by the entry port, abstracted, uneasy.

Phizackerly appeared, dark topper in hand, on *Thunder*'s deck. With the other hand he whisked a garishly printed handbill from a sheaf in the tail pocket of his coat and slapped it in the hand of the boy manning the side. He whispered hoarsely, "Special rates for young fellers." And winked lewdly. The boy gaped.

Phizackerly tucked the topper under his arm and ducked his head in a little bow. "G'morning, Captain." He swept the ship in one swift, fore and aft approving glance. "Ah! What a pleasure to tread the deck of a king's ship again. Fine ship you 'ave, sir. Fine ship. Does you credit, sir."

Smith said cautiously, "Thank you, Mister—?"

"Phizackerly, sir." He stepped forward and held out a skinny hand. Smith took it. "Arnold Phizackerly. A prominent member of the British community here. Entrepreneur an' impresario."

"What?"

Garrick came stalking down from the bridge and rasped in cold explanation, "Brothel keeper, sir."

27

"Oh?" Smith was off balance a second, then amused. As he stared at the cheekily absurd little man he had a strong temptation to laugh. It seemed a long time since he had laughed.

Phizackerly sensed a lack of animosity and seized the opportunity. A number of men had found work in the vicinity and were listening. He said, "It takes all kinds, as you might say, sir. And the door of my 'ouse, Fizzy's Palace of Entertainment, is always open." It seemed that in an abstracted moment the handbills slipped from his fingers and scattered in the breeze, to be rescued by the men. "I reckon I provide a little bit of old England, a little bit of 'ome, for these lads and that means a lot."

Garrick said, "Any lad I catch coming out of your whorehouse will certainly find it means a lot. It's out of bounds."

Phizackerly pretended not to hear. "So when I had to leave the seafaring profession my first thought was to use my little bit o' savings to make a little bit of England out here."

Smith asked, "You were a seaman?"

Garrick said, "He was a river pilot."

Phizackerly finally acknowledged him. "That's right, Mr. Garrick, pilot." And to Smith, this time with genuine pride, "I was the first pilot 'ere back in 'ninety-two when they opened the copper mines. I found the channel an' brought the first ship in with me own 'ands and after that it was me an' the pilots as worked for me, apprentices like, an' nothing moved in or out of this port without us. Not until they bought the dredger and 'ad the short channel dredged out, that's the one they use today."

He had to pause for breath and Garrick admitted grudgingly, "That's true. Only he and his pilots could thread that channel and he made a fortune before the mining company decided it would be cheaper to buy the dredger."

Phizackerly had finally made a point but he threw it away. Smiling paternally at the young commander he said, "Why bless you, sir, I've 'ad more fine ships through my hands than you've 'ad fine women." He saw Smith's lips tighten and the pale blue eyes grow hard. He knew he had gone badly wrong. He said cheerfully, but watchful, apprehensive, "Just a joke, sir. To make me point, as it were."

Smith smiled at him and Phizackerly did not like it. "You've

made your point, Mr. Phizackerly, and now I'll make mine. The next time you set foot on this ship I will throw you into the cells or over the side. That is a promise."

Phizackerly lifted the topper before his narrow chest like a shield and mumbled, "Time I was getting away." He retreated to the ladder and dropped from sight. In the launch he mopped his face with a handkerchief. "That's an honest man," he said.

Vargas started the engine. "Ah. That is too bad."

Up on deck Smith turned and found his signals officer waiting with Cherry's telegram, now decoded. Knight seemed excited. Smith read the telegram and said only, "Very good," in dismissal.

He read the telegram again. Then laughter broke into his thoughts and he saw Cherry and Sarah Benson attended by a little group of grinning officers who shredded away as he looked up at them. He said flatly, "Signal from Admiralty to be passed to all HM ships. The German cruisers *Wolf* and *Kondor* are now known to be at sea and to have been at large for some weeks. Their location and destination are unknown."

Cherry burst out, startled, "Good Lord!"

Smith stared past him. They would have slipped through the North Sea blockade in vile winter weather, not an easy feat but by no means impossible for two fast ships. *Wolf* and *Kondor*. He needed to be given no details nor to consult the silhouette book. He had seen these two.

On a wild black night they had obliterated his ship and his men and thrust him to the point of death. They haunted his dreams.

Cherry was saying, "Commerce raiders. . . ."

Raiders. Aimed at Allied shipping. They could wreak terrible destruction. They might be on their way to Africa or preparing to slash across the Atlantic trade routes, or— His mind took a leap in the dark: Sarah Benson had said the Germans were watching *Thunder*. The Pacific was the last place but . . . His thoughts raced and then were still.

Cherry murmured vaguely, "Maybe the African coast, but more likely the Atlantic. . . ."

Smith said with certainty, "No."

Sarah Benson stared at him. "You think they're coming here?"

"Yes. The Germans are watching this ship, following her movements. There are two ships, the *Gerda* and the *Maria*, flying neutral flags but in fact German and loaded with Welsh steam coal. Yes?" And as Cherry hesitated, then nodded, Smith said, "They're tenders. *Wolf* and *Kondor* are coal-burning ships."

Cherry was silent a moment, then he said doubtfully, "It's possible, I suppose."

Smith was to see that look of disbelief on many faces but he did not see it on Sarah Benson's. She asked, "You know these ships?" And when he nodded: "What are they like?"

"Of a size with this one but only half her age. They're slightly faster and decidedly better armed."

"Then you can't fight them." She said it with cold common sense. "Either one could run rings around this old tub and blow her out of the water!"

Smith's smile was bleak. Sarah Benson had summed up the situation with brutal clarity.

There was an uncomfortable silence until Cherry asked, "What will you do?"

Smith would not add to his worries. He said slowly, "I will sail now, heading north again but only for the sake of appearances. I have a rendezvous with a collier but I can't keep it now. Will you see she is sent here to wait for my orders?"

"Of course. And you will patrol these waters?"

Smith sidestepped the question. "It seems the obvious course."

THUNDER SAILED.

Every man aboard her knew something was afoot. But Smith conned his ship and was silent.

As *Thunder* slid past the signalling station at Punta Negro and out to sea, Garrick ventured, "The wardroom would be pleased if Miss Benson and yourself would join us for dinner this evening, sir."

Smith's lips twitched. "I'd be delighted and I'm sure Miss Benson will be. Will the gunroom be present?"

"Yes, sir. We rather thought that, as this will be your first visit as captain, it would be suitable."

"It will suit very well. I have one or two things to say."

31

He glanced at the log and read the entry, "weighed and proceeded". He laid his finger against the figure of coal remaining and did the sum in his head: sufficient for seven days at an economical ten knots.

Garrick said, "We'll complete with coal from the *Mary Ellen*, sir?" The *Mary Ellen* was their collier.

Smith said absently, "I hope so."

He left the bridge, and went down to his cabin. He had to make a decision. He had a cold knowledge inside himself that the cruisers were racing for these waters, and why.

On the Pacific seaboard the defence of Britain's trade, and there was more than a hundred thousand tons of British shipping on this coast, rested on one ship: *Thunder*. The cruisers could sweep British trade from this coast and their marauding would draw war ships from the Atlantic, maybe as many as fifty ships that were already desperately needed to blockade the High Seas Fleet and fight the growing submarine menace. And hunting the cruisers in the vast Pacific wastes would be a heartbreaking business, a thousand times worse than seeking a needle in a haystack.

But that would be later. *Thunder* would come first. They would know about *Thunder;* she was under observation. She offered them a victory that would resound around the world. They could annihilate her or bottle her up in some port so that *Thunder* was interned, humiliated.

He would not have to search for these cruisers. They would hunt him down like the wolfpack they were. . . .

There was a tap at the door and Horsfall entered. "Sir. Wondered if you'd like a—"

Smith snarled at him, "Get out!"

Horsfall got out.

IT WAS A pleasant evening. For the second time since they had sailed from Esquimalt the gunroom were present *en masse,* and Wakely brought his gramophone. Sarah Benson wore a simple dress, shattering in its effect on the wardroom. Smith thought with surprise that he supposed she was a very pretty girl, but that she was flirting outrageously with poor Garrick.

32

Benks, the steward, leaped nimbly, arms loaded with plates. Daddy Horsfall, pressed into service for the occasion, creaked around with bottle and napkin in stiff best boots and a pained expression.

Smith had been in good humour all evening, smiling, joking, a textbook demonstration of total relaxation when duties were ended. But his mouth was dry and he drank only one glass of water. The food almost choked him.

They drank the loyal toast. Sarah Benson caught Smith's eye and stifled a feigned yawn. "Well, me for me haybag." There were groans of disappointment, for it was still barely dusk. But she went. Smith had seen her before dinner and been polite but explicit on that and she had, as stiffly, agreed.

Benks and Horsfall withdrew to the pantry.

"Now then, gentlemen." It was said quietly but it cut through the buzz of conversation and the voices were stilled. Daddy Horsfall found, without any surprise, that the bottle he held was half-full. He and Benks saw it away while they listened to Smith beyond the pantry hatch.

Daddy listened, then left, walking forward to the mess-decks. The captain's cold assessment of the situation and his flat statement of his intentions had taken the wardroom's breath away. The first crowded mess Daddy came to was that of Nobby Clark, leading seaman and captain of a six-inch gun. Nobby stared at him and said, "Siddown you poor bastard before you fall down!" He indicated the wardroom aft with a jerk of his head. "What's going on back there?"

Daddy told them, and as he did so *Thunder* heeled and turned so they had to grab for a handhold, and still she turned.

3

There was a brooding hush about the night, black, close. *Thunder* lay once more off Punta Negro, the signalling station, while Guaya was a glow against the sky far inland.

Thunder swayed gently in a long, slow swell, without a light save the occasional blink from a shaded lamp. Smith's party were forming up in that black dark as the pinnace and whaler were hoisted out, men all in navy boiler-suits and blackened canvas shoes, their faces smeared with soot until only the eyes showed. There was always plenty of soot to be got on *Thunder*. They were a little sheepish. It all seemed unreal.

Every man was armed with a revolver; one chamber of each was unloaded and the hammer lay over that with the safety catch on. There would be no careless, accidental shot. Smith checked every pistol himself, then he spoke to them, his voice harsh and urgent. "I want no noise at all! No shooting except in direct defence of your lives!"

Someone guffawed, the laugh cut short as Smith stood before him. "What's the joke?" The question came softly.

The man grinned uneasily. "Just seemed a bit funny, sir."

He was Rattray, a hard case with a reputation as a brawler. Smith caught the whiff of rum. "Master at arms!" he rasped. "This man's been hoarding his tots. Take him to the boiler room. He can work the grog out with a shovel."

Rattray was hustled away. Smith glanced round, saw young Gibb in one of the deck parties. "Get some soot on your face and fall in."

Lieutenant Kennedy, a Reserve officer recalled from the mercantile marine and a man with knowledge of explosives, was in the pinnace with the midshipmen, Manton and Wakely, and ten seamen and ten marines under Sergeant Burton. The tow was passed from pinnace to whaler. Midshipman Somers was in the whaler with a dozen seamen. Smith, standing by Manton who had the helm, was taking as few officers and men as possible. If something went badly wrong, and it easily could, *Thunder* must still be able to function. He lifted one hand, saw Garrick's acknowledgement on the deck above him, and said quietly, "Carry on, Mr. Manton."

Garrick, he knew, was worried, even shocked. Smith's cold assessment of the situation had taken the wardroom's breath away. Cruisers? It seemed so unreal. And what Smith intended was too big a gamble for them. For Smith it was a risk they had to take.

The pinnace eased away, towing the whaler and steering for the signalling station at Punta Negro. Smith leaned with his arms on the coaming, relaxed, as if this was just one more item in the day's work. When they were a mile from the mouth of the river he said laconically, "Steer a point or two to starboard." Manton was expecting the order. The pinnace moved over to the right bank of the estuary, so when they entered it they were tucked right in under that bank, invisible to the men in the signalling station if they watched, though there was no reason why they should.

They passed Stillwater Cove, keeping to the shadows and the greatest darkness by the shore, avoiding the deepwater channel. The pinnace made an easy three knots despite the drag of the tow because the tide was flowing now. They rode smoothly through the night with only the slow, dull churn of the engine, the muffled scrape and clink of Jenner's shovel in the tiny engine room and the clump of the closing furnace door. Smith ordered an increase in speed and, as the shovel clanged like a bell below: "Quinn?"

The signalman started. "Sir?"

Smith's tone was mild but had an edge. "Tell Jenner that if he does that again his shovel goes over the side. And him with it."

"Aye, aye, sir."

He maintained his attitude of calm throughout the long haul up the estuary. He found himself continually stifling yawns, but far from being drowsy he was strung to a tight pitch. This was an awful gamble. Success could ruin him while failure would be an ignominious disaster. He thrust the thoughts aside. His decision had been taken and he believed it right. He was committed.

They rounded the bend and entered the pool with an odd mixture of relief and heightened tension. The waiting was over and now the action would begin. Scattered lights marked the ships that lay there. USS *Kansas*, the battleship, was a floating mountain far across the pool. The collier *Gerda* was a squat shadow, barely lit but seen against the lighted backdrop of the shore. And something else showed against that backdrop. Smith called softly, "Stop engines." They closed the collier, slowing as the way came off the pinnace, stopped. They drifted in silence but for the burble of water under the bow.

Smith saw it again. A boat was rowing around *Gerda*. It was halfway along the port side and creeping towards the stern. He watched until the boat worked around the stern of the collier and disappeared. It was odd behaviour for a neutral vessel.

"A guard-boat. That does it." Kennedy had spoken his thoughts aloud: the operation was off. Like most of the officers, he regarded this enterprise as an act of madness.

Smith turned to look at him. "Not by a long shot, Mr. Kennedy. Bring up the whaler."

Wakely answered, "Already coming, sir."

The whaler sprouted oars. Then they came in again as it ran alongside the pinnace. Smith gave Kennedy his orders then stepped over to sit in the stern by Somers. He called, "Sergeant Burton! Come with me." Burton's square bulk rose from the block of marines and he picked his way lightly between them to swing over into the whaler. Smith ordered, "Give way."

The whaler headed across the pool, giving *Gerda* a wide berth, keeping out in the sheltering dark, passing her. So for another half-minute. Then the whaler turned and pointed back downstream, heading for the collier. Now Smith could see a dangling ladder on the starboard side. There was a light on the superstructure amidships but he could not see a man there. But there would be a look-out, somewhere. He could see the guard-boat creeping again up the port side of the collier towards the stern. He gauged the relative distances and speeds as the whaler slid down on the ship and saw that they would meet the guard-boat under *Gerda*'s stern and was content.

He spoke in a whisper but his voice carried down the length of the whaler: "No shooting except in self-defence, and at this moment no shooting at all. Mr. Somers, you will need four men." Somers picked them. They were closing the stern of *Gerda* now. The guard-boat had seen them, Smith could tell that from the accelerated beat of its oars and the swing of the bow towards them, before a voice lifted, the words incomprehensible but the tone inquiring, suspicious.

Smith drawled nasally, "*Kansas*! Have you fellers seen anything of a swimmer? The son-of-a-bitch went over the side because his furlough was stopped and when I get my hands on him—"

The whaler came from the direction of *Kansas*. The two men in the guard-boat waited, listening to Smith's impersonation, a poor one but good enough to get him alongside. Then, as the whaler swept down on them, Smith snapped, "Oars! Somers!"

The oars came in, the whaler thumped against the boat and Somers and his four men leaped over the side like frogs to smother the men from the collier.

"Shove off! Give way!" Smith left Somers in the guard-boat to drift away down the port side of the *Gerda* while he took the whaler skimming down to the dangling ladder. The oars came in again and he snatched at the ladder and started climbing. He heard a voice on the deck above him but right aft, a voice that called, puzzled. He was aware of Burton at his heels and that he had started climbing without taking his pistol from its holster. His head lifted above the rail and he swung one leg over then the other, took a pace forward and saw the man hurrying from the stern towards him. The man halted a couple of yards away, just in the pool of light that flooded over Smith. He gaped and the hand at his side lifted. It held a pistol.

Smith snapped testily, "Put that away. I am a British officer." For an instant the man hesitated, and Smith took a long stride and grabbed the pistol with one hand, the man's throat with the other. In panic the man jerked back, hauling Smith with him, and his free hand came up to claw at Smith's face. At the instant that Smith realized he was out-matched in weight and strength, Burton appeared. In one smooth movement he plucked the man away from Smith and threw him face-down on the deck, Burton's hand at his throat, Burton's knee in his back.

Men spilled around Smith, hurrying soft-footed forward and aft. He crossed the deck, fumbling the torch from his pocket, blinked it twice and got one flash in return from the pinnace. He turned and stared into the muzzle of a pistol, had the briefest gut-sinking impression of an officer's jacket pulled on over pyjamas, a bearded face and eyes that glared death at him. Then a figure plunged from the gloom and crashed into the officer, flame blinded Smith and the discharge of the pistol deafened him.

He rubbed his eyes and when the wheeling circles were gone he saw Somers crouched on the officer's chest, pinning him to the deck. Somers held the pistol. Smith's ears still rang and he swore. The cat was out of the bag. He ran forward and saw a door open below the bridge, a man framed in that door and behind him the lighted interior of the wireless office. He saw Able Seaman

37

Beckett leap for that door and have it slammed in his face. He added his weight to that of Beckett but the door was bolted solid and the port clamped shut. He swore again and snarled at Beckett, "Guard it. He comes out with his hands up or you shoot."

He reached out to grab another seaman as he raced past. "Get on top of this wireless office and rip all the aerials adrift!"

"Aye, aye, sir!"

Smith ran on and met Sergeant Burton. "All secure forrard, sir. And we've got all the officers, I think."

"Keep searching. One of the officers nearly got *me*. Mr. Somers is sitting on him. What happened to yours?"

"Made fast, sir. And a mouthful o' rope for him to chew on."

"Add Somers's man to your collection."

Then the pinnace thumped alongside and moments later Wakely led his party aboard, swarming across the deck. The ship was theirs. Kennedy came over the side with his two assistants carrying the wares of his trade and they disappeared below.

Smith was not happy. That damned shot! He could not see or hear any sign of an alarm being raised, except—was there activity on *Kansas*? He could not be sure.

He made a rapid tour of the upper deck and returned to find the captive crew lined up below that bridge, officers and men, most of them still dazed from sleep, shivering in the night air. Burton brought the bearded officer to join the others. He held his midriff, badly winded, and wheezed out: "I protest—"

Smith cut him short, savagely, "Shut up or I'll shoot you!"

Wakely, coming up then, flinched at Smith's words then said, "There isn't a safe in the captain's cabin, sir. Just a desk with three locked drawers." It had been Wakely's job to take the safe. "I broke them open and emptied them into a sack."

"Very good."

Jenner panted up from *Gerda*'s engine room. "She had steam up, sir. Could ha' sailed in half-an-hour if she'd wanted to."

"Thank you. Carry on."

Jenner swung over the rail and down to the pinnace.

Smith turned to the silent master. "This ship sinks in ten minutes but you will be clear of her by then. Lower your boats."

"This is a neutral vessel—"

"Or swim." Smith offered the choice.

The master bellowed an order at his crew. In German. They ran to lower the boats.

Smith glanced at his watch. They were on time, in spite of the enforced change of plan caused by the guard-boat. Just. He saw a rent in the left-hand side of his boiler-suit and used his torch to inspect it. The hole was surrounded by a powder-burn. As he switched off the torch he faced Somers. "Where did you spring from?"

The soot on Somers's face was now striped by sweat-drawn channels. "Checking on the look-outs, sir."

Smith said, "I mean before. When you came up from the deck like the demon king."

"We'd run their boat right in under the stern. Some chap in the stern shouted but he couldn't see us and went away. I shinned up a line that was hanging and came forward and there I was."

"Yes. And here I nearly wasn't."

"Sir. *Kansas* seems to be manning a boat."

Smith stared across at *Kansas*. There was activity on her deck, figures moving under the lights. The rest of the pool was quiet.

Kennedy reappeared, breathing heavily. "Five minutes, sir."

"Right. Call in the look-outs." He raised his voice: "Over the side, all of you. Five minutes."

It was time to go.

He called to Beckett where he guarded the wireless office: "Give him the word, then it's up to him!"

Beckett hammered on the door. "Abandon ship! Ship kaput!"

There was no reaction. Beckett hesitated and Smith shouted, "Come *on!* We can't hang about all night!"

Beckett started towards him. He had taken only three strides when the door swung open behind him and a man loomed in the doorway pointing a blue-gleaming finger that suddenly flamed.

Beckett cried out and fell forward. The man held the door open with his left hand, aiming the pistol with the other. Smith ran at him in black rage at the sudden attack, tugging his pistol from his belt. The man fired again, but his aim was wild, panicked by Smith's mad rush. Smith squeezed the trigger again and again and the hammer clicked on the empty chamber then fired three times. The other pistol fired only once more, the slug howling off the deck, then it fell, clattering. The man reeled back into the cabin. Smith moved to the door and saw him sprawled, eyes staring.

He turned and saw Burton bending over Beckett who was feeling his left side. Smith used his torch and saw little blood. The minutes were ticking away. "We'll look at it in the boat."

Beckett went down on Burton's back, clinging on grimly, and the pinnace eased away from the collier, towing the whaler again. Smith saw outlined against the lights of the shore that *Gerda*'s boats were well clear, then the pinnace swung around the bow of the ship and thrust out into the pool. Wakely's voice came from the bow: "Boat fine on the port bow!"

Smith saw a steam pinnace bigger than *Thunder*'s, moving at speed to intercept them. The hail came: "What boat is that?"

Kansas's pinnace. Smith answered: "*Thunder!*"

The American pinnace swung neatly on her heel to come around and for long seconds the two pinnaces ran side by side as the Americans peered fascinated at the bizarre parties in the opposite boats. Then the explosions came, dull thumps, seeming more physical vibrations than sounds. Smith saw the collier heave and then settle. Kennedy had blown the bottom out of her. Smoke and steam suddenly roared from her funnel and she began to list. Smith said, "Very effective, Mr. Kennedy."

A voice on *Kansas*'s pinnace cried, "What the *hell?*" She spun away and headed for *Gerda*. She was the last vessel they saw.

In the channel they met the flowing tide and the crew of the whaler spat on their hands and bent to their oars in earnest. With their efforts and the pinnace punching along at her best speed they passed the signalling station at Punta Negro before dawn. Running without lights as they were it was unlikely that they would have been seen from the station but before they reached Stillwater Cove the mist curled thick and dirty yellow over the channel and held them cocooned for a half-hour. Then the yellow turned pink shot with golden light and they ran out of the mist and were clear of the estuary, on the open sea in the dawn's light, and *Thunder* patrolled, cruising slowly across their course, a mile ahead.

There was a ragged cheer from the men. Beckett sat up to gaze at the ship. He looked back at Burton. "You should ha' seen the old man run at that feller. Run right *at* him! And the bastard firing away like mad. But he never faltered." He would not forget it. "What daft bugger said he was windy?"

Thunder rounded to and the pinnace ran alongside. Smith stared back at the estuary. He could see no sign of pursuit. Probably it was too early for the authorities to have assessed the situation, much less to react. But they would.

As he climbed aboard Smith knew he was very hungry and very tired and that before he ate or slept he had work to do. Garrick looked relieved to see him. Smith grinned wearily at him, and at Aitkyne behind him. "A course for Malaguay, pilot, and revolutions for fifteen knots." And: "Pass the word to Miss Benson. I would be grateful if she could spare me a few minutes."

He found cheerful words of congratulation for the crews of pinnace and whaler as the boats were swung in. He received Albrecht's report that the bullet that hit Beckett had entered his back on the extreme left side, run along the ribs and out. He would be sore for some days and Albrecht was keeping him in the sick-bay for twenty-four hours. Then the messenger returned and said Miss Benson was ready to see him and Smith walked aft.

Garrick watched him go then shot a haggard glance at Aitkyne, who said, "He's got his nerve. That's one rumour nailed for a lie. By God, he's got his nerve."

Smith had sunk a neutral ship in a neutral port. The enormity of the offence left them silent, tempering also the exuberance of the crew as they welcomed back the boarding party. But there was still a lot of back-slapping, and young Gibb got his share.

Rattray took no part in this. A night spent in backbreaking labour had left him exhausted and filthy. The captain had humiliated him, taking that green squirt Gibb in his place. Rattray was not yet sure how, but he would get even with both of them.

SARAH HAD WOKEN long before dawn. The previous night she had watched the boats leave. Now as Smith entered and she saw the strained, bloodshot eyes in the dirty face, the hair sweat-stuck flat to his head, she asked only the one question: "You sank her?"

"Yes."

She sat up in the captain's bed, wrapped in a silk dressing-gown lent by Aitkyne. It was too large and loose but her case had held no nightclothes.

He had expected her question and she expected his. "What can you tell me about Malaguay?"

They were polite to each other, business-like. Sarah replied: "Let's see. . . . A German gunboat was interned there late in 1914. She's been tied up in the river since then. Disarmed of course, but otherwise untouched. Her crew live aboard and the Chileans have a guard on her. That's only a gesture; there's nowhere she could go. Strong German influence, a large German colony. Usual few British, the usual British club. Some Americans." She shrugged.

Smith stood up, rubbed at his face and smiled stiffly, blearily at her. "I'm grateful for your help."

"You're welcome, Commander." The door closed behind him. Sarah stared at it. "You'll need all the help you can get," she said softly.

As Smith climbed to the upper deck he met Garrick, who said, "Young Wakely has a sack of stuff he brought aboard from the *Gerda,* sir. He's in the captain's—your deck cabin with it, sir."

Smith ignored the slip but it was a sign of the newness of his command; he was a stranger here still. "Right. You'd better come along and give a hand with it." And as they went: "I will mention them in my report. Manton, Wakely, Somers, Kennedy, Burton. They all did well. . . ."

Half an hour later all the probabilities insisted he had been a bloody fool. The sack held the *Gerda's* log, her master's diary, copies of manifests, letters from owners and agents and his wife, personal papers. And there was nothing at all to cast doubt on *Gerda's* neutrality.

Nobody wanted to look at Smith. He dismissed them. On the bridge later, Aitkyne asked Garrick, "Well? Anything?"

Garrick shook his head worriedly. "Nothing at all. As far as evidence goes that collier was as neutral as a Swiss hospital ship."

Aitkyne said, "If he's lucky they'll decide he's mad—and they won't shoot him."

4

They made Malaguay in the late afternoon, *Thunder* trudging in over a slow, leaden swell under a grey and lowering sky. There was a strong, gusting wind that snapped the crests from the waves in spitting spume. The weather was worsening.

Thunder came to anchor in the bay. There was a muddy river at the head of it, and wharves on either bank of the river.

Up on the bridge Garrick said, "Can't see the collier, sir."

Smith had already made his inspection of the vessels at anchor. "No. She must be up-river." Ships lined the wharves in the river, a small forest of masts, but it was impossible to pick out a particular ship at that angle and that distance. He could see two British ships at anchor, one a commonplace tramp but the other bigger, smarter. They called for another decision.

Garrick said, "That's *Ariadne*, sir. Commodore Ballard. This is her regular run, right up the coast to Vancouver. Usually around forty or fifty passengers and cargo."

"And the other one." Smith lifted his glasses and read the tramp's name. "The *Elizabeth Bell?*"

"Don't know, sir. She's a stranger to me."

"My compliments to them both. I must explain the situation to them and request neither will move without my protection."

As he spoke, a boat carrying Thackeray, the consul, ran alongside and he jumped for the dangling ladder and clambered up. He was obviously in a hurry.

Smith left the bridge and went to meet Sarah Benson and the consul on the upper deck. Thackeray was a thin man, thin-lipped. He eyed Smith severely. "You've stirred up a hornet's nest, Captain, if reports are correct."

"I don't know what reports you've heard. The truth of the matter is that there was a German collier lying at Guaya, masquerading as a neutral. I sank her." He went on to explain.

Thackeray listened impatiently, lips pursed. At the end he shook his narrow head. "They're outraged and I'm not surprised. It will get worse, I'm sure. The Germans are playing it up with all their might, of course. They're bandying around phrases like the wolf sneaking into the fold to murder the lamb."

"An unusual lamb—fitted with brand-new wireless!"

"So you say. Did you know they've had a gunboat, the *Leopard*, interned here since 1914? Now they're demanding her release or the internment of *this* ship."

"That's nonsense. If they try to intern this ship illegally they'll have to do it by force." And he looked around at the crowded port and the town.

Thackeray muttered, "It's an indication of the trouble you've caused. Over the years I've built up good relations, *very* good relations with everyone in this port. Now my friends cut me and peasants shout at me in the streets!"

Smith caught Sarah Benson's eye on him. Her face was impassive but one eye closed, opened. So Thackeray's cosy little world had been upset and Smith was to blame. He'd get little more help from the consul than from the Chileans. He said, "The collier in this port, the *Maria*, I want *her* interned. Where is she lying?"

"She isn't." Thackeray sniffed. "She sailed about nine hours ago, soon after the telegrams began to arrive with the news of your—er—*escapade*." He said the word with distaste but he was relieved. Smith could wreak no damage here. "She headed west."

So there it was. Smith was not surprised that the *Maria* had fled; like *Gerda* she must have been lying with steam up ready to sail when called. But it was a blow. It was one more piece of circumstantial evidence pointing to her guilt but that only added to his reasons for wanting her. He had considered the possibility of her running and her probable course and destination. There were several, scattered around half of the compass. North? South? West? She had steered west, but was that merely a ruse to gain sea-room so as to swing north well clear of *Thunder* as she had run down to Malaguay? Or a ruse before she turned south?

Garrick said, "The port captain wants to come aboard, sir."

The words sank in slowly and then Smith said, "Yes. Due honours." And he sent a messenger running to his cabin.

The guns banged out and the pipes shrilled and Smith stood on his quarterdeck and met the port captain, Captain Encalada, saluting, at the head of the accommodation ladder.

Encalada was big and full of bluster. He protested. A neutral vessel sunk in a neutral port; insolent violation of neutrality; representations in the strongest terms were being made to the ambassador, to London. . . .

South or north or west? *Maria* had nine hours start and she would be making eight, possibly nine knots. If *Thunder* sailed now and made fifteen knots she should overhaul *Maria* in nine or ten hours. *If* Smith was right about her course. If he was wrong he would have lost her.

The port captain paused for breath as the messenger returned and handed Smith the envelope from his desk. Smith passed it to the port captain. "This is a copy of my report of the incident."

"*Incident!*" The port captain exploded the word.

"Incident." Smith went on doggedly, "It details the reasons for my action, the evidence I had that the vessel in question was not a neutral but a tender of war manned by a German crew."

"A tender—?" That set Encalada back on his heels.

"It is all in my report."

Encalada turned the envelope over in his hands. "I will present this . . . document to the proper authorities. But meanwhile you are unwelcome in this port, you will receive nothing and no one from this ship will be allowed to land."

It was Smith's turn to protest. "Are you aware that this ship has neither coaled nor provisioned in a Chilean port for the last three months and that under international law—"

"In normal circumstances, Captain. These are not normal. Be sure you understand me. You receive nothing, no one lands, and you sail immediately."

Smith shrugged. "Very well. Please believe me when I say I am sincerely sorry that our former excellent relations have deteriorated to this point and I hope they will soon return to happy normality." If they wanted diplomatic waffle they could have it.

After that came the lengthy formalities of departure and all the time the alternatives competed in Smith's head. South? West? North? And *Maria* already over seventy miles away. *Thunder* had twice the speed of a collier, but Smith could not go in three directions at once. He had to commit himself to one. There would be three, maybe four hours of daylight. If he sailed now and guessed correctly, enormous assumption, it would be noon when he came up with *Maria*. If he guessed wrong? He dared not guess wrong.

The port captain descended and Smith swung on Thackeray, hovering nearby. "You heard what the port captain had to say; I'll get no coal in Chile and I must coal soon. The collier *Mary Ellen* is making for Guaya. Will you send for her to come here?"

Thunder had coal for six days of economical steaming but for the last ten hours she had steamed at fifteen knots and at that speed she ate coal.

As Thackeray nodded grudgingly and went down into his launch, Garrick stepped close to Smith and muttered, "*Ariadne* and *Elizabeth Bell*, both masters here to see you, sir."

Smith turned to the group that waited on him on his quarter-deck. Sarah was still there. "Miss Benson. Gentlemen. I don't want to appear perfunctory but you'll realize my time is limited."

Hands were shaken. Ballard of *Ariadne* was hefty and hand-some, his uniform well-cut. He looked the picture of what he was, the commodore of a line. Graham of *Elizabeth Bell* was short and solid with a little round paunch that shoved out his waistcoat with its looped watch-chain. He carried a bowler hat in his hand to go with the blue serge suit.

Ballard said, "What's this story about German cruisers being loose in these waters?"

Smith nodded. "My information is that two cruisers are out. I haven't time for a lengthy explanation, but among other factors I received information that a couple of colliers were on this coast, loaded with steam coal and manned by Germans. There is no doubt in my mind that the cruisers have this coast as their objective."

Ballard glanced at Graham. Neither seemed happy. Graham said, "Understand, Commander, we don't want to be unreason-able or rash but in the merchant service time is money. If I waste time idling here my owners will take a loss and they'll want to know why. All you're saying is that you *think* those cruisers are headed this way."

Smith nodded sympathetically. "I appreciate your difficulty." But he went on firmly, "I'm certain about the cruisers. Now look here, gentlemen. I expect to return to this port within thirty-six hours. If I do not, you may decide at the end of that time whether or not to sail in the light of the situation then. If you sail before without my escort then you do so against my advice."

Ballard glanced at Graham then turned to Smith. "Well, that seems reasonable. It will give us time—"

Smith added quickly, "Can you take Miss Benson as a passenger? I'd be very grateful." The request was also a broad hint that it was time to leave.

Ballard hesitated, "I'm afraid I'm already overcrowded. I will disembark a number of passengers at Guaya, but until then—"

Graham said immediately, "I've a cabin for the young lady and she's right welcome, but we're no liner, miss."

Sarah grinned at him. "Lor' love you, I'm no fine lady, either." She winked at him impudently.

Smith sighed with relief. "Excellent." He shepherded them to the head of the ladder and handed Sarah down.

"Good luck," she said. And they parted.

The captains' boats pulled away. The cloud ceiling was low now and clouds ran in on the wind. Smith retired with Aitkyne to the chartroom, leaving Garrick to take the ship to sea.

He stared at the chart and fiddled with a pencil. He believed that *Maria* had not sailed north or west. He believed that she had a rendezvous to keep with cruisers that had traversed the Atlantic and rounded the Horn, coaling secretly and precariously from colliers just like her. They would want to meet without delay. And there was the Gulf of Penas, a place the Germans knew and had proved in the far-off days of 1914 when Von Spee had cruised this coast. Smith's fingers were tight on the pencil now.

It was logic allied with intuition and faith.

It was all based on his conviction that the cruisers would come.

He jabbed the pencil down at the chart. "A course for the Gulf of Penas, pilot. Revolutions for fifteen knots."

Aitkyne glanced sideways at him and said, "Coal, sir?"

"I know. I asked Thackeray for help. The *Mary Ellen* will be waiting for us here."

Thunder headed south out of Malaguay and into the night and the storm. She was rolling and Smith was grimly aware that rolling was made worse by the lightness of her bunkers. The seas were black mountains in the night, capped with the snow of driving spray.

He went to his cabin below the bridge. A hot meal had been cooked while they lay at Malaguay, a stew of corned beef. Horsfall had kept some warm for him and brought it now. Smith wolfed the meal. He laid himself down fully dressed.

But sleep would be impossible. *Thunder*'s rolling and pitching and the continuous hammering of the sea on her hull would see to that if his thoughts did not, and they were black enough.

He was acting only on the evidence of one collier that had been suspect and another that seemed to fly at his approach. He had no scrap of evidence that the cruisers were or would be in the Pacific. It was like assuming a murder without a body.

If he was *right* there would be a murder and *Thunder* would be the victim. If he was *wrong* he faced professional ruin and worse. He would be the man who upset single-handed the pro-British feeling in South America at a time when Britain needed all her friends. There would be a clamour for his blood and no reason at all why that clamour should not be satisfied. If he was wrong.

And again, if he was right? The cruisers loomed huge in his mind and he twisted in the bunk and put a hand to his eyes. He had to sleep.

Sarah Benson. Only Sarah Benson believed he was right. But she was prickly, short-tempered. Her face when she killed that man. . . . Well, he was rid of her now. He was grateful for her help. God knew! She had brought the word that the Germans were watching *Thunder*, spotted the oddity of the collier with wireless and because of her *Thunder* would not sail unprepared into an ambush.

If ambush there was. . . .

He slept.

5

Dawn came in a full gale and as Smith clung on the bridge the seas broke over the bows to sweep aft like a green glass wall and smash against the conning-tower. Visibility was maybe three miles. There was no ship in sight.

He ate breakfast there, a sandwich of the inevitable bully beef

washed down by cold tea. The galley fires were out. There would
be no hot food until this weather abated. The mess-decks were in
chaos and awash. *Thunder* was reduced to ten knots and making
hard work of that. In the stokehold men were thrown about as
they fought to feed the fires.

Garrick said, "*Maria*'ll be no better off, sir. She'll be lucky to
be making more than five knots in this sea." His face was grey
as the sky under the prickling black stubble and there were
shadows around his eyes.

Smith grunted bad temperedly. "I suggest you turn in, Number
One."

"Aye, aye, sir." But Garrick hung on, reluctant, until Smith's
baleful glare caught him. He left the bridge.

Kennedy had the watch. He took one look at his captain and
ventured no comments at all. Smith swayed to *Thunder*'s heave
and roll and peered wearily out at the wild sea.

At mid-morning the visibility was scarcely improved, variable
as the squalls swept in over the mountainous seas.

For what seemed the hundredth time Kennedy hailed the look-
out: "Masthead! Anything seen?"

The answer came down from the man miserably wet and cold
on his swaying, swooping, dizzying perch: "Nuffink, sir!"

Smith had been on the bridge for four hours. Waiting. Wait and
see. But would they see? They could pass the *Maria* within a few
miles and not see her in this weather. They should see her if
Smith was totally, completely right, but if her course varied from
his by only a degree that divergence would take him past her. He
cursed the absence of a consort. If he had another ship with him,
any ship, an armed merchant cruiser, say, it would widen his
search and be another pair of eyes.

What if *Maria*'s rendezvous was not the Gulf of Penas, if she
was already lying snugly hidden in some sheltered inlet? *Thunder*
could sail on for ever like the Flying Dutchman.

No. At a point in time he would have to acknowledge that he
had made a mistake and turn back. That time would be soon.
They should have caught her by now but she would be running
for all she was worth. He would have to set a time. He did a sum
in his head, involving the speed of *Thunder* and the probable

speed of *Maria,* and the relative times of sailing, and he arrived at an answer. Noon.

If they had not sighted her by noon he must turn. He must return to Malaguay and give clearance to *Ariadne* and *Elizabeth Bell.* And make his report by cable. And wait for the cable in reply that would relieve him, break him.

Garrick came back onto the bridge.

Smith felt bleakly, briefly, sorry for him, for the mess he would inherit. Then he remembered again what his own state would be and grinned wryly at himself.

Garrick caught the grin and misconstrued it. "Sighted her, sir?"

Smith shook his head and saw the worry that dragged Garrick's mouth down at the corners and the glance he threw at Kennedy. Smith said, "There's time yet, Number One." Covertly he examined expressions on the bridge and decided they were not fools and had done their sums as he had. They knew that any chance of a sighting had slid into improbability and was sliding fast towards impossibility.

At 11.30 the weather worsened, visibility fell to less than two miles and spray burst continually over the bridge.

At 11.50 the bridge was ominously silent and they were all waiting as they had waited all through that long morning, but now they were waiting for the change of course. *Thunder*'s rolling seemed as heavy and sullen as the atmosphere on the bridge. Smith was cold to the bone.

At 11.55 the squalls swept by and visibility marginally lifted to possibly five miles.

At 11.58 the masthead look-out howled: "Masthead! Ship bearing green two-oh!"

Smith fumbled at the glasses hanging on his chest, swept the arc of sea over the starboard bow and thought he saw something through the spray, a shadow, a shape, but could not be sure.

"Masthead! I think she could be the *Maria!*"

Smith could make out a ship now. She was ploughing gamely into the seas, and they hid all but her superstructure. He lowered the glasses. "Steer two points to starboard."

Thunder edged around and started to close the ship ahead. She slowly came up through the rain until she was within a mile and they could see her with the naked eye, but Garrick used his glasses. "It's her, sir. The *Maria*."

If he expected Smith to be delighted and relieved then he was disappointed. If anything Smith looked grimmer. "Very good. Make: Heave to."

The signal was hoisted and on Smith's orders a searchlight repeated it in morse.

Garrick said, "Of course, we have right of board and search, sir, but launching a boat in this sea—"

"Yes." A boat would not live a minute. "We'll cross that bridge when we come to it."

Maria maintained her course and speed.

Knight said, "She's flying: I am a neutral, sir."

Smith said deliberately, "Make: Heave to or I will sink you."

Knight swallowed. "Aye, aye, sir."

The signal broke out, the flags laid flat as boards on the wind. The collier steamed on.

Smith said, "Close up the starboard twelve-pounder battery." And as the guns' crews scrambled to the guns and the "Ready" reports came in: "Put a shot across her bows, Number One."

A twelve-pounder cracked and sea spurted ahead of *Maria*. She sailed on.

A messenger came staggering. "Wireless reports signalling, sir. Very close, they think it's this ship an' it seems to be in code."

"Very good."

So *Maria* was signalling furiously, to someone quite possibly out of range of her wireless anyway. Or whoever it was could be within a few miles. The eternal guessing game. The two ships ploughed heavily on through the breaking seas, the driving rain.

Smith's thoughts crystallized, ending his hesitation. He had known what the end of this would be and that hesitation was only a faltering of nerve. He had been right in his reasoning from the start and he was right now. Or had been, and still was, wrong. "A wolf sneaking into the fold to murder a lamb".

May as well be hung for a sheep.

"Close up the upper deck six-inch batteries." The maindeck guns were unusable in this sea. "And sink her."

"*Sink* her, sir?" Garrick's voice rose on the word.

Aitkyne said, "Sir, if I might suggest, we could lay right alongside and hail her. I'll take a party of volunteers—"

Smith cut brutally across the protests. "They're playing for time! First hours, and now for minutes! Sink her and quickly!" His voice was harsh and flat, denying argument or delay.

The men waded across the deck through the seas that washed it and manned the six-inch casemates. They reported ready. Garrick exchanged an agonized glance with Aitkyne, but Smith would not wait. "Open fire!"

The two starboard six-inch guns bellowed bass to the tenor cracking of the twelve-pounders. At that range, the trajectory near flat, a miss would have been inexcusable. The six-inch bursts were clearly seen, one forward and one aft on the *Maria*, opening great holes in her on the waterline. She seemed to stop dead in her tracks and fall away before the sea. There were men forward and aft of the superstructure, struggling waist-deep in the seas that swept her, attempting to lower boats. She was listing badly and *Thunder* was drawing ahead of her.

"Cease firing. Starboard ten!"

Thunder swung ponderously around to head across the bows of the sinking collier. There was a lifeboat in the water, a dozen men in her and thrusting away from their ship. Then she broke in half, bow and stern lifting as the coal in her belly dragged her down, and sank. A billow of smoke and steam and she was gone.

Smith rubbed at his eyes. "Stand by to pick up survivors."

Thunder straightened on a course that took her down towards the wreckage and reduced speed until she rolled to the seas, barely making headway. There was flotsam: the wreckage of the lifeboat, a few splintered planks, a cap. *Maria* would have carried a crew of twenty or so but there was not one survivor.

The guns' crews stood down and *Thunder*'s company braved the seas to line her rails, staring silently. There was no jubilation.

The crew of the forward 9.2 made a little group in the shelter below the bridge. Chalky White, the gun-trainer, muttered, "He's gone off his rocker."

Farmer Bates, leading seaman and the gunlayer, snapped edgily, "Oh, shut it!"

"I mean it. Do you reckon he knows what he's doing?"

Farmer was silent.

Young Gibb opened his mouth to speak, but felt Rattray's hot eyes on him and stayed quiet. Rattray was making his life a misery. If they met in a crowd anywhere then Gibb got Rattray's elbow in his ribs or Rattray's foot crushing his own. And he did not know why. But he was afraid to tell anyone and so reveal his fear of the man. It was wearing him down.

Up on the bridge Garrick did not look at Smith, nor did anyone else. Then the messenger came running. "Wireless reports she's stopped sending, sir." Smith glared at him. The man flinched but carried on: "Reports another signal, sir. Distant and it's stopped now, but they think it was Telefunken."

Telefunken transmissions were distinctive. And they were German.

Smith took a breath, "Thank you." Now they were all looking at him but he had had enough. "Pilot, a course for Malaguay. Revolutions for fifteen knots."

He staggered to his cabin to stretch out on his bunk and pull a blanket around him. He was cold, cold, and his body ached with the constant strain of those hours on the bridge. There was a tap at the door and he groaned softly and called, "Come in!"

Albrecht entered, holding a glass. "I took the liberty of prescribing for you, sir." He held out the glass. "Brandy. It will warm you and let you sleep."

"I have nothing on my conscience," Smith rasped.

Albrecht did not answer.

Smith sighed. "Doctor, I had to sink that ship. They were signalling and they got a reply. I *had* to."

Albrecht said, "The surgeon's knife." And: "You're still certain that these cruisers—"

He stopped. Smith's weary grin stopped him. "This ship can offer them a smashing victory, Doctor. Then they can annihilate British shipping along this coast and that will draw forces to hunt *them*, not just from the West Indies but from the Atlantic and Scapa Flow." He took the brandy and sipped and sighed. "It will take a lot of ships to track them down and ships of force to deal with them. They can lengthen the war or even, by weakening the Grand Fleet, win it. But first they sink this ship." Smith drained the glass and handed it back. "Goodnight, Doctor. And if you can't sleep, try a drop of brandy. It's all the thing."

But, left alone, Smith did not smile. The brandy had warmed him, burning down into his stomach. His body was exhausted but his mind was only too active.

The signals had been distant. That might mean a hundred miles or more or even, flukily, a thousand; but surely not so far in these conditions. No.

A distant signal that the men on *Thunder's* wireless thought might be Telefunken. It was still not evidence of the presence of a German ship, let alone two warships. Garrick and the rest did not believe in their existence. While Albrecht was uncertain.

Smith was certain.

6

They called Smith at dusk. Garrick's voice came urgent down the voice-pipe: "Captain, sir! Ship in distress off the starboard bow! I'm altering course."

"Very good!" Smith could feel *Thunder* heel as she turned tightly onto the new heading. Still stumbling from legs asleep, he dragged his oilskin on as he climbed the ladder, the folds of it streaming out behind and clapping as the wind tried to tear it from him. The rain ran down his face and he was wide awake when he stepped onto the bridge gratings.

Garrick pointed. "There she is, sir."

Smith wrapped an arm around a stanchion to steady himself against *Thunder's* pitching and rolling. Her engines still rammed her on at that punishing and coal-devouring fifteen knots because Smith was certain the cruisers were somewhere astern of him and *Ariadne* and *Elizabeth Bell* waited in Malaguay for *Thunder's* protection. Such as it was. And her collier, *Mary Ellen*.

He lifted his glasses, focused, swept and found. She was a black ship on a wild, dark ocean as the night came down on her, and close inshore. *Thunder* was racing down on her.

Garrick said, "We signalled her by searchlight and she answered. Her engines have broken down and she's sinking."

"What ship is she?" Smith asked, thinking of the men aboard

her, with that awful sea waiting to swallow them. Whatever the cost he would take them off. He lowered the glasses. "I asked, what ship?"

Garrick licked his lips. "She's the *Mary Ellen*, sir."

Smith peered at Garrick, eyes strained. "The *Mary Ellen*? Our collier? That *Mary Ellen*?"

"Yes, sir." And Garrick lowered his voice. "We—we're only a couple of hours or so out from Malaguay but we'll barely have coal to go on to Guaya, sir. At fifteen knots—"

"I *know!*" Smith snarled at him. "What the *hell* is she doing here? I told Thackeray I wanted her at Malaguay not—" He pounded softly on the rail with his fist. Then he clung to the stanchion and scowled stonefaced at the *Mary Ellen* as they closed her.

Then at last he came alive. "Slow ahead. Make to her: Stand by for a line. I will tow you." He swung on the gaping Garrick. "Make ready to tow her."

They could not believe it. It was impossible! It was dark now, the *Mary Ellen* a tossing black bulk. From her a signal-lamp faltered through a reply.

Knight read: "She says: Ship is sinking. Will you take off crew?"

There were lights on her bridge and lights on *Thunder*'s deck now, and men milling aft where they worked frenziedly to rouse out the big towing hawser. Smith had read the signal himself and his answer was ready. "Reply: Negative. Stand by for line."

A ripple ran through the men behind him. He was aware of it, ignored it, eyes fast on the *Mary Ellen*. The lamp blinked again, still stumbling but faster now: Boats gone. Urgently request—

He did not wait for the rest of it. He could see for himself that her boats were smashed. She had taken a beating as she lay powerless under the storm. "Make: Negative. Stand by for line."

Again that ripple.

Smith sensed Garrick's hesitation. "Everything ready aft, Mr. Garrick?"

"Yes, sir."

The use of boats was out of the question in this sea. Smith said, "I want a man to throw a line from the stern. What about that big leading hand of yours—" he turned on Somers, "Buckley? Is he good?"

"V-very good, sir."

Smith turned back to Garrick. "We'll want fenders over the stern, and done handsomely. Better go aft yourself and see to it."

So Garrick took himself aft and Smith ordered, "Port four points."

"Four points of port wheel on, sir."

"Midships." *Thunder* steadied on the new course that would take her alongside the collier. He could see a light in the bows of the *Mary Ellen* now and figures moved on her fo'c'sle, crouched as the seas burst over them in spray. He snapped, "Starboard a point. And make to her that they should make fast the towing hawser to their anchor cable *and* make damn sure that's secure."

The towing hawser was wire, immensely strong but with little elasticity except the curve in its length. The anchor cable was far heavier, would steepen that curve and give more spring, more elasticity to the tow to prevent it breaking. "Starboard a point." He edged *Thunder* closer as she drew abreast of the wallowing collier and crept past her.

Smith was out on the starboard wing of the bridge now, eyes gauging *Thunder*'s crawling progress against the collier's dead rolling, narrowing on the strip of water that separated them. He was aware of the pale blur of faces on the bridge of the *Mary Ellen* and of one man who had to be her master, his mouth opening and closing and fists lifted and shaking at Smith.

Smith tore his eyes from the man and back to the task in hand. He shouted against the wind, "Port four points!" And: "Midships!" And: "Ease on port engine!" *Thunder*'s bow swung around to point seawards and her stern swung to pass across the bow of the *Mary Ellen*. Close. Close!

From behind him Aitkyne's voice came. "God Almighty! She—"

But Smith knew she wouldn't strike. The figures on the collier's fo'c'sle scrambled away from the sudden towering steel cliff of *Thunder*'s stern hanging over them but that cliff eased away as the weighted line was hurled. They tailed onto it and dragged it to the donkey engine. Both ships were driven towards the shore now, the *Mary Ellen* by the storm, *Thunder* because Smith held her close on the collier. The sea was setting *Thunder* down quicker than the collier because it exerted more pressure on *Thunder*'s vastly bigger hull and Smith had to keep just enough way on her to balance that pressure. "Slow ahead together! . . . Ease on port engine! . . . together! . . ."

The collier's donkey engine hammered faintly now and a messenger cable was bent to the line and drawn over to her because the first line would not take the strain of the towing hawser. That followed, bent on to the messenger cable, dropping over *Thunder*'s stern. And all the time came the steady stream of orders to engines and helm as Smith juggled with them and the pressures of wind and sea on *Thunder*'s twelve-thousand ton bulk and the three-thousand tons of the collier. A wrong order might throw *Thunder* astern onto the collier or so slacken the hawser that it was sucked onto and around her screws. Or send her lunging away to tauten the hawser and yank it out of the collier before it was secured and leave the whole painful business to be done again. Outside the dancing, swinging lights on the cruiser's stern and the collier's fo'c'sle the night was a howling darkness. But they could see the shore and it was close, the breaking surf marked by a line of phosphorescence.

An arm went up on the *Mary Ellen*'s fo'c'sle, waving excitedly. The donkey engine was silent. In confirmation of the signal Aitkyne called, "First Lieutenant reports 'Tow secured', sir."

"Very good!" Smith did not take his eyes off the tow. "Slow ahead together. Watch for the strain coming on! Ease on port engine. . . . Slow ahead together."

He saw the hawser slowly straighten, the slack loop of it lifting from the sea. It tautened as *Thunder* eased away from the collier, and they all felt the shudder and an instant's check before *Thunder* paid off again. Smith's orders went on as he watched the tow for the first signs of the collier yawing and ordered again and again to correct it. Someone aboard the *Mary Ellen* was doing his best to steer and that was helping but while *Thunder* pulled her one way sea and gale tried to shove her the other.

It took over an hour to tow her out and around the headland into the little bay beyond. Smith grew hoarse. Someone brought him a mug of cocoa. He gulped it down and then was hoarse again.

"Rig fenders and boarding nets. When we're secure I want a party of men forward and another aft, both under a good petty officer who knows what he's about on this kind of business."

"Aye, aye, sir." And Aitkyne hesitated then burst out, "Congratulations, sir!" He still could not believe they had plucked the *Mary Ellen* off the shore. Smith saw no reason for congratulations. He had done what had to be done. He said tiredly, "For God's sake get her people off as soon as you can." And: "Hands to coal ship!"

"Hands to coal ship". It was a fact of life for the ship's company that she coaled every week or ten days. It was heavy, filthy work and only the captain was excused. But this time they would remember. Because of the gale. And because the collier was sinking.

In the comparatively sheltered waters of the bay Smith laid *Thunder* alongside the *Mary Ellen* and anchored. The ships were bound together fore and aft with securing warps, and ground on the fenders hung between them. The searchlights blazed out on the collier's hatches and the working parties swarmed onto her deck. Aboard the collier they threw off the hatchcovers and jumped down into the holds with their shovels. The coal was packed tight and the devil to break into as always but now they worked in a gale that rolled both ships together so that the coal shifted and slid in an oily, mountainous flow and they staggered and fell as they worked. They shovelled the coal into sacks and these were swung up out of the holds by the derricks, ten sacks to a strop, swayed over and lowered to *Thunder*'s deck.

Between the coaling scuttles in her deck and the bunkers far below were the mess-decks. So canvas chutes were rigged between scuttles and bunkers. The sacks were wheeled on barrows to the scuttles and the coal fell down the chutes into the bunkers. Coal dust found its way anywhere, any way.

In the dust-filled gloom of the bunkers they worked in frenzied haste, because there was not a man who did not know what coal meant to the ship, and that time was against them. The crew of the collier were taken off as soon as she was made fast alongside, and Garrick brought her master to the wing of the bridge.

He was wild-eyed, his face haggard. "You should have taken us

off. She could have gone down any time. Man, you've only got to
look at her! Every minute I thought she might go. You could have
taken us off. I watched you handle this ship and, by God! you're
a seaman! So you could ha' taken us off. I *pleaded* with you to
take us off and you passed us a *bloody tow* instead! *Why?*"

Smith did not answer. Instead he asked, "Why did you sail
south when I asked that you wait for me at Malaguay?"   ·

The master peered at him, bewildered. "The consul said you
needed the coal and I was to find you. You don't suppose I put
to sea in this weather for sport, do you? I did it for you, you—"
He stopped. Then he said, "We're men like yourself. Sailormen.
I don't see how you could—" He shook his head.

Smith finally turned to him a face as haggard as his own and
eyes as wild. "I had to have coal. *I had to have coal!*"

The master stepped back. "You're mad! A bloody *madman!*"
Garrick took his arm and led him away.

Smith watched the collier sinking and his men slaving in her at
risk of their lives and the master's charges hammered in his
head . . . "*bloody madman.* . . ." But his answer was the same.
He had to have coal. Because of the cruisers. And because of
Ariadne and *Elizabeth Bell* and the other British shipping
along this coast. He knew that he was right but took no comfort
from the knowledge.

So he handed over the bridge to Garrick and went down to the
Mary Ellen to pace her deck and feel the sluggish, water-laden
dying of her under him. He went down into the holds where
despite the searchlights the men laboured in a reeling near-
darkness and the coal slithered and slid around.

They saw him.

Somebody coughed and spat and croaked, "What's he doin'
here? Don't say our old cow's goin' down faster nor this one!"
And they laughed and coughed, and the shovels ripped at the
coal.

He said nothing but he grinned at them through a mask of
coal dust. On deck he told Aitkyne and the petty officers: "When
it comes you must be quick. Get them out and back on board
Thunder." And to the two men, one forward, one aft who stood
with axes where the big warps came down from the warship to

the collier: "When I give the word, cut her loose and jump! Understood?"

"Aye, aye, sir."

He paced the deck of the *Mary Ellen* as the loads soared up from the holds, until the collier's winches faltered and died and only the winch of the boat derrick hammered on aboard *Thunder*.

The *Mary Ellen* was settling.

He felt a sudden, sick lurch and his mouth was open when one of the party on the warp forward leaned over *Thunder*'s rail to scream through the clatter of the winch: "*She's going!*"

Smith shouted, "Cut her loose! Get those men out and accounted for!"

The axes flashed. The hands came clambering out of the holds, yanked out by the petty officers. They jumped at the nettings and clawed their way up *Thunder*'s side like flies caught in a web.

"Get aboard!" He shouted at them. "*Get aboard!*"

He stood by the after hold with *Thunder*'s boat derrick projecting above him like a gallows tree with its dangling wire. The *Mary Ellen* was going down.

He snapped at Aitkyne, the only man left on her deck, "How many men in the hold?"

"Two, sir. Kennedy and young Manton."

Smith could see them down there, securing the sacks on the strop. One of them yelled, Aitkyne lifted his arm and the wire drew taut.

Smith shoved him towards the side. "Get aboard!" He saw Aitkyne on the nettings as the warps parted to slam against *Thunder*'s side and be hauled inboard. He saw the two men with axes throw them away, jump at the nets and scramble up.

He was a solitary figure on the collier's deck under the glare of the lights as the sea seemed to hang above him. The load came swinging up with Kennedy and Manton clinging to the sacks and as it soared past he caught hold and Kennedy's fist clamped on his collar. He was snatched off the deck of the collier as the sea smashed around his waist.

They swung like a pendulum above the boiling sea. The *Mary Ellen* had gone. Then the derrick swayed them in and down onto *Thunder*'s deck.

At risk of their lives they had torn a hundred and twenty tons of coal out of the *Mary Ellen*—at most another twenty-four hours of life for *Thunder*. Now she had coal for just two days' steaming.

THUNDER raised the scattered lights of Malaguay at midnight, seen dimly through recurrent rain that drove in on the gale that thrust at her, rocking her badly. She still heaved lumpily in the shelter of the roadstead as she came to anchor. The pinnace set out for the shore with the crew of the *Mary Ellen* and the searchlight blinked to *Ariadne* and *Elizabeth Bell:* "Prepare to sail with me forthwith."

Ariadne acknowledged at once, *Elizabeth Bell* after a delay. There was a hail from the deck and a moment later Wakely reported: "Boat alongside, sir. Mr. Thackeray coming aboard."

In a glistening wet yellow oilskin that reached to his ankles Thackeray went with Smith and Garrick to Smith's deck cabin. His face even longer than usual, Thackeray asked: "Did you find her?"

Smith nodded. "She refused to heave to and continued to claim she was a neutral. Have you heard any report that she was calling the shore stations?"

"None."

"She was sending hard enough to someone, and in code. And our wireless picked up a reply that was a Telefunken transmission. That scarcely sounds neutral to me." He paused as Thackeray stared at him, then: "I sank her!"

Thackeray's lips tightened till they became a thin, sulky line. Smith pushed on, his voice dangerously quiet.

"She was not the only collier to sink. I met the *Mary Ellen* south of here. Her engines were broken down and she was being driven onto a lee shore where she had no damned business to be and her master said *you* sent her! She sank!"

A nerve twitched a corner of Thackeray's mouth. "It seemed best."

"Best? If her engines hadn't broken down I'd have missed her altogether!"

"You asked me to bring her down from Guaya because you badly needed coal. You didn't say she was to wait."

62

"I didn't need to! Because you couldn't send her anywhere because you didn't even know where *I* was going."

"I knew you sailed south."

"That is a very general direction in a very large ocean."

"I am no seaman. I was simply repeating your instructions."

"I told you—"

"I remember very well what you told me, Captain. I only wish I had a witness to the conversation."

Smith was silent. There was a little gleam of triumph in Thackeray's eyes and Smith had not missed the point of his words. Smith did not have a witness either, so it was his word against Thackeray's. Three ships sunk in forty-eight hours, two of them claiming to be neutrals and the master of the third believing him to be a madman. . . .

Smith rubbed his hands across his face. He said tiredly, "There will be a Court of Inquiry." He was done with Thackeray.

Thackeray was not done with him. He said with satisfaction, "No doubt. The attitude of the Chileans has hardened even further. They're very hostile. My protest about the German breach of neutrality was accepted and that's all."

"What breach of neutrality?"

"The *Leopard*, the gunboat interned here. There was no sentry aboard her, only one on the quay and last night, after you sailed, she got up steam and slipped away."

"*What?*"

"There's quite a strong German faction here. So when she was interned her crew were left aboard. All her ammunition was taken off, however, and put in bond in the naval arsenal."

"So she went to sea toothless." Smith scowled but it was a comforting thought in one way. "With what object?" He supplied the answer himself. "She can't sail to Germany and in her present state she can't fight. She's gone to meet the cruisers."

It was one more piece of evidence, circumstantial no doubt, but it fitted. Garrick looked thoughtful.

Smith said, "The cruisers can supply her with ammunition, and what's more she will be one more pair of eyes for them. . . ." He found he was on his feet. He said brusquely, "I must ask you to excuse me now. *Ariadne* and *Elizabeth Bell* should be ready to sail soon and it's important we leave for Guaya as soon as possible."

And he wanted to be quit of Thackeray with his narrow mouth and narrow cunning, his stupidity.

Thackeray did not move. Smith saw a twist of his lips as he spoke. "I received a cable. It said that *Wolf* and *Kondor* have been sighted in the Indian Ocean and the hunt has started there." He looked up at Smith and the eyes glittered. He had held it back to the end though it made the rest irrelevant.

Smith could not speak.

Garrick said, "Could easily be a mistake, sir. Some of these merchant chaps. . . ." His voice trailed away.

Thackeray said, "They're searching."

"I think it's time you went ashore, Mr. Thackeray." Garrick's voice held distaste.

Thackeray pulled his oilskin about him. "I'm not going ashore. I've booked a passage in the *Elizabeth Bell* as far as Guaya. I think it's time I compared notes with Mr. Cherry, particularly as he may be called home over this—this unfortunate affair."

Smith asked quietly, "Have you told Graham and Ballard?"

Thackeray knew what he meant—the cruisers being sighted in the Indian Ocean. He smiled. "No. I thought I'd leave that to you."

Garrick shouldered out of the cabin after Thackeray and Smith climbed up to the bridge. Aitkyne turned his back to the wind that hurled the rain in driving sheets and shouted, "They're both of them on the move, sir! Must have steam up!"

Smith nodded. He was aware that Garrick had muttered to Aitkyne and now both were watching him. They looked—sorry.

He said flatly, "*Elizabeth Bell* to lead at five knots, then *Ariadne* and we'll bring up the rear." The tramp was the slowest vessel. These were the dispositions he had decided before he reached Malaguay. He would play the game out to the end. "Make to *Elizabeth Bell:* Act on instructions from *Ariadne*. And to *Ariadne:* Pass all my orders to *Elizabeth Bell*."

THUNDER weighed and left her brief shelter and went to sea again, moving dead slow as she waited for the other two ships. They came beating out of the anchorage and plunging into the

64

big seas outside. In *Elizabeth Bell*'s lighted wheelhouse Smith saw Graham lift his bowler, and abaft the bridge a figure clung to a stanchion, skirt whipping out like a flag. Sarah Benson. He wondered why she was on deck in this weather.

Thunder was increasing speed and Smith ordered, "Make to *Ariadne* and *Elizabeth Bell:* Darken ship." Then he left the bridge and went below. He wanted to be alone.

HE WAS BACK ON the bridge before dawn and Garrick came to stand beside him and together they drank hot coffee and watched the blackness over the tossing sea turn to grey. Then it was full day and he could see his little convoy clearly, *Ariadne* heaving solidly, *Elizabeth Bell* plugging into the seas. Visibility was fair, no better than that, but it was enough.

Garrick hailed the masthead and the reply came back: "Nothing, sir, only *Ariadne* an' *Elizabeth Bell.*"

Smith heard it poker-faced. That was all that was left of his calm pose. He could not converse casually because he did not want to face his officers and to see their embarrassment and pity. They were at last on his side but now he had to stand alone. The whole ship seemed to tiptoe around him. He passed the long hours of the morning in thought and at the end could remember none of it. Only at the end his thoughts turned to coal and his need of it.

He had sunk two colliers filled with prime Welsh coal. And men. *My God, men!* But he still could not believe that his whole reasoning had been wrong.

It was long past noon and they would reach Guaya shortly after sunset. A sun that was bright but robbed of heat by the wind tightened his eyes. It seemed to smile on *Thunder* and on himself but it brought him no warmth nor comfort.

The call came down from the masthead: "*Ship bearing green one-six-oh!*"

7

The gale was blowing itself out. *Thunder* still rolled wildly but the sky was clearing and visibility was good.

On the bridge they could just see the ship now, a speck under the marking black banner of her smoke. The masthead look-out could see her better. *"She's a gunboat!"*

Garrick said, "She's making up on us, but slowly."

Knight ventured: "Maybe she isn't the German."

That was a possibility. Smith did not believe it. He turned away and lowered his glasses. He would know soon enough. *Elizabeth Bell* wallowed ahead, barely making eight knots. *Ariadne*, riding the waves better than either of the others could make another four or five knots in this sea. *Elizabeth Bell* had a crew of twenty-two. *Ariadne*'s crew and passengers totalled a hundred and thirty.

Once more the hail from the masthead: *"She's that German! Leopard!"* The look-outs had all seen the gunboat when she lay at Malaguay.

Smith said, "Mr. Knight. Make to *Ariadne*: Proceed independently at best speed'."

Knight was startled. There was only one gunboat, only just escaped from internment, unarmed. Smith could be sending *Ariadne* away in panic flight while the Germans laughed at the success of their bluff.

"*Ariadne* acknowledges, sir. And *Elizabeth Bell* signals: Am making best speed."

He was only too aware of it. Another man might have contrived a humorous reply but he did not feel humorous.

Ariadne's smoke thickened and she swung out to starboard and surged past the tramp and on towards the distant coast.

"Masthead! Smoke bearing green one-seven-oh! Astern of the gunboat!"

He could see the rest of his officers grouped on the after bridge with glasses and telescopes.

"Masthead! Looks like a four-funnel ship!"

Garrick bawled up, tight-nerved. "What the *hell* d'ye mean? *Looks like?*"

"She's near bows-on, sir, an' the smoke from that gunboat—"

Garrick fumed. Then the look-out bawled again, *"She's a four-funnel ship!"*

There was the end of doubt. A four-funnel ship meant a warship was closing on the gunboat. No doubt at all now. Smith thought that somehow they had got the word from Malaguay of the course he had taken out to sea and they had spread out in a wide, sweeping line with the gunboat taking the inshore station.

"*Masthead!* Two *four-funnel ships!*"

He stared up at the look-out then his eyes came slowly down. Once he stopped to fight he would never escape. *Thunder* faced impossible odds.

He found he was staring at Garrick and that the first lieutenant was grinning like an overgrown schoolboy. Aitkyne too. And Knight. All his officers seemed delighted, and then he realized it was for him, because he had been right about *Wolf* and *Kondor*. He caught a glimpse of young Wakely, flushed with excitement and laughing. Garrick said, "God knows who they're chasing in the Indian Ocean." He guffawed. There were few hours of daylight left but Smith thought they could all be dead by sunset.

On the bridge, throughout the ship, they expected orders. He gave none. He waited until he knew he would see the German ships. Only then did he lift the glasses to his eyes.

He saw them coming up under the smoke, a great deal of smoke, they were steaming for all they were worth. Bows on and superimposed as they were he could not distinguish their silhouettes, but he knew them. He lowered the glasses fractionally until the bucketing gunboat lurched into focus. Only nine hundred tons and with barely ten knots of speed, *Leopard* carried just a pair of four-inch guns. Except for them, with her flush deck she might be taken for a rich man's yacht. Yet she had sighted them, had pointed the finger. Without her he might have got away.

He turned his back to the enemy to stare ahead. *Thunder* plodded on at a laden eight knots while the pursuit, an enormously superior force, roared down on her at more than twice that speed. The reason, of course, was the *Elizabeth Bell*. She hung around his neck like an albatross. . . .

He could always abandon *Elizabeth Bell*.

Looked at coldly and logically it was the obvious course but he knew he could not do it. The sun was going down, already in his eyes as he turned aft again. The sun was going down but it would not set soon enough to save them.

Very well, then. "Number One!"

"Sir?" The reply was jerked out of Garrick. The jubilation on the bridge had turned to tension.

"I will want steam for full speed, and I want every man fed. There's time for a quick bite, say fifteen minutes."

Garrick ran from the bridge and Smith started to follow but paused by Aitkyne to say casually, "I'll be in my cabin, pilot. If there is any change in the situation no doubt you will let me know." He made his way below in leisurely fashion.

Boat-deck and upper-deck were crowded by the watch below, all eyes astern. One or two saw him stroll by and nudged each other. He was a cool one! But once in his cabin, alone, he opened the silhouette book and stared at it. That was not necessary. Now he could have drawn the silhouettes faithfully from memory.

They were faster and each of them carried eight 8.2-inch guns that were equal to *Thunder*'s 9.2-inch and she had only two of them. Sixteen to two. In a broadside fight they could fire twelve to two, even in a stern chase like this they would bring eight to bear against one. Between them they carried twelve 5.9-inch that outranged *Thunder*'s elderly six-inch guns. It was Sarah Benson who had said: "You can't fight them."

There was a tap at the door and Horsfall entered with a tray. "That there Benks, he's made sangwiches for all the gennelmen, bully beef an' a bit o' pickle an' I thought you might fancy a bottle o' pale ale." He set the tray on the table. "Looks as if we'll be busy later on. Anything particular you want?"

Smith shook his head. "No, thank you." Except another ten knots.

"Well. Might see you later on, sir."

Might. Smith looked up at Daddy's long horse-face. Daddy was under no illusions. Smith tapped the book. "Know this class of ship?"

Horsfall breathed over Smith's shoulder, then said simply, "Too bloody true, sir."

"Good luck, Horsfall."

"And the same to you, sir."

Smith drank the beer thirstily but he could not face the sandwiches. He returned to the bridge and moved out to the wing, staring aft. The two big cruisers were overhauling the gunboat

68

now. Ten miles away, maybe a little more. They were racing down in line abreast so both could fire with all guns that would bear forward. He grimaced and swung around. The coast looked no nearer and the sun seemed suspended, refusing to move down the sky. Neither sanctuary nor night to save them.

He ordered, "Sound 'General quarters'."

Thunder's crew boiled into life and ran to their action stations. The reports began to come in as the guns' crews closed up, magazines were manned and all the hundred and one posts necessary to *Thunder's* functioning as a fighting ship were filled.

Garrick went to the fore-top. *Thunder's* fire control like everything else about her was outdated. She had a rangefinder and a device to calculate deflection and that was all. The guns received range and deflection through navyphones and from then on it was up to the layers and trainers to lay and train the gun. Garrick in the fore-top watched for the fall of shot and issued orders to correct it if it was over or short.

Smith stayed on the bridge. In the conning-tower below they would have the protection of that eleven-inch-thick armour plate but Smith wanted to see as much as he could. If he could neither run nor fight with any hope then he would have to seek an alternative. He thought this was the place to seek it.

"Make to *Elizabeth Bell:* Copy my changes of course." *Elizabeth Bell* acknowledged. The reports were finished and the ship was quiet, her decks deserted.

The sea was moderating. It was a lovely evening. Smith stared at the two four-funnelled ships, eyes narrowed against the sun but still able to make them out under the thick black smoke. God! They were steaming! He lowered the glasses. "Steer four points to starboard."

"Four points to starboard, sir."

Thunder's bow swung through the arc, pointing away from *Elizabeth Bell.*

"Midships."

"Midships, sir."

Thunder steadied on the new course. Smith glanced at the *Elizabeth Bell*, she was turning to parallel *Thunder's* course and was now on the port bow. Smith saw light flicker on the cruisers again and smoke shred. The first salvo howled down and the sea erupted astern of *Thunder* in four tall columns.

"Hard a'port!"

"Hard a'port, sir!"

"Midships!"

"Midships, sir!"

Now *Thunder* was on the opposite leg of the zigzag. *Elizabeth Bell* should follow. She didn't. Smith snarled, "Come on, damn you!" The second salvo was on its way, plunging now. He snapped, "Make to *Elizabeth Bell*—"

He did not finish. The second salvo rushed over them and burst, water lifting, noise beating at them. And Knight shouted, "God! She's copped one!" The *Elizabeth Bell* had taken a direct hit amidships and another forward, each from a two-hundred-and-forty pound projectile plunging at a near vertical angle. She listed immediately and her bow went down; smoke billowed, sparks flying in it and flames leaping beneath it.

"Hard a'starboard!" And: "Midships!" And *Thunder* raced down on the *Elizabeth Bell*, now lying like a log and going down by the head. Smith rattled off orders to a string of rapid acknowledgements. "Slow ahead both! Dead slow! I want to edge alongside . . . ! Mr. Knight, I want lines over the side and strong men on them. Warn the doctor to expect survivors."

"Aye, aye, sir!"

"Open fire!"

He heard that last passed to Garrick. Seconds later the after 9.2 recoiled, spat flame and smoke and the *crack!* racketed through the ship.

Thunder closed the *Elizabeth Bell*, slowing. He could see a party on her superstructure just forward of the gaping hole in her deck that poured forth smoke. They were trying to lower a boat as the ship tilted, her bows already under water. He snatched the megaphone and ran out to the port wing of the bridge. He lifted the megaphone as a third salvo crashed down into the sea beyond *Elizabeth Bell*, hurling more tons of water aboard her to hasten her already horribly swift end. She was awash as far aft as the superstructure and sinking before his eyes. *Thunder*'s bow slid by her stern, creeping along her starboard side. Knight and his men were swarming along the rails right forward and hurling the lines far ahead, fishing for the survivors on the tramp's heeling superstructure. Smith picked out the flutter of a skirt. The Benson girl. He bellowed through the megaphone, "Take the lines! We'll haul you aboard!"

He moved up to them, over them, as *Thunder*, dead slow, ground forward. Through the swirling smoke from *Thunder*'s four funnels and the huge hole in the deck of *Elizabeth Bell* he saw the skirt fly like a flag as the girl seized a line.

The after 9.2 roared again. The stern of the *Elizabeth Bell* lifted and Smith saw Sarah Benson tying the line around a man who lay on the deck. He saw through the smoke another man leave the deck of *Thunder* at the end of a line and run down her side, as the seamen above him paid out the line. It was Somers and Smith saw him lunge at the girl as the man she helped was whipped away on the line and as the stern of the tramp reared and she went down.

A salvo burst and Wakely said behind him, "Short!"

They had dawdled only minutes but that was too long, far too long.

The *Elizabeth Bell* stood on her head, slid down with a roar of escaping steam and dull thumping explosions. Leaning far out Smith could see only six, no seven, figures swinging on the lines as they were hauled in and one of them was Somers and another Sarah Benson.

Another salvo roared over and burst in high spouts of upflung water, off the port bow and over by less than a hundred yards.

One under, one over. It was time; high time. He bellowed through the megaphone, "Mr. Knight! Get 'em *aboard*!" Knight and the men with him were doing their best but he could give them not a second more. "Full ahead both! Hard a'starboard!" He strode across the bridge as the helm went over.

That was when the shell burst right before the fore-turret. The impact was a hammer blow, shaking the ship, deafening. The flash seared his eyes and splinters whined around the upper works of the ship. Smith was thrown against the telegraph, bounced off, staggered, grabbed at his cap. There was smoke and flames but the fore-turret seemed intact. Forward the deck was ripped open. Petty Officer Miles and his damage control and fire-fighting party came running towards the hole, canvas hose snaking behind them.

Wakely squeaked, "Engine room reports no damage, sir!"

"Very good. What about the fore-turret?" And: "*Messenger!* Ask Mr. Miles for a report on the damage forward, and quick!"

Hit or no hit, *Thunder* was working up speed now. Smith turned to peer through the smoke astern and saw the cruisers grown larger, orange flashes prickling together. "Hard a'port!" . . . "Midships!"

From the wing of the bridge he could see Knight and his party and the survivors from the *Elizabeth Bell.* Sarah Benson was there, bent over someone lying on the deck. Knight knelt beside her.

Smith bellowed, "Mister Knight! What the *hell* are you doing?"

Knight jumped to his feet. "One of the survivors, sir. A splinter got him. I think he's dead."

"You won't do anything for him laying on hands! The doctor's below. Get them all down to him and yourself up here." Sarah Benson's white face turned up to him, outraged. Smith bellowed, "This ship is in *action*, for God's sake!"

To underline his words the after 9.2 out-bellowed him and another salvo howled down into the sea to starboard, close enough to hurl water in tons across *Thunder*'s deck, knocking the damage control party from their feet but helping to put out the fire they fought.

Smith swung back to the centre of the bridge. "Hard a'starboard!" *Thunder* turned on another leg of the zigzag. Starboard, port, starboard . . . *Thunder* was steaming for her life and closing slowly on *Ariadne*, running for the coast and safety.

But *Wolf* and *Kondor,* running straight, were overhauling *Thunder*. They had left the gunboat astern. He watched the cruisers and their firing and ordered the changes of course.

In the fore-turret young Gibb stood at his post, pale but trying to be still. Rattray grinned at him madly and looked right into his terrified soul, and Gibb knew it.

Knight returned to the bridge and Smith was aware of him without looking as a salvo fell to starboard and spray slashed across them. "Hard a'starboard! Mr. Knight! What was young Somers doing over the side? He was ordered closed up at his station in action."

"He says he knew there was no question of his gun firing because it was out of range."

Smith said grimly, "I'll see him later." And dress him down because it would be good for his soul, but it had been an act of deliberate bravery, a decision coolly taken and executed with speed and determination. He would mention Somers in his report.

If he made a report.

Aitkyne said, "I think that boy will make an admiral."

Smith grunted. Aitkyne might be right.

He saw the cruisers fire and ordered the change of course as the after 9.2 fired. He had noted the fall of its shot the last three times it had fired and was certain it was within range of the cruisers now but off for line. He could guess at the gunners' frustration—who were they? Hill—Corporal Hill and Private Bowker of the Marines. They had the same low, blinding sun that hurt Smith's eyes and on top of that *Thunder*'s smoke, belching out now she was running at full speed and rolling down over the after-turret and astern, blacking out the target. Add to that the continual sharp changes of course that meant big switches on the gun, continual relaying and training and an unstable platform. Conditions for gunnery were appalling. Another salvo burst frighteningly close.

Aitkyne said, "They're shooting very well."

"Yes, they are." And they were alive to his tactics of evasion and trying to anticipate them.

He ordered no change of course. The coxswain on the wheel shifted restlessly when it did not come. Corporal Hill, muttering under his breath, expecting it, found instead that his target was in sight for all of ten seconds and the 9.2 got off a round.

The next salvo plunged into the sea a quarter-mile away and Aitkyne yelled, "Fooled 'em!" And seconds later: "Hit her!"

Smith had seen it, too. He lowered his glasses. "Hard a'port!" And to Aitkyne and Wakely and the others, "Not a hit." The waterspout had been right on the bow of the leading cruiser but there had been no flash or smoke of impact. A very near miss. "But good shooting."

The sun was slipping below the horizon. The Guaya coast was close now but not close enough. *Ariadne* was a deal closer and her

73

lead being cut every second; *Thunder* was making all of her top speed of nineteen knots so Chief Davies had proved his claim. Smith estimated *Ariadne* would not enter neutral waters for at least fifteen minutes. Before that they would be up with her and the cruisers might well allot her a share of their fire. At the moment they were concentrating on *Thunder*, their prime target. He had another decision to make, and soon.

The sea was moderating and the ship was making better speed. Down in the belly of the ship where that speed was created the stokers, stripped near-naked and oily with sweat that formed a glue with the coal dust, laboured to feed the roaring red furnaces. In the magazine below the forward 9.2, Benks the steward sweated coldly, waiting for the inevitable hit, his job to load the charge into the gun-loading cage to be whisked up the hoist to the turret above. Seeing only the thick steel above his head that sealed him in, he prayed.

Thunder twisted her old frame at thrashing full speed, swerving, heavily jinking, like some lumbering old nanny playing tag with her charges. But effectively. Barely effectively. The cruisers astern had her range and were firing well, very well indeed. Time and again only the change of course hauled *Thunder* clear. At times she seemed to steam through a forest of tall trees, dark green in the trunk and blossoming dirty grey, through a fog of spray.

She bore a charmed life; or maybe she had a wizard on the bridge. On the bridge they thought so as they braced against the heel and turn. They lived from second to second and he gave them each second and they knew it.

He had to make his decision. The luck was running out as the range closed. Knight said, "They're firing their secondary armament, sir."

The fire had intensified. Now added to the four 8.2s that each cruiser fired were the two 5.9s that would bear forward in this stern chase. *Thunder* could reply only with the after 9.2, her elderly six-inch being still just out of range.

The coast was close but so was *Ariadne*, very close, with a hundred and thirty souls aboard her. Sunset was upon them, the darkness rushing in over the sea. Smith watched and gave his orders. They had to give *Ariadne* a little more time.

He snapped, "Hard a'starboard!" and *Thunder*'s bow swung and this time kept on swinging until, when he ordered, "Midships!" she ran at a right angle to her previous course and that of the pursuit. The turrets were already drumming as they trained round. And the sun was down. Smith took a breath. Now then. "Broadsides!"

Thunder still charged along at her maximum nineteen knots but she was running straight. She still belched smoke from the labour of the gasping, sweating stokers but now it rolled away to port on the wind and at last the layers and trainers could see. The sun was down, no longer sending shafts of blinding light directly into their eyes, but leaving instead just a red afterglow against which the pursuing cruisers stood out stark, clear black silhouettes, beautiful targets for gunners and the rangefinder.

She left one more salvo plummeting into her wake as the guns rose and fell like a blind man's questing fingers but *Thunder* was no longer blind. The long barrels steadied and an instant later the salvo bells rang and the broadside crashed out in tongues of flame and jetting smoke. *Thunder* heeled to it, recovered as the guns had already recoiled. In turrets shells were rammed, charges inserted, breeches closed, trainers and layers spun madly at their wheels then slowly as the sights came on. The layers' fingers went to the triggers.

Thunder fired again, heeled again.

Wakely said, "They're turning, sir, turning broadside."

Smith nodded. The cruisers were matching his manoeuvre to return broadside for broadside. It was what he expected and Garrick in the fore-top would be expecting it. The cruisers had an overwhelming advantage in firepower, but they were no longer closing the range. That was what he wanted.

Now it was up to the gunnery jack, Garrick, and the long chain of men that stretched down from him in the fore-top to the layers with their fingers on the triggers. He had given them a target they could see and a stable platform.

He had given *Ariadne* time.

Given? Nothing was free. Somebody would have to pay.

Thunder got off three broadsides and two salvoes fell in return, one short but close, briefly interfering with vision, one very short.

They were laddering, of course, in *Wolf* and *Kondor*, one salvo at the rangefinder range, one below it, one over. The third would be over—or a hit. This clicked through his mind as that second salvo hurled water at the darkening sky and as *Thunder*'s broadside heeled her again and the flashes of the cruisers' salvoes rippled with awful beauty along the black silhouettes.

"Hard a'port!" *Thunder* heeled again but this time turning in her tracks to plunge back along her course as the turrets hammered round. The third salvo came down on the port quarter, where *Thunder* would have been but for the violent change of course, but one rogue shell burst so close that the blow was felt through the hull. Corporal Hill felt it in the after-turret and swore. Benks felt it in the magazine and quivered.

Thunder steadied on her new course.

In the fore-top Garrick was a happy man. He had a good target at last and his guns were shooting well. He also noted with professional appreciation that the enemy cruisers were firing well. He could not judge the "overs" that fell somewhere behind him but the "shorts" were well together with little spread. It was good shooting, frighteningly good. He was aware also that *Thunder* was a broadside target. Out on the wing of the bridge Smith lifted the glasses again to watch for the next salvo's fall. It dropped into the sea well astern.

Wakely said tentatively, "Their shooting's going off a bit, sir."

"No." Smith's eyes were clamped to the glasses. "He's having trouble seeing us." The glow behind the cruisers was dying but they were still clear against it, while to them *Thunder* must be a ship lost in the darkness, only a black pall of smoke against the black background of the coast and the night sky.

Wakely yelped, "A hit!"

"Yes!" Smith saw the flash on the leading cruiser that was not the flash of a gun, and a second later the thread of smoke that trailed on.

But the salvo rippled again down the silhouette.

Thunder fired.

Knight called, "Signal from *Ariadne*, sir: Am in Chilean waters under escort. Looks like a Chilean destroyer lying off there, sir, lit up like a Christmas tree!"

Smith swung on his heel, staring. He could barely make out the bulk of *Ariadne* but the other ship was easy to see, a blaze of light. A Chilean destroyer.

Aitkyne said, "She's not taking any chances of somebody dropping one on her by mistake."

And Wakely reported, "Enemy's turning, sir."

Smith swung back. The black silhouettes were blurring now as the last of the light went but they had foreshortened, were again pointing at him, again in pursuit trying desperately to close the range. They, too, had seen the Chilean ship and knew what her presence signified. They fired.

As did *Thunder*.

Smith rubbed at his face. *Ariadne* was safe. He stared around him, at the wake creaming phosphorescent in the dusk, the dark ship. Black humping sea and black sky, tongues of orange flame, the ensign snapping a pale blur against the smoke that swirled down from the funnels and rolled away downwind, mixing with the acrid grey-yellow of the gunsmoke. The last glow almost gone from the distant rim of the ocean, the cruisers almost invisible.

One more broadside. These men of his had earned that.

He saw the cruisers' winking fire and then *Thunder*'s broadside heeled her for the last time. As the echoes crashed away in a concussion of air, Smith ordered, "Starboard ten! Cease firing!" The cruisers were no longer a target, hardly seen. The only way they would see *Thunder* would be from the flashes of her guns. He would not give them that opportunity.

He watched for the fall of the last broadsides.

The cruisers' landed first. Familiar spouts rose off the port quarter but the shells that counted were the ones that hit them. There was a blinding burst of livid flame and shock that sent him grabbing for handhold. He recovered his balance and gaped aft. There was smoke abaft the bridge but no flames. The unmistakable long figure of Miles ran aft with huge strides, his damage control party at his heels.

Smith thought he should have turned sooner and not hung on for their own last broadside. He lifted the glasses, looking for it.

Aitkyne shouted, "Hit her, by God!"

Smith saw the winking yellow flash on the cruiser to port, right

77

forward, the ship seen in that one camera-blink of light, then almost lost in the darkness as the night swept down over the sea. But flames flickered, tiny with distance, again. She had a fire.

Aitkyne crowed, "Gave 'em a bloody nose to remember us by!"

A seaman panted up the bridge ladder. "Mr. Miles, sir, says two hits, fire's out, wireless office wrecked but no casualties." A grin: "Sparks was away for a run-off when it 'it. An' no serious damage."

Smith took a deep breath and let it out. They had been lucky. He wondered if the rest of them really knew how lucky. . . .

Soon they came abreast of the Chilean destroyer lying in her pool of light. *Thunder*'s speed fell away. She was opening the channel into Guaya now. *Ariadne* lay ahead of them, dawdling, beyond her were the lights of the signalling station. *Thunder* ran down on *Ariadne* whose rails were crowded with crew and passengers and as *Thunder* slid past, smoke-blackened, torn, filthy, they cheered her.

Thunder's decks were alive with men now, swarming like bees, wide-eyed and short of breath but they cheered also and kept on cheering when *Ariadne* was left astern.

Their faces were turned up to the bridge.

Smith realized they were cheering him.

Garrick was down from the fore-top, grinning at him. Aitkyne and Wakely and Knight, all of them on the bridge wore the same drunken grin. Smith thought how they had settled the colliers, brought *Ariadne* safe to port, rescued at least some of the people from the luckless *Elizabeth Bell* and fought a long action against a faster and vastly superior force. They had survived to fight again, and were legally entitled even as a fighting ship to shelter for twenty-four hours. They had a lot to be pleased about.

He felt sick and his hands were starting to shake as they always did at such times. He jammed them in his pockets. He wanted his voice to be casual but it came out harsh and abrupt. "I'm going below, Number One. Set the men to work on the damage." At the head of the ladder he paused to say, "And well done."

He saw Garrick's expression had changed and that a messenger was with him. Garrick said, "Report of a casualty, sir."

"Yes?"

"It was when we were hit aft, sir. A section of plate must have

78

ricocheted and flew in the open door of the port after casemate." Smith stared at Garrick as he fumbled for words. "A chance in a million, sir. Young Somers. . . ." Then he put it brutally simply. "It cut him in half."

Smith turned, desperate to be away, and descended the ladder.

Somers. That last hit aft. If he had turned away before . . .

He strode the deck until he walked his bitterness away. He was sick at Somers's death, but it was a fact to be faced. He had a duty.

He went to the sick-bay and Albrecht greeted him with, "Oh, sir. The girl we picked up from *Elizabeth Bell*. My sick-bay attendant dug up some clothes for her, stuff that she left behind; she went over the side at Malaguay at short notice." Albrecht went on: "I put her in your cabin to get dressed. Hope you don't mind, but there was nowhere else, a lot of the cabins are in a mess and I could hardly ask. . . ."

Smith grunted. Then he got down to business. "What have you got?"

"One crushed finger and two cases of mild concussion. That's the crew. There are five survivors if you include the girl. One deck officer and three deck-hands. Shock, all of them. Except that girl. She's tough."

A picture of her rose in his mind. Tough indeed. He came back to the matter in hand. He saw the cases of concussion and the survivors and spoke to them briefly. Neither Captain Graham nor Thackeray, that twisted, bitter man, was among them. To his crew: "Well done." To the survivors: condolences, awkward sympathy and a promise to get them ashore and into hospital as soon as possible.

He returned to the deck. *Thunder* cruised steadily up the deep-water channel past the little scatters of lights that marked villages. The ship was not darkened now. Garrick had lights rigged forward and aft and men milled in urgent, disciplined confusion. He encountered Wakely. "I want the fires lit in the pinnace, Mr. Wakely, ready to put her in the water as soon as we anchor."

"Already seen to that, sir. Manton thought you might want her."

"Good."

Both forward and aft the damage was at first sight horrendous. Forward a hole gaped in the deck and below it the mess-deck was a devastated area, filthy with soot from the fire, dripping with water. Aft a huge bite had been taken out of deck and side. There was a great deal of work to be done, most of it ultimately dockyard work, but there was nothing that could not be patched by *Thunder*'s crew well enough to render her a fully effective unit, appearances not withstanding. He found the work well in hand, which he had a right to expect, but when he ran into Garrick he made a point of saying, clearly and loudly, with a score of men in earshot: "Very good, Number One. The ship's company have behaved in very satisfactory fashion." It sounded pompous to Smith as he said it but Garrick seemed pleased, as did the men.

Garrick said, "Chaps are in good spirits, sir."

Smith nodded. He was keenly aware of it. They were working hard and cheerfully. Joking. There was occasional laughter, some of it a little high-pitched, still excited, but laughter.

Then they rounded the turn in the channel, and opened the port and the pool. Smith took his ship to her anchorage neatly, with his usual insistence that a job be well done, but he was preoccupied with the thought that his ship was not welcome here. A reminder was there in the way the masts of the *Gerda* poked out of the water where she had settled on the bottom. They would be attacked, not with crude force but certainly in diplomatic terms.

He was not inclined to wait for that attack. So that, as *Thunder* anchored, the telegraph rang "stop engines", and the derrick yanked the pinnace over the side, he said, "I'm going ashore."

Garrick followed him down to the entry port. "You're going alone, sir? Do you want Knight as interpreter?"

"No." The port captain would make his feelings clear without an interpreter and it would be unpleasant so he would go alone.

It was night, now. Darkness hid the hills but the town twinkled with the yellow cats-eyes of a thousand lit windows. Half a dozen ships lay in the pool but *Kansas* loomed over them all. The picket-boat, at Smith's order, headed for the quay which was lit by one big lamp. He could see a crowd there. He stood quiet, still, alongside Wakely who had the helm.

The cruisers waited for him outside. His choice was to fight them or be interned. He had coal for only twenty-four hours' steaming. Suicide or surrender.

80

They ran in on the quay. Two boats already lay there, tied up clear of the steps. One belonged to the Chilean admiral, the other to *Kansas*. *Thunder*'s pinnace slipped between them and Smith climbed the steps. At their head he found the crowd and in the forefront stood a little party. There were several women, all in evening dress. The men were also in evening dress or full-dress uniform, black or navy-blue. The Chilean admiral and the American, Rear-Admiral Donoghue. And Donoghue's flag-captain and two young men who were obviously the respective Chilean and American flag-lieutenants. All glittered with decorations.

He saluted and smiled at them all. "Good evening. I seem to have interrupted a party. I'm sorry." Soot streaked his face and his eyes were red-rimmed and staring.

Encalada, the port captain, fluent in English, almost choked at that opening remark, and for a moment was bereft of speech. The Chilean admiral had not understood a word, but he scowled at Smith all the same. The American flag-lieutenant slipped into the gap. "If I may be permitted, sir, I have some Spanish."

He made the introductions, rolling off the titles in English and Spanish spectacularly: "Contra Almirante Gualcalda, the Navy of Chile, Rear-Admiral Donoghue, United States Navy, Captain Encalada . . ." One of the party was Herr Doktor Müller, the German Consul, tall and stiff, bald and hook-nosed. The flag-lieutenant came to the end of the titles and ranks. Then he stumbled, "And Commander—?"

Smith supplied it for him, tersely. "Smith."

Donoghue grinned, noticing the contrast. He said, "You didn't exactly interrupt. We were having dinner when we heard the firing, but in the tradition of Drake we finished the meal. Then we came down to see what we could." His eyes moved from Smith to *Thunder* lying in a circle of light out in the pool, aswarm with men. Through the hole torn in her side he could see the men labouring in the smashed interior. His eyes moved back to Smith.

One more contrast. Donoghue, tall, broad-shouldered, strongly handsome, saw a slight, young man, too thin, the face drawn. He cut a frail and lonely figure as he faced them all. And yet—there was something about the man, a restlessness, an energy that could be sensed even now when he stood unmoving.

They eyed each other warily.

Donoghue said, "I see you brought your consort safe to port."

"*Ariadne*? Yes. But we lost a merchantman, the *Elizabeth Bell*. She was hit and sank in minutes. I'm glad I was able to take off some of her crew before she sank, but the others were lost."

Donoghue thought about it. Smith had been able to take some off. The American thought there was a deal left unsaid.

But that saw the end of the courtesies. Encalada asked, "What is your business here, Captain?" He was still angry. Forty-eight hours before he had been outraged.

Smith met the attack coolly. "I escorted *Ariadne* to this port. As you know and can see, I have been in action and I need to make repairs and coal—"

Encalada brushed that aside with a wave of his hand. "Your presence here is effrontery! You have flagrantly violated the neutrality of this port!"

"This port harboured a belligerent for—"

"That has *not* been proved."

The Herr Doktor put in quickly, "I reiterate, neither my government nor myself accept responsibility for the collier, whosoever she was."

Smith rapped at him, "Responsibility or no, the *Gerda* was a belligerent and that was proved by the action of her sister ship, the *Maria*. She ran when I approached Malaguay." Müller smiled thinly, and shrugged. Smith said, "I caught her and sank her."

This time the Doktor's eyes flickered, his head twitched. Small signs but enough for Smith, who went on, "And before she sank I intercepted signals between her and a German warship, and two German cruisers lie outside this port now. That is a *fact*, Herr Doktor." He swung on Encalada. "As was also the matter of the *Leopard*, a German gunboat supposed to be interned at Malaguay but allowed to slip away to fight again and *she* is outside now! What kind of neutrality is *that*?"

"Do not lecture *me!*" Encalada shouted it. He swallowed, took hold of himself and said more quietly, "She was not allowed to slip away. She escaped because of gross negligence and indiscipline on the part of one junior officer and he will be dealt with. And that gunboat's violation of neutrality does not excuse

82

yours, which preceded theirs and I believe made theirs possible. Cruisers there are but I refuse to accept their presence as proof that *Gerda* was a belligerent." He took a breath. "I tell you this, Captain. Under international law you may claim shelter in this port for twenty-four hours to make your repairs. That you may have, but nothing else. You will not be permitted to land nor to receive supplies of any kind, coal, water—*nothing!*"

Smith said equably, "Very well." He would not beg. No, that was a lie. He would have begged for his ship and his crew if it would have done any good. But they did not need water or supplies. He had coal for only twenty-four hours' steaming but that was sufficient because he would not be allowed to steam for twenty-four hours or anything like it. The cruisers waiting out in the darkness of the Pacific would see to that.

Encalada took out his watch. "The time is twenty-one-ten hours. At this time tomorrow you will get under way and quit this port."

"That is understood. I ask for nothing, except—"

"No exceptions!"

Smith carried on as if he had not heard. "There is a boy—a man—I must bury. He was killed in today's action."

Encalada stared at him. Smith's face was grey under the lights, a tired face, a hard face, closed now, seeming to give nothing away, yet the port captain felt the stirring of an alien sympathy. But he kept his voice hard as he replied. "I see. That will be permitted but only a small party, the minimum necessary for due honours. Officers may wear swords, but no other arms."

"That, too, is understood." Smith thought there might be an element of sympathy lurking in Donoghue's eyes. An idea floated, bizarre, into Smith's mind. He said straight-faced, apologetic but patently sincere, "I'm afraid I've spoiled a pleasant evening for many of you. In normal times I would have extended the hospitality of my ship, at least to attempt to make some recompense, but these are not normal times. However. Despite the times my officers and myself will be taking tea tomorrow afternoon and we would be delighted to welcome all of you. At, say, four in the afternoon?" Then he added, "With, of course, one obvious exception." He grinned at Müller.

Those who understood him looked suspicious, as if this was

some sort of practical joke, or like Encalada suspecting a trap, but not Donoghue. As Smith saluted and went down into the pinnace Donoghue thought it was almost an actor's exit. An unusual young man. He wasn't going to drink their goddam tea, but he wanted to look at that ship and her crew.

The pinnace sheered off and headed out towards *Thunder*, still functioning with a jaunty efficiency despite the dents in her stumpy funnel and her woodwork down one side showing charred-black through the blistered paint. Donoghue gazed after it and thought with surprise: Well, now.

SMITH SAID, "They've given us twenty-four hours and at the end of that we sail. That's all they'll give us. No coal, no supplies, no assistance—nothing. It simplifies matters, anyway."

Garrick breathed heavily. "They know what's waiting for us outside and they'll send us out with barely enough coal—"

"It will be enough."

"Damn their bloody eyes!"

Smith blinked at this explosion from the stolid first lieutenant, and said mildly, "You can't blame them, you know. On the facts as they see them, as they know them, they're more than justified."

One of the midshipmen called up, "Boat coming alongside, sir."

It was Cherry, and Smith took him to the little sleeping cabin under the bridge. There was a certain amount of peace there from the hammering all over the ship. "I didn't see you at the party."

"No." Cherry shrugged. "The British are in bad odour at the moment. But I heard about your meeting with Encalada."

"Oh?"

Cherry nodded. "Twenty-four hours. And the rest of it. I'll intercede and protest, of course. I'll telegraph to Santiago, but frankly, I think their government will back him up."

"So do I."

Cherry said helplessly, "Well, is there *anything* I can do?"

"One or two ways you can help—Somers."

They discussed the matter in practical terms and Cherry said he would see to all the necessary arrangements. "Anything else?"

"Newspapers, as always. Any English papers you can get hold of, we'll be delighted to see."

84

"Can do."

"And last, but most important, the *Gerda*. The Chileans regard my action as indefensible, but if I can *prove* she was German they might change that." He told Cherry the details of the sinking of the *Gerda* and the papers they had taken from her. "Somewhere aboard that ship there must be proof. Has a diver been down?"

Cherry shook his head, puzzled. "No. One of my men has been watching her. Nobody's been near her." He finished definitely, "But tomorrow I'll see somebody goes down. If the proof is there we'll have it."

Cherry left, on his way to see Sarah Benson.

THEY HAD SET Gibb to work with the others in the clanging bedlam forward and every hammer blow was a nerve-wrenching echo of the hits on *Thunder*. There was no peace. And he had found Rattray's eyes on him once and knew that Rattray only waited his time. . . . He needed solitude and he could think of only one place in the ship where he could find it. He slunk round and into the fore-turret and in the airless steel gloom he squatted on the deck under the breech of the gun, head down, eyes closed, trying to blot it all out.

At that moment light flicked briefly over him as the door opened again, then clanged shut. Gibb blinked and focused on the figure that stood smacking right fist into the palm of the left hand. Rattray.

He took two long strides to stand over Gibb. "Home from home," he said savagely. "Just you and me and a bit of peace and quiet where we can sort things out without a lot of interference from nosey parkers, nor your God Almighty Captain Smith." The words meant nothing to Gibb.

Rattray reached down and grabbed him by the front of his overalls, swung him out from his hiding place. He hesitated for a second, seeing Gibb's face contort beyond recognition. It was a fatal second.

Gibb exploded in his hands. Gibb himself could never recall the few seconds that followed. It was a moment of black-out for his mind that under stress briefly ran away from its duties. The body functioned on its own.

A flailing fist caught Rattray in the eye and another in the lower abdomen, a boot smashed against his right shin and knocked that prop from under him. Then his back banged against the breech of the gun and he bounced from it into another hail of blows that landed at first on his body and then, as he fell, on his face and head. He was already unconscious and toppled back limply, his shoulders propped awkwardly against the side of the turret.

Gibb had nothing to hit. The curtain lifted and he saw Rattray. He stared, then retched, ran blindly from the turret, and brought up against the ship's rail, staring at the lights of Guaya. Rattray was dead and he had killed him.

Voices shouted hoarsely in the clamour forward, sounding like a pack at his heels, but the water moved oily black below him. He went over the rail and dived.

There was a crowd on the waterfront staring at *Thunder*, so he had to swim a long way down-river before he could drag himself out of the water without being seen. He skulked across the quay and into the shelter of an alley. The water ran off him. He found a dark corner and collapsed there, shuddering spasmodically.

Now at last he had quiet—but he knew he had to get away from prying eyes. He had never been to Fizzy's out-of-bounds bar but he knew where it was. He made his way through the alleys until he found the rear of Fizzy's Bar, and climbed the wall at the back of the house, and tapped at the first window he came to. He was lucky, a girl was in the room, alone. She pulled back the curtain and stared at him, a hand to her mouth. Then came recognition that he was a seaman and she smiled.

She opened the window and he climbed in. She threw up her hands in horror at his condition and rattled a spate of Spanish at him. His legs gave way under him and he sank down on the bed. He held up a hand weakly to stem the flow and laid his head on the pillow, miming sleep. She nodded and held out her hand. He fumbled money from his belt and she took it all. He said, "No tell. No one." And put a finger to his lips.

The girl peered at him, puzzled, then shrugged, hid the money, undressed and blew out the lamp. She climbed into bed, shoving him over, and in minutes she was asleep. It was not until dawn that he sank into an uneasy doze.

· Aboard *Thunder* the work went on through the night and into the day, the crew working watch and watch. At Smith's orders he was called when the watch was changed and inspected the work and talked with the men.

Garrick reported unhappily, "Able Seaman Rattray and Ordinary Seaman Gibb are missing from this working party, sir. They could have gone over the side. Gibb was a very good swimmer."

Smith bit his lip. He did not want to believe it. "Together? They don't sound a likely pair."

"No, sir. That's a fact."

"Well, make a search but quietly. I don't want this blown up." There could be others who might find desertion preferable to facing the cruisers. God knew he could sympathize but he had a duty, and so did his crew.

It was Albrecht who first found Rattray, on his way to the sickbay. "What happened to you?" he said, staring at him.

"Accident, sir. Fell down in the fore-turret."

Albrecht did not question the fatuous excuse: Rattray could have fallen a dozen times in the fore-turret and sustained fewer injuries. Albrecht said only, "Very well." And it was some time later before Rattray thought there might be some ambiguity in that simple remark.

Smith was at his desk before dawn. There was a letter to be written to Captain Graham's widow, another to Somers's parents. Then he wrote his report, adding his commendations of Garrick for the gunnery, and Somers. He was uncomfortable in full dress now with his cap and sword on the desk because later he had a formal duty.

As he finished he thought cynically that it would bring none of them honour or glory. It was a bald recital of a ship that had run for cover, been hit only twice and suffered but a single casualty—a decidedly unspectacular affair to the reader. It did not mention that every man aboard and many ashore thought he had performed a miracle, for the simple reason that he did not know it. But he would not have said so anyway.

He thought the next report would be a very different matter but he would not be writing it. He wondered what those men of his would think of him then, if any of them survived. They would know he had failed them. They followed him and asked for nothing but they were entitled to a fighting chance and they would not get it.

He pulled his head from his hands as Garrick knocked and was straight-faced though cold-eyed when the first lieutenant said, "Burial party ready, sir."

"Very well."

"And Leading Seaman Bates and Sergeant Burton ask to see you on a personal matter, sir. They say it's very urgent."

Smith said, "Send them in." And when they stood before him, "I hope this is a serious matter."

Bates said, "It's about young Gibb, sir. There's more to it than meets the eye. I don't reckon him as a deserter. Course, he had the wind up like all of us but I reckon there's more to it than that."

"What?"

"Dunno, sir. But I reckon I could get him to tell me. If we could sneak ashore and bring him back, 'cause I know where he'll be, I could get the truth out o' him. *Please*, sir." Bates was pleading because Smith's head was already moving in a slow negative.

It was too wild a scheme. Smith sympathized—like Bates he sensed that Gibb was no deserter. But—

Burton broke in. "There's only one place he *can* be, sir. Fizzy's Bar. That's the only place he'll know and the only one as might hide him. We'd land downstream, clear o' the town and we could get to the place by the back way. We'll wear old clothes. Should be easy."

Smith pushed up from his desk and shifted restlessly across the cabin to stand at the open scuttle staring out. He stood there a long time. Then he turned. "It will not be as easy as you think. Now, listen to me. . . ."

When Smith took up his cap and sword and went on deck he found the day again in mourning with scarcely a breath of wind and the sky overcast, grey. The flag-draped coffin rested aft by the accommodation ladder. The party was a small one. There were eight pallbearers, seamen from Somers's battery, at their own request. There was Kennedy and a boy bugler, sixteen years old, even younger than Somers had been.

The bugler sounded the "Still", work ceased and the ship's company froze into immobility. They lowered the coffin into the pinnace and the burial party went ashore and disembarked on the quay under the eyes of a considerable crowd, who were curious but quiet. There was a glass-sided hearse pulled by a pair of black-plumed, black horses, and a large escort of Chilean soldiers, seeming more guard than escort. And there was Cherry. As the seamen loaded the coffin into the hearse, Smith muttered to him, "I need more time."

Cherry shook his head. "They won't—"

"I think they might. My essential repairs will barely be completed at dusk. I want until six in the morning, but tell them I'll move up to Stillwater Cove as soon as repairs are complete and I'll leave the river by six."

"It will be broad day!"

"What difference does it make? They have a gunboat patrolling the mouth of the river and I can't pass her unseen, however dark the night."

"It will make a difference to *them*, surely?" And Cherry was talking about the cruisers. "They will be able to lie off and engage you at extreme range, twelve guns to your two."

"Then Müller won't oppose such a request. And the Chileans don't want a night engagement virtually on their doorstep."

Cherry murmured thoughtfully, "Ye-es. It might well be. . . ." He stopped, then finished apologetically, "Of course you know your own business best."

"I hope so."

The cortège was ready.

They marched behind the hearse out to the cemetery, that was the graveyard of the English church. The parson droned through the service. The soldiers fired a salute. The bugler boy's lip was trembling and big tears rolled down his cheeks. Kennedy's savage whisper snapped him upright. The first notes quavered but then he got hold of it and did it well.

They marched back to the pinnace with Smith at their head, stone-faced.

THE SUN WAS HIGH, but it was far too early for Phizackerly. Again. He woke reluctantly, bemused, to Olsen's determined shaking of his shoulder.

Olsen said, "There is a sailor downstairs from the British ship. If the police find out there will be trouble."

Slowly the words sank in. For seconds Phizackerly lay dumb, blank-faced. Then he reached out to claw at Olsen's arm. "Sailor? From the cruiser?"

"He came last night. Over the wall at the back."

Phizackerly groaned. "Give us a hand," he whispered huskily. Then he dressed and headed for the door, still moving stiffly, but drawn on by the emergency that caused him to leave his teeth grinning in their cup.

He and Olsen entered the girl's room. He glared at Gibb with hatred and jerked his thumb at the trembling girl. "Out." She fled.

Gibb's uniform lay on a chair. Phizackerly yelled at him with an old man's shrillness. "You're off the cruiser!"

Gibb muttered, "Yes."

Phizackerly chewed it over and his toothless jaws moved in time with his thoughts. His head ached. But this was a personal matter, between Englishmen."

He said to Olsen, "Fetch the rum." And when it came, "Give us half an hour, an' keep that girl's mouth shut."

Phizackerly poured the rum, got Gibb to drink it, nodded to himself as he refilled the glass. He poured, and he talked—about England, the Navy, duty . . . and the rum gave him a marvellous sincerity. But his little sharp eyes watched Gibb keenly as the rum sank its teeth into his empty belly.

Olsen returned, and together they got Gibb into his clothes. He moved dazedly, did as he was told. Olsen brought a coat to hide Gibb's uniform and Phizackerly muttered, "Right. He's going back. I'll see to him."

At that moment the window was thrust open and a burly man in overalls swung a leg across the sill. Another half-dozen crowded behind him. "'Ere! What's all this?" Phizackerly said, startled.

Farmer Bates said placidly, "All right Fizzy, me old son. It's the Navy claiming its own."

Phizackerly blew out his cheeks. "Cripes! I'm glad to see you." He knew a tough bunch when he saw them, and he knew everything was going to be all right.

WHEN THE PINNACE reached *Thunder* Smith said, "Stay alongside, Mr. Manton. I'll want the picket-boat in ten minutes." He ran up the ladder, returned Garrick's salute, went to his cabin and shifted out of his dress suit and into his shabby old uniform. He snatched his binoculars and as he stepped into the pinnace he asked Manton, "You've got the boat lead?"

"Yes, sir."

"Very well. Take her to sea, Mr. Manton. I'm curious to see our friends outside."

"Aye, aye, sir."

Once more they ran down the broad deep-water channel with its steep, forest-clad walls, down to where Stillwater Cove opened up to port and opposite, a bare quarter-mile to starboard, beyond the old channel, stood the signalling station. Smith saw light wink there as a telescope or binoculars was trained on them. They would be reported by telephone. He shrugged and lifted the glasses to his eyes. The cruisers were in sight.

One lay close outside Chilean waters, the gunboat alongside. The limit of Chilean waters was clearly defined because the Chilean destroyer was steaming slowly back and forth along a line outside the mouth of the river.

The pinnace plugged on out to sea against the flowing tide. Smith picked out the other cruiser, standing three or four miles farther out to sea, hove to. Saving her coal. She was running on a short rein that got shorter with every minute. Smith had seen to that when he sank the colliers.

He lowered the glasses and rubbed at his eyes. Theoretically they could well have entered Guaya at *Thunder*'s heels and coaled there. But if they had entered, and then *Thunder* had sailed, they would have had to give her twenty-four hours start. That was international law.

So they waited outside for *Thunder*, and a victory that would shake the world with the length of the German Navy's arm, and its strength.

Smith lifted the glasses again. He could see the nearer cruiser, and the gunboat alongside her, clearly now. He watched for a minute then handed the glasses to Manton and took the wheel himself. "Take a look." He waited until Manton lowered the glasses and then asked him, "Well?"

"It looked like ammunition they were loading on the *Leopard*, sir."

Smith said, noncommittally, "Yes." He had been quite certain of what he had seen but he had wanted confirmation. It was one more point to be borne in mind, that now the gunboat had teeth.

But she was no threat set beside the cruisers. He turned over the wheel to Manton and reclaimed the glasses. The farther cruiser was too far away to be seen in detail, but the nearer—he thought the fore-turret looked very odd, one gun of the pair bent at an angle. He let Manton see. "As Mr. Aitkyne put it, we gave her a bloody nose."

"By Jove, yes, sir!" Manton stared a long time until Smith said, "We'll return to the ship."

They did not return directly. Having run in under the signalling station and its watchful glass, Smith said, "Steer four points to starboard. Slow ahead." They crept into Stillwater Cove and on Smith's order Buckley took station in the bow with the boat lead. They took soundings for the length of the cove and proved deep water, or near as deep as the main channel. They chugged back to the centre of the cove and anchored. Smith stood over the compass, checking bearings, and then stared for a minute or two at the forest wall that climbed sheer from the water of the cove, then across the channel to where the signalling station was just visible around the right-turning curve of the main channel. As he was visible to them. They could not see this stretch of the channel but they could see the cove and himself. Just.

He cast one last look around at the cove, the forest, the channel, then smiled at Manton. He knew now what he must do. "Home, James."

They ran back up the channel.

As they opened up the pool his eyes went first, of course, to *Thunder*, appraising the work done and finding himself well content. She was grimy still but a sight cleaner than that morning.

Then his eyes drifted across to *Kansas*, lying massive, ugly in her menace but lovely in the clean lines of her.

Manton said, "She's enormous."

Smith smiled thinly. The cruisers could set a trap across the river mouth, he could act out defiance, but there was no argument as to where sea-power on this coast ultimately rested, whenever she chose to take it. *Kansas* seemed to doze in the late afternoon.

Five minutes later he faced Garrick and Bates. A look at Bates's face was enough, but he asked, "All well?"

"Took a time getting him back, sir, but all's well."

Garrick added, "In the cells now."

Smith only said, "Very good."

When Bates had gone Smith stood lost in thought, smiling faintly. That was one worry out of the way. As for the rest. . . . He turned the smile on Garrick.

"Now, about this bun-fight. Mr. Wakely will be in charge of the gramophone. All officers, except for watch-keepers, will be present and I want it understood that this is a *party*. Anyone who does not enjoy himself will answer to me." He grinned. "And a word to the paymaster. I have no doubt at all that the recent action will have destroyed some of his canteen stock, notably beer and probably of the order of two bottles per man, and I will expect to sign a certificate to that effect." He would do so with a clear conscience. The stock would be a total loss inside twenty-four hours.

As Garrick knew perfectly well, but he returned Smith's grin; it was infectious.

Then Smith told Garrick about the *Leopard* and how she had been armed by the cruiser. He told him of the soundings in the cove and that he wanted steam for sunset. And then he gave one last order that startled Garrick, that would have to be passed to the chiefs and petty officers and would mean more work for the men—after they had their beer.

He had half an hour to sluice himself down, change into clean clothes and then sit quietly in his cabin. Far below in the stoke-hold they would be starting already on the long job of getting up steam. But most of the other hands were fallen out below, and cooks piped to the galley for the evening meal. It was quiet.

The tick of the clock was a background to his thoughts as he re-examined his plan. He was not smiling now, for he knew, as he had known from the beginning, that he would have to fight. They had hunted him down though he had gone half across the world. . . .

He thought that when there was only one course you could take it became terribly simple. He was smiling as he went to join his officers where they waited in a well-scrubbed, shining group, neat in their best dress.

THUNDER'S CREW sweated together on her mess-decks in a grousing matiness, talked, and wondered.

Chalky White ate furiously, shovelling the food into his mouth. Through it he mumbled, "What can the skipper do? What? I *ask* yer! Too slow to run away, and either one o' them's got twice the big guns we have. So what can he *do?* I just want to *know."*

At that moment Daddy Horsfall hobbled through in his best boots that were crippling him and a starched white mess-jacket that threatened to choke him, on his way aft to the wardroom.

Chalky seized on opportunity. "Hey! Daddy! What's he goin' to do? The skipper, I mean."

"Do?"

"*Do!* About—this! He's got to have a plan, ain't he?"

"Ah! Plan." Daddy nodded, understanding now. "Well, that's simple enough. He's made no secret of it."

"What?"

Daddy said, "Get them to drop one on us."

Chalky gaped at him. "*What?*"

Daddy nodded. "An' when the bloody great cloud of rust goes up we can sneak away through it like it was a smoke screen." He hobbled away through the guffaws.

Burton squeezed in beside Farmer Bates and glanced at the bottles of beer. "You're not going to drink all that at your age?" he asked.

Farmer said amiably, "You're a scrounging bastard." He shoved along a bottle. They drank. Farmer asked, "What do you think?"

"Smith? Deep, that one. Dunno what he *can* do but he won't back down."

Farmer nodded in agreement. "Just have to wait and see."

They had talked to Rattray, who said indifferently, "I'll leave the little swine alone if they ever let him out. Doesn't matter now, does it? Not with what's coming off tomorrow."

Farmer and Burton sat in companionable silence in the midst of the teeming life around them. The moments of comparative peace would not last much longer.

NO BUGLE NOR PIPE sounded but the crew of *Thunder* had finished their brief breathing space, and their beer, and now turned to under the petty officers and chiefs. They swarmed below decks, and the din they created came in bedlam waves and went on and on.

In the wardroom the Chilean admiral and Encalada were stiffly polite, but their ladies openly excited. Neither officer mentioned Smith's request for more time but Cherry whispered, "They've agreed. You have until six tomorrow morning but not a minute longer. And here!" Cherry handed him a telegram.

It was a signal from Admiralty. Cherry was to inform the *Thunder*'s commander that a sighting of the cruisers had been reported in error, and if the cruisers arrived in the Pacific he was to avoid action until joined by a stronger force.

Cherry said bitterly, "They're a little late."

Smith shrugged and put the signal away in his pocket. The party had an air of unreality as Smith had suspected when he issued the invitation but he was glad he had done so. The white-jacketed stewards served tea, cake and wafer-thin sandwiches. Wakely's gramophone rag-timed away, muted by one of Wakely's socks stuffed down its horn. Wakely himself scurried between it and the group of officers who surrounded Sarah Benson.

She looked anything but a survivor now. She had moved to *Ariadne*, and during the day she had made demands of Mrs. Cherry and that lady had met them nobly so that Sarah's hair shone and her dress was expensive.

Ballard, *Ariadne*'s captain, was openly elated by *Thunder*'s performance and Smith's handling of her, but after Smith spoke briefly with him he became preoccupied.

Donoghue and his flag-captain had looked frankly at the damage, appraising it and the work done but saying nothing. For a coal-burning ship that had recently passed through heavy weather and hostile action the ship was remarkably clean. She still stank of burnt cordite and smoke.

Smith laboured at small talk. He was a poor hand at it and with the Chileans it was hard work. They all avoided mention of the war and Smith knew little of Chile. Encalada finally noticed the racket below deck. "Your men are still working very hard. I understand you were hit fore and aft—but not below."

"That is correct." Smith could have left it there, but he continued disarmingly, "It sounds as though someone's trying to steal the engines! In fact we have a small engine repair, and of course, we are trimming bunkers. But we will sail on time and shift our anchorage to Stillwater Cove tonight."

Encalada nodded, but Ballard blurted out eagerly, "Captain, there's a mist at dawn—" He bit his tongue.

Smith said quickly, "You came aboard in more comfortable style this evening, Miss Benson. It is a pleasure to open our doors to you." He felt like a tight-rope walker, and he was enjoying it.

When the party ended and the guests departed Ballard stood for a moment at the head of the ladder with Smith, and muttered, "Was that all right?"

"Perfect."

Thunder was left to herself. Smith paced the deck of his ship, his mind busy. Davies had raised steam and the smoke hung low on the still air. Soon, now.

He remembered Sarah Benson going down into *Ariadne*'s boat. He would have liked to see her again. But the chance was gone.

8

Sarah Benson had gone to the party as a duty and she had hated it. Tomorrow was in her mind. *Thunder* would sail out in the dawn, and the cruisers would be waiting for her. If only *Thunder* could gain more time.

She stood on the deck of *Ariadne* and stared across at *Thunder* as the night came down. Cherry found her there, a small, dejected figure.

She turned to him with hope. "Any news?"

Cherry shook his head gloomily. "No diver. There are two working out of this port but both were hired by Müller for a job up the coast and went the day before yesterday. They must have gone because Müller doesn't want a diver operating here until he has one he can trust to keep his mouth shut. And *that* means there *is* something in the wreck. Before I suspected it. Now I'm certain. But without a diver I can't *prove* it."

Sarah asked, "What kind of proof?"

"I've thought about that." Cherry paused. "She was a collier for the cruisers and she had a first-class wireless. So—she'd send in code."

"A book!"

"Right! And one of the places Smith didn't get the chance to search was the wireless office. It's in the superstructure and that's where the book will be. If I only had a *diver*—" He groaned in frustration.

They were silent a moment, then Sarah said quietly, "I'm a good swimmer."

"I dare say, young lady, but I'm talking about diving."

"So am I."

Cherry snapped hastily, "I mean diving to a depth of ten or twenty feet into the superstructure!" He was worried and on edge.

She snapped back at him. "I'm not a damn fool. I know the diving you're talking about and I can do it. I've swum in that depth of water plenty of times."

Cherry did not like the idea at all and his face showed it.

Sarah stared at *Thunder* and she spoke her thoughts aloud. "The Commander and I never got along very well. Maybe I'm partly to blame. But there's a man who can make a decision. We can either sit on our rumps and do nothing; or—"

THE SUN DIED in a red glow. The town twinkled with lights and *Thunder* lay in a pool of her own radiance. Men worked on her decks, seemingly still repairing the ravages of the fighting. Donoghue stood on *Kansas*'s quarterdeck, his flag-lieutenant by his side said, "So he's hauling up to Stillwater Cove tonight. He's not going to be interned. He's going to make a running fight of it."

The lieutenant sniffed. "He can't run. Those cruisers can give that old lady two or three knots. It sounds like he hopes to use the mist that comes up just before dawn, but. . . ." He shook his head.

"That's right. But." Donoghue scowled. "That mist hangs around the river and its mouth and that's all. It'll give him a few minutes of cover, just a little time. They'll be out there waiting for him when he comes out of the mist. The light will be behind him and he'll make one hell of a target."

"He's just trying everything he can."

Donoghue said heavily, "God help them."

CHERRY'S BOAT took him ashore and then returned to *Ariadne*. His boatman, Francis, handed Sarah Benson into the boat when she descended the accommodation ladder. He was an expatriate Geordie, squat, barrel-chested, and smelling strongly of the tobacco he chewed. Cherry had told him all about it and he disapproved.

As he swung the boat away from *Ariadne*, Sarah sat on a thwart and said tonelessly, "I think we can do without the lights."

Francis shrugged heavy shoulders. "Don't suppose anybody'll take any notice of us; they'll all be watching her." He jerked his head at *Thunder*. "Still, does no harm to be careful." He extinguished the boat's lights.

Francis was mistaken. One pair of eyes followed the boat as it slid softly across the dark water. A German, Friedrich Kaufmann, who sat in his own boat below the quay, was there to watch *Thunder*, but now he watched Cherry's boat and saw it drift in to the stub of *Gerda's* funnel that still showed above water.

Across the harbour Francis clambered forward with the light line coiled in his hand. "You did say you've done a lot of this, miss?"

"I can swim better than most men, and that includes diving." She stood up, rocking the boat gently. "Let's get on with it."

She pulled the dress over her head. Under it she wore only drawers and a short chemise that tucked into the waist of the drawers. She took the line from Francis and knotted it around her waist while he muttered, "Remember, I keep it pretty taut so it won't foul your legs. And if you get into any trouble—"

"I tug and keep tugging."

"Right."

Sarah wondered what he could do about it if she did run into trouble down there. She knew that Francis could not swim. Now he was muttering, "Remember what Mr. Cherry told you about the wireless cabin, the layout; it should be something like that."

"I remember." She was shivering uncontrollably now although the night air was not cold. She said again, "Let's get on with it."

Francis hesitated. He had an idea of the dangers involved in entering a submerged wreck, without an air line, in pitch blackness, and he did not like it. He said, "Take care, lass. And good luck."

Sarah lowered herself over the side, gasped as the chill water took her breath, hung on and breathed deeply, then went under. Francis saw her legs waving pale below the surface, and then they were gone leaving a trail of bubbles.

She had expected blackness but it was far worse than her fears. She worked by touch alone, striking down until one hand scraped on iron and she fumbled her way along the superstructure, passed one door, closed, reached the second that was the wireless office and found it open.

She dared not enter. She kicked up for the surface, broke into the air five yards from the boat and stroked towards it and clung to the side, gasping. "About over there," she panted. "But look, when I go down again I'll have to find the thing all over again. Take off this line, will you?"

"You've got to have a line!"

"I need it for something else. The only way I can do it is to use the line as a guide."

"I don't like it." Reluctantly he picked at the knot, and she took the end of the line from him. She breathed deeply, then was gone again.

That dive sufficed to mark the wireless office and she tied the line to the handle of the door.

On the third dive she followed the line and entered the office. After long seconds of awkward groping she located the desk and a drawer beneath. It was open and empty. She turned to re-surface and found she had lost her bearings and went bumping around in the steel cell, fumbling for the door. She found it only when her lungs were bursting and lights wheeled across her eyes. She kicked clumsily through the door and up.

Paddling feebly to the boat, she clung to the side, exhausted. Francis said, "Good God! Here, let's have you in." He reached for her but she flapped at his hands.

"No! Leave me alone! Just give me a minute."

He had to wait while she tried to fight down fear and fixed her mind on *Thunder* and the six hundred men aboard her. . . . She said, "All right. I should have taken the slack of the line in with me. That's what I'll do. I found the desk and a drawer but it was empty. Must be another one."

Francis said, "Wait a minute. The drawer was open?"

"That's right. Key in the lock. Why? What is it?"

Francis said slowly, "If the feller in there had thought the ship was in danger he would have got the book out ready to ditch it."

"So it could be kicking around on the deck in there."

"It'll be heavy, weighted so it would sink—"

"I know *that!*" She dived, and he waited.

She entered the office, taking the slack of the line with her in a loop around her wrist, feeling the light strain kept on it by Francis in the boat. She felt below the desk, around the chair bolted there, moved back towards the door . . . She felt rough canvas, a bag. It was weighty and rested on something. The thing moved, touching her arm as she lifted the bag. She felt at it, meaning to push it away, but her hand clasped another, fingers groping.

Air exploded from her with shock. She kicked and went hand over hand up the line, banging through the door, its iron frame stripping skin from her shoulders.

On the surface Francis felt her tugging and hauled in on the line, only to be checked as it tautened between him and the door below. Then Sarah burst up scarcely a yard away, threshed wildly one-handed, spat and took a whooping breath.

Francis thrust the boat away from the collier's funnel and as it moved to her he reached over, and manhandled her in over the side to lie gasping, shuddering. She still held the bag and Francis took it from her. "What happened?"

He had an arm around her, lifting her. With his free hand he reached to his hip pocket and pulled out a flat bottle. She gagged on the rum but felt it burn inside her. "There was a—that bag was lying on—a man."

Francis said softly, "Oh my God."

Then the faint light around them was snuffed out. They turned to stare across the pool and saw *Thunder*, now a dark bulk except for her navigation lights, slipping gently towards the channel.

Francis said, "She's on her way." Crouched in the bottom of the boat, in the glow of an electric torch he sliced through the straps of the bag. The bag was waterproof and the book was dry. He grinned up at Sarah. "You got it. This is it. Their code-book."

As he started the engine Sarah stared after *Thunder*, and thought, "This will make a difference, all the difference. This is a justification, this will give them time."

FRIEDRICH KAUFMANN BLINKED as *Thunder* slipped away, but his eyes went quickly back to the boat moored over the wreck of the collier. The boat was also moving and there was no stealth about her now. She ran straight for the quay.

His engineer asked, "We go?"

Their orders had been to observe *Thunder* and report but Kaufmann shook his head. He could catch the old cruiser at Stillwater Cove.

"No. You wait here." He leaped from the boat, ran up the steps to the quay and crossed quickly into the shadows of the buildings. From here he watched the boat sweep in, and a second or so later a girl climbed onto the quay, her dress clinging to her. She called down to the boat, "I'm heading straight for the consulate. You follow when you're ready." She hurried across the quay.

Friedrich Kaufmann hesitated only briefly. The girl carried a bag that had come from *Gerda* and she was hurrying to the British consulate. The mere possibility that she had found proof of *Gerda*'s real purpose was enough to merit action and therefore his course was clear. He broke into a run.

Once he tripped and fell, but rose immediately and ran on, limping now. He came to the tree-lined square on which the consulate stood. Ahead of him the girl was opening the gate of the consulate. As she stepped onto the path leading to the front door that door opened and Cherry came out. Kaufmann stepped from the trees, the revolver held two-handed at arm's length. It was a distance of thirty feet and he missed Sarah by inches, but Cherry spun and fell as the shot crashed out.

Sarah was still for a shocked instant but Francis, who had disobeyed orders and belatedly decided to follow her, yelled and sprinted. She threw herself down so that the second shot slammed into the doorpost. Kaufmann did not get another chance. Francis piled into him in a flying tackle that crashed his head on the cobbles and sent the revolver skidding away.

Servants showed at the open door, peering out nervously. Sarah shouted at them from where she knelt on the path over Cherry, "Get a doctor! Quick!"

Cherry had been hit high in the chest and she snatched the handkerchief from his cuff to press on the wound. Then she saw a slip of paper sticking from Cherry's pocket. She opened out the telegram, read it, then crumpled it savagely. She peered down into Cherry's unconscious face and whispered, "We got the proof Smith wanted and I'll see the Chileans have it." *Thunder's* wireless was wrecked but they could send a signal by the station at Punta Negro to *Thunder* where she lay in Stillwater Cove, waiting for the dawn. They could call her back. As for the telegram balled in her fist, she would find it—later.

The telegram was to relieve Smith of his command of *Thunder* and place him under arrest.

9

Aboard *Thunder* the activity below decks bore fruit. As she slipped slowly down-river towards the sea, the men began to bring up the furniture, the stores. Everything that could be ripped out and moved was brought up and heaved over the side. She left a thick trail. At the end of twenty minutes, down to coal for twenty-four hours anyway, she was down to stores for that same period and her inside scoured clean as a washed corpse.

Benks and Horsfall and a party of seamen staggered on deck with the wardroom piano and shoved it jangling into the river.

Benks groaned, "Going too far it is. He's barmy."

"No, he ain't. He knows what he's doing." But to himself, Daddy added, "I hopes." Because stripping for action was one thing and this was another.

On the bridge Garrick said, "They've thrown everything overboard but the galley stoves."

So Smith answered laconically, "See to it, Mr. Wakely."

"Aye, aye, sir."

They stripped the galley except for one stove.

Smith left the bridge and made his way down into the bowels of the ship until he came to the marine sentry and the door of the cell where they had put Gibb.

"Open up." Smith waited while the marine fumbled with the keys. Then he walked in. Gibb stood to attention.

Smith said, "You were in a fight with someone before you—left the ship?"

Gibb noted the choice of words. "Aye, sir." He knew now that Rattray was alive.

Smith stared at him. "We will shortly be in action," he said. "Would you rather be aloft doing your duty, or down here?"

Gibb swallowed, and whispered, "Aloft, sir."

Smith turned to the sentry. "Give me the keys and report for your normal duties." The marine looked at him oddly, but handed over the keys and left.

Two minutes later the cells were empty and Smith returned to the bridge. He had sent two men back to duty. No superfluous weight.

Thunder slipped down between the dark shadows of the forest, lights again sprinkling her decks. Then to port lay Stillwater Cove. *Thunder* edged over and into the cove, dead slow now, barely making headway against the tide that was beginning to flow. A cluster of shore lights crept into view over the starboard bow, set on a low hill: they marked the signalling station. *Thunder*, lit up as she was, would be clear to the watchers there. Her anchor roared out, her engines stopped and she hung at the end of her cable. As her pinnace had done that morning.

Then the deck lights went out, and there were only the riding lights to mark her position.

A lamp blinked a question from the signalling station. They had known she was coming but they put the formal question: "What ship is that?"

Thunder replied.

Voices called softly along the boat-deck and Garrick reported, "Whaler's away, sir." And then: "Gig's away, sir." The boats had been lowered by hand in near silence.

Smith nodded and looked at his watch.

One minute. Two. . . . Ten minutes.

He was watching the shore to port and saw the brief blink of light there that was Midshipman Wakely, who had taken the whaler and a dozen men, reporting that he was ready.

Now they waited for Kennedy, who had gone off in the gig.

Smith's eyes turned to starboard and he waited again. The night was overcast, without moon or stars, black dark here under the hanging wall of the forest.

There came another blink of light, down at water level.

Garrick said, "Kennedy."

"Seen." Smith ordered, "Slow ahead both. Douse the lights."

The riding lights went out and fresh lights blinked on, duplicates, where Wakely and his men had tied up their lanterns in the forest. *Thunder*, in total darkness now, eased up on her cable until a crewman forward rasped, "Up 'n down!" And the blacksmith knocked out the pin from the shackle and that length of the cable fell softly to join the anchor on the bed of the cove.

"Hard a'starboard!" The wheel went over and *Thunder* swung out of Stillwater Cove and cut across the main channel. Wakely and his men tumbled into the whaler and chased after her.

Kennedy stood on the shore, the water of that channel nudging the stern of the gig where it was drawn bows onto the sand. He could not see the seaman high above his head in the tree, nor those strung out, kneeling in a half-circle behind him. They were his sentries, armed with nothing more lethal than thick ropes' ends; his orders were not to be seen, let alone taken.

He saw *Thunder's* looming, barely drifting bulk lift huge out of the dark and inch into the side channel. She moved past him with the only sound the slow beating swash of her turning screws. Not a voice, not a whisper, not a chink of light. She passed into the darkness of the side channel and was gone.

"Right," Kennedy said huskily, "it's time we were out of this. Recover that wire."

The two seamen with him on the bank began hauling in on the signalling station's telephone wire that those in the trees had earlier lowered so that it lay on the bed of the channel. *Thunder* had passed over it. One of them ceased hauling at Kennedy's word and with Kennedy ran out the gig and rowed to the centre of the channel. The men perched in the trees were hauling on the lines attached to the telephone wire so that it emerged from the channel. It hung, not in a sagging loop, but in a sharp V because of the weights Kennedy had made fast to it to make sure it sank and was not cut. He cut the weights free and the wire rose into the night sky and was lost. By the time he reached the shore again the seaman was down from the tree. "All secure, sir."

Kennedy pulled in his sentries and they manned the gig. Halfway across the side channel the rowers were still. They heard the creak of oars then the whaler slid across their bow, the men in her pulling strongly after *Thunder*.

Almost at once *Thunder* grew out of the dark where she lay, just enough way on her to hold her against the still flowing tide. She was lowering her boats, all of them, again by hand and every man aboard who was not absolutely essential to the running of the ship at this time was going down into them. Enough stokers and engine-room staff remained to move *Thunder*, and men for her bridge and look-outs. Two cooks laboured in the almost denuded galley, sweating with every scuttle tight closed.

Near five hundred men went down into the boats, going over the side in the same way that every removable part of the inside of the ship had gone, from stoves to stores to partitions to beds to the wardroom piano and Wakely's gramophone, in the same way and for the same reason. Weight, taken out of *Thunder* for this one passage. The men and the boats might make a difference of a half-inch or more to *Thunder*'s draught. It could be vital.

The picket-boat crept up past *Thunder*'s length and took station ahead of her, Manton at the wheel, Buckley with the lead already swinging from one fist as he balanced in the bow, getting the feel of it. *Thunder* inched into the side channel, the forest and the mist and the night reaching out to wrap her round.

The hail came softly from the bow, repeated from the pinnace: "By the mark, five!" And Phizackerly stepped onto the bridge. When Smith had let him out of the cell next to Gibb's he had gone straight to the galley. Now he nursed a mug of cocoa as he said with hollow cheer, " 'Evening, gennelmen."

Smith said, "Five fathoms. Do you know where you are?"

Phizackerly peered out at the night, to port, to starboard, ahead, his head thrust out on its scrawny neck, questing. "Aye. Five fathom as I remember right."

"You'd better remember right."

"Aye. Starboard a point." The night was chill. Phizackerly buttoned his jacket around him and shivered. He was like to catch his death of this. Lucky he hadn't died of fright already. The bastards had shanghaied him! *Him!* They had shoved him in a cell but they'd fed him like a fighting cock, wine with his meal an' all. But Lord! He'd been worried. And when Smith finally opened his cell and told Phizackerly what he wanted he hadn't felt any better. It had been a long time.

"You said she would draw less'n twenty-five feet, Captain?"

"She's drawing twenty-four feet three inches."

"Fore and aft?"

"Fore and aft." Smith did not add that thirty tons of coal had been moved from forward to aft at cost of sweat and cursing on the part of the stokers to achieve that trim.

"Ta." Phizackerly was only slightly encouraged. He thought that it was one thing to stand safe in the sun and boast. It was another matter to prove that boast. He glanced furtively at Smith then quickly back to their heading. Smith seemed cool but that had to be an act, Phizackerly knew it. No master, no seaman could take his ship into this sort of trap without a sickening apprehension.

"Ease her a point to port." His voice was husky but there was a new note in it that brought a quick glance from Smith. The whine was gone and the authority lost for fifteen years was back. He was the pilot and this ship was his charge. "Steady."

"And a half, five!" The hail came back from the bow. Phizackerly nodded. That was right.

Thunder crept on through the desperately narrow channel

where the deep water lay. Fractional changes of course, minute adjustments, with the bridge sparsely staffed by rock-still figures and the only sounds the slow-turning screws and the regular muted hail from forward, "By the mark, five!" . . . "And a half, five!" . . . "A quarter less five!"

They touched, the barest tremor rubbing gently at the skin of the ship beneath them and away. Touched again. And again. But always *Thunder* slid on.

They passed a village on the bank, the red glow of a fire's embers there and a dog that howled and barked, startling the hand in the bow so his call came: "By the mark—*Bloody hell!*—by the mark, five!"

And Smith said, "By the bark, five." Nobody laughed. They grinned nervously in response to his tight grin, wondering how he could find a joke, however weak, at this moment.

Smith was aware that if he failed in this then at best he would somehow have to try to take *Thunder* astern into the main channel and to the fate that awaited her there. At worst *Thunder* could be stranded and interned, probably to lie for ever in this swamp to rot. . . . But they were better than halfway through and with time in hand. He had taken one more calculated risk and it was going right. In three hours or less it would be dawn but by then—

"*And a half, four!*" There was an urgency about that hail. *Thunder* was running into shoal water.

Phizackerly said, "'Ere!" And: "Stop her!"

Smith snapped, "Call back the picket-boat!" And to Phizackerly: "Silted?"

Phizackerly scowled. "Sounds like it. Should be deeper."

Thunder drifted with the little way on her, stopped. The pinnace slid alongside and Smith called down, "You're certain about that last sounding?"

Buckley's voice came up, "Dead sure, sir. Straight up an' down. And we got another after: four an' a half fathoms."

The tide was at the full, slack water. Soon it would start to ebb and *Thunder*'s chance of running the channel would drain away with that ebbing.

Phizackerly said heavily, "She's silted. Never did afore, though it was always a chance, like, 'cause the channel forks here. Straight

108

ahead there—see that light?" And as Smith nodded, "Another village on the right-hand bank where the channel goes on, that's what that light is, but the true channel turns to port near ninety degrees and she's silted out from that *left*-hand bank. So there just ain't the *room* to make that turn. Of all the bleeding luck—"

Smith cut him off. "We'll take a look at it."

They went down into the pinnace and Manton took it creeping away from *Thunder*'s inert bulk to sound the channel. Phizackerly's forecast was proved depressingly correct. Over the years a bar had built up, running out from the left-hand bank and cutting into the channel. The deep water was still there, just. If *Thunder*'s length had been less by fifty feet she might have worked around that tight turn. As it was, she could not. They explored the channel where it ran straight ahead, the false channel, and proved it to be just that. The water was deep for about forty yards but then shelved rapidly. Phizackerly thought exploring it was a waste of time anyway. "It peters out. Another three, four hundred yards and you can walk across."

Smith said, "Back to the ship, Mr. Manton."

It meant feverish activity. They cast off the boats that they had towed thus far and *Thunder* nosed slowly ahead into the blind channel, and ran gently aground. Labouring they took a heavy cable aboard the pinnace, dragged it to the right bank of the true channel and made it fast to a rock outcrop. *Thunder* went astern on both engines till she slid her bow off the bottom, then slow astern on the starboard engine and dead slow ahead on the port while the capstan aft hauled in on the cable. It tautened, straightened and as *Thunder* came out of the blind channel her stern came around.

Smith gave all his orders from the port wing of the bridge where he could see the channel and the slow-swinging stern and the pinnace anchored at the point of the spit that ran out from the far bank. The ship was still in darkness but he could see the water of the channel, slack water still—or was it ebbing now, pushing gently at the pinnace? He ordered, "Stop engines!"

Thunder was not clear of the blind channel. She still drifted astern with the way on her, still turning and with the cable dragging her around in an even tighter arc than before. Yet the stern edged across the channel until it hung over the pinnace and Manton broke out his anchor and shifted from under with Buckley sweating and swearing. The stern touched, dragged with that shiver through the ship and as the stern swung so did the bow as the capstan hauled her around and now the bow stroked sand, and stopped. The stern hesitated in its arc. The cable was bar-taut and the rock outcrop groaning out of the earth. *Thunder* was aground fore and aft across the channel.

The stern shivered again, moved on as the cable strained, coming around. The rock tore out of the bank like a tooth and the cable sagged and the capstan stopped. But *Thunder*'s stern pointed towards the sea and she floated.

Phizackerly breathed, "Gawd almighty!" He voiced the sentiments of many.

A party in the whaler recovered the cable and the boats were taken in tow again. The pinnace took station ahead and *Thunder* headed once more towards the open sea—stern first.

The channel ran straight. Only once she struck, hesitated for a second on a bar right under her until the engines went full astern and dragged her, grating, over into deep water beyond. Smith thought he could see the faintest wash of phosphorescence where the sea broke at the mouth of the channel and Phizackerly leaned wearily on the rail. "There she is, then. She's yours, Mister." He felt washed out, limp, drained by nervous tension. He thought that Smith and his men laboured like madmen for the privilege of having their heads blown off.

The dinghy was hauled alongside. Smith scribbled in his notebook, and tucked the page in the pocket of Phizackerly's jacket. "A note for Mr. Cherry to say that you've done us all an enormous service tonight. Thank you." He held out his hand and Phizackerly shook it. "The dinghy is yours. Away you go."

"Thank you, sir." Phizackerly sniffed and cleared his throat. "God bless you, sir. Good luck to all of yez." He was properly embarrassed so that it came out in an awkward mumble as he headed for the ladder but they heard it, and his sincerity. He was their last tie with the land. He went down into the dinghy and the seaman holding it there thrust it clear and climbed the ladder as the dinghy and Phizackerly bobbed away astern.

110

The boats came alongside and the men poured aboard and went straight to their action stations. Smith shouted at Kennedy. "Cast off the boats!" They could not waste a second now let alone the time needed to recover them. The pinnace they towed.

A minute later they were clear of the widening channel. For minutes more *Thunder* steamed out to sea as they strained their eyes against the darkness, but there was no challenge, no sudden salvo smashed out of the dark.

There was a gradual easing of tension. For the first time they were aware of the chilly night, of weariness, thick mouths and gummy eyes. There was no sense of achievement. Only slowly did it come to them that they had slipped through the net.

Thunder was free.

CHERRY WAS SHOT at on the stroke of midnight. The German consulate was only minutes away but it was nearly three before his staff woke Müller with news that Kaufmann had been arrested.

He could not believe it. That fool was under orders to watch *Thunder*. He went hurrying down to Kaufmann's boat and got the story from the yawning engineer. Despite Müller's efforts the British had found a diver and dragged up from the *Gerda*— what? He did not know but he could make a guess. They had gone running with it to their consul. That was enough. The British would demand more time for *Thunder* and would probably get it, though he would fight them. But he was in a bad position now.

One thing was clear: the cruisers must be informed.

Kaufmann's boat cast off and headed for the channel. When they sighted the signalling station at Punta Negro they also sighted the lights that marked *Thunder* where she lay in Stillwater Cove. As they came abreast of the cove Müller glared in, then stared.

10

Thunder was free, the Pacific open before her.

Free? It was an illusion. Smith left the bridge to Garrick and went down to give Manton his orders. It was still night but the day was not far off and Smith thought it would not be a long one.

He gave Manton the orders for the pinnace. "You'll be running north along the coast, full speed ahead and you must not attempt to conceal it. No stoking restrictions now. You will maintain course and speed until you are recalled. Is that understood? Repeat the orders."

Manton repeated them. Smith asked, "Any questions?" And when Manton hesitated, Smith told him why.

A messenger trotted up with a paper-wrapped bundle of sandwiches in one hand, a kettle of tea in the other and lowered them down to the pinnace. The two cooks had prepared a mountain of bacon sandwiches as *Thunder* had crept through the channel. A low cheer came up from the pinnace.

Smith held out his hand to Manton. "Good luck."

"Thank you, sir. And to you, sir."

Smith watched him climb down into the pinnace. He was sending Manton away with only Buckley and Quinn, the signalman, Rudkin the engineer and Jenner the stoker. He heard Manton give the course, saw the pinnace sheer off and heard Buckley's pained protest: "Bloody *'ell!* We'll be seen for *miles!*"

Smith returned to the bridge and stood on the starboard wing as *Thunder* headed out into the Pacific. They had forced the channel and slipped the cruisers, but got clean away? That was too much to dare to hope for.

Smith swept the sea astern of *Thunder* once more with his glasses. There was light astern but it was the glow against the cloud base from the lights of Guaya. And to starboard? He stared at the light between *Thunder* and the coast, a trail of sparks and a recurrent whiff of flame that pointed to the pinnace's funnel and her position as plain as any pointing finger.

Kennedy said involuntarily, "A bleating lamb."

Smith said quietly, "Yes." It was true enough. He had staked out the lamb. He would have to live with that decision. If any of them lived.

He ordered, "Starboard two points. Steer three-five-oh."

Thunder came around until she was running north at eight knots, parallel to the coast and to Manton's course; he could still see the pinnace, just, a blinking red light, leading by about eight thousand yards. As Smith wanted it.

He turned aft once more.

The ship was closed up at action stations. Garrick had gone to the fore-top, and Smith held the bridge with Aitkyne, Kennedy, Knight and Wakely. He was coldly aware that this ship, though preparing to fight for her life, had not been intended to fight any such action. She only had crews for her turrets and her four upper-deck six-inch. The eight six-inch guns below on the main deck were unmanned while the effective range of any of the six-inch guns was only six thousand yards.

He snapped irritably at Aitkyne, "Keep a good look-out astern!" And hid behind the glasses. Searching. Searching.

WAS THERE A first faint lightening of the sky in the east? They had been running for nearly fifteen minutes.

Smith stood waiting, outwardly calm, inwardly cherishing a wild hope. They might have got clean away. He still could not believe it. The chances of the decoy lights remaining undiscovered in Stillwater Cove dwindled as the night wore away and it was incredible they should not be found. *Thunder* was only matching the eight knots of the pinnace, she could run faster than this if she was going to run and now it looked as if the chance was there.

They could reach Peru in twelve hours. He had coal enough. There was a chance to escape annihilation. . . .

It was time to commit himself but he still waited, though forced now to pace the bridge restlessly. Tension seemed to still all life on the ship. The voice cracked urgent from the masthead: "Smoke bearing green one-six-oh!"

The men on the bridge jerked to life. Smith croaked, "Full speed ahead!" His glasses swept an arc on the approximate bearing and found first the faintest blink of funnel flame that marked the smoke beneath.

Aitkyne quietly reported, "Smoke bears green one-five-nine. Range six thousand."

The smoke lay five-and-a-half thousand yards astern of *Thunder*, was on the same course as the pinnace and maybe ten thousand yards astern of *her*. He was certain the ship, whoever she was, would not see the pinnace—yet.

The minutes ticked away and the softly called bearings and

113

ranges marked the minutes like the hand of a clock as the cruisers made up on the pinnace and more slowly, on the accelerating *Thunder*.

"Bearing green one-five-five . . . Green one-five-oh. . . . Green one-four-five, range three thousand."

Ten minutes. Fifteen. Twenty. All the time *Thunder* was working up to her full speed and all the time Smith watched the cruisers' smoke. In the sky to the east the mountains now stood vague but black against the background of the coming dawn.

It would be a fine day.

He caught the flickering white of broken water that was bow-wave and wash below the pall of funnel smoke and the ships came up.

There were two of them. With less than half the cruisers' speed, *Leopard* would be trailing far behind. They were in line abreast, the farther a fraction astern of the closer, seaward vessel. So that both of them could see the chase ahead and both could fire. They *had* to see the pinnace now; they were about five thousand yards astern of her—

They fired! The long tongue of flame ripped the night and Smith snapped his eyes shut against that glare. "Starboard ten!" He opened his eyes and the flames had died and out of the dark came the slamming bellow of the cruisers' guns. *Thunder* was heeling under him as he strained his eyes, peering for the cruisers and saw them take shape again off the starboard beam.

"Midships!"

Thunder was near her full speed and driving down on a course to intersect that of the cruisers and take her across their bows.

"Bearing green seven-oh! Range two thousand!"

The cruisers fired again, and this time he saw them lit in that split second of brilliance, surging along at full speed, swift, deadly. They were still astern of *Thunder* but edging up to draw level. Unaware of her; intent on the target ahead, banking on the chance that it could be no ship other than *Thunder*, a certainty.

The target. Smith remembered the target was the boy Manton and his little crew in their tiny cockleshell. Wakely reported, "Picket-boat's still in sight, sir."

"Thank you." Of course Wakely would be watching out for the

pinnace, for Manton. The first salvo had landed and they had survived it. But they would have to survive others.

"Range one-seven-double-oh!"

"Port ten! . . . Midships!"

"Midships, sir!"

Thunder heeled then straightened, paralleling the cruisers' course but leading them, on their port bow. It seemed they *must* see *Thunder*, but while they stood against that first faint light *Thunder* was out in the black void, and they were not looking for her there, eyes locked on the prey ahead.

"Range one-thousand! . . . Bearing green-nine-five!"

The cruisers fired and now the crash of discharge followed only a blink after the flash. They were that close.

Through the shadows Wakely's voice came clear, edgy, "Picket-boat still in sight, sir."

So they had survived the second salvo but there was still the third, hurtling towards them now.

He could, *must* forget them. This was the time.

"Open fire!"

Thunder heaved as she fired her broadside. Simultaneously the searchlights flooded across the thousand yards of dark sea to bathe the nearer cruiser in light—as the broadside struck her.

This was "Smith's game" that they had played so many times with the pinnace, and they had learnt the rules by heart.

The broadside could not fail to hit, fired at point-blank range, the trajectory virtually nil and the time of flight of the shells less than two seconds. Their impact was seen.

Smith was certain that it was *Wolf* that took the broadside from the two turrets and the six starboard six-inch guns that were manned. He shouted, "Douse!" The searchlights expired and the darkness rushed in to smother *Thunder* but he could still see *Wolf*. She was afire in three places. Flame painted her black and yellow, very clear, very close. She would be closer yet.

"Hard a'starboard!" *Thunder* heeled as the helm went over. "Port torpedo tube stand by!" *Thunder* pounded along, still heeling in the turn. The 9.2 fired from the forward-turret, the searchlights' probing fingers showed *Wolf* leaping at them broadside out of the dark, fresh columns of yellow flame soaring

115

and smoke balling up. She was rushing at them but *Thunder*'s helm was still hard over.

Kennedy shouted, "Torpedo running, sir."

Smith lifted one hand in acknowledgement and shouted in his turn, "Midships!" *Thunder* hurtled down past *Wolf* at an acute angle, passing at their combined speeds of forty knots. In those swift-flying seconds he saw that *Wolf*'s forward-turret had swung to meet *Thunder*'s attack but too late. As her searchlights chased *Thunder* a thumping explosion came from forward on *Wolf*. Then one more leaping flame.

Wakely screamed, "Torpedo hit, sir!"

They were barely a cable's length apart. *Wolf* seemed to stumble in her headlong career as the torpedo struck, then her guns fired and there came a crashing impact as a shot hit *Thunder*. But now they were charging right past *Wolf*'s stern and the after 9.2 and port side six-inch guns fired right into her.

Smith did not see the result. As they cleared *Wolf*'s stern he ordered, "Hard a'starboard!" and *Thunder* heeled again.

Wakely yelped, "God!"

Kondor was also heading to cross *Wolf*'s stern, seeking for a sight of the attacker who had burst from the night and was masked from her by *Wolf*. *Kondor* and *Thunder* were on a collision course. All of them on the bridge grabbed hold and hung on. There was nothing they could do. But they missed *Kondor*, it seemed by only feet, and swept past her in the blinking of an eye. But in that blinking the forward-turret hurled a shell into her. And Smith saw that already *Kondor*'s forward-turret had a gun pointing drunkenly; *Thunder* had done that thirty-six hours before. Guns fired on *Kondor* but they fired blind at a ship already storming away into the night.

Smith clawed his way out to the starboard wing of the bridge. They had been at it only minutes but mad, hell-filled minutes. *Thunder* had been hit, one of the port six-inch being put out of action and the after-bridge wrecked but she had come off relatively unscathed compared to the damage she had inflicted on *Wolf*. Lit by flames from end to end, she looked down by the head and scarcely moving. He could see *Kondor* too, clear of *Wolf* now and heading out to sea in pursuit of *Thunder*. He could see her against the growing light in the east but they would have their work cut out to see *Thunder* in the outer dark.

"Starboard ten . . . Midships! Hard a'port . . . Midships!" The guns recoiled and bellowed. *Thunder* dog-legged erratically out to sea and she was scoring. *Kondor* was firing hard, but at a dimly-seen, jinking target. Smith saw the waterspouts of the falling salvoes and some were close but none hit. *Kondor*'s course was diverging from that of *Thunder*, trying to claw her way out of that stretch of sea between *Thunder* and the growing light that marked her in sharp silhouette for *Thunder*'s rangefinder and layers.

That diverging course meant that the range was opening, nearing the extreme effective range of *Thunder*'s old six-inch guns. She fired her starboard broadside and Smith ordered, "Hard a'starboard!" And this time she kept on turning through sixteen points and headed back into the light, and towards *Wolf*.

Smith could see all of his ship now in that grey light and the faces of Aitkyne and Kennedy and Wakely, all the bridge staff, all their faces strained but excited. *Thunder* was fighting a good fight and they knew it.

He had a bleak moment in that dawn. He conned his ship, keeping her jinking to confuse *Kondor*'s guns, but he looked ahead with cold certainty. The element of surprise was gone, the advantage of the dark was going and *Thunder* was still badly out-gunned. And *Kondor* was shooting well, very well indeed. A salvo plummeted into the sea close alongside, emphasizing the point as the hurled water lashed across the bridge.

Finally, *Kondor* would have the edge in speed.

And *Wolf*? *Thunder* was racing down on her and she was still burning and not moving at all. Away to port *Kondor* had also turned and was roaring back towards her consort.

He said, "We'll shift to the conning-tower," and himself passed the word to Garrick before leaving the bridge. From the circular conning-tower below it, with its eleven inches of armour, their view was restricted to what they could see through the observation slits. It would have to serve. In the darkness he had risked fighting his ship from the bridge because he had to see. But now it was senseless to stay there.

They were under fire from both *Kondor* and *Wolf* now though

117

the latter's firing was ragged. *Thunder* scored hits but was hit herself. And again. A starboard six-inch gun was reported out of action with the loss of its crew of ten men.

Smith warned, "Pass the word to look out for torpedoes!" *Wolf* still had teeth.

They ran down past *Wolf*, pounding her. She was not only down by the head but listing to port. Fires sprouted all along her hull and they saw her through rolling clouds of smoke. *Thunder* fired into her twice more, then turned from her. They were done with *Wolf*, she had served her purpose. *Kondor* was driving inshore of her to chase *Thunder*, and she was firing hard. Smith could see the salvoes as the flashes rippled along her hull in awful beauty. But she, too, had been hurt, her speed reduced, her second funnel leaned crazily against the next astern and—

And then the salvo hit them.

They had left *Wolf* astern and Smith's mouth was open to order yet another change of course when the salvo roared in like a train. It skittled them all except the coxswain at the wheel. Smith pawed his way to his feet and felt *Thunder* listing. From the rear of the conning-tower he saw the cause of that list, the after funnel a battered cylinder of wreckage hanging over the starboard side. It slipped, and then ground over the side with wire stays parting and flailing, and *Thunder* righted herself.

She steamed on and Smith croaked, "Starboard ten!" And: "Midships!" *Thunder* headed out to sea once more, the smoke-wrapped hulk of *Wolf* came between them and *Kondor*— and the guns fell silent. He called up the voice-pipe to Garrick: "Engage the ship astern of us!"

Garrick's voice came back, rusty and metallic, "Port an' starboard batteries don't bear on this course, sir, and the after-turret is out of action. No contact with them and I can't see much because of this damn smoke—" *Thunder*'s three remaining funnels still rolled it out—"but I think they took a direct hit. Can't see the other cruiser."

Yet. Smith said, "You will. You're doing very well!"

He found Kennedy at his elbow, who said, "After-turret a total loss, sir. We've a fire aft—" Smith could see that, flames leaping pale in the sun—"and damage in the after boiler room."

Thunder's speed had fallen away.

Smith ordered, "Port ten! Steer one-seven-oh!" He stepped to the voice-pipe and called the engine room. "What speed can you give us, Chief?"

A second's hesitation, then Davies said, "I can maintain revolutions for fourteen knots."

"Thank you!" Smith called to Garrick. "Engage the enemy when sighted."

"Sir!" And Garrick added: "This light is hell."

It would be lancing into Garrick's eyes as he strained them towards the land. Smith said, "Do your best." He had *Kondor* where he wanted her, and the bad light was a price they would have to pay. They would pay far more before they were done.

Kondor thrust out from behind *Wolf*, pointing at *Thunder* who steamed broadside to her on the new course, and opened fire as *Thunder* heeled to her broadside. The battle closed around them.

They entered a world of thunderous discharge and shuddering impact as hits ripped into the old ship's frame. Smith conned his ship, swerving her to try to unsight the enemy, listening to the endless reports of damage and death, to the ranges calling "Double-five-double-oh! . . . five-six-double-oh! . . ."

The range was opening. "Port four points!" Smith set to closing it again. The enemy was edging away, trying to open the range and make it a big gun battle. *Thunder* had only one big gun now.

Minutes later *Kondor* opened the range again, and again Smith ordered a closing course. The message he sent was clear: if *Kondor* edged away he would follow her until she ran aground. But he knew the captain of *Kondor* would not just accept that.

"Torpedo red-four-oh," Wakely shrieked.

Thunder turned towards the enemy, and the torpedo ran down her side, clear away. Smith held the turn, then: "Midships!"

So they were running again on parallel courses five thousand yards apart and *Thunder* a steel door between *Kondor* and the open sea. *Kondor* hammered at the door; the nerve-battering, brutal slogging match went on.

In the conning-tower, thrown about, deafened, bruised, Smith took the reports as they came in. The twin after six-inch casemate on the port side received a direct hit from an 8.2-inch shell that wrecked the guns and decimated the crew. The port forward casemate took a freak hit on the muzzle of the gun that left its crew tossed about like dolls but still alive. That was Nobby Clark's gun. The upper-deck was a nightmare obstacle course of ripped plates, jagged-edged; piled wreckage and tangled rigging; sprouting fires fought by ghosts that came filthy out of the smoke, trailing hoses, and were lost in it again; over all rolled the smoke, from the fires, the clanging guns, and *Thunder*'s belching funnels.

Clark fought his way through and herded his crew along to a solitary six-inch gun that was still unmanned. They reached the gun moving like automata. The shell and the charge came up after Clark talked on the voice-pipe with Sergeant Burton who now seemed to be running some of the magazines. The ammunition that came up the hoist, which was worked manually because the power had failed, had travelled half the length of the ship from a port side magazine. The men of the ammunition parties carried those shells and charges along narrow ammunition passages in almost total darkness.

Elsewhere in the 'tweendecks men toiled in the smoke and frying heat, hauling at canvas hoses as they fought the fires. Duty was something to hold on to in a world being blasted apart around them.

Clark in the layer's seat squeezed the trigger and the gun slammed into action.

In the conning-tower the reports came in. "Hit forward, sir! Torpedo flat and prison flat flooded!"

Smith acknowledged and altered course again in that continual erratic weave trying to outguess the enemy guns. Occasionally he saw *Kondor* through the drifting smoke and saw she was badly mauled. As a raider she was finished; she needed a dockyard and that meant internment. *Wolf* was in at least as bad a case and probably worse, lying crippled, miles away.

But as *Thunder* fired her remaining guns, there were only three now, it was evident that *Kondor* had the whip hand. She was firing more guns, four or five, in regular salvoes.

The beating went on. An explosion right over the conning-tower sent them sprawling for the twentieth time, there was a rending crash and as Smith dragged to his feet with blood running from

120

his nose he saw that the mast had gone, fallen back along the length of *Thunder*'s deck, thrusting the tilted, riddled funnels to an even crazier angle.

Garrick's voice, hoarse and urgent, no longer echoed down the voice-pipe because the fore-top was now just part of the wreckage heaped in the waist. *Thunder* had only one six-inch gun still in action besides the forward-turret. She took a direct hit on the turret. The orange flash split the smoke-filled drum of the conning-tower. As the flame blinded them, the blast rattled them around the drum but Smith kept his feet as did the coxswain at the wheel. As Wakely rolled to his knees Smith hauled him upright, croaked, "Get a fire party on that turret!" And thrust him, staggering, on his way. That was the most Smith would do. The turret and the men in it, Gibb among them, he must now forget. He looked again for the enemy.

Thunder's speed was falling away. *Kondor* was starting to turn, slowly, to creep across ahead of *Thunder* and so out to sea. She was trying again to make it a big gun battle and *Thunder* did not have a big gun. She would haul out of range of the lone six-inch and then smash *Thunder* to pieces. Smith could not stop it.

"Steer four points to port!"

Thunder started to turn so that at least that one six-inch would bear. He could feel the sluggish response with the ship's speed down below ten knots and falling still.

She was dying beneath his feet.

WHEN THE HIT smashed the mast below Garrick it threw him onto his back in the fore-top, which then fell and Garrick fell with it. He clung on with arms wrapped around the mast as the fore-top smashed against the funnel and then onto the boat-deck. He was hurled loose to roll and almost plunge the ten feet to the upper deck but he grabbed half-dazed for handhold, and found one.

He was winded, bruised, disorientated. He could not move his left arm. But he realized his danger out there on the boat-deck where splinters whined. So he rolled over the edge, and dropped to the deck and collapsed as *Thunder* was hit forward.

Flame licked at the conning-tower, blinding him. His legs felt numb. He tried to stand, and succeeded at the third attempt. He

121

had to reach the captain. He started to stumble aft, felt the shock and slam of a six-inch firing and thought there was one gun still firing, and then somehow broke into a shambling trot.

ALBRECHT HAD seized on his expression of professional detachment and stamped it on his face and mind. And still the casualties came down; vicious splinter wounds, hideous burns, the wounds more terrible, the task impossible. The sick-bay filled as he operated. The ship rocked and lurched around them. Then the light flickered and went out and gave way to the emergency lighting.

The firing ceased. Albrecht thought, "Maybe he's surrendered". But he did not believe it. Looking up for an instant he saw Daddy Horsfall and a stoker black with coal dust stumble in, a body between them. They found a space and carefully laid him down.

Albrecht called, "Horsfall! Has the action ended?"

"Dunno, sir."

"If it has I want to move out of this. I want a place with light and air—" *Thunder* came out of a turn and opened fire again. The ship shook. Albrecht finished: "—as soon as it's over."

"Aye, aye, sir." Daddy went away, thinking: "You'll be bloody lucky, old cock. D'yer suppose some referee'll blow fer time?" The ship still shook but Albrecht tried to keep his hands steady until the job was done. And the next one. And the next . . .

Until he stopped. Everything stopped. He stared across at Purkiss, similarly frozen.

Purkiss said dully, "Engines have stopped, sir."

SMITH FELT the heart stop, as they all did. Now *Thunder* lay inert to be destroyed at will.

Another salvo shrieked in.

NOBBY CLARK, eye glued to the layer's telescope, held his breath, feeling the heart stop, and the sight-setter croaked, "Engines have stopped."

Nobby sighed. Oh, God. He bellowed, "Where's that flaming round?" He stumbled back to the hoist and bawled down, "Where's the ammunition? What're you doing down there, for Gawd's sake?"

There was silence, then he heard movement in the passage below and saw at the bottom of the hoist a face turned up to him, unrecognizable under the filth and in the gloom but the voice was unmistakable. It came up, gravelly, calm, "Noisy bastard, ain't you?" Burton the indestructible.

"Just give us the round."

The hoist creaked and the round came up, was rammed.

The charge was inserted. As the breech clanged shut Nobby slipped back into his seat, rubbed at bloodshot eyes and peered through the telescope again.

He could see the cruiser as a ghost ship almost hidden by the smoke she made and trailed; he could see she was burning, great gouts of flame leaping through holes in her hull. He thought that *Thunder* was sinking but she'd savaged the cruiser. Or Smith had.

He laid the gun. The way had fallen off *Thunder* and she was still in the water so that he was firing from a rock-steady platform. He squeezed the trigger.

Recoil. Flame and smoke and fumes.

With his eye glued again to the telescope, watching, he ordered automatically, "Load!"

"No bloody round to load."

He heard them shouting huskily down the black steel well of the hoist. He saw the flash on the hull of the distant ship and thought, "Hit her—"

He recoiled from the telescope, hands to his eyes. A flash like a great burning sun had blotted out the cruiser. The explosion came rocking across the sea in great shock waves. A ball of smoke climbed up from the German, rolled up and up, sparks and debris soared in that smoke, soared and then fell.

He whispered, "She's blown up."

11

Sunlight sparked on a quiet sea. Smith stood forward of the conning-tower, clear of the twisted wreckage of the bridge. He was numbed. The deck on which he stood was unrecognizable. Forward of him the turret smoked thinly, the barrel of the gun askew; the fore part of the ship was a moonscape of craters. Aft was a scene of tangled wreckage laced with licking pools of flame fought by men who stumbled over and around the wreckage, weaving like drunken men. It was a cat's-cradle of twisted steel, riven plates. Of *Thunder*'s four funnels only one stood, riddled. The two aftermost had fallen in on each other, joined by the mast and the whole steel mountain sagged over the port side, canting the deck. She was down by the stern.

Garrick was alive. His face was streaked with blood, one arm hung limp and his face was drawn with pain but he had returned to duty. So had Davies, his boiler-suit half-burned from him, his grizzled hair singed. And Petty Officer Miles, who seemed to bear the mark of every fire aboard.

And Smith had gone to see for himself. The steering compartment was wrecked and flooded right forward to the engine-room bulkhead. There was no power at all.

Davies summed it up, hugely understated the obvious: "It's a dockyard job."

That meant a tow. No doubt a tug would come, hurrying, a vulture. It meant internment. For the ship and her crew, for Smith himself.

But the fires were under control and *Thunder* was not sinking.

Wolf was sinking.

They could see her by squinting against that sun that was still low, across the miles of sea. Smith, with his glasses, was watching, when her stern lifted and her bow went under and she slid down. A rush of steam and smoke from the funnels hung in a spreading pall like a shroud.

It covered the men in the water. There were no boats to be seen and Smith had none to send. The pinnace had crabbed alongside to weak cheers, Manton at the wheel and all hands baling. When Manton stood swaying before Smith he had explained, "One dropped rather close, sir." She leaked in a dozen places and now she hung in the water, not floating, where they had made her fast at *Thunder*'s side. She was no more seaworthy than a colander.

Albrecht had contrived to clear a space on the upper-deck abaft the bridge to which he was evacuating his wounded. They carried them up, coughing, from below. "I'm setting up here," he told Smith. "The sick-bay is impossible."

124

"I know. Do what you can."

"I've blankets, bandages and cold water for one-hundred-and-forty-seven cases of everything from concussion to amputation, to severe scalding, to burns. The burns—" He shook his head. "There are more. They're still finding them. . . ."

He stopped at sight of Smith's face, sighed and went on wearily, "I'm not blaming you. I know that if you hadn't fought those cruisers they'd have run wild all along this coast, and all the rest of it. I know. It had to be done. You did it and still saved most of us and the ship though only God knows how. I still can't believe it. The surgeon's knife. I only wish my surgery was as successful as yours, but we both have to live with it."

Smith knew that; he had laid one ghost only to raise another. He said, "Anything you want, anything I can do . . ."

"I know. If you have time, later, you ought to come and talk to the men." Albrecht smiled wryly. "They call you all kinds of a tough, mad bastard, but they love you, all of them."

That silenced Smith. He looked at the men where they lay uncomplaining, silent or weakly joking on the deck and beyond them to the others who laboured like filthy spectres, and beyond them in his mind's eye to the others below, out of his sight in the smoke-filled reeking darkness. And to *Thunder*'s seventy-three dead. So far. And he wondered for the thousandth time or more in his life how he could deserve men like this.

Albrecht cleared his throat. "And I'd like to see that boy Wakely. One of my lads put a dressing on him but I want him as soon as you can spare him." Smith had seen him working on the deck below, the once plump and pink Wakely now haggard and grey, skull wrapped in a bloody bandage.

Albrecht started to turn away and a shell shrieked in and landed aft in the centre of a working-party. Smith winced against the flash, rocked by the burst and saw men tossed like bloody dolls. He stared stupidly, then his eyes searched as he cursed himself for forgetting, knowing what he would find.

The *Leopard* was coming in from the sea. *Thunder* had left her behind guarding the mouth of the river, a cork in an empty bottle, but she had followed the cruisers. He had forgotten her. She was coming in from the sea because she would have set that

125

course while *Kondor* still fought, not risking going inshore of the bigger ships. Now she was left with nothing but vengeance and she would take it. She must know *Thunder* hadn't a gun that would fire seaward. She only had two four-inch guns herself and they would not sink *Thunder* quickly but they would steadily tear her to pieces.

There was nothing to stop her. Garrick was trying with a party to clear a midships twelve-pounder that looked as if it *might* have survived. If he succeeded that pop-gun would not stop *Leopard*. The men were ready to fight again but they stumbled with fatigue.

He saw Benks standing among the wounded where they lay in rows on the deck. "Benks!" He spoke briefly to the hollow-eyed steward and Benks disappeared below and Smith climbed to the fore-deck to stand by the conning-tower, eyes fixed on the gunboat. Like a rich man's yacht. He flinched as her forward gun fired again. The round burst close alongside.

Smith had thrown himself to the deck but he scrambled up as Benks called to him and he took the bundle from the steward. He jammed it inside his jacket and started to climb painfully up through the tangle of wreckage to the top of the conning-tower. A shell burst on the useless fore-turret and blast plucked at him. He hung on, looked down and saw Garrick standing by the abandoned twelve-pounder, staring dumbly up at him. Smith climbed again.

He stood up on top of the conning-tower, blinking at the gunboat as he fumbled at the big, white tablecloth tucked inside his jacket. Garrick's face showed agony but Garrick knew as well as he that Smith had no choice. The gunboat came on. She would turn soon so that she could fire both the fore and aft guns, and then . . .

The waterspouts rose in white towers, a line of them that hid the *Leopard* behind a curtain of water that hung for seeming seconds as the sound of that salvo came rumbling across the sea. As the water fell and the spray blew away he could see her turning, turning away from that sudden enormous salvo from out of the blue. The sound wave rumbled in bass over the sea and staring aft he saw *Kansas*, unmistakable, huge, roaring up from the south.

126

ABOARD *KANSAS* the messenger from the wireless room said, "Signal, sir."

Donoghue took it, read it and handed it to his flag-captain who muttered the words as he read: ". . . 'commence hostilities' . . . Came just a trifle late."

Donoghue growled, "I didn't commence hostilities. I said we would come out in case survivors needed assistance but once here I wasn't going to sit and watch murder done. However. Order that gunboat to heave to or we'll sink her. And make to *Thunder*: United States at war with Germany. Where are the enemy cruisers?"

On the signal bridge a yeoman with a telescope to his eye drawled, "Feller on top of—the bridge—I think. Signalling with a couple of white flags. He's hellish slow, even for a Limey."

Smith was rusty.

The answer came. "*Thunder* replies, sir: 'Sunk. Can you tow me?'"

Donoghue groped for some noble phrase, some stirring reply but then he remembered the slight, lonely figure on the quay naming himself simply, "Smith."

And Donoghue said, "Affirmative."

SMITH STARTED the climb down to the deck. There was work to do but there would be help for all of them now, for Garrick, for Davies, for Albrecht and the men. For the ship. His mind already worked on the details of the tow, of the bulkheads that needed to be shored up. *Kansas* could lend them divers. . . .

He found himself wondering about Sarah Benson and the destruction wrought this day. There was good reason for that destruction, for him at least. When she had raised the pistol and fired in cold blood, what was the reason? He had never asked her. . . .

The battered hulk that was *Thunder* wallowed in the seaway. On *Kansas* as she swept down on her every man who could stared at her in silence.

The guns were silent.

IN GUAYA, Sarah Benson had waited, listening to the rumble of the distant guns. Now she listened to that silence, cold. And waited.

Alan Evans

How is it that an author comes to write a book like *Thunder at Dawn*, surely the Hornblower of the First World War? Alan Evans claims that it all began most unromantically in a London suburban train. He suddenly "saw", apparently quite unprompted, a massive cruiser creeping through a swamp. It was definitely a Great War cruiser and a South American swamp. Why so?

Evans believes that the vision may have sprung unconsciously from a book he had been reading about the Battle of Coronel, during which, in 1914, British ships in South American waters had been blown out of the water by superior German ships. He had wondered then if there was any way in which they could have won. Perhaps part of the answer lay in that vision. Perhaps it could make a book.

Alan Evans was already a part-time writer of thrillers and short stories, and was also writing children's books, but he had never written of war, of ships, or of any historical subject. Still, as a Territorial soldier he had always been fascinated by gunnery and could still recall his father's tales of his life in the navy seventy-five years ago. So he settled down to years of research in the hope that a book might result.

With a young family and his job at the Inland Revenue taking up most of his time, research went slowly. No old cruisers have survived, but pictures and models of them do, and the memories of those who served in them. On these he built his story.

The book became an obsession. There were no more thrillers, no more short stories. There were first drafts, second drafts, revisions—then suddenly offers for paperback, translation rights on a scale he had never dreamed of before; then, finally, a Condensed Books choice.

Thunder was well and truly launched—and even if she has fought her last battle in this book, her brilliant captain has deservedly survived to fight again, and is surely destined for further, even more challenging commands. In which we at Reader's Digest offer him every good wish. And predict a distinguished future, both for him and his talented author.

TISHA

The Story of a Young Teacher
in the Wilderness of Alaska

a condensation of the book by

Anne Hobbs with Robert Specht

Illustrated by Tom Hall
Published by Michael Joseph

Anne Hobbs was a schoolmarm of nineteen when she trekked into the wilds of Alaska, bound for a one-room schoolhouse in a tiny settlement with the unlikely name of Chicken. It was the adventure of a lifetime for Anne, but the inhabitants of Chicken found her independent ways disturbing—especially when she took up with Fred Purdy, who was handsome, gentle and half Eskimo. Then Teacher—pronounced "Tisha" by the young ones—proceeded to take two half-Indian children into her home, and the atmosphere became explosive.

This is the spirited true story of a spunky young woman who was blessed with more than her share of courage and humour.

I've lived in the Forty Mile country of Alaska for a long time, but even now, every so often when I'm out rock hunting, I get lost. Sometimes I'll have to wander around for a while before I get my bearings. That's what happened to me when I started to think about telling this story. I wasn't sure which direction to take, until I finally realized that the only way to tell it was the way I might have told it when I first came to Alaska.

That was back in 1927, when I was a prim and proper young lady of nineteen. I'd always been thrilled with the idea of living on a frontier, so when I was offered the job of teaching school in a gold-mining settlement called Chicken I accepted right away.

The first time I heard the name Chicken I laughed. I didn't believe there could really be such a place. Sure enough, though, when I looked at a map of Alaska there it was (and still is), right up near the Yukon Territory and the trading center of Forty Mile, about forty miles northwest of Dawson.

Green as goose grass and full of lofty ideals, off I went, thinking of myself as a lamp unto the wilderness. The last thing I expected was that the residents of Chicken wouldn't think of me that way at all. All that was forty-eight years ago, yet I can still remember how excited I was the day I set off for Chicken by packtrain. It left from a village called Eagle. . . .

SEPTEMBER 1927

I

Even though the sun had just come up, practically the whole town of Eagle had turned out to see the packtrain off. Counting the Indians, who'd come down from their fish camp for the dance the previous night, there must have been close to a hundred people: miners in hip boots, old sourdoughs in battered stetsons, women and children. In a few minutes I'd be going off into the wilderness. I was scared and I must have shown it, because Mrs. Rooney, the schoolteacher in Eagle, asked if I was feeling well.

"Yes, ma'am," I said. "I guess I just didn't expect there'd be all these people."

Mrs. Rooney dismissed them with a wave of her hand. "It doesn't take much to collect a crowd in Alaska. As for the trip, it's only ninety miles and Mr. Strong will take good care of you."

But it really wasn't the crowd that was bothering me. It was the horse I'd be riding for the next four days. He was called Blossom, but it was the last thing he looked like. He was so huge that even if I stood on my toes I wouldn't have been able to see over the saddle, and he was scarred and wild-looking. I'd ridden a horse on my grandmother's farm back in Missouri as a child, but he was so gentle you could have gone to sleep on his back. This one was mean. From the minute Mr. Strong handed his reins over to me, Blossom started rolling his eyes and trying to nip me.

From the corner of my eye I could see Mr. Strong moving toward me down the line of horses and mules tethered together. Besides the U.S. mail, the animals were loaded down with washboards, sacks of dried beans, bolts of canvas, even windowpanes.

I wished I weren't the only passenger. In another minute I'd have to mount up, and I was sure I'd make a spectacle of myself.

Then Mr. Strong was beside me. He was a tall, stoop-shouldered man, who had come to Alaska in his twenties to look for gold. He had been in the Forty Mile country for twenty years. He had a courtly way about him that seemed very out of place in this rough country. When I'd asked him the day before if he could take me to Chicken he'd said, "Yes, madam, I can. My packtrain leaves on the fourth, the fourteenth and the twenty-fourth of each month. I shall, therefore, be leaving tomorrow. Eight a.m. sharp."

"I'd like to go," I'd told him.

"The rent for your horse will be ten dollars per day. That will include your meals and your lodgings. The journey will take four days. I hope that will be satisfactory."

I'd told him it would be fine and that was that.

"If you are ready, madam," he said to me now, "I shall assist you to mount."

He took the reins and dropped them over Blossom's head, then bent forward with his hands locked together. I grabbed the saddle horn and he boosted me up. Once I was in the saddle the ground looked pretty far down. Blossom started to dance around and a few people laughed. As soon as he settled down, I saw they were laughing at my legs. The saddle was so wide that they stuck out like wings.

"Better do somethin' about them pins a hers, Walter," somebody called out, "or she'll be knockin' down every tree in the Forty Mile."

Mr. Strong shortened the stirrups until I could get my feet into them, but I was still spread out pretty wide. He looked at my clothes skeptically. "Are you sure, madam, you will not reconsider the coat?"

A little earlier he had offered to lend me a coat, saying that the weather was very changeable. But I'd told him I didn't think I'd need it. "I'm really very comfortable," I said now.

If I were back in the States I'd have felt ridiculous, but here in Alaska nobody cared how you dressed. I was wearing the jacket of my pink Easter suit, a pair of boy's corduroy knickers, cotton stockings and some old sport brogues. I knew that the flowered hat I'd bought in Portland would end up crushed if it were put on the pack animals with my other things, so I wore that too. My ensemble was completed by a nickel-plated revolver that a fellow had given me at the dance last night.

Mr. Strong started for the front of the packtrain and I looked around, able to see the whole crowd for the first time. A few old men were sitting on the rail of the schoolhouse porch. Aside from the stables, the sturdy log schoolhouse was the only building here at the edge of town. I was looking forward to teaching in it when I took over from Mrs. Rooney next year. Lester Henderson, education commissioner for the territory, had told me I could when he interviewed me in Juneau. I hoped the schoolhouse I was heading for now would be as nice as the one in Eagle.

Farther up the line of pack animals a few men were checking the loads, but most people were just gathered around talking. The Indians stood apart from the whites. Compared to the whites, who were laughing and joking, the Indian men were quiet, just watching what was going on.

"How's the weather up there, Teacher?" "Cabaret" Jackson—who bragged he'd been in every cabaret from Dawson to the Bering Sea—grinned up at me. "Hate to see you leavin'," he said. "Don't suppose you'd change your mind about what I asked you last night?"

"Thanks, Cab, but I don't think so."

He was the one who'd given me the revolver, telling me that I shouldn't be going into the wilds without a little protection. Last night, before he got too drunk and into a fight, he'd proposed to me, promising me everything under the sun. He'd been a real gentleman, but when he got drunk he turned mean. He wasn't the type I'd want to keep company with.

"Well," he said, "I'll be mushin' out there to Chicken after the freeze-up, and I'll just try you again."

"Teacher?" A girl with a sweet smile had come up near me along with her husband. I couldn't remember her name, but there was something so nice about her when I'd met her the day before that I'd liked her right away. She was going to have a baby, and she kept stooping over to hide her stomach. She said, "Teacher, do me a favor, will you?"

"Sure." I liked that—the way everybody called me Teacher.

"My ma runs the roadhouse out to Chicken—Maggie Carew.

Tell her I'm comin' along real good an' that I'm expectin' middle of December."

"And tell her it'll be a boy," her husband said.

"Tell her it's gonna be a girl. I know it. My name's Jeannette Terwilliger. And this here's Elmer."

"Maggie Carew," I said. "Middle of December. I'll tell her."

At the front of the line Mr. Strong had mounted up. Holding a coiled bullwhip, he wheeled his horse and slapped a few of the animals on the rump, and the packtrain moved out. Someone gave Blossom a whack and I grabbed for the saddle horn as he plunged forward. I held on for dear life as he caught up with the packtrain and kept going. I felt my hat lifting from my head, and then it was gone. By the time we passed Mr. Strong I was sliding off and I braced myself for a fall. Then Blossom stopped just short of a corridor of birches that led into the forest.

Shaking, I watched Mr. Strong ride up. "Madam," he said graciously, "since you're not familiar with the trail, I think it better if you allow me to lead."

As he went past I looked back at Eagle and the green waters of the Yukon River. There were a few people waving good-by, and I felt sad. For the past two weeks I'd done more traveling and met more friendly people than ever before in my life. Up to now the longest trip I'd ever made had been from Colorado, where I was born, to Oregon, where I'd been teaching.

Even though I'd heard that there weren't too many women in the North, I hadn't expected to be treated like a raving beauty wherever I went. But I was. In Whitehorse and Dawson there'd been dances given in my honor. A couple of times I'd looked at myself in a mirror, thinking that maybe I was really prettier than I'd thought. But after a good examination I knew I was just the same plain Anne Hobbs: same gray eyes, not a bad nose, good white teeth. One of the front ones was a little crooked, so about the best I could say was that if my hair were long I might have a faint resemblance to Mary Pickford.

The last of the pack animals passed me, and Blossom started to move, following them into the birches flaming with autumn colors and growing so thick on each side of the trail that I couldn't see the mountains beyond. It was warm enough to open my jacket, and I found it hard to believe this was Alaska. Even though it was only the fourth of September, I'd expected to find snow on the ground.

The trail suddenly narrowed; trees and buckbrush pressed in on each side and branches tore at my jacket. Now I realized why Mr. Strong had offered me the coat. If I could have, I'd have ridden forward and asked for it, but the trail was too narrow and uneven for me to pass the animals ahead. I kept slipping and sliding all over the saddle. My legs were aching from trying to hold on. When I pulled on the reins to try to make Blossom slow down, he turned and tried to bite my foot.

An hour later the land dipped suddenly, and Blossom started down a canyon side so steep I was afraid I'd go tumbling over his head. By the time we were halfway down, I could barely hold on to the saddle horn. My jacket was ruined and all I wanted to do was cry. Then without warning the sun disappeared and everything was gray and chill. A few minutes later big feathery snowflakes were drifting down and it was like the middle of winter. When I finally reached the bottom of the canyon my teeth were chattering. My hands were so numb I couldn't move my fingers.

The packtrain had stopped and Mr. Strong came riding back, an olive-drab army coat over his arm. He shook his head when he saw how I looked, but he didn't say anything. He helped me on with the coat and we went on. If he'd asked me how I was I would have started crying. Snow kept drifting down, melting as it hit the ground. Finally it stopped. Once Mr. Strong rode back and complimented me on how much better I was sitting. "You're not sliding all over the place now."

"Thanks," I told him, "but it's not me. The snow melted on the saddle and my pants are stuck."

He smiled for the first time since I had met him.

We stopped for lunch at Gravel Gulch, where the slopes were thick with willow and tamarack. After that the going was easier. The country smoothed out into a series of gently sweeping hills, and I wished I weren't so saddle sore, so that I could really appreciate it. It was all so big that it made me feel as if something exciting was going to happen, yet so quiet and lonely I felt lost in it. But big as it was, when we'd stop to water the horses at a creek and have a drink ourselves, there'd always be an old tin cup hanging from a nail driven into a tree.

Darkness came slowly after a long twilight. It was past eight o'clock when we reached Liberty. There was nothing to see but an old sagging cabin with a stable nearby, and I was so bone-weary I lay down in a bedroll on the cabin floor by the stove and fell into an exhausted sleep.

We left early the next morning and rode for most of the day through creek land and hills. In late afternoon, when I was so sore I could hardly sit in the saddle, we came to a high ridge and Mr. Strong said, "Walk your horse over there." He pointed to a spot about a hundred yards away and I nudged Blossom over to it.

What I saw made me forget every ache and pain. The sun was below the distant mountains, and the land in between was covered with a strange veil of gray. Pine and spruce loomed up from the slopes below, and beyond there was so much land, all of it bursting with spruce and tamarack, that I felt like a speck of dust that could be swept away in a second. Winding through it for as far as I could see were the waters of the Fortymile River, which empties into the Yukon at the town of Forty Mile. Directly below, on the other side of the river, looking almost unreal, were twenty acres of tilled farmland. A big red barn was set to one side, and near that was a log building with bright patches of flowers around it.

"Steel Creek," Mr. Strong said, riding up beside me. "That's the creek, branching into the river down there. And that's the Prentiss roadhouse." I couldn't wait to get there. Mr. Strong had told me I'd be able to take a hot bath when we reached Steel Creek.

At the roadhouse, Mrs. Prentiss, a stocky woman with gray hair and a bossy manner, took me in charge. She told a girl with braids down her back to unfold the canvas tub, and then she ushered me into a room to take off my clothes. She came back a few minutes later with an old flannel bathrobe, steered me into a bathing room and eased me into the tub, which was full of steaming water.

"This is my daughter, Nancy," Mrs. Prentiss said. She said to the girl, "You stay with her. I got supper to make and I don't want her falling asleep."

I slid down along the rubber lining of the tub and let my head rest against the wooden frame. Nancy sat down in a chair. She was uncomfortable. Her green eyes kept looking everyplace but at me. I told her she didn't have to stay. "I won't fall asleep."

"You sure?"

"Positive. It feels too good."

I stayed in the tub until Mrs. Prentiss came for me. She handed me a suit of boy's long underwear. "It's scratchy," she said, "but it's warm."

She ordered me to stay awake until she brought me some dinner. The meat was bear cub, but it tasted like pork and was delicious. No sooner had I finished it than I fell asleep.

At breakfast the next morning Mrs. Prentiss asked, "How long you been teaching?"

"Two years."

"What do you think of somebody who's had plenty of schooling and still can't read?"

"I don't know," I said. "There could be a lot of reasons."

"I got a favor to ask you," she said. "I want my Nancy to stay with you at Chicken."

I was too surprised to answer.

"I'm willing to pay," she went on. "I'm not asking nothing for nothing."

"But Nancy and I don't even know each other, Mrs. Prentiss."

She brushed that aside. "That doesn't matter. My Nancy can't read too good and I think you could help her."

"But I don't even know if I'll have room for her."

"If there isn't room she'll sleep on the floor. Look, Teacher, you're a cheechako. You don't know the first thing about this country. Nancy could be a big help."

Cheechako, I had already learned, meant greenhorn—greenest of the green. "Let me think about it," I said, wanting to get away.

Mrs. Prentiss' tone changed. "I'll give it to you straight, Teacher.

I think you'd be good for Nancy. I'm talking to you because she asked me to. I could send her to school in Eagle, but she doesn't like Mrs. Rooney."

I had the feeling Nancy was behind the door, listening. I got up. "Let me think about it," I said again.

Mr. Strong was in the stable, ready to lead the animals out. When I told him about the proposal, he said, "It's a good idea. Living in the bush isn't easy for anyone, madam, much less for someone like you. Nancy can teach you a great deal."

It was true. Having someone like Nancy to show me the ropes would make things a lot easier. I could help her and she could help me. Before the packtrain left I told Mrs. Prentiss that it was all right, and she said she'd send Nancy out with Mr. Strong sometime in the next few weeks.

We were a few miles out of Steel Creek when a settlement appeared in the distance—a line of about fifteen cabins set back from the banks of the Fortymile River. "An Indian village," Mr. Strong said. "We'll stop there."

When we drew near I was shocked. My father had been a coal miner, moving from one ugly Colorado mining town to another, but this was a shantytown, worse than any of the coal towns I'd lived in. There were three or four decent-looking places, but the rest were hovels, sagging shacks patched with tar paper, scraps of iron, old animal hides. Rusting cans, bottles and fishbones littered the ground. The stench was nauseating.

As we rode in, people stared at us from doorways. I'd thought that the Indians at Eagle were poor, but these people had nothing. Worn dresses hung like sacks on the women, patched and baggy overalls on the men. Mangy dogs, chained to stakes, snarled and leaped at us as we went by. Barefoot and in rags, a few children kept pace with us. Some had running sores on their necks from glandular tuberculosis.

We stopped in front of a frame house with peeling paint. "*Skooltrai* here?" Mr. Strong asked a woman. She nodded as the door opened and an Indian and a white girl came out. The girl was beautiful, but the Indian was one of the ugliest men I'd ever seen, tall and thin, his neck covered with scars. They were followed by a little boy about eight years old, skinny as a rail. You could see he was part white.

"Good day, Miss Winters," Mr. Strong called to the girl. "This young lady is bound for Chicken and she needs a short rest. I would appreciate it if you would accommodate her."

"I'll give you a hand," she said, reaching up to me. She was lovely, with bright blue eyes, and long black hair tied back with a red bandanna. Her dress was homespun, embroidered with Indian designs around the hem and sleeves.

"I'm Cathy Winters," she said as she helped me down.

"Thanks," I said. "I'm Anne Hobbs."

She indicated the tall Indian beside her. "This is Titus Paul." I could see she was pretty fond of him. He wore a beaded leather vest, and he did look kind of dashing in an ugly way.

Cathy asked the little boy to get her mail, then took me into the house, to a dingy room with cracked brown linoleum on the floor. The little boy came back and put her mail on a table.

"This is Chuck," Cathy said. "He'll be keeping you company the rest of the way. He's going to his mother in Chicken. Chuck, I'd like you to meet Miss Hobbs."

He was too shy to look at me.

"Oh, come on," she encouraged him. "Is that the way I taught you to say hello? She won't bite you. She's a teacher just like me."

"Please . . . to . . . meet you," he said gravely.

"I'm pleased to meet you too," I said.

Over a cup of coffee I found out that these were Cathy's living quarters. The rest of the house was the school. She didn't have much of a place, but she'd made it comfortable, with books all over and Indian ceremonial masks on the walls.

When we went out, we saw that Mr. Strong had untied a load on one of the animals and laid the contents on the ground. The Indians who'd ordered stuff were stooped around it. They had their money ready as he handed them their goods: a frying pan for one, kerosene lantern for another, canned milk, a teapot.

Cathy introduced me to them in their own language. I caught the words *skooltrai* and Chicken. The girls giggled shyly. The older women, like most of the men, looked listless and tired; many had the hectic flush of TB. Cathy told me half the village had it.

She pointed to the storage caches in back of many of the cabins, which should have been packed with dried meat and fish. Most held pitifully little. "They won't be empty in the winter, though," she said bitterly. "We'll keep the dead there until we can bury them in the spring."

"Why do they live this way?" I asked.

"Because they're weak. Before the whites came, about forty years ago, these people were hunters. Their diet was almost all meat and fat, practically raw. They had the strength to go out and take game when they needed it. Now they eat the white man's flour, sugar, canned goods, junk. And they drink his liquor. . . ."

"What kind of Indians are they?" I asked her.

"Athapaskans. That's the general designation for all the Indians up here. Then that's broken down into tribes. These people are Takhud Kutchins."

She told me she was a graduate of Columbia University and was writing a thesis on the Athapaskans of the Forty Mile for her doctorate. She said Titus Paul was one of the few Indians the whites couldn't boss around. He was the unofficial chief of the village.

Nearby we saw an old crone with bowed legs, and only a couple of teeth in her mouth. "That's Lame Sarah," Cathy said. "Chuck, the little boy who's going with you, has been living with her. She can barely take care of herself. Thank God he's getting out of here."

When we were ready to leave, the old woman and Chuck were standing by one of the mules, which had an old saddle on it. She hugged the child to her, murmuring endearments, but his frightened eyes were on the mule. It towered over him the way Blossom did over me. Mr. Strong grabbed the back of his mackinaw, lifted him bodily and plunked him down on the mule's back. "You stay put," he warned him, "savvy?"

Terrorized, Chuck didn't answer.

Cathy said, "Look after him, will you, Anne? He's hardly ever gone more than a few miles out of this village and he'll be scared to death."

"I'll look after him."

"Remember," Cathy said to him, "if you need anything you speak English. You tell the teacher here, savvy?"

"*Aha*," he said.

"No more *aha*," Cathy said. "From now on it's yes, understand?" He nodded. "I say yiss and I tell Tisha."

The packtrain moved out. We followed the curve of the river, and the last I saw of the Indian village was the white wooden cross on top of the church. Then that disappeared over the tops of the trees. I was glad when it was gone. The poverty and sickness of the place was awful.

Chuck made out all right on the mule as long as we stuck to the riverbank, but when we veered off and started going through rough country, the mule jumped over a dead tree and he went tumbling off. He scrambled to his feet and ran after the mule; but it wouldn't stop, and Chuck stood in the trail, tears of anger streaming down his face.

There was a big boulder a short distance away and I headed Blossom over to it and called to Chuck, "See if you can climb up and get on with me." He came over and clambered on in back of me. Then we rode on, his arms tight around my waist. Up ahead, Mr. Strong appeared with the mule. He looked at me questioningly.

"He asked if he could ride with me for a while," I said. "I'm getting pretty good now. I don't mind."

Mr. Strong rode off without saying anything. Chuck's head leaned against my back.

"Tisha?"

"Yes?"

"You one helluva good white woman," he said, tightening his grip on my waist. It made me feel good.

At the next rest stop, I spent some time showing Chuck how to ride the mule. "You say whoa when you want him to stop, say giddap and give him a kick when you want him to go." It took a little while, but once he saw he could control the animal he stopped being afraid. By the time we were ready to go, he was having fun. The longer we rode together, the more I liked him. If he was sore— and he had to be—he didn't complain. Instead he'd jump down every so often and lead the mule along.

We stopped overnight at the O'Shaughnessy roadhouse. It was run by a pleasant Irishman with a thick accent. I shared the bed with his wife, a plump Indian woman, who saw to it that Chuck was well fed and bedded down in a warm sleeping bag in our room. I tucked him in and was going out when he called to me. "Tisha . . . you talk me?"

I sat down on the sleeping bag. "I bet you'll be glad to see your mother."

"Oh yiss. She beyoodeeful, Tisha—like you."

"I'll bet. Is your father in Chicken too?"

"Yiss. He big man. Got plenty guns. Got big glass eyes see far." He curled his fists in front of his eyes to make binoculars. "I no like him," he added.

"Why not?"

"He no like me and Et'el."

"Is Ethel your sister?"

"Mmm. . . . You got nice school?" he asked drowsily.

"I don't know. I haven't seen it yet."

"You let me come?"

"Sure. Do you like school?"

"School plenty warm. Miss Wintuhs make good grub for kids. You make good grub you school?"

"I probably could. What do you like to eat?"

He didn't answer. He'd fallen asleep.

II

AROUND noon the next day Mr. Strong stopped the packtrain as we were making our way through a dense growth of cotton-wood. The cowbells that had been clanking around us all the way down the line were suddenly quiet, and all I could hear were the waters of the meandering creek we'd been crossing and recrossing.

"There it is, madam," Mr. Strong said. "That is Chicken."

I could barely make it out through the trees—a settlement about a mile away and a little below us. I looked at the distant cabins, my stomach doing flip-flops. This is it, I thought. I'd come to a far place, just as my grandmother Hobbs used to tell me I would. When I was a little girl back in Colorado I used to hate the places I lived in: mining towns full of company shacks. I felt sure I'd be living in them forever, but Granny said no I wouldn't.

"You be a teacher, Annie," she used to tell me, "an' you can go anywhere in the world you want."

I could see her as clearly as if she were right in front of me. She wasn't like anybody else in our family. The rest of us were light-skinned and had blue eyes—or gray eyes like mine. But Granny was a full-blooded Kentuck Indian and her face was brown and broad, with black eyes that sparkled and laughed. If it weren't for her I can't think what might have happened to me. My parents had never cared much about me, but Granny had adored me.

Every time my father lost his job or left the house I was sent to live with her. She had a ramshackle little farm in the backlands of Deepwater, Missouri, and I thought it was wonderful. It made me smile just to think about it now. She must have been close to seventy the last time I was there. I'd lived with her a whole year that time, and I felt terrible when my mother wrote me to come home because my father was working again. Granny couldn't read, but although I wanted to, I couldn't lie to her about what was in the letter. She felt as bad as I did.

That last night we spent together we went to bed right after supper and I read to her from the Book of Psalms, her favorite. She had decided she couldn't abide beds after my grandfather died, so we were lying on thick patchwork quilts on the floor. She was a tiny little thing, and she was curled up beside me, her hair in a long braid down to her waist. Her eyes were closed. Her face was so dark and looked so Indian that I could imagine her living in a tepee. Thinking she was asleep, I put the Bible away. Her eyes popped open and she took my hand and squeezed it. "I'm gonna miss you, Annie."

I started to bawl as if I would never stop. Granny got up and held on to me the whole time. When I was done, she said, "Annie . . . you know I never told you a lie."

"I know."

"Then you know if I tell you you're a lucky girl, that's the truth. 'Cause you're smart. When a person's got brains they got a ticket to the whole world."

"What kind of a ticket?"

She tapped her head. "Right up here. Didn't you tell me that if you was to really study hard you could be teachin' school by the time you're sixteen?"

"That's what my teacher said."

"Then that's what you got to think about—bein' a teacher an' gettin' outta them dirty minin' places. Listen to me, 'cause I ain't gonna say this twice. You're gonna do real big things someday, Annie. But you can't do them if you go round feelin' sorry for yourself." She stopped for a second and she looked a little sad. "Your pa's my son, child. He ain't an easy man, but he always stood on his own two feet an' he learned you the same. Maybe him and your ma ain't been too understandin', but they fed you good an' give you a roof. That's more than many's got. . . ."

"But they don't really want me, Granny."

"Yes they do. They jus' don't know how to show it. But never mind that. If you got just *one* person in the whole world who loves you an' believes in you, why that's wonderful, don't ya see. An' you got one—me. So anytime you get to thinkin' you ain't gonna make it, or that you can't do somethin' for your own self's sake, you do it for my sake. Promise?"

"I promise."

"You'll see, Annie. Someday you're gonna go off to a new land just like a pioneer—like your grampa an' me did. 'Cause you're a big person. An' that's the kind that goes to a new land."

"But there's no new lands, Granny. They're all gone."

"Shoot, child, there always be new lands."

"Where?"

"California maybe. Or Alaska. . . . Now there's a new land."

As the packtrain began to move again, I thought of that last morning with Granny. When we hugged each other good-by she'd felt like a little bird. I was only eleven, but I was bigger than she was. I'd never seen her again. My mother wrote me during my first year of teaching that she had died in her sleep, and that she had left me a legacy. She sure had, but it wasn't the legacy my mother had written about. It was one she'd given me a long time ago, when I needed it most. And for that I'd never forget her.

As soon as we broke into the open, the packtrain speeded up and we descended into a small, level valley. About a quarter of a mile ahead were twenty-five or thirty buildings strung along the creek.

"Is that all of it?" I asked Mr. Strong.

"Just about."

I'd imagined Chicken would be a town like Eagle, but from this distance it looked more like the Indian village. It couldn't have been built in a better place, though, set down snug on the valley floor. Low hills ringed the valley, rolling away into a blue haze of high mountain peaks. The creek was deep and narrow, spilling down from the slope behind us. It got wider as it went, and in the middle of the settlement a wooden bridge arched across it.

It had rained recently, and halfway there we started winding around craters filled with muddy water. Mr. Strong cautioned me when Blossom came close to one, and I asked what they were.

"Prospect holes," he said. "Some go down forty feet. These miners don't bother to fill them up after they've dug them."

The ground got muddier as we went on. "Looks like everybody's waiting for us," I said. Just ahead was a crowd of twenty or thirty people gathered in front of the post office, a tiny cabin with an American flag fluttering over it.

I started grinning. The fragrance of woodsmoke wafted over and I felt proud enough to burst. I'd really done it. I'd traveled through the wilderness to a frontier settlement just the way Granny Hobbs had done. Mr. Strong saw the look on my face and he smiled.

"It looks wonderful," I said.

It wasn't like the Indian village at all. The street between the

148

creek and settlement was wide, with patches of late grass here and there. I could see vegetable gardens in a few backyards, along with dog kennels and stacks of corded wood. As we neared, the crowd started calling and waving. Between their hollering and the sled dogs barking you'd have thought it was the Fourth of July.

The whole place was about three city blocks long, the post office right in the middle, opposite the wooden bridge. The first few cabins were rotted skeletons or boarded up. Some of the others down the line weren't lived in either. The ones that were, though, were solid and sturdy, with traps, harness and washtubs hanging from posts and railings.

As we passed the first cabins Blossom broke into a jog for the stable and I couldn't hold him back. A man in knee-length boots ran out to cut him off, waving a fedora. Blossom gave up. A little old man appeared under him and grabbed his rein. "Steady as she goes." He smiled up at me, his teeth stained from chewing tobacco. "Hop right on down, little lady."

"Damn fool," another old man with a beard like a weeping willow said to him. "Can't ya see she can't make it by herself? Wait'll I get a box."

Everybody who hadn't moved out to stop the pack animals stood around and stared up at me. Chuck had found his mother, I saw—a slight dark Indian woman who had a little girl by the hand. From the glimpse I caught of her as she knelt to hug him she looked like a beauty.

I kept smiling and getting smiles in return. I tried to figure out which building was the schoolhouse and realized that it must be the big frame house with a homemade flagpole in front of it, opposite the stable. I knew my living quarters were in it, so I was glad to see that it was larger than Cathy's place.

The second old man came back with a box and set it down. "Here you be, missis." He helped me down. A big burly woman pushed him aside. "I'm Angela Barrett," she announced. "You're the new schoolmom, I take it." I nodded.

She led me over to another woman, who was wearing a long navy-blue coat buttoned up to the neck. She had a broken nose.

"I'm Maggie Carew," the woman said. "What's your name, honey?"

"Anne Hobbs."

"Let's get you over to the schoolhouse."

I'd been right about which building it was. When we stepped up onto the porch, Angela Barrett moved to the first of two doors. It was studded with mean-looking nails that stuck out about three inches. "This here's the schoolroom," she said, opening it. "The other door's to your quarters."

As I followed her in, my heart sank. The room was big, but it wasn't like any schoolroom I ever saw. It was in a shambles. Dust and dirt were everywhere, and yellowed papers littered the floor. Light came in through windows fogged with smoke and grime.

"Needs a little cleaning up," Maggie admitted.

The other room, the same size as the schoolroom, was neater, but except for a brass bed with no mattress, two chairs, and a big potbellied stove, it was empty.

"How do you like 'er?" Angela Barrett asked in a rasping voice. She must have weighed two hundred pounds and she towered over me. I tried to think of something nice to say.

"It's a good big room. Will it take much time to get it ready?"

"What do you mean ready? It's ready now."

Both women were staring at me as if there were something wrong with me. I was almost afraid to ask the next question. "Don't I have to have a mattress?" I said. "Or blankets, or a table?"

It took a moment before they realized that I had a point.

"Where'na hell'd it all go?" Angela said, as if she'd turned her back for a minute and somebody had snatched everything away. "It's your fault, Maggie, you're the school janitor."

"When there's no school there's no janitor," Maggie said tartly, "and there ain't been a school here in over a year."

"What are we gonna do?" Angela asked.

Maggie thought for a minute. "Come on," she said finally. Angela and I followed her to the post office, where the stuff everyone had ordered was lying on the ground: boxes of candles, flashlight batteries, sacks of flour, crated cans of kerosene, and parcel post packages.

150

"This is Anne Hobbs, our new teacher," Maggie said to the crowd. "And she's got a problem that needs everybody's attention. Some of you mutts have borrowed everything in the teacher's quarters. I ain't sayin' who took what, but it's got to be packed back here pronto. The poor girl's got an empty cabin."

"I can spare a couple of Hudson's Bay blankets," said a tall good-looking man who was trying on a fleece-lined jacket.

"We got a set of tin dishes she can borrow," a girl of about ten said. She was with two older girls who looked like twins, both of them rawboned and husky. "Can she, Pa?" she asked. A red-haired man beside her nodded.

After that the offers came thick and fast—a broom and pan, a rocking chair, a washboiler. People kept trooping in carrying things, and within a few hours I not only had a firm straw mattress but also a blanket, a pillow, a table and even a water barrel. My prize possession was a wood-burning cookstove with nickel-plated fittings, which took four men to carry in.

Granny sure knew what she was talking about, I thought. People who go to a new land *are* big—kind and generous. I didn't even have to clean the place alone. Five of my pupils showed up to help. The three Vaughn girls were first—Elvira, the girl who'd asked her father for the tin dishes, and her older, twin sisters, Evelyn and Eleanor. Then Maggie Carew's two boys, Jimmy and Willard, came over. While we were working, the good-looking man who'd promised me the blankets rode up. "I'm Joe Temple," he said. The two blankets were almost new. I offered to pay for them, but he said forget it. "Use them for as long as you like."

I'd unpacked my dresses and hung them on nails. "I haven't been Outside in a couple of years," he said, looking at them, "but I thought they were wearing dresses shorter than that."

"They are. I guess I'm pretty conservative."

"Not all the time, I hope." I didn't know how to take that. "You'll have to let me take you out to dinner," he said.

"Maybe after I get settled."

"How about tomorrow night?"

"All right, you're on."

"See you around six," he said, going out.

Things really happen fast around here, I thought. I haven't been in Chicken more than a few hours and already I have a date.

Maggie Carew came by a little before dark. "Joe Temple tells me you're comin' over to my roadhouse with him tomorrow night. Fast worker, that one."

"What does he do?"

"Mines, like everyone else. Do 'im good to go out with a white woman for a change."

She went to the back of the room and opened the door that led into a small storage room—the cache. "You'll have plenty of room for your outfit," she said.

"Outfit?"

"Your grub for the winter—flour, sugar, all that."

Now that she mentioned it, I realized I didn't have a bit of food.

"Don't worry. Walter Strong'll bring in an outfit for you. We'll help you out in the meantime."

Just then I remembered her daughter. Her face lit up when I told her what Jeannette Terwilliger had said. "Thinks she's gonna have a girl, eh? Well, if she's anything like Jennie, that'll be two good things I got outta this life."

As she went out, I asked what all the nails in the doors were for. "Bear," she answered. "Last teacher threw a fit when one came sniffin' at the door."

Alone, I sat down on the bed and looked the room over. In some places the floor had dropped below the walls and I could see the ground outside. The walls were just rough planks with canvas stretched over them. But I didn't care. This was the first place I'd ever had to myself. When I fixed it up, it would look a lot nicer than Cathy Winters' place.

There was no water left, so I took a pail and went to fill it from the creek. Standing there outside, the darkness falling fast, I felt lonely all of a sudden. Except for the sounds from the Vaughn cabin next door, everything was quiet. There weren't as many people here as I had thought there'd be. Of all the buildings on each side of me there were maybe only six that had people living in them—the Vaughns', the Carews' roadhouse, Angela Barrett's cabin, and a couple of others down at the far end. Most of the people who'd been at the post office lived on outlying creeks.

It was a little like being in a ghost town. Thirty years ago this had been a thriving settlement, men had streamed in looking for gold, built these cabins and dreamed about making a big strike.

I filled the pail with water and started lugging it back, stopping halfway to rest. I felt a little scared. Maybe it was because everything looked so rough and bare. Back in Oregon the nights were made for a nice walk or a soda at the drugstore. Here it was all wilderness. I picked up the pail and hurried back into my quarters.

Inside, it was almost too dark to see. I thought about going next door to the Vaughns to wait for Mr. Strong, who was bringing dinner. But if I was going to get used to being on my own, I might as well start now. Lighting a couple of candle stubs I found in an empty fruit box, I put one on the counter and the other on my table. They made shadows jump all over.

The door to the schoolroom was open and it looked like a big dark hole, so I closed it. I realized suddenly that I had no protection here at all. I didn't even have locks on the doors. Anyone who wanted to could walk right in. My nickel-plated revolver in its holster lay in a box beside the bed. Tying it around my waist, I felt better.

A half hour later one of the candle stubs flickered out and the other had only two inches to go. Once it was gone, I'd be in complete darkness.

Then I heard footsteps outside.

I knew they didn't belong to Mr. Strong. He'd gone to make some deliveries on outlying creeks and I'd have heard his horses. The footsteps padded closer, moving around the side of the house and up onto the porch. Then there was a soft knock at the door.

Taking the revolver out, I stayed still as a rabbit. When the knock came a second time, I decided that whoever was there could get in just by turning the doorknob. He'd be less antagonized if I invited him in. Holding the revolver in both hands, I pointed it at the door. "Come in," I said, "but be careful."

I could just make out a dark man with thick black hair staring at me from the porch. As soon as he saw the gun he raised his hands. He was nervous, but he smiled. He was darker than a Spaniard, and his teeth looked deadly white.

"You better be careful," I said. "I shot a bear with this once." I was so scared I didn't know what I was saying.

He stopped smiling. "I can believe that," he answered.

"Did you come to see me?"

"Yes. My mother sent me over to see if you'd like to have supper with us."

I could see now that he wasn't much older than I was, and I realized how silly I was being. He was embarrassed. So was I.

I said, "I'm sorry. You can come in if you want."

"That's all right. I'm sorry I scared you. My mother thought maybe you'd like to eat with us."

"That's awfully nice of her," I said, "but Mr. Strong is coming back and he'll be bringing dinner with him."

He looked uncomfortable. "Well, my mother said to tell you that if you need any help at all just let us know."

"Do you live here in the settlement?" I asked him.

"No, a little further up Chicken Creek," he said.

Now that I wasn't afraid of him I wished he would keep me company. But he said good-by and closed the door before I could even think to ask him his name.

"That was young Fred Purdy," Mr. Strong said when he finally came back. Later, as we were finishing the cold chicken he had brought, he smiled when I told how I'd held the gun on Fred.

"You'd have been more than safe with him. Fred will never amount to anything, but he is a fine young fellow. . . ."

"Why won't he ever amount to anything? He seemed very nice."

"Couldn't you see? He's a half-breed. Mother's Eskimo, father's white. When you mix the races—the offspring have to suffer."

He made it sound as if anybody who wasn't all white had some disease. I wondered what he'd think if he knew my grandmother had been Indian.

"What is Chuck's father like?" I asked, changing the subject.

154

"Joe Temple? Good miner, good trapper. You can bet he regrets ever having involved himself with a native woman."

"Joe Temple is Chuck's father?"

"Why do you look surprised?"

"He's supposed to take me to dinner tomorrow night."

"Well, it's nothing for you to be concerned about. Mr. Temple is a gentleman and he will treat you like a lady."

"But he's married."

"No, he is not, and I'm sure he thanks God for it."

Married or not, I felt funny about going out with him.

THE next morning Mr. Strong took me to his store, a small log building about five cabins away. Looking the shelves over, I felt better. There was everything here, even tins of butter. I loaded up two sacks with canned goods, flour, sugar and other staples. A little later, after I'd rustled up some bacon, eggs and hot coffee for us on the potbellied stove, Mr. Strong paid me a compliment. "It is heartening to know, madam, that there are still girls around who can make a proper breakfast." He gave me the key to the store, something he said he'd never done with anyone else. I was to take what I needed, and we'd settle up once a month. In return, if anyone wanted anything while he was away, I would give it out and keep a record of what was bought.

At midmorning I was working in the schoolroom when I heard footsteps on the porch. It was Fred Purdy and what I thought were two younger sisters with him. But only one was his sister. The other was his mother. She was even smaller than Granny Hobbs. I doubted she weighed more than ninety pounds. She was Eskimo for sure—round dark face, wide mouth and strong uneven teeth. She seemed to light up when she saw me and I liked her right off.

"Ah, the teasher," she said. "I am happy to meet you. I am Mrs. Purdy, and this is my daughter, Isabelle."

She put a hand out and it felt small and capable. "My son Frayd have tell me how pretty you are," she said. "Now I see for myself. Indeed, you are very lovely."

She was like a little queen, dressed beautifully in a cloth parka that looked like a Fifth Avenue design, and a soft fur hat. I invited them in and we all sat down and had a cup of tea. I told them about the trip out and my troubles with Blossom. It hadn't seemed funny at the time, but it amused Fred. I never heard anybody laugh the way he did—with so much fun and enjoyment that it made me laugh myself. By the time I told how I'd walked in here to find hardly a stick of furniture, we were all doubled over.

Then Mrs. Purdy went around the room, shaking her head. "There is mush work to do, Ahnne. You must have home that is comfortable, warm." She pointed to the baseboard where light was coming in. "This must be fixed or in winter you will freeze to the death." She reeled off the things that had to be fixed—sagging shelves, loose floorboards, crippled tables in the schoolroom.

"You will work here," she said to Fred, "and Father will do your chores at home."

Fred grinned. "Yes, boss."

"You wish to open school when, Ahnne?"

"In a few days, if I can."

"You will do it in a few days, Frayd, no?"

"I will do it, boss, yes."

Before they left, Mrs. Purdy asked me to supper the next night. A couple of hours later Fred came back driving a wagon loaded with rough boards and a big toolbox. We were a little shy with each other at first, but after we worked together for a while we were gabbing about everything under the sun. People dropped by to lend me more things: a kettle, some spoons and knives, even an old encyclopedia. I told Fred that I knew people in Alaska were hospitable, but I hadn't expected it to be like this.

"Everybody wants to make you stay," he said.

"Why should they think I won't?"

"For the same reason the last teacher didn't. This is tough country, especially for a cheechako."

"When do I stop being a cheechako and become an Alaskan?"

He looked at me almost the way Mr. Strong did when he'd offered me his army coat—as if I were a foreigner. Only Fred's look was a little different. It was the way one forest animal might look

157

at another to see if it was its own kind. It gave me a funny feeling.

"Well," he said, "some people never really become Alaskans. They never get to like it. They just tolerate it."

"I don't know what you mean."

"It's something you have to feel inside. All these old sourdoughs around here—they're real Alaskans. They came here when there was nothing but raw land. They went hungry, froze their feet and their hands and hardly ever took enough gold out of the ground to keep themselves in grub, but they made it."

"You think I'll make it?"

"No reason why you shouldn't. Just make sure you've got good footgear and warm clothes—and take people's advice. If somebody tells you something, you have to listen the first time. They won't tell you twice. That's the way they are."

I asked, "Is Mr. Strong an Alaskan?"

"He sure is. He's skookum—he's got guts. Twenty-four days out of every month he mushes that trail alone, and no matter what it's like—flooded or frozen—he's usually here like clockwork."

I wondered if he knew what Mr. Strong thought of him and his family, and I had a feeling he did.

Joe came for me a little after six and was surprised I was ready. "You'll have to get used to Alaska time," he said, helping me on with my coat. "An hour or two early or an hour or two late, depending on the weather. If somebody doesn't show up at all, they'll be along the next day or the next."

"I hope the school won't work that way," I said.

The roadhouse was about six cabins down from me. It had rough plank floors, a ceiling black with woodsmoke, a couple of long tables covered with oilcloth, and a bunk room and stable in the rear. Maggie gave us a small table against the wall. The boiled moose tongue was delicious, and while we ate I found out that Joe had gone to Washington State University. He'd come to Alaska in 1920, after he got out of the army. We finished eating, and Maggie and her husband sat down with us.

"How's the Purdy kid comin' along fixin' your place up?" Maggie asked me.

"Fine. It won't look like the same place when he's done."

"He's a good kid for a half-breed," she said.

"Mr. Strong didn't seem to think too much of him or his family."

"I'm no crazier about half-breeds than he is," Mr. Carew said. "Siwashes either." He was a small, intense man and he kept clicking his false teeth.

While we were talking Mr. Vaughn came in. A widower, he told me he'd raised his three girls practically by himself. Living next door to him, I'd heard him yelling at them once or twice. He asked me what kind of teaching I was going to do. "Are you going to get fancy, or are you going to teach the three R's?" The way he said it put me on the defensive.

"I'll teach the best way I know how, I guess. Arithmetic and reading are important, but there are other things too."

"Such as?"

"Literature and poetry. Civics, music."

"Sounds pretty fancy, all right," Mr. Carew put in.

"Hey, give her a chance, will you?" Joe said. "She hasn't even started yet."

"What's wrong with us being interested?" Mr. Vaughn said. "That's why we have a school board."

"Does the school board meet often?" I asked.

"When we think it's necessary," Mr. Vaughn answered. "We'll let you know when we think we should have a meeting."

A little while later Joe walked me back to my place. "What's a Sy-wash?" I asked him.

"Siwash? An Indian."

"Is it an Indian word?"

"French. *Sauvage*. Savage. The old-timers weren't too finicky about their accent."

He came in with me and built up the fire in the stove. I thanked him for the supper. "My pleasure," he said. "We'll have to get together again soon."

"I'll tell you the truth, Joe. I feel a little funny about going out with you."

"Why?" He saw I was embarrassed. "I see . . . Mary Angus?"

159

"I guess so."

"Don't let that worry you. We split the blanket a while back."

We dropped the subject and after a couple of minutes he left.

The next day while Fred and I were working I asked him about Joe and Mary. "It's pretty much of an old story," he said. "Mary lived in the Indian village and Joe was mining nearby. They fell in love and took up housekeeping like man and wife for a long time. They finally broke up about a year ago. Then a few months ago Mary came out to be with him. I don't think he wanted her to, but she's still in love with him."

"Where does she live?"

"About a half mile from here, on the way to my house."

Later we stopped off at her cabin, when Fred took me over to his house for supper. It was a lovely walk, the sun settling behind the mountain in a sea of liquid gold.

We followed a wide trail along Chicken Creek, then turned north. Mary Angus' place was stuck back off the trail, hidden in the buckbrush and willow. Fred said it was an old line shack put up by a trapper to stay in overnight as he moved along his trapline. It was awful—an old weathered shack that looked as if one good wind would blow it over. A stovepipe leaned out of the roof and a couple of broken windowpanes had rags stuffed in them.

Mary Angus was out in front sawing some wood, and it was hard to believe she was the same woman I'd glimpsed a few days ago. I'd had the impression then that she was beautiful. At one time she must have been, with a lovely long face and slanted dark eyes. Now, although she was probably in her mid-twenties, she looked old and tired, and there were dark circles under her eyes. She was flushed and perspiring from the work she'd been doing. When Fred introduced us she smiled. "I ... am ... happy ... to ... see ... you," she said in English, like a little girl reciting.

Fred had told me she didn't speak English too well, so I spoke slowly. "I'm glad to meet you too," I said. "Is Chuck around?"

"In cabin. He sick."

"Can I say hello to him?"

She gave Fred a quick questioning look and he nodded slightly.

White women didn't usually go into Indians' cabins. Inside, it was like being in a tiny foul hell. The floor was dirt, and Chuck was lying on a fur robe, a couple of dirty blankets pulled over him. His sister was asleep on a small wooden frame lashed together with leather strips. There was some gray stew bubbling in a coffee can on top of the Yukon stove. The smell from a slop jar was so foul I had to breathe through my mouth. Chuck had a cold. I stooped down alongside him. "How are you feeling?"

"Bad sick," he murmured.

He looked it too. If I could have, I'd have taken him home with me right then and there. He needed a clean bed, some good nourishing food and a place where he could breathe.

"I'll see you in school," I said, "when you're better."

He didn't answer. He wasn't in any shape to be interested in me, school, or anything else. I went outside, so furious at Joe Temple I wanted to scream. "How can he let them live like that?" I asked Fred when we went on. "Couldn't he move her into one of those empty cabins in the settlement?"

"The people there don't want her."

"Fred, that's inhuman. Joe lived with that woman. Those are his children. It's all wrong."

"There's nothing anybody can do about it. What Joe does is his business—his and Mary's. That's the way it is." He didn't want to talk about it, so I didn't say anything more.

His own house was beautiful, a log cabin built on a knoll, and telescoping out from the rear were two smaller cabins. I'd seen other cabins added onto like that. I asked him why people did it.

"The only time you can build is during the season—that's about four months. So you build your main cabin, then keep adding on every year."

As soon as I walked in, I realized why his mother had thought my place looked so terrible. Potted plants and herbs lined the windowsills, and braided rugs lay on the highly polished floor. The Purdys had made everything themselves, from the glass-fronted cupboards in the kitchen area to the bright curtains on the windows.

It was a nice evening, with everybody good-humored—and a

delicious dinner. The only one who didn't have much to say was Fred's father. I asked him where he was from. "New England," he said. That ended the conversation between us. After dinner he excused himself and went into the next room, where I could see him working on a crystal radio.

Before I left, Fred asked if I'd ever seen gold in the raw. I said no, and he took a preserve jar down from a shelf. He handed it to me, and everybody laughed when I nearly dropped it. It was filled with dull yellow flecks mixed with black powder and it was about ten times heavier than I'd thought. "That's flour gold," Fred said. Another jar was filled with nuggets, ranging in size from pinheads to little pebbles. The two jars held their whole season's cleanup— maybe two thousand dollars' worth of gold. To get it, they had spent four months shoveling pay dirt into a wooden sluice box open at both ends, and diverting water from a creek through the box. As the water sent the dirt and rocks rushing through, whatever gold there was in the dirt dropped to the bottom of the box and was caught in grooved wooden slats.

"You've got to wash tons of dirt to get a few ounces of gold," Fred said. "No water, no mining. You can have the richest ground in the world, but if you can't pipe water to it, it's not worth a cent. There won't be enough water for mining again until the winter's over and the snow starts to melt."

"What will everyone do now?"

"Trapping'll start in November, as soon as there's snow."

"Why wait so long?"

"When you go out trapping," he explained, "you've got to use sleds to tote food and supplies and bring the furs back. And for sleds you need snow."

We worked for another two days before my quarters and the schoolroom were finished. You could see the difference right away. Fred had painted the walls a pale green, the tables and chairs in the schoolroom were sturdy, and I even had a "blackboard"—a couple of dark green window shades tacked to beaverboard. He'd also made a couch for me by nailing three boxes together. Maggie Carew gave me a mattress for padding, and covered with a blanket and pillows it looked fine. The day we finished, Fred stayed for supper.

"I'm really grateful to you," I told him. I meant it too. He'd done just about all the work.

"Forget it," he said. "I was glad to help out."

We sat talking for a while. He didn't want to go and I didn't want him to either, which really surprised me. Usually I never knew what to say to boys, but I felt I could have gone on talking to him all night. I'd never met any boy like him. He'd only gone as far as the sixth grade, but he read everything he could get his hands on and was interested in history, current events, even metallurgy.

After he'd gone, I went into the schoolroom again and stood behind my table. Looking at the empty tables and chairs, I thought of so many things I wanted to say to the class—like our being as much a part of America up here as any of the forty-eight states, and how important it was for all of us to be fine, well-educated citizens. I went to my quarters and started jotting them down.

III

SCHOOL was supposed to start at nine the next morning, but by a quarter to, my nine pupils were all outside. One of the Vaughn girls had brought over a flag, so I went out and ran it up to the top of the pole and we all said the pledge of allegiance.

Once we were in the schoolroom I couldn't say anything at all. I had stage fright. For a full minute the whole class stood staring at me silently, and, completely tongue-tied, I stared back at them. The only sound was everybody's breathing and the squeak of the floorboards. I shivered. "Before we choose seats, does anybody know how to build a fire in that stove? I can't make it work."

The oldest boy, Robert Merriweather, stepped forward and began to put kindling in the squat black Yukon stove, which was a little bigger than an orange crate. "You didn't use enough kindling," he said, "and you didn't open the damper enough."

After that we found seats for everyone, and then I wrote my name on the blackboard and said I was glad to be here.

One thing I didn't have to worry about was keeping their attention. Everything was new to them and they were hungry to learn.

Their big problem was reading. The only pupil who could read well was Isabelle Purdy. The rest of the class had trouble reading orally from a third-grade reader. The Vaughn twins were thirteen, but their sister, Elvira, three years younger, could read better than they could. Joan Simpson and Willard Carew were six and I'd have to teach both of them to read. Four-year-old Lily Harrington already knew some of the alphabet.

It had been almost a year and a half since there'd been a teacher here, and except for Isabelle and Robert, none of the children knew anything about history or geography or social studies. I'd have to figure out some way of getting them interested in those subjects. Before that, though, I'd have to get them to feel like a class, not just a bunch of kids that happened to be in the same room. What I needed was a project they could all work on together. I told them about the one I already had in mind.

"We're going to make a map of Chicken," I said. "We're going to use one whole wall for it. Everybody can draw a little picture of their own cabin and we'll put it up in the right place."

They liked that idea—having the place they lived in and their name right up where everybody could see. "But that's only part of the project," I said. "We'll find out all about Chicken—its geography and history. For instance—does anybody know how Chicken got its name?"

Nobody did, so I asked Robert Merriweather if he'd ask the old prospectors and write a report on it. Then we decided that the next day we'd go on a field trip to collect leaves and rocks.

For the next few days everything went fine. We decided that since we had a whole wall to use for our map, we ought to show not only where everybody lived but some of the things we'd found on our field trip. We'd come back loaded with birch and cottonwood leaves, samples of willow and alder, and rocks galore. We decided to put some of them up on the map. The rest we'd make up books about—leaf books, fur-sample books and animal-picture books. When the project was finished we'd invite everybody in Chicken

164

to come and see what we'd done. The class was so enthusiastic that I had trouble bringing them back to their regular lessons.

Robert Merriweather's report turned out to be excellent and I tacked it on the wall.

HOW CHICKEN GOT IT'S NAME

Chicken got it's name from the first prospectors who came here. There was a lot of Ptarmigans here and they thanked God for it because they were hungry. They were so grateful they wanted to name this place Ptarmigan, but they couldn't spell it. They named it good old American Chicken instead. This is what Uncle Arthur Spratt said.

By the time the first week was over, the class was really interested in what they were doing. The only trouble I could see I might have was teaching Robert arithmetic. He was good enough to do seventh-grade work, and I'd have to do some studying to keep ahead of him. Aside from that I was pretty optimistic.

I shouldn't have been, though, because on Monday I was in trouble. It was over Chuck. He showed up Monday morning before school when I was in my quarters. Outside, Jimmy Carew was tossing a ball against the porch with the Vaughn girls. All of a sudden he stopped and said, "Where'd *you* come from?"

"From Louse Town," Evelyn Vaughn said.

"Who is he?" Jimmy asked her.

"Mary Angus' kid."

"Whattaya want here?" Jimmy asked him.

"Come school."

"Like hell you are," Evelyn said. "This is a white school."

"I come here. Tisha, she say I come."

"Tisha?"

"He means Teacher."

"I know what he means."

I went outside. "Good morning, everybody," I said. "Hello, Chuck—nice to see you here finally. How are you feeling?"

He looked down at the ground and mumbled, "Good."

He looked anything but good. He was thinner than ever and his lips were all chapped. His clothes were dirty and smelled awful. His mackinaw was so small his wrists stuck out, and his pants were so big the bottoms were ragged from scraping the ground.

We had the pledge of allegiance and then I introduced Chuck and started everybody working. When they were all busy I took him over in a corner to read for me. He did fine when I tried him with a first-grade reader. His arithmetic wasn't bad either.

The class was restless that morning, many of them preoccupied with giving each other looks about him. During vocabulary I gave Evelyn Vaughn the word intelligent to put into a sentence.

"Siwashes aren't very intelligent," she recited. A few of the older kids giggled.

"Can you tell me what the word Siwash means?" I asked her.

"Sure. It's a dirty low-down Injun."

More giggles. "There are certain words," I said, "which I don't want to hear in this classroom. One of them is Siwash."

Eleanor Vaughn asked, "How about if I said *Indians* aren't very intelligent?"

"Do you really think that's true? All Indians?"

She nodded.

"How about people who are only part Indian?"

"You mean like half-breeds? I guess so," she said.

"I should tell you," I said, "that my grandmother was an Indian. That makes me part Indian too. Do you think there's anything wrong with my intelligence?"

Eleanor shifted uncomfortably. "No."

"Is that really true, Teacher?" Jimmy asked.

"Yes, it is."

"What kind of an Indian was she?" Elvira Vaughn asked.

"Kentuck."

"I never heard of that kind."

"They're like Comanche or Sioux, any kind of Indian."

"Oh, well," Jimmy said. "They're *American* Indians. They're different from the ones we got here."

"Indians are Indians, and there are all kinds."

"Was your grandmother like these Indians?"

"I'll tell you the truth," I said. "If you saw her in the Indian village you'd think she was one of them."

"How come you don't look Indian then?"

"I guess I take after my grandfather. He was white."

Robert Merriweather raised his hand. "If your grandmother was an Indian, then your father was a half-breed."

"I guess that's right. But you know something? Where I come from, nobody cared about it. As a matter of fact, whenever anybody found out I was part Indian they thought that was a pretty interesting thing to be. . . . Now we've got work to do, but just remember, what people are doesn't matter, whether they're Indian or Irish or Negro or anything else—they're just people."

When school was over, Chuck hung around for a few minutes. "You tell truth, Tisha?" he asked me. "You Indian?"

"I'm part Indian, yes."

"You make moccasin?"

"No. I don't know how to do that."

"Cut fish? Trap?"

"I'm afraid not."

He thought it over. "Funny Indian," he murmured.

Just before six that night Jimmy Carew knocked at my door. "My mother says is it all right if the school board comes over after supper?"

"Sure. Tell her seven thirty would be fine."

The three of them came in looking solemn—Maggie Carew, Angela Barrett and Mr. Vaughn. They turned me down when I offered them tea. Mr. Vaughn cleared his throat. "We'd like to know on what grounds you've taken Joe Temple's half-breed into the school."

"The same grounds on which I'd take any pupil in, Mr. Vaughn."

"He doesn't belong here. If you weren't a cheechako you'd know that. He belongs in the Indian village school."

"But he's not *in* the Indian village now."

"That has nothing to do with it. He shouldn't be in the same school with our children. According to the law, this school is open to, and I quote, 'white children and children of mixed blood *who lead a civilized life.*' That kid isn't civilized. None of those Indians from that village are."

"Isn't that your interpretation, Mr. Vaughn?" I asked. "Chuck can read, he can write, he's like any other little boy. I can't tell him to get out of class for no good reason."

"You've been given the reason. We're not running a school for uncivilized Siwashes and the law will back us up. Now are you going to tell him?"

"I can't."

"Then I'll do it for you. We'll take a vote to show we're doing it lawfully. I move that the half-breed child known as Charles Temple be excluded from the school on the grounds that he does not lead a civilized life. How do you two vote?"

Maggie and Angela said aye.

"That settles it," Mr. Vaughn said.

Maybe it settled it for them, but it didn't for me. I was so mad I could have thrown the stove at them.

"We don't want any hard feelin's, Annie," Maggie said. "We're just tryin' to show you what's best. You're still new, ya know."

"I know."

"I'll take that tea if you're still offerin'."

I served her and Angela some. Mr. Vaughn didn't want any.

"If there's no further business," Mr. Vaughn said, "we can close this meeting."

Not as far as I was concerned. Mr. Henderson, the education commissioner, had told me in Juneau that he believed that where there was even one child who needed schooling—not ten, as the law said there must be—there should be a school for him, which was why he had overlooked the fact that we did not quite meet enrollment. But the board didn't know that. I heard myself say, "It's too bad I had to come all the way out here for nothing."

"How's that?" Mr. Vaughn said.

"I'm going to have to close the school."

Mr. Vaughn's eyes narrowed. "What are you talking about?"

"I don't have enough of an enrollment," I said, trying to keep my voice even. "Under the law there has to be ten pupils. There's only nine."

"So what?" Maggie said. "That's just a technicality. If you hadda rely on a full enrollment there'd never be a school in the bush."

"I don't know about that," I said. "This is my first teaching job in Alaska and I don't want to break the law." My hands were sweating and my heart was pounding.

Maggie stared at me for a long moment. "You telling us you'd pack up and git?"

"That's what I'd have to do, Mrs. Carew."

"You're bluffing," Mr. Vaughn said.

"No I'm not. You told me yourself—the law is the law."

"Will somebody tell me what's going on?" Angela yelled.

"We're being blackmailed, that's what's going on," Mr. Vaughn said. "We've got a second Catherine Winters here—another Indian lover. I heard you're part Siwash," he said to me. "Now I believe it. For my part you can just pack up and get the hell out right now. As far as I'm concerned this meeting is adjourned." He walked out without saying another word.

Angela had her arms crossed in front of her. Her expression was pure hate. "Angela, you go on back to the roadhouse," Maggie said. "I'll be there in a few minutes."

When she was gone, Maggie said, "You're expectin' to teach in Eagle next year, I take it."

"Yes."

"They got a school board there too. If they don't want you, they don't have to take you. They're not gonna like this."

"There's not much I can do about that."

170

She got up. "You got more gall than a government mule, I'll say that for ya. You're a good kid and I like ya, but I'm gonna tell ya something—don't go too far or you won't be teachin' in Eagle or anywhere else in Alaska next year. People are goin' to be writin' to the commissioner about this."

"I don't want any trouble, but that little boy is entitled to—"

"Never mind what he's entitled to. Maybe you don't want trouble, but you got a peck of it right now."

She buttoned up her coat. "I'd advise you to watch your step. I'm willin' to look the other way on this. Other folks won't."

The next morning I was a nervous wreck wondering if the class was going to show up. They all came, though, even the Vaughn girls, and when we had singing that morning you could have heard my voice clear over to Steel Creek I was so glad.

But I found out right away what Maggie meant about people not looking the other way. There was a little birdlike woman named Mrs. Dowles, who'd loaned me a washboiler. She scuttled in during the morning and said she needed it. About eleven thirty an old sourdough came in and said would I mind letting him have the two chairs he'd loaned me; he was expecting company. My dishes went next, when Elvira came up to me before she went home to lunch. "My father says could you give us back the set of dishes we lent you? We need 'em for our own use."

I tried not to let the way people felt bother me, but it did. Here I'd been in this place no more than ten days and already I'd made them antagonistic.

Not everybody, of course. Lily Harrington's father, Jake Harrington, gave Mr. Vaughn an eloquent cussing out. Joan Simpson's parents invited me over for supper a couple of nights after it happened and told me they thought it was funny. I spent a nice evening with them. "Don't pay it any mind," Tom Simpson said. "That Vaughn is just a blowhard."

The one person who surprised me was Mrs. Purdy. "I think you have make mush trouble for yourself, Ahnne," she said when I was over at their house one night. "It is bad for this Indian boy to be in the school."

"Why, Mrs. Purdy?"

"Can you not see, Ahnne? He is dirty, ignorant. What you call a . . ." She tried to think of the word.

Fred leaned his cheek on his fist. "Bad example," he said.

"Yes. Thank you. It will be different, Ahnne, if Chuck is clean, neat. He is not. He is dirty and smells bad."

"That's simple," Fred said to me. "Give him a bath."

"I've been thinking of it."

Mrs. Purdy shook her head. "People look at him and think all native children are like him."

Fred groaned. "Ah, Ma . . ."

"'Ah, Ma,' you say. I say I would like Mary Angus to go back to Indian village and take her children with her."

"Yeah," Fred said dryly. "You want her to go back so bad you were the first one to say I ought to bring her over some wood. Tomorrow I'll go over and haul it all back."

Mrs. Purdy didn't think it was funny. "We must help those who need our help. We cannot let her freeze. But she does not belong here and the boy does not belong in this school. Ahnne, you are young. You do not know what is in the heart of people here. I know. My children know. You must be careful."

She was really upset, and it made me realize something. She wanted to fit in, be like everyone else, and any native who didn't was a reflection on herself. And suddenly I realized why Mr. Purdy acted the way he did, never saying anything when I was around and just going off by himself. He was ashamed that Mrs. Purdy was Eskimo, and she knew it. It was hard to believe, but I knew it was true, and I felt sorry for him.

Later on, Fred walked me home. The ground was as hard as concrete and slippery with leaves. The trees were so bare now that during the day you could see the game trails running through the woods. I put the hood of my parka up. "Your mother really worries about what people think of her, doesn't she?" I asked Fred.

"Well, it took her a long time to make friends around here."

I slipped on some leaves and he grabbed me. When he let me go, we were both a little self-conscious. We kept trying not to bump

172

into each other all the rest of the way. When we reached the school-house we were walking a couple of feet apart.

"Anything you need to have done in the classroom?" he asked me. "I've got plenty of time till trapping season."

I told him I could use some cubbyholes for the kids to put their stuff in, and he said he'd come by in a few days.

Chuck stayed.

How he was able to put up with the way the other kids treated him, I didn't know. If they talked to him at all, it was just to make fun of him. They mimicked his accent and called him Ol' Man Yiss. It wouldn't have been so bad if he could have held his own, but when they made him mad he couldn't think fast enough in English to talk back. He'd just stand there getting red in the face with fury, and wind up stomping off. And he *did* smell so awful that no one wanted to sit near him in class.

One afternoon I took him to my quarters and did what I should have done when he first came. I got all my pots out, filled them with water and put them on the stove. Then I took him over to the store. We picked out a couple of good warm flannel shirts, two pairs of bib overalls, long underwear and some socks. He loved them, but back in my quarters, when I told him he was going to have a bath before he could put them on, his jaw dropped.

"Aw no, Tisha."

"You want those new clothes?"

"Yiss."

"You want to come to school?"

"Yiss."

"Then you're going to have to take a bath."

In he went, and when he was finished and all dressed up, he looked like a different boy. I let him see himself in my mirror. "Like yourself?" I'd given him a shampoo and combed his hair.

He smiled. "Look too much good."

"We're going to do this once a week," I said. Even with scrubbing we hadn't been able to get all the dirt off him. Some of it was just too deep.

"Why them kids they no like me?" he asked.

"They don't know you yet, Chuck. You'll just have to give them time. When they get to know you better and see what a fine boy you are, they'll like you a lot."

"You know me?"

"I think so."

"I wait. Pretty soon them kids they know me too."

When the kids saw him the next day they almost didn't recognize him. It didn't make them any friendlier, though. When they found out I'd got him the new clothes they called him teacher's pet. But he kept coming. Whatever he had to put up with, it was better than hanging around that awful shack he lived in. I had to admit that I was fond of him. There was something so good and steady about him that it made me furious when the kids picked on him.

He dropped over to see me on Saturday and brought his sister with him. She was a beautiful little thing, long black hair, delicate nose and big brown inquiring eyes. "She name Et'el," Chuck said. He tried to get her to say hello to me, but she was too afraid.

I cut a slice of bread I'd baked that morning, smeared it with butter and honey and gave it to her. She gobbled it down, and two more slices disappeared the same way. Chuck took her into the schoolroom and showed her his leaf book, a couple of spelling papers and a picture of a moose he had drawn.

Before they left, I asked Chuck where he liked it better—the Indian village or here.

"Indian village," he said. "Kids no play me here. I wait and wait, Tisha, for them kids know me."

"Sooner or later they will."

He sighed. "I hope you be right. I wait too long I be old man like Uncle Arthur Spratt."

IV

"Is it time yet, Teacher?"

I looked at my watch. It was one minute to twelve. "Almost. Everybody's books and papers put away?"

They all answered yes, excited and anxious to get out. The packtrain was due in after lunch. I'd told them they could have the afternoon off. I was pretty excited myself, because Nancy was coming in. From now on I wouldn't have to eat all alone and I'd have somebody to talk to at night. "School's out for the day!" I yelled, and a minute later the classroom was empty.

The packtrain didn't come in until almost three. Fred was playing softball with some of the kids, batting easy flies to them. I was playing too, when suddenly the dogs all over the settlement began to bark and howl in their kennels. It meant that Mr. Strong was pretty near. We kept playing while everybody started straggling out of their cabins. I yelled for Fred to pop one to me, and the ball hit the side of the Vaughns's storm entry just as Mr. Vaughn came out. He walked over to me.

"'What are these kids doing out of school?" he asked.

"I gave them the afternoon off because of the packtrain," I said. "I didn't think there was anything wrong in it."

"The next time you want to take time off, you get permission from the school board," he said, pointing a finger at me. "You're too damn smart for your own good."

"You have no right to speak to me that way, Mr. Vaughn."

"I'll speak to you any way I damn please." He pointed that finger at me again. "One more word out of you and I'll smack all that smartness right out of you."

I was too scared to move.

Fred's hand touched my arm. "C'mon, Anne." He started to lead me away, and I went willingly.

"Your boy friend has more brains than you have," Mr. Vaughn sneered. "I was just getting ready to take you over my knee."

Fred whirled around. "You won't lay a finger on her," he said.

"What did you say?" Mr. Vaughn walked over to us with blood in his eye.

Fred drew back the baseball bat without a word. "You touch her or me and I'll let you have it," he said.

Mr. Vaughn was a full head taller than Fred and he'd have chewed Fred up if he could have. He was afraid of that bat, though. He gave Fred a contemptuous look and went over to the

175

post office. Fred and I drifted over along with everybody else, but I was so upset I could hardly say a word to anybody.

I felt a little better as soon as I saw Nancy. At my quarters, while she put away her things, I read a note from her mother that Mr. Strong had handed to me. Mrs. Prentiss had had second thoughts about her offer to pay me. "I heard you don't have a food outfit," the note ended. "Since it won't cost anything for Nancy's room, maybe we can work out something where I send you some grub for her keep."

Nancy didn't have much with her, just a few pairs of bib overalls and a couple of washed-out dresses. After we found a place for everything, I told her how much I'd looked forward to having her with me and asked about her schooling. "What grade have you gone through?"

"Eighth."

"Without being able to read?"

"I can read somewhat."

I gave her a fifth-grade reader. She studied it and spat the words out like pits, but she did well enough.

"You read fine," I said. "I don't see why you need me."

"I know how to read this book 'cause my ma tutored me with it for a whole year. I can only read if somebody reads it to me first and shows me the words."

I handed her a book of fairy tales. "Have you ever read this?"

She shook her head. I opened the book to the beginning of a story. She studied the page for almost a minute before she began to read. Later I realized that she had guessed at the first few words. "'Once . . . upon a . . . time . . .'" She paused, and what came next was gibberish. "Three . . . was . . . a . . . title . . . tar . . ." I looked over her shoulder. "There was a little tailor," the words read.

She went on, the rest of it just as senseless, until finally she gave up. "I don't know what I'm reading." When I questioned her I found out that she had never memorized the alphabet. To her a word was just a bunch of letters in a certain order. She was able to memorize the key words and guess at the rest. I'd never seen anything like it.

176

Her teachers had pushed her through to the eighth grade, I guessed, figuring it wouldn't do any harm. She couldn't go any farther, though, because in order to get out of the eighth grade she had to pass the territorial examination. And she wasn't able to read it. "I gotta pass the exam," she said. "If I do, my mother promised I could go to high school in Fairbanks." After quizzing her for a while I found that she was smart, no doubt about it. We decided that she would attend classes and I would give her extra help at night.

I blessed Mr. Strong for advising me to take her. Nancy pitched in with the chores so willingly that in a few days my quarters were spick-and-span. I didn't know what I'd have done without her when it came to water. The snow was two feet deep and the creek was running thick with slush ice. Then all of a sudden the temperature dropped to thirty below and the creek froze up. Nancy had piled snow high alongside the door, and there was our water supply. I didn't care much for the taste of it. It was flat, until Nancy dumped oatmeal in the barrel, and that improved it.

"We'll have to go easy on the water now," she told me. The trick, she showed me, was not to throw away any water until it was thoroughly used—first for personal washing, then for clothes. If necessary it could be used a third time to scrub floors.

After the first week or so, problems began to come up between us. She didn't like it when I gave Chuck a bath, acting as if he were just about the lowest thing she ever saw. "You can't even turn around here without runnin' over 'im."

"He likes it here."

"Between him and all them other kids you'd think this was a roadhouse."

She didn't like the idea that the kids were always trooping in and out after school, so I tried to discourage them from coming into my quarters. But things kept going from bad to worse between us. It was her job to see to it that we always had enough wood and water on hand. But when we ran low on them a couple of times, I had to remind her. Finally we took turns washing the linens, sweeping, doing the dishes and everything else.

I hadn't planned it that way at all. I was in the schoolroom almost all day and I'd sometimes be working long after supper, planning lessons and activities. I'd thought that Nancy would help me out, but I had as much to do as I had before, and besides that, I had to put up with someone I liked less every day.

I'd told Nancy that before she could learn to read she was going to have to learn how to recognize all her letters and the sounds they had. She buckled down at first, memorized the letters in no time, and even started to write simple three-letter words. But a couple of the older kids made fun of her, and soon she wasn't even completing her assignments. Once when I asked Jimmy Carew to read aloud, he did an imitation of her—slumping down in his seat and staring at his book, which he held upside down.

The situation came to a head near dismissal time one afternoon when Nancy rose from her seat, went over to Jimmy and smacked him hard across the ear. Then she walked out the front door, slamming it behind her.

It was well after supper when she came back. She sat down on the couch and stared into space.

We were silent for a few moments, then she said, "You don't like me, do you? 'Cause I won't do all the scrubbin' and cleanin' you want."

"Nancy—"

"Well, that's not what I come here for," she went on, deliberately using poor grammar. "I do enough a that at home. I come here so you could teach me to read and you ain't done it."

"No, I *ain't*," I said, beginning to lose my temper, "and the way you're acting I'll never be able to. You're so busy being angry, you haven't got room for anything else inside."

"My mother ain't payin' for me to cook and clean," she said stoically. "She's payin' for you to tutor me."

"Nancy, your mother isn't paying me anything."

"What are you talkin' about? I heard 'er tell you when you first came through that she'd pay you for takin' me."

"Yes, she did. But I sent her a note back on the day you arrived. I told her she could forget about paying me."

178

She went pale. "Why'd you do that?" Her voice seemed to come from far away.

"I was glad to have the company," I said honestly. "I was afraid being here all by myself."

She got up and went to the window. She slowly rubbed some moisture from a pane and stared out into the darkness. Then she cried for a long time.

From then on, Nancy was a dynamo—doing so many chores that I had to tell her to slow down. "You're doin' more for me than anybody in my whole life," she said. "And I'm not forgetting it."

She started being nicer to the other kids. When a few of the "books" the children had made started falling apart, she sewed the pages together, then shoved them at the kids with a gruff "Here." She was tops in arithmetic, so one morning I asked her if she'd help Jimmy with his multiplication tables. Neither of them looked too keen about the idea. I sent them into my quarters to work, and when I glanced through the door a few minutes later she was tutoring him as if she'd done it all her life.

After she helped Jimmy the class was less leery of her and in a couple of weeks some of the kids were taking a shine to her. During recess I let her supervise the older kids outside while the little ones played in the schoolroom. In private I told her that I'd appreciate it if she watched out for Chuck.

She watched out for him better than I could. During one recess I heard him start to cry, and I went to the door just in time to see Nancy give Eleanor Vaughn a shove. She'd have done the same with Evelyn, but Evelyn danced out of the way. They must have washed Chuck's face with snow because it was all red and wet.

Nancy put a mitten on Chuck's shoulder. "If you two lay your hands on this kid again," she said, "I'm gonna bash your heads in."

They left Chuck alone from then on.

I guessed I was never so happy in my life as around that time. Everything just seemed the way I'd dreamed it would be—the settlement and the entire countryside hushed under a thick white blanket, the snow dry enough so you could walk outdoors in moccasins and never get wet. Now I realized what the North was really

like. Winter was when everything went on. You could ski anyplace you wanted to and get there twice as fast as you could before
there was snow. The whole country was so quiet and open and free
that it was like being let out of prison. It put everybody in good
spirits and they went around looking the way the country did—
clean and fresh.

I learned how to ski in no time at all, and I wanted to learn
skijoring—holding on to a string of dogs and letting them pull you.
Fred was expert at it and said he'd teach me. "Be ready next Saturday morning," he told me. "I'll be by around ten."

On the dot I heard him call my name, and when I opened the door
he was out there on his skis. He'd brought his favorite lead dog, Pancake, and two others. He'd fitted an extra pair of straps on his own
skis so I could stand behind him. Nancy watched from the doorway
while I got on, and I had the barest second to wave before he
yelled "Mush!" and we were off.

Once we were on the trail, Fred started singing "Sweet Rosie
O'Grady," and the dogs began to pull like sixty. Everybody had a
different way of making sled dogs pull. Some used a whip. Others,
like Angela Barrett, yelled and cursed at them all the time. Fred
sang to his and they loved it.

"Fred!" I yelled. "We're going too fast. We'll fall!"

"No we won't! We haven't even started."

I held on to his parka as tight as I could, his skis crunching under
us. The dogs were thirty feet ahead, the full length of the lead rope.
If they geed or hawed, I knew I was going to be dumped.

But I hung on. Skiing was fun, but it wasn't anywhere near as
exciting as this.

After a while I started to congratulate myself. I leaned into
turns easily and could key my movements to Fred's, as if we were
on a bicycle built for two. We must have gone half a mile before I
got so cocky I didn't look where we were going. The trail took a
sharp turn. Fred leaned to the left, I dragged him off to the right,
and we went flying.

We ended up in a drift, laughing. "You all right?" Fred asked.

"Perfect. Maybe I'll take a nap." I propped myself up on my

elbows, watching the dogs. They'd taken a spill too, and a couple were tangled in the lead lines. They were well trained, though, and didn't get excited. Pancake was a beauty, a Siberian husky, with a brown mask over a gray wolf face and slanted ice-blue eyes. Panting, he went to Fred, his tail down and his rear end moving from side to side.

"Look at that. He thinks it was his fault," Fred said. He sat up and started untangling the rope.

"Well, whose fault was it?"

"Yours."

"I knew I'd be blamed." I picked up a gob of snow and tossed it at him. He blocked it easily; then, shoveling up a bigger gob, he hefted it high in the air. It plopped down on the hood of my parka.

"You look like a tree," he said.

"Nicest thing you ever said to me."

I looked up at the blue sky. It was still early, but the sun was low, skimming the distant mountaintops and sending out long blue shadows from the trees.

I watched Fred while he straightened out the harness. I'd really liked being so close to him on the skis and I wondered if he felt the same about me. I had a feeling he did, but he didn't show it. So far all he'd done was hold my hand when we were alone. We never talked about it, but I knew full well he'd swallowed a lot of that half-breed talk and it made him keep his distance.

He got up now, brushed himself off and gave me a hand. Then we were on our way again.

A couple of minutes later we were in sight of Mary Angus' place. There was smoke coming from the stovepipe, which meant she was all right. A couple of weeks ago when I'd seen her on the trail near Fred's house, I'd been scared she might die. She was pulling a hand sled and was probably heading for her trapline. We waved at each other, but before she went on she doubled over, coughing. When I crossed the place where she'd stopped, I saw blood splattered all over the snow. I wondered now if we should stop and see how she was, but decided we'd just be bothering her.

A little later, when we started home, we took a shortcut across some fresh snow, figuring we'd pick up the trail again just past Uncle Arthur's place. The dogs had to break trail, leaping forward like fish breaking water, so we walked. Fred slung the skis over his shoulder. I took his arm. "When are you going to take me on that snow picnic you promised?"

"I was thinking we'd go in a couple of weeks. Have to go out on the trapline in a few days."

He hated trapping. Most of the time the animal was still alive when he got to it. It had to be clubbed, then skinned before the carcass froze. The only reason he did it was because his family needed the money.

"I wish you didn't have to go," I said.

"Me too. I'm going to miss you."

"I feel the same way. I'll miss you too."

He dropped the skis on the snow, looking very serious, and put his arms around me. He was still holding on to the dogs' lead line, and I thought that if one of those dogs pulled on the line now I'd kill it. But they all stayed quiet. And then Fred's mouth was on mine, and my heart was pumping like a steam engine. After he kissed me he held me away from him a little and the way he looked at me I knew he'd always cared for me a lot more than he'd let on.

His parka was open at the neck and when I laid my head against his shoulder I could feel the heat from his body. He smelled of woodsmoke.

"I shouldn't have done that, Anne."

"Why not?"

"You know why. There's a lot of difference between us."

"Does that mean you want me to become a Democrat?"

He laughed, and then he kissed me again.

We found a place to sit down on a small shelf of rock over a creek bottom. Fred cut some spruce boughs for us to sit on and I leaned back in the crook of his arm. It was a cozy spot and we snuggled together for warmth.

We started talking about what he wanted to do in the future. He'd worked for wages a few times and hadn't liked it. What he wanted more than anything was to be on his own. He and his

182

father had plans to buy a tractor. With it, he said, he'd do ten times the mining they were doing now with pick and shovel. If everything worked out, he might try farming. He felt that anything done in the States could be done here. He loved it here.

"You just look out there," he said. "It's so big and beautiful it makes you feel wonderful just to be alive. I couldn't even think of living anyplace else."

We were still talking when a sudden gust of cold air hit me. It was as if a giant box of dry ice had dropped on us. "We'd better get back," Fred said. "Temperature's starting to drop."

Ten minutes later we were on our skis and back on the trail, ice fog swirling around us. I could feel the cold nipping at my body, almost like teeth. The ice fog became so thick that we had to depend on the dogs to stay on the trail. But as long as I was with Fred I wasn't scared. All the way back I felt as if I were part of him, his body against mine, lean and strong.

By the time we reached my quarters the thermometer outside the window read thirty-five below zero. It had been zero when we started out. Nancy had a roaring fire going in the stove, but even so there was frost along the far walls. Fred stayed long enough to warm up, then headed for home. "See you when I get back from trapping," he said.

I felt so good I wanted to sing and dance around the room. I had more energy than I knew what to do with, so I washed some clothes. I sang "Row, Row, Row Your Boat," scrubbing on the washboard to keep time.

"Boy, are *you* happy," Nancy said.

"Of course I'm happy. Fred and I had a nice time."

She didn't say anything, but I could tell something was on her mind. She waited until after supper to bring it up.

"You mind if I tell you something, Anne?" she asked while we were doing the dishes.

"Go ahead."

"Well . . . there's a lot of talk goin' around about you and Fred. Some of it's pretty salty. . . . You know what I mean."

"Who's doing the talking?"

"Mr. Vaughn, Angela—all of 'em. A couple have already written to Juneau about you."

She'd been washing the same plate for the past minute. Finally she handed it to me to dry. She rested her hands on the rim of the washtub. "Anne," she said, "that man's a breed. The way you act towards 'im is, well . . . like somebody who's more than a friend."

"Is that the only way you think about him, Nancy—that he's a half-breed? Does that mean he's less of a person?"

"I never thought about it much."

"I'm pretty fond of him—and more than just as a friend."

She picked up a cup and started washing it, looking unhappy.

For the next couple of days it stayed so cold that Nancy and I warmed up the bed with hot rocks before we got in. Even then, when we woke up in the morning the blankets were stuck to the wall. On Thursday it dropped to forty below, and we moved the whole class into my quarters and let the little ones sit in the bed.

People began to say that if it was this cold in November, we were probably in for a three-dog winter. In a one-dog winter you stayed warm at night with just one dog in bed with you. A two-dog winter was tough, but a three-dog winter—well, that was so cold that the smoke froze in the stovepipe. An exaggeration—but close.

V

WHEN Fred got back from the trapline he invited me to a snow picnic at West Fork the following Saturday. But before Saturday came, Mrs. Purdy paid me a visit after school. When I opened the door she smiled up at me from under a beautiful hat of otter fur. She needed something from Mr. Strong's store, she said.

Now with the freeze-up Mr. Strong was able to use his big sled and the store was full of stuff he'd brought in, but all she wanted, she said, was a can of peppercorns for a pepper-pot stew. She stuffed the pepper in the pocket of her fur coat, and as I was writing it down, she said, "You are going on snow picnic with my Frayd he tell me."

"On Saturday."

"He like you very mush, Ahnne."

"I feel the same way about him."

"I understand why he likes you. You are pretty, Ahnne. Someday you marry man who have mush money, give you *big* house, many things. . . . Frayd, he give you nothing." She said it as if he were a dismal failure, and I almost had to smile.

"Mrs. Purdy, why don't you tell me what's really on your mind?"

She laughed, a lilting laugh full of good humor. Then she was serious. "Please, Ahnne, do not like him. It is not good. . . . You savvy what I say?"

"Mrs. Purdy, do you think that Fred and I have done anything wrong?"

"No. I not say this. I say only that now there is mush trouble. Three days ago Mr. Strong come see me. He tell me Frayd like you too mush. People know, and it is very bad. I am shocked he tell me this, Ahnne. I not know. When Frayd he come home I talk with him. He say it is true, and I weep. I am afraid, Ahnne. People here not like see white woman, dark man. Better to close book on that. Too many tears come your eyes, too many pains in your heart. . . . I ask you—I tell Frayd you not like him anymore. Yes?"

I didn't want to hurt her for anything in the world. "Mrs. Purdy . . ."

"Ahnne, I beg of you."

"I'm sorry . . ."

She was angry, but she collected herself.

"I say good night to you, Ahnne," she said, "but first I tell you something make me sad almost to cry. You must come my house no more." She turned and went out the door.

"Mrs. Purdy!" Locking the door after me, I followed as quickly as possible. I called to her again, but she didn't turn around.

As her tiny figure kept moving off, I felt the same way I had years before when my grandmother Hobbs had stood in the road and waved good-by to me.

For the rest of the week I was afraid that Fred wouldn't be able to make it on Saturday. I knew he'd want to hurt his mother even less than I did.

When Saturday morning came, though, he was outside with his sled at nine. I saw that Pancake wasn't his lead dog this time. He'd put Pancake directly in front of the sled and harnessed all the malamutes up front, with Shakespeare in the lead. Fred had taught me enough about sled dogs so I knew why. It had snowed a few days before and the dogs would have to break trail part of the way. The heavier dogs like Pancake would be more likely to break through the snow and have tough going. The lighter malamutes would pack it down.

As soon as I was tucked in the sled and Fred yelled "Mush!" that team took off. Riding the runners, Fred launched into a chorus of "Oh! Susanna" and the dogs pushed into their collars. For the first hour we moved along at such a good pace and it looked so easy that I asked him to let me try driving.

"Might be a little hard for you," he yelled. "We'll be hitting some hummock ice soon."

"I'll bet you I can do it."

We changed places and I started singing "Ta-Ra-Ra-Boom-Dee-Ay." But between having to jump off the runners to keep the sled from tipping, and trying to manipulate the lead lines, I found out that it took a lot more strength than I thought to keep the sled on trail. When we hit the hummock ice I decided to give up. It was like going over slippery rocks. Sweating and hardly able to breathe, I said, "Fred, maybe you ought to take it."

"You sure you want me to? You're not doing bad at all."

"I'm getting a little tired." It was all I could do to hold on to the handles.

"There's only another quarter mile, then it'll be downhill." He was trying to keep a straight face, but he couldn't.

"Fred, I mean it. My hands are killing me. . . . Whoa!" I yelled to the dogs. It came out like a whisper and they didn't pay any attention. "Fred—"

He was laughing so hard he could barely yell whoa to the dogs. He stumbled out of the sled, trying to stop laughing, but every time he looked at me he'd start all over again. Finally he took me in his arms and gave me a big hug, then held me away from him. I couldn't think of anybody who ever looked at me the way he did then, and I had all I could do not to tell him I loved him right then and there. Because I did. I knew I'd never felt this way about anybody and that I never would again about anybody else. And I saw in his eyes that it was that way with him too.

Once the hummock ice was behind us we moved fast, and finally we reached the crest of a hill from where we could see West Fork joining the Fortymile River. Ahead of us stretched endlessness.

Months before, the river below had been rushing along so fast that there didn't seem to be any force on earth powerful enough to stop it. But now something held it in a mighty grip, freezing West Fork all the fifteen miles back to where it began, freezing the Fortymile all the way to Steel Creek and beyond. The sun was just coming up over the mountains—blood red and cold. I felt as if I were standing in the mightiest cathedral ever built. There was no end to it, and no beginning. All I could do was look at it and worship.

We found a picnic spot at the base of a soaring face of rock, and Fred tied the dogs. In a little while, with the fire and the bright ball of sun, it was warm enough for us to take off our parkas. I made some tea and we sat drinking out of tin cups.

He took my hand and held it. There were cuts all over his from the cold steel of the traps. Mine were chapped and rough, but compared with his they were slender and soft. "Look at the difference," he said. "How light yours are—how dark mine are."

"I like your hands."

"You know what I'm talking about. We shouldn't even be here."

"What can anybody do to me, take back more pots and pans?"

"It's no joke. They can be a hard set, these people. When I told my mother we were going on this picnic . . . Well, she told me she went to see you. She's really upset."

"How about you?"

"I'm worried. If I had any sense, I wouldn't have taken you out here all alone."

"Do you want to go back?"

"No."

He put some more wood on the fire and then I moved into his arms. I could have kept on kissing him all day, except that my lips started to burn after a while. "I just learned something," I said.

"What?"

"Why Eskimos rub noses. Their lips are always chapped."

"I don't rub noses."

"You're only half Eskimo."

He smiled at that, then a moment later his eyes flicked to someplace in back of me. "We're being watched."

I tried to sit up, but he held me tight. "Don't move too fast. Just turn your head slowly. There, standing by that rotted spruce."

I saw him—a shaggy-coated moose. He'd been feeding on some willow, but now he was still, looking our way. He was tremendous, with racks maybe six feet wide and covered with white winter fuzz. He didn't seem to see us.

The sled was only about ten feet away, Fred's rifle slung across the handles. He started to ease away from me.

"Let him go, Fred."

"Anne, that's fresh meat—eight hundred pounds of it. You'll have enough for the whole winter."

"But we won't have a picnic." He'd have to butcher it then and there and it'd be a mess. He thought about it, then waved a hand toward the moose. "Have a good dinner," he said. The moose dipped his head and shambled off.

After we ate we took a walk out onto the river. It had frozen smooth in the center, but near the banks it was a mass of twisted shapes that looked like a sculptor had gone crazy. When we got back to the sled I was all for building up the fire and staying there, but it was dark already and Fred said we should go.

On the way home, I kept imagining that we'd just go on and on through the moonlit night. I leaned back in the sled and stared up at the heavens, imagining that we were on our way up to them, gliding into the stars on a trip to the Milky Way.

It was after six when we reached the settlement. Fred said good night to me on the porch. "See you at the Thanksgiving party Friday night," he said.

188

A few minutes later I'd changed into some slipper moccasins, and Nancy and I were preparing supper when she told me we were going to have a visitor.

"Who?"

"I'll give you one guess. He's from Eagle."

"I can't imagine."

"Really? From the way he talked you'd think you were engaged to marry him. Cabaret Jackson."

A little later Cab stomped in with a heart-shaped box of candy. He was all dolled up in his Saturday-night cowboy clothes. He'd taken a bath at the roadhouse and pomaded his hair so that he smelled like a barbershop. He was as loud and brassy as when he'd given me the revolver at the dance in Eagle. I offered him coffee, but he said he was drunk on love and didn't want to sober up. "Cab," I said, "I can smell what you're drunk on and it isn't love."

That made him whoop up a storm. "Ain't she somethin'?" he said to Nancy. "Teacher, what I need is a good woman like you. I'd take a vow that nary a drop would I touch, and I'd build you a cabin that'd be a palace."

I told him thanks, but I intended to stay single.

"I tell you, if you say yes, you won't be sorry."

It was all a game to him and he was enjoying it. He said he would be coming back through Chicken for the big Thanksgiving party and would try again. "I got all this money ajinglin' in my belt, and if I can't spend it on the most beautiful gal in the Forty Mile, what's it good for?"

"You must have struck it rich."

"I sure did," he said craftily. "What I got on that sled a mine's more precious than gold, grub or fire."

He was running liquor, Nancy told me after he left. "He runs it all over the Forty Mile."

"Isn't he afraid of getting caught?"

"Not him. He's got the fastest dog team around."

I saw his team the next day, kenneled in back of the roadhouse. They were a mean bunch, but they looked fast—lean in the flanks and heavy in the shoulders. If Cab had wanted to make money

190

honestly with them, he could have. There were always people willing to pay top dollar for a man who knew the country and had a good team of dogs—metallurgists or businessmen who wanted to be mushed into the interior. But all he was interested in was wasting his time drinking and bragging about his sled racing.

We'd planned the Thanksgiving party for weeks, and by the time Friday rolled around, the schoolroom really looked festive. The class had cut turkeys and pumpkins out of colored paper and pasted them on the windowpanes. Streamers and paper chains hung from the ceiling. By four o'clock there were so many people in the schoolroom that even though an icy mist rolled in every time someone opened the door, we hardly needed the stove. Except for Fred's mother, who was down with a cold, and his father, just about everybody showed up.

Nancy was the hit of the party. I had cut her hair short and marcelled it that morning. She wore the new dress we'd made for her and I'd helped her put on a touch of lipstick and rouge. When she looked in the mirror it was all I could do to stop her from washing it off.

"Anne, I look like a flapper! Everybody's gonna laugh at me."

"You look beautiful," I told her. And it was the truth.

When the first few people came in, Nancy pretended to be busy at the stove and wouldn't even turn around. Jimmy Carew didn't recognize her. "Who are *you*?" he asked.

"Who do you think I am?" Nancy said grimly.

"Holy cow!" He stared at her, his mouth gaping. "Nancy, you look beyootiful!" She blushed beet red, loving it.

As soon as everybody was there, the class put on a pageant about the landing of the Pilgrims at Plymouth Rock. After that we had supper, and everybody helped themselves to bear soup, moose spareribs, pickled caribou and dried king salmon. Along with a load of oranges and apples, we'd had corn on the cob freighted in from Fairbanks. Willard Carew was sitting alongside me. He'd never seen whole corn before and was eating the cob and all.

"I sure don't think much of this," he whispered to me.

"Try eating just the yellow part," I told him. "Most people don't bother with the rest of it." He liked it a lot better after that.

We topped it all off with dried-apple pie and ice cream. Then we cleared the tables from the schoolroom, Fred took out his banjo and the square dancing was on. I had as much fun watching as dancing, especially when Lily's parents, Rebekah and Jake Harrington, were on the floor. Rebekah was almost as heavy as her husband, but she swung around and do-si-doed like a young girl.

Cab Jackson breezed in about nine, with a bottle of whiskey in one hand and a bottle of gin in the other. After a while I didn't even want to dance with him, he was getting so wild.

The square dancing ended and an ancient gramophone was set up for us to dance to until the "Home, Sweet Home" waltz would signal it was time to go over to Maggie's roadhouse for midnight supper. I should have known something was going to happen when I heard a few of the men talking with Cab about how fast Fred's dogs were. Cab buttonholed Fred and was all for having a race with him. "I just mushed 'em fifty miles to here and I'll put 'em up against yours right now."

"Thanks, Cab, but I'm not a racing man."

Cab had that stubborn look that said he wasn't going to be talked out of it. "Hell, I hear them's all Indian dogs you got anyway. Ain't worth the fish ya feed 'em."

Fred walked away from him, but Cab was back to the same song again right after Fred and I danced a fox-trot. By this time his eyes were bloodshot and he was getting mean. I was hoping that even if I didn't end up with Fred when the "Home, Sweet Home" waltz went on, at least I wouldn't end up with Cab. When the waltz did go on, Fred was right beside me.

That was the loveliest waltz I'd ever danced with anyone. For the first time in my life I really felt beautiful. Just having Fred look at me the way he did made me whirl around that floor as if we weren't in a little schoolroom out in the wilds but in the grand ballroom of a palace.

At the roadhouse, Fred and I sat at one of the long tables. I wished we could have had a table for two, but just having midnight supper with Fred was enough. We could hear Cab yelling over on

192

the other side of the room, still challenging anybody in the house to a dog race. Then I heard somebody say something about Fred and a few men laughed.

When we were almost finished eating, Nancy came over. She leaned down close to me. "Anne," she whispered, "somethin's goin' on. You and Fred better go as soon as you can."

We looked over at the other table. Angela Barrett was staring at Fred and me with hate in her eyes. There was something in the air, all right. Fred and I got up and he went to pay for our supper.

"You ain't leavin' so early, are ya, Teacher?" Cab yelled.

"Sure am, Cab. I'm dead tired."

He got up from the table and made his way toward me. Fred brought my coat and Cab tried to take it from him. "I'll take care of 'er. Lemme have that," he said.

"It's all right, Cab," Fred told him.. "I'll take her home."

"You will like hell," Cab said. "Let it go." Cab shoved him and Fred fell against the counter.

I was scared now. The whole place had gotten quiet, and everybody was watching to see what was going to happen. They were waiting like a pack of wolves for Cab to do their dirty work. And Fred knew it. I could see by the way he was looking at everybody. He was cornered, being forced into a fight with Cab.

"Now you hightail it outta here, half-breed," Cab said to him. He was wound up like a spring. He wanted to fight bad, you could see it in the way his shoulders moved, as if he would shake himself apart if he didn't start lashing out. I felt sick.

"Cab, I don't want to fight with you," Fred told him.

"Thought so," Mr. Vaughn said. "He's going to crawfish."

Fred moved away from the counter. He'd gone dead white around his mouth and he was all tightened up, so I was surprised he could walk so easily. He went over to get his parka where it was hanging on a hook. Cab rushed over to him and gave him another shove that sent him flying into a bunch of men. They pushed him back and Cab's fist went out and hit Fred in the mouth. Fred's lip started to bleed and the punch kind of stunned him. That did it. Mr. Carew and another man grabbed Cab, two others grabbed Fred, and they hustled them both out the door. I kept trying to get them to stop, but nobody was listening to me.

So there Fred was, out in the middle of the snow, his parka still hanging over his arm and Cab staring at him wild-eyed, going into a slight crouch, telling him to get ready. Everybody was really having a good time now. "Slam 'im in the mush, Cab. Chew 'im up!" Not one of them was rooting for Fred.

Fred wasn't doing anything but watching Cab. Then Cab started to move in.

I was really scared. I thought Fred would be too, but he wasn't. I almost didn't recognize him for the expression on his face. It was the strangest expression I'd ever seen, the look he might have had on trail when he was alone and in trouble and it was only him against an enemy. At that moment I didn't know him at all.

I tried to go over to him, but Angela Barrett grabbed me.

What happened next made everybody jump. There was a big explosion and I caught a flash of flame out of the corner of my eye and smelled the sharp odor of burned powder. It was Jake Harrington, standing there holding Mr. Carew's thirty-aught-six over-an'-under. Everybody froze and my ears were ringing. He'd fired into the air, but now he was pointing that shotgun straight at Cab. "Go on back inside, Cab," he told him quietly.

Cab wasn't so drunk that those two barrels staring him in the face didn't sober him a little.

"This is none a your business," he said to Jake.

"Only tryin' to do you a favor, Cab," Jake said.

"It's not him you're doing any favors," Mr. Vaughn said. "It's the breed."

"It's him," Jake said. " 'Cause if he tries to hit that boy I'm gonna kill 'im. What do you say, Cab? It's cold out here."

Cab slouched back inside. I pulled away from Angela.

"C'mon, Fred." I took his arm.

At my quarters, we stood on the porch. "I'm glad you're not hurt too bad," I said. He didn't say anything.

"Why are you looking at me like that?" I asked him.

"No reason."

I wanted to say, I love you. Instead I said, "Can you kiss me good night or does your mouth hurt too much?"

He leaned down. His lips just barely touched mine, but he hugged me so tight it took the breath out of me. Before he walked off the porch, he stared at me in a way that gave me the most awful feeling, as if he'd pushed me away or shut me out. I wanted to call him back. But I didn't. I just stood there.

Monday morning I asked Isabelle Purdy about Fred, and she said he'd gone over to Steel Creek. Every time I thought of the look on his face when he left Friday night, I'd had a sinking feeling. I had the same feeling now.

His father showed up for the mail when Mr. Strong came into the settlement a few days later.

"How's everybody in the family?" I asked him while we were standing in line outside the post office.

"Fine," he said. "They all say hello."

"What did Fred go to Steel Creek for?" I asked him.

"See some people. He ought to be back in a few days."

I couldn't bring myself to pry anymore.

There was a letter for me from Lester Henderson, the education commissioner. He'd received the first monthly report I'd sent him and he was very satisfied with it. Then he went on to say that he'd received letters from a few people in Chicken.

The general tone of them is that you are a good teacher. I've received letters from parents, however, who mentioned that you have been teaching the children about the Indians and that you seem to be fond of a young man of mixed blood. I want you to know I have faith in you and your abilities, and your personal life is your own. I do wish to advise you, however, to be as diplomatic as possible, especially if you wish to teach in Eagle next year.

The week dragged by. Every time I'd hear footsteps outside I'd think it was Fred, but it was always somebody else. Then right after dark Friday afternoon there he was. He'd come back from Steel Creek a few hours ago, he said.

"Can you stay for supper?" I asked him.

"No, I haven't been home yet." He went over to the potbellied stove while I poured coffee. I heard him open it up, then take a couple of pieces of wood from the woodbox and heft them in.

"Anne . . ."

I didn't turn around. I braced myself, waiting.

"I'm going away," he said. "To Steel Creek. Some guys doing winter mining there can use another hand. Till June."

Till June. School would be over by then and I'd be gone.

I picked up his cup from the cookstove and put it down on the table. I was numb.

"When are you going?"

"Tomorrow."

The gas lamp threw our shadows on the wall. I was almost surprised to see mine there. I felt as if I'd faded away to nothing.

"I don't want to go, Anne. But I have to. I don't want to see you hurt. Once these people turn against you, you won't have a job in Eagle or maybe anywhere else in Alaska. They can write letters to the commissioner that'd curl your hair."

"They already have. I'm not scared of them."

"I am. Not for me. For you, for my mother and my sister."

I think I must have groaned then, I felt so awful. "Oh, Fred . . ."

He was as miserable as I was. "Don't you see, Anne? I can't do you anything but harm. I can't give you anything. I can't take care of you. You see what I'm trying to say?"

"No." I knew he was doing it for me, but he was wrong. And yet I didn't know how to make him see it.

"I'd better go," he said finally.

I moved over to him and my arms went around him. "Please, Fred. Don't."

"I have to." He gripped my arms and held me away from him. "Anne, will you try to understand . . . !"

"You don't have to go right now," I said desperately. "We can talk awhile. Just stay until Nancy comes home."

He hesitated. But then he was moving to the door. "Please, Fred," I asked him, "don't go. I love you so much."

196

"Anne, don't," he said, his voice hard. "I'm going."

That stopped me as if he'd slapped me. He said something else before he went out, but I didn't listen. I heard him walk off the porch. I'd never loved anybody as much in my entire life and now he was going away from me for the stupidest reason in the whole world. "It isn't fair," I said, starting to cry. "It isn't fair at all."

It wasn't until after Nancy came home and we were in bed that I realized what he'd said before he went out. He'd said *I love you.*

VI

THE next morning when I woke up, the blankets were frozen to the wall, as usual. Wearing a couple of heavy sweaters, Nancy was sitting alongside the stove, a book open in front of her. As soon as I tugged the blankets free I felt the cold. The stove had a roaring fire in it, but there were dots of white all over the walls where the nails were frost-covered. Nancy called them frost buttons.

"What's it down to?" I asked her.

"Fifty-four."

Fifty-four below zero. I hung some bib overalls and a shirt over the stove to warm them, then dressed quickly. I rubbed a hole in the thick layer of frost that covered the window and looked at the thermometer. "It *was* fifty-four. It's fifty-six now."

I thought about breakfast but had no appetite. Nancy knew how I was feeling I'd told her last night that Fred was leaving.

I did some washing just to keep busy, but I couldn't shake off the feeling of being trapped. Finally I couldn't stand being cooped up any longer and put on my parka. I started to walk without even thinking about where I was going. Gray and still out, it was so cold that my parka was white with the frost from my own breath.

After a while I found myself near Mary Angus' shack. It looked so lonely and forlorn I almost started to cry. For the first time I really understood why she was staying here, how even though she was sick she could keep on living in a place like that. If you loved somebody enough, you could live anywhere.

Nancy went home to Steel Creek for Christmas, and all through the holidays I took long walks—once as far as the Fortymile River. I was feeling so sorry for myself that I even went out on the ice, hoping I'd find a spot thin enough to break through. All I managed to do was stay out so long that I wound up with frostbite. The pain was agonizing before circulation came back, and I knew I'd never do that again.

Finally, Nancy came back and Maggie invited us to a New Year's Eve party at the roadhouse. I didn't feel like going. Instead I stayed home and wrote a letter to Fred. I missed him badly, I wrote him, and all I did was think about him. I told him that I was mad too, because he was wrong. "You may say you did it for me," I wrote, "but I wonder if maybe you just didn't really care about me that much, so when it came down to it you just took the easy way. If you did, then I want you to write and tell me. I can take anything as long as it's the truth. . . ."

When I finished the letter I stamped and addressed it before I could change my mind about sending it.

I sat and read for a while after that. Occasionally I'd hear the square-dance music from the roadhouse. When twelve o'clock came, everybody started hooraying and whistling and banging on pots. Then they started singing "Auld Lang Syne," and it made me feel so lonely. Someone came running toward the schoolhouse as they got near the end. Nancy burst in and there were tears in her eyes. "Anne," she said, "I just wanted to come over and wish you . . . wish you a—" That was as far as she got before she threw her arms around me and then we both started crying. She kept saying over and over how bad she felt for me.

After that I made a New Year's resolution that from now on I wasn't going to think about anything but teaching, and I was going to do the best job I knew how. When school opened again, I could feel from the first day that something was different about me. We had as much fun as before, but I made the children work harder. They only had till June to get all the schooling they could, I figured, and they were going to get it.

People must have noticed I'd changed, because they acted differently toward me, as if I weren't a kid or a cheechako anymore. They

198

stopped asking me whether it was cold enough for me, and what I wanted to be when I grew up. I felt different, all right—as if all my life I'd been trying to be what other people wanted me to be. From now on, they were going to have to take me for what I was. It was as if I'd grown up all of a sudden.

A couple of weeks after school started I got a letter from Fred. He hadn't been trifling with my affections, he wrote. He cared for me more than he'd ever cared for anybody.

> I did what I thought was right, Anne. I can't tell you how much it turned me inside out to come here, but I did it because I love you so much that there was nothing else I *could* do.
>
> If I can take it, I'll be staying here until summer, so I won't be seeing you for a long time. Maybe never again. I just want you to know that I love you deeply, but I am not going to take up any more of your time. You'll be going to Eagle to teach and you'll probably forget all about me. And maybe that's the best thing.

I read the letter over and over, and every time I saw the words "if I can take it" I winced. I'd asked Nancy how Fred was doing at Steel Creek and she'd told me he was lonely. "The other miners don't like to work alongside half-breeds," she'd said. "They won't let him bunk with 'em, so Ma and Pa rented him the work shed back of the roadhouse. It's not too bad, Anne, nothing like Mary Angus' place. It's got a wood floor and it's clean."

Fred lived in a work shed all by himself when here he had the most beautiful home of anybody and a family that loved him. And it was my fault. He hated working for wages, and on top of it he had to work with men who didn't want him.

I wrote him a letter telling him I thought he should come back. "We don't have to see each other at all," I ended it. "I promise you that. I won't even say hello to you. I know how you feel now and I'll respect your feelings, so please don't stay there because of me." I signed it "Your friend (and I mean just that), Anne."

That was the most peculiar time I ever went through. I'd never felt more alone in my life, and at the same time I felt more whole than I ever had. I didn't seem to need anybody; it was as if there were a protective shell around me and I couldn't say or do anything wrong. Not that I didn't feel things. I did. I just felt them in a different way. The night that Nancy finally accomplished what she'd set her heart on, for instance, I was so composed I hardly recognized myself.

Nancy was looking through a third-grade reader and I was practicing on the harmonica. Since I didn't have a piano, I figured I could play it when we needed music for songs and games. I was playing "Home on the Range" and not doing bad at all when I heard her say, "Anne?"

I looked over at her and there was just no way to describe the wonderful smile on her face. "I can read," she said.

"You sure?"

She nodded.

"Go ahead."

"'Once-upon-ay-time,'" she read, "'ay-crab-left-thee-sea-and-went-out-upon-thee-beach-to-warm-himself-in-thee-sunshine. . . .'"
It was the first time she'd ever read anything without my help, and she read it perfectly. When she finished she was glowing.

"Was that reading?"

"That was reading."

We tried her with some headlines from the Fairbanks *Daily News–Miner* just to be sure. She didn't do too badly with a few paragraphs from *Collier's* either. She was so happy about it she almost started to cry. A couple of months before, I'd have joined her. But I wasn't surprised. It was as if I'd known all along it was going to happen.

The next morning Nancy could barely wait for the class to show up to tell them all, and before the day was over, everybody in Chicken knew she could read. Maggie Carew invited us over to supper to celebrate. Now that Fred was gone she acted more kindly toward me, or maybe she was even sorry for what had happened. After supper she asked if I was looking forward to teaching in Eagle next year.

"I don't know," I said. "I hear the school board has some doubts about me."

200

"Well, I oughtta have something to say about that. End of spring we're movin' there. I bought the roadhouse alongside the dock. I'll put in a good word for you—unless you got other plans."

I didn't have any at all. I was just waiting. There was an empty space inside of me, but what was going to fill it up I couldn't say.

Come February, I almost wondered if I wanted to teach any-where in Alaska at all, because suddenly the weather turned so mean it felt as if God had gone away from this part of the world. The sky stayed so dark you couldn't tell whether it was day or night. For almost a week the temperature dropped to fifty below and stayed there. All the moisture was sucked out of the air, leaving everybody thirsty all the time—no matter how much tea or water we drank we still felt dry.

People began to get as mean as the weather. With the holidays over, everybody had cabin fever—aggravation from staying indoors day after day—and they started quarrels with each other over everything. Sometimes I'd find myself getting annoyed about small things, but most of the time I was just kind of detached, as if I were still waiting for something to happen.

When it did finally, it was a day I'd never forget.

It was sixty below that day and the little children were using my bed again. I was beginning to think the bed was the most important article of furniture I had. Besides the kids using it when the floor was too cold, Nancy and I had put our sack of potatoes in it because it was the only place they wouldn't freeze.

We were in my quarters when we heard three distant rifle shots, one after the other. We all knew what they meant. Someone was calling for help. Nancy put on her coat and went outside to see if anyone knew where they'd come from. She came back a few minutes later. "The Carews think they came from over towards Mary Angus'," she said. "Your mother and father's goin' over," she told Jimmy. "They said you and Willard could go along."

After that, there was no keeping the rest of the class. Three more shots came as they all ran out. Nancy and I started for Mary Angus' shack too. The cold made it impossible to talk, so we trudged all the way in silence, moving fast enough to stay warm, slow enough to avoid perspiring. Some of the kids from my class were playing outside the shack when we got there. As soon as they saw Nancy and me they came running over.

"Mary's dead, Teacher!" Jimmy yelled.

"Dead as a doornail," Willard chimed in.

Jake Harrington was standing outside the door with Rebekah. "Is it true?" I asked. Jake nodded.

I pushed the door open. There were a lot of people inside, but only a sputtering candle for light, so at first I could only make out Mr. Vaughn, Angela, the Carews and Joe Temple. Then I saw Ben Norvall, a wrinkled old basset hound of a man, in a corner with Chuck, the two of them bending down over what must have been Mary's body. Ben was covering her up with a wolf robe.

"What happened?" I asked Maggie.

"She musta hemorrhaged," Maggie said. "We're tryin' to decide what to do," she went on. "Joe here's gonna get his sled and mush the body over to our place. We'll keep it in the extra cache till Strong can tote it up to the Indian village, but we ain't figgered out what to do with the kids."

Now that my eyes had adjusted to the darkness I saw Ethel. She was sitting on a box, wide-eyed and scared. I went over to her.

"How about it, Joe?" Angela asked. "You gonna take the kids?"

"I don't know anything about taking care of kids," Joe said.

"All you gotta do is keep 'em a week or so," Maggie said. "Then Strong'll mush 'em outta here."

Ben and Chuck straightened up. There was blood on the edge of the mattress. Chuck was in shock. I put an arm around him and he just let me hold him without making a sound. "This one had it the worst," Ben said, putting a hand on Ethel's head. "I was going by and didn't see any smoke coming from the chimney. Came in and she was sitting alongside Mary there." He patted her head. "If ol' Ben hadn't happened by," he said to her, "you'd liable to have froze to death."

"Maybe she'd of been better off," Maggie said.

"She sure ain't got nothin' to look for'ard to in that Indian village," Angela said.

Mr. Carew spoke up. "Unless we're gonna stand here jawin' all day, let's decide what we do with the kids."

Angela said, "I vote Joe takes 'em. Teach 'im a good lesson."

"That's not funny," Joe said. "I told you I wouldn't know what to do with them."

"How about you, Maggie?" Angela asked. "You got the bunk-house."

"I got my own to look after."

I stood listening to them. Nobody had ever wanted me either when I was a kid—except Granny. Chuck and Ethel needed somebody to take care of them, and I could do it.

"I'll take them," I said to Joe.

"*You'll* take 'em!" Angela said.

"Yes."

"That's fine with me." Joe seemed relieved. "Thanks, Anne."

"I don't think it's right," Mr. Vaughn said.

"I agree," Maggie said. "She's just a kid."

"Then why don't you take them?" Joe snapped at her. She didn't answer.

"They're all yours," Joe said to me.

I picked up Ethel. "You take Chuck," I said to Nancy.

"Sure." She was a little surprised.

Nobody made a move to get out of the way. They just stared at me.

"Anybody else want them?" I asked.

Nobody answered.

"Then if nobody minds, we'll take these children home."

Ethel was quiet until we reached the door. Then she realized that I was taking her away and she began to scream. By the time we were outside, she was fighting me tooth and nail. She was just too young to realize her mother was dead. Ben got Mary's hand sled, then helped me tuck a blanket around Ethel and tie her into the sled. It was the only way we could get her home.

Harnessing myself to the sled, I started pulling, but it was hard going, the dry snow tugging at the runners like sand. After ten minutes Nancy took over, and all the way back to the house Ethel kept screaming and struggling. When she threw her head back the first time and I saw her face, I thought something terrible had happened to her—until I realized it was her tears. They'd frozen all around her eyes. By the time we were inside, Nancy's cheeks and nose had turned white, and from the numbness I felt I knew mine had too. Ethel ran straight under the table and sat there crying. And Chuck started crying too.

I tried to console him. It took a while before he was able to stop, and then he wanted to know when his mother was going to wake up. I had to tell him that she wasn't going to, that she was dead. Even though he knew what the word meant, he couldn't accept it as meaning he'd never see her again.

"When my mudda come?"

"She's not going to. You're going to stay here with me and Nancy. Chuck—" He looked as though he were going to cry again. "I need your help. We have to explain to Ethel that she has nothing to be afraid of here. She doesn't understand what's happened. You're going to have to tell her. Can you do that?"

He went over to the table and knelt down beside his sister. She was still sniffling, but she listened to him. They exchanged some words, and then she let Chuck lead her out from under the table.

Her parka was covered with grease, her hair matted and her face caked with dirt. "We'll have to give her a bath," I said.

While the water was simmering on the stove, there was a knock at the door. It was Maggie and her husband with Chuck's and Ethel's things, some moccasins, a .22 rifle and a couple of pairs of children's snowshoes.

After we had enough hot water in the washtub I tried to take off Ethel's clothes, but she pulled away and began to cry.

"She not like take off clothes," Chuck said. "Nevuh take off."

"You better tell her she has to," I said. "She has to have a bath."

That did it. He explained, and the next moment Ethel dived under the bed. I got a bite on the hand and Nancy a good healthy kick before we dragged her out, screaming to high heaven. Chuck put his fingers in his ears, and while Nancy held on to her I took off her clothes—knee-length moccasins, a light jacket and two calico dresses. Her undergarment had me stumped. It was like a union suit, with a drop seat, but there were no buttons up the front. "That's Indian-style underwear," Nancy said. "The mothers sew 'em up in it around October and it stays on till April."

I got a pair of scissors to cut it off while Nancy held Ethel, but she struggled and screamed so loud it made my eardrums ache. It scared Chuck, and he began to cry in sympathy.

Finally it was all off. "Ugh," Nancy said. The drop seat was soggy and foul. Nancy and I lowered Ethel into the tub. As soon as we did, all hell broke loose. She let out a shriek, started striking out at us, and before we could stop her, water was flying in all directions and she was out of the tub. We went after her and finally got her back in. She sat there sobbing, all the fight gone out of her. Nancy and I started to wash her, and when we'd finished, even Nancy was taken with her. "Gee, Anne, she's a beauty."

She was too, with skin like a dusky rose, and shining black hair. When we stood her up and started to dry her, she looked so frail and helpless I'd have given anything to be able to tell her she was safe, but of course she didn't speak English. We put her in bed to keep her warm, then rummaged through the stuff Maggie had brought, but there were no clothes for her. Whatever she owned she'd had on.

"I'll go over to the store and see what I can dig up," I told Nancy. I couldn't find much to fit her—a pair of bib overalls, some long underwear, socks and a corduroy shirt—but at least she had clean clothes. We had to roll up the bottom of the overalls and she was lost in the shirt, but she really looked cute. Even Chuck thought so. He said, "She one pretty girl, Tisha." He went over and sniffed her. "Smell good too," he added approvingly.

We didn't have trouble getting Ethel to eat. She wolfed down two thick slices of bread for supper and a good helping of moose roast and beans. Maggie Carew came by right after supper. "Joe brought the mother over," she said quietly. She looked at Ethel admiringly. "Kid doesn't look half bad now." She put a paper sack on the table. "Some of Willard's old clothes. They might fit her."

I thanked her, and before she went out she said, "Nice of you to keep 'em here."

"I don't mind a bit."

We put both children in the big bed so that Ethel wouldn't be scared. When Nancy and I were ready for bed we'd transfer Chuck to the couch. They tossed and turned for a while, murmuring to each other, then they were quiet. I thought they were asleep, but Chuck wasn't. He called to me, and I went over to him.

"My mudda, she all by herselfs in cabin. Priddy lonely, I t'ink."

"They've taken her out."

"Where they take?"

"They put her in the cache—in back of the roadhouse." I tried not to get choked up, but it was hard.

"Still priddy lonely." He started to get up. "Maybe I go see. She not be lonely."

"She's not lonely, Chuck. She's sleeping. And she's very happy. She'll never again be cold, or hungry, or sad."

"You no tell lie? She never be hungry, be cold?"

"Never. That's the truth. Her spirit is up in heaven now."

"She have big fat moose to eat?"

"Oh yes. She has everything there."

"I like dat. She one good mudda me. You good mudda me too, Tisha. You take care me now like real mudda."

"You're a fine boy, that's why. Now go to sleep."

My eyes were so wet that I could hardly see. I looked over at Nancy. Her face was all twisted up and she was trying her best to hold back her tears. She went into the schoolroom. I went in right after her and the two of us stood crying silently so that Chuck wouldn't hear us.

Later we transferred him to the couch, then we both got in on

206

each side of Ethel. We left the oil lamp burning so they wouldn't be scared if they woke in the night. Ethel was in a deep sleep, a lock of long black hair curled across her check. I pushed it back. She was lovely.

Outside, a wind rose and little drafts of freezing air nipped in. I thought of Mary Angus lying cold and alone in the dark cache. There was nobody to take care of Chuck and Ethel now. They were all by themselves.

"You awake, Nancy?"

"Uh-huh."

"What do you think about keeping Chuck and Ethel here? I don't want to send them back to the Indian village."

"How long do you want to keep 'em?"

"I'll give you one guess."

"Anne—you saying you want them for your *own?*"

"Yes. What do you think?"

"I don't know. . . . That's up to you," she said.

I asked her not to tell anybody about it. Besides the fact that it was going to start a ruckus, they were still Joe Temple's children and I'd have to talk to him before I could keep them.

The kids in class were much nicer to Ethel than they were to Chuck. She wasn't any competition for them and they knew she was an orphan. Having them around all day helped her a lot, and in a few days she was repeating words—book, sandwich, eat, dish. She and Willard Carew took to each other from the beginning. The first morning he wanted her to sit at his table. By afternoon he had her coloring with crayons. He also had her licking the window. It was his favorite sport, getting his tongue to stick to the window just enough so he could still pull it away easily. He'd lost a sliver of tongue doing it once and I stopped it fast.

I kept putting off my talk with Joe Temple. Finally, a couple of days before Mr. Strong was due in, I skied over to see Joe after supper. He lived about a mile from the settlement, on Stonehouse Creek. I didn't have any trouble finding it.

There was no wind, and a bright crescent moon shone down. Every twig, every bush that pushed up through the whiteness

207

stood out in the pale moonlight. When I reached Stonehouse Creek, Joe's dogs began to howl. He came out and I waved to him.

"Tea or coffee?" he called.

"Tea!"

He had a nice place. There were a few guns on the wall—a high-powered rifle with a telescopic sight, a shotgun and a revolver—and they all were clean and gleaming with oil. Some painted boxes nailed to the wall were filled with books: Dickens, Fitzgerald, Milton. A can of tobacco and a rack of pipes sat on a crate beside a rocking chair.

He handed me a steaming cup of tea. "Now tell me," he said, "what this visit is all about. You didn't come for my company, I'm sure of that."

"It's about Chuck and Ethel," I said. "Can I have them?"

"Are you serious?"

"Of course I am."

He laughed. "What do you want them for?"

"What's the difference?"

"You're asking me to give you something. I want to know why you want it."

"Joe, I just want them."

"Good enough. Take them."

"You mean it?"

"Sure. You know you're going to get people all riled up, though, don't you?"

"I guess so."

"Then why not avoid a whole mess and let those kids go to the Indian village where they belong?"

"Joe, you know what that Indian village is like. It's no place for a dog, much less children. Don't they mean anything to you?"

"No."

"How about Mary—did she?"

"Mary and I were finished over a year ago. Maybe you don't like the way I treated her, but what do you know about her and me? She knew what she was doing. I never told her I was gonna marry her, even though I thought about it. But what was I gonna say when the two of us went Outside? 'Meet the wife. She knows everything about making jerky and drying fish, just don't talk to her about literature, current events, art.'"

I got up to leave.

"I've got a couple more things to say," he went on. "You stepped on a lot of toes since you've been here, and if you weren't as nice a kid as you are, you wouldn't have gotten away with it. If people don't like Indians they don't like Indians, and that goes for half-breeds too. Fred Purdy did you the biggest favor in the world when he pulled out of here. He did the right thing by you. You ought to be grateful. Instead you have to stick your foot right smack in people's faces again and take these kids."

I said, "Joe, all you've told me is that people around here don't like Indians. Well, if I want to like them that's my right—and I'm getting sick and tired of people looking at me as if I'm a nut because of it."

He smiled. "It hasn't stopped you so far. Go ahead, take the kids. Just remember they're still part savage."

"If they are, it's probably the part they got from you."

I thought he'd get mad at that, but he didn't. He was still smiling.

"Will you do me a favor?" I asked. "Don't say anything. There's no use in anybody knowing until Mr. Strong comes."

He said he wouldn't.

I felt good all the way home. "What do you think Mr. Strong will say?" I asked Nancy when I got back. He'd be expecting to take Chuck and Ethel back to the Indian village with Mary's body.

"He'll be speechless," Nancy said.

VII

THE dogs started barking right after lunch. We listened as the barking became more excited. And finally someone yelled out, "Wahoo-o-o-o! The dogs say Mr. Strong's comin'!"

Fifteen minutes later everybody in Chicken, including the class and me, was waiting outside the post office, stomping around to keep warm. Soon the sled materialized, rocking and tinkling and crunching its way toward us. Mr. Strong was standing up looking like a big bear, furred from head to toe, cracking his whip and urging the two horses on. They'd had a rough trip, you could see. Their blankets were hung with icicles. The two of them were just one big cloud of steam.

There was somebody sitting alongside Mr. Strong. As soon as the sled stopped, the passenger jumped down and yelled at the men who were crowding forward. "Just hold on, lemme get my wife and baby out."

It was Elmer Terwilliger, Maggie Carew's son-in-law, who had brought his new family from Eagle for a visit. He moved to the back of the sled, where somebody was already pushing up the covering canvas from underneath. There was Maggie's daughter, Jeannette, swaddled in a cocoon of furs. She started to hand Elmer a little bundle wrapped in blankets, but Maggie was already alongside of him. "Give 'er to me!" While he helped Jeannette down, Maggie headed right over to the roadhouse with the baby, not even taking a peek. She wasn't about to let it catch its death out there in the cold, she said.

After supper Nancy started to get dressed up to go to the roadhouse. With everybody coming in from all over to send out their furs with Mr. Strong, there was going to be a dance. I went to the store to go over the accounts with Mr. Strong. I was hoping he would be alone, but Mr. Vaughn, Harry Dowles and a couple of other men were sitting around the oil-drum stove. Harry shifted his quid of chewing tobacco and asked me if I was coming to the roadhouse.

"I don't think so," I said. I didn't want to drag Chuck and Ethel over there, tonight of all nights.

"Too bad." He spat into the big tin can sitting by the stove. "Fred Purdy's liable to show up."

"Fred came in with me," Mr. Strong said. "He jumped off at Stonehouse Creek."

Harry Dowles chuckled. While I went over the accounts with Mr. Strong I knew the men were giving each other know-it-all looks in back of me. I just kept hoping they'd leave before I talked with Mr. Strong about Chuck and Ethel, but they stayed put.

"Too bad about Mary Angus," Mr. Strong said.

"Yes, it was."

"It was commendable of you to look after the two youngsters. I'll pick them up before I leave tomorrow."

"You won't have to," I said. "I'm going to keep them for a while. I don't think they ought to go back to the Indian village yet."

He peered at me over his glasses. "Madam, I'm sure your intentions are good, but those children belong among their own people."

"I want to keep them with me, Mr. Strong. I already spoke with Joe Temple about it. He said it's all right with him."

"How long do you intend to keep them?"

"For quite some time."

"Quite some time!" Mr. Vaughn mimicked. He took his parka from the wall and walked out. He'd be headed for the roadhouse to tell everybody. The others stayed put.

"I would be doing you a service, madam, if I were to go over to your quarters right now and take them forcibly."

"I don't think you'd do something like that, Mr. Strong," I said. I walked out, shaking.

Nancy asked me right away how it had gone and I told her what Mr. Strong had said. "You go on to the dance and have a good time. I'm not worried," I lied. I didn't mention the news about Fred.

After Chuck and Ethel were in bed I sat down to write to Mr. Henderson about them. "I'll be keeping them with me at least until June," I wrote, "and I have the feeling you'll be getting some letters about them."

While I was addressing the envelope, there were quick footsteps on the porch and the door was flung open. I was scared out of my wits, thinking it was a bunch from the roadhouse come to take the kids, but it was Nancy. She had tears in her eyes and a big red welt on her cheek. Maggie Carew was in back of her, fuming mad. "What are you up to now?" she yelled.

"What happened?"

"What does it look like?" Maggie said. "She nearly got her head knocked off on account a you."

"The kids are asleep, Mrs. Carew." We went into the schoolroom and closed the door.

"Are you keepin' those kids?" Maggie demanded.

"Yes, Mrs. Carew—"

"Do you have any idea what you're doing? Goin' daffy over that half-breed was bad enough, but this takes the cake. Do you realize you're lousin' up your whole future?"

"I'm not worried about it."

"Well, you better worry about a lot of things from here on in. There's talk over to the roadhouse about comin' over here and takin' those kids whether you like it or not."

I saw red. "I'll be right back," I said. I went into the cache and got the revolver from the high shelf where I'd hidden it.

"What are you gonna do with that?" Maggie said when I marched back into the schoolroom.

"If I have to, I'm going to use it. You tell anybody who has a mind to set foot in here and take those children that if they try to, so help me God I'll shoot them dead."

"You'd be crazy enough, wouldn't you?"

"You are absolutely right."

"Then that's the blow that killed Father. I wash my hands of the whole thing. I'll tell you one thing, young lady. This ain't over yet—not by a long shot."

As soon as she was out the door I asked Nancy what had happened. "Angela Barrett was saying things about how you and Fred carried on. I told 'er she oughtta mind her own business and she walloped me."

"We better stay out of her way."

Nancy and I didn't sleep too well that night. Every time we heard somebody go by we expected them to come charging in. But nobody bothered us.

The next morning while I was giving a spelling test I heard Mr. Strong swinging open the doors to his stable, which was across the road. "Yah!" he yelled to the horses. Everybody looked up as the jangle of bells sounded outside and the sled was on its way. I sat back and relaxed.

After lunch the weather turned so cold that at dismissal time I kept Isabelle and Joan in. They were both too young to go home alone in this cold. Joan's mother picked her up a few minutes after school was over, but no one came for Isabelle until a half hour later.

I had a feeling it was going to be Fred, and it was. I'd made up my mind to be levelheaded and poised when I saw him again, but as soon as he walked in, I felt the kind of lurch you get when you walk downstairs in the dark and think there's one more step and there isn't.

Nancy took the kids into the schoolroom so we could talk by ourselves, and at first we just sat there like two blocks of ice.

"I guess you're glad to be back," I said.

"I sure am," he answered.

"You heard about my taking Chuck and Ethel?"

"Me and everybody else in the Forty Mile," he said.

"What did you think?"

"That it was just the kind of thing I'd expect you to do. That's the way you are." The way he said it made me glow.

"Why'd you come over?" I blurted out.

"I wanted to see you one more time."

"You going away again?"

"No. I just came over to say good-by."

"That's stupid," I said, afraid I'd start to cry. "I mean can't we even be friends?"

He shook his head. "I just can't make you understand."

"No, you can't," I said. "I can't understand why two people who like each other aren't even entitled to look at each other."

Impulsively I put my hand on his. "Oops," I said, pulling it back. "See, I'm learning already."

He almost smiled. "Do you know why I left Steel Creek?"

"Because they treated you lousy there."

"That was only part of it. I went there to take the pressure off you and my mother, but after a while I realized that I could do the same thing here. All I had to do was make sure that you and I

213

stayed away from each other. That way everybody'd be happy."

"Except you and me."

He shrugged, then he got up.

"I guess you won't be at the next dance, then."

"I'll be out on the trapline."

I got up too. "How about the one after?"

"Same thing."

His parka was untied at the throat and his neck was the color of coffee and cream. I remembered how he'd smelled of woodsmoke every time he held me. He said, "Anne, if you ever need me for anything at all, I'll be here."

"Thanks. Should we shake hands now or something?"

He just stared at me without saying anything for the longest time; then he went past me to the schoolroom. A couple of minutes later he left with Isabelle.

"What did he say?" Nancy asked me.

"Good-by."

Even though the weather was foul that February, people wouldn't pass up the slightest opportunity to get out and go somewhere. At the next dance the schoolroom was as crowded as it had been at the Thanksgiving party.

Elmer and Jeannette Terwilliger had come with the Carews and they brought the baby along. She was about two months old and just about perfect, but blanket and all I bet she didn't weigh more than nine or ten pounds.

"Nine and a half," Maggie said, holding her while her daughter and Elmer were dancing. Everybody'd been oohing and ahing. There was something about a baby that just made you feel good, especially here. Her name was Patricia.

"Can I hold her?" I asked.

Maggie handed her over to me. She was sleeping and I rocked her a little. "Like to have one like that?"

"I sure would."

"You won't as long as you got those two," she said, nodding toward my quarters, where Ethel and Chuck were fast asleep.

When the "Home, Sweet Home" waltz was played, I ended up

with Joe Temple. I went over to the roadhouse with him, leaving Robert Merriweather to watch Chuck and Ethel. Maggie gave us a table by ourselves.

I wasn't very good company. Joe tried to cheer me up, telling me not to blame myself for the way people felt about my taking Chuck and Ethel. "I shouldn't have let you have them in the first place," he said. "It's not doing you or anybody else any good."

"It's keeping them out of that village."

"And you in the doghouse. I'm even getting the cold shoulder for giving them to you. Everybody's getting crankier and crankier. There's no telling what they're liable to do."

I didn't think things could get worse, but I was wrong. The next time Mr. Strong came in, he brought me a letter from Nancy's mother. Mrs. Prentiss didn't mince words.

I want you to send Nancy home with Mr. Strong right now. I don't want her staying with you any more. You ought to be ashamed of yourself. First you take a halfbreed lover then you go and adopt two siwash brats you got no business to. You aren't decent company for self-respecting white people. You do what I say and send Nancy home to me.

I told Nancy some of what her mother had said and she burst out crying. I was hit pretty hard myself. Nancy had become almost like a sister to me.

I went to see Mr. Strong. He listened to what I had to say; then he said, "Be honest with me. Do you think she could pass the eighth-grade exam if she were to take it today?"

"I think so."

"In that case she is better off at home. She can continue studying on her own."

"You really think I'm a bad influence on her."

"I am under the impression, madam, that you do not care one way or the other what I think." He cleared his throat. "There is nothing I can do," he said, "and that is the plain truth."

The next morning, after I told the class that Nancy was leaving, we didn't even pretend to work. When we heard the stable door bang open, we all went out to see her off. "You make sure you study," I said to her. I'd given her a couple of books and marked the pages for her.

When she said good-by to Chuck she told him to be a good boy. "With me gone," she said, "Anne's gonna need all the help you can give her, you savvy?"

"I help plenty."

"By, sweetheart," she said, giving Ethel a hug.

"You'll be back to take that exam before you know it," I said.

She swallowed hard, then we hugged each other. "Thanks for everything, Anne," she whispered. "You were right to take Chuck and Ethel. They're good kids. I hope it works out."

A few days after Nancy left, Jeannette and her husband started back for Eagle, with Jeannette and the baby tucked into the Carews' sled. The Carews had a fairly good string of dogs, but there was an awful lot on the sled for them to pull. Since Maggie would be closing the roadhouse, she was trying to move as many things to Eagle as she could. There must have been seven or eight hundred pounds there.

Ben Norvall said they oughtn't to go with so much packed on the sled. "There's a storm comin' down," he said, "and you're liable to run right into it."

A few hours later Ben was proved right. A freeze came in so fast you could hear the nails in the walls snapping as they contracted. The wind swept down from the north, driving sleet against the windows so hard I thought they'd break.

When I was putting Chuck and Ethel to bed that night somebody knocked at the door. It was still sleeting out and I could hardly see beyond the porch. Right in front of the threshold was a fancy little box all done up with gleaming ribbon and cellophane, and there, hugging the wall, was Cab Jackson. He gave me a big grin, then picked up the box and held it out. "Howdy, Teacher."

It was too cold to do anything but invite him in. The children wouldn't go to bed until I'd let Chuck open the box and take out the bottle of perfume that was in it. I gave them each a smell, then hustled them off to sleep, with Chuck getting the cellophane wrapping and Ethel the ribbon. Then I gave Cab a cup of coffee. "I'm sorry 'bout what happened last time," he said. "I don't hardly remember any of it, but I sure wish you wouldn't be mad at me."

"I got over it."

"You wouldn't maybe want to splash a little of that perfume on and come over t' the roadhouse a spell, would ya?"

"I can't leave the kids alone, Cab."

He looked over at them and I could feel a sermon coming, so I changed the subject. "D'you come in from Eagle?"

"I was in Nulato doing a little business. I'll be mushing over to Eagle tomorrow mornin'. . . . Teacher," he said, "you mind if I tell you somethin'?"

"I'll have to hear it first."

"There's some mighty loose talk bein' spread about you. You're ruinin' your whole career, people are sayin'."

"Look, Cab. I won't say anything to you about whiskey running if you won't say anything to me about what I do."

"I got to," he said. "The only thing stoppin' that school board in Eagle from givin' you your walkin' papers right now is old Strong. He's atellin' 'em to wait an' see. . . . And Teacher, I don't want you to lose that job. Shucks, I was bankin' on you bein' there."

"I appreciate everything you're trying to tell me, Cab, but I know what I'm doing."

"No you don't, Teacher. You got a heart big as all outdoors and you're lettin' it rule out your good sense. Now you just let me mush them two kids outta here and you'll wind up the happiest female in the Forty Mile."

"It's getting kinda late. I've still got some work to do."

He got up and took his mackinaw down from the drying rack. "I guess you think I'm kinda wild and not smart. But I got deep feelin's and I wanta be a help to you. You know what I mean?"

"I think so. . . . I appreciate it."

"Good night."

It was gloomy and foggy all the next day, so we didn't go outside for recess. A little after school was over, Harry Dowles knocked at the door and said he needed a couple of things from the store. I peeked into the schoolroom. Chuck and Ethel and Joan were playing so well that I didn't see any harm in leaving for a few minutes. I told them to stay in the schoolroom.

In Mr. Strong's store, Harry said he needed some blue thread. The color he wanted wasn't on the rack, so I had to hunt through some boxes before I found it. Then he asked for a tin of tea and five pounds of sugar. After I weighed out the sugar he looked around, scratching his head. "Somep'n' else I wanted," he said.

"Maybe you'll think of it later," I told him. I'd been gone over five minutes and wanted to get back. From outside I heard Cab yell out, "Yah-h-h-h—mush!" I wondered why he was leaving so late. Last night he'd told me he'd be leaving in the morning.

"Well," Harry Dowles said, "I can't think of it. You go ahead and tally up." He put a hand on the counter and it was shaking. I looked at him and his eyes shifted away.

And then it came to me. It was written all over Harry's face. I ran out the door and along the path to the schoolhouse in time to see Angela Barrett ducking into the roadhouse storm entry. Cab's sled was already speeding up the trail beside Chicken Creek, and he was yelling at his dogs to move faster. He was running in back of it, so I couldn't really see the sled at first. But then the dogs swung to the left and the sled was in full view.

Chuck and Ethel were in it.

"Cab, come back!" I yelled. "Come back!"

I started to run after him, but it was useless. The sled was moving too fast. Cab didn't so much as turn around. In a minute the sled disappeared. I stood dazed, hearing Cab urge the dogs on, and then I didn't even hear that anymore. I turned back.

Except for little Joan, standing on the porch of the schoolhouse, shivering, no one was out. The settlement could have been deserted. Inside my quarters, I asked her what happened. "They just came in here, Teacher," she stammered, "and took Ethel and Chuck away. Mr. Vaughn. And Mrs. Barrett. And that man whose sled it is."

I looked around. The bureau drawers were open. At least they'd

218

taken the children's clothes. Ethel's dresses were gone from the wall too. The room looked empty, as if nobody lived in it.

I heard Joan's mother come up on the porch and knock. The sound seemed to come from another world. Joan ran to her and told her that Chuck and Ethel had been taken away. She looked at me and asked me if it were true, but something was sticking in my throat and I couldn't answer her.

"Anne, that's terrible." Her hand touched my shoulder. She asked if she could do anything for me. I said, "No. Thanks. You take Joan home. I'll be all right."

After she left I sat listening to how quiet it was.

My feet began to get cold, so I got up and shut the bureau drawers, arranged the chairs neatly around the table and then went into the schoolroom.

I couldn't cry. If I cried I wouldn't be able to think, and I had to do that. I had to figure out how to get Chuck and Ethel back. That's what I had to do, I realized—get them back.

Tomorrow was Friday. After the weekend I'd get someone to take me to the Indian village. I probably wouldn't be back until Tuesday or Wednesday, but I'd get the children.

Somebody came up on the porch and knocked. It was Maggie Carew. She came in and stood in front of the closed door in her long blue coat, with her arms crossed. She made some sound that could have meant anything from sympathy to "That's that."

"Did you know they were going to do this?" I asked her.

"I heard about it," she said. "It wasn't my idea, if that's what you're thinkin'."

"Whose was it?"

"What's it matter?"

I said, "You can tell them there won't be any school on Monday. Tuesday either. I'm going up to the Indian village. I'm bringing Chuck and Ethel back."

"You can save yourself the trip. Those kids are there to stay, thank God. When Cab gets through tellin' those Injuns what'll happen if they let you have those kids, they'll scalp you before they let you so much as touch 'em."

"What can he tell them?"

"That if they so much as let you *look* at those kids, that's the end of 'em. A couple of 'em get work at the Prentiss roadhouse and some more at Eagle. If they let you have those kids, they won't ever work for anybody around here again. He's also gonna tell 'em that Strong won't tote a damn thing in or out of their village. If that ain't enough, he'll tell 'em he'll get the marshal after them. So like I say, save yourself the trip."

I felt weak.

"Good riddance to bad rubbish, if you ask me," Maggie said. Then she softened a little. "They did you a favor, Annie. I know you liked them kids, but one day you'll see how much better off you are without 'em."

"You could have stopped it," I said. "Don't you realize what that Indian village is like? Don't you realize that you might as well have sent those children to the electric chair?"

"I mind my own business."

"Is that what you'll tell Jimmy and Willard if they ask—that you let two kids be taken away to starve or freeze to death because it was none of your business?"

She walked out.

My hands were sweating and cold. My mind was going a mile a minute. Cab had probably gotten to Stonehouse Creek by now.

VIII

I T TOOK me twenty minutes to get to Fred's house. Isabelle answered the door. "Is Fred home?" I asked.

"Out in back, Miss Hobbs."

I went around the back to the stable. He was working the treadle of the grindstone, sparks flying from the axe he was holding. He looked up, and I blurted out, "Fred, they took Chuck and Ethel away from me," and then I was in his arms, crying. When I was able to control myself I told him the whole story, including what Maggie Carew said about my not ever getting Chuck and Ethel back once they were in the Indian village.

220

"'They didn't have any right at all to do that," he said.

"Fred, will you go after Cab with me? Right now? Please, Fred. If we can catch him before he reaches the Indian village I'll be able to reason with him. I know he'll let me have them back if I can just talk to him."

He didn't say anything. "Fred, please help me, otherwise I'll never get them back."

"When did Cab leave?"

"About an hour ago."

"Is he toting anything else on the sled?"

"Whiskey."

He thought about it. Then he said, "Go home. Put on your warmest clothes and pack some spares—parka, moccasins, socks. I'll be by as soon as I can."

I nearly knocked him over I hugged him so tight. "Get going," he said.

I was ready in twenty minutes. I put together some tea and some meat and beans, then sat down to wait. After a half hour I wondered if Fred's parents had persuaded him not to go. I heard a shout and the sound of a sled, but the sled pulled up at the roadhouse, and the driver and his passenger went inside.

I was ready to give up after another half hour went by. And then suddenly there he was.

I told him what food I'd packed, but he said he had everything we'd need for a week.

"A week!"

"I don't know how long it'll take us to catch up with Cab. If the trail is bad we may need everything we have."

"Two men just mushed in to the roadhouse. Let's ask them."

The sled that had come in was a freighter, carrying a Dawson banker to Fairbanks. The two men were eating when we walked in, and the driver was trying to wolf down a steak and answer Maggie Carew's questions at the same time. Angela Barrett was there too.

"You didn't see a sign of them at all?" Maggie was asking. She was worried about Jeannette and Elmer and her grandchild.

221

"Only sled I seen was Cabaret Jackson's, an' that was about two hours ago," the driver said.

"Maggie," her husband put in, "they coulda hit bad weather and holed up any number of places."

"You bet your boots they did," the driver said. "There was a stretch back there day before yesterday where I didn't make more'n a mile the whole day."

"What's the trail like through Franklin?" Fred asked him.

"Drifted in. Unless you got somethin' won't wait, I'd advise you to stay put."

"You're goin' after Cab," Maggie said to Fred.

Fred nodded and Angela Barrett said, "I hope he kills ya."

"Shut up!" Maggie snapped at her. She was so upset about the Terwilligers she didn't give a hoot now about anyone but them. "Be on the lookout, will you, Fred?"

"I wouldn't be worried if I were you," he said. "Elmer knows this country."

"I know," Maggie said, "but they should've at least been at Steel Creek when this man went through there. He says they weren't. Last time anybody saw 'em was at O'Shaughnessy's. You keep a sharp eye out."

Fred said he would, and we went out to the sled. "Mush!" he yelled, once I was in. And we were off.

For the first few miles we moved along fast. Then the trail toughened, and I got out to trot alongside or help push the sled through scrubby spruce, down and up sharp banks and across hummock-littered tundra. Then one of the runners ran over a rock slick with ice, and the sled tipped into a drift. The two of us struggled to get it out, but the runner was caught.

"We'll have to unpack some of the load," Fred said.

We worked at unpacking slowly—too slowly, I felt. I tried to work fast, but Fred kept stopping me. "Slow down," he said, "and keep that scarf over your face."

I knew he was right. You had to pace yourself, not move so fast that you started breathing through your mouth, taking freezing air into your lungs. It was the first rule of the trail—don't exhaust

222

yourself. We had to take off half the load to free the runner, then reload, working at the same maddening slow pace.

Once we left the tundra behind, it was like moving along in a slow-motion dream, following a trail that wound ahead without any end, dipping across a creek, narrowing around one hill, then another. The dogs never let up, trotting along at a fast, willing pace when we hit the flats, digging in as if they enjoyed it when the going was rough. Night came on fast and the northern lights billowed like curtains across the starlit sky. We didn't talk. We were on the trail—sometimes snowshoeing across snow ten feet deep, sometimes sailing along when the way was smooth.

Two hours later we reached a saddle between two hills, a long slope of white marked with the twin lines of Cab's sled running up as far as we could see. Alongside were the small footprints of Chuck and Ethel. Halfway, Ethel's footprints stopped and I could see where she'd sat down. Cab had gone on a short distance, then come back, picked her up and brought her to the sled.

I thought that when we got to the top of the pass maybe we'd be able to spot Cab's sled, but it was too dark to see anything except the endless forest and the dark outline of the river.

From the top of the pass, for two miles straight down, Fred rode the runners, the only sound the squeaking of the sled and the *plop plop* of the white clods the dogs threw up behind them. We rode down to the river; then once we were on it we went like an express train, swinging around big drifts and patches of rough ice. Again, Fred was able to ride the runners for long stretches and I didn't have to get out. Two hours later we pulled up by a small cabin buried up to the eaves. A path had been dug to the door, and there was smoke coming from the stovepipe. Inside, a dog growled threateningly when Fred knocked.

"Who's there?" a gruff voice asked.

"Fred Purdy. Did another sled mush by here recently?"

"Yeah. Maybe three hours ago. Cab Jackson it was."

"Thanks." Fred came over to the sled. "He'd go on to the O'Shaughnessy roadhouse. It's eight miles. Can you make it? Or should we stop and rest here?"

"I can make it," I said.

Those eight miles to the roadhouse took almost four hours. Even though Cab was following the trail the freighter had broken for him coming in, and he was breaking it even more for us, it was still hard going. The wind didn't help. It beat at us so hard that we were pinching ice off our eyelashes every few minutes. Then one of the lead lines broke and we had to spell each other mending it, each of us working till our fingers were too cold, then the other taking over.

When the O'Shaughnessy roadhouse came into view I felt I'd never seen anything so warm and inviting as the yellow lights in its windows. We pulled up to the welcome yips of dogs, and a bundled-up figure came out of the roadhouse door. It was Mr. O'Shaughnessy. "Inside with ye," he yelled over the wind.

I went to the door so sure Cab would be on the other side of it that my stomach started doing flip-flops. When I opened it the heat hit me with a lovely warm sting and the quiet made me reel. Mr. O'Shaughnessy's Indian wife took me by the arm. "You sit down quick, Teacher. Get warm." I was surprised she remembered me. I hadn't seen her in over five months, when I'd stopped on the way to Chicken with Chuck and Mr. Strong.

I looked around. The only other person in the room was a neighbor, Joshua Potter, who'd dropped by for a visit. There was no sign of Cab. Some blankets were strung across part of the room to shield the bunk beds and I wondered if he and the kids were behind them.

I kept my voice low. "Is Cab Jackson here?"

Mrs. O'Shaughnessy shook her head. It was clear that she knew why I was asking.

"Ye'll not catch oop with *that* bludy rascal bafore he's ta the Indian village," Mr. O'Shaughnessy said in his thick accent. "He stayed only long enough ta warm up an' eat. 'It's an outrageous hardship for the little tykes,' I sez to 'im. But he sez, 'Oi makes no stop till Oi've done whut Oi've set out ta do.' He's an hour an' a half hid start on ye already!"

Mrs. O'Shaughnessy gave us some hot food, but I could hardly touch it. "Oi'm sorry, lass," Mr. O'Shaughnessy said to me after Fred and I had changed our clothes. "Ye'll never catch 'im. Thim dogs a his are greased loightnin'."

I looked at Fred. There were dark circles under his eyes. "Suppose we went over the drop?" he asked Mr. O'Shaughnessy. "It would save us two hours."

Mr. O'Shaughnessy looked at the other man. "Phwat do you think, Josh?"

"You might catch him," he said to Fred, "if your sled holds together."

"You have some chain I can borrow?" Fred asked.

"All ye need," Mr. O'Shaughnessy said.

Fred glanced at me. He was tired. We both were. He looked away quickly. "If you'll tell me where it is, I'll get it," he said.

"I'll go with ye."

Fred collected his clothes. As he was about to go out, I said, "Hey, you're forgetting mine." I collected my own clothes and gave them to him. "What's the drop?" I asked Josh after they went out.

"Ptarmigan Drop. A pass. Bad one." He raised one hand and tilted it steeply. "This time of year it's half ice."

I thought about Chuck and Ethel. "Is there any chance Cab would take it?"

"Not when he's carrying whiskey."

"How about children?"

"Be glad he's got the whiskey," he said.

I heard the dogs yipping as Fred and Mr. O'Shaughnessy led them out of the barn. I sat back and closed my eyes, enjoying the last few moments of warmth and thinking how nice it would be to sleep. It was almost two in the morning and we'd been on trail for over eight hours. Suddenly I thought of the way Fred had almost walked out without my clothes. I was up like a shot.

The dogs were all harnessed and as soon as I reached the sled I knew I had been right. The tarp was lashed down over the load and Mr. O'Shaughnessy had my clothes bundled under his arm.

"You were going without me," I said to Fred.

"Anne, it's going to be tougher now, and you're tired. . . ."

"You're not going to catch him all by yourself. I mean that."

I stood my ground and he gave in. We repacked the load to make room for me, then went back in and said good-by.

I was able to ride for about a mile, and every time I thought about what he'd intended to do I'd get a lump in my throat. When we came to the bank of a slough we had to cross, I got out.

"Fred"—I pulled my scarf down—"I'm so proud of you."

He put his arms around me and held me for a few moments. "I feel the same way about you," he said.

I'll never forget those next six hours. Old-timers had told me dozens of stories of forced mushes they'd made, and of how they'd almost frozen, but I found out I hadn't had the least idea of what they meant. Twice, for stretches of a quarter of a mile, Fred had to put on snowshoes and break trail across snow that would have swallowed us up to the waist, while I stayed at the handlebars inching the sled forward. Time and again we had to push from behind as the dogs labored up a steep bluff or the sharp bank of a creek. Bushes caught in the runners and tore at our moccasins.

"There it is!" Fred yelled finally. "Ptarmigan Drop!"

I didn't see anything that resembled a drop. "Where?"

"The other side of that hill."

The hill looked pretty steep from where we were, but not half as steep as it did when we reached the base of it. It was an obstacle course of ledges, clefts and boulders.

I got behind the sled with him and we both started pushing to help the dogs. It was like trying to roll a boulder uphill—shoulders behind the handlebars, struggle upward a few hundred feet, then rest. Finally we reached what seemed the top of the world, and even as played out as I was, my spirits lifted. The gray wide line of the Fortymile River wound northeast through mountains whose sides were shrouded in mist. Above the mist loomed white pinnacles that stood out sharp against a midnight-blue sky spangled with stars. Stretching below us was a long sweep of slope.

"That couldn't be the drop," I said.

"No. It's down below. Couple of miles."

We took them easily, leaving the wind on the other side of the hill. The air was clear and tingling, the moonlight sparkling off bushes laced with frost. The slope ended in a plateau, and we came out onto a narrow ledge. There below was the drop—one long cascade of snow and ice-covered rock that ended half a mile below at Ptarmigan Creek.

"Fred, we can't go down that in the sled—it's suicide!"

He was already untying the dogs. "*We're* not. I am." He'd done it before, he said as he unharnessed the team, then swung the sled around to face the drop.

We were almost finished rough-locking the runners with chain when Fred pointed to something way off. "Look. It's Cab," he said. My heart skipped a beat. "There on the river. See?"

Then I saw it—a faint long speck, darker than the gray around it. From this distance it looked as if it was barely moving. "You sure it's him?"

"It's him," Fred said. "He may be a little ahead of us when we hit the river, but not much."

We finished chaining the runners quickly, then Fred told me to start down with the dogs. "I'll catch up with you."

"Fred . . ."

"Go on," he said. "I'll make it, don't worry."

I started down with all the dogs except Pancake. Fred needed him to keep the sled pointed straight. I didn't have to walk. All I had to do was keep my balance—and slide. I was halfway down when Fred let out a yell. I made the dogs whoa and sat down fast, bracing one moccasin against a rock.

By the time I looked up, the sled was moving. Pancake was on a long lead, and the line was taut. Chains jingling, Fred on the runners, the sled nosed down in a straight line. Underneath the soft surface snow was hard crust, greasing the way. The sled picked up speed fast, even rough-locked as it was. A shower of sparks flew out from under the right runner as the chains scraped across a slab of rock. Once over the rock the sled jumped forward and a spray of white flew out from behind as Fred rode the brake. Pancake had to run like sixty to keep the line from going slack. It was either that or get out of the way.

227

"Mush, Pancake!" Fred yelled. "Yah-h-h—mush!"

By the time it was close to passing me the sled was rocking from side to side. It hit a bump that sent the front of it two feet in the air. It came down with a punishing *whump* that I felt in the soles of my feet, and Fred was bounced off the runners. I screamed, sure he wouldn't be able to get back on, that he'd end up tumbling like a rag doll, neck broken. But somehow he got one foot back on. In a kneeling position, he grabbed at the lashings and pulled himself up. Then he was standing, foot on the brake again, yelling to Pancake.

Once he was past, the sled disappeared in its own boiling mist. The next moment I was jerked forward by the dogs running after the sled, dragging me with them. It happened so fast I didn't have time to try to free the line from around my mitten. All I saw was a violent white world flying around me. Then my mitten was pulled off and I slid to a stop.

By the time the world stopped spinning, the dogs were a snarling mass of confusion, tangled in the lines, rolling and fighting their way down the hill. I didn't give one hoot about them, though, because there, all the way at the bottom, was Fred. He'd made it and was already scrambling up toward the dogs.

Twenty minutes later we were on our way again, mushing down Ptarmigan Creek. When we spilled down a cleft and onto the river, Cab was nowhere in sight.

"How far ahead is he, Fred?"

"Maybe half a mile."

"How far is it to the Indian village?"

"Another ten, maybe."

"We've got to catch him!"

"We will—don't you worry. Pancake!" he yelled. "Domino! Samson—mush!"

They mushed. They had picked up the scent of the dogs ahead and dug into their collars as though they knew they were in a race. We sped down the river like the wind.

We caught our first glimpse of Cab's sled when it was going around a bend in the river. A few minutes later when we rounded the bend he was no more than a quarter of a mile away. We kept narrowing his lead until Fred called out to him. "Cab!" The hills picked it up and echoed it: *Cab! Cab! Cab!*

He slowed his team and I saw him rub his eyes, trying to see who we were. "Howdy there!" he called when we pulled alongside. His scarf muffled his voice. Between that and his furred hood I could only see his eyes, but I knew he was grinning. Chuck and Ethel were all bundled up. Chuck looked at us as if we were ghosts. "Tisha!" he called out. Ethel waved. The two of them were all right.

"Cab," Fred shouted, "hold up a minute, will you?"

For answer Cab speeded his dogs up.

"Cab, please stop," I called.

"You got a hundred dollars, Fred?" he yelled back. "A hundred spondulicks says I make it to Cross Creek before ya!"

"Take the kids off."

"No race, no stop. C'mon, boy, it's an easy mile, nary a bump. How about it?"

"You're on!" Fred called back.

Cab let out a bloodcurdling screech. "Mush, you buzzards," he roared. "Yah-h-h!" At almost the same time, Fred let out a yell of his own and our sled jumped forward. We'd gone fast a few times, but nothing like the way we went then. We flew across that snow with the wind behind us and the sled rocking like a cradle.

"Down!" Fred yelled at me. The sled was a bare two feet wide, and with someone sitting up, it could tip over from the slightest bump. I slid down until I could just barely see ahead.

I looked over to Cab. We were running almost neck and neck, with him a few feet ahead. "Yah, Pepper!" Cab called to his lead dog. "Pull, you damn crow bait, or I'll skin your hide! Yah!"

The teams knew they were in a race and they were pulling their hearts out. A few seconds later both sleds separated to avoid a jag of rough ice. Cab came around his side too wide and lost a few feet. Once we were straightened out, we were a little ahead of him. Chuck and Ethel were scrunched down as far as they could and were probably enjoying the ride.

A half mile later Cab was a little ahead, but then his dogs had

to veer around some frozen branches and we were two team lengths ahead of him. Cab and Fred were yelling up a storm, the echoes bouncing off the hills. Neither of us was going in a straight line. We veered all over the river, trying to keep to the smooth. One minute Fred and I would be in the lead, the next it would be Cab. When we both hit a stretch of soft snow and slowed down, Fred and Cab were off the runners and pushing. Cab moved ahead of us.

Once we were through it, both men on the runners again, Cab was still ahead. We were off to his left, closer to shore and gaining on him, when all of a sudden a rabbit appeared out of nowhere, dead ahead. Pancake saw it, broke stride for a moment and stumbled. The dogs piled into each other and we ran into the wheel dog. He went down with a yowl and we plowed into three more before we could stop. None of them was hurt, but by the time Fred got all the harness straightened out, Cab was too far ahead to catch. He reached Cross Creek a full two minutes before us.

Fred stopped the sled far enough away from him so the dogs couldn't get to each other, then he just stood for a couple of minutes trying to get his breath back. I got out and went over to Chuck and Ethel. They weren't any the worse for wear, but they were scared. Ethel put her arms out to me.

"Leave 'er be, Teacher," Cab said. "Sorry you came all this way, but I can't let you have 'em. I ain't gonna let you ruin your life."

I tried to convince him that he was wrong. No matter what I said he shook his head. He was doing it for my good.

"Let her have them, Cab," Fred said, coming over. "If Anne wants those kids it's her right to keep them."

"I wouldn't butt in if I was you," Cab said. "I'm takin' them where they belong." He spoke so softly that if you didn't see his eyes you'd have thought he was being friendly.

"Fred . . ." I tried to take his arm, but he shook me off. He went to the sled to lift Ethel out. He never got to touch her. Cab's left

231

fist streaked out. Fred tilted his head back, but Cab hit him on the side of the jaw with his other fist and Fred fell down, stunned. He sat there shaking his head for a few seconds, then spat out a tooth. I started to go to him, but Cab said, "Leave 'im be, Teacher." He stood over Fred, fists ready. "You get up, boy, and you're crazy," he warned. "You just say uncle now and we'll call it quits."

Fred wiped his mouth and smeared blood all over his chin, then he looked down at his tooth. When he looked up again I hardly recognized him. It was that same expression he'd had when he'd almost fought Cab back in Chicken. I'd seen him get it on the trail when we had tough going. There wasn't any fear in it. It was calculating and deadly.

He didn't get up fast, but when he did a sound came from deep inside him that I didn't know a human being could make. Cab didn't have a chance. One second he was standing there with his fists weaving and the next there was blood spurting out of his nose and he was backing off with Fred wanting to kill him. I don't know how many times Fred hit him before he just toppled over backward and his head hit the ice with an awful sound. Then Fred pounced on him and started pounding him as if he'd gone insane. He didn't care where he hit him, just as long as he could hit him. I kept trying to pull him off, but he didn't stop until Cab's head was lolling like a dead chicken's.

We sat him up against his sled and then Fred set about trying to wake him up. We bathed his face with snow. He looked terrible. His nose was broken and one eye was almost closed.

He didn't come to for ten minutes, and one thing you had to say for him was that he didn't hold any grudge. In fact he told Fred he truly admired him, that he hadn't any idea Fred could handle himself that way. Fred said that Cab was pretty good himself and that he hoped he hadn't hurt him too much. It was almost funny; they were carrying on like buddies. Cab even got out a bottle of whiskey and offered Fred some. "Half-breed or not," he said, "you're a white man."

Fred turned down the drink and we put Chuck and Ethel into our sled. We were about ready to go when Cab's dogs started sniffing the air, growling and baring their teeth. They were all looking back up the river. A tiny patch of white fog was moving toward us, then a dotted black line that turned into a string of a dozen dogs. There was a man riding the sled behind them, another one trotting alongside.

"Indians," Cab said. "My dogs don't take to 'em."

They were Indians, and one was Titus Paul. They were on their way back from their trapline and their sled was loaded with furs. They stopped some distance away, their dogs as ready for a fight as Cab's. Titus walked over.

I'd never thought about why Indians and Eskimos ornamented their parkas with bright beadwork and plenty of color until I watched Titus walking toward us. His caribou parka was a beauty, white fur speckled with brown, topped by a wolf-fur hood. As he came nearer I suddenly realized that after being on trail all this time I'd become tired of seeing green and white. Looking at Titus was like seeing the whole world take on color, the slash of it at the hem of his parka, even the braided leather mitten string attached to his collar. He looked like a northern prince.

"Howdy, Titus," Cab called. "You make good catch?"

Titus nodded, taking in Cab's condition without changing expression, then his eyes went *flick-flick-flick*, taking in me and Chuck and Ethel. Then they flicked to Fred and the dogs. Fred took off a mitten and offered his hand. "Fred Purdy," he said.

Titus took off his own lynx-paw mitten. "Titus Paul. You come see Cathy?" he asked me.

"No, Fred and I are going back to Chicken." Titus looked at Chuck and Ethel, then asked them something in Indian. Chuck pointed to Cab, explaining, then to me.

"You take kids from *skooltrai?*" Titus asked Cab.

"Yeah. I bring 'em back to Indian village where they belong."

Titus looked at Fred. "Why *you* take from *him?*"

"Anne wants them and they want her."

"Why you want?" Titus asked me.

"Because I love them."

The minute I said it I felt tears coming and I was furious with myself. I needed to be tough, so I screwed my face up and gave Titus the meanest look I could manage. "What's wrong with that?" I said. "Is that a crime?"

"Titus," Cab said, "you have law in village—no brave go way from village without council say yes. This boy belong in village until council say he can go. Am I right?"

Titus nodded.

"Well, then, I think you better take him and the girl too."

Cab came over to our sled and started to undo the ties. "No!" I cried. "These children are mine and nobody is going to take them away from me. Titus, please, let me keep them. What chance will Chuck have in that place—the chance to grow up speaking broken English and get a job sweeping in a roadhouse? What chance will Ethel have except maybe to wind up living with some white miner the way her mother did?"

"They belong Indian village," Titus said grimly.

"I'll make you a promise. Let me keep them and I swear I won't let them forget their own people. I'll never let them forget where they came from. Titus, I can make them strong. I can help them to be proud and stay proud. Let me do it."

He stared at me for the longest time, then he asked Chuck a question in Indian. "*Aha*," Chuck answered. Yes.

Then, just like that, Titus turned on his heel and headed back for his sled. It happened so fast I didn't realize for a few seconds that Chuck and Ethel were mine. Cab did, though. "You know what you're doin'?" he called after Titus. Titus didn't pay him any mind and Cab took a few steps after him. "Titus! Are you deef?"

Titus finally turned around when he reached his sled. I thought Cab was going to start more trouble, but he was as unpredictable as he was stubborn. "You wanna race to the village?" he called.

"You give me start," Titus called back.

"Give you a quarter mile an' betcha fifty dollars."

"Bet," Titus answered. "I fire two shot."

Titus' sled drove off. "Teacher," Cab said, coming back, "I was doin' what I thought was right. So how about lettin' bygones be bygones?"

234

"All right."

He smiled at me. "I'll tell you somethin' and I mean it from the bottom of my heart. You're an Alaskan."

"Thanks, Cab."

Fred released the brake on the sled and I got on the runners.

And that's the way we parted.

IX

FRED and I took turns riding the runners and trotting alongside the sled. We'd take the route Mr. Strong followed, Fred said, along the river. If the weather held we could make the O'Shaughnessy roadhouse in seven hours.

We traveled for almost an hour. It must have been around nine o'clock and the sun should have been coming up. Instead it was growing darker and the wind was getting worse. I was trotting alongside when all of a sudden a blast banged at us so hard I was nearly bowled over. Fred stopped the sled, and the dogs immediately dropped on all fours and started curling up.

"We're in for it!" Fred yelled. The snow drove at us like a wall. The two of us got down behind the sled to wait the blast out.

"Is it over?" I said after it died down.

"It hasn't started," Fred said, getting up. "This is just a lull. There's a cabin a little farther on. We can hole up there."

A few minutes later the wind was at us again, meaner and colder than ever. I began to feel thirsty, and I had to stop myself from eating some snow. In this kind of cold it would be the worst thing to do, sucking precious body heat and giving nothing in return. Fred headed the sled for a big cleft in the bank, a slough. "Cabin's about a quarter mile up!" he yelled.

It was a long quarter mile. Fred had to get out his and Chuck's snowshoes, and the two of them moved ahead, breaking trail, while I drove the sled after them at a snail's pace. Finally, Fred stopped. "I can't find that cabin," he said. "It's probably drifted in." He pointed over Chuck's shoulder. "Take a look over towards that rise," he told him.

Chuck went off in one direction, Fred in another. The dogs had been lying quietly, noses tucked into tails in the driving snow, as contentedly as if they were in a warm room. Now, one after the other, they got to their feet, sniffing the air. Pancake uttered a low growl, the ruff around his neck bristling. Some of the other dogs began to whine. I called Fred and he snowshoed over. Chuck joined us.

"What is it, boy?" Fred asked Pancake.

Pancake hung his head and kept growling. He was scared. Fred grabbed his collar and jerked him forward, but Pancake braced his forelegs and wouldn't budge. When Fred tried to pull him again, he snarled and bared his fangs. I could feel the hair on my own neck start to rise. Then Pancake simply lay down and whimpered. *Do what you want to me,* he was saying, *I'm not going.* The other dogs did the same. It was eerie.

"Stay here," Fred said to us. He moved along the edge of the slough, and I saw him stoop and pick something up. He came back with it—a length of dog harness. It had been chewed. "There's what's left of a dog over there, a few bones and some hair."

"Bear?" I asked him.

"Wolf," Chuck said.

Fred chained the dogs to a tree, then took his rifle out of the sled. "You stay with the kids," he said to me. "I'm going to take a look around."

"Oh no. We're going with you." Nothing was going to keep me there with him gone. I took Ethel out of the sled. We slogged after him. I knew that wolves didn't attack living people—but I held Ethel's hand tight. Instead of going straight up the slough, Fred made a wide circle, then started working back toward it. Before we reached it we found the remains of another dog. Chuck found something else snagged in a bush—a small length of polished hardwood. It was part of a sled.

We went on a little farther until we all stopped at almost the same time. There above us was some kind of a ledge where there shouldn't have been one, right in the path of the slough, as though someone had built a curved platform across its banks. But

236

it wasn't the ledge that made us stop. It was what was on it: a pack of wolves circled around something. We were downwind, so they hadn't caught our scent, and they hadn't heard us approach.

I counted seven of them. The smallest wasn't under a hundred and fifty pounds. They looked like ghosts through the flying drift, all of them staring at something, milling around as if they didn't know how to get to it. And that was the weird part. There was nothing there, at least nothing I could see.

They saw us a few seconds later. They didn't want to leave whatever it was that interested them, so they waited to see what we were going to do. The way they sized us up made my skin crawl.

Fred went down on one knee, took aim, and his rifle cracked. The biggest of them, which must have weighed close to two hundred pounds, went down. He rolled to the end of the ledge, then disappeared into a bed of snow below it. The rest of them took off.

Fred made his way up along the border of the slough, then moved out onto the ledge on his hands and knees. He stopped at the place where one of the wolves had been peering down and I thought I heard him call out to somebody. He turned and waved me over. "Leave the kids there," he said.

I followed, stepping in his tracks. The ledge was bigger than I'd thought, bulging up a little toward the center. There was a big jagged hole in the middle of it, maybe four feet wide and three times as long. The whine of a dog was coming from it.

Fred pushed himself back from the hole before I reached him. He pulled his scarf down, and his expression was awful. "Take a look," he said, "but be careful. . . . It's Jeannette and Elmer."

I crawled to the edge of the hole and peered in. Underneath me was a huge domed ice cavern, and there in the darkness a dozen feet below lay Jeannette Terwilliger, her eyes boring into mine. I thought she was dead until her eyes blinked, and I saw the glint of tears. I heard myself say, "Oh dear God."

She was lying on her side among the rocks of the slough bed, a fur robe wrapped around her. Beside her was the smashed sled. Elmer was a short distance away. I could only see his legs. He'd crawled up the side of the slough, where he lay now, not moving.

In a split second I saw it all as it must have happened: the loaded sled moving across the innocent-looking snow, the domed roof of ice giving under it, shattering like an egg, and the sled crashing to the ravine below. Two dogs had been pulled down with them. One of them had clambered onto the overturned sled as if to jump up at me, whining in eagerness. The other dog lay still among the rocks. Jeannette hadn't taken her eyes from me.

"Jennie?" I managed to croak out her name.

She made some sounds. That was all.

"We'll get you out," I said. Then, afraid I'd burst into tears, I inched back from the scene.

Chuck and Ethel had come up on the ledge and Chuck started to edge forward. "Stay away from there," Fred said. "I need you with me."

We followed him to a big fallen spruce, where he started scooping snow out on the side that was out of the wind. "You'll stay here," Fred said when there was a hole big enough for Ethel and me to huddle in. He gave me his rifle. "I'm going to find that cabin."

He and Chuck went off to get the sled. From where Ethel and I were we could see the whole ledge. I thought about the baby. I hadn't seen her. Terrible images crept into my mind. She could be under the sled, crushed, or she could have been thrown out. Finally I couldn't stand it anymore. "Stay here, Ethel," I said. I crawled back to the hole and looked down. Elmer was in exactly the same position as before. He must have been dead.

"Jennie . . . Jennie?" She turned her head a little.

"Patricia—where is she?"

Her arm moved under the robe that covered her, then her mittened hand pulled down her scarf. Half of her face was white as snow, dead-looking. It was frozen. She groaned.

"Is she with you? Nod your head and I'll know it's yes."

Her head moved slightly and I thought, Thank God. Then I wondered if the baby was alive, but I couldn't ask Jennie that. "Hang on, Jennie," I said.

238

I went back to Ethel and while the two of us huddled together, I wondered how long Jennie had been down there. It could have been as much as three days, three days of lying in a frozen dungeon with hardly the barest chance of being found, and the wolves circling around above.

Over an hour must have passed before Fred came back with the sled. "We've found the cabin!" he said. It was drifted in and he'd left Chuck to finish clearing the door. He'd brought a strong, slender birch trunk that he'd chopped down. Tying a rope around the center of it, he placed it across the narrowest width of the hole. After he made sure the ice on each side would hold, he let himself down the rope.

The dog that was uninjured was overjoyed, jumping all over him. Fred put another robe over Jennie before he looked around. The slough was flat at the bottom, the banks sloping up gently to where the ice met them. He picked up a mattock that had spilled from the sled and chopped a rock loose from the frozen ground. "Anne, move over that way about ten feet." He pointed to where the ceiling arched down to meet the top of the bank. "Tell me if you can hear this rock hitting." His voice sounded hollow, as if it came from a tomb.

I did as he told me, listening. *Thump. Thump.* I scrambled back to the hole.

"I heard it."

"I'm going to try to dig out of here."

"Fred, what about the baby?"

"She's under her parka."

"Can you hand her up to me?"

"Jennie's arm is broken. I don't want to touch her until we can get her out." He moved out of sight and I heard him start chopping.

When Chuck came back I told him what Fred was doing and he went to the hole, swung himself over the birch trunk and disappeared. I kept looking toward the spot where I thought Chuck and Fred would come out. Finally I saw a small hole appear. Chuck's head popped up and he levered himself out of the hole as Ethel and I headed toward him. "We digged out!" he yelled excitedly.

239

The dog scrambled out after him, yelping. I lowered myself into the hole slowly. My feet touched the solid bank and I felt Fred grab me. Then I was below the ice.

It was like a gloomy world where time had stood still. Overhead was a dome of ice that stretched from one bank to the other and maybe thirty feet up and down the slough. Outside, the wind was howling, but it was quiet in here, snowflakes drifting down through the opening. Elmer was stretched out on the bank opposite, his head almost touching the ice above him. He was frozen, one hand upraised. There was a hunting knife in it, and you could see where he'd tried to chop away at the ice. He'd managed to crawl up the bank, and he'd died there.

I went over to Jennie. "I'm going to take the baby to warm her," I said. She nodded and her eyes closed. I pulled away the furs and lifted her parka. The baby was lying against her stomach, still wrapped in a blanket. When I lifted the corner of the blanket my heart sank. Her face was a sickly blue, her little body still. The barest wisp of vapor curled from her mouth. I put her inside my own parka, a cold little thing that didn't move.

Fred set Chuck to work making the hole wider, then he knelt beside Jennie. "She's out," he said. "Thank God." He picked up a man's shirt that lay in a pile of clothes thrown from the sled. "Rip that up," he said. "I'm going to set her arm."

He went after the sled with an axe until he had two lengths of wood. After that he eased the broken arm out of her parka. He sat down and braced one foot against her armpit, then pulled on her wrist slowly. I heard the bone snap into place. While he set her arm in the splint I walked up and down the slough bed, hoping I could jostle the baby into making even the smallest move. She lay still, though.

When Fred was finished he climbed up the bank alongside Chuck and chopped some more ice away. Then he looked over at me wearily. "How's the baby?"

"She's not moving." She's going to die, I thought.

"You'd better give her to Chuck. I'll need your help with Jennie."

I handed the baby over. "Hold her tight," I said. I could have saved my breath. He was eight years old, but if ever I'd seen a boy act twice his age, it had been him.

Fred lifted Jennie's shoulders and I took her legs. Halfway up the bank her foot dropped onto a rock, making a horrible sound—as if it were a rock itself. I glanced up at Fred, cringing inside. His mouth set itself in a tight line. Only one thing could have made that sound—a foot that was frozen solid.

We managed to get Jennie up through the hole and into the sled. We made a few trips back in to bring out food and things for the baby. There'd been some traps on their sled, and before we left, Fred brought five of them out and set them around the hole to keep the wolves away from Elmer's body.

When we reached the cabin I wondered how Fred had found it. It squatted so low against a hill that I didn't even see it until we were practically on top of it. Inside, the sloping ceiling was too low for Fred or me to stand up straight except by one wall. It was shelter, though. There was oil in a dusty lamp. After Fred lit it we brought Jennie in and laid her on a rickety canvas cot. Then Fred started a fire in the small Yukon stove.

I took Patricia from Chuck. Her face and hands looked violet in the light of the oil lamp, and there wasn't anything I could do for her except sit by the stove and hold her close under my parka.

I started some stew thawing while Fred and Chuck went to work on Jennie. Fred filled a small washtub with snow, then took the moccasin and socks off her frozen leg. It was hard as marble, white up to the knee. He put it into the washtub and began to bathe the leg with snow while Chuck bathed her face. She hadn't regained consciousness and I hoped for her sake that she wouldn't for a while. Once feeling came back she'd be in terrible pain.

"How bad is she, Fred?"

"Her foot's frozen to the bone. The leg may be too. We've got to get her to a doctor."

Outside, the wind was blowing hard, making the stovepipe hum. "How can we?"

"I could take her as far as Forty Mile," he said. "Someone could get her to the hospital in Dawson from there."

Forty Mile was the first town across the Canadian border, but it was still ninety miles away. I didn't see how he could make it, as tired as he was. "That's a long trip, Fred."

"I'd have to get some sleep after we eat, but I could do it. There are some places to stop on the way. You'd have to manage here alone, though."

It was a grim meal. I hardly tasted the stew. When Chuck and Ethel finished we bundled them together in a sleeping bag we'd taken from the sled and they fell asleep at once. Fred and I had a cup of tea.

"I hate to leave you alone," he said. "Mr. Strong's due up the river in a day or two. I'll leave word at Steel Creek that you're here."

"You better get to sleep," I said.

"You think you can stay awake?"

"I'll have to." Fred laid out another sleeping bag and told me to wake him in three hours.

I took Patricia out of my parka. She was losing the blue color she'd had. Her little hands were pink. I brushed her cheek with my lips. It was warm, soft as a flower petal.

I'd gone over her carefully and outside of some chafing from wet diapers she seemed all right. I sat on a stool by the stove and rocked her and she squirmed a little, then she yawned. Excited, I got up and walked back and forth with her. I had a bottle filled with diluted condensed milk, all set to be put in a saucepan if she woke. "Come on, Patricia," I said. "Just wake up and start yelling. You can do it."

But she lay still. There was a small fruit crate lying by the stove with some kindling in it. I emptied it, then wrapped a blanket around Patricia and placed her in the crate. After that I put some more wood in the stove and sat down on the edge of the cot. For the next couple of hours I kept putting snow on my face and neck to stay awake.

A half hour before I was supposed to wake Fred, Jennie began to scream. It happened so suddenly that I was terrified. One moment everything was still and the next I was wrestling with Jennie and sobbing hysterically for Fred. She thrashed around, scream-

242

ing in pain. And finally, Fred was holding her in a firm grip, talking to her while she stared at us wild-eyed. "Jennie, you're with Anne and me," Fred kept repeating. "You're safe."

The wild look went out of her eyes. She stopped struggling and fell back in exhaustion. Her eyes closed and tears of pain welled up from them.

"Patricia's here, Jennie," I said. "She's sleeping. Do you want to hold her?" She nodded. I brought the baby and laid her in the crook of Jennie's arm. She raised her head, then slumped back and closed her eyes.

"Jennie," Fred said, "I have to get you to a doctor. . . . Anne'll stay here with the baby and take care of her." She only made the barest movement. She understood.

Chuck and Ethel hadn't waked up. They'd lived in close quarters all their lives. They were used to noise.

While Fred made preparations to leave I warmed up a chunk of vegetable soup and fed a little of the broth to Jennie. We carried her out and lashed her into the sled. Gray sleet drove at us, the cold pressing like water. I leaned over Jennie. "I'll take good care of the baby, Jennie."

She moved one mittened hand feebly and pulled the scarf from her mouth. She tried to smile.

Fred was ready to go. There were so many things I wanted to say—how much I admired him, how deeply I loved him. But there was no time. I kissed him hard so that maybe it would keep him warm and safe all the way he had to go. Then he was gone, the sled disappearing in a gray swirl. I turned back into the cabin.

I knew I couldn't stay awake any longer. I'd kept walking back and forth with Patricia, coaxing her to wake up. She'd move a little, open and close a tiny fist, and that was all. Now I felt myself caving in. I put some more wood in the stove, then crawled into Fred's sleeping bag with the baby.

I don't know how much later it was that I woke up, thinking there was an alarm clock ringing somewhere. Then I realized it was a baby crying. Beside me, Patricia was spluttering in rage— the most wonderful sound I'd ever heard. I was out of the sleeping bag in a moment and put the bottle I'd prepared into the saucepan. Then I turned up the oil lamp.

Chuck's head popped out of the other sleeping bag. He eased himself out, slipped on his parka and watched while I tried to get Patricia to take the bottle. She took it, then spat it out and started crying.

"Baby no hungry," Chuck said.

"She is hungry, Chuck. That's why she's crying. She hasn't eaten in two or three days. Maybe she is too weak to hold on to the nipple. Get me the first-aid kit from the shelf."

There was a medicine dropper in it. I pulled some milk up into the dropper and put it in her mouth. For I don't know how long, the milk kept dripping out of her mouth. Then she began holding on to some of it. First just a few drops, then more. When she fell asleep she'd had hardly more than a couple of mouthfuls, but at least she'd taken something.

I put her back in the fruit crate and set about getting a meal ready. Ethel woke up and the three of us sat down and ate biscuits and stew. I couldn't seem to get my mind going. What I needed was about twelve straight hours of sleep. I felt as if I was going to burst out crying. I wondered how Fred was making out. Sleet was needling at the window. If the weather kept up like this it could take him four or five days to reach Forty Mile.

Time passed. We couldn't go outside, so we played games—hot and cold, hide the thimble. Each time Patricia woke up, every hour or so, she took a little more milk. It must have been almost a day later when she took the nipple. She was getting stronger, but she couldn't sleep for more than a few hours at a time. She'd cry, and I'd walk up and down with her in a daze until she settled into an uneasy sleep and I'd do the same.

After two days the time came when I couldn't bring myself to wake up. Patricia began to cry, and I asked Chuck to put the bottle in the saucepan and wake me when it was ready. That was all I remembered until I woke up some time later to hear her crying again. Ethel was sitting on the sleeping bag, holding Patricia. Chuck was at the stove, warming a bottle.

244

"Chuck, how long have I been asleep?"

He shrugged. "Long time, I think. I give baby milk. He go sleep, I go sleep. I wake up, Et'el wake up, baby wake up. I give milk. You have one good sleep."

I took Patricia from Ethel. "You and Ethel fed her?"

"Yiss. I do good?"

I hugged him. "You did marvelous."

He beamed. "You happy me, I glad."

"Happy? I adore you. And you too," I told Ethel.

Only then did I notice how quiet it was. The wind had stopped blowing. I went to the door. Outside, the sky was bright with stars, the air still. It was so bitterly cold that my breath snapped into crystals. I came right back in.

From then on I wasn't worried about a thing. I knew we'd make out and that someone would come for us eventually. All we had to do was wait.

The next day the weather was lovely. The sun shone bright in a cloudless sky and it was warm enough to walk around with parka hoods down. Chuck and Ethel went out early and busied themselves building a "roadhouse," then played hunter for a while. In the afternoon I brought one of the sleeping bags outside, laid it against a stump and sat taking in the sun with Patricia on my lap. The sun felt so good that I started to drowse. Then I heard another sound coming from the direction of the river, one I'd become familiar with. I opened my eyes to see Chuck and Ethel standing stock-still, listening.

It was Mr. Strong's sled. Chuck let out a yell and ran down toward the river. A few minutes later I heard him calling to Mr. Strong, and the bells on the sled sounded louder and louder. I ran into the cabin and put Patricia on the cot, then went out to wait until the two of them appeared. Chuck was hopping and jumping like a sparrow, Mr. Strong clumping along after him. I was so happy to see him that I threw myself into his arms and almost knocked him over.

"Now, madam," he cajoled, "don't take on so. The situation is well in hand. We'll be out of here in no time."

WE STOPPED only once on the way back—at O'Shaughnessy's—
to take a hot meal and rest. When we rode into Chicken
everybody was out waiting. The whole place looked strange to me,
as if I'd been away much longer than five or six days—as if I'd left
as a girl and now I was coming back grown up.

As we neared the post office Mr. Strong halted the sled and there
everybody was, staring up at me and the children, nobody saying a
word. I had Patricia in my arms, swaddled in a wolf robe. As soon
as Maggie Carew saw what I was holding, the life seemed to drain
right out of her. I handed the baby down and she took her from
me, her eyes making the questions she couldn't bring herself to ask
out loud.

Mr. Strong lifted me down and then everybody was pressing
forward, Mr. Carew asking in a croaking voice where Jennie and
Elmer were, Mrs. Purdy wanting to know about Fred, all the
faces around me stunned.

Eight days later Fred pulled into the settlement in the early
afternoon, and in a few minutes we were all at the roadhouse
listening as he told us what had happened. He'd mushed Jennie
as far as Forty Mile. There he ran into Percy de Wolfe, who was
known as the Iron Man of the North. He carried the mail up and
down the Yukon, and he had the fastest team in that part of the
country. Minutes after Fred arrived, they had transferred Jennie
to Percy's sled and he'd mushed off with her to Dawson. There
was a telegraph station at Forty Mile and they'd wired ahead to
the authorities. "Before I left," Fred said, "Dawson wired back
that there'd be a doctor at the hospital ready to work on her right
away."

It wasn't until the end of March, three weeks later, that Maggie
received a telegram from her husband, who had gone to Dawson to
be with Jennie. By then the days were sunny, and gentle chinook
winds were melting the snow. Mr. Strong brought the telegram in
on his last sled trip of the season. It said that Jennie had been in

very serious condition for a while, but that she was going to pull through. Mr. Strong would tell her the details, the telegram ended. Mr. Strong broke it to Maggie as gently as he could. They'd had to amputate Jennie's foot above the ankle.

Maggie took it pretty hard and it worked a change in her. She became a little more tolerant. She even had Chuck and Ethel come over to the roadhouse every so often to play with Jimmy and Willard. Everybody else kind of eased up too. Maggie swung weight in the settlement. Then one night when I went over to the roadhouse to pick up Chuck and Ethel, Maggie asked me a question right out of the blue. "You done anything about buying yourself a cabin in Eagle?"

"No," I said. "I still don't know whether I'll be teaching there."

Angela and Mr. Vaughn were playing cribbage and they didn't look up from their game, but they were listening to every word.

"I know everybody on that school board," Maggie said, "and if they got any objections I wanna hear about it. How big a cabin might you want if they take ya?"

"Well . . . big enough so maybe Chuck and Ethel could have their own room."

She didn't bat an eye. "Think it'll be easy to find one, Arnold?" she asked Mr. Vaughn.

He mumbled something and Maggie said, "I didn't hear ya."

"I said probably," he said.

"We'll find you one," Maggie said.

Having Maggie on my side went a long way. Sure enough, come mid-April Mr. Strong brought me the news from Mr. Henderson that I'd been accepted to teach at Eagle. Chuck and Ethel were with me for good. The only thing that didn't change was the way things were between Fred and me. I didn't see him again for weeks after he got back, and then only once, when he came in to pick up some hardware he'd ordered from Mr. Strong. He'd made up his mind he was going to stay away from me for my sake and that was that. It didn't matter that he had saved Jennie's life and even risked his own; he was still a half-breed and I was still pure northern womanhood.

Then in May spring exploded. The sun came and stayed, and soon we were able to open the schoolroom windows to the tangy smell of running sap and the spicy odor of willow. Great flocks of Canadian honkers passed overhead, the beating of their wings making the air seem thick as water. And suddenly the snow was gone. Tender shoots of grass sprinkled the hills, and wild canaries flashed through trees haloed in green.

At the end of May, Nancy came back to take the territorial exam in hope of going to high school in Fairbanks next year. She took it in my quarters on the last morning of school, while I rehearsed the class in the schoolroom for the pageant we were going to put on after lunch. For the whole time she sat behind the closed door I was on pins and needles. When she was finished she came in and handed the test to me, then went outside while I looked it over. I couldn't grade it for her. That would have to be done in Juneau, but I could tell her whether she'd passed or not. She passed, all right, and when I yelled for her to come back in and hear the good news the class let out a cheer.

Before the pageant started we had an exhibit of work the class had done over the school year. Everybody made a point of admiring the map of Chicken on the wall. As big as it was, they'd never seemed to notice it before. Now they said they'd never seen anything like it, and how clever the kids were to have made it. Drawings and book reports also decorated the walls. Set out on the shelves were fossils and birds' nests, pot holders and samplers, papier-mâché masks—everything the class had made and collected. Watching the kids showing it all off to the parents, I felt proud. Without any fancy equipment, without even all the books they should have had, they'd worked hard, helped each other, competed and cooperated. And they'd learned.

The pageant was about the gold-rush days and it went off without a hitch. We served ice cream and cake, and when it was over, everybody helped clean up for the dance that night. Maggie Carew was the last to leave.

"Well, that's the end of 'er," she said, looking around the room. "She's gone now."

She meant the school. With Chuck and Jimmy and Willard leaving, there just wasn't enough enrollment to keep it open. "You did a good job," she said.

"Thanks." Coming from her it was a high compliment.

It was still light out at eight thirty, when everybody started showing up for the dance. It would stay light until about eleven, when dusk would set in for a couple of hours. The sun came up again in the middle of the night. Sometimes, unable to sleep, I'd get up and start the day at three in the morning.

Everybody kept crazy hours. Miners would be out working their claims right through the night, setting up sluice boxes, excavating ground. They only had three good months to get their work done and they didn't want to waste any time. A few didn't even bother with dress-up clothes when they came to that last dance. Sprouting beards for protection against mosquitoes, they showed up in clean work clothes, all ready to go back to their diggings when the dance was over. Fred and his mother came, and that made the evening for me.

Everybody kept wanting to know if I was having a good time. I was, but I couldn't help feeling sad. In a few days I'd be leaving, yet when I looked around the room it seemed as if it was only yesterday that I'd arrived. In less than a year I'd lived a whole lifetime here. One of the green shades had a message written on it, left over from the class party: "Farewell, Miss Hobbs." Under it Jimmy Carew had scrawled a PS: "See you in Eagle."

With Fred playing the banjo during most of the square dances, I only got to dance with him once. When the gramophone was wound up, Fred ambled over to me. He looked grand. He had on a starched blue and white striped shirt, and the sun had tanned him really dark. He had a big smile on his face.

The "Home, Sweet Home" waltz began to play. His arm slipped around my waist, and like the first time we danced that waltz together, the walls of the schoolroom moved right back and everybody disappeared. I was so far away in my mind that not until the record was over and everybody began to clap did I realize no one else had danced. All of them had stopped to watch Fred and me.

Chuck and Ethel were asleep, so Robert Merriweather stayed with them while we all went over to the roadhouse. It was almost two in the morning when a couple of chords sounded on the piano. We all turned to see Joe Temple point a finger at the kitchen, and while he played a march Maggie Carew came out carrying a huge chocolate cake with a candle in the center. She set it down in front of me. "Good Luck" was written on it in icing. Beside it was a beautiful farewell gift of an expensive camera. Everybody yelled for me to make a speech.

"I wish I could," I said, "but I'm not very good at making speeches. All I can say is, thanks—I appreciate it."

"No more than we appreciate you, Teacher," Ben Norvall said. "There isn't a soul in this room that doesn't think you're a fine, honest girl and a true-blue Alaskan to boot."

Joe started to play "Auld Lang Syne," and then Fred and everybody were singing. By the time they got to the end I was on the point of crying. I wasn't the only one either. Maggie's and Nancy's eyes were wet.

It was almost three in the morning when Fred and I went over to my quarters to see if everything was all right. Robert was asleep on the couch, Chuck and Ethel on the bed, so I tiptoed out and Fred and I went for a walk.

As soon as we were out of sight of the settlement, Fred took my hand. The woods were as quiet as if the sun in the sky was just pretending to be there and it was really night. We talked a little about Eagle and what it would be like living there with Chuck and Ethel. Fred said he wanted to come and see me after the freeze-up. We went on until we came to the creek. Before we sat down on the grassy bank we scooped up a drink. The water was cold and sweet, dyed clear amber from roots and dried hillside moss.

"I guess you're relieved that I'm going," I said, lying back on the bank. The ground was warm.

"Why should I be?" Fred lay down on his stomach and leaned on his elbows.

"You won't have me chasing after you anymore."

"You didn't do that," he said.

250

"Yes, I did. I'm doing it right now. I'll be leaving in a few days, so what does it matter? It's the truth. I've been chasing after you almost from the time we met." I didn't have a bit of shame left in me and I was glad of it. He could be a gentleman if he wanted. I was sick of being a lady.

That made him squirm. "Anne, if I had money enough to take care of you, I'd ask you to marry me right now."

I felt like shaking him to make him wake up and realize I didn't care how much he had or how little, that all I wanted was him. There was no point to it, though. We'd been through all that, so I just stared at him long enough until he couldn't do anything else but kiss me. I ran my fingers along the back of his neck and he started kissing me in a way he'd never done before. He murmured my name and for the first time in my life it didn't sound plain to me. It sounded lovely, all mixed in with the rush of water running below us, and the sweet smell of the earth.

I didn't want to open my eyes, but when I finally did and looked into his I loved what I saw. He wasn't thinking about being noble. He was just being *him*. And he wanted *me*. He said, "Anne," his voice husky and deep.

My fingers went to his lips. "I want to say something to you," I told him.

He waited while I got it all straight in my mind, and I said, "I don't know what you think you have to have before you want to keep company with me, but you just remember this. I love you. I won't be chasing after you anymore, because we're going to be far away from each other, but someday, when you get ready, you better come and marry me. Because I'm never going to marry anybody else. I mean that, Fred Purdy. If you don't marry me someday I'm going to be an old maid."

"No you won't," he said.

"Is that a promise?"

"That's a promise."

A little later we started to walk back arm in arm, stopping every so often to linger and embrace. We went on that way until we came in sight of the settlement, then we let each other go.

That's how Fred and I parted those many years ago, with a promise. We didn't get married until over ten years later, on September 4, 1938, the eleventh anniversary of the day I'd started out by pack-train from Eagle. By that time Chuck had graduated from high school, Ethel had entered it, and I'd adopted three more children.

It was worth all the waiting, though. We had a grand life together. Fred mined in the summer, and in the winter sometimes we stayed home, sometimes we packed up the family and went Outside. We did whatever we liked. One winter, maybe the finest we ever spent, we took on the jobs of teacher and custodian in an Indian village. As for children, Fred loved them as much as I did, so we adopted four more.

I'm sixty-seven years old now. Fred passed away ten years ago, and although I've since gotten over the sharp pain of losing him, I still miss him badly at times, mostly when there's a gentle rain falling. I think of it falling so quietly all over the hills, soaking into the ground to bring out new life, and it's hard for me to accept that I'm never going to see him again or hear his laugh. It's like trying to imagine springtime without the sound of birds.

Then I think about the wonderful years we had together. Every time I do, I realize how fortunate I've been, because as much as I love children and sunlight, I know that the sun would never have shone as brightly for me, nor children's smiles seemed so lovely, had I spent those years without Fred.

ANNE HOBBS PURDY
Chicken, Alaska

Anne Hobbs Purdy

"Before my eyes, she turned into a nineteen-year-old girl in Alaska." This is author Robert Specht describing his first meeting with Anne Hobbs Purdy. Specht was then an editor with a Los Angeles publishing company, and Anne had come to talk over a book about life in an Indian village.

"She had this fantastic ability to become a young girl again, and as she began to remember Alaska, and Chicken, in 1927, I fell in love with her. I wanted to tell her story."

It was not until 1965, when Specht had left publishing to become a free-lance writer of television scripts and screenplays—work which he still does today—that he was able to begin *Tisha*, his first book. Work continued intermittently over the next eleven years, and it took Robert Specht to Chicken, where he retraced Anne's steps. He says, "The book was possible only because Anne was able to remember everything so vividly—beginning with the packtrain and Blossom."

Anne often spends the winters in California. The rest of the year she lives with one of her adopted daughters, Anlynn, in the house Fred built on a hill above Chicken. Robert Specht met Fred not long before his death. "He was a magnificent human being," Specht recalls, "wonderfully warm and amiable."

And what happened to everyone else? Beautiful Ethel grew up to marry and live in the States. Chuck died of tuberculosis several years ago. The schoolhouse has become a rooming house for Indians who work with gold-dredging equipment at Chicken.

Just how were Fred and Anne reunited eight years after she had gone to teach at Eagle? "They met by beautiful accident in Fairbanks, Alaska. One look and they knew they would marry. But that," says Specht, "is another story—the sequel to *Tisha*—and I just may write it."

THE
LONG LONG
DANCES

a condensation of the book by

ERIC MALPASS

Illustrated by Eric Stemp
Published by Transworld

For young Derek Bates, the proud owner of a new motor bike, girls were of only two kinds: if they were too young to be impressed then they were small enough to be terrorized.

And eight-year-old Julia, dancing alone in the water meadow, inevitably came into that second category.

But John Pentecost also was down by the river that day, with his shot-gun. And his small grandson not far behind him, hurrying to catch him up, because Grandpa appeared to be pointing his gun at a Martian. . . .

It was a small enough beginning. Certainly out of all proportion to the terrifying drama it was to bring in its train.

Two delightful earlier books by Eric Malpass about the hilarious Pentecost family—*Morning's At Seven*, and *At The Height Of The Moon*—have already appeared in Condensed Books, in 1970 and 1971. Now, once again, he writes of the Pentecosts' innocent eccentricities. And of their courage also, blundering perhaps, but steadfast.

The little girl dances alone in the meadow.

She is beautiful, and grave, and eight years old.

When Julia dances, her toes are filled with delight. Her black hair hangs down to her waist. Her arms float like weed in a lazy stream, like a mermaid's tresses. . . .

IN THE HOUSE, her father is writing a letter: "John Pentecost, Esq. Dear Sir, In answer to your advertisement for a farm manager . . . graduated at Aberdeen University . . . considerable experience . . . only fair to tell you that owing to my wife's death, I have the sole care of a young daughter. But this is my problem, and I can assure you I shall find ways of dealing with it. Yours faithfully, Duncan Mackintosh."

THE GREAT CRUISE SHIP ploughs northward. Behind it lie the sun and colour of the Mediterranean; before it, the gathering cold of a northern winter. In the dining room Miss Dorothea Pentecost looks as happy as any maiden lady sipping champagne under the admiring gaze of an elderly but handsome Frenchman ought to look. He says, smiling, "What are your family going to say?"

She chuckles deliciously into her Dom Ruinart Blanc de Blancs. "I don't think they're going to be very pleased, dear."

"Oh!" From deep in his chest comes that exquisitely modulated cry of concern that only a Frenchman can produce. "Why not?"

She looks puzzled. She often looks as if she is waiting for the mist to clear. "Bea and John don't need *reasons, mon cher.* They just react, like that stuff we used to have at school."

"Litmus paper? And you think I shall turn them red? Tell me about them," he says.

She ponders. "Well, there's Bea. She's my sister. And Brother John has a farm, and my nephew Jocelyn and his family live with him, and Jocelyn writes books. I keep meaning to read one of them sometime."

THE SHIP DRIVES on towards an England where Mrs. Agnes Thompson, all alone, suddenly breathes her ladylike last. And *that,* she thinks grimly as she passes over, will teach Wendy to leave me alone while she goes gadding. But her daughter Wendy is in a fool's paradise, having just been appointed Speaker Finder of the Ingerby Writers' Club. And Madam Chairman, who thinks it is high time Wendy stopped devoting her whole life to her old mother, says "Why don't you have a run out to Shepherd's Warning, dear? Fix up with Jocelyn Pentecost the date of his lecture. . . ."

AND, IN THE SAME town of Ingerby, Derek Bates lives with his parents. Their house has every comfort known to the television commercials. Derek is a lucky lad. But is he happy? No. Because, for Derek, one more thing is necessary—a motor bike. Given a motor bike, his cup of happiness would be full. Without it, the cup makes him puke. "Oh, give over," says Mrs. Bates. "You're not having one, that's flat." But Mr. Bates will be master in his own house. "Who says he isn't?" he demands, glaring. Master Bates hugs himself, knowing that the battle is won. . . .

THE LITTLE GIRL dances alone in the meadow. Joy flows along her arms, along her outstretched fingers. It flutters away from her finger tips like butterflies—flutters away into a dangerous and violent world. . . .

CHAPTER ONE

May Pentecost was disliking herself. Her father-in-law had told her about the new farm manager and his motherless daughter, clearly hoping she would say, "Well, they'd better come and live in the house. Leave it to me, Father-in-law."

She had stayed silent. Why? Because, she thought severely, like everyone else nowadays, I don't want to get involved. Every man is an island. Don't bother to send to know for whom the bell tolls. So long as you can hear it tolling, *you're* all right, Jack.

Non-involvement, that was what she wanted. So that she could go on looking after a big house, an irascible old man, a busy and absorbed husband, a boy of seven and a baby girl, she thought defensively. But it was no good. Conscience was a cruel judge.

She went into her husband's study. "I've got problems," she said.

Jocelyn Pentecost looked up warily. He could do without problems: he'd got enough in his fictional world without having to worry about real-life ones. But May was looking a bit upset. "Your father's going to ask this Scotsman to manage the farm. And the Scotsman has a young daughter—and he's a widower."

All the characters who had been working away so cooperatively in Jocelyn's head put their hats on and went home. He wondered sadly when he would see them again. He said gently, "And you can see yourself becoming responsible for the child?"

"I can't stand by and watch a man coping on his own."

"What's the Scotsman like?"

"As reliable as Aberdeen granite, your father says. And about as talkative."

"And they'll take the cottage, of course?"

"Yes. I think your father was hoping I'd say they could live here. But—I didn't."

Rather to his surprise Jocelyn heard the Jocelyn-he-would-like-to-be saying, "Of course not. Leave it to me, May. I'll speak to my father. You've got quite enough to do."

May gave him a brilliant smile. "Thank you, darling. I would be grateful."

Reluctantly, Jocelyn went to see the old man. "Er, Father, this manager chap and his daughter. I think May feels it's a bit of a responsibility for her."

"Oh, a most capable woman, May. She'll cope." John Pentecost was a great admirer of his daughter-in-law.

"But—" This was difficult. "But she shouldn't *have* to, Father."

"Look! I'm not damn well giving up a man with most excellent references just because—" The telephone rang and he grabbed it. "Pentecost. Yes? . . . I'm very pleased to hear it, Mr. Mackintosh. That sounds most satisfactory." He put back the receiver and looked up at Jocelyn with one of his rare smiles.

"Mackintosh has persuaded his sister to move in to the cottage with them and look after the girl."

"Oh, good. May will be relieved."

"So am I relieved. So ought you to be, Jocelyn." He looked at his son sternly. "Must admit you sometimes take May's good nature too much for granted, you know."

Jocelyn went into the kitchen. His wife looked up from the stove, smiled: she was always pleased to see Jocelyn, and it took a lot to get him out of his study during working hours. "I've, er, had a word with Father," he said. "I told him I didn't want you getting involved with the little girl."

He looked, she thought, like a small boy who has just scored his first goal.

"Darling, *thank* you."

"So he had a word with Mackintosh on the telephone, and Mackintosh is going to get his sister to live with them."

"Jocelyn, that *was* clever of you." She kissed him fondly. Yet there was an amusement in her smile that left him uneasy. If he *had* slightly manoeuvred the telling in his own favour, could she have realized this? He had to admit that he had never yet succeeded in pulling any wool over his wife's eyes.

GAYLORD, if pressed, would have admitted to knowing that girls existed, but they were not creatures a chap expected to meet. And certainly, if you *did* come across a girl, you couldn't be expected to acknowledge her socially.

He was trying, not altogether successfully, to dam the River Trent when his grandfather's voice said, "Oh, and this is my grandson. Gaylord, this is Mr. Mackintosh, who is going to look after the farm for me. And this is Miss Mackintosh. And Julia."

Julia smiled. Gaylord scowled. Miss Mackintosh said, "The laddie's awful wet."

Gaylord looked up into the utilitarian features of Elspeth Mackintosh, all carbolic and Calvinism. He was affronted. He expected Momma to go on when he got wet, but if complete strangers started doing it you'd have chaos.

The man, with what seemed something of an effort, said, "What are you doing, laddie?"

"Damming the Trent," said Gaylord.

The man looked unimpressed. Grandpa said, "You'll cause consternation down-river in Nottingham." He turned to the little girl. "Now, Julia, are you going to stay and help Gaylord devastate the Eastern Counties?"

Gaylord could scarcely believe his ears. Grandpa had always been his friend; he was bitterly disappointed in him.

"May I?" Julia's voice was soft, and sweet.

"You can if you like," Gaylord said.

But now Miss Mackintosh was putting her oar in. "Och, the lassie's not dressed for splashing about in water."

Splashing about in water, indeed—a major engineering project! Deeply hurt by this belittling of his efforts Gaylord swiftly said, "She won't get wet, Miss Mackintosh," and gave Julia a spade and a grudging smile.

"Now come and see the milking parlour," said Grandpa. The adults moved off.

"If that lady's your mother, why is she a Miss?" Gaylord asked.

"She isn't. My mother died last month. Daddy asked Aunt Elspeth to come and look after me."

Gaylord went on shovelling mud. This needed thinking about. It had never really occurred to him that God could let anyone as vital to the scheme of things as Momma, die. He couldn't imagine Poppa left to bring up him and Amanda—he liked Poppa very much, but he'd no illusions about his practical abilities. "I'm sorry your mother's dead," he said, keeping his head down. He was annoyed with himself for being unable to think of anything helpful to say. "I bet it's awful."

"It is a bit." The little girl was looking sad and forlorn. Now she looked anxious as well. "Shall we really devastate the Eastern Counties?"

"I don't know. Grandpa might have been joking. He does sometimes."

She said, "That big log. If we used that—"

Gaylord tried not to look impressed, and wondered why *he* hadn't thought of it.

DEREK BATES straddled the shiny, powerful machine. He twisted the throttle, pulled down his perspex visor, and roared off; a knight on his great stallion, a Cossack mowing down his peasants. His parents watched him go. "He'll kill somebody," said Mum.

"So long as it ain't himself," said Dad philosophically.

MISS WENDY THOMPSON sat in the Corporation bus and thought wistfully how nice it would be to drive out in the Mini to ask Mr. Pentecost in person when he could speak to the Club. But she knew Mother would be opposed to the idea. When Mother was opposed to an idea, Wendy just gave up because Mother had such an array of weapons at her disposal, from accusations of ingratitude and thoughtlessness to sick headaches and nasty turns. She was utterly ruthless in using her armoury, while Wendy was good-natured and friendly, and really very fond of her.

She let herself into the house. "Only me," she called. No reply. That was always ominous: it sounded as though she was in trouble for something. She went into the living room, where Mother sat, as always, in her rocker. . . .

Mother was past impatience and irritation, past sick headaches and nasty turns: her weapons of war were perished. She was a pitiful old woman, sprawled in death.

And Wendy did a shameful, outrageous thing—she pirouetted round the room, before she fell weeping bitterly onto the sofa.

She'd been very fond of Mother; but her death had given Wendy two wonderful, lucent gifts—her own thirty-year-old life; and the bright world. No wonder she was a maelstrom of emotions. Her dear companion, gone! Herself, free, looking with fear and misgiving at the open door of her cage.

The autumn was long and lovely; the golden, mellow days mocked Miss Thompson in the bijou residence from which she still hesitated to venture. Every day she vowed she would write a little note to Mr. Pentecost. Every day she decided to wait, and drive over tomorrow. It is not easy, she found, to make decisions when they have always been made for you.

"A MONTH AGO I too was puny, ineffectual. Now I am a giant among men." Such might have been Derek Bates's testimonial to the motor cycle company.

A month ago, he'd been nobody; just a spotty youth, pushed around by his mates, nattered at by his mother, cursed by his dad. But now, what a transformation! Booted, encased from head to toe like a deep-sea diver, his acne hidden by a merciful bowl of perspex, he straddled his bike. A roar, and he was off; young men and maidens, old men and children, scattered from his path. He had discovered the secret of power!

But soon it was no longer enough to send some old woman scuttling for the pavement. More and more he demanded attention. Anyone who did not look up when he roared by deserved to be punished. So that when he saw a small girl so absorbed in her dancing that she refused to notice him, even when he pulled up and angrily revved his engine, he decided to teach her a sharp lesson. Especially since she was quite obviously alone. . . .

The October noontide was a distillation of the summer's glory. Golden, high-piled clouds were seen as through a gauze. A late dragonfly quivered and darted in the sunshine, a living rainbow. Julia became a dragonfly: motionless, on tiptoe, arms outstretched, fingertips a-quiver. She did not notice Derek Bates, and furiously he turned his machine into the meadow, gave the throttle a savage twist, and charged at Julia.

The girl screamed. Derek drove to within a yard of her, then turned suddenly and went into a tight circle round and round her. Behind his visor his mouth stretched tight in angry triumph as she collapsed in a sobbing heap on the grass. She'd noticed him now, by God. *And* she wouldn't forget him in a hurry.

Derek did one more circle, near enough to give her a farewell kick *en passant*, and then with a roar of triumph made for the gate.

But he saw, with a quick stab of fear, that the gate was now shut, and that a powerful-looking old gentleman was leaning on it. The grimness of his face was complemented by a certain menace in the way he held his double-barrelled shot gun. Derek slowed down and stopped.

John Pentecost stared at him with loathing, his trim, white moustache bristling with rage. "Switch that noise off!" he roared. Derek did as he was told. Grandpa looked at him and winced. Poor, miserable little devil, he thought; but out of the corner of his eye he saw Miss Mackintosh carrying Julia back to the cottage. "Now, young man," he said furiously. "You're going to dump that iron-mongery in the river."

For perhaps ten seconds the silence was absolute. Then: "You mean the bike?" asked Derek belligerently.

"I mean the bike," said Grandpa. And slipped the safety catch.

"But. Mister—?"

"Push it! I shall walk behind. And don't imagine I'm not capable of peppering your backside."

It is doubtful whether Abraham, bidden to sacrifice his son, felt as bad as Derek. Derek was being told to sacrifice the only thing in the whole world that could make him feel important. He looked at the face of the old man and began pushing. But on the river bank he turned. "Please, mate. I didn't mean to frighten the kid."

"Push!" said Grandpa.

"No—I can't. I *can't*." Derek was near tears.

"*Push!*"

It was the first time in his life, either at home or at school, that Derek had heard the true voice of authority. With a great cry of rage and despair, he pushed: the lovely, shiny machine splashed mightily into the ooze. Derek peered down at it, unbelieving. Life couldn't be so cruel. . . .

"What's that motor bike doing in the river, Grandpa?" an interested voice said. Seeing Grandpa talking to what he had at first taken for a Martian, Gaylord had approached at a rate of knots; and found the motor cyclist something of an anti-climax.

Grandpa ignored him. He said magnanimously to Derek, "If you want a garage to salvage it, they have permission to cross my land."

"You're not from Mars, are you?" Gaylord asked, always hopeful.

"Mars?" said Grandpa. He turned back to Derek. "I suppose you're disturbed, or maladjusted, or whatever the current claptrap is. But to me you're just a nasty little thug who kicks children. So get off my land."

Humiliated Derek might be, but he had seen an antagonist more suited to his metal. He looked down at Gaylord. "I'll get you," he sobbed. "Me and my mates'll carve you up." He turned to John Pentecost. "*And* you. You don't think you'll get away with this, do you?" He was weeping, trembling with rage and self-pity. "And how do I bleeding well get home?" he demanded.

"You bleeding well walk, dear boy," John Pentecost said suavely.

With her well-known propensity for rubbing salt in wounds, Fate arranged for Derek to meet a mounted posse of his mates as he trudged home. "Hey, Derek, where's your bike?"

He told them, playing down his humiliation, playing up the panache of his attack on the girl, and leaving the old bastard writhing in agony on the ground from a well-aimed kick in the crotch. His pals applauded: old geezers who took the law into their hands had to be taught a lesson. And so the trail of powder that led ultimately to destruction and death, began its slow burning.

BACK AT THE HOUSE, John Pentecost telephoned Mackintosh, then called May and Jocelyn. He said, "We're waiting for Mackintosh."

As the silence stretched to breaking point, May and Jocelyn looked at each other anxiously. Even May daren't question him when he was in this mood. Then Mackintosh came in, ignoring them, and dragged up a chair. "Now," he said.

John Pentecost said, "May, Jocelyn. Mr. Mackintosh already knows something of what has happened. Julia was playing in the meadows. A young thug drove into the field on his motor bike, terrified her almost into a faint, and then kicked her."

They both gasped with horror. "How is she?" they asked simultaneously.

Mackintosh said, "She's badly frightened, but not physically hurt, I think. We shall know more when the doctor's seen her."

Jocelyn said, "You *saw* it, Father?"

"I did. And I took it upon myself to make the punishment fit the crime. And what I did may involve me in difficulties and all of us in danger. I made him chuck his motor bike in the Trent."

May crowed with delight; but Jocelyn looked grave. "How did you persuade him, Father?"

"Stuck an unloaded gun in his ribs."

Was there even a flicker about the grey granite mouth of Mackintosh? If so, it was but fleeting. The Scotsman said, "Legally they can throw the book at you, Mr. Pentecost."

"If they've the wit," the old man replied blandly. "But when I spoke of danger I meant this. The youth went off swearing vengeance on me and—I'm sorry, May—Gaylord."

May slipped her hand into Jocelyn's, and was silent.

"Now this youth daren't say 'boo' to a goose—unless four of his pals were holding it down. But they have the pack instinct and I think that for the time being we have all got to be very watchful. Anyone approaching the farm has to come along the river road: they're clearly visible."

May's mouth was dry. "I think we should tell the police."

"What exactly can we tell them? That a teenage youth uttered some vague threats?"

May sighed. "Oh, Father-in-law, you do make life difficult."

He said gravely, "What would you have had me do, May?"

She stood up and put a hand on his shoulder. "Exactly what you did do, you reprehensible old man." She turned to Mackintosh. "I *am* sorry about Julia, Mr. Mackintosh. It's—not a good beginning, is it?"

"She has to learn to take the rough with the smooth, Mrs. Pentecost."

She looked at him. Grizzled hair, grey skin taut over a strong bone structure; Aberdeen granite! He might have been talking about a pony, rather than his own daughter.

Jocelyn Pentecost had been sitting, hunched and silent. Now he said, "What is it about beauty? Some men give their whole lives to its creation. Others must destroy it whenever they see it. I wonder why."

Mackintosh rose. "They also destroy public conveniences, and telephone kiosks, Mr. Pentecost. How does that fit in with your wee theory?"

May said, very stiffly indeed, "I do hope your little daughter will soon be better, Mr. Mackintosh."

"Aye. Thanks," said the Scot. He turned to the old man. "I'm glad *you* dealt with it and not me, Mr. Pentecost. *My* gun would have been loaded."

May looked at Mackintosh quickly. There was no shift in his expression yet she decided he was not perhaps the cold stone she had imagined.

EVERY MORNING, at nine o'clock, the Gas Lane complex of schools sucks in children like a vacuum cleaner: neat children, loutish children; children who come to learn (or anyway to be taught) about poetry and the binary system and the Counter Reformation and the use of a chisel and a needle. As well as children, the vacuum cleaner also sucks in a large number of staff, most of whom attend daily with a mixture of resignation, distaste, apprehension, and even downright fear. But there are some who still retain some faith in their work, and in children; such a one is Miss Wendy Thompson.

Since her mother's death, in fact, Wendy had become even more absorbed in her job. It saved her from making decisions about the house, about Christmas, about arranging with Jocelyn Pentecost the date of his visit to the Writers' Club. Meeting strangers was never easy for her. So that when the Headmistress of the Primary said, "We've a new little girl for you, Miss Thompson, I'll leave her with you," and Wendy saw a slim child clinging anxiously to the hand of a grey, lonely-looking man, she said happily, "Splendid. And what's your name?"

The child was silent. The man said, "Julia Mackintosh. We've just moved down here from the Mearns, Kincardineshire."

"I see. And where are you living now, Mr. Mackintosh?"

"World's End Cottage, Shepherd's Warning."

Mr. Pentecost lived at Shepherd's Warning. She would have liked to ask more, but she did not think Mr. Mackintosh welcomed chat. She said to Julia, "And is Mummy at work?"

The child hung her head. The man said, with rough incongruity, "Her mother's with the angels." The child began to cry.

"Oh, dear. I *am* sorry. That was very foolish of me."

"You weren't to know," he said casually.

But Wendy was down on her knees, comforting the child. "Now Julia, what do you like to do best in all the world? Tell me, dear, and we'll see whether we can do it."

Julia said something through her tears. "Did you say dancing?" Wendy asked gently.

The child nodded, staring at the floor.

The man said, "Her mother was a ballet dancer. She sent the child to ballet lessons. But—this is no' a world for ballet dancers."

"What is it a world for, Mr. Mackintosh?"

"Och, women policemen, hairdressers, shorthand typists."

Wendy Thompson straightened up, suddenly very sad. "I hope you're wrong, Mr. Mackintosh," she said quietly. She looked at the Scotsman, wondered what fantastic combination of chance and attraction had brought a ballet dancer to the Mearns. She said, "And you are quite opposed to her attending ballet school? Even if she shows great promise?"

He nodded. "I'm a practical man, Miss Thompson. I wouldn't want my daughter earning her bread doing dying swans. Just teach her her three R's, that's your job. Goodbye to you. Goodbye, Julia." He stooped down, kissed the child with sudden tenderness, and was gone.

Rude man, thought Miss Thompson. But her mind wasn't really on him. She was remembering another girl who had wanted to be a ballet dancer, who had known she had both the ability and the perseverance, who in dreams had heard the applause for the Prima Ballerina, and seen the stage strewn with flowers; who would have thought even the chorus very heaven; yet who also had not been allowed to go to ballet school; in her case by a selfish and possessive mother, God rest her soul.

She took Julia's hand. "Did you like ballet lessons?"

"Oh *yes*, Miss. It was wonderful."

Poor kid, thought Wendy. To lose her mother, and have to give up ballet lessons, it must have seemed like the end of the world. Wendy said, "I wanted to be a dancer too."

At last the child looked at her. Wendy saw the beautifully etched brows, the long sensitive mouth, the proud set of the head. "Why weren't you?"

"My mother wanted me to be a teacher."

Julia thought this over. Then she gave Wendy a quick, sudden, friendly smile.

CHAPTER TWO

Gaylord was watching Momma feed Amanda when Grandpa burst in, letter in hand. "May, I—Oh, sorry. Didn't realize Amanda was refuelling."

"It's all right, Father-in-law," said May, cutting off the infant (who thought it was anything but all right) from her source of supply. "Whatever's happened?"

"It's my sister, Dorothea. She's taken leave of her senses."

"Why, whatever has she done, Father-in-law?"

"It's not what she's done, dammit. It's what she's going to do." His voice was awestruck. "She's marrying a Frog."

"Dear me," said May, trying to look suitably grave.

"'Dear me'? *That* all you can say?" The old man was taken aback. "Not only is he a Frog. She met him on a Mediterranean cruise." He waited for this to sink in. "Quite obviously one of these fellows who make a living out of making up to rich old ladies on cruises. Why, his name's enough to prove it." He glanced at the letter. "Edouard St. Michèle Bouverie. Can you imagine a chap with a name like that *not* being a crook?"

"It could happen," said May.

Grandpa looked disappointed in her. "Anyway," he said gruffly, "she and Bea want to bring him over to stay for a few days in early December. That's all right with you, I suppose?"

"Of course," said May, who had been telling herself that this year she would try to take things easy before the Christmas rush really began; and who, unlike Grandpa, visualized Edouard St. Michèle Bouverie as an aristocrat of the old school, who would refuse to eat if anything, from the seating arrangements to the temperature of the wine, displeased him.

"Good girl," said Grandpa. That was what he liked about May. Took things in her stride. To show his appreciation he said, "And listen, May. Don't you go wasting your time on Froggie food for the chap. If he can't eat the sort of plain, nourishing stuff you give us, he can damn well go hungry."

"Very well, Father-in-law," said May, who spent much of her time and thought producing meals for the family from her Cordon Bleu Cookery Book. "We'll have roast beef and Yorkshire pud and semolina every day."

He gave her a wary look. It seemed to him his daughter-in-law was in a funny mood today.

MAY SLID AMANDA into her pram. She looked at her drowsy child with a moment's envy—clean, well-fed, lapped in comfort, with nothing to do or think about until her next feed. "Would you like to wheel her outside, Gaylord?" she said.

Gaylord was pleased to do so. He liked Amanda; not as much as he liked the dog Schultz, of course. But his fondness for her often surprised him. Today, however, he had far too much on his mind to pull funny faces to amuse his sister. Great Aunt Dorothea marrying a Frog!

He was not only intrigued, but uneasy. He knew Princesses often married Frogs, if only because Frogs could usually be relied upon to turn into Fairy Princes; but Great Aunt Dorothea was no Princess, and the idea of her turning up with a Mr. Jeremy Fisher didn't fit somehow.

Besides, Gaylord had been beginning to fear that fairy tales were one thing and life was another, and that Frog Princes belonged to the fairy-tale side. Yet he had just listened to Momma and Grandpa quite seriously discussing what to give the Frog to eat. Could it be that fairy tales *were* real?

He saw Miss Mackintosh and Julia in the distance, and decided to test their reactions. He parked Amanda by the dustbins and fell in with them. "My Great Aunt Dorothea's going to marry a Frog," he announced casually.

There was a silence. It must, thought Elspeth Mackintosh, be an English joke. "Och, awa' wi your daffin'," she said sternly.

But Julia, eyes shining, said, "Is she *really*, Gaylord? I bet he's a Fairy Prince, then."

"Yes," said Gaylord. "That's what I thought." He went and sought out Poppa, who was taking a walk to try to unravel his current plot. "Poppa, Great Aunt Dorothea's going to marry a Frog. *Why* is she?"

"I suppose they've fallen in love with each other." Jocelyn's duty to his son clashed with his duty to his public. He put the plot from his mind long enough to say, "Actually, old man, I think the Race Relations Board would prefer you to say: a Frenchman."

Questions multiplied in Gaylord's brain like rabbits. "I don't see where the Frenchman comes in."

"He's the man your aunt's going to marry."

Gaylord pondered. "Not a Frog?"

"No." He laughed. "Ladies only marry frogs in fairy stories, old chap."

Gaylord felt depressed. If only grown ups would say what they meant! In spite of himself, he had rather been looking forward to meeting a Mr. Jeremy Fisher. But no. As usual, life had come down on the side of the humdrum.

A YELLOW VAN, equipped with lifting gear, hoicked Derek's machine out of the river, and trundled it back to its owner. He did not attend the exhumation. He might meet the old man again and that he did not want to do until he'd got his mates with him.

John Pentecost strolled across to watch the operation. "Crazy coot," said one of the men. "You'd wonder how he managed to run into the river."

"You would indeed," said John Pentecost. As he strolled home he thought: no police action then. Well, perhaps he was sorry. Now he was left with an enemy that knew no rules, that could strike anywhere, and at any time.

The garage did what they could with the bike to clean it up, and make it serviceable. "There you are, mate," they told Derek. "We've got the tiddlers out of the carburettor. It's as good as new."

But it wasn't as good as new. It could still do a hundred miles an hour, but it no longer gleamed like a knight's charger. It looked, in fact, like a motor bike that has spent some time at the bottom of a river. Worse. It had once been the symbol of Derek's pride and manhood; now it was the reminder of his humiliation—and the call to vengeance.

A FRIDAY AFTERNOON in December: the winter's dark already turning the river to gunmetal; the lights of John Pentecost's farmhouse the only cheerful thing in a grey scene.

The farm stood on a slight rise, overlooking the river valley. It would have made a good fortress. There was only one approach, and that was from a lane running beside the river. And Gaylord was watching this lane like a hawk: both his Great Aunts, and the Frenchman, were coming to stay, and as soon as he saw the Mini coming along the road he would do his disappearing act. He was lying on his stomach in the hayloft, gazing out through a very convenient knothole. Fifteen feet below was the stackyard; beyond that the paddock, the meadows and the river.

Now there were lights coming along the lane, flashing in and out as the Mini passed behind trees and hedges. Any time at all now, Great Aunts Bea and Dorothea, those compulsive kissers, would be out of the car and crying, "Where is the young scamp? Where is my precious?" Gaylord crossed to go down the ladder into the big barn, pulling his iron rations out of his pocket—a Mars Bar and a bottle of Coca Cola. He hadn't *much* hope of staying hidden till the aunts went home—who *could* have, with a mother like his, hearing all, seeing all, knowing all?—but it was worth trying.

From his study, Jocelyn could not see the road. He could only wait until the house was filled with the clamour of the aunts' arrival.

But once that happened, he could no longer shut himself away. Hushed voices saying, "The master is not to be disturbed," were unknown in the Pentecost household. Well, he supposed it was his own fault. Too amiable by half. Other writers just didn't seem to have domestic lives: you couldn't imagine, "Just give me a hand with the second best bed, Will. Ben Jonson's coming for the weekend," any more than you could imagine Wordsworth going round Dove Cottage with a duster. No. Most other writers, it seemed to him, divided their time between writing masterpieces and dallying with their mistresses. But he, Jocelyn Pentecost, had clearly started off on the wrong foot.

Grandpa, snoozing in the drawing room, heard the sound of tyres on gravel. He opened a baleful eye, shut it again, and began breathing deep and steady. He knew that, fond though he was of his sisters, that fondness had got to last over at least a weekend: no point in meeting them until it was absolutely necessary.

Besides, he was still mulling over what May had said. "Now, Father-in-law, it's most unfair to assume that this Frenchman is a crook, just because Aunt Dorothea met him on a cruise."

He had glared up at her with that aggressive sheepishness that meant she had struck home. "My dear May, you're not suggesting that I of all people could treat a guest with anything but courtesy?" He was hurt. John Pentecost prided himself on his courtesy and his tact. But he wasn't letting a French crook think he could pull the wool over *his* eyes.

May, too, heard the car and braced herself. We're off, she thought. A whole weekend; with everything and everybody, even Father-in-law, under my control: cooking, entertaining, electric blankets, glasses for teeth, morning tea; and those wildly disparate characters, Jocelyn, Father-in-law, Gaylord and the aunts, to say nothing of an unknown Frenchman; even little Amanda who could yet create a mayhem peculiarly her own. She felt like a captain whose ship, stealing out of harbour, gets its first vicious slap from the mighty Atlantic. Nevertheless, she put on a bright smile and threw open the front door with a cry of "Welcome, Aunts!"

It wasn't the aunts. It was a young lady who, at this strange greeting, seemed prepared to leap back into her Mini as the startled fawn leaps back into the brake.

May said, "I'm terribly sorry. I was expecting—someone else."

"Oh, dear. But—Mr. Jocelyn Pentecost said it would be quite in order to call some time."

May was intrigued. Jocelyn had mentioned no young woman. She looked at the visitor more closely. Very feminine, with her small bones and rather fine grey eyes; despite her anxious expression, she had a certain quiet authority. "Do come in," said May. "I'll tell him. What name shall I say?"

"Wendy Thompson."

May marched into the study. "Are they here?" Jocelyn asked, like one hearing the tramp of feet outside the condemned cell.

"No. But Wendy Thompson is."

"Who's Wendy Thompson?"

"*I* don't know. But she says you told her to drop in any time."

Quite obviously, May regarded Miss Thompson's visit as both an irritation and a source of innocent merriment. Jocelyn wished his wife's sense of humour was a little less astringent. He stood up. "I'd better see what she wants."

May went back into the hall. "Do come this way," she said. But her voice was drowned by the hideous crash of metal on metal, the prolonged tinkle of glass, followed by the awful voice of Great Aunt Bea demanding to know what damn fool had left a car without lights just where she would run into it.

The effect on the household of this clatter was rather like that of a boot on an ant heap. Gaylord, flinging discretion to the winds, was out of the barn and gleefully running for the house. When disaster struck, Gaylord wanted to be in the front row.

Miss Thompson quite literally wrung her hands and cried, "It

274

must be my car." May hurried outside and Grandpa abandoned all pretence of slumber and rampaged towards the hall crying, "What the devil does Bea think she's playing at?"

Miss Thompson sank into a chair. A small boy dashed in, bright-eyed. "Is anyone hurt?" he asked eagerly.

"I—I *do* hope not."

Gaylord listened. "I can't hear any screams. So perhaps whoever it is, isn't—unless they're dead."

He rushed out. A fierce-looking old gentleman rushed in. "Where's May? What's happened? Who are you?" he barked.

"So terribly sorry," said Miss Thompson. "I—I just never thought—leaving my car without lights."

"My dear madam." Grandpa's sudden access of old-world courtesy was almost as disconcerting as his rudeness. "My dear madam, don't give it another thought. My sister Bea would have run into it had it been floodlit like Buckingham Palace. Let's go and look at it."

She seemed to be having difficulty in rising. He looked at her with sudden compassion, feeling an emotion he had not felt for years: a desire to slip a manly, comforting arm round those frail shoulders. He said, "No, you stay here. I'll go and find out for you." He went out into the dusk of the drive.

The two cars appeared to be locked together, like stags in mortal combat. A large, formidable woman was shaking them violently to get them apart.

"Well, Bea?" John said sweetly. "Still carving a trail of devastation, I see."

From the middle distance a voice said, "I bet that lady won't half be cross."

The moment he had spoken, Gaylord realized his mistake. Aunt Bea dropped the pair of Minis, and peered into the dusk. "Why, it's my little pickle." She held out her arms. "Come and give your old auntie a kiss, dear."

Gaylord, sticking his lower lip out, edged a little farther into the encircling gloom. Using every bit of cover, he was soon lost in the shadows.

John Pentecost remembered something. "Hey, Bea? Where's this chap of Dorothea's?"

"May took him and Dorothea into the house. Come on. I'll introduce you."

"Never thought you'd let Dorothea fall for a crook," he said reproachfully.

Bea stopped in her tracks. "One thing I admire about you, John. You've never let complete ignorance of a subject stop you being dogmatic, tendentious and self-opinionated about it."

The old man fumed. First May, then his elder sister: both lecturing him as though he was some sort of monster, instead of one of the most reasonable men you could meet in a day's march. Of *course* he'd be polite.

But he wasn't having any Frog crooks in the family.

MAY SAT in the comfortable, cottage living room. With her was Great Aunt Dorothea: frail, her mind and body seemed to sway and drift like gossamer in the breeze; yet she smiled with ineffable sweetness in her late-flowering love. Monsieur Edouard St. Michèle Bouverie was there too, smiling at his loved one, gazing with frank and unabashed admiration at May.

But where was Gaylord? Was Amanda sleeping safely? Was Jocelyn at his desk, pretending he hadn't heard a damn thing? And what about poor Miss What's-it? To leave a guest in this way was unpardonable, but Jocelyn must have done something by now—and May *had* to be here, to welcome her future uncle. She also had to witness the meeting between what Grandpa clearly thought of as East and West.

The door opened. Here we go, thought May. But it still wasn't the old man. It was, to her relief, Gaylord.

It had been no light decision of Gaylord's to come into this aunt-infested room. But his plan to remain hidden had been destroyed by his own curiosity: he wanted to see the Frenchman.

Yet, once again, he was disappointed. A picture of Napoleon, the only Frenchman he knew about, hung on his classroom wall, and to find that Aunt Dorothea's lover had neither white breeches nor a cocked hat was a sad anti-climax.

"This is my pickle, Edouard," cried Dorothea. "Come and give your auntie a kiss, boy."

Well, there was no help for it. He advanced reluctantly and was

276

enfolded in what felt like a spider and fly embrace. But worse was to come. "Now kiss your Uncle Edouard," said Dorothea.

Gaylord was affronted. But Edouard earned his undying love and devotion by saying, "Oh, men don't *kiss* each other in England, Dorothea," and shook hands gravely and firmly.

Gaylord was won over. He said chattily, "Isn't it funny. I thought at first you'd be like Mr. Jeremy Fisher."

"Indeed? And who is Jeremy Fisher?" Edouard wrinkled his brow. "A politician?"

May said hurriedly, "He's just a character in a book, Monsieur."

"He's a frog gentleman," said Gaylord.

The room was silent. Edouard looked puzzled; then suddenly, he saw the light. He shouted with laughter and drew Gaylord to him. *"Oh, mon brave. Que tu es gentil."* He pointed to his stout but immaculate shoes. "You thought I had webbed feet, yes?"

Gaylord thought him the nicest man he'd ever met.

John Pentecost entered with Bea, wearing a grim and wary look. He went and kissed Dorothea, who embraced him fondly. Out of the corner of his eye he took in the French chap.

But this chap didn't fit the picture in his mind at all. His brown tweeds were as rough as John's own, his complexion looked as though it spent more time in sun and wind than in the salon, he was laughing, and his arm lay affectionately round Gaylord's shoulders. At this stage John Pentecost was prepared to pay him the greatest compliment he could pay any foreigner: after a couple of whiskies, and with the light behind him, you could almost forget he wasn't English.

Dorothea said, "And now, John, I want you to meet your new brother-in-law, Edouard St. Michèle Bouverie."

John nodded stiffly and growled, "How do you do?"

To his surprise the Frog also bowed stiffly and said, "How do you do?"

Fight against it as he would, John couldn't help feeling mollified. Chaps, it seemed to him, were divided into two types: those who said, "How do you do?" on being introduced, and those who said, "Pleased to meet you," or even "Hi!" And anyone who used any but the first, whatever his nationality, was fit only for treasons, stratagems and spoils.

277

"Dorothea tells me you fish, sir," Edouard said.

"A little trout. Don't suppose you'd know anything about that, though."

"Oh, I've fished some of the Scottish lochs."

It had never occurred to Grandpa that Frenchmen could do anything but eat, drink and make love. (That they also played Rugby Football always seemed to him one of the most bizarre facts in nature.)

The gathering began to break up. But the two elderly gentlemen seated themselves, their chairs comfortably close.

"Dorothea tells me you work in a bank," John remarked casually.

There was a moment's silence. Then: "I *am* a bank," Edouard said with just a suspicion of hauteur. "Bouverie et Cie, Paris."

Good Lord! "My dear chap, I beg your pardon."

Edouard shrugged, and smiled. "And now I suppose I should ask your formal permission to marry your sister?"

"Nothing would give me greater pleasure. And I wish you both every happiness. When—had you thought?"

"April. If that would be convenient to yourself?"

"April. *Dear* Dorothea! If I may say so, Monsieur, you are a very lucky man." He blew his nose loudly. He was greatly affected.

CHAPTER THREE

Miss Wendy Thompson was demoralized. It had taken all her courage to come out to the farm in the first place: and look where it had landed her! She hadn't even seen Mr. Pentecost yet. Instead, she had been greeted by a woman whose beauty and serenity immediately made her feel she was back in the Lower Fourth. She had heard her car suffering untold indignities. Then, she had met a crazy small boy, and an old man who had frightened the life out of her; she had inspected her car and found the front wheel wrapped up in the wing like a badly tied parcel; and finally, back in the hall, she had collided with a tall, mannish woman who had said jovially, "You the chick who left that car slap in the middle of the drive? Damn stupid thing to do. Never mind."

It was at this point that Wendy Thompson's hackles began to

rise. It was outrageous—here she'd been, on a perfectly civil errand, and they'd smashed her car, left her waiting in the hall, forgotten about her. Well, she wouldn't stay another moment. She marched out of the front door and slammed it behind her. Metaphorically she shook the dust of the Pentecost household off her feet for ever.

A light had been switched on in the drive. Beyond that, it was now quite dark. Already her anger was beginning to ebb and her fear to return, but she set her small jaw and marched resolutely on into the darkness. Her solicitor would act for her over the car, she need never go back to the farm.

There was a harsh, aggressive noise on the windless evening. A motor cycle was thundering past, half blinding her. She saw the rider crouched, toad-like and menacing, on his machine.

As soon as he had passed, he slowed down and stopped. The machine turned and began to follow her, slowly. Its headlamp threw her shadow on the road before her.

She wanted desperately to run, but she made herself walk. On her left, the river glinted in the light. There seemed to be a ploughed field on her right, fenced by wire. Her nerves were near breaking point as the cyclist followed, grimly, surely.

Then suddenly the driver accelerated and swept past her. Thank heaven! But twenty yards on he stopped, turned his bike so that the headlamp illuminated her, and switched off his engine.

The silence was appalling. She put up a hand to shield her eyes, and moved across to the darkness at the side of the road. The light followed her. She crossed to the river side; the light followed her again. She was trapped by it.

Wendy Thompson was small, and fragile, and certainly not very brave. But now she made a decision that surprised her. She would march boldly up to this youth and tell him to leave her alone. Resolutely, she walked towards him. Perhaps, she thought, with just a glimmer of hope, I shall be able to walk past. Perhaps he'll let me go when he sees I'm not some young girl.

Then he spoke, his voice harsh and flat. "You live at that farm?"

She had to make several attempts to speak, so dry was her mouth.

"No. And—you should be ashamed of yourself, frightening people."

"I bet you do," he said. "I'll throw you in the river if you do. I'm going to throw in anybody who lives there, and hold them down."

"I *don't*," she said piteously.

"Well, you've been there." He dismounted. "That's good enough for me."

He was still in darkness, she in the one patch of light in the whole brooding countryside. Suddenly a gauntleted hand shot out, seized her wrist, and began dragging her towards the icy river. She screamed. It was at this moment that she heard a sound in the distance. It *could* be footsteps, coming from the farm.

Clearly the motor cyclist had heard it too. His grip faltered. "Help!" screamed Miss Thompson. With a swift movement she jerked her arm free, and began to run on unsteady legs back to the farm. And as she ran she heard the motor cycle starting up and fading into the distance. But had it faded? Or had it stopped again?

The footsteps were nearer now, light and quick. "Hello," said a friendly voice. "Where are you going?"

It was the boy. "Hello," said Wendy, relieved. "I was going to Shepherd's Warning—but I heard your footsteps, and waited."

Gaylord was agog. "I heard the White Nun of Shepherd's Warning. 'Help, help', she was screaming." He gave a lifelike imitation. "Did you hear her?"

Suddenly, all Miss Thompson's fears for herself disappeared in her fears for this boy, who lived at the farm, and was therefore, in the motor cyclist's genial expression, due to be drowned. She had to get him back to the farm and warn his parents. In the distance she could see a glow among the trees: she was almost certain the motor cyclist was still lurking in the lane.

"Come along," she said. "We must get back to the farm."

Suddenly Gaylord felt very big, and grown-up, and protective. "You can hold my hand if you like," he said.

Miss Thompson grabbed his little paw and dragged him towards the farm. She'd heard the motor bike again.

"Wasn't someone silly, leaving their motor car where Aunt Bea could run into it?" he said chattily.

"*I* was. Very silly."

"Oh, was it you? Grandpa says that if Great Aunt Bea *must* drive a car, she ought to have men with sticks running in front, clearing the way."

The lights of the farm were quite near, now. "I'll race you home," said Miss Thompson.

He was off, like an arrow from the bow. She followed. They reached the doorstep almost together, laughing and panting. The motor cycle droned away in the distance.

MAY CAME IN to Jocelyn's study. "Well blow me!" she said. "Chaos is come, and there you sit."

"I'm waiting for Miss Thompson," he said patiently.

"You'll wait a long time. She's disappeared."

"Well, that's all right," he said. "Probably didn't need to see me. Saw someone else."

"But her car's still here, or what's left of it." She saw his puzzlement. "Bea biffed it. What did you think the uproar was?"

"Oh, Lord. Anyone hurt?"

"No, thank goodness. Miss Thompson was safe in the house when the crash occurred, but now she's disappeared. And—Jocelyn, I don't want to be alarmist, but—" her voice was suddenly bleak "—I don't know where Gaylord is."

He stared at her. "He's probably gone to ground to avoid Bea's kisses."

"That's what I thought. But I've looked everywhere—all his favourite haunts. I'm worried. Especially after that motor cycle business."

"I shall telephone the police," he said and reached for the telephone. "Wait!" said May. They listened. "Gaylord!" They hurried down to the front door.

MAY WAS NOT overjoyed to find Gaylord and Miss Thompson enjoying themselves hugely on her doorstep. "Gaylord! Where *have* you been?" she snapped. Miss Thompson she ignored.

Miss Thompson sobered up quickly. "I met your little boy down by the river, Mrs. Pentecost, and brought him home as quickly as I could. I thought you might be worried."

"You're dead right, I was worried. But—thank you, Miss Thompson," she said, a trifle grudgingly. Then she realized how dreadfully she had neglected this uninvited guest. She said, "Do come inside. Miss Thompson, you—weren't—*walking* home?"

"Well, I did realize I'd called at a very inconvenient time. . . ."

Wendy Thompson's eyes were sparkling from her exertions, her face was still alight from her triumph in having brought the boy back safely. Jocelyn, who had come into the hall, saw a very different Wendy from the frightened creature of May's first meeting. He said, "I'm afraid I've treated you very badly indeed, Miss Thompson."

"Of course not, Mr. Pentecost. It was ridiculous of me to turn up like that." She saw a very different person from the one she had imagined: a great bull of a man, glaring at her over a simmering typewriter. She smiled at him gratefully.

"Momma, I heard the White Nun," Gaylord broke in. He gave a realistic rendering of her cries.

"Gaylord, be quiet. You'll bring out the fire brigade." And then, in the way that one thing *always* led to another with Momma, "And what were you doing down by the river?"

"As a matter of fact," Miss Thompson said quietly, "he was protecting *me*. If I could have a word—"

"Off you go Gaylord," said Momma, firmly. "Now, Miss Thompson. Let's go into the small sitting room."

THE BLACK SKY brooded over the silent earth. A flake drifted down out of the blackness, feather-light, then another, and another, dancing and whirling. John Pentecost heard the rising wind. But no one heard the snow, wrapping a winding sheet of white about the lonely farmhouse, industriously blotting out the lanes.

Derek Bates rode home through the swirling flakes. He felt frustrated; knowing in his heart that that woman (and he'd recognized her—she taught in the Primary. *And* she lived just down the road) had got the better of him. Still, if it hadn't been for someone else coming he'd have had her in the river, and they'd have been getting the tiddlers out of *her* carburettor. He slammed into the house, threw off his gear and slumped in front of the telly. He stared at the screen. Some bloke with a stocking over his face had gone into a room where an old woman was asleep. Any minute now the old woman was going to wake up and see him. Here she went!

282

Mouth open, eyes popping out of her head. Derek rolled about in his chair. Funniest thing he'd seen for ages. He'd like to do that to that schoolteacher bitch.

AS THEY CAME OUT of the sitting room, May said, "We really are grateful, Miss Thompson. Even though it does confirm our fears."

"Very grateful," said Jocelyn. He smiled down at her. Pretty little thing! Thinking of her out there, at the mercy of that youth, made him feel very protective. "Stay and have dinner, Miss Thompson. Then I'll run you home."

May might be very grateful to Miss Thompson, but she'd seen Jocelyn looking fond and fatherly. Much as she loved him she didn't trust him not to get even more fond and fatherly alone with Miss Thompson on the Ingerby road. Then she heard something that sounded very much like manna falling from heaven. A soft, insistent pattering on the window. It was. And Gaylord confirmed it by running in and crying, "Momma! It's snowing bucketfuls."

She opened the door and looked out. She saw the swirling snow. She saw, as always, the situation: her husband, Miss Thompson, the implications, the required moves. She said, "Goodness! Another hour of this and the roads will be blocked. You'd better be getting home, Miss Thompson. Perhaps my father-in-law will run you in."

"Oh, I couldn't ask Father to turn out in this," Jocelyn said nobly. "I'll take you—then we can discuss my lecture."

A rapturous voice cried, "Poppa, can we have a snowball fight?"

"My dear Gaylord," said Jocelyn, "I have to run Miss Thompson home. And it's almost bedtime."

It sounded exciting. They might be marooned for days. "Can I come?" he asked, expecting, as always, the answer "no".

"No, I don't think so," began Poppa. But to Gaylord's utter astonishment Momma said, almost eagerly, "Of course, dear. I'll just fetch your coat."

She hurried off. You could have knocked Gaylord down with a feather. Nearly bedtime, and Momma letting him set off on a long and perilous journey! He didn't understand it. Asked, he would have said that Momma was one hundred per cent predictable. Yet he knew that, just very, very occasionally, she would do something completely unexpected.

283

"I'VE NEVER SEEN IT snow as hard as this, have you, Poppa?" That was Gaylord, bouncing happily up and down on the back seat.

Miss Thompson said, "I'm afraid Mrs. Pentecost will never forgive me, dragging you out on a night like this."

The car lurched and slithered. Jocelyn had become an infinitely delicate instrument, a part of a machine coping in demented surroundings. But he was aware of Miss Thompson's pale face and her frail hands, folded demurely in her lap. It was exhilarating to bring her safely through the storm. He said gallantly, "I'm only too pleased to be of use, Miss Thompson."

"*Course* we are," said Gaylord. Not to be outdone in gallantry he added, "I bet Sir Galahad never let ladies walk home."

Miss Thompson felt quite touched. And it was at this point that she suddenly realized she was enjoying herself! The evening had been so embarrassing, yet everyone had been *so* nice to her.

"We haven't discussed your lecture, Mr. Pentecost," she said, almost coyly.

It was not the best of moments. Jocelyn was beginning to realize two very unpleasant facts: that, blinded by the snow, he had missed the turn for Shepherd's Warning, which left him the choices of turning in this narrow lane, or backing an unknown distance, or driving miles across the bleak upland of No Man's Heath. The other even more unpleasant fact was that the engine had begun to sound as though it was choking on a fishbone.

Confirmation came from the back seat. "Poppa, you've missed the turn. We're nearly at No Man's Heath."

Jocelyn drove grimly on. "It won't half be blowing on the Heath," said Gaylord with relish. "I bet it could blow us over." Then, "Poppa, I think your engine's going to stop."

Jocelyn said nothing. It seemed as though all his being was centred in the ball of his right foot—coaxing, wheedling, urging. All to no avail. The engine spluttered and died.

Gaylord said, "No one ever comes along this road. We could stay here for days and days and days, if you ask me."

"Oh, Mr. Pentecost, it's all my fault, dragging you out," said Miss Thompson. "I'm so sorry."

Jocelyn was trying the starter. It ground drearily. Gaylord said cosily, "I've been thinking. If they send out a search party they'll

284

never think of coming this way. They'll go to Shepherd's Warning. Henry Bartlett's Uncle Fred—"

"Oh, *blow* Henry Bartlett's Uncle Fred," said Jocelyn.

Gaylord sounded hurt. "I was only going to say that he broke down once and rang up the A.A. and when they came they found he'd run out of petrol. Henry Bartlett's mother said he didn't half feel silly."

Jocelyn had already got one leg out of the car. Now he quietly pulled it back and closed the door. He looked bleakly at the fuel gauge and said, "Miss Thompson, I have done something utterly foolish. I've run out of petrol."

She said, with feeling, "To anyone who can write as well as you, Mr. Pentecost, a great deal can be allowed. It happens to everyone, sooner or later."

But Gaylord struck a less soothing note. "I bet Momma won't half pull your leg, Poppa. If we ever see her again, that is. It won't surprise me," he went on ecstatically, "if there are wolves. Teacher says hunger can drive them down from the hills they live in. Or they could have escaped from that circus we went to."

"Gaylord, *do* try not to end *all* your sentences with a preposition."

Weren't grown-ups hopeless! Mention something really exciting, like wolves, and before you could begin to savour its rich possibilities you found yourself switched on to prepositions. But he wasn't one to give in easily. Pressing his nose against the window he peered out into the snowy waste. "I *think* I can see an Abominable Snowman," he said hopefully.

Miss Thompson looked at the small, eager face. She was already beginning to know Gaylord. Normally she would have tried to reassure the child, pointing out that the existence of Abominable Snowmen was open to question, even in Nepal. Now she said, "Just behind that bush. Look. I saw him move."

She and Gaylord looked at each other and chuckled happily. All right for some, thought Jocelyn. He said, "I still haven't discussed the date of this lecture, Miss Thompson." Not that he cared, he ought to show some interest in her affairs.

"I do realize now that it was very wrong of me to barge in on you, like this, Mr. Pentecost. I should have written."

"Not at all. I'm only sorry I've made such a hash of getting you home."

"Mr. Pentecost, please don't apologize. I ought not to have come. Only—it was a temptation because I admire your books so much and—well, I think your work's terribly significant."

"Significant of what?" To Jocelyn, flattery was a sweet-smelling savour.

"Well, of—LIFE," said Miss Thompson.

Jocelyn said, "One tries to reflect life, of course. But—good Lord, something's coming." He jumped out of the car.

Gaylord was bitterly disappointed. This promising adventure, it seemed, was coming to an end. Already he could see the Land-Rover slowing down, and drawing up beside them.

Mr. Duncan Mackintosh jumped down, and came across, unsmiling. "I thought it was yourself, Mr. Pentecost. You'll be in some kind of trouble, maybe?"

If Jocelyn had been given a list of the fifty million people in the British Isles, and had been told to choose the one he would least like to be rescued by, there is no doubt that Mr. Duncan Mackintosh, who made him feel like a feeble-minded child, would have been first on his list. He said, sulkily, "I've run out of petrol."

Mackintosh peered round at the dashboard and tapped the fuel gauge. "Aye, it's empty all right. You'd better transfer to the Land-Rover."

They got in, Gaylord looking back enviously at the little car already half submerged in snow, the setting for a life and death adventure ruined by this interfering Scotsman.

Jocelyn said, "Miss Thompson, this is Mr. Mackintosh."

Mackintosh said, "Miss Thompson teaches my lassie."

"One feels so silly, running out of petrol," Jocelyn said.

"I never let *my* tank get below a quarter full. Stick to that simple rule, Mr. Pentecost, and you can't go far wrong."

How absolutely right he was. And how impossible! But now a determined voice said, "I think *everybody* ought to run out of petrol at least once in their lives. Stop them getting priggish."

Mackintosh drove a little way in silence. Then he said, "I'd rather be priggish than daft, Miss Thompson."

Angry on behalf of Jocelyn Pentecost, she said, "When are you going to let your daughter do what she wants with her life, Mr. Mackintosh?"

A sudden increase of speed showed that he resented the question.

"May I remind ye, Mistress Thompson, that I'm her father and ye're just the person paid to teach her to read and write."

Jocelyn said, "That's an uncalled for remark, Mr. Mackintosh."

"You don't need to protect me, Mr. Pentecost," Wendy Thompson said gratefully. "Why won't you let Julia go to ballet school, Mr. Mackintosh?"

"Och, awa'," he muttered. "Because she'd be tired of it in a week. And because I don't want any daughter of mine daffin' half naked in front of gawping fools."

"We're discussing ballet, Mr. Mackintosh. Not strip-tease. Anyway, presumably you were content that your wife should—"

He looked round furiously. "Ye'll leave my dead wife out of this, Mistress Thompson."

"I'm sorry. I shouldn't have said that. But I still think to stop Julia dancing will be like caging a skylark."

He was silent. They were nearly at the farm. Then he sighed, and said, "Ye're a rare fighting cock, Miss Thompson, for all your size. But ye're not to fill my Julia's head with your fancy ideas."

"Her head's full of them already."

"Aye. So. Well, there you are, Mr. Pentecost." They got out of the Land-Rover. "And you remember. Whenever you're down to a quarter, fill up. Goodnight to ye." He drove away, his rear lights disappearing among the dancing snowflakes. "Rude man!" exclaimed Miss Thompson. Then she looked at Jocelyn with alarm. "Oh dear, I'd meant to ask Mr. Mackintosh whether he could possibly run me into Shepherd's Warning. But—I got so cross, I forgot."

"My dear Miss Thompson, you'd never have got to Ingerby, anyway. No, my wife will fit you in somewhere."

"Oh, *do* stay, Miss Thompson," cried Gaylord, who was still feeling very protective.

Spend a night, with this alarming family? Miss Thompson thought of her cosy bijou residence with the doors shut and the curtains drawn, but it was separated from her by miles of snowy waste. She had not, it seemed, much choice in the matter.

MAY, FINDING Miss Wendy Thompson on the doorstep for the third time in one evening, had a not unsurprising sense of *déjà vu*. She said, "Oh you're back, Jocelyn. Well, I'm not surprised. Now, Gaylord, straight up to bed." Slight pause. "Hello, Miss Thompson."

Jocelyn said, "I've told Miss Thompson you'll find her a bed, May." He gave a light laugh that rang as hollow as a cracked bell.

May, without looking at anybody, said, "Of course, Miss Thompson, we shall be delighted to have you."

Gaylord, wishing to divert Momma's attention from his bedtime, said, "Momma! I saw an Abominable Snowman when we were broken down."

"Jocelyn, did you break down?"

"It wasn't Poppa's fault that we ran out of petrol, Momma," Gaylord said hurriedly. "There must have been a hole in the tank."

"Jocelyn, darling, you *didn't?* On a night like *this?*"

"It was *all* my fault," said Miss Thompson.

Then to Jocelyn's relief May gave her sudden, joyous laugh and said, "What on earth does it matter, whose fault? You're all safe. Except poor Miss Thompson, who's adrift in a house of strangers."

She gave Wendy a smile that made the poor girl her slave for life. "Never mind, Miss Thompson. You'll find us friendly, when you get to know us. Even my father-in-law doesn't actually bite. And now, Gaylord—off to bed."

And to her astonishment he went. But then she saw what Gaylord had seen a second before her, and she understood his sudden submission: Great Aunt Bea, just coming out of the living room, followed by Dorothea, Edouard, and John Pentecost.

May made vague introductions. "Miss Thompson is staying the night with us," she announced.

The Frenchman gave the impression that this was all he needed to make his cup of happiness full, and May said, "Well, now, shall we say supper in half an hour?"

"That's all right for you, old man?" Grandpa demanded of Edouard. "Don't go expecting anything grand. Just pot luck." He grinned at his daughter-in-law. "That's right, isn't it, May, old girl?"

She turned to the Frenchman. "Actually, I've done a *Coq au vin* with *Pommes Anna* and aubergines. And I did wonder—?"

"And you'll have a glass of good English beer to wash it down, eh," said Grandpa.

May said, "Actually, Monsieur, I have cooled some Meursault Clos de Bouches Chères—the 1971. But—" for a moment she looked the helpless female "—I know so little about wine, and if you would prefer beer—?"

Edouard, who thought English beer flat, warm and quite undrinkable, turned to John Pentecost. "My old friend, you will forgive me. For no other wine would I refuse your beer. But for the Meursault—" he kissed his hand to May. "It is what the gods drink on Olympus, my charming niece-to-be."

CHAPTER FOUR

By next morning the English climate had turned one of those somersaults for which it is justly famous. The sun edged up into a flawless dome of icy blue steel. The world was a feather bed of snow. In that scene there was no hint of the chaos that was about to descend from a clear sky.

Wendy Thompson rose to a day of unanswered questions, though, whatever happened, she was almost certain to spend some time with Mr. Pentecost who was tall, and quietly spoken, and whose eyes lit so quickly into a kindly smile.

Never before had she breakfasted with a crowd of strangers. The last thing any of them seemed concerned about was the fact that Miss Thompson was stranded; and she was far too shy to bring up the subject herself. So she sat nibbling her toast with downcast eyes, wondering how and when she could get back to the peace of her little house.

May Pentecost watched her, and thought: poor little mouse, with the detached kindness of a good hostess. But that was where the kindness stopped. Miss Thompson was a woman of thirty, not unattractive: and, as such, made the tigress that sleeps in every woman stir uneasily.

Jocelyn thought how vulnerable she looked. "I wondered whether you'd like to see my study after breakfast, Miss Thompson," he said. "Not much to see I'm afraid, but—"

She looked up at her name, flushed with pleasure. "Oh, Mr. Pentecost, I'd *love* to."

"Oh, don't expect too much, Miss Thompson," May put in. "It's only one of the small bedrooms, tarted up with a desk and a dictionary or two."

Miss Thompson said blissfully, "But that's not what matters. It's a—it's a sort of *power house.*"

"Good God," said Grandpa, who thought he'd never heard such damn nonsense in his life. But May was silent. It had never occurred to *her* to think of her husband's workroom as a power house—and yet things *were* created there. She felt a belated pride —and kicked herself for having left it to another woman to open her eyes.

But now breakfast was drawing to a close. They all strolled into the living room and across to the French windows, drawn by the brilliance of the morning.

The windows opened onto a white lawn, which fell away to meadows and the black snake of river. They stood in the pleasant warmth, separated by a frame of wood and glass from snow and ice and pinching cold. The only moving thing in that world of brilliant blue and white was a tiny figure trudging along the river road, pulling a sledge.

"Looks like a page who's lost his Good King Wenceslas," said Grandpa, lighting his dear friend Edouard's first cigar for him.

Gaylord didn't think *that* sounded very likely, though one could never be sure, of course. He looked more closely. "It's Henry Bartlett," he said. "I knew it wasn't a page. Momma, can I go and meet Henry? And take Schultz?"

"Yes. Wrap up. It's icy out there."

He set off. The snow was crisp, dry, sparkling: the most wonderful and extravagant gift a benevolent heaven could give a small boy. What with the way the snow fluffed up in front of his wellies, and the braggadocio antics of Schultz, and the thought of snowballs and snowmen and sledging—Gaylord felt like bursting with happiness.

He went along sizzling like a kettle that is just off the boil, kicking at the snow, and watching the round, smooth, pink, bespectacled face of his dear friend Henry approaching like another little sun in that white waste.

They met. "We nearly perished in the snow last night," said Gaylord. "If Mr. Mackintosh hadn't rescued us we should have done."

Henry Bartlett looked impressed. "I nearly fell in the river," he said, in a half-hearted attempt to keep up. But it was no use. It wasn't like perishing in the snow.

"I bet you'd have frozen to death straight off if you had," Gaylord said kindly.

Henry Bartlett nodded, then said, "Sledges. You can't ride and pull at the same time. I don't think there's much point in a sledge when you're on your own." This feeling had been growing on him all the way from Shepherd's Warning.

"No," said Gaylord. An idea struck him. "*You* could pull me," he said. "Then," he added a little less enthusiastically, "I could pull you."

It was a brilliant solution. Gaylord sat on the sledge and Henry pulled. And the runners hissed and rang, and Schultz cavorted beside them. And Henry thought how wonderful it was to have a brilliant, clear-minded friend like Gaylord Pentecost.

"YELLOW THE LEAVES," said Miss Thompson, looking at the shelves in Jocelyn's study. "It's a lovely title, for a lovely book." Her lips were parted, her eyes shone. "So this room is where it's all done," she said.

"Actually," he said, "I'm afraid it isn't at present. I just don't seem to feel things any more. I've become—anaesthetized. My new novel just won't grow."

She looked horrified. "But it *must*. The world's waiting for it."

He gave a hollow laugh. "If I never wrote another line, the world wouldn't even notice."

She crossed to the window. Outside, two small boys and a dog, in a timeless Brueghel landscape. After a moment she turned and looked up at Jocelyn, taking a deep breath. "Mr. Pentecost, you're not fair to yourself. You can write wonderful books. And a lot of people are waiting for your next one—you've *got* to write it."

"So what do you recommend?" he asked. He was already beginning to see himself in a new, and more impressive, light.

"Why, that you take yourself more seriously." The vague, fluttering Miss Thompson of yesterday was growing in stature as quickly as Jocelyn's mental image of himself. "I shouldn't have asked you to waste your time on our club," she went on. "Foisting myself on you last night, talking to you now when you should be writing."

He said, "I do not regard addressing your club as a waste of my time." He too was gazing out of the window, now, at the timeless game of boys and dog and snow. "And, as for this morning—" he turned and gave her a grave, searching look "—it has been a great pleasure, Miss Thompson." Then, to his astonishment he heard himself say, "Let's go and join the boys."

"But Mr. Pentecost, I must be getting back. I—"

"See you in the hall in five minutes," he said. "Booted and spurred."

SCHULTZ had already forgotten that there had been a time when the earth was green. The snow had become his natural element. He tossed it, burrowed in it, rolled in it, worried it, ate it. And when he spotted two more playmates coming across the lawn he cavorted off to meet them. With Miss Thompson he went straight into what

May called his window-cleaner act, propping himself against her chest and licking her face with intemperate delight.

The boys too seemed pleased to see them. Jocelyn said, "This is Henry, Miss Thompson."

Henry went pink.

Miss Thompson said, "How do you do, Henry?" Gaylord thought he ought to tell Miss Thompson that last night he had decided to marry her, but thought this wasn't quite the moment. "I don't suppose anyone would like to make a snowman?" asked Jocelyn.

Gaylord looked eager, then doubtful. "Do you think Momma would let us?"

It was not the sort of remark Jocelyn would have chosen for Miss Thompson to hear, but he said, smiling, "Don't worry, Gaylord. I'll take full responsibility."

"I'll get some shovels and things," he said, and disappeared towards the farm buildings in a flurry of snow.

GRANDPA, glancing out of the window, said unkindly, "Good Lord, Jocelyn doing a bit of manual work!" He opened the window, called, "Jocelyn! You'll be knocking yourself up."

Jocelyn grinned and waved. Today, so rare was the morning, so pleasant was it to have an admiring companion, he was amused by everything—even his father's belief that writing books was the world's most effete way of earning a living.

Aunt Bea cried, "*That's* not the way to make a snowman. They're not *organized*. They're just *playing* at it."

"It certainly does look nice out there," said Aunt Dorothea wistfully. "Let us take a stroll, Edouard."

Edouard rose courteously, and gave his arm to his beloved.

John Pentecost, muffled to the eyebrows, and with snow on his boots, marched into the kitchen where May was toiling over a hot stove. "Hello, my dear."

It was, she realized, the affectionate, yet slightly sheepish greeting the old man used when he wanted something. "Hello, Father-in-law," she said non-committally. "Come to lend a hand?"

"Well, actually," he said, "I've come to ask a favour. We're all making a snowman. And I wondered—" he paused "—a bowl of hot punch would go down awfully well, May."

293

She straightened up, looked at him in silence, unsmiling. Then: "Give me twenty minutes," she said.

"Good girl," he said, touching her shoulder as he went. That was what he liked about May. She made everything so easy. An extra little job or two meant nothing to her.

JOCELYN was wishing the snowman in Hanover. What had begun as a *jeu d'esprit* had developed into a major construction job with a whole army of advisers, critics, foremen and overseers. Why, they'd only just started when Duncan and Elspeth Mackintosh had appeared with Julia. Julia had flung herself happily into the fray, but Mackintosh and Elspeth had watched with dour disapproval until Mackintosh found a shovel and, with a look of martyrdom, began clearing the drive; and, after a few minutes, Miss Mackintosh had called to Julia to "go and help Daddy with something useful."

The child looked forlorn. "Mr. Pentecost wants me to help with the snowman, Aunt," she pleaded.

"Ye heard what I said, Julia," said Elspeth primly.

Julia looked at Jocelyn for guidance.

Jocelyn was one of those people who have the misfortune to see the other fellow's side in every argument, but others did not suffer from the same disability. Gaylord, seeing the longing in Julia's eyes, said out of the side of his mouth, "You stay here. This is *ever* so useful."

But Miss Mackintosh knew insubordination when she saw it. "What did ye say, laddie?"

Gaylord gave her a dirty look. "Och, awa', woman," he said. He didn't know what it meant, but he sensed that it just about summed up his feelings.

Miss Mackintosh planted herself in front of Jocelyn. "Did ye hear, Mr. Pentecost? Your son's a rude wee laddie."

"*Were* you rude to Miss Mackintosh, Gaylord?"

"Aye. I was that," said Gaylord, in what was undoubtedly an embryo Scottish accent.

Jocelyn was horrified. "When you mean yes, *say* yes. Not that dreadful Aye sound."

"And what's wrang wi' the dreadful Aye sound?" demanded the

affronted Miss Mackintosh. She called to her brother. "Duncan, get Julia to help you."

"Come and give me a hand, Julia," he called.

Ill temper seemed to be infectious. Miss Thompson strode over to the drive and glared at the Scotsman. "Can't you see how she's enjoying it with the other children?" she demanded. "Can't you let her enjoy herself, just for once?"

For a long moment they stared furiously at each other. Then he slammed his shovel into a foot of snow. "Pentecost can clear his own drive," he muttered. He joined his sister.

That, however, had been only the beginning. Aunt Bea was treating Jocelyn like one of the slaves on the old plantation. " 'Tote dat barge, lift dat bale'," he was just muttering to himself bitterly, when he saw a sight that instantly restored his good humour: his wife, May, looking absolutely radiant in a suede coat and fur-lined hood, carrying a large tray. On the tray a great steaming bowl, glasses, and a plate of mince pies—and on her face the smile whose serenity and friendliness embraced them all. He thought: eight years married, and my heart can still leap at the sight of my wife.

Nor was Jocelyn's the only heart to leap at the sight of May. Edouard's did, as it always did at the sight of a pretty woman. Grandpa's did, as it always did at sight of a bowl of punch. Schultz's did, as it always did at sight of another playmate.

The dog bounded joyfully forward to meet her.

"Jocelyn!" screamed May. "Quick! Get the dog! He'll knock the tray for six."

"Down, Schultz!" yelled Jocelyn. "Down I say."

But "Down" was not one of Schultz's few key words. He continued to bound.

Jocelyn became the man of action. He grabbed the tray from his wife, and carried it safely to a wrought-iron table. He turned to find May lying in the snow with Schultz standing on her ecstatically licking her face.

He sprang forward, but Mr. Mackintosh and the Frenchman were before him, Mackintosh dragging off the hound, Edouard helping May to her feet, uttering Gallic cries of concern and solicitude.

"May, are you hurt? What happened?" cried Jocelyn.

Mackintosh said, "The dog tripped her just as you'd upset her balance by taking that heavy tray."

Jocelyn tried to get near his wife; but Edouard was protecting her like a mother hen. "You must lie down," he was insisting, "in a darkened room. And perhaps a smelling bottle—"

"I'm *hanged* if I will," laughed May. Though she had to admit her laughter rang a bit hollow. In the fall, her head had struck something hard with a force that surprised her. She was still seeing quite a firework display.

May ignored the fireworks. "Now then, everyone," she cried. "Let's have the punch before it's cold." They gathered round the table, laughing, chattering, stamping their feet. It was one of those rare moments when time seems to stand still, and love and happiness are caught like flowers in a glass paperweight; one of those moments when it is as though a spirit of harmony touches the world with its wings—and passes on.

And passes on. . . . May, having served the punch, said, "Now Gaylord, see what your friends would like."

"What would you like, Julia?" he asked. "Lemonade?"

"Yes, please, Gaylord."

"Och, we don't want to chill your inside wi' that cauld stuff," cried Miss Mackintosh. "A wee glass of hot milk is what you want, child."

Gaylord thought he had never seen anyone look as sad as Julia. "*I'll* fetch you some lemonade," he said stoutly.

"She'll have milk or nothing," said Miss Mackintosh.

There really must have been something very abrasive about the Mackintoshes; for now Gaylord did something that shocked and astonished him as much as it shocked and astonished his parents. He put out his tongue.

Miss Mackintosh very deliberately smacked his head.

May strode furiously up to her. "How *dare* you?" Then she dragged Gaylord towards Miss Mackintosh and told him in an awful voice to apologize, but Gaylord stood mute.

Miss Mackintosh said, "Duncan! If the wean has not apologized by midday, I'm awa' w' ma bags."

"I think it would be as well if you did leave," said May. "Since you have so little self-control." She turned to her son.

"Gaylord, you've been a very rude little boy, and I'm ashamed of you. Now will you apologize?"

"No." He looked up at her piteously. His face was determined but apologetic, "I'm sorry, Momma."

Well, she certainly didn't blame him. "Come into the house, Miss Mackintosh," she said grimly.

Inside May turned to her. "Now, Miss Mackintosh. I apologize for my little boy's rudeness. But if ever you touch either of my children again, you'll leave immediately."

"Och, ye canna dismiss *me*, Mrs. Pentecost. And if ye're talking of dismissing my brother—ye'll have the old man to reckon with."

The two women faced each other. Then May said, "That will be all, Miss Mackintosh." The Scotswoman stared at her insolently; then turned and went.

May sat down, trembling. She hated giving way to anger, but there were times— Her head was aching. She really mustn't let Miss Mackintosh work her up in this way. After all, it looked as if the Scotswoman would be part of her life for a long time.

GAYLORD, Henry Bartlett and Julia went on toiling away at the snowman. The Frenchman smiled at Wendy and gave her a little bow. "She is beautiful, the little one."

"Yes, indeed," said Wendy. "She's my favourite pupil, even though I know one shouldn't have favourites."

"So? You are her teacher?"

She nodded. "Actually," she said confidentially, "she wants to be a ballet dancer. But her father won't hear of it—he wants her to be something useful, like a shorthand typist."

"*Mon Dieu!* But she is exquisite. I would like to meet her."

Wendy called Julia and introduced her.

He said, "Give me your hand, child."

Shyly, she held out her hand. He stooped, kissed it. "I salute," he said smiling, "the future Assoluta."

It was absurd, but Miss Thompson felt the tears in her eyes. It was the rum punch, of course.

"You have spoken to the father?" Edouard asked her.

"Yes. Twice. He was rather rude."

"So." He turned back to the girl. "And you really want to dance?

297

All day, every day, until your legs are like lead, and it is an agony to lift your arms, and your back is breaking?"

"Oh, *yes*, sir." Her face was radiant. But as she ran back to the others he sighed helplessly. "What can we do? The man *is* her father. And—who knows—she might lose interest after a week."

"I don't think so. I know she's a determined young woman."

He stared at her, then he shook his head. "It's no good, Miss Thompson. We cannot play God."

"We could have a jolly good try," she said.

Another long stare. Then he stooped and kissed her hand.

IT IS A well-known fact that grown-ups can never concentrate on anything for very long, so Gaylord was not a bit surprised when they drifted back into the house. Only Miss Thompson looked back wistfully at the two vast and trunkless legs of snow which were all they had achieved.

Once, on holiday, when she was seventeen, Wendy Thompson had gone down to the seashore before breakfast. The wind had whipped off the sea, slapping her cheeks to colour, laying salt on her lips and tongue; she had danced on the lonely shore, a dance of praise and exultation. That morning Wendy caught a glimpse of what life could be about. Since then, life with Mother had dulled the bright memory. The salt had been wiped from her lips; the wind still blew by the sea, but the dancing girl was gone for ever.

Strangely, her stay with the Pentecosts had reminded her of that faraway shore. And now it was time to leave them.

Jocelyn Pentecost saw her backward glance at the snowman. "'My name is Ozymandias, King of Kings'," he murmured.

Wendy Thompson laughed and said, "I do love your quotations, Mr. Pentecost."

He smiled down at her. It really was rather refreshing to have someone around who not only recognized quotations, but actually appreciated them. And Wendy thought how wonderful it must be to be *friendly* with someone like Mr. Pentecost and not just someone who had called to ask him about a lecture.

"It's been so kind of you and Mrs. Pentecost to put me up," she said. "But I must be finding my way home."

"Stay for lunch," he said. "Then I'll drive you back in the other

298

car. May," he called, "you can find Miss Thompson some lunch?"

"Of course," said May, doing mental arithmetic with prime steaks and slices of Pavlova, and wishing her headache would go away. Her confrontation with Miss Mackintosh must have taken more out of her than she'd imagined.

"And can Henry Bartlett stay, Momma?"

She looked down at her son's eager face, at Henry's pink and anxious one. "He *can*, dear. But I think he ought to go home. His mother will be worried."

"She won't, Momma. She told him it was all right to stay if he was asked."

All right for whom, wondered May. "Well, that's all right, then," she said.

Now if she could get it across to Jocelyn that he really much preferred biscuits and cheese to Pavlova—? "Say you don't want any Pavlova," she hissed. "It won't go round."

"What's—? Oh, I know. That meringue thing. No, that's all right, May. I'll have cheese and biscuits."

"Right. Don't forget to *say* so."

It was all very confusing. He had said so, hadn't he? Well, he'd just have to play it along and hope to recognize a clue.

"PAVLOVA, JOCELYN?" May stood, cake-slice in hand.

"Thanks, May," he said. He looked up, met a steely eye. CLUE! "No thanks, old girl. Biscuits and cheese for me." And then, improvising brilliantly, "Waistline and all that."

"I'm sure *you* don't need to worry, Mr. Pentecost," said Miss Thompson. Jocelyn positively smirked.

You keep out of this, Wendy Thompson, May thought rudely. "What about you, Henry?" she said aloud.

Henry swallowed, blushed and nodded. Gaylord said, "Henry likes Pavlova better than anything in the world except baked beans on toast, don't you, Henry?"

Henry nodded. Grandpa, who had been staring at the silent child for some time could stand it no longer. "Doesn't say much, does he?" he barked.

"He thinks a lot," said Gaylord.

May said, "After you with the cheese, Jocelyn."

He looked at her in astonishment. "Good Lord, you not having Pavlova?"

"There's none left, you fool," said Grandpa.

"Oh dear," said Miss Thompson. "That comes of my staying for lunch. Mrs. Pentecost, look, do share mine."

Gaylord said, "If you did Henry some baked beans, Momma, he'd give you his Pavlova. Wouldn't you, Henry—I bet you'd *rather* have baked beans, wouldn't you, Henry?"

"I'll fetch the coffee," said May.

DEREK BATES sat with two of his mates in his bedroom, planning his revenge. Night and day he had brooded over his humiliation and now his only pleasure was in savouring his hatred. "We could kidnap the boy," he said. "Dump *him* in the river."

The other two did not seem very keen. One said doubtfully, "If that old chap took your number he could trace you—I don't reckon we ought to let the kid drown."

"What about roughing up the old man himself?" suggested Norman.

Now it was Derek who didn't sound very keen. "Wouldn't trust the old bastard," he said doubtfully. "He looks tough. I reckon the kid's best."

Frank said, "I seen a bloke carve another bloke up with a broken bottle. On telly." He hugged himself at the memory. "Didn't half make a mess."

"I reckon you can't beat a broken bottle," said Derek thoughtfully. "And we could smash the place up a bit while we were waiting." Much as he longed for his revenge, he didn't want it to be over too quickly.

IT WAS TIME TO GO. Wendy Thompson walked with Mr. Pentecost to his car. She had thanked Mrs. Pentecost warmly for her hospitality and she had replied charmingly; yet Wendy knew that to this busy woman she meant no more than did a fleeting guest to a hotel keeper.

Only to the Frenchman did she seem more than thistledown blown on the wind. As he kissed her hand he said, "I wish you luck with your young pupil, Miss Thompson."

300

"Thank you," she said, moved. "It won't be easy."

He put his card into her hand. "All I can offer is money," he said deprecatingly. "But never be afraid—"

"Thank you," she had said again. While Jocelyn started his car she looked back sadly. The big gaunt house, the snowy lawns, the distant river, Ozymandias the Snowman. Then a voice at her elbow said, "I'm sorry you're going, Miss Thompson. I wish you could stay here always."

"Gaylord!" she said. She'd been wishing so much that the boy could find a moment to say goodbye.

But Gaylord wanted to say more than goodbye. "Miss Thompson?"

"Yes, dear?"

"I wondered if you'd like to marry me when I grow up?"

"I'd love to." She ruffled his hair. "But I shall be too old for you, my dear."

He looked doubtful. "Well, don't marry anyone else, anyway."

She was silent. "There's no fear of that," she said in a small voice.

She got into the car, looking back as they moved away at a forlornly waving Gaylord.

By the time Jocelyn reached Ingerby, the street lamps were lit, and Miss Thompson's bijou residence looked dark and cold. "I'll just see you in," he said, holding the front gate for her. She went ahead, and unlocked the front door. "Do come in," she said. "Let me make you a cup of tea."

"No, really, thank you. I must get back. The roads are still treacherous." They both seemed shy, ill-at-ease.

"Well, if you're sure." She held out a hand, smiled. "Mr. Pentecost, *do* forgive me for being such a nuisance. And thank you for being so patient and for—everything."

"I'm awfully pleased to have met you," he said. "And I'll see you in April." Then he turned and went. She waited while he started the car, then shut the door, and went into the front living room. It felt cold. She soon saw why. The window was smashed. A brick lay on the hearthrug. A piece of paper was fastened to it by an elastic band, on the paper was a crude drawing of a motor cycle.

CHAPTER FIVE

Night. In the river lands, the only lights were those from John Pentecost's farm, and from World's End Cottage.

Julia Mackintosh—curled up under the bedclothes with her most loved possession, her mother's coloured picture book of ballet—was reading it by the light of an electric torch (Aunt Elspeth disapproved of reading in bed). She gazed, fascinated, at pictures she had already devoured a hundred times. Pavlova, Fonteyn; the whole glamorous, thrilling world which she would know only through the pages of an old book. She was like a prisoner gazing out at a bright garden where free men walked.

Yet, being a child, she dreamed. Someone would see her dancing in the meadows, and would spirit her away to Covent Garden— where Nureyev would stride up imperiously to where she stood in the chorus and lead her to the front of the stage to dance the *pas de deux*. Being a child, she dreamed . . . But it was not Nureyev who came with imperious gesture. It was Aunt Elspeth who, stealing unheard into the bedroom and seeing the glow under the bedclothes, snatched the precious book and angrily tore it in two.

Julia, in her fury, bit Aunt Elspeth's hand. A strange act, for so seemingly gentle a child; but to Julia her book was far more than a book—it was her only window onto a life she could never know.

Aunt Elspeth screamed with rage and pain, and was beating Julia ferociously about the head when Duncan burst into the room. He seized his sister, grabbed the book, and saw her bleeding hand. "Ye'd best put some Dettol on that," he said quietly. "Then pack your bags."

"Aye. I will that," she said bitterly; and marched away.

Julia, hanging her head, began slowly picking up the pieces of her book. Her father watched her. "Did your aunt do that?"

The child nodded.

"And did you bite your aunt's hand?"

"Aye." There was no emotion in her big, dark eyes.

Wearily he sat down on the bed. "Oh, lassie, lassie," he said, drawing her close. She held herself stiff; then, slowly, she relaxed against him. "Is Auntie Elspeth really going?"

He nodded. "But who will look after you, child?" It was a bleak prospect. For perhaps the first time in his life Duncan Mackintosh realized that there *were* things that were too much for him.

MAY'S HEADACHE was no better on Sunday morning. Of course, no one realized she had a headache: she was as cheerful as ever, her appearance was as elegant, she saw to every detail of the household. Only Gaylord sensed that something was amiss. The All Seeing Eye was not quite as all-seeing as usual.

May was counting the hours. The visitors wanted to leave straight after lunch; that left two more hours of listening as through a blanket; and of hearing her own responses, courteous and seemingly intelligent, yet uttered without apparent thought.

Two more hours. But here came Mr. Mackintosh, all grim

303

granite, demanding to see her father-in-law. And, ten minutes later, here came her father-in-law. "May, are you busy?"

Since the joint, and the potatoes, and the greens, and the gravy, and the Yorkshire pudding had all reached one perfect moment of togetherness, she could be said to be busy. But she asked, quietly, "What is it, Father-in-law?"

"Mackintosh wants to give in his notice," he said, appalled. "It's damned serious—he's the best man I've ever had."

"Oh, dear. I am sorry."

"It's that sister of his. She's leaving. She's catching the six o'clock train tomorrow morning, and he says he can't be fair to the girl and to me." The old man waited hopefully.

"I see," said May, putting the joint back in the oven. She began to stir the gravy.

"Poor little kid," said Grandpa. "And I can't see he'll be much better off anywhere else."

"No," said May.

"Unless, of course, they lived with the family."

In came Gaylord. "Momma, I'm ever so hungry. Can we—?"

May said, "Your friend Miss Mackintosh is leaving, Gaylord."

"You mean—*really* leaving? Whoopee!" cried Gaylord.

She did not give him long to rejoice. "It means poor little Julia won't have anyone to look after her."

He thought this over. "Couldn't *you* look after her, Momma?"

Grandpa tried to keep the gleam out of his eye.

"It would mean them living here. You wouldn't want a *girl* about the place, would you, Gaylord?" May asked him.

No, he wouldn't. But if poor Julia hadn't anyone to look after her—? "*I* wouldn't mind," he said stoutly.

John Pentecost was looking astonished. "You mean—you'd have them *here*, May? Are you sure, my dear?"

She had just picked up a loaded tray. Now she put it down and looked coolly at her father-in-law. "Such an idea had never occurred to you, had it?"

"Good heavens, no. Still, now you have suggested it. It *would* be a solution, May."

Well, her headache wouldn't last for ever. A good night's sleep, and she'd be as right as rain in the morning.

But she had reckoned without two men, those unpredictable creatures: Jocelyn, who said flatly that *he* wasn't spending the rest of his life in the same house as Aberdeen Angus; the chap would be telling him how to write his novels in no time at all; and Duncan himself. "Mrs. Pentecost, this is most kind, and I can think of no one I would prefer to keep an eye on my lassie," he said. "But I'm a thrawn sort of man, myself, and would be ill at ease. So if I could stay at World's End, and Julia could stay here—I'd take her off your hands as much as I could." He actually smiled. His smile was that of a man who has discovered gratitude in his heart.

Julia was in her Sunday best—a blue coat, buttoning up to the throat, with a fur collar—very stiff, formal and ladylike. "Hello, my dear," said May. "Would you like me to show you where you will sleep when you are here?"

"Yes, please, Mrs. Pentecost."

As soon as the visitors had left, May had remade the bed in the guest room, which she now showed to Julia. "Gaylord's next door, and Mr. Pentecost and I are just across the landing, and look—through the window you can see Daddy's cottage."

Julia clasped her hands. "It's beautiful, Mrs. Pentecost."

"Through the window—you can see Daddy's cottage," said May.

The child looked at her with a touch of fear: May had a curious, set smile on her face. "Through the window you can see—" And she crumpled to the floor.

Gaylord and Jocelyn both heard Julia's screams, and came running. The sight of May lying helpless was curiously horrifying: it was a denial of nature. May was the life force, it was she who raised up the fallen. And if she had now become one of the fallen, then the world had lost its prop.

Jocelyn made a dreadful sound in his throat, and knelt beside her. She was very pale. Desperately he sought for her pulse. Nothing. But then he could never find a pulse, not even his own. Any sort of crisis he'd always left to May. And now? He managed to get a pillow under her head, and ran out onto the landing where Gaylord and Julia stood frozen with shock. Jocelyn telephoned the doctor, then called his father who diagnosed delayed concussion.

"Must have caught her head on something when that damn dog knocked her over."

305

Jocelyn had followed the ambulance with his still unconscious wife to hospital, where she was to stay under observation. He watched her with desperate concern.

John Pentecost determined to devote himself to his young charges. He said, "I tell you what. I'll have a game of 'Monopoly' with you if you promise not to worry." But nobody played very well: Gaylord, because he was following the ambulance along the Ingerby Road, and watching them slide that shrouded object that was unaccountably Momma out at the other end, just as they had slid it in *so* horribly at this; Julia, because her sweet nature lacked the dedicated ruthlessness the game demands; and Grandpa because he had a lot on his mind. He was truly sorry about May, but he didn't relish Jocelyn getting his meals for him. There must be someone who'd look after an old man, he thought pathetically. But there wasn't. It was at this low ebb in John Pentecost's thoughts that the telephone rang.

Wendy Thompson had looked at the broken window with a sense of fear and physical revulsion. She had telephoned the police, who came and seemed relatively unimpressed, even when she told them about the motor cyclist in the river lane; she slept badly, and spent Sunday wondering whether she ought to tell the Pentecosts.

There might be no connection. Mr. and Mrs. Pentecost might well think it was just an excuse to continue an acquaintance. On the other hand, it might be important to them to know that this menace still existed.

Decision-making was not easy. It was evening before she telephoned, hoping against hope that Mr. Jocelyn Pentecost would answer.

It was the boy—breathless, tense. "Hello. Who's that?"

"Is that Gaylord? It's Wendy Thompson. You remember me?"

"Course. I thought you were Poppa. He's taken Momma into hospital—she's unconscious."

"Oh, no! But how—?"

"When Schultz knocked her over. She must have banged her head."

"I *am* sorry, Gaylord. Could I please speak to your Grandpa?"

Grandpa remembered Miss Thompson—a nice woman. Yes, it would be a pleasure to speak to her again.

"John Pentecost here, Miss Thompson." No sucking dove ever cooed more sweetly.

She said, "Oh, Mr. Pentecost, I'm so sorry to hear your news. Is it serious, do you think?"

"Well, I'm afraid it will mean some time in hospital."

"How difficult for you all! Is one of your visitors staying on?"

"No. They'd already left. And of course they all have commitments, anyway." She heard a sigh. "Oh, we shall manage well enough. It's the children—especially the young baby."

"Well, I *am* sorry. If there *is* anything I can do—?"

He was deeply touched. "My dear Miss Thompson! How *very* kind. But I wouldn't think of asking you. No, we shall get by somehow. It won't hurt Jocelyn and me to rough it a bit."

She couldn't bear to think of Jocelyn Pentecost roughing it a bit. "I'm not a very capable person. But I should be only too pleased if there was something—"

The old man said firmly, "No, Miss Thompson. You have your own life to lead. Our problems are not insuperable."

"I do mean it, Mr. Pentecost."

"You do? You really do? I'll pick you up in half an hour then," said John Pentecost. "Where do you live?"

She told him. "Pack your things," he said and put down his receiver.

His capitulation had been both unexpected and sudden. Now, suddenly, Wendy Thompson seemed to have a household on her hands, including two men and a baby. And what did *she* know of either men or babies? She would do it, and gladly: it would be an honour to be able to help a man like Jocelyn Pentecost, and it might be an opportunity to work on Julia's stubborn father. But it frightened the life out of her.

John Pentecost was well pleased with himself. A few minutes ago, the future had looked bleak and uncomfortable; now, thanks to his decision and tact, the *status quo* was restored. He said, "I have to go out the moment your father returns, Gaylord."

Gaylord listened. "There's Poppa's car, now." He tore out of the front door. "Poppa! How's Momma?"

Jocelyn slipped an arm about his shoulders. "She'll be all right. She's all tucked up, ever so comfortable."

To his father he said, "She's still unconscious, and they're—not committing themselves."

"I'm sorry, Jocelyn."

His son looked forlorn. "We're in a hell of a mess, Father. And I just don't know how we're going to cope with Amanda."

The old man clapped his hand on his son's shoulder. "Everything's arranged, boy. I'm just off to bring help: housekeeper, nursemaid, call her what you will."

"Who?" Jocelyn was amazed. *He'd* been trying to think of someone all the way home, but there wasn't anyone.

"Wendy Thompson," said Grandpa smugly. "She volunteered. Look. I must go, she's waiting."

"Father, we *can't* have Wendy Thompson."

"Why not?"

Jocelyn didn't know why not. But when you've been married eight years, the heart has its reasons that the reason knows not of. He simply knew that May would just as soon have a boa constrictor about the house during her absence as little, inoffensive, not-terribly-attractive Miss Thompson.

John went, and Jocelyn had never felt so lonely in his life. The doctor had been fairly reassuring. Just a case of keeping her under observation, my dear fellow. But doctors could be wrong, especially when it came to blows on the head. It was unbelievable that only yesterday morning she had stood, radiant and beautiful, in the snow.

Gaylord slipped his hand into Poppa's. Suddenly he wanted to cry and cry. But he didn't. He mustn't upset Poppa.

"Julia and I can bath Amanda, Poppa," he said. "Can't we, Julia? And isn't it a good thing Momma was weaning her. We can give her her bottle, and put ourselves to bed. So if you just get Grandpa's and your supper, that will be everything. Julia and I can wash the dishes tomorrow."

Jocelyn looked at his son in astonishment. "When did you think all this out?"

"I didn't, Poppa. It sort of came."

Well, he supposed some were born organizers, and some weren't. He wandered into his study, slumped into his chair. He thought of all the days he had sat here so industriously writing, happy in the knowledge that May was bustling about the kitchen. If only those days would return, how he would revel in his wife's every smile, how his heart would leap whenever he heard her singing at her work! Never again, *never*, would he take such things for granted, if only—Come back, come back, oh days of long ago!

He heard his father's voice on the landing. "Now you may as well have your old room, Miss Thompson. Here you are." And then Miss Thompson: "Thank you. I do hope I shall be able to cope."

"Of course you will."

Jocelyn erupted from his room. "Father, can I—? Oh, hello, Miss Thompson. Father, can I have a word?"

"Of course, dear boy. You just sort yourself out, Miss Thompson." He followed Jocelyn into the study. He was in a strong position: by the time Jocelyn had said his say, Miss Thompson's nightie would be laid on her pillow, and her toothbrush perched in the tooth mug. And if all that didn't add up to a *fait accompli*, he'd like to know what did.

Jocelyn shut the study door. "Father, we can't *do* this."

"My dear boy." He put a hand on his son's arm. "It'll take her mind off her own troubles." He looked very moved. "Do you realize, Jocelyn, that that poor, lonely woman lost her mother only last month, and hasn't a soul in the world?"

"But—" Jocelyn was silent. He had another reason, one he had not really formulated to himself: ridiculous though it sounded, Miss Thompson was emotionally attracted by an author whose work she greatly admired. But he couldn't say this to his father. So he said firmly, "Well, I'll agree to her giving a hand with the children. But you and I can look after ourselves, Father."

"Of course we can, dear boy. Now. What are you giving us for supper?"

Jocelyn went off miserably to take a look in the kitchen. To him, the cooking of anything more exotic than a boiled egg was shrouded in a mystique he had never attempted to pierce. So in spite of himself he was very relieved when Miss Thompson came in, looking scared but helpful. "Now, Mr. Pentecost. Just let me ask about Mrs. Pentecost. Then tell me what I can do."

Jocelyn told her what little he knew about May; then said severely, "Look, did my father bulldoze you into this?"

She laughed. "Bulldoze me? I had the greatest difficulty in persuading him to let me come."

"You mean it was actually your suggestion?"

Her eyes were grey, and clear, and honest. "Of course, I'd love to do anything I can. If *you'd* like me to."

He said, "Quite frankly, I really don't know what I should do without some help. But that doesn't mean—"

"Then that's settled," she said. She was curiously excited. "You've got enough to worry about," she went on, "and something rather unpleasant happened last night." She told him about the smashed window. "So it's really rather nice to be out of the house for a day or two."

He felt very protective. "Miss Thompson, how very nasty for you. And—you think it's all connected with that motor cyclist?"

She was silent. "Since you ask," she said at last. "Yes. But—it's not your fault."

She was wrong. He knew it *was* their fault. His father had answered violence with violence. And from the old man's one act of violence the ripples were spreading out even as they had spread out from the submerged motor bike. He said, "We're all to blame. The world is as we have made it."

"No. Not you, Mr. Pentecost. You're so—good."

"Good? Me?" He was genuinely amused. "What does my middle class morality amount to? All over the world, people are starving to death. And do I really care, so long as they do it quietly, and don't trouble me?"

"But you can't take everybody's troubles on your shoulders."

"I don't see why not. Sometimes I remind myself that there are millions who would give everything they possess for one of the three meals I take for granted every day. Do I care?"

She looked at him with awe. "Mr. Pentecost, there are not many people doing more for humanity than writers like you—"

John Pentecost put his head round the door. He looked round the kitchen and said rather dubiously, "Supper about ready, is it?"

"I'm afraid it's not quite, Mr. Pentecost." Miss Thompson said with a little chuckle. "We've been discussing middle class morality instead of getting on with things, haven't we, Mr. Pentecost."

"Good God," said Grandpa, and disappeared back into the living room. "Don't know what the world's coming to," he muttered, angrily squirting soda into his whisky.

Jocelyn showed Wendy where things were, then said nervously, "Would you mind if I just go and telephone the hospital?" He loped off. When he came back he looked between tears and laughter. "She's conscious. They say I can see her for a few minutes. So—would you mind awfully if I left you to—?"

"Of course not," she said.

"Oh, good. Right." He looked round rather helplessly. "I'll get over there."

Then, without a backward glance, he was gone.

CHAPTER SIX

It was awful. Bed after bed, each containing a lady. Jocelyn didn't like to stare, but somewhere inside this assortment of Marks and Sparks nighties was his May, and he *had* to find her.

"Hey! Jocelyn!" called a voice. Yes, there she was. But how different she looked, in these drear surroundings. He hurried across.

"Jocelyn, you ass, that's not me," came the voice again. He checked, stared. The lady for whom he had been heading grinned, shook her head. "There's a pity. Been raising my hopes nicely, hadn't you, boyo."

He said, "I do beg your pardon," and veered a few points. And there at last was May, pale but beautiful. "You can talk to her if you'd rather," she said. The two women grinned cheerfully at each other.

He went and kissed her. Love and tenderness flowed out of him. He sat down, took her hand. "Darling, how are you? I've been *so* worried," he said anxiously.

"Oh, I'm fine. I just don't know what all the fuss is about. How are the children, and how are you, my darling?"

"Don't you worry about us. We're managing splendidly. But— are the doctors *really* satisfied with you?"

"Of course. Don't worry so." She gave him a too brilliant smile. She squeezed his hand, and he could feel the nervous tension in her grip. "Now listen carefully, I've got everything organized. I bullied them into bringing me the telephone trolley, and I rang up Elspeth Mackintosh."

"Elspeth *Mackintosh*?"

She misinterpreted the horror in his voice. "Oh, it wasn't easy. But when she'd rubbed my nose in the dust long enough, she agreed to unpack and move in tomorrow."

"But—?" he said.

"Oh, I know it's not ideal. But you *will* all be looked after." She lay back, and waited for the applause.

It didn't come. She looked at him sharply. He said, "As a matter of fact, May, it sounds an ideal arrangement, and it is wonderful of you to have done all this. I really do appreciate it."

"But—?" she said. He heard the tinkle of ice.

"Well, Father's gone ahead—you know Father—he's brought Miss Thompson in to housekeep. Sort of," he finished lamely.

"And she's actually installed?" He nodded. There was a long silence. "How very obliging of Miss Thompson," May said at last, in a rather tight voice. "The fact that I happen to have a jealous nature doesn't make it an any the less satisfactory arrangement."

"My dear May, you're *not* jealous of Miss T? A splendid woman like you, jealous of that fragile little creature?"

"That's what I'm afraid of, her fragility. Every man in the house has been just yearning to comfort and protect her, ever since she arrived. Even Gaylord. Still—" to his astonishment her eyes filled with tears "—so long as she sees my children fed, and looks after you, my darling—"

"May, don't torment yourself. You trust *me*?" he said hopefully.

"As much as I'd trust Amanda with the bleach," she said coolly. She took his hand and clung to it rather desperately, then said, "I *can* rely on you to telephone Miss Mackintosh and tell her she won't be needed after all?"

"Of course, darling."

"Frankly, I'm not sorry—I think she'd have established a dictatorship. But you will thank her, and apologize?"

"I will."

"Good. Now. The joint's in the fridge and there should be enough for you to have it cold for lunch tomorrow." She gave him a complete resumé of the household situation. Then she said, "But, darling, you will—help with Amanda? You know, I think I envy her Amanda almost as much as I envy her you." She looked bleak.

They stared at each other gravely. "Poor old May," he said.

"Why? Because I've got to give up for a few days something she has never had and may never have?"

It was his turn to be silent. Then he said, "Bless you, May."

A nurse appeared at the end of the ward, and rang a surly, sullen bell. It was time to go.

GAYLORD AND MISS THOMPSON had done a splendid job. Julia was already in bed, while Amanda—clean, warm, full of babyfood and bonhomie was snuggled drowsily against Miss Thompson's arm. Outside the warm room, the earth lay silent under its snow. Miss Thompson was in heaven. To hold this happy little creature in her arms was her moment of paradise. She looked across at Gaylord, sturdy and grave. She tried to imagine what it must be like to be May Pentecost, mother of these two, and wife to Jocelyn.

Gaylord, much as it went against his principles, said, "I think perhaps you ought to tell me to go to bed, Miss Thompson." To go to bed *without* being told was, of course, unthinkable.

"Do you, Gaylord? Right, off you go, I'll bring you up some milk."

She put a caressing hand on his head, put Amanda down, and went to the kitchen. When she came back with his milk he was perched up in bed in his red pyjamas, sleek of hair and scrubbed of face. "Is Poppa home?"

"Not yet, dear."

He sounded forlorn. "I hope Momma's all right."

"She will be." She longed to comfort him. "Night, night, darling." He held up his face to be kissed. She peeped into the nursery, where her other babe was sleeping peacefully. With a full heart, she tiptoed downstairs.

JOCELYN CAME HOME and went up to tell Gaylord of May's improvement. Over supper, Wendy said little, sensing his weariness. But afterwards she said, "It was wonderful for me, finding Julia. Is her father living here, too?"

"No, I think he's staying on at the cottage."

"Oh, well, he'll be around. I want to get that gentleman in a corner and talk to him."

The idea of anyone getting Duncan Mackintosh in a corner—especially anyone as diminutive as Miss Thompson, filled Jocelyn with amazement. "Did you know his wife was a ballet dancer?" Wendy went on. "He won't let Julia follow in mother's footsteps, and it'll break the child's heart. Still—I haven't worked on him properly yet."

He looked at her small, resolute jaw, and marvelled. But he was never one to underrate the power of women. She said, "What are you smiling at?"

"I was just feeling a little male sympathy for Duncan Mackintosh. But seriously, Miss Thompson, I wish you luck."

"Thanks." Then she asked the question she had been longing to ask ever since his return. "Did you tell Mrs. Pentecost I was here?"

"Yes. She's so grateful to you."

Wendy was silent. She didn't somehow think that gratitude would be Mrs. Pentecost's prime emotion.

Only Wendy Thompson heard the sound of the motor cycle in the lane. And snuggled deliciously in her bed. For almost the first time in her life, there were men in the house in which she slept; danger was no longer her responsibility. Besides, there were plenty of motor cycles around nowadays. No reason to assume it was her tormentor. She quickly drifted back into sleep.

Only Schultz heard the footsteps in the stackyard. He began to bark joyously. Now the latch on the door of Schultz's outhouse was being lifted. Schultz bounced forward eagerly to meet his new playmates. . . .

No one heard the silence when Schultz's barking ceased. Not even Gaylord. He slept peacefully, knowing that Momma would soon be home again; and that until that happy day came his dear Miss Thompson would be looking after him.

WENDY THOMPSON was preparing breakfast when Miss Elspeth Mackintosh marched in at the back door, dumped down a suitcase, and looked Wendy up and down aggressively. "Aren't you the schoolteacher who's always blethering about Julia and ballet school?"

"I am Julia's teacher," Wendy said bravely. "And I do think it will be a very great shame if she is not allowed to follow her bent."

"You do? And what are you doing with that frying pan, may I ask?"

"Mr. John Pentecost asked me to lend a hand—"

"Aye? Well, Mrs. Pentecost asked me to take over while she's in hospital. So ye can awa' hame."

"I'm hanged if I'll awa' hame."

Elspeth's rage then was cold as ice. Mrs. Pentecost's cry for help had meant she could stay on without losing face. She could knock a bit of discipline into the boy, and give the dreamy Jocelyn Pentecost the dusting around he so sorely needed. Power was in Elspeth's grasp, and she wasn't having any pale schoolteacher taking it from her. She said, "Don't you adopt that line with me, Miss Thompson. Everything's arranged."

Wendy felt quite capable of hitting Miss Mackintosh over the head with the frying pan. She was delivered from this temptation by the entry of Gaylord. "I thought you'd gone," he said in a disappointed voice.

"No. Your mother asked me to stay and look after you all."

"But Miss Thompson's looking after us." Momma, do a thing like that? Never! Momma would never put him and Poppa in *this* woman's charge.

Gaylord had left the door open. Julia came dancing through it on her toes, smiling.

She went down on her heels. The smile faded. "Aunt—I thought—?"

"Aye. You thought I'd go and leave you uncared for. Not me, lassie. I've got a heart in my body," she said virtuously.

It was at this fraught moment that Jocelyn Pentecost came warily into the kitchen.

THERE HAD BEEN only one thought in Jocelyn's head when he awoke: to telephone the hospital. He put through the call: Mrs. Pentecost was "satisfactory". The telephone had awakened an unidentified memory. He had to telephone—but whom?

Then the awful truth flooded in on him. Miss Mackintosh! The train from Shepherd's Warning had gone an hour ago, and she would not be on it, simply because he had forgotten to ring her. Far worse, she'd probably be lording it in the Pentecost kitchen.

He marched downstairs in his dressing gown. The dreaded Elspeth viewed him with a disapproval that amounted to contempt. "Lord save us, Mr. Pentecost, and is that the way to appear before two spinster ladies?"

Spinster lady yourself, thought Wendy. She said, "Mr. Pentecost, will you tell Miss Mackintosh that your father asked me—"

Jocelyn said, "Miss Mackintosh, I'm most terribly sorry. I should have telephoned you yesterday evening, but—I believe the 10.40 from Ingerby does connect with the London to Glasgow express."

"I am catching no train, Mr. Pentecost. Mrs. Pentecost asked me to stay and stay I will."

Wendy said, "If you really wish Miss Mackintosh to stay, Jocelyn, then there is no point in my staying."

"There is no question of your going," said Jocelyn. He turned to Elspeth. "As I explained, it was all a mistake. But for me, you'd have been on that train now."

Duncan Mackintosh came in, stamping the snow from his boots. "Och, it was cold before sunrise. I've been inspecting the drainage in ten-acre." He looked at the dishevelled Jocelyn. "You've no objection to my taking my meals here, as Mrs. Pentecost suggested?"

"Well, as a matter of fact—" began Jocelyn.

But Duncan wasn't listening. He seemed in an unusually good humour this morning. He hugged Julia and said, "And what are you doing here, Miss Thompson, wielding a frying pan instead of a primer?"

Jocelyn said, "There's been a mix-up, for which I am afraid I'm responsible."

Duncan looked as though *that* didn't surprise him. At this moment Grandpa appeared. "Morning, Miss Thompson. My breakfast ready yet?"

Wendy said, "It would have been. Only Miss Mackintosh seems to think she's in charge."

Jocelyn explained once more. "Well, that's soon settled," said Grandpa. "Miss Mackintosh can look after the children, and Miss Thompson after the cooking."

316

"I don't *want* Miss Mackintosh to look after me. I want Miss Thompson." That was Gaylord.

"Mrs. Pentecost put me in charge, and in charge I will be," said Elspeth.

Grandpa said, "*I* put Miss Thompson in charge. And in charge *she* will be. And it's *my* house," he finished, bristling.

Wendy said, "If Miss Mackintosh really wishes to do all the cooking, I shall be very happy to look after the children."

"Oh, very well." He turned and stabbed a finger at Elspeth. "But I will not eat haggis, mind."

She said contemptuously, "Och, I ken fine what the English eat. Dinna fash yerself, man."

So taken aback was John Pentecost by this curt dismissal that he stumped off to the living room. He was a little put out to find that the fire had not yet been lit, but he didn't complain; one couldn't expect everything to go like clockwork immediately. After all, he reflected with some satisfaction, it wasn't every man in this sort of situation who would have *two* women fighting for the honour of looking after him. It couldn't all be his tact and courtesy. It must also, he decided, have something to do with his personal magnetism.

But on the lower deck there was near mutiny. As soon as breakfast was over, Julia, Gaylord and the faithful Henry began digging.

"And what have you been doing, Gaylord?" asked Miss Thompson later on that morning.

"Well, we started digging an Aunt Elspeth trap. But then we decided not to."

Wendy stifled the question "why?" and just smiled understandingly.

Gaylord said, "So we dug a bit deeper and went to Australia instead. Miss Thompson, I've lost Schultz. His door was open, and he's gone."

"Well, he can't be far away, can he? Shall we go and look for him?"

"*Oh, yes*, Miss Thompson."

They set off briskly through the snow, in the morning sunshine. They kicked up the snow with their wellies, they laughed, they chattered. "One man went to mow," they sang. "Went to mow a

317

meadow." Their hearts, even Wendy's, were light and gay as the hearts of children.

But they didn't find Schultz.

THE FOOD AT LUNCHTIME was copious, nourishing and enjoyable. Elspeth, having served everyone, went and sat herself down in May's chair. This irritated and distressed Jocelyn; though he had to admit there was nowhere else she could sit.

Gaylord was less fair-minded. He said hotly, "That's Momma's chair."

"And Momma's in hospital," Elspeth said coolly.

"But it's *Momma's* chair." He was crying.

This wasn't like Gaylord at all. Jocelyn, secretly sympathizing, said sternly, "Stop being silly, Gaylord."

To everyone's astonishment Duncan Mackintosh rose, went and nudged his sister out of her seat. "Change places, lass." They all watched with bated breath.

Elspeth sat tight. Then, slowly, she picked up her plate and went and sat in Duncan's place. "Pandering to a neurotic child," she muttered.

"What's neurotic?" asked Gaylord, interested in spite of his tears.

"You are," said Elspeth.

"Oh no he's not," said Wendy. "*I* think he's been very brave."

More than ever did Gaylord want to marry Miss Thompson. He smiled tearfully. Duncan sat down. "Is that better, laddie?"

"Yes, thank you," said Gaylord.

Duncan addressed himself to the old man. "Mr. Pentecost, I wanted to store some potatoes in the small outhouse, but there's a Mini in the way. Do you know anything about it?"

"Oh, dear," said Wendy. "It's mine. The garage people are supposed to be collecting it today."

"Aye. Well, if they've not been by this evening, I'll have a look at it for ye."

"That's awfully kind of you," said Wendy.

As, on a cloudy day, a thin gleam of sunshine will flit for a moment across the high corries of the mountains, so now something that could almost be called a smile flickered over Duncan's features. "I'm thinking of my potatoes, Miss Thompson," he said.

318

CHAPTER SEVEN

The day passed, and the group of comparative strangers who now inhabited the farmhouse already began to take on a certain cohesion, to decide that they might as well look for each other's good points, if any.

Gaylord, really worried now that Schultz had not appeared at feeding time, formed himself into a search party, complete with rope, electric torch, and dog biscuits. John Pentecost went and snoozed in his easy chair before the now bright fire, congratulating himself. Today, without his initiative, he and Jocelyn might well have been facing each other miserably across a plate of cold mutton. Instead, after a splendid breakfast, and an excellent lunch, here came Elspeth bustling in with what she called a "fly cuppie": a pot of tea, fortified with an assortment of baps, scones and pancakes. This was to keep him going until high tea: like all her race, Miss Mackintosh believed that the human frame cannot survive unless it is nourished at two-hourly intervals.

Jocelyn went to visit his wife.

May was less buoyant today. "Darling," she greeted him. "You look pinched and hungry. Has that woman not fed you?"

"Actually," he said, "I had egg and bacon for breakfast, then a fairly substantial meal at eleven—brought, mark you, to my study —and an excellent lunch at one."

There was a long silence. "Are you asking me to give in my notice?" she said at last.

"No." He laughed. "You have other qualities which the dreaded Elspeth lacks, my love."

"Elspeth? But she's in Scotland."

It was his turn to be silent. "I forgot to tell her," he said at last.

"Jocelyn. You idiot. So you had to get rid of Miss Thompson instead?"

"No. They're both there."

Silences, it seemed, were the order of the day. At last she said, "And which of my duties has little Wendy taken over?"

"The comfort and solace of your children."

"Not the comfort and solace of my husband?"

"No."

"Honestly," she said. "I'm out of the way for five minutes, and you get *two* of them running after you. How *are* the children?"

"Fine. Gaylord's a bit worried because Schultz has gone off again. Oh, and he took considerable umbrage when Elspeth sat in your chair."

"Bless him. Quite right too."

"How *are* you feeling, May?"

"Frustrated. Bloody-minded. Jealous." Suddenly she drummed her fists on the bedclothes. "I want to get out of here."

"Have they given you any idea?"

"No. There are still some tests they've got to take—I'll just have to wait, I'm afraid."

"TELL ME ABOUT your mother," said Wendy.

Julia, sitting at her feet, her arm across Wendy's knee, stared at the carpet. "She was ever so pretty," she said.

"Did you ever see her dance?"

"No. But—one night—she came in when I was reading, and—" Now the dark eyes were looking up solemnly at Wendy.

"And—?" said Wendy.

"She'd put on her ballet dress—bodice, tutu, shoes, everything. And combed back her hair. Oh, she—" the child's hand gripped Wendy's knee. "She was the most beautiful thing I shall ever see."

"What did she do?"

"She just stood there, smiling down at me. And she had diamonds in her hair. They sparkled in the candlelight."

Wendy, strangely moved, could see it all: the homely bedroom; the wonder and love in the child's eyes; the woman, moved by who knows what hunger or frustration to try to recreate a beauty that was past.

"What happened?" she said.

"She said, 'One day, Julia, you will look like this. Only more beautiful.' Oh, I wanted to jump out of bed and hug and kiss her. But she was so—strange. I was shy, and afraid."

"So you didn't?"

"No. But I always wish I had." She was thoughtful. Then: "She died soon after," she said in a matter of fact voice.

"SCHULTZ!" cried Gaylord. "Schultz! Where are you, boy?"

The afternoon stayed silent and still. Melting snow, black trees, a brooding sky. A heron flew lazily into the still reeds. Nothing else moved in the whole wide world. Gaylord trudged on through the darkening afternoon, anxious and cold at heart.

He came to the river. The water ran black and chill. "Schultz," he called. "Schultz!" The river moaned, and sighed. That, and the cold dripping of the snow, were the only sounds. Gaylord peered down into the swirling waters. There was a piece of weed, drifting and curling, brown, in shape almost like an ear.

To any small boy, any water weed has only one purpose: to be prodded. Gaylord found a stick and prodded the piece of weed. It had a curiously heavy texture. And when he looked closer, it seemed to be attached to something, large and brown, that heaved very slightly with the current.

Gaylord walked home, gravely and thoughtfully. "Poppa," he said, "I think—"

"What, boy?" his father said gently.

"I think Schultz is in the river," said Gaylord. And just managed to reach the bathroom before he vomited his heart up.

Jocelyn, heavy-hearted, telephoned the police. They said they would deal with poor Schultz, but they were unimpressed by suggestions that the affair could be connected with their other inquiries.

Gaylord wanted to go and watch. "*Please*, Poppa," he said.

Jocelyn gave in. The child would grow up in an increasingly brutal and bitter world, he thought sadly. So he might as well see the results of violence early. "I'll come with you," he said.

The police worked by the light of car headlamps. The water looked black and oily, the snow starkly white. Gaylord held Poppa's hand very tight. "Don't look, son," called the sergeant as they prepared to pull the dog out. Jocelyn put a hand over Gaylord's eyes, but Gaylord pulled it away angrily and stared. Up came Schultz, limp and lifeless, water pouring from him and out of him. Gaylord made a little noise in his throat, but remained silent. "Bleeding throat cut," muttered someone. "Shut up," said an angry voice. They covered Schultz with a blanket, put him in a van, drove him away. This was the first time Gaylord had seen a dead friend. Though he would never have admitted it to a soul, he rather wished he hadn't come. For he knew that the dead Schultz would be with him all his days.

GAYLORD SAID, "I bet Schultz is in Heaven now." He had a beatific vision of Schultz doing his window-cleaner act against St. Peter, while the Pearly Gates rattled to the thumping of his tail.

"Aunt Elspeth says animals don't go to Heaven," said Julia. She caught Wendy's eye. "But *I* think she's wrong."

Gaylord thought it was just the mean sort of thing Miss Mackintosh *would* say. Nevertheless, it depressed him. "Well, I bet Schultz will, anyway," he said loyally.

At that moment Duncan Mackintosh came in. "I see your car's still there, Miss Thompson," he said without preamble, but gazing down at Julia, who had come running into his arms. "I'll take a look at it for you."

"Oh, thank you, Mr. Mackintosh. Can I come and hold things?"

"Ye might as well." Gently he released himself from his daughter, and went out of the room.

She ought to help. But she couldn't leave Gaylord to his nightmare thoughts. She said, "Let's all go. But wrap up well."

They ran hand in hand to the outhouse. Inside, an inspection lamp cast black shadows about a beamed roof, lit brilliantly the earth floor. Duncan had got the bonnet up, and was touching wires and points with gentle precision.

Wendy got into the car and turned the starter. It made a flat, grinding noise, sounding to her as though the car were in its death agony. But Duncan seemed unperturbed.

"Is it serious?" Wendy asked.

"No. You wouldn't understand, so I may as well save my breath to cool my porridge. But it'll take about an hour. Then I'll straighten that wing for you."

"*Thank you*, Mr. Mackintosh."

"Och, it's nothing. Now if you can hold the lamp so—?"

In the flickering light of the inspection lamp, Julia looked wonderingly round the barn. "What shall we play at?" she said.

Gaylord didn't think he wanted to play at anything. He said, "They wrapped him in a blanket. Like they did Momma."

Julia wanted to cheer him up. "I know," she said, leaping to her feet with a very creditable *entrechat*, considering she was wearing Wellingtons. "Let's do a *pas de deux*."

"What's a pahdidah?" asked Gaylord glumly.

"Dancing. See." She took his hands. "I stand so, and you—"

Gaylord was affronted. Boys didn't dance. He stood, feet firmly planted on the English earth, arms grimly folded. Yet it was at this defiant moment that he had an idea so exciting that it drove out his nightmare memories; and what gave him this brilliant idea was the sight of Miss Thompson and Mr. Mackintosh standing with their heads close together under the bonnet of the car.

Miss Thompson was saying, "Did you see that *entrechat* of Julia's? Most children would have done a hop skip and jump. She's a born dancer, Mr. Mackintosh."

He ignored her. "See if you can find a washer," he said. "I dropped it down there somewhere."

She found it. "She's got the right figure. *And* the right temperament."

He said, "Miss Thompson, I think you are the most irritating woman I have ever met."

"I know I can be," she said. "But it's only when I get a bee in my bonnet." She took a deep breath. "I know I shouldn't say this, Mr. Mackintosh. But—it's what your wife wanted."

He straightened up, stared at her. In the stark light from the lamp, his eyes glinted out of deep shadows. "I'll thank you to keep Jeannie's name out—" he began furiously; and broke off. "How do you know?" he said quietly.

"The child told me." She repeated Julia's story, yet hating herself for twisting the knife in his wounds. She said, "I know I've said a lot of things I shouldn't. But it's only for Julia's sake."

"*My* daughter," he reminded her bitterly. "Just try the engine again."

She turned the starter. The engine ran sweetly. He began hammering, tapping at the wing of the car. The noise precluded conversation. At last he said coldly, "That'll do."

"Thank you," she said. "It's been very kind of you."

He pulled on his jacket. They would both be thankful to go their separate ways: she because she knew she had said quite enough for one evening; he because, ridiculous though he knew it to be, this woman had shaken the convictions by which he had lived.

But: "Where are the children?" she said.

"Probably slipped out while I was hammering. You go and open the door. Then I'll unplug the lamp."

She crossed to the door, lifted the latch. The door would not open. "Hurry up!" he called.

"I can't get it open," she said.

"Oh, let *me* do it." He strode across, pushed. Pushed again. The door would not budge. "It's locked," he said, surprised.

"Perhaps they did it for a joke," said Wendy. "Gaylord," she shouted. "Come and unlock this door. At once, do you hear!" She was beginning to feel panicky.

"Joke!" he muttered.

A terrifying thought struck Wendy: *I might have to spend the night here with him.* In an agony of embarrassment she said, "There *must* be some way." She heard the nervousness in her voice.

"Of course there's a way, woman. Smash the door down. But I don't want to damage property if that boy's just playing a *joke*. We'll go and sit in the car until he tires of it."

"I'd rather wait here," she said.

"You'd be quite safe," he said contemptuously.

She supposed, miserably, that she'd given him the right to speak to her like that. She said humbly, "I only meant—I could call from here." She bent down to the keyhole. "Gaylord. Come and open this door."

The country night stayed silent. She walked across to her car and joined him in the front seat. He said, staring hard in front of him, "I'm sorry—my last remark was very rude. I'd never thought of myself doing or saying anything so cheap."

"I wouldn't have expected it, knowing you," she said generously.

They sat on. There was nothing left to say.

THE IDEA had flooded like a spring tide into Gaylord's mind. He said, "I've been thinking, Julia."

"Yes, Gaylord?"

"If Miss Thompson married your Poppa, she'd be your mother—

well, stepmother—and Aunt Elspeth could go back to Scotland." It meant, of course, that he himself would have to marry someone else; but for Julia's sake he was prepared to sacrifice all. And it wasn't, frankly, just for Julia. No one would be happier than he to see Miss Mackintosh on the train for Scotland.

She looked at him with sudden, dawning hope. It faded. "They might not want to marry each other."

Gaylord couldn't see why not. Nevertheless, it was a good point, and he considered. He said, "I *think*, if a lady and a gentleman spend a night alone together, they have to get married. It's a Law of Nature."

Julia remained unconvinced. "How do you know?"

"Poppa told me," said Gaylord who, while usually taking his father's pronouncements with a pinch of salt, was always prepared to accept them as *ex cathedra* when it suited his purpose.

"But they *don't* spend the night together," Julia pointed out.

"They would if we locked 'em in," Gaylord said triumphantly.

AT NINE O'CLOCK, Grandpa and Jocelyn were just tucking into another of Elspeth's "fly cuppies", when Duncan marched into the room, followed by Miss Thompson. He stood before the old man, and said formally, "Mr. Pentecost, I have to report breaking down the door of one of your outhouses."

"Well, don't stand there, man, like a bally army sergeant. Sit down and have a cup of tea."

Mackintosh sat down. "I have reason to believe your grandson —and my daughter—locked Miss Thompson and me in," he said.

"Gaylord wouldn't do a thing like that," Jocelyn said without total conviction. "And I'm sure Julia wouldn't."

He went to the door and called his son.

Gaylord and Julia came in, Gaylord looking chagrined to see his plan so obviously in ruins. Julia just looked scared. "Gaylord, did you lock Mr. Mackintosh and Miss Thompson in an outhouse?"

"Yes," said Gaylord. "Sort of," he qualified, not liking the look in his father's eye.

"Why?" said Jocelyn coldly.

It wasn't an easy question. "It's a bit complicated, actually."

"Take your time."

Gaylord had never seen his Poppa so magisterial before. He supposed it was because he was having to stand in for Momma. He said, "If a lady and a gentleman spend a night alone together they have to get married."

"You surprise me," said John Pentecost.

"They *do*, Grandpa," Gaylord said earnestly. "It's a Law of Nature. So I thought if we locked Mr. Mackintosh and Miss Thompson in the outhouse all night they'd have to get married and then Miss Thompson would be Julia's mother and Miss Mackintosh could go back to Scotland. I thought Julia would like that."

Miss Thompson was scarlet. "I'm sorry, Mr. Mackintosh," Jocelyn said. "I'll admit Gaylord often does the wrong thing—but it's always from the highest possible motives."

"I know fine how *I'd* deal with him," Elspeth said grimly.

Jocelyn said quietly, "But it isn't for you to deal with him, Miss Mackintosh. I think it was agreed that Miss Thompson should be in charge of the children. Miss Thompson, would you like to take Gaylord and Julia, and deal with them as you think fit?"

"Come along, children," said Wendy. She looked at Duncan Mackintosh who was staring at one of his employer's hunting prints. She said tartly, "Goodnight, Mr. Mackintosh. It seems we can both congratulate ourselves on a lucky escape."

He turned slowly and looked at her. "Aye," he said.

As soon as they were out of the room, Wendy said, "I am absolutely furious with you both. Gaylord, have you *any* idea how you've humiliated me?"

"I don't see why," said Gaylord sturdily. "I thought you'd have liked to be Julia's mother."

"That's not the *point*," cried Wendy, exasperated.

Gaylord stuck his lower lip out. "Well, *I* think it was a good idea," he said.

WENDY COULDN'T SLEEP, for a number of reasons: her humiliation over that dreadful Mackintosh; her anger with the children; but most of all because she wanted to take a cold, clear look at her feelings for Jocelyn Pentecost before it was too late.

Jocelyn Pentecost! He was a man to whom she could devote her life with complete happiness. But—he was a married man, and if

326

she did not want to destroy her own happiness for ever, the sooner she took to her heels the better.

Wendy lay for a long time, staring up into the darkness.

ON TUESDAY JOCELYN took Gaylord to see his mother. He approached her bed with some trepidation, even when he saw her sitting there, smiling away and holding out her arms to him.

He stood and stared. In his mind she and the dog were strangely mixed: he could not believe now that Momma was alive and smiling, while Schultz was dead, wrapped in a dripping grey blanket.

"Oh, darling," she said, her voice breaking, and it did the trick. He ran into her arms. "Momma, Aunt Elspeth gives us baps and scones with our elevenses."

"Does she, my pet?" She grinned up at Jocelyn, who asked every visiting relative's 64,000 dollar question. "How are you?"

"Fine. Fine. Coming out tomorrow at eleven."

"No!" He felt his features crumpling. "You mean—everything's all right?"

"Perfectly. The doctor says he'd pass me for jet fighters."

They smiled at each other. "I'd rather you came home and looked after the kids and me," he said unsteadily. He began to discuss her homecoming in unnecessary detail: only later did he remember to fish in his coat-pocket for a small parcel. "This came for you this morning."

"For me?" She tore off the outside wrappings. Inside, an inner parcel; and a note. She read it, said: "A thank-you letter from Edouard Bouverie. And will I give the parcel to the little school-teacher whose address he does not know. Most intriguing."

She handed the parcel to Jocelyn. "If you give it to her without finding out what's in it, I'll never forgive you, never."

"I can hardly stand over her while she opens it."

"I don't care how you find out. But I'm fascinated. That little creature's got all you men eating out of her hand. Even Gaylord."

Gaylord actually blushed. "Gaylord has plans for Miss Thompson. Haven't you, old chap?" said Jocelyn.

May looked inquiringly at her son, who said: "I thought it would be nice if she could be Julia's mother. But it means her marrying

Mr. Mackintosh, and I don't think she wants to much. I think—"
He fell silent.

"You think what, dear?"

"Oh, nothing," he said, trying to sound casual.

"You think what, Gaylord?" said Momma.

"I think she'd rather marry Poppa," said Gaylord.

Clang, went the bell. "But she couldn't, could she," said Gaylord reasonably, "because he's married already."

"That bell woman's giving me a look," Jocelyn said nervously.

"She's not the only one," said May. "Gaylord, why do you think Miss Thompson wants to marry Poppa?"

"She sort of looks at him," said Gaylord.

"I see," said May. She kissed them both rather absently. The temptation to defy Sister, Matron, and if need be the entire Health Service, and insist on going home now, was almost overwhelming. But she overcame it. She thought it might give her husband the impression she was jealous.

"I'VE SOME SPLENDID NEWS," said Jocelyn. "May's coming home tomorrow. They can find nothing wrong."

"Mr. Pentecost, I *am* glad." Wendy beamed. She *was* glad; for him, but not for herself. Tomorrow. Tomorrow it would all end: the company, the sweet responsibility for the children, the gentle presence of this man who now smiled at her across the supper table. Tomorrow his wife would walk back into his life; and she, Wendy, would walk out of it, and out of his heart and mind, for ever. He would scarcely notice her passing. And that was how it had to be.

"I can't tell you how grateful we all are to you, Wendy," he said. "You really have been incredibly kind."

The sudden use of her Christian name brought tears to her eyes. She said, speaking slowly to keep her voice steady, staring down very hard at the tablecloth, "You could never understand what a privilege and a pleasure it's been for me to spend a few days among your family."

Jocelyn remembered something. "Oh, I've got a parcel for you from Dorothea's Frenchman. He didn't know your address, so he sent it to May."

She took the parcel in astonishment. "But—are you sure it's for me?"

"Certain."

She unfastened the paper, and found inside a battered shoe box. Inside was a pair of ballet shoes, well worn, and rather shabby. There was also a card, on which was written: "For you, or for your pupil, as you think best. They belonged to a girl who danced at the Bolshoi, long ago. Fight the good fight. E. St. M. B."

It was too sudden, too overwhelming. This kindness, this discovery that she had an ally in what she had assumed must be her private war, simply opened the floodgates. "Excuse me," she said rising, "I—"

"Can I help?" Jocelyn was on his feet, yearning to comfort and protect. But she groped her way, blinded and choked by tears, to the door, and, shook him off almost roughly.

"You—can't—help," she sobbed. "No one—can." And she went through the door and up to her room, clutching the crumpled paper, and the card, and the shoes of the dancer.

THAT NIGHT, Gaylord ran with Schultz in the summer meadows, laughing until his sides ached at the antics of his friend. But then, suddenly, his friend was no longer there, and there was only something wrapped in a grey sodden blanket, and when Gaylord pulled aside the blanket he saw the dead eyes of Momma staring at him out of a marble face. Wendy, hearing his screams, leaped out of bed and went to her door, only to see Jocelyn disappearing into his son's room. She made herself turn, and go back to bed, thinking: tomorrow night I shall say to myself bitterly, "Last night, you could have helped him comfort his son. What more innocent? Yet you didn't. Why? Because of your folly, or your integrity? Or your fear? Whatever the reason, whether noble or base, you will not have the choice again tonight, or tomorrow night, or ever."

DEREK BATES and his friends prowled about the farm. A petrol bomb lay in Derek's pocket. They weren't out to do damage this time. They'd had a few jars at the *Prince of Wales*, and were strangely relaxed. All they wanted was a giggle.

The most humorous thing, it seemed to them, would be to set fire to the hen roost. But while they were looking for it Derek suddenly threw up all over his gear, so they chucked the petrol bomb into an outhouse, where, disappointingly, it failed to explode, and made for home.

THE NEXT MORNING Jocelyn fetched May out of hospital. And by mid-day Miss Thompson was driving sadly along the river road in her little Mini, with the charmingly expressed thanks of Mrs. Pentecost still in her ears, and the memory of Jocelyn saying goodbye while just a little too obviously eager to get back to his wife; and trying hard to be sensible and adult about the fact that Gaylord had not shown up to say goodbye.

This was the spot where that horrible motor cyclist had appeared—so long ago, it seemed. And now a small figure was running towards her. She stopped, ridiculously pleased. "Gaylord! How nice. I thought—" She reached over, opened the passenger door. He climbed in, panting.

He said, "I wish you wouldn't go, Miss Thompson. First Schultz, and then you."

"But you've got your mother back. That's all that matters, isn't it?"

"Course." But he was looking doubtful. "Momma and I sometimes fail to see eye to eye." There was a pause.

Then he said, "I wish you *would* marry Mr. Mackintosh. Then you could be Julia's mother, and live at World's End Cottage, and I could come and have tea sometimes."

"Perfect. There's only one snag," she said.

"I know. You don't want to marry Mr. Mackintosh. That's what I told Momma and Poppa."

"Gaylord! You haven't discussed this with your mother?"

"Sort of. But *I* said you'd rather marry Poppa." He wriggled down more comfortably in his seat. "But you couldn't, could you."

At the back of Wendy's mind had been a foolish hope that one day she might meet this family again. Now she knew it was impossible. It was as though her most shameful longings had been revealed to the wife of the man she had wrongly, yet honourably, loved. She had been going home with heartbreak and loneliness; now she would take shame as well. "What did your mother say?" she asked.

"She said, 'I see'—in that voice she uses when we're failing to see eye to eye."

"I'm not surprised," she said. Then she suddenly turned and kissed him. "Oh, Gaylord, you little chump!"

Well, he didn't understand. But he thought Miss Thompson sounded a bit upset. "Never mind, Miss Thompson. You can always marry me, any time," he said comfortingly.

"Thank you, Gaylord," she said gratefully.

He got out. "Goodbye, Miss Thompson." He walked back along the lane, kicking moodily at the grass that lined the road. He was melancholy. It was strange how two friends, lost in so short a space, could empty the world.

He came home, and went poking about the stackyard, looking for buried treasure. He was too young to be called a conservationist, but he was an ardent protector of milk bottles: Grandpa had told him how scarce they had become. So that when he found one filled with what smelt like petrol, and stuffed with bits of dirty rag, he was incensed. He put the rags in the dustbin, emptied the

331

petrol down the drain, washed the bottle carefully and took it to Momma. "Momma, look what someone left lying about. All full of petrol and stuffed with rags."

"Petrol?" said May. "What did you do with the rags?"

"Put them in the dustbin. And I poured the petrol down the drain and I washed the bottle."

"When it comes to destroying evidence, Gaylord, you are in the premier class."

"Is that good?" he asked hopefully.

"It depends on the circumstances," she said.

Later she told Jocelyn. "It *must* have been a petrol bomb," she said. "But thanks to Gaylord the only evidence is a shining milk bottle—which wouldn't particularly impress the police."

They sat staring into the fire. She said, "They've frightened Miss Thompson twice. They've killed Schultz. And now—a petrol bomb in a stackyard. Jocelyn, they've frightened me."

"It's damnable," he said.

He found to his surprise that the controlled May was quietly weeping. He took her in his arms. "It was so—marvellous, coming home," she said. "And now? They've spoilt everything."

"The destroyers do," he said.

"Oh, yes. Your theory." She managed a smile. "But why? Why do they *want* to destroy?"

"Because of the darkness in our souls," he said.

CHAPTER EIGHT

It was the April meeting of the Ingerby Writers' Club.

Miss Thompson sat in the back row in a state of considerable ferment. She hadn't wanted to come—after Gaylord's revelations she felt that she could never look either Mr. or Mrs. Pentecost in the eye again. But come she had, telling herself it was her job as Speaker Finder to be present. She would keep in the background; with any luck Jocelyn wouldn't even notice her.

He came into the room, looking slightly nervous. Madam Chairman led him to his seat, and opened the meeting, while Jocelyn pulled his notes out of his briefcase and then sat looking rather hard at the members. As though he were searching for someone?

Jocelyn stood up to speak, and spotted her immediately, giving her his gentle, friendly smile. And as soon as the coffee break began he excused himself to Madam Chairman and came and sat beside Wendy. "Miss Thompson, I so much hoped you would be here," he said.

"I wouldn't have missed it for anything," she said. "It was a splendid talk. And how's Mrs. Pentecost?"

"Fine. No repercussions at all."

"And the children? Has Gaylord got over that horrible business of his dog?"

"He still has nightmares. But you know Gaylord. He only tells you as much as he thinks is good for you to know."

Then, suddenly they were silent. She felt longing flood through her, and she looked at him hard, trying to fix this last picture of him in her memory for ever. She said, "It was so kind of you and Mrs. Pentecost to send me those flowers. And, did you know? Your father sent me a large box of chocolates."

"It was the least we could do. Er—Miss Thompson?"

"Yes?"

"My Aunt Dorothea's marrying her Frenchman on the twentieth. We would very much like you to come, if—you would care to."

She was in a sudden panic. "But I couldn't possibly. Weddings are family affairs. I'm not even a friend of the family."

"You're very much a friend of the family, Miss Thompson. We shall send you an invitation and if you don't come we shall all be very disappointed." He rose, gave her a quick smile, and went back to his chair.

SPRING! Such a turmoil of cleaning and furbishing, of painting the April skies and the semi-detacheds, of hanging leaves on the black woodlands, and changing the gunmetal Trent to cloth of silver! And to what end? thought Jocelyn, who had never been world-weary before, and didn't like it. To the overworked birds and the bustling bees, to the travailing sheep and cows, it was just routine. Only man, foolish man, glorified the scene; and hailed absurdly the re-awakening of an earth he seemed all too eager to turn into a hell.

Derek Bates and his pals came out of their semi-hibernation. They polished and tuned and gloated over their machines; they bought new gear and assembled at street corners revving their engines. But Derek's machine gleamed a little less brightly than the others. There were patches of rust. His bike had become an ever-present reminder of his humiliation. And Derek's resentment spread into every fibre of his being.

Spring. Miss Thompson, after much careful thought, said, "Julia, that French gentleman who came to Mr. Pentecost's has sent you a present." She gave her the ballet shoes.

The child looked at them with delight. Wendy said, "They're not to wear, of course. Long ago, before you were born, a lady wore them to dance at the Bolshoi."

The child was still staring entranced at the shoes; Wendy didn't think she'd heard a word.

The next day, Mackintosh was waiting for her in one of the corridors when she finished school. "Miss Thompson, my lassie doesn't wear anyone's cast-offs."

"They're not cast-offs, you silly man," said Wendy, laughing angrily. "They're just a souvenir from someone who is very sad, as I am, that you won't let Julia dance."

"I'm sorry if I seem silly to you," he said stiffly. "But I want what's best for Julia."

"And you think being a typist will be best for her?"

"I didn't say that." He looked round rather helplessly. "Look. Is there somewhere we could talk, Miss Thompson?"

"Of course." She took him into her empty classroom; they both sat down. He was silent so long that she said, "How's Miss Mackintosh? Is she still with you?"

He sat, elbows on knees, watching his hands clasp and unclasp. "Aye, but it's not been a great success, Miss Thompson."

She waited. He said, "I thought I knew what was best for everything and everybody." He slammed his fist into his palm and turned and faced her. "And I do, in my job. But these last months —without Jeannie—it's in what ye might call personal relationships," he said helplessly.

The silence lasted nearly a minute. Then she said, very hesitantly, "If you did ever feel you'd like some information about ballet as a career—I imagine Mr. Bouverie might be very helpful. In fact, I think he'd be only too happy to help financially. But of course," she said hurriedly, "you're the last man to want that."

"Aye. If Julia did go in for ballet, she'd do it the way *I* could afford. I'm not a pauper, Miss Thompson."

"Good heavens, no." She rose. "Well, you must think about it, Mr. Mackintosh. No doubt you'll want to talk it over with your sister."

He too had risen. "I doubt that'll be necessary." Then, with a touch of the old arrogance, "I can make my own decisions, Miss Thompson."

"You don't need to tell me that, Mr. Mackintosh." She held out her hand. "If you do feel you'd like to take this a step farther, let me know. I might be able to be of some help. Goodbye."

"Aye. Thanks. Goodbye." He let himself be steered to the door, vaguely surprised that the interview should be ending here. Wendy shut the door behind him. Then she pirouetted solemnly round the classroom.

JOHN PENTECOST looked at himself in the glass with some complacency. There was no doubt about it. A certain portliness *did* something for a morning coat, gave it something to work on. He turned sideways. Yes. He had the figure of one of those well-groomed blackbirds who so obviously take such a pride in their appearance.

May, dressing, and with a hundred things on her mind, was worried about leaving the house empty. Still, she consoled herself, it was ages now since Gaylord found the petrol bomb. Perhaps their tormentor had found something else to occupy his mind.

At World's End Cottage, Aunt Elspeth poised a hat pin against her skull, and drove it home. The sight of her brother in his grey morning suit and carnation seemed to enrage her. "All this blether about an auld woman who ought to be thinking about hell fire instead of marriage."

He said, adjusting his tie, "You're a hard and intolerant woman, Elspeth."

"Aye. Well, there's one thing I'll tell *you*, Duncan. Ye've soon let the English corrupt *you*. Look at you. If Aberdeen Cattle Market could see you now!" She laughed, harsh and taunting. "And my lady here." Julia had come in, grave and exquisite. "All got up like a tattie-bogle."

Duncan looked at his daughter. "Take no notice of your aunt, child. You're very beautiful, and I'm proud of you."

"Man, that's no way to talk to a child. There'll be no living with her."

"I shall talk to my own daughter as I wish, Elspeth. And, since we are in good time, I shall ask you to go and wait in the car. I've something to say to Julia."

"That ye can't say in front of me?"

"That I'd prefer not to say in front of you, Elspeth."

She went off muttering. All these months, looking after them both, nothing but ingratitude. . . .

Julia looked up at him, scared. He said, awkwardly, "I just wanted to say, lassie. If you're really set on ballet school—I'll give it a wee trial."

She couldn't believe it. She went on looking scared. Then she flung her arms round his neck, pressed her face against his. "Daddy! Daddy!" It was all she could manage.

Gently he unwound her arms, straightened his rumpled carnation. He stared at her, said sorrowfully, "Julia, does it mean *so* much to you?"

"Oh, Daddy! Everything!"

"*I'll* tell your aunt," he said. "Later."

MISS THOMPSON sat, a church mouse, on the back pew of St. Saviour's, Shepherd's Warning. She had come early, so that she could tuck herself away out of sight of the main guests; and so that she could see them arrive.

Monsieur Bouverie, of course, was already in position with his best man. But now the others were beginning to arrive. Miss Thompson's heart gave a great leap as Jocelyn came in, looking unbelievably splendid in his grey morning suit; and on his arm the lovely, smiling May; and, a little way behind, achieving a dignified solemnity all his own, Gaylord.

336

Miss Thompson expected to cry at weddings, but not quite so early in the proceedings; and before she could compose herself a small figure slipped into the pew beside her and whispered, "Miss Thompson, Miss Thompson, Daddy says I can go to ballet school."

Wendy's delighted "No?" was heard all over the church. "Darling, I'm *so* pleased." But here came Elspeth, clucking Julia out of the pew like a bad-tempered hen.

Then, at last, the organ piped up a familiar note. The congregation rose. Dorothea entered on the arm of her brother: she, vague and fluttering, as though racking her brains as to what she'd come for; John, solid as a rock. Edouard St. Michèle Bouverie stepped out of his pew, turned and smiled at his bride. John Pentecost stood back. "Dearly beloved, we are gathered together—" began the priest, speaking the words that have brought more tears to more female eyes than any other words in the language. And not only female. John Pentecost was deeply moved. Little Dorothea! Why, it seemed only yesterday he'd let her share his first cigar. And now, here she was marrying a bally Frog, bless her.

At the reception, Edouard St. Michèle Bouverie bowed low over Wendy's hand. "My dear Miss Thompson."

"*Mes félicitations les plus profondes, Monsieur,*" she said. Then, sotto voce: "Julia's going to ballet school. A thousand thanks."

He looked at her radiant face. He too lowered his voice. "This is wonderful news."

"Yes. And the ballet shoes were what you might call the catalyst." She passed on.

Gaylord, strolling elegantly round the room, met Julia, who shocked him by saying, "Would you like to kiss me?"

"What for?" he asked suspiciously.

Her face was absolutely radiant. "Because I'm going to ballet school, and I just want everybody to kiss me."

Gaylord thought this sounded potty. "Oh, all right," he said grudgingly. He kissed her, wiped his lips. But now, something was happening. People were moving to the big, horseshoe table; laughing, chattering, as they searched for places. But there wasn't much laughter and chatter when Gaylord found *his* place, next to the dreaded Elspeth. And his first glass of champagne was one of the disappointments of his young life. It was horrible!

Yet *not* to drink it was unthinkable: at his age, to be allowed champagne was an event. In this dilemma, it was, surprisingly, Elspeth who came to his rescue. She too sipped her champagne and pursed her thin lips. "Sour, thin stuff," she muttered, and reached for the sugar basin. "Ye want some?" she said to Gaylord.

She gave him two heaped teaspoonsfuls, and stirred. It *was* an improvement. "Aye. There'll be a few uneasy stomachs after that acid stuff," Aunt Elspeth announced with satisfaction.

Gaylord was so grateful that he decided to chat. "Isn't it nice, Julia going to ballet school."

"What's that?" demanded Aunt Elspeth sharply. "Who says she's away to ballet school?"

"*She* does."

"We'll see about that," snorted Elspeth. She speared an anchovy with venom.

After the meal, everyone circulated most delightfully. Edouard Bouverie, smiling and relaxed, thought: it's true. After a few drinks the English can be almost human. He caught the passing Gaylord to him. "Well, my nephew. Did you enjoy the champagne?"

"Not much," said Gaylord frankly. Then, doing his usual balancing act between being truthful and not hurting people's feelings, he said, "It was all right with some sugar in, though."

Edouard shuddered. "Gaylord, now that I am your uncle, will you let me speak freely?"

Gaylord nodded.

Edouard said gravely, "There is a special hell reserved for those who put sugar in good champagne."

Gaylord was impressed; he didn't relish the thought of spending eternity with Aunt Elspeth, however special the hell. However, when he saw Aunt Elspeth having what looked like a very interesting conversation with her brother, he hove to. He didn't *listen*, of course. He just stood where he couldn't help overhearing.

And Elspeth was saying, "So ye've decided to put the wean to dancing?"

"Yes."

338

"And ye didn't think to tell your ain sister?"

"Not at this stage," he said coolly. "I should have told you in good time, Elspeth."

"Aye. And ye ken fine what I should have said. Well, I'll not give ye another chance to affront me, Duncan. I'm awa' the morn."

He said wearily, "I'm grateful for everything you've done for us, Elspeth. But I'll not stand in your way."

Gaylord turned into an intrepid explorer and hacked his way briskly through a jungle of light grey trousers. "Miss Thompson. Miss Thompson. Aunt Elspeth says she's awa' the morn. Does that mean she's leaving?"

"It sounds like it."

"Whoopee," said Gaylord. "Now you'll *have* to marry Mr. Mackintosh and look after Julia."

But before Gaylord could pursue this fascinating subject further, there was a surge towards the door, and Miss Thompson said excitedly, "Come on, the bride's leaving." They went out into the forecourt of the hotel where, it seemed to Gaylord, everybody was behaving very childishly, laughing and chattering and throwing confetti. He preferred to lurk in the background, rightly fearing a bout of kissing. And his prudence was rewarded: Aunt Dorothea was halfway to the airport before she remembered she hadn't said goodbye to her little pickle.

But Miss Thompson knew, sadly, that it would soon be time for *her* to go, too. But just as she was thinking of the loneliness of her house after this bright and happy day, an arm was slipped into hers, and May's voice said, "Come back to the house with us, Miss Thompson. I'm sure you're dying for a cup of tea. And I've never really had a chance to thank you for all you did for us."

"Mrs. Pentecost, I really couldn't. It will be a family occasion."

"Considering that you're Gaylord's intended, I think you could be regarded as family, don't you?" said May. "Now have you got your car, or can we take you?"

ON THAT CALM and perfect April evening, Jocelyn Pentecost, back in slacks and a pullover, sat in the garden with his wife and his father and watched the sun go down. It had been a good day, a happy day. He was as content as he could ever hope to be, now that words, his stock in trade as a writer, had changed from bright jewels to heavy stones.

John Pentecost was feeling rather pleased with himself. It wasn't everyone, he reflected, who'd have been broad-minded enough to let his sister marry a foreigner.

Wendy Thompson was content. She loved children: their darting minds, their gravity, their logical reasoning; and this evening she was with two of the nicest of them, she thought, having a picnic with Gaylord and Julia.

"Momma," Gaylord had said. "Can Julia and I have a picnic?"

"I'd rather you didn't, dear. Not on your own." Not after Schultz. Not with that sense of disaster flaring again at the core of her being.

Wendy said, "If *I* went with them, Mrs. Pentecost? Would you—?"

"Oh, *please*," cried Gaylord and Julia.

So Momma had agreed. And here they were. May and Wendy had cut sandwiches and cake, and found lemonade and glasses. Gaylord had found an old travelling rug to sit on, so that Miss Thompson's navy blue wedding suit would stay as good as new, and he had carried it into the paddock and spread it on the spring grass. Beyond the two young and eager faces Wendy saw a chequer board of fields glowing in horizontal sunlight, and all the peace of England. She put an arm round Julia. "I *am* glad your father's relented."

Julia rolled her cheek happily and fondly against Wendy's arm.

Gaylord said stoutly, "It's all Miss Thompson's doing. I bet she bullied him into it."

Wendy laughed gaily. "Can you imagine me, bullying anybody?" she asked. Nevertheless, it was pleasant to think that she had tilted the world just a tiny fraction towards happiness.

DEREK BATES had been mooning around alone, his mood vicious and idle. Listlessly, he took the Shepherd's Warning road; accelerated noisily and dangerously through the village; then ambled along the river road to the farm.

He parked his bike in a ditch, began wandering about the

340

outbuildings, but he found they gave very little opportunity for mischief. Great, heavy pieces of machinery were far beyond his capabilities to damage. And having hurt his toe by kicking savagely at a pile of beet in an outlying barn, he gave up.

So he flung himself down on a pile of hay, smoked a fag, and resigned himself to the thought that revenge wasn't going to be easy. Unless he met one of those kids on its own, of course. But that seemed too much to hope for.

Or was it? For now a small figure was coming stealthily into the barn. Alone? Yes, for she shut the door carefully behind her.

Julia knew exactly where she was going to hide. She remembered noticing a pile of hay in a dark corner of the great barn. And no one had said that the game of hide and seek was confined to the out of doors. So, while Gaylord and Miss Thompson sat in the paddock, covering their eyes and counting up to fifty, she ran across the field on those dancing feet of hers and into the barn.

It was then that the game of hide and seek became a nightmare reality. This little victim, walking straight towards him, was like an answer to Derek's prayer. His listlessness disappeared; he chucked his cigarette down in the hay, pulled his mother's stocking over his face, and waited till Julia was within reach. Then he stood up, and grabbed at her.

The sight of this faceless creature, coming at her out of the shadows, almost robbed Julia of her reason. Yet her dancer's body served her well. She twisted herself out of his grasp, and ran. But where? She had shut the door behind her, and now, in the half-dark, she did not know where to find it. She ran, as a hare runs, this way and that, whimpering piteously. And behind her, close at hand, were the heavy breathing and the footsteps.

One thing she saw: a ladder, leading up through an open trap door. The hayloft. She made for it, stamping desperately up the ladder. Once, for one dreadful moment, his fingers reached up and caught her left ankle. She kicked him off, and went on into the loft.

If only she could slam the trap door on him! She seized the edge of the heavy wooden square, heaved. But she was half a second too late. Derek was out, and grabbing the trap door to stop it slicing him. He let it fall into the closed position. Behind the nylon mask his features twisted into a triumphant grin.

"Please," she begged. "Oh, *please!*" He made a sudden grab, missed. She began again her pitiful, harelike running from this faceless creature—fingers caught at her, missed, caught again.

In the hayloft was a doorway, fitted with a windlass, for loading and unloading the hay. The door was usually left open, and it was open now, to the clean, free air of the world. The brilliant, evening sunlight streamed through this doorway. It drew the terrified girl as the candle draws the moth. She ran towards it, sobbing, knowing that it opened on to a twenty-foot drop to the field below.

She paused in the doorway, looked down, recoiled with a choking sob, turned.

Now, at last, she could see him. The level beams of the setting sun brilliantly lit every detail: the leather clad body, the hands hanging, gorilla-like, at his sides; the head, made bald and top-knotted by its stocking; the face which, behind its smooth veil, appeared de-humanized.

For a long moment they stared at each other, frozen. Then he lifted one heavy, booted foot, and set it forward, a few inches nearer his victim. Julia put up her hands before her face, and stepped backwards. Too late, she tried to steady herself. With a great cry she fell into the field. Derek looked down. She lay there, very still, very graceful.

"Christ!" said Derek. "Oh, Christ!" The sooner he got out of here the better. He ran back to the trap door, trembling in every limb. All he'd got to do, he told himself, was go down the ladder, slip out of the door, walk quickly to the old bike—and away. Once in the saddle, he'd run anyone down who tried to stop him. He bent down, grasped the trap door, and lifted it. But then a blast of hot air struck him in the face. He was suddenly frightened. He wrenched the trap door farther open, peered down—and discovered that his cigarette, so lightly tossed aside, had set the barn on fire. Flames crept across its floor like an incoming tide. The ladder, his only way of retreat, was already enveloped in them. And, even as he watched, the flames burst through the trap door like water through a broken dam. "Help!" cried Derek. "Help! Help!" Someone *must* come to *his* rescue.

But nobody did.

CHAPTER NINE

Jocelyn said, "There's something painful, almost unbearable, about an evening as beautiful as this."

"I know what you mean," said May, smiling.

John Pentecost never agreed with his son's more effete remarks, on principle. But, to himself, he had to admit there was some truth in this one. His own store cupboard of summer evenings was growing empty. One day soon, inevitably, he would open it and find it—bare!

"Listen," said May. "Someone's calling. I thought—a man's voice."

They listened idly. The silence was complete. It stretched into the far blue depths of sky. "I heard nothing," said Jocelyn.

Normally, May would have had to find out. But the evening was so calm, and the day had been so perfect, all she wanted was to rest in this blue peace of evening. They sat on. The sun edged a little farther down the sky. Soon they would go in to supper, and the lighting of the lamps. A perfect end to a long, perfect day.

"FORTY-NINE. FIFTY," said Gaylord. He opened his eyes. "Coming!" he called.

He and Miss Thompson set off. They searched the drive, various outhouses. They did not find her. "Perhaps she'll be like that girl they couldn't find and years later her mother went to the chest to get a tablecloth and found her skeleton," Gaylord said hopefully.

"I shouldn't think so," said Wendy, but with a touch of fear. "Julia," she called loudly. "Come out, now. You win."

Silence. Stillness. Then: "*Look!*" cried Gaylord.

They had come in sight of the distant barn. Smoke was pouring out of the hayloft door, eddying and billowing out of holes and crannies. And, as they watched, a great tongue of flame licked out of the high doorway. "Run! Tell your parents to dial 999. And wait —tell them we haven't found Julia."

He tore off. She ran towards the barn. "Julia!" she yelled. "Julia!" her voice dry and harsh. Even to herself she sounded a mad woman.

There was a new sound on the still evening, a yo-yo wail, coming rapidly nearer. She looked round as she ran. The great red fire-engine towered behind her. She stabbed her finger at the barn. "There's a child missing," she called. "She might—" They did not hear a word. They swept on. By the time she reached the barn they had run their hoses out. The flames spat and hissed, angry as serpents, as the water struck them.

For a few moments she stood, screaming the child's name. She ran up to one of the firemen. He ignored her. She tugged at his sleeve. "There could be a child in there," she sobbed.

"We're getting topside. Leave it to us, miss," he said calmly.

Sanity returned like a blow in the chest. The child had been left in her care, and her first duty was to warn the father. She ran to World's End Cottage and hammered on the door. Duncan came out. "It's yourself," he said curtly. "Go and stay with Julia while I help with the fire."

"Where is she?"

"In her room, of course. The doctor's on his way."

She ran after him, seized his shoulder. "What *happened?*"

He spun round, stared at her. "She must have been in the loft when the fire started." Wendy caught her breath. "Then she must have panicked, and jumped from the hayloft door." He went to see to the fire.

Miss Thompson went into the cottage, ran two at a time up the cramped stairs. A door on the landing was open. She went in. Julia lay there, pale, her eyes closed. Wendy sat down, took her hand. The child did not stir.

IT WAS, without doubt, one of the most exciting moments in Gaylord's life. He burst into the garden. "Momma! Poppa! Grandpa! Quick. Dial 999. The great barn's on fire."

They sprang to their feet. But at that moment they heard the approaching wail of the fire engine. Gaylord was bitterly disappointed. Someone must have beaten him to it. And he *had* wanted to dial 999.

"Mackintosh must have alerted them," said Grandpa, as they all started towards the barn. "But what would start a fire, Jocelyn? It's not as though everything's dry."

"Gaylord!" May's voice was sharp. "Where is Julia?"

"We hadn't found her yet, Momma—we were playing hide and seek. When we saw the fire we stopped the game, and Miss Thompson told me to get here as fast as I could and ring 999."

"I—see," said May. "But—where *is* Miss Thompson?"

"Well, there's Mackintosh, anyway," said Grandpa. For now they had arrived at the fire. And there were the firemen, busy with hoses and axes and ladders.

May rushed up to Mackintosh. "Where's Julia?"

"At the cottage. Miss Thompson's with her."

May had a cold feeling in her stomach. "She's—not *hurt?*"

"Aye, she is that." He strode forward to speak to the firemen.

May said, "Jocelyn, I'm going to the cottage."

Jocelyn nodded absently; but never took his eyes from the blazing barn. The leaping flames, the spurting smoke, the age-old struggle between water and fire absorbed him. Coming on this calm and lovely evening, it seemed to him a symbol of everything that had haunted his thoughts: the mindless violence of the flames was one with the mindless violence that threatened the world.

So he stood, until he was aware of an urgent voice: "That will be the doctor's car, Mr. Pentecost. Tell your father I'm away, will you."

Duncan joined the doctor and together they went to the cottage and up into Julia's room. May and Wendy rose and went down into the parlour. "She may be all right, Miss Thompson," said May. "It was a long fall—but she's young."

Wendy looked grateful. But said, "Yes," rather heavily.

May said, watching the schoolteacher closely: "And you think it's your fault. It's nothing of the kind. You mustn't even *think* that, Miss Thompson."

"But I do. Of course I do."

May put a hand on Wendy's and said, "I'm going to leave you now. This is *your* concern. But come and tell me when you know something."

Wendy smiled gratefully, and sat on in the fusty little parlour with its smells of upholstery and dried bulrushes. She waited a long time. And even when at last she heard the men coming down the stairs, her vigil was not over. There was a long, muffled conversation before finally she heard the door close behind the doctor, and Duncan's footsteps begin to ascend the stairs once more.

She ran into the hall. "Mr. Mackintosh, what does he say?"

He checked on the second step; turned and stared. He smelt of smoke and charred wood. His eyes were bloodshot and he looked tired and gaunt. "She'll be all right," he said.

"She will?" Her voice soared with joy.

He stood staring grimly down at her. Then he said brutally, "But she'll not dance again."

Wendy said furiously, "How can you know? How can anyone know at her age?"

He said, "All her weight went on her right leg." He turned, took another step up the stairs. He paused again, looked at her bitterly. "As far as ballet school goes, you could have saved your breath to cool your porridge, Miss Thompson."

"Has she to go to hospital?"

"Yes. The doctor's arranging it straight away."

"Will you let me help to—get her ready?"

"Thank you. That would be kind, Miss Thompson."

"I'll go with her if you like."

"Thanks. I'm not so good at that kind of thing." He gave his fleeting, thin smile. "Poor lassie! It'll be good for her to have a womanly body with her."

WHEN HE WAS driving her back from the hospital he said formally, "Miss Thompson, I wouldn't want you to think I don't appreciate all you've done for the lassie."

"Thank you," she said. She was still frozen with the horror of it —one bent and twisted limb destroying all the ecstasy of movement. And on this was piled another horror. She said, with a dry mouth, "Julia was in my charge when this terrible thing happened, Mr. Mackintosh."

His hands clenched on the wheel of the Land-Rover. He turned on her sharply. "You're *never* to think such a thing. Julia is *my* responsibility."

"Thank you," she said in a tight voice.

Later she said, "When she comes out of hospital, it won't be easy for you, will it? I did wonder whether you'd let her come and stay with me. She and I could go to school together in my car."

He was silent. She added pleadingly, "You know, I'm very, very fond of her, Mr. Mackintosh."

"I know you are, lassie," he said. "Aye. You'd make her a bonny mother," he muttered; he seemed to be speaking to himself.

It was Wendy's turn to be silent. He said, humbly for him, "But I doubt ye'd want *me* for a husband."

She was taken completely off guard. She gave a nervous laugh; "I don't think you'd want *me* for a wife, Mr. Mackintosh."

He sat, staring ahead; thoughtful, unsmiling. "It could be quite a satisfactory arrangement," he said.

She said, scornfully, "When I marry, Mr. Mackintosh, it will have to be much more than 'quite a satisfactory arrangement'. There'll have to be love, for one thing."

"Och, ye've been reading too many story books," he said. "But I'll not press ye. Just remember we've one thing in common."

"What's that?"

"Julia," he said quietly.

WENDY THOMPSON went back to the farm. She found May Pentecost in the kitchen. "Well?" asked May anxiously.

"They think she'll be all right. Except that—she'll never dance," said Wendy.

"They can't know," May said.

"Her father seems sure, after what the doctor said."

"I'm sorry." May looked up from her work, gazed at Wendy with a great sadness. "I really am, Miss Thompson. And I'm so sorry for him," May went on. "He's so helpless."

"Who?" Wendy asked in astonishment. "Not Mr. Mackintosh? But—he's terribly capable."

May put down the carving knife, smiled. "Which would you say was the more helpless? Duncan Mackintosh, or my husband?" She laughed. "You needn't be polite."

"Well. Of course, I admire Mr. Pentecost's *books* enormously. But—I would have thought—"

"Don't you believe it," said May. "Oh, I know Jocelyn relies a great deal on me. But he's got tremendous reserves. Whereas Mackintosh—outside farming, he's lost." She grinned at her

347

disciple. "He needs a woman to guide him, Miss Thompson."

Wendy felt herself blushing. But so taken was she with her understanding hostess that she said, "Between ourselves, Mrs. Pentecost, he did make a sort of proposal. But—I couldn't—"

"You'd be doing him a great service if you did," May said briskly. "And as for the girl—"

The two women smiled at each other. Wendy shook her head. "Thank you for being so understanding, Mrs. Pentecost. And now I really must be going."

It was already dusk as she returned home. But no one rose up to waylay her in the river lands. And her house was snug and safe at her homecoming.

THE BARN SMOULDERED and stank and hissed. But the danger was past. "I wish I knew what started it," muttered John Pentecost. "Could be arson, I suppose. That youth—"

Duncan Mackintosh came into the room. "Mr. Pentecost, I've found a motor cycle parked in a ditch, not far from the barn."

The machine was half hidden by the spring leaves. "Somewhere," said John, "I have a note of the number." He pulled an envelope from his breastpocket and, by the light of Mackintosh's torch, looked at something pencilled on it. "It's him," he said.

"Revenge," said Mackintosh. "Well, we'll give him revenge. If his bike's here, he's here. I'll nab him."

But Derek Bates never came for his motorbike.

THE PASSING of Derek Bates caused singularly few ripples. "Death by Misadventure" was the headline in the *Ingerby Advertiser*, which reported the inquest and published a smudged photograph. His mates weren't a bit surprised. This was just the sort of thing the silly devil would do.

His dad blamed Society, full stop. Mrs. Bates blamed everyone: his friends, his teachers, his dad, the police, the old man for his carelessness in not locking a barn with all that dry hay in it; everyone, in fact, except Derek and herself.

But—if I hadn't, all those months ago, made him chuck his bike in the river, he'd be alive now, thought John Pentecost. Alive to harass and terrify more children. But no one appointed *me* his executioner. What did I start, when I answered violence with violence? A boy's pet, a girl condemned to walk instead of fly, a youth dying horribly before he started to live.

May said briskly, "This is absolute nonsense, Father-in-law. It's a terrible and horrible business, I know. But it didn't begin with you and the motor cycle. It began with his tormenting Julia in the river meadows. And *that* began—when? In his childhood, in his conception—"

"You'll be quoting Freud at me next," muttered Grandpa.

Later, alone in his study, Jocelyn thought: the old man could be right. Should violence ever be the answer to violence? Did not a creator, once he resorted to violence, however righteously, join the destroyers? For he saw even more clearly now, that all mankind was divided into two, and that the world's future rested on the creators retaining the balance; yet every time he saw a smashed telephone kiosk, a trampled flower bed, his heart failed him; for he knew that the destroyers were on the march. And, if they could not be opposed by violence, then where in God's name lay the answer for a threatened world? He didn't know. All he knew was that, if there *was* an answer he could find it only by letting it come out in his writing. With a creative excitement he thought had deserted him for ever, he turned to a blank page, and took up his pen. . . .

SUMMER CAME EARLY that year. The mornings proudly seeming to say, "Look, O man, what another brilliant day we have created for your delight and happiness." The noontides saying, "Here is warmth, and shade, for your rest." The evenings saying, "See how the daylight lingers; now you may sip your wine, and talk, and dance the long, long dances."

One day May and Jocelyn put Gaylord in the car, refusing to answer any of his questions, and took him to a nearby farm where, in an outhouse, a sheepdog fussed over a litter of puppies. And Gaylord chose one, crooning over it tenderly. And though he wept a little at the memory of his dear friend Schultz, he really thought this was the happiest moment of all his young life.

Miss Thompson was often at World's End Cottage, loving and caring for Julia, and remaining placid when Duncan pointed out where she went wrong with her cooking or her washing up;

349

occasionally dropping in for a chat with her friends May and Jocelyn Pentecost, or taking Gaylord for a walk or a picnic, and feeling her unacknowledged and unrequited love for Jocelyn become mellow and tender like an October sun. Duncan had not mentioned marriage again; but her woman's instinct told her that one day he would. And, when he did, she thought she might say yes. There were worse things than honesty and plain speaking and dourness. There were worse materials than granite. And May had been right. He *did* need her, perhaps even more than Julia did.

AND THE LITTLE GIRL danced, alone, in the water meadows.

She was beautiful, and grave, and eight years old.

She danced alone. No one, not even her dear Miss Thompson, was allowed to see her dance.

For she danced as a broken grass dances in the wind, or as a lame bird flutters to reach the treetops.

Eric Malpass

Eric Malpass was born in 1910. At the age of seventeen, he went to work in a local bank where, apart from his war service in the RAF, he stayed for thirty-nine persevering years. But since 1947, when he first began writing, he had dreamed of becoming a full-time author. During those years he wrote innumerable short stories—and one of those stories featured a small boy called Gaylord. It was Mrs. Malpass who persuaded her husband to turn the story into a novel, and in 1965 *Morning's At Seven* was published, the first in the Pentecost series.

When Eric Malpass gave up his job the following year he took a considerable financial risk; all he hoped, he says, was to make ends meet with his writing. Then, six months later, *Morning's At Seven* shot onto the best-seller lists in Germany, and his future was secure. "But I'm always rather glad that I did take that risk," Malpass maintains. "I'm a cautious sort of person by nature, and it feels good to have taken one real gamble before I knew of the book's success."

Morning's At Seven was followed by *At The Height Of The Moon* (both Condensed Books selections), and now the unpredictable Pentecosts have made their author famous all over Europe. Malpass seems as bemused by their behaviour as his readers are: apparently, he never knows what they are going to do next. "This may sound rather haphazard," he says, "but to me, writing a novel is like driving on a long journey in fog, with no idea of whether one is going to Penzance or Aberdeen. . . . I just put my characters in a certain situation and see how they will react."

Success has not much changed Eric Malpass's lifestyle. He and his wife still live near Nottingham in an area he has loved all his life, enjoying the nearby countryside, making trips to the theatre, and pottering around their well-kept garden. Are they anything like the Pentecosts? Malpass admits that his own wife largely inspired May Pentecost; but their son Michael (now the father of two teenage daughters) hotly denies being the original Gaylord!

THE
R
DOCUMENT

a condensation of the book by

Irving Wallace

Illustrated by Robert Lavin
Published by Cassell

Vernon T. Tynan was a young government agent when John F. Kennedy was in the White House. But that was long before the opening of this dramatic novel. Now Tynan is director of the FBI and determined to end the crime wave which is ravaging the United States. How? With a controversial amendment to the American Constitution which would impose the next thing to martial law on the country.

With Tynan's amendment on the brink of ratification, Christopher Collins, the newly appointed Attorney General, receives a deathbed warning from his predecessor about the amendment: "The R Document—dangerous—must be exposed. . . ."

Collins's search for the missing document projects him into a crisis which could destroy his career, his marriage and the nation itself.

1

THE visit had been quite unexpected—he had forgotten that he had made the appointment, had forgotten to cancel it after he'd promised to have dinner with the President—and now he was trying to get it over with as quickly and gracefully as possible.

Yet Christopher Collins didn't want to hurt the man sitting opposite him, because this was apparently a sensible and gentle man, and at another time Collins would have enjoyed talking to him. He'd have to handle this carefully, Collins decided. Not merely because he didn't want to hurt his feelings, but because he didn't want to offend FBI Director Tynan. Obviously the director had encouraged this man to interview Collins for the autobiography of Tynan he was ghostwriting. No one was foolhardy enough to offend the FBI director, and Collins, in his new position, least of all.

Collins' eyes went to the portable cassette tape recorder his visitor had placed on the desk ten minutes ago. It was still recording, although nothing of consequence so far. Collins' eyes rose to take in the writer, Ishmael Young, who was studying his list of questions. He was a short, pudgy person, perhaps in his mid-fifties, and he bulged out of his rumpled gray suit. Except for the horn-rimmed glasses that needed cleaning and the charred brown briar pipe, he did not look like a writer at all. But then Collins had never met a ghostwriter before. He was a successful one, too; had written books for an actress, a black Olympics hero, a military genius. Collins hadn't read any of the books, but Karen probably had, and he would try to remember to ask her about them.

Ishmael Young had lifted his head and was now posing his next question. Listening, Collins saw an out, a way to terminate this interview. It simply required honesty. "What do I think of Vernon T. Tynan?" Collins said, repeating the question.

He immediately thought of the physical Tynan: a man almost as tall as himself, with a rasping voice. Of the inner Tynan he knew next to nothing. He need only say so and let Ishmael Young look elsewhere.

"Frankly, I don't know Director Tynan very well. I've been on this job just one week."

"You've been Attorney General just one week," said Young, correcting him nicely, "but you've been in the Department of Justice almost eighteen months. You were Deputy Attorney General under the last Attorney General, Colonel Noah Baxter, for thirteen of those months."

"That's true," admitted Collins. "But as Deputy Attorney General I saw Director Tynan very little. It was Colonel Baxter who saw him—quite often. They were friends, after a fashion."

Ishmael Young's eyebrows went up a notch. "I didn't know Vernon Tynan had any friends. At least that's my feeling, from my talks with him. I thought only his assistant, Harry Adcock, was a friend. And I regarded that as mainly a business relationship."

"No," Collins insisted, "he was also close to Colonel Baxter. Though I suppose Director Tynan is actually a loner. It's in the nature of the job. Anyway, I never got to know him at all."

The writer would not be put off. "But Mr. Collins . . ." He paused. "Or should I call you Attorney General Collins?"

Collins smiled. "Mr. Collins will do."

"Very well. What I was going to say was that after Colonel Baxter suffered his stroke five months ago, you were unofficially the head of Justice, until it was made official a week ago. The FBI is under you. The director of the FBI, Tynan, is your subordinate, so you'd have contact—"

Collins was forced to laugh. "Director Tynan my subordinate? Mr. Young, you've got a lot to learn."

"I'm here to learn, Mr. Collins," said Young earnestly. "I can't ghostwrite an autobiography for the director of the FBI without knowing his precise relationship with the Attorney General, the President, the CIA. You might think I should ask the director. I have, believe me. But he's surprisingly vague about the governmental process and his own place in it. Not that he won't tell me. It's just that he's not interested, and rather impatient. What he is interested in is talking about his exploits in the FBI. I'm interested in those, too. They're the meat of the book. But I'm also interested in where he stands—in relation to his colleagues—in the power structure."

Collins made up his mind to clarify this. "All right, Mr. Young, let me level with you. It says in the *Government Manual* that the FBI director is under the Attorney General. But it's not that way at all. According to law, the Attorney General doesn't appoint the FBI director, the President does, with the advice and consent of the Senate. The President alone can remove him. So, except on paper, Director Tynan is not my subordinate. Therefore, to go back to your question—I haven't had much contact with him, not even as Deputy Attorney General, when I was in charge here after Colonel Baxter was taken to Bethesda Naval Medical Center. I'm sorry I can't be more helpful. In fact, I can't imagine why Director Tynan sent you to see me."

Young sat up slightly. "Oh, he didn't. This was something I wanted to do on my own."

"Then that explains it." Collins felt relieved. He could cut the interview short without giving offense to Tynan. Still, he wanted to send Young off happy. "Anyway, you wanted to hear what I thought of Director Tynan for your book—"

"Not for my book," said Young hastily. "For Tynan's book. It'll be by Tynan."

"All right, let me give you my impression of him," said Collins, searching for something bland and safe. "The director is plainly a man of action, a doer, a no-nonsense guy. He's probably just right for investigating federal violations. His job is digging up facts and reporting them. My job is to do the prosecuting based on his findings."

357

"Then you're the man of action," said Young.

"Not really. I'm strictly a lawyer among lawyers in Justice. We go the slow, careful route; Tynan and his agents do the direct, dangerous stuff. Now, for your purposes, my only other judgment of him is—well, when he's into something he believes in, he won't stop pushing for it. He's dogged, in the best way. Like the new amendment to the Constitution that's out there for ratification. Once the President originated it, Tynan got right behind it—"

Ishmael Young interrupted. "Mr. Collins, the President didn't originate this 35th Amendment. Director Tynan did."

Collins stared at the writer. "Where did you get that idea?"

"From the director himself. He speaks of it as his baby."

"Whatever he thinks, it isn't his. But what you've said makes my point exactly. When he believes in something, he makes it his own. And now, indeed, he's as responsible as anyone, maybe more than anyone, for putting the 35th over."

"It's not been put over yet," said Young quietly. "It's not been ratified yet by three-fourths of the states."

"Well, it will be," said Collins. "Only two more states have to approve it."

"And there are only three left to go."

"Two of the three are doing their final voting tonight. I think the 35th will be part of the Constitution tonight. However, that's neither here nor there." He glanced at his watch.

"Mr. Collins, just one more thing. I know this has nothing to do with the interview, but I'm interested to know the answer." Young swallowed and then said, "Do you like that 35th Amendment?"

Collins was momentarily silent. The question had been unexpected. Moreover, he had never clearly answered it for anyone—not even for his wife, Karen, or for himself. "Maybe I have some reservations about it," he said slowly. "But I can't suggest anything better. Do you like it, Mr. Young?"

"Strictly between us?"

"Strictly."

"I hate it," said Young flatly. "I hate anything that wipes out the Bill of Rights."

"Well, that's something of an overstatement, I'd say. The 35th

358

is meant to supersede the Bill of Rights, but only in the event of extreme internal emergency that might threaten to destroy the country. Obviously we're heading in that direction fast, and the 35th will give us something with which we can organize order out of chaos—"

"It'll give us repression. It'll sacrifice liberties as the price for peace."

Collins was annoyed. "Mr. Young, you know what's going on out there in the streets. The worst crisis of crime and violence in our history. Take that attack on the White House two months ago. Bombing, machine-gunning—killing thirteen guards and Secret Service men, murdering seven helpless tourists, gutting the East Room—nobody's done anything like that to the White House since the British sailors did it in 1814. But we were at war with the British. This attack two months ago was by *Americans*. No one is safe. Did you see the news this morning?"

Young shook his head.

"Then let me tell you," said Collins. "Peoria, Illinois. The police department. The morning shift finished its briefing, and the officers started outside to their motorcycles and squad cars, when they were ambushed. At least one-third of the force dead or injured. We've never had a crime crisis like this in our entire history. How would you solve it?"

Ishmael Young was ready with his answer. "I'd put our house in order by rebuilding it. From the bottom up. Crime is the consequence of poverty. I'd take drastic measures to get rid of economic oppression, inequality, injustice."

"There's no time for the total overhaul now. I don't disagree with you on what must be done in due time."

"It'll never come about once the 35th Amendment is passed."

Collins wanted no further debate. "I'm curious, Mr. Young. Do you talk like this when you work with Director Tynan?"

Young shrugged his shoulders. "I wouldn't be here now if I did. I talk like this with you because you seem to be a nice guy. And—I hope you don't mind my saying this—I simply can't figure out what you're doing with that crowd."

This hit a nerve. Karen had made the same point over a month ago, when he had decided to accept the job of Attorney General. "Would you like to see someone Director Tynan recommended in this job?" he said. "Why do you think I took it? Because I believe nice guys can finish first." He stood up. "I'm sorry, Mr. Young. We've run out of time. Look, I'll know a good deal more a few months from now. Why don't you give me a ring then?"

Ishmael Young was on his feet, taking up his tape recorder and shutting it off. "I will call you. Thanks a lot."

Collins reached over and shook the writer's hand. "By the way, how long have you been working with Director Tynan?"

"Once a week for six months."

"Well, you haven't told me—what do *you* think of him?"

"Mr. Collins, I'll cop the Fifth." Young grinned. "This work is my bread and butter. I never risk that."

After he had gone, Collins remained standing, thinking about their exchange. Finally he settled down in his chair and rolled up to his desk. Soon he had forgotten his visitor, absorbed by cases that required his immediate attention.

Some time later, in the stillness of the huge seventy-foot office, he heard the brush of footsteps on the thick Oriental rug. He looked up to see Marion Rice, his secretary, coming hastily toward him with a large manila envelope. "Just came in—hand delivered—from across the street."

Across the street meant across Pennsylvania Avenue—from the J. Edgar Hoover Building and the FBI.

"It's marked confidential and important. It must be from the director." She handed him the envelope. "Unless there's something else, Mr. Collins, I'll be leaving now."

He was surprised. "What time is it?"

"Twenty after six."

"I'm not even half through yet." Ruefully he looked down at the stacks on his desk. "Okay, Marion, you can lock up and go."

"You'll have no more time for work now. Don't forget, you have a dinner date tonight, seven fifteen, the White House."

He grimaced. "That may be work, too."

She hesitated, and then a reticent smile surfaced on her face. "I—I just want to say, Mr. Collins, congratulations on your first week's anniversary as Attorney General. We're all happy you're here. Good night."

"Good night, Marion. I appreciate that."

After she had gone, he considered the envelope she had given him. There was rarely good news from the FBI these days, so it was with reluctance that he unsealed the package.

He withdrew a half dozen pages of typed statistics. Attached to them was a handwritten note. From the impatient abbreviations and punctuation, he knew that the note had been written by Director Vernon T. Tynan even before the signature confirmed it.

Dear Chris—

Heres the latest figures on last months nat'l crime statistics—the worst in our history by far—I'm sending a copy to the Pres and one to you so that you get it before we see the Pres tonight. Note the jump in murders, riots, armed robbery, interstate kidnapping. See my addendum on leads to probable conspiracies and organized revolutionaries—we're really in a stew, and the only thing that can pull us out is final passage of the 35th Amend—pray for it tonight. I already had these latest statistics phoned in to legislators in Albany, NY, and Columbus, O, so they know the true situation before they vote tonight. See you at the TV dinner in a few hours.

Best,
Vernon

Collins glanced through the Uniform Crime Report. In the past month violent crimes, including murder, had gone up eighteen percent, forcible rape had gone up fifteen percent, robbery and aggravated assault up thirty percent, riots up twenty percent.

Thoughtfully he laid down the pages. Because of the growing lawlessness, prisons were filled to bursting. Despite the forty-five thousand lawyers and FBI agents working for the Department of Justice, despite three special divisions of army troops assigned to domestic control by the Pentagon, despite the twenty-two billion dollars that would be spent on law enforcement this year (it had been only three and a half billion back in 1960), the crime rate continued to spiral upward.

It was the darkest period in America since the Civil War, of this he was certain. Anarchy and terror dominated every new day. When you woke in the morning, you did not know whether you would see the night. When you went to sleep at night, you did not know whether you would wake in the morning. Every day when he kissed Karen good-by before going to work, he felt the frightening uncertainty that he might not find her (and the child she was carrying) alive when he came home.

His telephone was ringing. He lifted the receiver. "Collins here."

"Darling. I hope I'm not interrupting. . . ." It was Karen's voice.

"No, no. I was just going through some last-minute things. How are you, honey?"

She didn't answer directly. She said, "I wanted to check on the time your driver is picking me up for the dinner tonight."

"Twenty to seven. You'll be meeting me at seven. We're due at the White House fifteen minutes after that. The President wants us to be on time. We're watching the TV specials from New York and Ohio. Are you dressed?"

"I'm all made up. I just have to slip into something. Can I wear the red knit?"

"Wear whatever is casual. His secretary said this was going to be informal."

"I guess the red knit will do. It's almost the last time I can wear it before my stomach starts showing."

"Any action today?"

"A few tentative kicks."

"Good. The Redskins need a punter. How are you otherwise?"

"I'm fine, I guess. All things considered."

"What things?" He knew, but he had to ask anyway.

"Well, you know how I feel about these affairs. I've been to the White House only once, that time when we went with the Baxters. That was bad enough. But you said this one was a small affair, intimate—that's doubly scary. I won't know what to say."

"You won't have to say a thing. We'll all be watching television."

"Why do you have to be there?"

"I told you this morning," he said impatiently. "First of all, the President wants me there. In the second place, I *am* the Attorney

General. The 35th Amendment is up for a crucial vote in the New York and Ohio lower houses tonight, and that falls in my province. Since only two more states are needed to pass the 35th and make it part of the Constitution, this is a big deal."

"I understand. Don't be angry with me, Chris." She paused. "Do we want it to pass? I've read some bad things about it."

"So have I, honey. I really don't know what's right. The amendment can be good if good people are running the country. It can be bad if there are bad people. I can only say, if it passes, it'll make my job easier."

"Then I hope it passes." But her voice carried no conviction.

After hanging up, he sat thinking of Karen. He was sorry he had been gruff with her. She deserved better, his best. He knew the evening ahead would be an ordeal for her. She had been against the job as Deputy Attorney General, against the move from his private practice in Los Angeles to public office in Washington, and, recently, even more vehemently against the Cabinet post as Attorney General. While she pretended to be apolitical, he knew where Karen stood. She did not trust the people he would be associated with in the Justice Department. She had tried to tell him, it was a loser's job. The country was going rapidly downhill, and he'd be at the wheel. Above all, Karen did not want the forced socializing and the nakedness before the news media demanded by his position. She had been against that from the start; they had been newly married then—the second time for each. Now two years married and in her fourth month of pregnancy, she still wanted privacy, and she did not want to share him.

He rose from his chair with the resolve to be by her side all evening, no matter how difficult that proved, and to be kind. He stretched to his entire stringy six feet two, until he could hear his bones crack. He briefly considered his not unhandsome visage and rumpled dark hair in the mirror, then went to his private sitting room to wash and change.

WHEN his Cadillac limousine entered the White House driveway, Collins could see a great number of news people with their lighting equipment on the lawn across from the north façade.

Mike Hogan, his carefully handpicked bodyguard, twisted around in the front seat and asked, "Do you want to talk to them, Mr. Collins?"

Collins squeezed Karen's hand and said, "Not if I can help it. Let's go right inside."

They left the car at the North Portico and were escorted to the Cabinet Room, in the West Wing, where a dozen or so people were gathered. Along the wall that faced the French doors to the Rose Garden, a large color-television console had been installed. Several persons were watching the picture on the screen, although the audio had been turned down low. The black leather-covered chairs usually around the long, shining Cabinet table had been placed to face the television set. Standing between the United States flag and the presidential flag, President Andrew Wadsworth was engaged in an animated conversation with the Senate and House majority leaders and their wives.

As Collins, with Karen clutching his arm, surveyed the scene, the President's chief aide, McKnight, hurried forward to welcome them. Quickly they were taken on the rounds of the Cabinet Room, to greet Vice-President Frank Loomis and his wife; Miss Ledger, the President's personal secretary; Ronald Steedman, the President's private pollster, from the University of Chicago; Secretary of the Interior Martin; the congressional leaders and their wives, and then President Wadsworth himself.

The President, a slight, dapper man, suave and urbane, with dark hair graying at the temples, took Karen's hand, shook Collins', and was at once apologetic. "Martha"—he was referring to the First Lady—"is so disappointed she won't be here tonight to get to know you better. She's in bed with a touch of the flu. But there'll be a next time. . . . Well, Chris, it looks like a happy evening."

"I hope so, Mr. President," said Collins. "What do you hear?"

"As you know, the senates in New York and Ohio ratified the 35th early yesterday. Now we're entirely in the hands of the New York assembly and the Ohio house. Immediately after yesterday's votes, Steedman had his pollsters swarming over Albany and Columbus, buttonholing state legislators. Ohio looks like a cinch. New York could go either way. Most of the legislators polled were undecided or no comment, but among those who did reply, there's been a definite gain over the last poll. Also, I think Vernon's latest FBI statistics— Hello, Vernon."

Director Vernon T. Tynan had joined them, occupying all immediate empty space, a formidable presence. He was shaking the President's hand, Collins' hand, complimenting Karen on her appearance.

"I was just saying, Vernon," the President resumed, "those figures you sent over should have great impact in Albany. I'm glad you got them in on time. Two hours from now I'm confident we'll have thirty-eight out of fifty states, and a new amendment to the Constitution."

"It wasn't easy," said Tynan. "But you're right. They should help."

Collins nodded in the direction of the television set. "When does it start, Mr. President?"

"Ten or fifteen minutes. They're just warming up with some background. Why not get yourselves drinks before it begins?"

As Collins guided Karen away, he realized that Tynan was in step beside him. "I think I can use a drink, too," said Tynan.

They went toward the end of the Cabinet table where the President's valet was supervising the drinks. Tynan looked past Collins at Karen. "Are you feeling okay these days, Mrs. Collins?"

Surprised, Karen raised her hand to smooth her short blond hair, then automatically lowered it to touch her loose chain belt. "I've never felt better, thank you."

"Good, good to hear that," said Tynan.

After Collins had got a glass of champagne for his wife and a Scotch and water for himself and started her toward the television set, he felt a tug at his sleeve.

"Did you hear that?" Karen whispered. "His concern about how I feel? He was practically telling us that he knows I'm pregnant."

"He can't know. No one knows."

"*He* knows," whispered Karen.

"But even if he has found out, what's the point?"

"Just to remind you he's omniscient. To keep you and everyone else in line."

"I think you're overreacting, honey. He was just being social. It was an innocent remark."

They had reached the chairs almost directly in front of the large television set, and they both sat down to watch. A distinguished network commentator was recapping the procedure of adding a new amendment to the Constitution.

"Once a resolution proposing a new amendment is made in Congress," he was saying, "hearings are held on it by the Rules and Judiciary committees. After approval by these committees, the amendment goes to the floors of the Senate and the House. When approved by a two-thirds vote of each legislative body, it is sent to the state legislatures for debate and vote. If three-fourths of the legislatures—thirty-eight out of fifty—ratify the amendment, it becomes an official part of the Constitution. The most quickly approved amendment in our history was the 26th, back in 1971,

giving eighteen-year-olds the vote. Only three months and seven days after it came out of Congress, it was ratified by three-fourths of the fifty states. Which brings us to the latest amendment, the 35th, which we may see killed or made the law of the land tonight."

Collins heard the scraping of chairs as guests began to crowd around the set. Then he devoted himself to the television screen.

"The controversial 35th Amendment, designed to supersede the first ten amendments—or the Bill of Rights—in time of internal national emergency, grew out of a desire by congressional leaders and President Wadsworth to forge a weapon to impose law and order on the nation if required."

"Weapon?" interrupted the President, who had just sat down in back of Collins. "What does he mean, weapon? If ever I heard prejudicial language, that's it. I wish we could pass an amendment to take care of commentators like that."

"We're passing one," Director Tynan boomed from his chair on Collins' other side. "The 35th Amendment will take care of those troublemakers."

Collins caught Karen's sharp glance, and squirmed uncomfortably toward the television screen again.

"Despite vocal—but limited—opposition from the liberal blocs," the commentator was continuing, "both bodies of Congress gave the 35th Amendment overwhelming approval. Then the amendment was sent out to the fifty states. That was four months and two days ago. After a relatively easy passage in the first states voting on it, the voyage of the 35th became increasingly stormy as opposition was organized against it. To date, forty-seven of the fifty states have voted upon it. Eleven have turned it down. Thirty-six have approved it. It is still two states short of approval. As of tonight, there remain three states that have not voted—New York, Ohio, and California. New York and Ohio are concluding their voting this very night, and California has scheduled its vote a month hence. But will California be needed? If both New York and Ohio turn down the amendment tonight, it will be dead. If both ratify the amendment, it will become part of the Constitution immediately, and President Wadsworth will have his arsenal to combat the growing lawlessness that is strangling the nation. Now we take you to the state assembly in Albany, New York, where the floor debate is just concluding before the final roll-call vote."

The telecast cut to a close shot of a dignified gentleman, identified as Assemblyman Lyman Smith. Collins listened.

"And while the United States Constitution as written by our forefathers is a noble instrument of law," the speaker was saying, "it was meant to be sufficiently flexible to meet the needs of each new generation and the challenge of progress. Remember, my friends, this Constitution of ours was written by a group of largely youthful radicals who came to its signing in horse-drawn carriages. They never heard of atomic bombs or space satellites. And certainly they never heard of the Saturday-night special. But they built into their Constitution the instrument for adjusting our federal laws to whatever the future might bring. Now the future is here, and the time has come to modify our supreme law to suit the

368

needs of our present citizenry. The old Bill of Rights, as set down by our founders, is too ambiguous, too soft to meet the onrush of events conspiring to destroy the structure of our democracy. Only passage of the 35th Amendment can save us."

As the speaker returned to his seat, the camera roved over the assembly, showing the thunderous applause. In the Cabinet Room there was also hearty applause.

"Bravo!" the President exclaimed. "McKnight," he called out to his chief aide, "who's that New York assemblyman who just spoke? Somebody-or-other Smith? Check him out. We could use a person on the White House staff who thinks that straight and is eloquent besides." His gaze went back to the screen. "Everybody, attention. The roll call is about to begin."

Collins could hear the names of the assemblymen, and their yeas and nays. Behind him, Steedman's clipped voice observed it would take awhile for the verdict since there were one hundred and fifty members in the New York assembly.

Collins allowed his attention to drift from the screen. He fastened on Tynan, who was now standing, his face flushed with anxiety, his eyes hooded, as he followed the voting. He looked over his shoulder at the President, whose countenance was granite as he concentrated on the screen.

Honest, dedicated men, Collins thought. No matter what others said on the outside—carpers like Ishmael Young, or even doubters like Karen—these men were responsible human beings. At once he felt comfortable in this circle of power. He felt he belonged. He wished he could thank the person who had put him there— Colonel Baxter, who was missing, who was lying in a coma on a hospital bed in Bethesda.

Collins had believed he owed everything to Colonel Baxter, but actually, examining it, he saw that it was a series of accidents and mistakes that had elevated him to Attorney General. Colonel Baxter had been Collins' father's college roommate at Stanford and his closest friend after graduation. His father, who had wanted to practice law, had turned to business instead and had become a wealthy electronic-parts manufacturer. Collins remembered the great pride his father had taken in his lawyer son. His father had kept Colonel Baxter apprised of his son's growing legal reputation.

Two events had further brought him to Colonel Baxter's attention. One was his brief but well-publicized tenure as an American Civil Liberties Union lawyer in San Francisco. He had successfully defended the civil rights of a thoroughly Fascist right-wing American organization, because he believed in free expression for all as a matter of principle. Colonel Baxter, a conservative, had been impressed for the wrong reasons. Shortly after, when serving as the new district attorney in Oakland, Collins had gained national attention by successfully prosecuting three black killers who had committed particularly horrendous crimes. This had impressed Colonel Baxter even more, showing that he was no bleeding heart meting out more compassionate justice for blacks than for whites. What had never gotten into print was Collins' true feelings: that these impoverished, ill-raised blacks had themselves been victims of society.

The fact that Collins, in private practice in Los Angeles, had also successfully defended several organizations of blacks and Chicanos and dozens of white dissenters had been regarded by Baxter as a sop to a rising young attorney's conscience. Thus, backed by a few headline achievements and his father's old friendship, Collins had been summoned to Washington to become Colonel Baxter's Deputy Attorney General; so, by chance, when Baxter was incapacitated, he had become Attorney General of the United States and a part of this elite company.

Suddenly, Collins saw the President leap from his chair, and heard a tremendous cheer go up around him. Bewildered, he looked at the screen, then at Karen, who whispered, "It just passed the New York assembly."

Collins' view of the screen was momentarily blocked by Steedman, who was addressing the President. "Congratulations, Mr. President!" the pollster was saying. "I admit that was a surprise."

Director Tynan gripped Collins' shoulder until he winced. "Great news, old boy, isn't it? Great news!"

"Vernon—" It was the President addressing Tynan. "You know what swung New York to our side? It was that last speech, delivered by that Smith fellow. That speech was perfect. It was just as if you had written it yourself."

Director Tynan grinned broadly. "Maybe I did." Others around them laughed knowingly.

A shrill voice interrupted. "Buffet dinner is ready!" It was Miss Ledger, the President's personal secretary, directing the guests to gleaming copper chafing dishes at the far end of the Cabinet table. Collins and Karen filled their plates and went back to the semicircle of guests around the television set. From the podium of the Ohio house of representatives, someone was droning.

"Resolved that the First to Tenth Amendments to the Constitution shall be superseded in time of internal national emergency by the following new amendment:

"Section one, number one: No right or liberty guaranteed by the Constitution shall be construed as license to endanger the national security. Number two: In the event of clear and present danger, a Committee on National Safety, appointed by the President, shall meet in joint session with the National Security Council. Number three: Upon determination that national security is at issue, the Committee on National Safety shall declare a state of emergency and assume plenipotentiary power, supplanting constitutional authority until the established danger has been brought under control and/or eliminated. Number four: The chairman of the committee shall be the director of the Federal Bureau of Investigation. Number five: The proclamation shall exist only during such time as the emergency is declared to be in effect, and it shall be automatically terminated by formal declaration upon the emergency's resolution.

"Section two, number one: During the suspensory period, the remainder of all rights and privileges guaranteed by the Constitution shall be held inviolable. Number two: All committee action shall be taken by unanimous vote."

Collins had read all this before, but somehow hearing it aloud made it seem harsher, and he sat worried, picking at his food.

"They're beginning the roll call of the ninety-nine legislators," he heard the President say. "Well, this one's a cinch. The 35th is in the bag."

Collins set down his plate, fully attentive. He could see the close-ups of the various representatives on the Ohio house floor pushing the buttons at their desks—the votes being registered on a huge board at one end of the chamber. Ayes and nays about even, very close. The Cabinet Room was silent. Minutes ticked away. Aye. Nay. Nay. Nay. Aye. Nay.

The announcer's voice broke in quickly over the voting: "The nays have just gone ahead. This is a surprise. An upset seems in the making."

More minutes. More votes. As suddenly as it had begun, it was over. The 35th Amendment had been rejected by the Ohio house of representatives.

There were audible groans in the Cabinet Room. Unaccountably, Collins felt his heart pounding fast. He cast a sidelong glance at Karen. She was composed as she suppressed a smile. Collins frowned and looked away.

Everyone was beginning to rise. Puzzled, most of the guests gathered about the President, who looked to his pollster. "I thought it was in the bag, Ronald. What went wrong?"

"We had projected a win by a comfortable margin," said Steedman. "But our last sampling of the house members was thirty-six hours ago. Who knows what may have happened among the members during the last thirty-six hours?"

The President's aide, McKnight, was waving his arm. "Mr. President, the announcer—he seems to have some kind of answer."

The President and his guests turned back to the set. The network newsman was saying, "And this word has just come up to us here in our booth. Several legislators indicated to our floor man that there had been an intensive lobbying campaign last night and throughout this morning here in the state capital—a blitz effort by Anthony Pierce—Tony Pierce, head of Defenders of the Bill of Rights, that national group known as DBR—who only a month ago started a campaign among legislators of the most recent states to vote on the amendment and who has just had his most resounding success in Ohio. Tony Pierce, as most viewers will remember, is the onetime FBI agent who turned successful author, lawyer, and civil rights advocate. His record—"

A bellowing voice drowned out the television audio. "We know his record!" roared Director Tynan, bounding in front of the television set, shaking his fist at the screen. "We know all about him!"

He whirled around, red-faced, fixing on the President. "We know he headed a radical activist group at the University of Wisconsin. We know how he got a medal he didn't deserve in Vietnam. We know how he weaseled his way into the FBI, playing the war hero. We know he was negligent in his duties—freeing criminals he was supposed to detain, doctoring his reports, being insubordinate. That's why I kicked him out of the bureau. We know the names of four radical groups his wife belongs to. We know at least nine subversive organizations his law firm has represented. We knew Tony Pierce was bad medicine before all this started. We should have demolished him the minute he headed up DBR—but we didn't want to give a former FBI agent such negative headlines, hurt the image of the bureau—"

"Never mind, Vernon, that's all water under the bridge," said the President, trying to calm him. "He's done his damage, if indeed he was responsible. We'll just have to see that it doesn't happen again."

Observing the scene, Chris Collins found himself embarrassed and upset. Tynan's venomous outburst had revealed an inquisitor's side of the FBI director that he had never seen before.

Collins saw the President signaling him. He pushed between McKnight and the Senate majority leader to reach the President, who had already been joined by Tynan.

For a moment the President stood rubbing his jaw thoughtfully. "Well, gentlemen, we won one by an upset, and we lost one by an upset. There's only one state left. All our marbles are on California. Ronald tells me we're ahead in the Golden State poll. That's not enough for me. You know how unpredictable they are out there. It's our last shot, and I'm staking everything on it. I want you, Vernon, and you, Chris, to give it everything you've got. We've *got* to win."

Both Collins and Tynan nodded vigorously.

The President turned to Collins. "I have one idea, to begin with, Chris. You come from California, don't you?"

"Yes, I do. I'm from the San Francisco Bay area, but I also practiced in Los Angeles."

"Perfect. I think it might be worthwhile for you to get back out there in the next week or two. You can do some subtle lobbying for the cause."

"Well," said Collins, troubled, "I don't know if I'd have that much influence. The only really popular native son is Chief Justice Maynard."

The President shook his head. "No, Maynard wouldn't do. I have it from good sources he's not on our side. But we should have someone in California. You—or perhaps someone who's been in the Administration longer. Let me think about it."

Uncomfortable as he was with the idea, Collins knew that he dared not resist. "If you feel it's important—"

"Nothing more important," Tynan broke in. "This is the most crucial piece of legislation ever voted on by the states. Without it, we'll have no country at all."

"Vernon's right," the President said. "We're not going to lose this one. I won't let things go on the way they have. You know those trained Doberman pinschers they made me put on the grounds? Last night we lost our sixth one to snipers. Now I'm being advised to allow an electrified barrier to be installed around the White House—to make me a prisoner in my own home, the way most decent citizens of this country have been forced to confine themselves behind dead bolts and alarms. When the President's house isn't safe, we know we're in trouble. Well, gentlemen, we're going to bring civilization back to this land of ours with the 35th Amendment. And we're going to do it by winning in California."

At that moment Miss Ledger appeared. "Pardon me, Mr. President. Mr. Collins, your bodyguard is at the door. He has to speak to you. He says it is urgent."

"Thank you," said Collins. He turned back to the President. "I'm prepared to do whatever I can."

"I'll let you know next week. You'd better go now and attend to your urgent business."

Collins hastily crossed to the doorway where his bodyguard, Mike Hogan, was waiting. "What's the problem?" he asked.

374

"It's Colonel Noah Baxter, sir," said Hogan in an undertone. "He's come out of his coma. But he's dying. The word came from Mrs. Baxter herself to the Justice switchboard, and it was relayed to me in the car. Colonel Baxter's first words were that he wanted to see you about something urgent. Mrs. Baxter begged me to get you to his bedside before it's too late."

Collins went back into the Cabinet Room and took Karen's arm. "Sorry, honey. I have to get over to Bethesda and we'd better not waste a minute."

A short while later, the limousine braked to a halt before the white tower that was the main building in the Bethesda National Naval Medical Center complex.

Bidding Karen to remain in the car with Hogan and Pagano, the driver, Collins hastened into the building. As he entered, a navy officer quickly intercepted him. "Attorney General Collins?"

"Yes."

"Follow me, sir. They're on the fifth floor."

As they ascended in the elevator, Collins inquired, "How is Colonel Baxter?"

"When I came down twenty minutes ago, he was hanging on by a thread."

"I hope I'm in time. Who's with him?"

"The missus, of course. And their grandson, Rick Baxter. He's staying with his grandparents while his parents are in Kenya on government business. We tried to reach them tonight. No luck. Then, there are two doctors and a nurse in attendance. And Father Dubinski is standing by. He's from Holy Trinity Church in Georgetown. . . . Here we are, sir."

They proceeded quickly up the corridor. When they reached a room with an open door, Collins' guide gestured toward it. "In here, sir. The colonel has two adjoining rooms, and this one is used as a sitting room. He's in the other."

Entering the sitting room, which was empty, Collins heard a soft sobbing and saw that the door to the next room was ajar. He could see only a portion of the bed, but then he made out a tableau in a dim corner. There was gray-haired, dumpy Hannah Baxter, for whom he had great respect, seated in a chair, weeping inconsolably. There was the grandson, Rick—he was twelve, Collins recalled—clutching her arm, looking pale. Standing over them was the black-garbed priest.

"Please wait, sir," said the officer who had escorted Collins. "I'll let them know you're here." He disappeared into the next room, closing the door behind him.

Collins lit a cigarette and paced nervously around the small, cheerless room. He wondered what Colonel Baxter had to tell him that was so urgent. Although Collins knew the colonel and his wife from occasional social functions, most of his relationship with the colonel had been of a business nature. What could the colonel have to say to him in these fading moments?

Presently the door to the adjoining room opened and the officer emerged, followed by a nurse and young Rick. They went past Collins and out into the corridor. Seconds later the doorway from Colonel Baxter's room was filled by a short, stocky figure with jet-black hair, surprisingly light blue eyes, sunken cheeks; a man perhaps in his mid-forties. He shut the door carefully behind him, gave Collins a nod, then crossed to close the corridor door.

"Mr. Collins? I'm Father Dubinski."

"Yes, I know," said Collins. "I was at the White House when I got the message from Mrs. Baxter that the colonel had something important to tell me. I came as quickly as I could. Is he conscious? Can I see him now?"

The priest cleared his throat. "I'm afraid not. I'm sorry to say it's too late. Colonel Baxter died just ten minutes ago."

"That—that's tragic," Collins said. "I can't believe it."

He did not know whether it was proper, in this immediate period of mourning, to try to find out why the colonel had summoned him. But, proper or not, he knew he must inquire.

"Father, was the colonel lucid before he died? Was he able to tell anyone—you or Mrs. Baxter—why he wanted to see me?"

"No, I'm afraid not. He simply informed his wife that it was urgent that he speak to you."

"And he said nothing more?"

The priest fidgeted with his rosary. "Well, after that, he did speak briefly to me. I advised him that I was present to administer

376

the Sacraments if he so wished. He requested that I give them to him, and I was able to do so in time for him to be reconciled with God before he died."

"Father, are you saying he made a deathbed confession?"

"Yes, I heard his final confession."

"Was there anything that could give me a clue to what he was trying to tell me that was so urgent?"

"Mr. Collins," Father Dubinski replied gently, "confession is a confidential matter. I can reveal no part of it. Now I'd better return to Mrs. Baxter." He paused. "I'm sorry, Mr. Collins."

The priest started for the adjoining room, and Collins walked slowly out into the corridor. Minutes later he settled into the back seat of the limousine beside an anxious Karen. He ordered the driver to take them home to McLean.

As the car began to move, he turned to Karen. "I was too late. He was dead when I arrived."

"That's terrible. Did you find out what he wanted to tell you?"

"No, I haven't the faintest idea." He slumped deeper into the seat. "But I intend to find out—somehow. Why would he waste his last words on me? I wasn't even a close friend."

"But you succeeded him as Attorney General."

"Exactly what I was thinking. It must have had something to do with my job. Or with the country's affairs. Something that might be important to all of us. I don't know how yet, but I've got to learn what he wanted to tell me."

He felt Karen's hand tighten on his arm. "Don't, Chris, don't get involved further. I can't explain it. But it scares me. I don't like living scared."

He stared out the window into the night. "And I don't like living with mysteries," he said.

2

THEY buried former Attorney General Noah Baxter on a wet May morning in one of the few plots left in the four-hundred-and-twenty-acre Arlington National Cemetery, across the Potomac from Washington, D.C., as Father Dubinski intoned the final prayer.

Director Vernon T. Tynan, his assistant, Associate Deputy Director Harry Adcock, and Attorney General Christopher Collins, who had come to the rites together, were now leaving together. They walked silently in step down Sheridan Avenue, past the gravestones of Pierre Charles L'Enfant and General Philip H. Sheridan, past the eternal flame over the grave of President John F. Kennedy, to Tynan's official limousine. Moments later they were heading over the Memorial Bridge and on into the city.

Tynan was the first to break the silence. "I'll miss old Noah," he said. "You don't know how close we were. I enjoyed the old curmudgeon."

"He was a good guy," agreed Adcock.

"I'm just sorry," said Tynan, "he didn't hang around long enough to see the fruits of his labor on the 35th Amendment come into being. Everyone gives the President credit for coming up with the 35th. But, actually, Noah was responsible for getting it off the ground. He believed in it like a religion. We owe it to him to push it over in the last lap."

"We'll try," said Collins.

"We've got to do more than try, Chris." He gave Collins an appraising look. "I know old Noah would be counting on you to put it over in California. I tell you, Chris, Noah Baxter considered the passage of that amendment the most urgent priority of all."

Collins caught the word *urgent*. Instantly his mind went back to the night in the hospital when the priest had confirmed that Colonel Baxter had wanted to see him about something *urgent*. Could it have had to do with the 35th Amendment? Maybe Tynan, who had been so close to Colonel Baxter, could offer a lead.

"Vernon," Collins said, "apropos of the colonel's priorities, remember how I had to leave the White House in a hurry the other night? Well, I got a message from Bethesda that Colonel Baxter was dying, and he wanted to tell me something of vital importance. I rushed to the hospital, but he'd died just minutes before."

"Oh, yeah?" said Tynan. "Did you find out what he thought was so important to tell you?"

"That's the point. I didn't. Just before dying, he made his confession to Father Dubinski, the priest who was at Arlington today.

I thought maybe in his last moments the colonel might have got something off his chest that he wanted to speak to me about. But Father Dubinski wouldn't say. He only said confessions are confidential. I'm wondering," Collins continued, "if you have any idea of the kind of information Colonel Baxter might have wanted to communicate to me—some unfinished business in the department he might have discussed with you that I should know about. It really puzzles me."

Tynan stared at his chauffeur's back a moment. "I'm afraid it puzzles me, too. I can't think of anything outstanding we discussed before Noah had his stroke five months ago. I can only repeat what had been uppermost in his mind. That was getting the 35th Amendment ratified and made into law. Maybe what he had to tell you had to do with that."

"Maybe. But exactly what about the 35th? It had to be something special if he summoned me to his deathbed. You know, I was thinking of going back to that priest and giving him another try."

Adcock leaned across Tynan. His face was solemn. "If you knew priests the way I do, you'd know you'd be wasting your time."

"Harry's right," Tynan agreed. He peered out the window. "Well, here we are at Justice."

Collins glanced outside. "Yes. Time to get to work. Thanks for the lift." He opened the door and stepped out in front of the Department of Justice.

Tynan and Adcock watched him enter the building. As their car rounded the block toward the rear of the FBI building and the director's private parking place, in the second of three basements beneath, Tynan's eyes met Adcock's. "Harry, what do you think old Noah wanted to say to him that was so urgent?"

"I can't imagine, Chief. Or maybe I can, but don't want to."

"You think maybe Noah Baxter got religion at the last minute and wanted to spill his guts?"

"Could be. No way ever to know. Anyway, thank God, he didn't have time to babble."

"But he did. He babbled something to the priest."

"That was a holy confession. A dying man making a confession, he doesn't talk business."

Tynan screwed up his face. "How do we know? Call it what you want, a confession or whatever, the fact is that Noah *talked* to someone before croaking. I want to know very much what Noah talked about and how much he talked."

The limousine had dipped down the ramp leading beneath the building. "That's a tough one, Chief," Adcock said.

"They're all tough ones, Harry. Tough ones are our meat. The bureau's profession is making people talk. Especially when they have information that endangers government security. There's no reason that priest Dubinski should be an exception. Pay the good father a friendly visit. Find out what old Noah said to him with his last words. If he knows what he shouldn't know, we'll find the means to shut him up."

"Chief, you know I'll do anything. But on this one, I don't think we have a chance."

"Oh, no? We've got every chance if you handle it right. Have the department run a thorough check on Dubinski first. You know our axiom. Everybody's got something to hide. So has this priest. He's human. There's always something. You go to him with what *he* hasn't confessed, and he'll talk all right. You won't be able to shut him up. He'll trade anything for our silence."

The limousine had drawn to a halt in the director's parking slot. Tynan stared ahead, motionless for a moment. "I'm serious about this, Harry. We're too close to home to have anything go wrong. Clear your slate. This is priority one."

At Justice, trying to make up for the time he had lost attending Colonel Baxter's funeral, Collins worked straight through lunch. That evening, seated with his wife and two of their closest friends, Ruth and Paul Hilliard, in the upstairs dining room of the 1789 Restaurant in Georgetown, he finally began to relax. He regarded the man across the table with affection. He had known the junior Senator from California when Hilliard had been a San Francisco city councilman and he himself had been an ACLU attorney. Hilliard was a pleasant man, bespectacled, scholarly, moderate, soft-spoken.

"How do you like the wine, Paul?" Collins asked. "It's California, you know."

"Just look at my glass." Hilliard indicated his empty glass. "The best testimony for our vineyards."

"Want more?"

"I've had enough of California wine," said Hilliard, lighting his pipe. "But not enough of California. I was waiting to discuss it with you. I guess that's where it's all going to be happening from now on."

"Going to be happening? Oh, you mean the 35th."

"Ever since the Ohio vote the other night, I've been getting calls from California. The whole state is buzzing with it."

"What's the word?"

"The odds are the bill's going to be ratified. The governor'll be announcing his support of it later in the week."

"That'll make the President happy," said Collins.

"Between us, it's a deal," said Hilliard. "The governor is going to run for the Senate after this term. He wants Wadsworth's backing, and the President's always been lukewarm about him. So they've made a trade. The governor'll come out for the 35th if the President will come out for him." He paused. "Too bad."

"What's too bad?" Collins asked.

"That the big guns are lining up behind the 35th in California."

"I thought you were for it."

"I wasn't for it or against it. I sort of played the innocent bystander. But now that the decision is in our backyard, I'm inclined to get involved."

"On which side?"

"Against it. Based on what I'm gradually learning of the situation back home, the provisions of the 35th amount to overkill. Too heavy an armament aimed at too small an enemy. That's what Tony Pierce thinks, too. He's coming into California to fight the amendment."

"Pierce's motives are suspect," said Collins, remembering Director Tynan's tirade against the civil rights advocate. "He's made the 35th a personal vendetta. He's fighting Tynan as much as the amendment, because Tynan fired him from the FBI."

"Do you know that for a fact?" said Hilliard.

"Well, that's what I've heard. I haven't checked it."

"Check it, because I've heard different. Pierce became disillusioned by the FBI when he was part of it. He threw his support to some special agents Tynan was manhandling. In retaliation, Tynan decided to exile him to Montana or some such place—and so Pierce resigned to fight for his reforms from the outside. I'm told Tynan spread the story that he was fired."

"No matter," said Collins with a trace of impatience. "What matters is that you've decided to side with those opposing the 35th."

"Because that bill troubles me, Chris. More and more I feel its provisions could be abused. Frankly, the only thing that makes me feel safe about its passage is that John Maynard is on the high bench as Chief Justice. He'd keep it honest."

"There's a positive side, Paul. It'll keep crime from overwhelming us. Crime in California alone is just becoming too much. You read the FBI statistics as well as I do."

"Statistics, figures." Hilliard put down his pipe and looked directly at Collins. "Actually, that is something I've been wanting to discuss with you, too. I've been a little hesitant about bringing it up, because it's your department and I was afraid you might be touchy."

"What do I have to be touchy about? Speak your mind."

"All right. I had a disturbing call yesterday. From Olin Keefe, a newly elected state legislator from San Francisco. He's a good guy. You'd like him. Anyway, he's on some committee that required him to talk to a number of police chiefs in the Bay area. Two of the chiefs wondered aloud why the FBI was trying to make them look bad. They claimed the figures on crime that they submitted to Director Tynan were nowhere near as high as the figures you put out."

"I don't put out any figures, except technically," said Collins. "Tynan gathers them from local communities and computes them. Formally, my office releases them. Anyway, that's not important. What are you telling me, Paul?"

"That Keefe—Assemblyman Keefe—suspects that someone, probably Director Tynan, is doctoring those national crime statistics, especially the figures from California. We've been given a bigger crime wave than we actually have."

382

"Why should he do that? It makes no sense."

"It makes plenty of sense. Tynan is doing that—if he is the one who's doing it—to scare our legislators into passing the 35th Amendment."

"Look, I know Tynan is gung ho on getting the amendment passed. But why do a risky thing like falsifying figures? What does he have to gain?"

"Power."

"He already has power," said Collins flatly.

"Not the kind of power he would have as head of the Committee on National Safety, if the emergency provision of the 35th were ever invoked. Then it would be Vernon T. Tynan *über alles.*"

Collins shook his head. "I don't believe that. Paul, I've been part of Justice for eighteen months. I know what goes on in the department. You're removed from it. And that young assemblyman of yours, Keefe, he's also on the outside. He doesn't know a thing."

Hilliard would not be stopped. "There are some other things he knows, too, and they're not pretty. You don't have to take it from me, Chris. Find out for yourself firsthand. You said you might be going to California soon. Why don't you let me have Olin Keefe look you up? Then, just hear him out." He paused. "Unless for some reason you don't want to."

"Cut it out, Paul. You know me better than that. There'd be no reason I wouldn't want to hear facts—if they are facts. I'm as interested in the truth as you are."

"Then you're willing to see Keefe?"

"You set up the meeting and I'll be there."

THE following day, exactly at noon, as he had done once every week for six months, Ishmael Young arrived in the basement of the J. Edgar Hoover Building after a drive from his rented bungalow in Fredericksburg, Virginia. Even though it was Sunday, he knew that in these critical times everyone in Justice, in the FBI, was on a seven-day week. Tynan would be expecting him. Young parked in the basement, with effort pushed out of the front seat of his secondhand sports car, and met Special Agent O'Dea in front of the director's private-key elevator.

They rode up to the seventh floor, there parted company, and Young walked alone—carrying his tape recorder and briefcase—to Director Tynan's suite.

Presently, in Tynan's spacious office high above Pennsylvania Avenue, Ishmael Young rolled an easy chair close to the low circular coffee table, faced it toward the sofa where the director would soon sit, took out his papers, and made himself ready. By twelve fifteen Tynan's secretary, Beth, had placed a beer on the coffee table for the director, a Diet Pepsi-Cola for his ghostwriter, and two plates with lunch from a nearby delicatessen. Then she left. A minute later Tynan got up from behind his desk and secured the office, locking both doors from the inside. He dropped down on the sofa to gulp his beer.

Tynan enjoyed these sessions. Ishmael Young did not.

Young admired the FBI because it was flawlessly, smoothly efficient, which Young was not. He got things done mostly with a pencil, a typewriter, a mess of papers and tapes, in fits and starts, with nervous tension, and it was no way for a man to live.

He had respected the FBI as an organization from that time, before his first session with Director Tynan six months ago, when Associate Deputy Director Adcock had taken him on a backstage tour of the bureau—off limits for tourists—to give him "the feel." Ishmael Young had been enamored of the FBI files. In this clearinghouse for criminal apprehension, there had been over two hundred and fifty million fingerprint sets. Among the other eighty-seven hundred gray file cabinets there had been the Typewriter Standards file, a record of the typeface and make of every typewriter ever manufactured (he would never again fantasize the typewriting of an anonymous letter).

And there had been much else—the Serology section, where body fluids and blood were tested; the Chemistry department; the Spectrograph room, where particles of paint were examined. He had found it hard to tear himself away from the Hairs and Fibers unit. "When people get into a fight," Adcock had explained, "the fibers of their garments may adhere to each other. We shave all fibers off the garments, separate them, and test them to learn which belonged to the assailant and which to the victim."

When he left, Young's mind had been bursting with ideas. It had been a writer's heaven.

And then he had been brought to his first official book-writing session with Director Vernon T. Tynan. Tynan had wanted an autobiography, and Young had been recommended. Tynan had read two of Young's ghosted books and approved. Young had somehow expected that some of his admiration for the bureau would rub off on its director, but it hadn't. From hearsay, he had known Tynan's reputation, his egomania.

Now six months of weeks had passed, weeks which had only served to confirm, not only the egomania, but also a frightening ruthlessness. In these weeks Young had grown to hate the man whose life story he was writing.

As Tynan gulped down the last of his beer, Young knew it was the signal to begin. He leaned over, simultaneously pressed the RECORD and PLAY buttons on his tape recorder, and reviewed the notes in his lap. A week ago the director had announced the subject of this session. Young reminded himself to show restraint.

"We were going to talk about how things have deteriorated and what the President thinks of the job I'm doing," Tynan said. "Write this down carefully to be sure you get it with no mistakes."

"Well, sir, I have the tape on. There's no need to write it down—"

"Oh, yeah. I forgot. Okay. Now, you listen. The President took me aside a month ago and said, 'Vernon, no one could have accomplished what you've managed to accomplish.' His very words."

"That was quite a tribute," said Young.

Just then the buzzer sounded from the director's desk.

Tynan got quickly to his feet and tramped toward the desk. He picked up the receiver. "Yeah, Beth?" He listened. "Harry Adcock? Well, ask him what's so important." He listened more intently. "Baxter what? The Holy Trinity matter— Oh, yes, of course, the Collins thing. Okay, tell Harry I'll be ready for him in a minute."

He placed the receiver back on the cradle, lost in some reflection. At last he turned away from the desk and saw Ishmael Young. "You— I forgot you were here. Did you hear that conversation?"

"What?" said Young, pretending bewilderment as he studied his list of questions.

"Nothing," said Tynan, satisfied. "I'm afraid some pressing business has come up. Sorry to shortchange you this time, Young, but I'll give you an extra half hour next week."

"Certainly. Anything you say, sir."

As Young obediently shut off his tape recorder and stuffed his papers into the briefcase, he made a mental note to replay the tape when he returned to his bungalow. What was it that the director had not wanted him to hear? Something about Adcock having to see him at once concerning Baxter—that would be the former Attorney General who had been buried yesterday—and the Holy Trinity matter. Holy Trinity Church in Georgetown? The Collins thing. That would be Christopher Collins. What could be important about all that? He determined to file away carefully these pieces of an interesting jigsaw puzzle which might give him a better picture of Tynan's activities. How he'd like to withdraw from this rotten project with integrity.

With a wheeze, he came to his feet and started across the office as Tynan finished unlocking the second of the two doors. Tynan held the door open for his ghostwriter. "Next week we'll talk about some of my contributions to the bureau. How's that?"·

"That's great," said Ishmael Young. "I can't wait."

"Hold any calls," Tynan ordered a few minutes later on the intercom, "unless they're from the White House." He hung up and swiveled to face Harry Adcock. "Okay, Harry, what is it?"

"We ran the check on Father Dubinski of Holy Trinity. There wasn't much. Just one item, way back. He was involved in a drug case in Trenton once, but the police dropped it."

Tynan straightened in his swivel chair. "That's more than enough. You go in and spring that on him, and then we'll see—"

"I already have, Chief," said Adcock. "I've just come back."

"Well, what did he say? Did he spill Noah's confession?"

Harry Adcock made careful notes and never gave answers out of sequence in his narratives, because he felt it led to distortions. Tynan drummed his fingers on his desk and listened impatiently.

"I phoned Father Dubinski early this morning and told him I had to make an inquiry on a matter of government security," said Adcock, consulting his notes. "I saw him in his rectory at five after eleven. At my request, we were alone. I told him it had come to our attention that he had been Colonel Noah Baxter's confessor the night Baxter expired. That Baxter had spoken to no one but him just before dying. I asked him if that was true. He said it was, then he asked if I had obtained this information from Attorney General Christopher Collins. I said no."

"Good."

"Then I said, 'As you must be aware, Father, Colonel Baxter was privy to some of the government's highest secrets. Anything he had to say to anyone outside government, when he was not in complete control of his faculties, would be of extreme interest to the bureau. We've been trying to trace a leak on a matter of utmost security, and it would be useful for us to know if Colonel Baxter spoke to you about it in his last words.'" Adcock looked up. "Father Dubinski said, 'I'm sorry. His last words were his confession. The confession is privileged.'"

"What did you say to that?" muttered Tynan.

"I said this was information desired, not by an individual, but by the government. He reminded me of the separation of church and state. I saw I was getting nowhere fast, so I toughened up."

"Good, Harry. That's better."

"I said that despite his clerical collar, he wasn't above the law. I reeled off the evidence we had of charges against him for possible drug possession in Trenton fifteen years ago. He didn't deny it, didn't even answer, as a matter of fact. I said while he had no formal arrest record, this information—if made public—would make him look pretty bad today. I could see he was angry all right. He said, 'Mr. Adcock, are you threatening me?' I was quick to tell him the FBI doesn't threaten anyone, the FBI merely collects facts. I knew we had no real offense to hang on him. We could only cause him trouble with his parishioners."

"All priests are vulnerable in the public relations area," said Tynan sagely.

Adcock went on. "That's what I was counting on. I told him that if he withheld vital security information, it was inevitable that his name and past might come up when the security leak was probed. 'But if you cooperate with your government now,' I said, 'then your past is no issue.' He flatly refused. I told him that if he didn't cooperate for the good of his country, we'd have to speak about him and his past behavior to his ecclesiastical superiors."

"And still he didn't crack?"

"Nope. My evaluation is that nothing will make him talk. Even if we aired his dirty linen, I think he'd prefer minor martyrdom to betraying his vows." Adcock shoved his notes into his pocket. "What do we do next, Chief?"

Tynan rose, thrust his hands into his trouser pockets, and paced behind his desk for a few moments. He stopped. "Nothing," he said. "If Father Dubinski wouldn't talk to you, despite what you could have done to him, he won't talk to anyone." Tynan exhaled. "Whatever he knows doesn't matter. We're safe."

The buzzer sounded. Tynan started for his telephone. "You've done good work, Harry. Just keep tabs on Dubinski from time to time to keep him in line."

As Adcock left the room, Tynan picked up the receiver. "Yes, Beth? . . . Okay, I'll take it. Hello, Miss Ledger." He listened. "Fine. Tell the President I'll be right over."

As Appointments Secretary Nichols ushered him into the Oval Office a few minutes later, Tynan had a feeling of déjà vu, of reliving an earlier experience. This was because President Wadsworth had restored the Oval Office to the way it had been long ago, when Kennedy was Chief Executive. Director Tynan, as a young FBI agent, had on several occasions accompanied J. Edgar Hoover to the Oval Office when the director had been summoned by Kennedy to witness the signing of some crime bill. For a half second Tynan thought there was President Kennedy behind the elaborate Buchanan desk, speaking to someone, and Director Hoover beside him, and Tynan was a young man once more. But the moment he was announced, the past was dispelled. The man beside him, now backing away and leaving him, was Nichols, not Hoover. The man behind the desk was President Wadsworth, not President Kennedy. And the someone he was speaking to was not a Kennedy aide but Ronald Steedman, the President's personal public-opinion pollster.

"Glad you could make it, Vernon," President Wadsworth said. "Pull up a chair. You, too, Ronald." He wheeled toward Steedman.

388

"Those latest figures you have from California. Review the results again, so Vernon can hear them."

"Certainly," said Steedman. He held a computerized printout before him and began to read. "The results of our public-opinion poll of 2455 registered California voters, taken two days following New York's passage and Ohio's rejection of the amendment, are as follows: forty-one percent in favor of passage of the 35th, twenty-seven percent against, and thirty-two percent undecided."

"That's a lot of undecideds," said the President. "Now read your poll of the California senate and assembly."

Steedman held up a new printout. "This one was even less satisfactory. The legislators are obviously being cautious, waiting to hear from their constituents. Here we have forty percent who were undecided or refused to express any opinion. Then, of the sixty percent of the legislators who did express an opinion, fifty-two percent favored passage, forty-eight percent were against it."

The President shook his head glumly. "Too many fence sitters. I don't like it. That's why I wanted you here, Vernon, to discuss strategy. . . . Thank you, Ronald. When do I see you again?"

Steedman stood up. "Per your instructions, Mr. President, we're running a new poll in California every week now. I should have this week's results for you next Monday."

After collecting his papers, Steedman departed, and the President and Tynan were alone. "Well, there you have it, Vernon," the President said. "Our fate is entirely in the hands of people who haven't made up their minds. We have to instigate every stratagem, exert every pressure, to make them see things our way—for their own good, of course."

"You're right, Mr. President. I've already notified all local police officials in California to Teletype their latest crime statistics every week instead of every month. We'll now be releasing the FBI's Uniform Crime Report every Saturday for media coverage on Sundays. We'll saturate California with the rise in its crime rate."

"Excellent," said the President. "The only problem there is that people become inured to the repetition of mere figures. A speech can dramatize the situation far better. And get more coverage. I was thinking of having a number of Administration people speak at conventions or meetings already scheduled in California cities."

Tynan pushed forward in his chair. "There's only one person who could be really effective. You, Mr. President. You could rally the people around the 35th, and implore them to put pressure on their representatives in Sacramento."

President Wadsworth shook his head. "No, Vernon, it might have just the opposite effect. The legislators and citizens might look upon an address from me about a decision that belongs to them as federal interference. They'd resent the President's telling them what to do. We have to be more subtle. As I mentioned, I've been thinking of Chris Collins. An Attorney General would be regarded as objective and reasonable."

"Umm. Collins. . . . I'm not sure about him. I don't know if he's strong enough or has the conviction—"

"Exactly. His weaknesses can be assets in this case. Give him more credibility. Actually, Vernon, I have no real doubts about him. He's clearly on our side. He understates, yet he carries the authority of his office."

"What do you have in mind—a speaking tour up and down the state?"

"No, that would seem too much like programmed propaganda. Something less obvious." The President snapped his fingers. "If Collins *had* to be in California on other business, it would appear more natural. One second."

He buzzed for his secretary. Almost instantly she appeared.

"Miss Ledger, yesterday I asked you to look into any conventions in California next week where it might be logical for the Attorney General to speak."

"You're in luck, Mr. President. The American Bar Association is having its annual national meeting in Los Angeles from Monday through Friday."

Wadsworth came to his feet, beaming. "Perfect. Get right on the phone to the president of the ABA—he's an old friend—and tell him I'd appreciate it very much if he could book Attorney General Collins as their main guest speaker the last day of the convention."

Miss Ledger looked troubled. "It won't be easy, Mr. President. The main guest speaker on Friday is Chief Justice Maynard."

"What's the difference?" said the President. "Now they can have two speakers. Tell him I'd consider his doing that a personal favor."

After Miss Ledger had gone back to her office, President Wadsworth remained standing. "Well, that's taken care of. I'll inform Collins. He can give a very generalized speech on the 35th Amendment as the hope of the future, and the historic role California will play when it ratifies. I think a fair number of the state legislators will be in the audience. Maybe Collins can hold an informal cocktail party for them afterward, do a little low-key lobbying. . . ."

He was looking down at the memorandums spread on his desk. Suddenly he snatched up one he'd received from his chief aide, McKnight. "I almost forgot, Vernon. There's another matter. A national network television show that originates from some locale prominent in the news each week. A Miss"—he squinted at the memorandum—"Miss Monica Evans, the producer, phoned McKnight. The end of next week they want to tape a debate in Los Angeles on whether or not California should ratify the 35th Amendment. The program is called 'Search for Truth.' They have two guests, each giving his side to some controversial issue. They want you on this one, Vernon, to present the arguments in favor of the 35th. It would be on the same day Chris is addressing the ABA. You could fly out together. I think this exposure would be important for us."

"Who's taking the other side?" asked Tynan.

The President consulted the memorandum. "Tony Pierce."

Tynan bolted upright in his chair. "Mr. President, forgive me, but I think it would be a mistake for the director of the FBI to appear on the same program with a former agent who's been a traitor to the bureau. Why not Collins? He'll be in Los Angeles anyway. He could do the show as well as make his speech. The Attorney General should be welcome on the program."

President Wadsworth seemed pleased. "Good idea," he said. "I'll have McKnight confirm Collins as your substitute. Well, that gives Collins plenty to do out there for our cause."

He extended his hand, and Tynan scrambled to his feet to shake it. "Thanks for everything, Vernon." The President grinned. "California, here we come." He reached for his telephone.

IN HIS OFFICE, the phone receiver caught between his ear and shoulder, Chris Collins busily wrote down the President's instructions. Although making the obligatory agreeable sounds to the proposals, Collins did not like what he heard. He did not mind going to California. It would be old home week, a chance to see his grown son, Josh, by his first marriage, catch up with friends. What he did not like was being forced to defend the 35th Amendment publicly, before a nationwide television audience. He felt equal distaste at the idea of appearing at the ABA convention on the same platform with Chief Justice Maynard, whose civil rights decisions he admired, and being forced in Maynard's presence to take a stand in favor of the 35th Amendment as the President's pitchman.

After hanging up, Collins stared gloomily out the window for a while. Finally he resumed his work and soon was immersed in legal briefs. The next time he lifted his head, he saw that darkness had fallen.

The telephone rang. Then he heard Marion's voice coming through the intercom. "Mr. Collins, there's a Father Dubinski on the line. He says it is important that he speak to you."

Collins recognized the name at once. He took up the receiver. "Father Dubinski? This is Christopher Collins."

"I don't know if you remember me." The priest's voice sounded very distant. "We met the night Colonel Noah Baxter died at Bethesda."

"Certainly I remember you, Father. In fact, I had considered getting in touch with you."

"I'm calling because I would like to see you. The sooner the better. It's about a matter that may be of some interest to you. Nothing I'd wish to discuss on the telephone."

Collins was alert, his curiosity aroused. "I can make it tonight. In fact, within the next half hour."

"I'm glad." The priest sounded relieved. "Would it be an imposition to ask that you come to the church to see me? It would be, well, rather awkward for me to call on you."

"Of course I'll come. Holy Trinity in Georgetown, isn't it?"

"Yes. Actually, I'd prefer that you come to the rectory, where we can speak in privacy." He paused. Then he added, "The front entrance of the church is being watched. It would be better for both of us if your visit is not observed. You'll understand once we've had a chance to talk. In a half hour, then?"

"Or sooner," said Collins.

All the way to Georgetown, in the back seat of the official limousine, Collins speculated about why Father Dubinski wanted to see him. His remark that the front entrance of his church was being watched was unsettling. Watched by whom and for what?

It was baffling. Collins wanted to try out the riddle on the two men in the front seat. There was Pagano, an ex-prizefighter Collins had successfully defended in a criminal action in Oakland and had brought with him to be his driver. Beside him was his bodyguard, Hogan. Both men were thoroughly trustworthy.

But then Collins could see that they were already nearing the rectory. He leaned forward in his seat. "Pagano, drop me off on the next corner. I don't want anyone to see this car."

When they reached the corner, Collins hastily stepped out and said over his shoulder, "Take the car north about a block and park wherever you can. I'll find you."

He stepped away from the limousine, and Mike Hogan was right beside him. "Okay, you can come with me to the rectory, but I'll go in myself. Wait outside, and don't be too conspicuous."

They crossed the thoroughfare and proceeded a short distance. Collins pointed. "There it is." The rectory was a red brick building trimmed in white. "I'll leave you here."

As Collins neared the door, it was opened by an unseen hand. He heard and recognized the voice. "Come right in, Mr. Collins."

He entered a tiny vestibule, dimly lighted, and found himself confronting the dark-haired priest. After a handshake, Father Dubinski and Collins passed through a doorway into a hall. Midway down the hall there was a door. The priest opened it. "Our parlor," said the priest, adding, "It's soundproof."

Inside, Father Dubinski directed him toward a sofa.

"No one saw me come in," said Collins. "Who is it that's watching the front entrance?"

"The FBI."

"The FBI?" Collins repeated incredulously. "Watching you? For what reason?"

"I'll explain," said Father Dubinski. "Do sit down."

Collins sat at the end of the sofa near a small lamplit table. Briskly, Father Dubinski settled on the sofa a few feet from him. The priest wasted no time. "I had a visitor this morning. A Mr. Harry Adcock, whose identity card showed he is assistant deputy —or is it associate?—to the director of the FBI."

"He's Director Tynan's associate. What was he doing here?"

"He wanted to know what Colonel Noah Baxter confessed to me the night he died. He said it might involve a matter of internal national security. I might have accepted the inquiry as well meaning, except for one thing. When I refused to repeat Colonel Baxter's confession, Mr. Adcock threatened me."

"Threatened you?" Collins repeated with disbelief.

"Yes. But before we go into that, I'm mystified by one thing. How could he have known that Colonel Baxter *did* have time to speak to me before dying? Had you told him?"

"As a matter of fact, I did speak of it to Tynan and Adcock as we were driving away from Baxter's funeral. I thought they might have a clue to what Baxter wanted to tell me." He paused. "Tynan actually sent Adcock here to find out Baxter's confession from you? That's incredible. How did Adcock threaten you?"

Father Dubinski fixed his gaze on the coffee table. "The threat was open and direct—well, blackmail. Apparently the FBI had run a thorough check on me and unearthed an unhappy incident in my past. When I was a young priest—I had a church in a Trenton, New Jersey, ghetto—I started a drug-control program. To stop my crusade, some of the hard-core delinquent youngsters planted a small cache of drugs in my rectory, and then informed the authorities that I'd been peddling drugs. It could have ended my service. Fortunately my bishop prevailed upon the chief of police to let me testify at a private hearing. Based on my testimony, I was cleared. Since the culprits were never found, the case rested entirely on my word. I can see how, reviewing the incident today, someone might consider my guilt—or lack of guilt—as unresolved. Somehow the whole abortive affair got into the FBI files.

This is what Mr. Harry Adcock confronted me with this morning."

Collins was stunned. "I—I can't believe it."

"You had better believe it. Mr. Adcock threatened to make this information about my past public if I continued to refuse to divulge the details of Colonel Baxter's last confession. I told Adcock I would not cooperate with him. Afterward, I was enraged at the strong-arm methods being used by a government agency against the very citizens it is supposed to protect."

"I still find it incredible. What could have been so important about Baxter's confession to make Tynan go to such lengths?"

"I don't know," said Father Dubinski. "I assumed you might know. That's why I called you. You shall know some of what Colonel Baxter told me. Because I'm going to tell you."

Collins felt a thrill of excitement. He waited.

"I spent several hours today reconsidering my position," Father Dubinski said. "I knew I could not cooperate with Mr. Adcock or Director Tynan. But I began to see your own request in a different light. Obviously, Colonel Baxter had trusted you. When he was sinking, it was you alone he sent for. I began to see that much of what he told me was probably meant for you. I realized more clearly that my duties were not only spiritual but temporal, and that perhaps I was merely the caretaker of information that Colonel Baxter wished passed on to you. That is how I came to my decision to do so."

Collins' heartbeat quickened. "I deeply appreciate that, Father."

"Dying, Colonel Baxter was reconciled with God," said Father Dubinski. "Once his confession was completed, he made a final effort to address himself to one remaining earthly matter. His last words, spoken almost in his dying breath . . ." The priest searched the folds of his cassock. "I wrote them down after Mr. Adcock left, when I came to believe they were meant for you." He read from a slip of paper: " 'Yes, I have sinned, Father—and my greatest sin—I must speak of it—they cannot control me now—I am free, I no longer have to be afraid anymore—it's about the 35th. . . .'

"He was momentarily incoherent, and then I caught this. 'The R Document—danger—dangerous—must be exposed at all costs at once— The R Document, it's . . .' He drifted off, then tried again.

Very difficult to make out what he was trying to say, but I'm almost sure he said, 'I saw—trick—go see . . .' Moments later he was dead."

Collins sat chilled. Confused and troubled, he said, "The R Document? That's what he spoke of?"

"Twice. Clearly he wanted to say something about it. He couldn't."

"Father, do you have the faintest idea of what the R Document might be?"

"I'd hoped you might know."

"I never heard of it before," said Collins. He considered Colonel Baxter's last words. "He was saying he had sinned by being involved with this—whatever it is. He had been forced to be involved. Whatever it was concerned the 35th Amendment and something called the R Document, a trick which was dangerous and had to be exposed. He'd sent for me to tell me that."

"His legacy to the living, a desire to right a wrong."

"His legacy to me, his successor," said Collins, half to himself. "Why not to the President? Or to Tynan? Or even to his wife? Why to me?"

"Maybe because he trusted you more than he did the President or the director. Possibly because he felt you would understand where his wife would not."

"But I do not understand," said Collins desperately. "The R Document. What could it be?"

Father Dubinski was rising to his feet. "Perhaps you had better find out as soon as possible." He handed Collins the slip of paper. "Now you know all I know of what Noah Baxter meant to tell you in his last agony. The rest is in your hands. There is danger here. I will pray for your success and safety."

3

HE HAD awakened early the following morning, the R Document on his mind. How to find it?

He had decided not to tell Karen about Father Dubinski, because he knew it would worry her, as it had worried him. Later, at his desk, he continued to mull over the matter. When Marion arrived with his cup of strong tea, he had made up his mind where to start.

"Marion, Colonel Baxter's files. Where are they?"

"The main files are in my office. Then he kept more personal files—private correspondence, memorandums—in a fireproof cabinet in his sitting room."

"Is it there now?"

"Oh, no. About a month after he went to the hospital, that file was moved to his home in Georgetown."

"So that's where it is now?"

"Yes. If there's something you want, I could call Mrs. Baxter."

Instantly he knew the person he would interview first on the R Document.

"Yes, call her and ask if she's up to seeing me for a few minutes this afternoon." As Marion started to leave, he added casually, "By the way, I've been looking for a memorandum called the R Document. Does that ring a bell?"

"I'm afraid not."

"It was a memorandum related to the 35th Amendment. Do you want to take a look in our regular files?"

"Right away."

Drinking his tea, Collins disposed of the morning's messages in rapid succession. By noon he had heard from his secretary. She had searched the general files. There was no reference to anything named the R Document. She had contacted Hannah Baxter, and Mrs. Baxter would be glad to see him at two o'clock.

After lunch, Collins was ready to begin his private investigation of the R Document.

Pagano drove him, and Hogan accompanied him, to the familiar white brick nineteenth-century house in Georgetown. Leaving his chauffeur and bodyguard behind, Collins rang the bell and was admitted by the maid.

"I'll fetch Mrs. Baxter," she said. "Would you like to wait on the patio? It's such a lovely day."

Collins went out on the flagstone patio, settled into a padded wrought-iron chair, and lighted a cigarette.

"Hi, Mr. Collins," he heard a young voice call.

He looked over his shoulder and saw Rick Baxter, Noah and Hannah's grandson, on his knees on the flagstone, fiddling with a portable tape recorder.

"Hello, Rick. How come you're not in school today?"

"The driver was sick. So Grandma let me stay home."

"Are your parents still in Africa?"

"Yup. They couldn't come home in time for Grandpa's funeral, so they're staying there for another month."

"You seem to be having trouble with that contraption. Anything wrong?"

"I can't make it work," said Rick. "I'm trying to fix it for tonight so I can tape a TV special, 'The History of Comics in America.'"

"Let me see it, Rick. Maybe I can help."

Rick brought his machine over to Collins. He was a brown-haired boy with alert, wide-set eyes, and braces on his teeth. He was, Collins remembered, bright and mature for a twelve-year-old.

Collins got up and took the tape recorder, checked all the buttons, and then opened up the machine. In a moment he saw what was wrong, made a simple adjustment, and tried it. It worked.

"Thanks!" exclaimed Rick. "Now I can take down the show. You should see my collection. I tape TV and radio shows and interviews. It's my favorite hobby— Hi, Grandma."

Collins turned and greeted Hannah Baxter affectionately. She was a small, plump woman, aging now but with a shiny, warm face, all the features generous.

"I'm sorry," Collins said to her. "I'm really sorry."

"Thanks, Christopher. I'm just glad it's over with. I couldn't stand seeing him suffer. You don't know how much I miss him. But that's life. We all have to face it." She half turned. "Rick, please go inside and leave us."

After the boy left, Hannah spoke nostalgically about Noah Baxter for a while, but at last her voice trailed off. She sighed. "Don't let me go on," she said. "How are you doing with your work?"

"Not easy. I can appreciate what Noah went through."

"He used to say it was like having an office in quicksand. No matter what you did, you sank. Still, if anyone can handle it, you can, Christopher. Noah always had great faith in you."

"Is that why he sent for me the last night, Hannah?"

"Of course."

"What did he say to you?"

"When he came out of the coma he was desperately weak. He whispered, 'Bring Chris Collins here. Urgent matter. Must talk to him.' It wasn't that clear, but it was what he was trying to say."

"Hannah, why didn't he tell you what he wanted to tell me?"

"He wouldn't do that. It was business, I'm sure. He didn't discuss business with me."

"I wish I could have talked to him," Collins said. "He could have straightened me out about a lot of things. For instance, there are some files I can't find in the office. My secretary says Noah's personal file cabinet was sent here after he became ill."

"That's right. I kept it in his study."

"Could I spend a few minutes going through it, Hannah?"

"I don't have it. It was moved out the day after Noah died. Vernon Tynan asked if he could borrow it for a month or two, to be sure there was no top-security material in it."

Odd, Collins thought. What did Vernon T. Tynan want with Colonel Baxter's private papers?

"Actually, Hannah, what I'm looking for is connected with the 35th Amendment. Do you remember if Noah ever spoke to you about something called the R Document?"

She shook her head. "No, not that I can recall."

Disappointed, Collins continued. "Can you think of anyone—any friends—he might have confided in, spoken to about it?"

"Noah didn't have many close friends. He was a very private person. A personal friend?" She broke off, lost in thought. "Well, I guess the only one would be Donald Radenbaugh. He and Noah were the closest of friends. But after Donald was convicted of extortion and sentenced to Lewisburg Federal Penitentiary, well, Noah couldn't see him anymore, of course. Considering Noah's position, it would have been awkward. He had to disqualify himself. But all along, he believed in Donald's innocence. He felt the whole case was a miscarriage of justice."

"Donald Radenbaugh," said Collins. "I remember his name. A money scandal of some kind."

"Donald was a lawyer practicing here in Washington when he became a presidential adviser in the previous Administration. He was indicted for conspiracy to extort a million dollars from big corporations with government contracts. Actually, the money came from illegal campaign contributions. He had nothing to do with conspiring to extort money from anybody. When the FBI zeroed in on a man named Hyland, this Hyland turned state's evidence to get a lighter sentence, and laid all the blame on Donald Radenbaugh. He claimed that Donald was en route to Miami Beach to deliver the money to a third conspirator. When the FBI picked up Donald in Miami, he did not have the money. He insisted he'd never had it. Nevertheless, based largely on Hyland's testimony, Donald was tried and found guilty of extortion."

"Yes, it's all coming back to me now," said Collins. "I think he got a heavy sentence, didn't he?"

"Fifteen years," said Hannah. "Noah always said Donald was used as the fall guy by the aides to the last President, to keep that Administration looking clean. I know he hoped to get Donald a parole after he'd served five years, but now Noah isn't here to help him. Anyway, Donald Radenbaugh is the only person I can think of who might help you. If this document was a project Noah was concerned with, he very well might have discussed it with Donald. He often asked his advice on difficult matters." She paused. "You might visit Lewisburg in your official capacity, arrange to see Donald, say you want to help him the way Noah meant to. He might give you the information you need. I could write him and tell him he can trust you, that you were a protégé of Noah's."

"Would you do that?" Collins asked eagerly. "Of course I would try to help him."

"I certainly shall. I intended to write Donald a few words anyway, about what happened. I don't think he gets much mail anymore, except from his daughter, Susie, who lives in Philadelphia now. I'll tell him you'll be visiting him. Do you know when?"

"I have to be in California the end of the week to deliver a speech. I should be heading back a few days after that. Tell Mr. Radenbaugh I'll be seeing him in a week or so. It's a good lead,

Hannah, and I appreciate it. If there's anything Karen or I can do for you, please call."

Heading for the car, he felt much better. Radenbaugh was a real possibility. But then his mood dampened. First he would have to confront Vernon T. Tynan with the mystery of the R Document. Since meeting with Father Dubinski, Collins had entertained a growing suspicion about his FBI director, but it would have to be done—the sooner the better.

The following morning Collins met with Tynan in the director's seventh-floor conference room. There, Tynan had insisted that Collins take the chair at the head of the table, while he sat in a chair to the Attorney General's right.

"Okay, Chris, what can I do for you?"

"I just need a few minutes," said Collins. "I'm reworking my speech for Los Angeles. I'm including the reports on crime in California that you sent over yesterday." He studied the topmost sheet in his hand. "I must say the statistics are unusually high compared with the other large states." He looked up. "And they are absolutely accurate?"

"As accurate as the police chiefs in California want them to be," said Tynan. "You'll be quoting their own numbers back to them."

"Just want to be sure I'm on solid ground."

"You're on solid ground, all right. Presentation of those figures will be perfect groundwork for going into the 35th Amendment."

Collins said, "I'll be going into the 35th, of course. Although I'll be careful not to overdo it. Frankly, I haven't had time to study the bill closely since becoming Attorney General."

"You did well enough on the 35th during your congressional hearings," said Tynan airily. "You know as much as you need to know."

"But"—Collins hesitated—"maybe I don't know *everything*."

Tynan displayed a flicker of fretfulness. "What else is there to know?"

The moment had come. Collins plunged. "There's something— some kind of supplement—called the R Document. How much does it have to do with the 35th Amendment?"

Tynan's eyes were blank. "The what?"

"The R Document. I thought you could brief me on it, so that I'm prepared for anything."

"Chris, I have no idea what you're talking about. What is it?"

"I don't know. I was cleaning out some of Noah Baxter's old papers and saw mention of it in one of his memos on the 35th. Something about checking it out in relation to the amendment."

"Do you have the memo? Seeing it might refresh my memory."

"It went into the shredder with a lot of Noah's dated papers. But it stuck in my mind, so I thought I'd mention it."

"Could have been Noah's synonym—or whatever you'd call it—for the 35th Amendment," said Tynan. "I can't imagine anything else. Anyway, you can be confident you have all the information you require to do a bang-up job in California. You do your job, we'll do ours, and you can be certain California will ratify. It's all our chips on one bet in another month—and Chris, I don't intend to see us lose the pot."

"Nor do I," said Collins, packing his papers. "Well, I guess I'm in pretty good shape."

As he walked toward the elevator, Collins reviewed the meeting. There had been nothing in Tynan's behavior to indicate that he had knowledge of a dangerous paper known as the R Document. Well, Collins decided, there was still California, where he might learn more. And after that, there was Radenbaugh in Lewisburg, from whom he might learn even more about Tynan and the R Document. Noah Baxter would not have directed him on this blind odyssey unless there were a door somewhere.

He vowed to find it fast.

Tynan stood grimly in the center of his office, awaiting his deputy. When Adcock entered, Tynan was staring absently at the carpet. Without raising his head, he said, "He just left."

"What did he want?" asked Adcock.

Tynan snorted. "He tried to play games with me. He said he was here to get some help on his Los Angeles speech."

"What did he really want, Chief?"

"He wanted to know if I'd ever heard about something called the R Document."

"Where did he hear of such a thing?"

"He talked about seeing it on one of Noah's memos." Tynan snorted again. "He was lying." He met Adcock's eyes. "He's a pretty nosy fellow, our Mr. Collins. I thought he was one of those lightweight intellectuals, still wet behind the ears. I also thought, considering that Noah brought him in, he was a team player. I'm not so sure of that anymore. I think he's definitely looking for trouble. Like thinking he can outsmart Vernon T. Tynan."

Tynan moved around his desk and settled into his swivel chair. "You know, Harry, this building is J. Edgar Hoover's monument. I want my own monument to be the 35th Amendment ratified as part of the Constitution. I don't care if I'm not remembered for anything but that."

"You will be remembered for it, Chief," Adcock said fervently.

"Well, I want to be sure our Mr. Collins understands that, too. I think we better keep an eye on him. Especially in California."

4

TWO DAYS before his departure from Washington, Collins telephoned his nineteen-year-old son, Josh, in Berkeley. He had not seen the boy in eight months. Their phone conversation included the obligatory questions and answers.

"How've you been, Josh? Still excited about political science?"

"Sure, if they didn't make it so boring—and too much homework. I've got lots of outside activities."

"Have you seen your mother lately?" To Collins, his first wife, Helen, was simply Josh's mother. His love for Karen was natural and mutually giving in a way he had never enjoyed with Helen.

"I went to Santa Barbara for her birthday. She's fine."

"How's her husband?"

"I guess they get along. Me, I have nothing to talk about to an over-the-hill tennis pro with arthritis. And worse, he insists on calling me son."

Collins could not resist laughing. Physically, Josh was very unlike his stepfather and much like his real father: over six feet tall, wiry, with a thin face. Josh began to laugh, too. Then he inquired about Karen, whom he'd met only twice. Collins told him he would have a brother or sister in five months.

To his relief, Josh was delighted and full of congratulations. "When am I going to see you both?"

"That's why I'm calling. You'll be seeing me this week if you're free. I'm flying out on Thursday. Karen doesn't feel up to coming along." He went on to outline his agenda in California.

After a brief silence, Josh asked, "Are you going to be plugging the 35th Amendment in the speech, Dad?"

Collins hesitated, sensing storm warnings. "Yes, I am. There are some good things to be said for the 35th."

"I can't think of one," Josh retorted. "I'll be honest with you. I've joined Tony Pierce's group; I'm an investigator for Defenders of the Bill of Rights. We're going to make a fight of it in California. The advocates of the 35th are always arguing it'll never be invoked except in a serious emergency. But, Dad, I think the people behind the bill—I'm not saying you, I mean Tynan and his gang—intend to do much more with it, once they have the amendment. I don't want to discuss this on the phone. But the DBR can prove it."

"Prove what?" Collins demanded.

"I'll show you. I'll take you there. You've got to see it for yourself to believe it. Do me a favor, Dad. Meet me in Sacramento on Thursday before you go to Los Angeles. I want to take you to a place called Newell."

"Well, maybe I can make the time."

Because he was a father as well as the Attorney General, Collins rearranged his plans and arrived in Sacramento just before noon on Thursday. Josh—clean, sunburned, beard neatly trimmed—was waiting. They embraced briefly, then went straight to a rented Mercury with a driver, accompanied by Hogan.

After hours on the road—Josh still keeping secret what he intended to show his father—Collins asked, "Are we almost there?"

Josh peered through the windshield, over the shoulders of the driver and Hogan in the front seat. "Yes."

Collins looked out the window into the glare. This was America at its most desolate. In the past hour he had seen little except dry lakes, alkali beds, abandoned farms overgrown by scrub. Now

they were passing through a forbidding terrain, mostly old lava
flows without any signs of life.

Suddenly there were a few people chatting in front of a store, a
few others gathered near a gas pump, some shanties, and a
weather-beaten sign reading NEWELL.

Josh gave the driver directions and told him when to stop.

Collins was bewildered. "Where are we?"

"Tule Lake," Josh announced. "One of the concentration camps
created in 1942, eight weeks after Pearl Harbor, by President
Roosevelt's order. Eighteen thousand Japanese-Americans were interned here, even though most were United States citizens!"

"I don't like that blot on our history any more than you do,"
said Collins. "But what's it got to do with the 35th Amendment?"

"You can see for yourself." Josh opened the back door of the
Mercury and stepped outside. Collins followed his son, standing
in the dry, hot wind, trying to get his bearings. They were near
what appeared to be a huge manufacturing plant—a series of brick
buildings and corrugated huts in the distance, set behind a new
chain link fence.

"This was our toughest concentration camp," said Josh. "Built
on a twenty-six-thousand-acre dry lake bed. Now it's something
else, and that's why I brought you here. First let me show you
something." He opened a large manila envelope, extracted a half
dozen photographs, and handed them to his father. "Look at these
photos of the old camp, taken just one year ago by the Japanese
American Citizens League. What do you see?"

Collins studied the photographs. He saw a broken-down chain
link fence, with rusted barbed wire on top. Behind the fence, some
decaying remnants of barracks and a crumbling watchtower.

Collins returned the pictures. "There's nothing to see."

"Exactly," said Josh. "That's the point." He gestured toward the
scene in front of them. "Now, a year later, what do you see? A
brand-new security fence with electrified wire, set in reinforced-
concrete foundations. And out there a spanking-new brick watchtower with searchlights. Three new cement-block buildings, four
more going up. What does that tell you?"

"That there's construction work going on."

"But what kind of construction work? I'll tell you. It's a secret government project taking place. It's a new Tule Lake concentration camp. And it's being prepared for the victims of mass arrests when the 35th Amendment goes into effect."

Collins was taken aback and irritated. "Come on, Josh, you don't expect me to buy that. Wherever did you dream that up?"

Josh's mouth tightened. "We have our sources. It *is* a government project. It's new. It's plainly some kind of internment camp or prison. If it isn't, why the renovated watchtower?"

"Hundreds of government projects have towers for security." Collins saw that behind the fence a man in military uniform was walking toward the entry gate. "I'll disprove your notion about this project," he said determinedly. "You wait here."

Collins strode toward the gate. "Are you a guard here?" he asked the uniformed man.

"That's right."

"Is this private property or federal?"

"It's federal. Anything I can do for you, sir?"

"I'd like to have a look at your facility." Collins was tempted to display his credentials, but thought better of it. "I'm with the Justice Department—Washington."

"You'll have to have clearance from the Pentagon or the navy. This is a restricted area."

"The navy, you said."

"That's no secret," the guard said. "It's an arm of Project Sanguine. Called ELF—Extremely Low Frequency. A U.S. Navy communication system to contact submerged submarines. It's been in all the papers. Come back with proper clearance and we'll be glad to show you around."

Feeling foolish, Collins trudged back to where Josh was waiting in front of the car. He repeated exactly what he had been told. "So much for that. Now you can tell Pierce and your DBR friends it's a U.S. Navy facility and nothing more."

Stubbornly, Josh persisted. "Dad, why all those barracks? Navy personnel doesn't need that kind of setup. Why the electrified fence? You just won't face up to what the President and the FBI are planning to do. They're duping you all the way."

Collins started for the car. "Maybe you're the one who is being duped. Come on, let's return to civilization."

The long ride back was a silent one. Only when they had reached Sacramento Municipal Airport and were about to say good-by— he to proceed to Los Angeles, his son to return to Berkeley via Oakland—did Collins offer a smile. He placed his arm around Josh's shoulder. "Look, I don't object to your being an activist. I'm proud to have you that involved. But you've got to be positive about your facts before making accusations."

"I'm positive about this," said Josh.

The boy's obstinacy was maddening. With an effort, Collins maintained his good humor. "Okay, okay. What if I can prove to you that what we saw was a legitimate navy project? Will that convince you?"

For the first time Josh smiled. "Fair enough. You prove it, Dad, and I'll admit I was wrong."

"You have my word that I will. Now I'd better catch that plane. I've got to meet with a state legislator tonight who's on your side. But he's going to have to prove a few things, too."

In Los Angeles, Collins had his bags taken to a private three-room bungalow at the rear of the Beverly Hills Hotel, washed and changed, and hurried to a waiting Lincoln Continental.

His appointment with Assemblyman Olin Keefe, which Paul Hilliard had arranged, was at the Beverly Wilshire Hotel at ten o'clock. When Collins entered Keefe's small living room, he found two other men also rising to greet him.

Keefe pumped Collins' hand enthusiastically. "I hope you don't mind," he said, "but I took the liberty of inviting two colleagues from the assembly. Since we're lucky enough to have you here, I thought the more input the better."

"I'm delighted," said Collins, somewhat disconcerted.

"This is Assemblyman Yurkovich." He appeared to be a serious young man with a flowing rust mustache. Collins shook his hand.

"And this is Assemblyman Tobias, a veteran of the legislature." Tobias had bulging brown eyes and a bulging waistline.

"Here, why don't you take the armchair?" said Keefe. "You must be tired—all that flying today. We'll try not to keep you too long. In fact, we'll start right in."

"Please do," said Collins.

The other two seated themselves on the sofa, and Keefe hauled a chair to the coffee table across from Collins. "I understand our mutual friend, Senator Paul Hilliard, filled you in a little last week," said Keefe.

"Yes, he did. He wanted me to see you about some discrepancy in California's crime statistics. Do I have it right?"

"Yes," said Keefe. "We three—as well as many more in the California State Legislature who are afraid to speak out—are gravely distressed by the tactics you and your Department of Justice are employing to win this state in the 35th Amendment vote."

"I've employed no tactics whatsoever to influence the vote here. You have my word for that."

"Then someone else has," interjected Tobias from the sofa. "Someone in your department is trying to scare the legislators of this state into ratifying the 35th."

Collins scowled. "Do you want to be more specific?"

"We're talking about your statistics reports of violent crimes and conspiracies," Keefe said. "I've personally interviewed fourteen community police chiefs. More than half agreed that the figures they send to the FBI are not the figures released by the Department of Justice. Somewhere along the way the real statistics have been doctored, exaggerated, even falsified."

"That's a grave charge," Collins said. "Have you got written statements from these police chiefs to back it up?"

"No, I do not," said Keefe. "They won't go that far. They're too dependent on the goodwill of the FBI to antagonize the bureau. They spoke to me only because they resent being made to look incompetent. You have asked us to take your word that you are not involved in this. You in turn will have to take our word about the tactics being used by the FBI. I've tried to get it in writing, but it's no use."

"Maybe I could. They might be willing to file a complaint with me, as Attorney General, where they would refuse to do so with you. Do you have their names?"

410

"Right here." Keefe tore out three pages from a notebook and handed them to Collins. "The police chiefs who wouldn't talk are crossed out. The other eight talked. The addresses and phone numbers are there. I hope you have some luck."

Collins folded the pages and put them in his jacket pocket.

"The problem is," said Keefe, "that some faceless person or persons in your department seem determined to shove the 35th down our throats at any cost. Tampering with statistics, Mr. Collins, is the least of it. Someone in Washington is tampering with our very lives."

Collins sat up. "What do you mean?"

"I mean there's been a concerted campaign by the Federal Bureau of Investigation to intimidate certain members of the legislature by using blackmail—"

Blackmail. Collins' mind went back to the meeting with Father Dubinski, who had also spoken of blackmail. He listened for what was next.

"The attack has been directed primarily at legislators who have not made up their minds about the 35th and who might have something in their pasts that they don't want made public. Assemblyman Yurkovich and Assemblyman Tobias—while they thought it unwise to denounce the FBI—were prepared to come here and protest to you personally. At first they worried that you might be part of the plot. But Senator Hilliard convinced me— even before I met you—and I convinced them, that you were honest and trustworthy and perhaps too new to your job to know what's going on behind your back." Keefe paused. "I hope this estimate of you is correct."

Collins found a cigarette and brought it to his lips. He was not surprised to find that his hand was trembling. "Honest and trustworthy, yes. But what's going on behind my back?"

Yurkovich spoke up. "Let me tell what happened to me. Mr. Collins, I was an alcoholic until eight years ago. I finally had myself confined in a sanatorium for treatment. I licked it. I've been straight ever since. It's been known to no one except my immediate family. A week ago two FBI agents—one named Parkhill, the other Naughton—visited me in my Sacramento office. They said that they

411

needed my help on a difficult investigation—that such inquiries into the breaking of federal laws would be made easier once the 35th was passed, but for now they had to do it the slow way. They required information on a certain sanatorium involved in illegal drugs, where, they had learned, a California legislator had once been confined for five months. Perhaps I could tell them more about the proprietors of this sanatorium."

Yurkovich wagged his head in disbelief. "It was diabolical the way they let me know. My absolute secret was in their hands. I was sickened."

Collins was sickened, too. "What did you say to them?"

"What could I say? I told them what I had heard and seen while I'd been confined. When it was over, one said, 'You may be called upon to give public courtroom testimony.' I told them I couldn't do that. The agent said, 'Well, you might speak to the director, if you wish. He might come to some understanding with you.' Then they went away. And I had the message. Vote for the 35th and the director won't let your hospitalization be made public."

"What are you going to do?" asked Collins.

"I struggled to get where I am," said Yurkovich simply. "I'll have to vote for the 35th. I'm taking no chances."

"Neither am I," said Assemblyman Tobias.

"You mean the same thing happened to you?" asked Collins.

"Almost the same," said Tobias. "It was a day later. Only the FBI didn't come to me. They went to— Well, I have a lady friend, and they called on her. I'm a solid married man with kids—on the surface. Actually, my wife and I were through long ago. But for the kids' sake we continue to maintain a front. And it helps me in government life. For years I've had a woman on the side, a separate residence. No one knew about it except the three of us. Then, last week, the FBI called on my woman friend. One agent's name was Lindenmeyer, I remember. For a while they talked about other things—even the 35th Amendment—oh, very casually. Finally they got down to business. I was on a committee concerned with government contracts. They were investigating someone on the committee who was under suspicion. They wanted to know if I ever discussed government contracts with her. She tried to say she

412

didn't know me very well. They ignored her protests. They knew how many days a week I spent with her for how many years. When they left, they emphasized that 'if it came to it,' they might have to subpoena her."

Collins let out his breath slowly. "I can't believe it."

"*I* believe it," said Tobias. "So I'm changing my vote. I despise the 35th. But I'm going to declare aye loud and clear when it's my turn to vote. There, now you know it all, Mr. Collins."

Collins let it sink in. "Has this happened to other legislators?"

"I don't know," said Tobias. "It's certainly nothing we want to talk to each other about. We each have our private lives."

"Can you do anything about it?" Keefe wanted to know.

Collins stood up. "I'm not sure. Again, we have no hard evidence. These visits may have been actual inquiries with a sound basis for investigation. Or—they may have been a form of blackmail."

"How are you going to find out which?" Keefe asked.

"By investigating the investigators," Collins said.

BACK in the Beverly Hills Hotel, Chris Collins picked up his bungalow key and went to the pay phone booths in the lobby to begin his search for facts.

He had promised his son that he would prove the Tule Lake facility was not a future internment camp. There was also the manipulation of California crime statistics to look into. And the business of FBI agents' probing California state legislators. Above all, there was the R Document.

The pay booths were vacant. Closing himself in the nearest one, he dialed the Deputy Attorney General, Ed Schrader, at home. It was almost three in the morning in Virginia, but he wanted information as soon as possible.

A sleepy voice answered the phone.

"Ed, this is Chris. Listen, there's something I want you to do for me this morning. Got a pencil? Find out what you can about a U.S. Navy land-based submarine communication facility called ELF or Project Sanguine, under construction at Tule Lake in northern California. I'm not leaving for the television show until noon. Ring me up as soon as you have the facts."

413

Leaving the phone booth, he picked up his bodyguard, Oakes—who was spelling Hogan—led him along the walks bordered with foliage to his bungalow, bade him good night, and went inside.

He was tired to the marrow of his bones.

Briefly he rattled around the bungalow living room, removing his suit coat and tie, trying to get some perspective on the events of the day. Taking off his shirt, he walked through the darkened bedroom and on into the bathroom, turning on the light. He undressed, then reached for his pajamas. They weren't hanging on the back of the door. The hotel maid had probably laid them out on the bed.

Turning off the bathroom light, he groped his way naked toward the bed, where a strip of illumination from a crack in the living-room door fell on his pajamas. He had reached down—when suddenly something warm and fleshy touched his thigh.

"What the hell—" he blurted.

"Come to bed, darling," he heard a feminine voice purr.

He fumbled for the lamp, desperately trying to find the switch. In a moment the dim light threw a half circle of yellow on the bed. He was too incredulous to speak or act. She was young, perhaps in her early twenties.

"Hello," she said. "I'm Kitty. I thought you'd never get back."

"You've made a mistake," he burst out. "You're in the wrong—"

"This is the bungalow number I was given. I was told to wait for Mr. Collins."

"Who told you to come here?" he demanded.

"I'm a present from a friend of yours. He gave me two hundred dollars. He said this was to be a surprise, that you'd like it."

"How did you get in?"

"A few of the employees know me. I tip well." She studied him. "Aren't you cute? I like tall men. But you talk too much. Now come here like a good boy—I promise you a good time. I'm staying all night."

"The hell you are!" he almost shouted. "Get out, right now." He grabbed her arms and yanked her to a sitting position. "Get dressed and leave here immediately." He snatched up his pajamas. "By the time I'm out of the bathroom, I expect you to be gone."

414

When he emerged from the bathroom, she had just finished fastening her blouse.

"Hurry up," he said. He took her arm and spun her toward the door. "Get moving."

"Let go, you're hurting me."

He eased his hold, but pushed her into the living room and propelled her hastily to the front door. At the door, breathing heavily, he relented slightly. "I'm sorry somebody used you this way in a childish practical joke. It was wrong, and I'm sorry. Good night."

"No loss," she said.

He jerked open the door, and as she passed in front of him to go, he saw a shadowy figure pop up from behind the hedge below the bungalow. It was a man lifting a camera.

Acting on instinct, Collins ducked behind the door just as the strobe flash went off. He fell against the door, slamming it shut; lay against it, panting, knowing the photographer had caught Kitty but missed him.

Somebody had tried to set him up, compromise him. But who? And why? Proponents of the 35th Amendment? Unbelievable, since so far he had been publicly on their side. Unless they wanted to be sure he remained on their side.

Morning brought definition to the murky things that had filled his mind during his restless sleep. He had intended to call the eight police chiefs who had complained to Assemblyman Keefe. He spoke to only three, and then called no more. Once convinced they were talking to the Attorney General, they had become guarded in answering his questions. All three had refused to acknowledge that they had complained about exaggerations in the statistics, saying, each in his different way, that Assemblyman Keefe had misunderstood him.

Collins had jotted down the names of the FBI special agents who had interviewed Yurkovich and Tobias. He put in a call to his secretary. "Marion, I want a query made of the FBI. It's not to come from me. Just a run-of-the-mill check from anyone in the Office of Legal Counsel to someone on a lower level in the bureau. Have them ask if two of the FBI's special agents in California, one named Parkhill, the other Naughton, interviewed Assemblyman Yurkovich last week.

"Then have them ask if a Special Agent Lindenmeyer interviewed anyone in Sacramento during an investigation of a California assembly committee on which Assemblyman Tobias sits. I'm in the hotel. Get right back to me."

In fifteen minutes the phone rang. It was Marion. "The FBI says it has no special agents named Parkhill or Naughton or Lindenmeyer in California. In fact, it has none by those names in the entire country."

Weird! It could mean that both Yurkovich and Tobias had gotten the names wrong. Unlikely. Or it could mean that the FBI had a special corps of secret agents—names unlisted—deployed to intimidate California lawmakers.

Normally, Collins, a factual, realistic person rarely given to flights of fancy or melodrama, would have dismissed this possibility as too sinister to treat seriously. But his predecessor in office had saved his dying words to warn him of a terrible danger called the R Document. If one could accept as fact that the existence of a document could menace the security of the country, one could also accept the possibility of unknown FBI agents threatening California assemblymen. It was a fact that a known agent had threatened Father Dubinski.

All of this, one way or another, had been engendered by the efforts to ratify the 35th Amendment. What, he thought, would it be like if the 35th actually became the law of the land?

He was about to leave to tape the television show with Pierce when the telephone rang and he heard the voice of Ed Schrader on the line from Washington. "Chris, about the assignment you gave me last night. I have this from authoritative sources at the Pentagon. The navy's Project Sanguine—or ELF, as they call it— was completed three years ago. There are no new installations under construction or any being repaired. None of their facilities is anywhere near Tule Lake."

He couldn't believe his ears. "But, dammit, *some* government project is being built up there."

"Well, it's certainly not what you heard."

416

"No, I guess not," he said slowly. "Thanks, Ed."

For the first time he admitted to himself the possibility that his son, Josh, might be right. And Keefe, Yurkovich, and Tobias, too.

All during the drive to the network studios he reviewed the mounting evidence of something sinister. But finally it was the smallest event of all that unsettled him the most—the photographer planted outside his bungalow, trying to catch him with the girl who had been planted inside. That had not been hearsay. That had been experienced firsthand.

He was filled with suspicion and distrust toward those around him, the advocates of the 35th Amendment, as well as toward the amendment itself. Above all, he was in no mood to defend the amendment on national television. He was sickened by the role he had to play. He wanted to turn around and run. But it was too late. He could see the network studios up ahead.

He was met by the producer of "Search for Truth," a tailored young woman named Monica Evans.

"I hope you're running on schedule," Collins said. "Right after this, I'm due at the Century Plaza for a speech to the bar association. It's going to be close."

"You'll be out in plenty of time," she assured him. "Tony Pierce is already on the stage with our moderator, Brant Vanbrugh."

He followed her quickly into the vast television studio. Cameras were focused on a small platform dressed as a private library set, with three swivel chairs grouped around a table. Two men were conversing on the platform.

Although Collins had never met Pierce, he recognized him from his newspaper pictures and television appearances. For the debate Collins wanted an enemy, and what he saw instead was a disarming and winning human being. Pierce had sandy hair and a freckled, open face alive with enthusiasm. Collins' heart sank. What had brought him here to champion the horrendous 35th Amendment? The only enemy he could find now was himself.

Monica Evans introduced them.

"I'm glad to meet you at last, Mr. Collins," Pierce said. "The little I know about you is from what I've read and from your son, Josh. He's quite a boy."

417

"He speaks highly of you," said Collins.

Vanbrugh led them to their respective chairs on either side of him. As someone fastened a small microphone around Collins' neck, he heard the moderator say, "We'll be taping in two minutes. This edition of 'Search for Truth' will air coast to coast on prime time tonight. What you do here goes on as is. No editing. I'll open with the proposition: 'Should California ratify the 35th Amendment?' You'll each make an opening statement. After that you can start your debate. When the red light goes on above the middle camera, we're taping. Good luck, gentlemen, and let's keep it lively."

The red light above the middle camera began to shine.

Feeling ill and fuzzy-headed, Collins heard his name and knew he was being introduced. He summoned up a sickly smile for the camera.

Next, he heard Tony Pierce's name. Pierce's face was grave.

He heard his own name again, and the opening question. From a distance he heard himself speaking:

"At no time since the Civil War have our democratic institutions been so seriously threatened as they are today. Violence has become commonplace. Back in 1975, ten out of every one hundred thousand Americans died by murder. Today, twenty-two out of every one hundred thousand Americans die by murder. It was out of a need to stop this upward spiral of violence that the concept of the 35th Amendment was born."

Laboriously he continued until he saw the fifteen-second card, and with relief concluded his opening statement.

Now he heard Tony Pierce speaking, every sentence a blow, and he winced inside and tried not to listen.

Two minutes more and he knew the debate had begun.

He heard Pierce speaking once more. "If the 35th Amendment is passed, freedom will end in America. Overnight, at the whim of the director of the FBI and his Committee on National Safety, the Bill of Rights could be suspended indefinitely—"

"Not indefinitely," Collins interrupted. "Only in an emergency, and only for a short time, perhaps a few months."

"That's what they said in India in 1962," said Pierce. "They had

418

an emergency and they suspended their Bill of Rights. It remained suspended for six years. Then they suspended it again in 1975. Who can guarantee that won't happen here? You are arguing for an amendment to void the Bill of Rights, and I am saying to do so is to void democracy itself."

Collins felt cornered and helpless. He compensated with anger. "Mr. Pierce, it is to *preserve* democracy that I am supporting the 35th," he said heatedly. "What will void democracy is permitting our present plague of lawlessness and anarchy to escalate totally out of control."

"There are better ways to control crime than by offering dictatorship," retorted Pierce. "We might begin by offering people food, jobs, housing, justice, compassion, equality."

"I believe in all those things, too, Mr. Pierce. But we must stop the killing first. With order restored, we can start attending to our other priorities."

Pierce shook his head. "We'll be able to attend to nothing once our human rights are lost. I was rereading a book last night"—he plucked a paperback off the table and opened it—"called *Your Freedoms: The Bill of Rights* by Frank K. Kelly, vice-president of the Fund for the Republic. Listen to what he has to say: 'If we lost our Bill of Rights, what would happen to our way of life? . . . The government could keep young men in the military services for indefinite periods, without giving any justification for this policy. Young men and women leaving school could be assigned to jobs in industries where the government asserted that workers were needed. Young people could be forced to take these jobs. Students protesting against government policies . . . could be thrown into federal prisons by order of the President. Americans, young or old, could be required to give up their property for public use without compensation. . . .'"

Pierce was going on and on, and Collins unconsciously began shrinking in his chair. The fight he had tried to fake had gone out of him. He didn't belong here, not on the side where he sat.

He waited. He listened. He attempted a few more halfhearted defenses. He did his duty. The endless thirty minutes passed, and finally the torture was over.

He fumbled to remove his microphone, went hastily into the hallway, found the bathroom, and rushed inside. He made it to the basin just in time.

After a while, he washed his face and hands and tried to regain his composure. He stared at himself in the mirror. If he had wondered where he stood on the Bill of Rights, he knew now.

An hour later he had made up his mind what he must do. It wasn't what he wanted completely, but it was a start.

While his bodyguards and local police helped him push through the mob of press photographers and spectators at the Century Plaza Hotel, Collins crossed the vast lower lobby and entered the Los Angeles Room.

Clutching the leather folder that held his speech, he came onto the dais, where officers of the American Bar Association rose to welcome him. A scattering of applause followed him as he was directed to his seat beside Chief Justice John G. Maynard.

Shaking hands with the Chief Justice, Collins was once again impressed by the idol of his youth. Maynard's mass of white hair, deep-set, probing eyes beneath thick brows, hooked nose, and square jaw gave him the appearance of an honest Caesar. His carriage, ramrod straight, added an air of vigor and youth remarkable for a man in his mid-seventies.

For Collins, the next move was difficult. He barely knew Chief Justice Maynard, who had sworn him in so recently as Attorney General. Aware that the president of the American Bar Association had gone to the podium and that the proceedings were about to begin, Collins touched Maynard's sleeve and leaned toward him. "Mr. Chief Justice, I wonder if I could have five minutes alone with you in private after we leave here?"

"Why, certainly, Mr. Collins. We have rooms upstairs. Mrs. Maynard is out shopping, so we can be quite alone."

Collins sat back again, feeling better. On his lap rested his speech recounting the acceleration of crime in the United States and the ways the judiciary had developed to meet it. At the beginning and end were pleas for the necessity of constitutional revision, when required, with particular emphasis on the importance of the 35th Amendment.

Taking out his pen, Collins quickly cut three paragraphs from the opening pages. What remained was still an argument for consideration of new laws to handle new problems, but now the argument was milder, watered down—more a suggestion offered for debate.

Then he heard the president of the ABA from the podium. "Ladies and gentlemen, the Attorney General of the United States —Christopher Collins!" He rose to speak.

Two hours later, his own turgid speech behind him, the Chief Justice's brilliant words still ringing in his ears, Collins sat on the edge of a straight-backed chair in the quiet of Maynard's suite.

"Mr. Chief Justice," Collins began, "I'll come directly to the point and tell you why I wanted to see you alone. I'd like to know your views on the 35th Amendment."

The Chief Justice, relaxed on the couch, filling his pipe with tobacco from a pouch, raised his head with a frown. "Your question—is it inspired by the Executive Branch, or is it your own?"

"It is my own, growing out of my personal concern. I have great respect for your opinion," continued Collins. "I'm eager to know your thoughts on what might be the most controversial and decisive bill ever put before the American people."

"The 35th," murmured Maynard, lighting his pipe. He puffed a few seconds, then studied Collins. "I'm very much against such drastic legislation. Improperly applied, it can turn our democracy into a totalitarian state. The 35th Amendment may buy safety. But it will be at the cost of human liberty. It's a bad bargain."

"Why don't you come out and publicly say so?" asked Collins.

Chief Justice Maynard eyed Collins shrewdly. "You are the Attorney General. Why don't you speak out against it?"

"Because I'd no longer be the Attorney General and I think I can do more good where I am. Besides, my voice wouldn't be listened to as yours would. Surely you saw the recent California statewide poll on the most admired Americans. You polled eighty-seven percent. People will listen to you here, and so will the state legislators."

"I'm afraid you've thoroughly confused me, Mr. Collins," said Maynard, setting down his pipe. "When you asked why I am not speaking out against the bill, I responded by asking you the same question. I expected you to say because you are all for it. Instead, you indicate you're on my side. Yet you want me to be the one to denounce it publicly. I simply don't understand. I thought you, as well as the President, the congressional leaders, the FBI director, were all supporters of the 35th. Even in your speech today you seemed to indicate the 35th should be given careful consideration."

Collins nodded. "I've been confused myself. The speech was written before today, and delivered at the instigation of President Wadsworth. Since yesterday I've become increasingly fearful of how the amendment might be misused. I now agree totally with you about it. I would resign rather than defend it again. But for now, I'd prefer to stay in office. I'm faced with some unfinished business before I can take a stand. Meanwhile, time is running out here in California. That's why I urge you to speak out. You, alone, could kill it."

"All right, I'll tell you why I can't speak out," said Maynard. "The justices of the high court have an ethical agreement not to speak out on political matters."

"I see," said Collins in despair. "I guess there's no way for you to tell the public what you really think of the 35th."

"No way as long as I'm on the bench." Maynard was thoughtful a moment. "Of course, I could resign. Then I'd be free to speak out." He shook his head. "But present circumstances don't seem to warrant such a drastic step."

"Can you envision any future circumstances that might make you want to resign and speak out against the 35th?"

Maynard considered the question. "Well, yes. If I were convinced that the men and the motives behind the 35th were evil, if I were certain that in their hands the 35th would present a true and immediate danger to the country, I would step down and raise my voice immediately. In short, if there were more to it than meets the eye—"

Collins thought of the R Document and Noah Baxter's deathbed warning. "Chief Justice Maynard," Collins interrupted, "have you ever heard of something called the R Document?"

"The R Document? No, I think not. What is it?"

422

"I'm not sure. Let me explain." Slowly he related to Maynard the circumstances of Colonel Baxter's death and his portentous last words. "As far as I can deduce, it seems to be a paper or plan which is involved in the 35th Amendment in some way. As you heard, it is something Baxter considered dangerous. It may be the something that does not meet the eye."

"It may be," said Maynard. "It certainly sounds ominous."

"If I uncovered it and it proved to be a danger, could that make you act?"

"It might," said Maynard cautiously. "Let me see it—and then I'll give you my answer."

"Fair enough." Collins stood up. "I'm resuming my search. If and when I find the R Document, you'll be the first to hear."

Chief Justice Maynard rose. "Once I've heard from you, I'll be ready to make a decision."

As Collins left Maynard's suite, his mind felt clearer. He knew where he stood on the 35th at last. He knew there was an ally to help him stop it, if he came up with the elusive missing evidence against it. And he knew one source that might give him a clue. He must return to Washington. But after that, he must go calling on someone at Lewisburg Federal Penitentiary in Pennsylvania.

THE following morning, behind the locked doors of the office of the director of the FBI, two immobilized figures sat listening to a tape spinning slowly on the large silver recorder set on the coffee table between them. Vernon T. Tynan and Harry Adcock had been listening, wordlessly, for nearly a quarter of an hour. The last of the tape was playing:

"Fair enough. I'm resuming my search. If and when I find the R Document, you'll be the first to hear."

"Once I've heard from you, I'll be ready to make a decision." Silence, except for the rubbing of the remainder of the blank tape.

Tynan jumped to his feet, his face livid. "That dirty, rotten Collins. I'm going to have his neck for this. He won't get anywhere trying to subvert us. We'll put him out of the way fast. Maynard's the one that bothers me. He can be real trouble if he goes back to California to bad-mouth us and the 35th. I'm not taking any chances with either of them. We're going to beat Maynard and Collins to the punch."

"Collins will be easy," said Adcock. "Take this tape over to the President—he'll fire his Attorney General in one minute flat."

Tynan held up his hand. "No, Harry. You and your boys did a great job in Los Angeles. The tapes are precious, but I don't think it would be wise to let the President in on our procedures. He can be pretty square. Besides, he doesn't want to be involved. I think it would be better to handle Mr. Attorney General Collins and Mr. Chief Justice Maynard in our own way. We can start by having the bureau run a quiet check on Collins."

"But he was checked out thoroughly before Congress confirmed him as Attorney General," Adcock protested.

Tynan waved his hand. "That first investigation was routine. I want an elite strike force assigned to this investigation, with you in charge. Go after everyone ever connected with him. Go after his first wife, Helen Collins—or whatever her name is now. Go after their son. Go after his second wife, Karen Collins, and their housekeeper. Run down close relatives and friends. Don't overlook anyone. I want the investigation completed in one week."

"One week," Adcock promised.

"Okay. Next, John G. Maynard. Have our task force investigate every step he has made; his every statement, letter, investment, activity gone over with a magnifying glass. If Collins went public against us, he might hurt us a little in California, but not fatally. If Maynard decided to turn against us, he could destroy us."

Adcock came forward to the desk. "Chief, even if we found something on Maynard, it would never be enough to stop him once he made up his mind to oppose the 35th."

Tynan reflected on the matter. "You're right, Harry. If Maynard resigned to come out against us, he'd go all the way." Tynan's countenance darkened. "Then we'd have to go all the way, too. It would be him or us. There's one thing . . ."

He had drifted off into deeper deliberation. "It'll take money— lots of it. We need a war chest from a source that can't be traced." Suddenly he hit the palm of his hand with his fist. "Harry, I've got it!"

Tynan sat down in his chair and dialed his secretary on the intercom. "Beth? Get me the file on Donald Radenbaugh." He hung up and lay back, beaming at his assistant.

Adcock was plainly puzzled. "Radenbaugh is locked up in Lewisburg."

"I know."

"I thought you were looking for a lot of money?"

Tynan grinned. "I am. Just have trust."

In minutes, Beth appeared with the file. Tynan opened it and began skimming the sheets of paper. "Extortion . . . To deliver money in Miami Beach, according to Hyland . . . No money . . . Then the trial . . . Guilty. Fifteen years . . . Two years and eight months served."

Tynan looked up at his assistant with a smack of satisfaction. "Perfect," he said. "If this works, I'm a genius. If our Chief Justice interferes, we'll be ready for him."

"I don't understand, Chief."

"You will, soon enough. You can get on to the Collins investigation after this. First call Warden Bruce Jenkins at Lewisburg. Tell Jenkins it's in absolute confidence. He can be trusted. The warden owes me plenty. Tell him I want to see one of his inmates, Donald Radenbaugh, outside the prison walls tonight—say, two o'clock in the morning. Find out a place to meet where I can have a nice private talk with Mr. Donald Radenbaugh. Everything's at stake, Harry, so get it right."

5

VERNON T. Tynan squinted ahead through the windshield at the heavy foliage and trees guarding the little-used side road. "How much longer before we get there?"

"Any minute, Chief," Harry Adcock assured him.

They had flown in a small private jet plane from Washington, D.C., to Harrisburg, Pennsylvania. In Harrisburg, a rented Pontiac sedan had been waiting for them at the airport. Adcock had taken the wheel, with Tynan beside him, and a red-marked topographic map of the Lewisburg quadrangle between them. It had taken an hour and a half, covering approximately fifty miles. Now they were moving at a snail's pace through forest.

"Jenkins said there would be a clearing between some trees to the right," Adcock muttered. "Yup, right on the nose. Here it is."

He swung off the road and parked. Some distance ahead they could make out the concrete wall surrounding Lewisburg Federal Penitentiary. Adcock cut off the headlights. He indicated the wall beyond. "There are some tough cookies in there."

"Some," said Tynan. "Donald Radenbaugh isn't one of them. He's a political prisoner. He knew too much about what went on in high places. That can be an offense, too."

Adcock tugged at Tynan's sleeve. "Chief, I think I see them coming."

Tynan peered through the windshield intently and made out two specks of light approaching head-on. "Must be Jenkins. He's using only his parking lights. Here's how we'll do it. I'll get in the back seat to meet him. You stay where you are, behind the wheel. I'll do all the talking. You just listen."

Tynan opened the front door of the Pontiac, stepped out, got into the rear, and slumped in the far corner of the back seat. The other car had entered the clearing and drawn up ten yards behind them. A door closed. There was the crunch of footsteps.

The wizened face of Warden Bruce Jenkins came down to appear in the window next to Adcock, who jerked his thumb over his shoulder. Jenkins moved back, and now his face was at the rear side window. Tynan rolled the window halfway down. "Hi, Jenkins. How've you been?"

"Good to see you, Director. I got who you want with me."

"Bring him here," said Tynan. "Remove his handcuffs and let him in through the other side, so he can sit next to me. After we're through and he gets out and you secure him, you come back here. I may want you to do a little more."

"Sure."

"One more thing, Jenkins. This meeting never took place."

The warden's face cracked into a smile. "What meeting?"

In a minute or so, Jenkins had brought the prisoner over and was saying, "You can get in the back seat."

Donald Radenbaugh stooped to enter the car. He hadn't changed much in his nearly three years of incarceration. Thinner, perhaps. He had a bald head, eyes made smaller by the bags under them behind steel-rimmed glasses, a thin, sallow face and pointed nose, with an untidy blond mustache beneath it. He was pale and sullen. He climbed into the car and sank into the back seat as far away from Tynan as possible. He didn't like the director and made no effort to hide it.

Tynan, in turn, made no effort to shake his hand.

"Hello, Don," Tynan said. "It's been a long time. Would you like a cigarette? Harry, give him a cigarette and your lighter."

Radenbaugh held out his hand to accept them. He lit the cigarette, drew heavily on it, exhaled a cloud of smoke, and seemed more relaxed.

"Well, Don," Tynan resumed, "how've you been?"

Radenbaugh grunted. "That's a helluva question."

"Is it that bad?" asked Tynan solicitously.

"I'm in jail. Cooped up like an animal, and I'm innocent," said Radenbaugh bitterly. "How would you like to spend your best years in a cage six feet by eleven? The big event is getting a haircut. Or maybe a letter from your daughter. It stinks. There's just no hope."

He lapsed into angry silence.

Tynan studied him in the gloom. "Yeah, the lack of hope—I guess that's the worst of it," he said sympathetically. "Too bad about Noah Baxter. I guess he was your second to last chance to get out of here earlier."

Radenbaugh glanced up sharply. "My second to last chance?"

"Yeah. I'm your last chance, Don. I came here to offer you a deal. Strictly business, and between us. I can give you something you want. Freedom. You can give me something I want. Money. Are you ready to listen?"

Radenbaugh did not speak. But he was listening.

"Okay," continued Tynan, "let me give it to you all at once, short and sweet. You've got a million dollars in cash stashed away somewhere in Florida. I've read the record over carefully. A reliable witness swore you left Washington with the money. You were to deliver it in Miami. You knew you were fingered, so you never delivered it. When you were picked up, you didn't have it."

"Maybe I never had the money," said Radenbaugh calmly.

"Maybe," said Tynan agreeably. "Again, maybe not. Let's just go on the assumption that there's a nice cool million in cash hidden somewhere down there in Florida. It should be worth something to you—not twelve years from now, but right this minute, today. What can money like that buy? Freedom. It can get you out of this rotten, stinking prison. I can't make you innocent of extortion when the court said you were guilty. But I can make you a free man. Do you want to hear more?"

Radenbaugh rolled down the window and threw away the butt of his cigarette. "Go on," he said.

"That million dollars," said Tynan. "I need part of it—let's say for an investment. In return, I'll cut your fifteen-year sentence down to what you've served, as of a few nights from tonight. It's not easy, but I can arrange it. For your part, you'd go down to Miami, retrieve your money, deliver seven hundred and fifty thousand dollars to an intermediary, and you'd keep the remaining two hundred and fifty thousand to get a fresh start. How does that grab you?"

Radenbaugh gave no response. He sat staring straight ahead, lips compressed, face tight.

"There's one catch that you'll have to go along with," Tynan said. "Or the deal's off. I told you this wasn't easy. I'm not empowered to parole you or free you. I can't get Donald Radenbaugh out of Lewisburg Federal Penitentiary. But I can get *you* out."

Radenbaugh looked at the director now.

"You'd have to take on a new identity the day you were released. It's been done successfully before. Since 1970, at least five hundred informers, government witnesses, persons who turned state's evidence have been given new identities by the chief of criminal intelligence in the Department of Justice, and they've been secretly relocated. It's worked every time, and it can work again. Only this time I'd have to handle it myself."

There was no reaction from Radenbaugh.

"First," Tynan continued, "we'd have to get rid of Donald

428

Radenbaugh. Warden Jenkins would put out a story that you were dead. That you died of natural causes—say, a heart attack. Next, we'd release you. We'd get rid of your fingerprints, alter your appearance, give you a completely new identity, and papers to back it up. From next week on you'd be totally free, with a fat bankroll. But remember, there'd be no more Radenbaugh. I know you have a daughter, some other relatives, friends, but they'd be in mourning. They could never know the truth. It's part of the price you pay for the deal—that and the money.

"There you have it," Tynan said. "You've got five minutes to decide yes or no. If it's no, then you can open that door and get out, and Jenkins will be waiting to take you back to your cell. If it's yes, in a week you'll have a quarter of a million dollars and a free life. When you leave prison, you'll only have to follow the simple instructions that'll be in the pocket of your new suit."

Tynan paused, waiting for Radenbaugh's decision.

IT was not until five days later that Chris Collins got to Lewisburg Federal Penitentiary. Demands on his time after he got back to Washington had made an immediate trip impossible. At last, through his subordinates in the Bureau of Prisons, he had arranged the trip, saying that he was working on recommendations for a revised Prisoner Rehabilitation Act and must make a tour of the federal institution.

And so, in step with Warden Bruce Jenkins, he was making a hasty inspection of the prison. Now the tour was over, and for Collins the most important part of it was to begin.

"Is there anything else I can do for you?" Jenkins inquired.

"You've done quite enough," said Collins graciously. "I have everything I need. I'd better . . ." He hesitated effectively. "As a matter of fact, there is one more thing. We have a tax case going, and the name of one of your inmates has come up constantly. I wonder if I could see him in private for five or ten minutes?"

"Tell me who it is," said Jenkins, "and I'll have him brought in."

"His name is Radenbaugh. Donald Radenbaugh."

Warden Jenkins did not hide his surprise. "You mean you didn't see this morning's paper?"

"I'm afraid not."

"Donald Radenbaugh died three days ago of a heart attack. We withheld the story until his next of kin could be located. It was announced early today."

"Dead," said Collins hollowly. He felt ill. Then his one high hope of learning about the R Document was dead also. In despair, Collins was preparing to leave when a thought struck him. "Did you say you withheld the news because you had to locate Radenbaugh's next of kin?"

"Yes. He had a daughter in Philadelphia. She happened to be out of the city. We finally found her. With her consent, we buried him locally at government expense."

"How did she take the news?"

"Naturally, she was pretty broken up by it."

"Are you saying Radenbaugh was close to his daughter?"

"Except for former Attorney General Baxter—who'd been a friend—Susie was the only one who stayed in touch with him regularly."

"Do you have her address?"

"No. But she has a post office box at the main post office in Philadelphia. We wired her, and when she got it, she phoned us."

"Can I have her post office box number, Warden?"

"Why, yes." He went to his desk, peeled through a series of folders, opened one, and read off the information.

"Thanks," said Collins. "Maybe she knew some of his business and could help me."

So FAR it had gone without a hitch. Seated in the cabin of the sleek motorboat as it zoomed across the channel that separated the southern tip of Miami Beach from Fisher Island, he reviewed the events of the past week.

Six nights ago, outside Lewisburg Federal Penitentiary, he had parted from FBI Director Vernon T. Tynan, agreeing to make the bizarre deal offered to Donald Radenbaugh, convict. Two nights ago, crouched in the rear of the warden's car, he had been driven out of the sleep-stilled prison as Herbert Miller, citizen and free man.

430

After his meeting with Tynan, he had been placed in solitary confinement. There had been four visitors: Tynan's assistant, Harry Adcock, and three others. An elderly man with a limp had applied acid to change—painfully—his fingerprints. An optician had taken away his spectacles and fitted him with contact lenses. A barber had shaved off his blond mustache, and fitted him with a black hairpiece. Finally there had been Adcock, with papers to transform him officially into the respectable Herbert Miller, aged fifty-nine.

There had been Adcock's oral instructions. Immediately after his release, he was to proceed to Miami and the Bayamo Hotel, located on West Flagler Street. The following day he would be free to dig up his hidden one million dollars. He would not be followed. Late morning of the next day he would meet with a real estate broker named Mrs. Remos in the suburban community of Coconut Grove and from her get the name of a safe plastic surgeon, who would perform cosmetic surgery around his eyes before he left Miami. That night he would go to a waiting motorboat at the Municipal Pier in Miami Beach and be taken to Fisher Island. There, at the first oil-storage tank, he would be hailed as Miller. He would give the password—Linda—twice, drop the package containing three-quarters of a million dollars, and return to his boat. Back in Miami Beach, he could proceed with his surgery. After that, he would be free to go where he wished, do what he liked.

"You'll get a new suit just before you leave prison," Adcock had said. "In the right-hand side pocket there will be an envelope with an air ticket to Miami, the location of your rendezvous with the motorboat, and a map of Fisher Island showing you where the drop is to be made. Don't get any tricky ideas. They'd only endanger your health. Got it?"

He had got it all. He knew that people who could invent a new human being were people not to be crossed.

He had arrived in Miami and checked into the dilapidated Bayamo Hotel on schedule. He rented a car, constantly making certain he was not being followed, and drove into the Everglades west of Miami. There he made his way on foot to the bank of the mangrove swamp where he had secreted the million dollars in a metal box over three years ago. He emptied the cash into a large suitcase and retraced his steps to his car.

The rest had gone easily. In his hotel room, he removed his share of the money and placed it in a second suitcase. At night he went to Miami International Airport and shoved the second suitcase inside a locker. Leaving the airport, he picked up a copy of the next morning's Miami *Herald*. Scanning it, he found his obituary. It felt strange to read of his own death, to learn how little he had achieved and how overshadowed it had been by his felony trial and conviction. It was unfair. And he grieved for his beloved Susie, left with such a legacy.

The next day he had only one appointment before the critical evening's mission. Late in the morning he drove out to Coconut Grove for a brief meeting with Mrs. Remos, who expected him. "Be free tonight after ten o'clock," she had said. "Dr. Garcia will be waiting for you in your hotel room at ten fifteen to examine you and arrange for surgery. We would rather he not ask for you at the desk. Let me have your door key. Your hotel will have an extra one for you in your mailbox."

When night had fallen, Radenbaugh took his heavy suitcase and proceeded by taxi to Miami Beach and the Municipal Pier. By eight o'clock he had found his contact and boarded the motorboat. Now, as planned, he was en route to Fisher Island for the climax of his deal. He tugged the hand-drawn map out of his coat pocket once more and committed it to memory.

Fisher Island was an abandoned two-hundred-and-thirteen-acre piece of land bearing thickets of wild Australian pine trees, a rotting mansion, and two oil-storage tanks.

The motorboat was slowing and sputtering to a stop. Radenbaugh saw the pilot signaling to him. Nervously he gripped the suitcase and, bending low, made his way out of the cabin and stepped up onto the wooden dock.

Setting foot on the island, he began to ascend the trail. The landmarks he had memorized were clear. The only difficulties were the darkness and the burden of the suitcase with three-quarters of a million dollars in cash inside. After a while, he made out the first of the oil-storage tanks, left the trail, and started through woods toward the area of the drop.

He was a dozen yards from the tank when he heard a rustle.

A voice—high-pitched and with a Spanish accent—said, "You are Mr. Miller?"

"I am."

The accented voice came out of the darkness again. "What is your word?"

"Linda," he called out. "Linda."

"Leave right where you are what you have. Go back to the boat the way you came."

He lowered his suitcase to the ground. "All right," he said. "I am going."

He turned away quickly and tried to make haste through the woods as he sought the trail. After a few minutes, he stopped to catch his breath. Then he caught something else. The drift of voices, two voices, chattering cheerfully somewhere in the woods off to his right.

Suddenly, for the first time as a free man, he allowed himself to wonder why Tynan wanted so great a sum of money, without strings. Maybe personal financial troubles. He wondered who these people were to whom it had been entrusted. Possibly FBI agents. He decided to have a look.

Instead of continuing on the trail, he cut diagonally through a scattering of pine trees and in a few minutes saw a light. He crept closer, slipping from behind one tree to the next, until he was no more than thirty feet away. He stopped and watched and listened.

There were two of them, all right.

One, plainly illuminated by his partner's lantern, was kneeling beside the open suitcase, counting the money. The man standing over him with the lantern asked, "It is all there?" He spoke an unaccented English.

The one kneeling, busy, said, "It is here."

The man with the lantern said, "Ah, you will be the rich Senor Ramon Escobar."

"Will you shut up, Fernandez?" barked the one who was kneeling, and then he looked up fully into the direct light of the lantern and sputtered something in Spanish. Radenbaugh could see his curly jet-black hair, long sideburns, ugly face with deeply sunken cheeks and a livid scar along his jawbone.

The two men continued talking, but now only in Spanish. Radenbaugh backed away and gingerly started toward the trail. He could not believe this pair, Escobar and Fernandez, were FBI agents. Who were they, then? What did they have to do with Director Tynan?

He found the trail and resumed walking to the landing. The passage back to Miami seemed faster and was infinitely more relaxed.

Ashore on the mainland again, there remained one final piece of unfinished business—the meeting in his hotel room with the plastic surgeon Dr. Garcia at ten fifteen—a half hour away. Radenbaugh was now ravenously hungry and in a celebratory mood. He was sure Dr. Garcia would not mind his being a little late, since he had a key to his room and was able to make himself comfortable. The important thing was that this evening he had fulfilled his part of the deal, and Tynan had fulfilled his. It was time to celebrate.

An hour and fifteen minutes later, a full meal under his belt, Radenbaugh was ready to meet with Dr. Garcia. Aware that he would be three-quarters of an hour late, Radenbaugh hastened to catch a taxi and directed it to the Bayamo Hotel. As his cab swung into West Flagler Street and headed toward the Bayamo Hotel, he saw a crowd up ahead—people in the street, a fire truck backing away, two police cars. The commotion was in the vicinity of his hotel.

"You can let me out here on the corner," he told the cabby.

He made his way rapidly up the block toward a scene of frenzied activity. When he arrived at the fringes of the crowd, he saw that all the attention was centered on the Bayamo Hotel. Helmeted firemen were dragging their hoses out of the lobby. Smoke was still curling out of shattered third-floor windows. Radenbaugh realized with a start that his own room was on the third floor.

He turned to the spectator nearest him. "What's happened?"

"There was an explosion and fire on the third floor about an

434

hour ago. Destroyed four or five rooms. I think I heard them say someone was killed and a couple of people were injured."

Radenbaugh searched ahead and saw four men—one with a microphone, obviously reporters—interviewing a fireman. Hurriedly, Radenbaugh shoved his way through the mass of people until he reached the front line of spectators. He was directly behind the spokesman for the fire department.

"You say one fatality?" a reporter was asking.

"Yes—as far as we know, only one. The occupant of the room where the blast occurred. He must have been killed instantly. His name—let me see—yes, here, we found some shreds of paper—his name was Mr. Herbert Miller. No further identification."

Radenbaugh had to cover his mouth to prevent his gasp from being audible.

Another reporter asked, "Was it a gas leak or a bomb?"

"Can't say yet. Too early to tell."

Radenbaugh turned away and pushed back through the crowd. Dazed, he tried to think about what had happened. Rarely did a man live to be a witness to one, let alone two, of his obituaries.

Tynan had killed Radenbaugh to resurrect him as Miller. Once Tynan had his three-quarters of a million, he had set out to kill Miller. Officially now, Miller *had* been killed.

The dirty, dirty double-crossing swine.

But there was nothing he could do about it, now or ever, Radenbaugh knew. He was extinct, a nonperson. Then he realized there was real safety in this, as long as he was never recognized again as Radenbaugh or Miller.

He would require a plastic surgeon as soon as possible. For that, he needed a place to hide and someone he could trust. And then he remembered there was someone.

He moved away to find a taxi to Miami International Airport.

THE next morning Chris Collins, at his desk in the Department of Justice, eagerly took the call from the Deputy Attorney General. "Well, Ed, what did you find out?"

"That post office box in Philadelphia is still rented to a Susan Radenbaugh. They gave me her address on South Jessup Street."

"Thanks, Ed." Collins jotted the address on his pad and hung up. There was one thin strand left that might lead to the R Document. Susan Radenbaugh, the bereaved daughter. She had remained in contact with her father. If he had known about the R Document, she might have heard of it, too. A very long shot, but the only shot.

Collins crossed the room and put his head into his secretary's office: "Marion, change any appointments I have for tomorrow, and book me on the earliest Metroliner to Philadelphia in the morning."

6

IT WAS a small, nondescript frame house tucked behind a larger residence on South Jessup Street, and had probably once been a guesthouse.

Before leaving Washington, Chris Collins had learned what he could about Susan Radenbaugh. She was Donald Radenbaugh's only child, twenty-six years old, a graduate of the University of Pittsburgh. She was employed by the Philadelphia *Inquirer* as a feature writer. When Collins had telephoned the newspaper to make an appointment, he had been informed that she was home ill, following the death of her father.

Once he had arrived in Philadelphia, he had directed the chauffeur of his rented car to take him straight to South Jessup Street. He had left the car, driver, and his bodyguard a half block beyond his destination and returned to the address on foot.

Now he crossed the yard and rang the bell. No answer.

He rang again, and had just about decided that she had gone out when the door opened a crack and a young woman peered out at him. She was attractive, with blond hair down to her shoulders and a scrubbed face that seemed unnaturally pale and set.

"Miss Susan Radenbaugh?" he asked.

She gave him a tentative, worried nod.

"I've come from Washington to see you. I want to talk to you briefly about your father. I'm sorry that—"

"I can't see anyone now," she said abruptly.

"Please let me explain. I'm Christopher Collins. The United

States Attorney General. I must talk to you. Colonel Noah Baxter was a close friend of mine, and—"

"You knew Noah Baxter?"

"Yes. Please let me in. I'll just be a few minutes."

She hesitated, and then pulled back the door. He went past her into the small but tasteful living room. An archway to the right revealed a dining table and an entrance to the kitchen.

"You can sit down," she said. He sat on the edge of the nearest object, an ottoman. She stood across from him, nervously brushing her hair back.

"I'm very sorry about your father," he said. "If there's anything I can do—"

"Thanks. Are you actually the Attorney General?"

"Yes."

"The FBI didn't send you?"

He smiled. "I send them. They don't send me. No, I'm here of my own accord. On a personal matter—because your father and Colonel Baxter were friends, too. The night Colonel Baxter died, he left a message for me about a matter I've been pursuing ever since. Mrs. Baxter felt your father might know something about it. She suggested I visit him in Lewisburg. I did go there two days ago, only to learn of your father's death. Then I heard you were the one person he had stayed in touch with. It occurred to me that your father might have spoken to you about the matter I've been investigating. I decided to track you down and see you."

"What do you want to know?"

He took a deep breath. "I wonder if your father ever spoke to you about something called the R Document?"

She looked blank. "What's that?"

Collins' heart sank. "I don't know. I had hoped you would."

"No," she said firmly. "I've never heard a word about it."

He rose wearily from the ottoman. "Forgive me for bothering you. You and your father were my last bets. Well, I tried and that's that." He paused. "Let me say just this. Colonel Baxter believed in your father. Before his stroke he was working on getting your father a parole. Since then I've reviewed his case, and I agree with Colonel Baxter that your father was not guilty of extortion.

Your father was a fall guy. I promised Mrs. Baxter I'd discuss a parole with your father when I went to see him about the R Document. She told me she would write him to cooperate with me." He shrugged. "Well, I guess I'm always too late."

He saw the girl's eyes widen and her hands go to her mouth as she looked past him, and suddenly there was a third voice in the room.

"You're not too late this time," someone said from behind Collins. He whirled around and found himself confronted by a stranger standing in the archway to the dining room. The man walked toward him and stopped. "I'm Donald Radenbaugh," he said quietly. "What do you want to know about the R Document?"

Incredulously, Collins sat down facing Radenbaugh on the daybed in Susan's living room. "Hannah did write me about you," Radenbaugh said. "And after overhearing your conversation with Susie, I know how you got here. But before I tell you about the R Document, let me tell you how *I* got here. It's quite a story."

Collins listened, mouth agape, as Radenbaugh related what had happened to him. He ended with his astonishment that Tynan had required a large sum of money so badly that he would take such a risk.

After Radenbaugh's recital, Collins had no more doubts about what had been going on in California.

"It has been Tynan!" he said aloud.

"He's behind everything," Radenbaugh agreed. "It's simple to see why. The 35th Amendment will make him the most powerful man in America. Yet I'd bet there's not one bit of concrete evidence against him."

"Unless he's involved with the R Document. Can we talk about that now?"

"We can. But before we do, I want three things from you."

"Name them."

"First, I want plastic surgery on my face. If I'm recognized, Tynan would see to it that I'd be dead for sure."

"No problem. I'll find a surgeon for you. When would you want it done?"

"Immediately. Like tomorrow."

438

"Done."

"Second, I need a new identity, new papers. I've got to be *somebody*."

"You'll have the papers in about five days. What else?"

"A solemn promise from you that if it is ever possible, one day, to tell the truth about what Tynan did, about my supposed death, you'll do so—and after I've returned my share of the money, you'll help restore to me my own name and get me a parole or pardon."

Collins briefly considered his dilemma. Could he, as a law officer, make a commitment involving the law to a convicted felon? He decided that his duty in the present situation transcended narrow legalisms. "Someday, if it is possible, I'll do it. I swear to that."

"Now I can tell you about the R Document."

Radenbaugh took a cigarette from his daughter, lit up, and swung around to face Collins.

"I don't know all about it," he said slowly, "but I do know something. The 35th Amendment—the R Document was an unwritten part of it not made public—came into being before I went to jail. The amendment troubled Noah Baxter very much. He was a conservative, and did not like to tamper with the Constitution. But as crime got worse and worse, he was backed into a corner. He had a job to do, and he thought it couldn't be done unless the laws were changed. He thought the 35th Amendment was too stringent. But despite his grave misgivings he went along. I always felt he regretted that. In the end, I suspect, he was in too deep to get out."

"I think you're right," said Collins. "In his last breath, he said, 'I must speak of it—they cannot control me now—I am free, I no longer have to be afraid anymore.' Afraid of whom or what?"

Radenbaugh shook his head. "I don't know. I only know he got in deeper than he wanted to, and he was much troubled, and had no one to confide in except me. So he would tell me what he wanted to, when he was in the mood. It was under those circumstances that he first mentioned the R Document. He brought it up several times after that. He wished Tynan hadn't got him involved with the 35th or the R Document."

"Tynan?" said Collins with surprise. "I thought President Wadsworth instigated the 35th Amendment and everything connected with it?"

"No, it was all Tynan. He was the author and creator of the 35th and the R Document. He sold the 35th to the President and the Congress. I don't know if anyone besides Tynan and Baxter—and me, of course—ever heard of the R Document. The R stands for reconstruction—the reconstruction of the United States. It was a secretly conceived plan to supplement and implement the 35th Amendment—a blueprint for turning the United States into a crimeless country under the 35th. The document fell into two parts. Baxter knew of only one part. The second, he told me, was then still being worked out by Tynan. The first part was the pilot program.

"I told you Tynan conceived the 35th Amendment. Here is how he did it. In trying to develop new laws to recommend to the President and Congress that might reverse the rapidly escalating crime rate, Tynan hit upon the idea of making a study of crimeless or near crimeless communities in the United States. He wanted to know which elements in the structure of such communities made their low crime rates possible."

"So far, sensible," admitted Collins.

"So far," said Radenbaugh. "Well, Tynan's aides fed the computers, and they came up with a handful of almost crime-free communities. In every case it was a company town."

"A company town?"

"The United States is full of them—communities in which every home, store, business building, even every public utility is owned by a single company. Now, not all company towns are crimeless. But those where crime was almost nonexistent were usually small, remote communities, totally dominated by just one company or person."

"A dictatorship."

"In a sense. At least, a place where there were powerful economic and social controls. Among these communities there was one that fascinated Tynan. It had the best longtime record. It suffered virtually no crime or disorder. It was called Argo City, and it was owned entirely by the Argo Smelting and Refining

440

Company of Arizona. Tynan made a thorough investigation and found that most of the freedoms under the Bill of Rights had been suspended there. The inhabitants did not seem to object so long as they were economically and physically secure. Using the legal structures of this town, Tynan developed his idea for the 35th Amendment. He decided that what could work in Argo City, Arizona, could work throughout the United States of America."

"Fascinating," said Collins. "And diabolical."

"Even more diabolical was what Tynan did to this town. He had to be positive that every aspect of the 35th Amendment would work in real life. He used the people of Argo City as his guinea pigs. How was he able to do this? He investigated the company running the town and found that Argo Smelting and Refining had been getting away with tax fraud for years. Tynan put pressure on the board of directors, and they were quick to make a deal. If Tynan would not report his findings to the Justice Department, they would give him and his aides a free hand in running the community. So Tynan, as he might run the Committee on National Safety under the 35th Amendment, ran a prototype safety committee in Argo City. It was his proving ground to see how the 35th would work in action."

"Incredible," said Collins. "You mean that city, without a Bill of Rights, exists today?"

"As far as I know, it does. Anyway, the results of that experiment represent the first half of the R Document."

"And the second half?"

Radenbaugh threw up his hands. "I don't know."

Collins pondered what he had heard. "What about the results? Did it work in Argo City?"

Radenbaugh stared at Collins. "You'd have to see for yourself." He paused. "Would you like to?"

"You're damn right I would. I want to get to the bottom of Tynan's plot. Is it safe to go have a look?"

"There aren't many visitors to that town, the last I heard. But just the two of us won't be conspicuous."

"There might be three of us," said Collins. "It would be worth the added risk."

THE MOMENT HE returned to Washington, Collins instigated a crash research project to investigate company towns in the United States in general and Argo City, Arizona, in particular.

Four days later he had the basic facts, and he began to review them. He saw at once that the American company town was a natural and innocent phenomenon connected with the nation's growth. They were a means to lure employees to work in remote areas, and to provide for them. Most seemed decent enough. And then there was Argo City, Arizona, owned by the Argo Smelting and Refining Company—and Vernon T. Tynan. The material on Argo City was suspiciously skimpy.

He picked up the telephone. "Marion, were these phones debugged today?"

"No longer necessary, Mr. Collins. The scrambler equipment you ordered was installed this morning." This meant all his outgoing calls would be rendered unintelligible until they reached their destination, where they would be unscrambled and rendered into intelligible conversation.

Feeling reassured by this precaution, he said, "Put through a call to Chief Justice Maynard. If he's not in, locate him. I must speak to him at once."

THEY converged on Phoenix, Arizona, by air, from three different places on a Friday morning in June.

Collins, his plane reservation made in the name of C. Cutshaw, arrived from Baltimore at eleven seventeen. Shortly after, Donald Radenbaugh, traveling under his new name of Dorian Schiller, arrived from Carson City, Nevada, where he had gone for the plastic surgery. Finally, Chief Justice John G. Maynard, answering to the name Joseph Lengel, was due to arrive from New York at eleven forty-six.

It had been agreed in advance that Collins and Radenbaugh would proceed to Argo City at once, to be followed by Maynard after his later arrival.

Collins waited impatiently in the air terminal until Radenbaugh's flight landed. He did not recognize Radenbaugh until the other was almost upon him. The plastic surgeon had done his work well. Something had happened to Radenbaugh's nose, which was still swollen. When he removed his sunglasses, it could be seen that the bags had been removed from beneath his eyes, replaced by bruises that were fading, and the eyes were smaller, almost oriental.

"Mr. Cutshaw?" Radenbaugh said with amusement.

"Mr. Dorian Schiller," said Collins, handing Radenbaugh a manila envelope. "Your official baptism is in there. And anything else you'd ever want to know about Dorian Schiller." He glanced at his watch. "John Maynard will be here in about twenty minutes. He'll be taking a taxi to Argo City." Collins gestured toward the exit. "I have a rented Ford outside."

They drove southwest steadily, in the direction of the Mexican border. Presently they came upon a road sign:

ARGO CITY

POPULATION 14,000

HOME OF ARGO SMELTING AND REFINING CO.

Radenbaugh, at the wheel, pointed across Collins' chest. "There it is—the copper-mine pit, a mile and a half wide and about six hundred feet deep, where most of the male population works."

In minutes they were in the center of Argo City—a single broad paved main street, with four or five intersections. There were a number of clean, well-maintained buildings; a vast, glass-fronted general store; a U.S. post office; a small park, neat, with walks leading to the Argo City Public Library; a steepled church; and a two-story brick edifice identified as the home of the Argo City *Bugle*, the town newspaper. The tallest building was the four-story Constellation Hotel, in good repair, of Spanish design.

They parked in the lot next to the hotel and entered the tiled lobby. At the desk they registered as Cutshaw and Schiller, from Bisbee, Arizona. They required adjoining single rooms, only until late afternoon, when they would be checking out. A bellhop led them to their rooms.

Now they were in Collins' room, waiting for Maynard.

"I only hope we can find what we want in four hours," said Collins.

"Everything will depend on how people buy our cover story," said Radenbaugh. "Do you have the letter?"

Collins patted the breast of his coat. "Right here. Someone in Justice got stationery with the Phillips Industries letterhead. Then I dictated the letter of introduction."

They rehearsed their story. It had them in Argo City as representatives of Phillips Industries of Bisbee, Arizona, which had secured permission from the Argo Smelting and Refining Company for an inspection of civic improvements to be considered in remodeling Bisbee.

"What's Maynard going to use for a cover?" Radenbaugh asked.

"He's registering overnight, even though he'll leave with us. He's a retired lawyer from Los Angeles, traveling to Tucson to visit his son and daughter-in-law. He's stopping in Argo City not only to get some rest on his trip, but to look into the possibility of buying a home here. He's been through once before and was attracted by the community."

"I'm not sure of that one."

"It should do for four hours. Trying to become a resident of Argo City could turn up plenty."

Ten minutes later Maynard rapped on the door and was admitted to Collins' room. In his broad-brimmed brown hat, sunglasses, open shirt, rumpled khakis, and ankle-high boots he resembled an old prospector rather than the dignified Chief Justice of the United States.

Maynard tossed his hat on the bed and sat down. He looked at Radenbaugh. "You, I gather, are Donald Radenbaugh. Your report on Argo City was shocking, to say the least. I hope it was accurate."

"I reported only what I had heard from Colonel Baxter," said Radenbaugh defensively.

"Umm. So we're here to see the future United States in microcosm, as it will appear after the 35th Amendment is passed and invoked. Well, Mr. Radenbaugh, I tell you honestly, I find it hard to believe. If it is true . . ." He lapsed into thought. "Well, that would certainly put a new light on everything. We'll have to find out firsthand. Mr. Collins, where do we begin?"

444

Collins took a list of places to investigate from his pocket. "I'd like to suggest, Mr. Chief Justice, that you start by visiting the Argo City Realty Company. You are supposed to be considering living here. Then, playing the role of a retired attorney, you might drop in on the local judge, possibly through him get to the sheriff. Also, look in on the Argo City *Bugle*. Go through some of the back copies. It might give you an opportunity to chat with a reporter or the editor."

"It's going to take some ingenuity," said Maynard.

"We'll be in and out of here before anyone becomes suspicious," said Collins. "Donald and I will work the library, post office, try to see the city manager. We should all talk to as many ordinary citizens as we can. At lunch question a waitress. Stop some people in the street to get directions, and try to engage them in conversation." He looked at his wristwatch. "It's now one fourteen. We should all meet back here in my room at five o'clock. We can compare our findings, and possibly by then we will know the truth. Shall we go? You leave first, Mr. Chief Justice."

Maynard picked up his hat and went out the door. Then in five minutes Collins signaled Radenbaugh, and they left the room.

Three hours later the city manager pushed his gold-rimmed spectacles higher on his nose and beamed at Collins and Radenbaugh across his desk. "That's about all I can tell you, gentlemen. Hope I was of some help. Remember this, an attractive community leads to attractive people and promotes peace. As I said, we've had no public disorders in five years, since we instituted the local law against public gatherings. Our civil servants are all content and productive. There's an occasional rotten apple, like that history teacher I mentioned, but we're getting rid of her quickly." He rose and led them to the door. "Good luck with your rebuilding in Bisbee. When you see Mr. Pitman at Phillips Industries, give him my regards."

As the city manager turned back into his office, he found that his secretary had followed him. Noticing her perplexed expression, he asked, "What is it, Miss Hazeltine?"

"Did I hear you say the two gentlemen who just left were here to get information to help rebuild Bisbee?"

"That's right."

"But it must be wrong, sir. Bisbee was thoroughly rebuilt just a few years ago. I have a file on it from the Bisbee Chamber of Commerce."

Minutes later the city manager had gone through the file of clippings, photographs, and maps extolling the rebuilding of the city. He looked stricken. Immediately he put through a call to Mr. Pitman of Phillips Industries in Bisbee.

After that, he phoned the sheriff. "Mac, two outsiders were just here posing as personnel from the Bisbee branch of Phillips Industries, asking all kinds of nosy questions. They had a letter from Pitman of Phillips. He never heard of them. I don't like this, Mac. Should we arrest them?"

"Not until we find out who they are. You know our orders. I'll get right in touch with Kiley. He'll know what to do."

Meanwhile, on the second floor of Argo City High School, Miss Watkins, a prim, middle-aged woman, had left her class to join Collins and Radenbaugh in the hallway. "The principal said you wanted to see me."

"We're from the school board in Bisbee, Miss Watkins," Collins began. "We are making a survey of your school system. We wanted to ask you some questions. We were chatting with the city manager, when he mentioned they gave you notice."

"Yes, today's my last day."

"Can you tell us what happened?" asked Radenbaugh.

"I'm almost ashamed to repeat it," she said. "It's too ridiculous. My tenth-grade history class was about to embark on a study of the Founding Fathers. To enliven the study, I read them an old clipping I'd saved from a newspaper in Wyoming, where I lived before I came here." She fished into her purse, drew out a yellowing clipping, and handed it to Collins.

Collins and Radenbaugh read the lead of the Associated Press story: "Only one person out of fifty approached on Miami streets by a reporter agreed to sign a typed copy of the Declaration of Independence."

Miss Watkins pointed to the last part of the story, remarking, "And you can see there, the reporter circulated a questionnaire containing an excerpt from the Declaration of Independence among three hundred members of a young religious group, and twenty-eight percent thought the excerpt had been written by Lenin."

She took the clipping back. "After I read it to my students, I told them I wasn't going to let them go through my course without reading the Declaration of Independence and the Constitution properly, or without understanding those classic documents."

"Did you mention the Bill of Rights?" asked Collins.

"Of course. I got into quite a discussion with my class about basic freedoms and civil rights. My students seemed highly stimulated. However, several went home and told their parents about it, and the head of the Argo City Board of Education came down on me as a troublemaker. I said I was only teaching American history. He insisted I was fomenting dissent and he would have to terminate me. Truly, I still don't understand what happened."

"Aren't you going to protest your dismissal?" Radenbaugh asked.

Miss Watkins seemed genuinely surprised at the suggestion. "Protest? To whom?"

"Surely there must be someone."

"There isn't. Even if there were, I wouldn't think of doing so. I don't want to get involved in such things."

"What are you going to do now, Miss Watkins?" Collins asked. "Stay in Argo City?"

"Oh, no, I couldn't. You have to work for the company or the city, and they wouldn't give me another job. I suppose I'll go back to Wyoming. It's very upsetting. I don't know what I did wrong."

"Do you want to tell us more about what goes on here?"

"Nothing goes on here, really nothing," she said too emphatically. "I think I'd better get back to my class. . . ." She disappeared inside the room.

Radenbaugh looked at Collins. "Who said it, Chris? If fascism ever comes to the United States, it'll be because the people voted it in."

"Amen," said Collins. He took Radenbaugh by the arm. "We'd better get back to the hotel."

By five minutes after five o'clock the three had reassembled in

447

Collins' room. Collins was the first to speak. "Well, Mr. Chief Justice, what did you find out?"

Maynard sat dazed. "It's—it's—shocking. I saw a lot of people, including the sheriff and the newspaper editor. They talk and they don't realize what they're saying. It's become a way of life. Never in my experience, here or abroad, since the Second World War, have I seen a population living such a robotlike existence. Who could imagine this going on in the United States?"

"It's going on, all right," said Collins grimly. "Let me tell you what Donald and I found out. The Argo Smelting and Refining Company owns the only food and clothing stores in town. The mining employees are paid salaries, but they are also given coupon books, with scrip, good in the company stores. When they run out of money, they can use the scrip to buy on credit. Thus, most wind up in hock to the company.

"The company also owns or controls every acre of land, the city hall, sheriff's office, schools, hospital, post office, church, city newspaper, this very hotel. The company librarian bans political and history books. The postmaster screens all incoming and out-going mail. The hotel allows no one to stay more than two days. Strangers are picked up for vagrancy after three days. The company censors the minister's sermons. Unmarried men and women are segregated into four company boardinghouses—which are probably filled with informers. As to general housing—"

"I looked into that," said Maynard. "Only employees of Argo City Smelting are eligible to buy homes. The company holds the mortgage on every house. Mortgage payments are deducted from salary. If the owner decides to leave town, he must sell his house back to the company.

"I have never encountered such blatant disregard for the Bill of Rights. Listen. The First Amendment guarantees freedom of religion, press, speech. In Argo City, you attend one church, read one newspaper. Outside newspapers and magazines are banned. Television consists of one local UHF station—company-controlled. All radios are sold with special band filters so they can't pick up other cities. No public gatherings and demonstrations permitted. The last one occurred five years ago. It was broken up and the workers were arrested. The jail was too small to hold them, but unbeknownst to anyone there is an internment camp outside of town in the desert—"

"An internment camp?" Collins said, remembering Josh and the trip to Tule Lake.

"Yes. Four weeks' confinement in that camp ended the protest." Maynard went on. "The Second Amendment gives the citizen the right to keep and bear arms for a militia. In Argo City, only an elite group of company employees can own weapons. The Third says no soldier can be quartered in a private residence without consent of the owner. A ruling here permits the police to move in and live under anyone's roof. The Fourth gives people the right to be secure against unreasonable search. An Argo City ordinance allows the sheriff to enter any home without a warrant. The Fifth protects the accused in a capital crime. In Argo City, there's no grand jury. A judge appointed by the company decides whether the evidence makes a trial necessary. The Sixth Amendment guarantees a speedy trial. In Argo City, you can languish in jail indefinitely before being tried.

"The Seventh Amendment guarantees the right to a trial by jury in suits of common law. This is entirely ignored in Argo City. The Eighth promises no excessive bail and protects the citizen against cruel and unusual punishment. Well, here, even for a misdemeanor, high bail and cruel and unusual punishment are the norm. Felonies send you to the internment camp. The Ninth Amendment safeguards other rights not specified in the Constitution. Argo City citizens apparently have no clear rights other than the right to eat and sleep. The Tenth Amendment reserves all powers not delegated to the federal government by the Constitution to the states and the people. Here, such powers are totally controlled by the company."

"Or by Vernon T. Tynan," said Collins.

"Or by Tynan, yes," Maynard agreed.

"We can't sit by and let this go on," Collins said. "As Attorney General, I've got to act. I can send a team of investigators in here—"

Maynard raised a hand. "No, that's not of immediate concern.

449

Argo City and its fourteen thousand people are merely part of the larger issue. There's far more at stake. We have today seen a preview of the entire United States in the years to come, if California ratifies the 35th and makes it part of the Constitution." The Chief Justice stood up.

"Gentlemen, I've made my decision. If it is up to me, California cannot and shall not pass the 35th Amendment. I'm going to speak to the President first and try to persuade him to reverse his position. If I fail, then I'll come forward and be heard. If my influence, Mr. Collins, is what you believe it to be, there will be no 35th Amendment, no more Argo Citys in America, and our time of agony will be ended."

Collins grabbed Maynard's hand and pumped it warmly. Radenbaugh nodded approval. "We'd better get moving," Maynard said. "I'll get my things and meet you in the hall in two minutes flat." He hastened out the door.

Jubilantly, Collins and Radenbaugh took up their effects and started to leave. At the door, Collins halted Radenbaugh. "Where are you going from Phoenix, Donald?"

"Back to Philadelphia, I guess."

"Come to Washington. I can't put you on the federal payroll. But I can put you on my private one. I need you. Once Maynard kills the 35th Amendment, we'll need a new and decent substitute program that will bring about a reduction in crime without sacrificing our civil rights."

"You really can use me? I'd be glad to, but—"

"Come on. Let's not waste time."

They met Maynard, checked out, and exited into the warm late afternoon. As Collins and Radenbaugh proceeded to the parking lot, Maynard halted to buy the latest edition of the Argo City *Bugle* from a bearded blind vendor seated on a box next to the hotel entrance. At the clink of the coins, the eyes behind his dark glasses remained vacant, but his mouth curled in a smile of thanks.

Maynard hurried to catch up with his companions. As Radenbaugh drove the Ford out of the parking lot, heading back through Argo City toward Phoenix and free air, the blind vendor got to his feet and placed his stack of newspapers on top of the box.

450

Tapping his white cane, he hobbled past the hotel, turned toward the filling station on the corner, and entered one of two telephone booths in the rear.

Glancing behind him, he removed his dark glasses, took the receiver in his hand, dropped a coin into the slot, and gave the operator a number. He cupped the mouthpiece of the phone. "Put me through to Director Tynan," he said urgently. "Tell him it's Special Agent Kiley reporting from Field Office R."

He waited only seconds. Tynan's voice came on loud and clear, and with equal urgency. "What is it?"

"Director Tynan. Kiley here at R. There were three of them. I recognized only two. One was Attorney General Collins. The other was Chief Justice Maynard. . . . Absolutely no question. Collins and Maynard."

7

IT WAS midmorning of the following day and President Wadsworth had twice unsuccessfully telephoned Director Vernon T. Tynan, who was with Harry Adcock behind closed doors. Tynan and Adcock had just finished listening to a tape taken an hour before of a telephone conversation between Chief Justice Maynard and President Wadsworth.

Tynan leaned back in his chair. "I must say I'm not surprised. After Kiley reported from Argo City last night, I suspected this would happen. Well, I'd better call the President and hear his replay of it."

Seconds later Tynan was connected with the Oval Office. "Sorry to have missed you," he said. "Just walked in. Is it something urgent?"

"Vernon," said President Wadsworth, "we're cooked. The 35th is as good as dead. I've had a call from Chief Justice Maynard. He wanted to know if I'd ever heard of Argo City, Arizona—the place you discussed with me last night when you were briefing me on the latest bureau activities. I told him that you were personally leading an investigation of federal crimes in that city, and would soon be submitting your findings to Attorney General Collins."

451

"Correct."

"Well, Maynard took another view of your activities in Argo City. He had the notion you had been using it as a test site for the 35th Amendment. And the results were horrifying to him."

"That's absurd."

"I told him so. But the old coot would not be swayed. He said he'd never publicly expressed himself on the 35th, but he was now prepared to do so. Then he tried to strong-arm me. He said if I publicly withdrew my support of the 35th, he would gladly remain silent. But if I refused to do so, then he would speak out."

"Who does he think he is, threatening the President?" said Tynan indignantly. "How did you answer him?"

"I told him I had consistently stood behind the 35th, and I would continue to."

"How did he take that?" asked Tynan.

"He said, 'Then you're forcing me to act, Mr. President. I'm stepping down from the bench so I can speak out while there is still time.' He said he was flying to Los Angeles this afternoon. He'll spend all of tomorrow at his Palm Springs home to prepare. The day after, he's holding a news conference in Los Angeles. He said, 'I'm going to announce my resignation from the Supreme Court, and my willingness to appear as a witness before the judiciary committees of the California assembly and senate to speak against passage of the 35th Amendment.' I tried to argue some sense into him, but to no avail. The minute he comes out against the 35th, we're finished. What can we do, Vernon?"

"We can fight him."

"How?"

"I'll try to think of something."

"Think of something—anything."

"I will, Mr. President."

Tynan hung up and smiled at Adcock. "We certainly will think of something, won't we, Harry?"

THAT evening Collins was in high spirits. When he returned home from work, there had been the expected telephone call from Maynard. The Chief Justice had arrived at Los Angeles Inter-

452

national Airport, and before he and his wife drove to Palm Springs he wanted to inform Collins of what had transpired that morning in his conversation with the President. He would spend a day in his Palm Springs study writing his resignation speech and his strongly worded statement to the state legislative committees.

"I hope this does it," he said.

"It will, it will," Collins promised. "Thank you, Mr. Chief Justice."

Karen had been hovering nearby, wondering, and the moment he hung up, Collins leaped to his feet, grabbed his wife, and kissed her.

Quickly he explained—without mentioning Argo City—the Chief Justice's decision to come out publicly against the 35th.

Karen was genuinely thrilled. "How wonderful, darling. Good news at last."

"Let's celebrate," Collins said. "Let's go out on the town. I'll make a reservation at the Jockey Club. Just the two of us. No business, just pleasure, I promise you."

A half hour later, as Collins was putting on his best navy-blue suit, the telephone rang. "Mr. Collins?" an urgent voice said. "This is Ishmael Young. I'm doing Tynan's autobiography, and you were kind enough to see me last month." He hesitated, then blurted out, "I know how busy you are, Mr. Collins, but if it's humanly possible I must see you tonight—"

Glancing at his wife, who was almost dressed, Collins interrupted. "I'm afraid I am tied up for the evening, Mr. Young. Perhaps you can call me at the office on Monday."

"Mr. Collins, believe me, I wouldn't bother you if it wasn't important. To you, as well as to me."

The tone of Ishmael Young's voice made Collins capitulate. "All right. My wife and I are having dinner at the Jockey Club at eight thirty. You can join us."

After he hung up, he saw Karen looking at him inquiringly.

Collins shrugged. "He's ghostwriting an autobiography for Vernon Tynan. He has to see me tonight. I guess I'm curious enough to want to know why. At least, he's a nice guy. I hope you don't mind, honey."

"Silly, I never expected it to be two." She pointed to the telephone. "Better call back and make the reservation for three. Besides, I'm as curious as you."

Ishmael Young arrived at the Jockey Club anxious and apologetic. "I hate intruding on your private evening like this," he said.

"We're delighted to have you," said Collins expansively. He held up his Scotch and water in a toast. "Here's to the defeat of the 35th Amendment." Setting down his glass, he said to Young, "You didn't know, did you, that I'm not supporting the 35th anymore?"

"But I do know," said Young.

Collins did not hide his surprise. "How could you? It's nothing I've made public."

"You forget," said Young. "I'm working with Director Tynan. The director knows everything. And I'm his ghost."

Collins' mood had sobered. "I see. So he knows, also. I should have guessed."

They fell into brief silence. Ishmael Young fiddled with his drink. At last he spoke. "I wanted to see you tonight to warn you about Tynan. He doesn't like you, you know."

"I'm not surprised," said Collins, "but how did you find out?"

"I'm there with him every week, but lately he doesn't seem to realize it half the time. He answers the phone. He makes calls. He leaves notes and memos lying around. Two weeks ago I got my hands on a whole new cache of material for the book—papers, tapes Tynan gave me to copy. Lots of it was from the late Attorney General's papers, lots was new material of Tynan's. I've been copying this research at my place in Fredericksburg so I can return the originals to Tynan. Well, yesterday, going through some of these papers, I came across a memorandum Tynan had written, setting up two topnotch investigative strike forces—one in the field, the other inside headquarters here." Young lowered his voice. "Tynan and the FBI have been investigating you."

"Oh, Chris," Karen gasped.

Collins waved her silent. "Naturally I was investigated the minute the President nominated me for Attorney General. It was routine."

"You misunderstand, Mr. Collins. I'm trying to tell you that

Tynan instigated a new investigation of you the other day. It's in progress right now."

"Are you sure?"

"Positive. Not the first time Tynan's checked on you, either. Once, last month, I overheard him speak on the phone about Baxter and the Holy Trinity Church and make a reference to the Collins thing—"

Collins interrupted. "I know about that. This is more important. You say you're positive Tynan is investigating me again?"

"Absolutely. Not only the memo. The last time I was with him he got this call. When I'm there, he usually takes calls only from the President and Adcock. The call wasn't from the President. While he was on the phone, I went into the bathroom, but I left the door partly open. I could hear his side of it. There was some reference that made it clear they were talking about you. It had to do with an investigation now going on. Tynan finally said to Adcock, 'Well, keep trying. And keep after the others.'"

"The others?" Karen asked. "What did he mean by that?"

"I have no idea," said Ishmael Young. He turned back to Collins. "Would there be any reason for him to investigate you now?"

"There could be," said Collins slowly.

"Well, I thought I shouldn't waste any time in warning you," said Young, "so that you can have your guard up."

"I appreciate it," said Collins sincerely. "Thank you."

Karen drew closer to her husband. She tried to repress her agitation. "What does all this mean, Chris?"

"Probably nothing, darling." He tried to comfort her. "Not all investigations are sinister. Sometimes they check on someone I'm associated with in order to protect me."

"But at least he ought to tell you," said Karen, "not do this sort of thing behind your back. I mean, you're his boss. Really, he's a horrible man."

Young lifted his glass. "That's something I'll drink to, Mrs. Collins. I can find no one who likes him except his mother and Adcock. Everyone else either fears him or plain hates him."

Collins became interested. "Does he have a mother around?"

"You wouldn't believe it, would you? That Vernon T. Tynan

could have a mother. Well, he has. Just a stone's throw away from here. Rose Tynan. Eighty-four years old. She's in the Golden Years Senior Citizens Village in Alexandria. Nobody knows this except Adcock and myself, but Tynan goes to see her every Saturday."

"Have you seen her?" asked Collins.

"Oh, no. Verboten. Once, when I was interviewing him about his younger days, he couldn't remember something, but he said his mother would know and he'd find out from her. I told him I didn't know his mother was alive. He said, 'Oh yes, but I don't talk about it for security reasons, for her safety.' He's afraid revolutionary conspirators would kidnap the mother of the FBI director and ask an incredible ransom, such as the freedom of all the left-wingers in federal penitentiaries. The only friend she keeps in touch with is Colonel Baxter's wife, who visits her now and then."

"Interesting," said Collins. "Hannah never mentioned her to me."

"I can't imagine Tynan's having a mother," said Karen. "It makes him sound almost human. . . . Does he do this sort of thing often? Interfering in people's lives?"

"With his investigative apparatus, he's Big Brother incarnate. I'm sure there is nothing in your life, Mrs. Collins, or your life, Mr. Collins, or my own life that Vernon T. Tynan doesn't know about. He's probably the most powerful man in the country. If he isn't, he will be, once the 35th Amendment is passed."

"It won't be passed," said Collins. "The day after tomorrow it'll be dead. So don't worry about Tynan. Tonight we celebrate."

At one o'clock in the morning Karen emerged from the dressing room into their bedroom. On the far side of the bed, already tucked in, her husband lay with his head deep in the pillow, his back to her. She lifted the blanket and slid into bed. "Thanks for a lovely evening, darling," she whispered. She put her lips to his cheek. "Good night, dearest. You're so tired. Sleep well."

She settled on her back and stared thoughtfully up at the ceiling. Her mind went back to the evening. Ishmael Young had said, "The director knows everything. . . ." She thought about the time in Fort Worth, Texas, and she was suddenly scared. She turned toward her husband, licking her dry lips. There was still time.

456

"Chris darling," she said loudly. "There's something I've got to tell you. I should have before. It's something you have to know. It has to do with not long before we met. Just listen. Just let me talk. Will you, darling?"

She waited for his response, and then she heard it. He was snoring softly.

With a deep sigh, she turned away, eyes open in the darkness. She shivered—remembering the past, wondering about the future.

She closed her eyes. Maybe, she thought—her last comforting thought—I'm being childish and silly to be afraid.

In the J. Edgar Hoover Building Sunday afternoon, Harry Adcock left his office and made his way to the elevator. His destination, as it had been every day since the chief had given him the high-priority assignment, was the vast computer complex—the FBI National Crime Information Center—in the rear of the first floor.

To date, the results of the strike force investigators had been miserably disappointing. Everything found out about Collins had been legitimate, confirming the bureau's original investigation. Wandering through the complex, Adcock searched for Mary Lampert, a senior communications officer and his major contact down here. She was not in her office, but an operator said she would be back in a few minutes.

Adcock found a chair and sat down to wait. Surveying the computer network—where arrest and dissenter data came in from forty thousand federal, state, and community agencies in fifty states—remembering the Identification division upstairs with its millions of fingerprint sets on file, Adcock knew that no human impurity could escape detection. It was merely a matter of time.

His reverie was interrupted by a feminine voice. "Hello, Harry." Mary Lampert had returned. "Come into the office."

He followed her in and watched her go to the fireproof file cabinet and unlock it.

"Here's the latest data covering the last twenty hours," she said, handing him a manila folder.

He opened the folder and scanned the pages. "Damn," he said. "Nothing. We've got to keep trying, Mary. The chief expects—"

The telephone jangled and Mary answered. "Oh, really?" she said. "I'll be right up."

Adcock looked at her questioningly.

"Identification division. I'll be back in a jiffy. It has to do with our case. I don't know what."

Minutes later she returned, beaming. With a flourish she handed him a fingerprint card and a sheaf of papers. "Good news, Harry. The Collins investigation. Just came through."

He examined the card and began to leaf through the papers.

Then suddenly he was beaming, too.

AT EIGHT o'clock the next morning Collins hummed as he stood before the bathroom mirror and finished shaving. Ever since the call from Chief Justice Maynard two days ago, he had been unremittingly cheerful. Tynan's mysterious weapon, the R Document, would be rendered impotent today. Drying his face, Collins calculated the precise moment of victory for democracy in the United States. It was now five in the morning in California. Soon, Maynard would be preparing to drive from Palm Springs to Los Angeles to hold his news conference. He'd stun the nation with his resignation and word that he was flying to Sacramento this afternoon to urge the legislature to vote down the 35th Amendment. There, at three in the afternoon—just as Collins was leaving his office for home and dinner—Maynard would be reading his statement against the 35th to the judiciary committees of the California assembly and senate.

Tomorrow the assembly would vote on the amendment; it would never reach the senate. It would die forever in its first test in California. Maynard's judgment, his influence and prestige, would have carried the day. As for Tynan's investigation of Collins, let Tynan play his useless game. There was nothing in Collins' past or present to hide. And with the defeat of the 35th, Tynan's dreams of dictatorial power would be over.

Collins had pulled on a shirt and knotted his tie, preparing to join Karen for a hasty breakfast, when he heard a knock on the bedroom door. "Chris?" Karen called. "There's a Mr. Dorian Schiller here to see you."

459

Collins opened the door. "I'll be there in a second."

Radenbaugh's appearance here was a surprise. Since their return from Argo City, Collins had met with Radenbaugh only once, although he had spoken to him daily on the phone.

When Collins entered the living room, Radenbaugh was pacing agitatedly up and down. He halted and stared at Collins, his face a picture of misery. "Bad news. Very bad news, Chris. I tried to call you, but I had misplaced your unlisted number."

Collins did not move. He had a premonition of disaster. "What is it, Donald? You look a wreck."

"The worst news possible. Chief Justice and Mrs. Maynard were murdered in their beds in Palm Springs around two thirty this morning. Killed by a common housebreaker."

Collins felt his knees go liquid. "Maynard—murdered? I—I can't believe it."

"It's been on television direct from Palm Springs since six this morning. Where's your set? Let's find out what's happening."

"In here," said Collins, leading him to the book-lined study. Collins turned on the TV.

The camera was panning the front of the contemporary desert house where the tragedy had occurred. A cordon of police was stationed before the walk to the house. Plainclothes detectives kept going and coming through the open front door. Neighbors, many still in nightclothes, stood stricken, observing the scene.

Now the camera moved in on the network's reporter. "Here, in California's most famous resort town," the reporter said, "the Chief Justice of the United States, the Honorable John G. Maynard, and his wife, Abigail Maynard, met death violently at the hands of an unknown assailant this morning. The bodies were removed a little over an hour ago. Not only the bodies of the Chief Justice and his wife, but the body of the as yet unidentified murderer, who was cut down by police bullets before he could escape. Let me recap once more what is known of what happened here in Palm Springs, California, not three hours ago. . . ."

Collins sat mesmerized before the screen, listening.

Apparently the intruder had been acquainted with the layout of the Maynard home. After coming through the service porch, he had headed for the bedroom, intent on getting Mrs. Maynard's valuables. His entrance into the bedroom had awakened Chief Justice Maynard. The police theorized that Maynard had half risen from his bed, reached out, and pressed a silent-alarm button on the wall. The police had been alerted at once.

Meanwhile, when the killer had seen Maynard move, he opened fire on him. Mrs. Maynard had sprung upright, and he had opened up on her. The two had been shot to death in a matter of seconds. Unaware that his first victim had set off an alarm, the killer had ransacked the bedroom for money and jewels, then retreated from the house the way he had entered. Once on the front sidewalk, he had started for his Plymouth, parked two blocks away. Suddenly he had been caught in the spotlight of a police squad car bearing down on him. He had started to run, stopped, spun about, and fired on the police officers as they left their car. They had answered him with a hail of bullets, and mowed him down on the sidewalk. Aside from the stolen goods in his pockets, he carried not a thing on his person. His identity remained unknown.

"Now," said the reporter, "we return to our newsroom in Los Angeles." A newscaster behind a desk picked up a sheet of paper just placed before him.

"Another late development," he announced. "Chief Justice John G. Maynard's arrival in Los Angeles the day before yesterday was unexpected. The next morning, from his Palm Springs residence, he contacted an old friend, James Guffey, speaker of the assembly, and stated that he would like to fly up to the capital the next day— that would have been this afternoon—and appear before the judiciary committee to discuss the 35th Amendment before it was put to a vote on the floor. Guffey said this morning that Maynard had not mentioned if he was going to come out for it or against it. Now death has stilled the Chief Justice's voice, and we'll never know what he intended to say in this all-important matter of the crucial 35th Amendment vote in California."

Collins heaved a sigh. The initial shock was over, and he felt only an overwhelming depression. He looked at Radenbaugh. "I guess it's our funeral, too, Donald."

Radenbaugh nodded tiredly. "I'm afraid so."

461

They both fell silent, concentrating on the television screen. The White House press secretary was reading President Wadsworth's condolences. Then FBI Director Vernon T. Tynan's name was announced. Tynan's familiar broad shoulders appeared on the screen, his face set in a look of grief and mourning. He began: "This brutal and senseless slaying of one of the nation's outstanding humanitarians has wounded America, but because of it America will become strong enough to survive all crime, all violence. I am sure Chief Justice Maynard would want us to view this tragedy in a larger sense. This systematic decimation of our leaders and our citizenry must be brought to a stop."

Tynan looked up into the camera. "Fortunately, Chief Justice Maynard's vicious slayer did not escape. He has met his own violent end. I have just been informed that the killer has been fully identified, and this will be announced shortly by the Federal Bureau of Investigation. Suffice it to say, for now, the killer was a former convict, a man with a long arrest record, yet he was allowed to roam our streets under the present ambiguous and loose provisions of the Bill of Rights. While the 35th Amendment would never be put into effect except in the case of conspiracy and rebellion, its passage alone would engender a positive atmosphere that would relegate slayings like these to the past. Ladies and gentlemen, we've learned a lesson on this day of grief. Let us work together, hand in hand, to make America secure and to keep America strong."

Tynan's face left the screen, to be replaced by that of a reporter in the network's Washington newsroom. "The killer of Chief Justice Maynard," the newsman said, "has just been identified as Ramon Escobar, thirty-two, an American citizen of Cuban extraction, a resident of Miami, Florida."

Immediately both a full-face and a profile shot of Ramon Escobar were flashed on the screen. The pictures revealed a swarthy young man with curly black hair, long sideburns, sunken cheeks, and a livid scar on his jawbone.

"That's him, Chris!" Radenbaugh shouted, leaping to his feet and shaking his fist at the screen. "The man who killed Maynard is the one I saw! Ramon Escobar. I heard that name on Fisher

Island. He's the man Vernon Tynan had me pass the seven hundred and fifty thousand dollars to. Chris, do you know what this means? Tynan had me sprung from prison to get his hands on enough money to pay a professional assassin, money that couldn't be traced. Tynan engineered the murder. He was ready to go to any length to prevent Maynard from killing the 35th, even to the length of killing Maynard himself. I can go to the police. I can tell them I gave this killer the money on Tynan's behalf. I can tell the whole truth."

Collins was trying to think, to sort it all out. He shook his head. "I believe you, but it won't work. Donald Radenbaugh could have told the truth. But there isn't a shred of evidence that Radenbaugh's alive. Only Dorian Schiller exists now."

Radenbaugh suddenly sagged. "I—I guess you're right."

As if transformed, infused with a new resolve, Collins came alive. "But *I* exist. I'm going directly to the President and lay it all out. When he knows the truth, he'll do what Chief Justice Maynard meant to do—speak out to the public, disown Vernon T. Tynan, denounce the 35th Amendment and have it voted down once and for all. Pull yourself together, Donald. Our bad dream is almost over."

8

THE President of the United States sat up straight behind the Buchanan desk. "Remove him?" he repeated. "You want me to fire the director of the FBI?"

They had been seated in the Oval Office for twenty minutes. Collins had been talking and the President listening.

In an impassioned monologue, Collins had recited the incidents he encountered from the time of Colonel Baxter's warning about the R Document to Donald Radenbaugh's identification of Chief Justice Maynard's slayer. He had spilled it out nonstop, with a trial lawyer's clarity, omitting no detail.

The President had remained remarkably unruffled throughout Collins' recital. He had listened quietly and without any display of emotion. Now his only movement was to lift an ornate letter opener, absently weigh it in one hand, then put it back down on the desk. He spoke again. "So you really think Director Tynan deserves to be fired?"

"Absolutely," said Collins emphatically. "The grounds for dismissal are unquestionable. Unlawful conspiracy. Misuse of his office in trying to get a bill passed that could invest him with superpower. He should be fired for blackmail and interference with due process. The only thing I'm not accusing him of is murder, because I can't prove that."

The President lifted himself from his chair, turned his back on Collins, carried his slight, erect frame to the window, and stood there gazing out at the Rose Garden.

Collins sat taut, waiting.

After what seemed an interminable interval, the President started back toward his chair. He stopped behind it, set his arms lightly on top of it, and rested his eyes on Collins.

"Well, now . . ." he said. "I've been considering everything you've told me. I've been examining it closely. Let me tell you how it strikes me."

Collins gave a short nod, expectant.

"Your grounds for firing Director Tynan," the President said. "Chris, let's try to be objective. You're the country's first lawyer. You know a person is innocent until *proved* guilty. What have you got but a fabric sewn together from fanciful speculations and conjecture? Your evidence is a tissue of talk, not facts. I respect facts. I listen to facts. Based on what you've told me, I don't see sufficient grounds for dismissing Tynan."

"Nothing I can say will dissuade you? You're determined to stand with him?"

"Yes," said the President flatly. "I have no other course."

"Then I have no other course, either, Mr. President," said Collins, rising to his feet, "but to resign as Attorney General. I'll go back to my office now and write a formal letter of resignation—and spend every hour of the next twenty-four fighting that amendment in the California assembly. If I fail there, I'll spend every hour I have left fighting it in the California senate."

He gave the President a curt nod, and had started for the door when the President called his name. He halted and looked back.

President Wadsworth was plainly distressed. "Chris, before you do anything you'll regret later, think twice about it. This is a critical period for the country. This is no time to rock the boat."

"I'm getting off the boat, Mr. President. I'll sink or swim on my own. Good day."

With that, he left the Oval Office.

President Wadsworth stared at the door a long time after Collins had departed. Finally he reached for his telephone. "Miss Ledger? Tell Director Tynan I want to see him alone, as soon as possible."

COLLINS' first task, upon returning to his office, was to telephone his wife. That morning, after viewing the news reports on the Maynards' murder, Collins had filled her in on the events of recent weeks. Karen had been aghast. And even more so when he said he was going to ask the President to fire Tynan. He had been confident that President Wadsworth would agree with him. Now, four hours later, he knew that he had never been more wrong in his judgment.

Karen answered the phone. Her voice was edgy. "What happened, Chris?"

"The President sided with Tynan right down the line. I told him I'm resigning."

"Thank God." He had never heard her sound more relieved. "We can put the house up for sale and move back to California—maybe next month."

"We're heading back to California tonight. I want to be in Sacramento in the morning to do some lobbying. The 35th goes to the assembly floor in the afternoon. If I fail, at least I'll go down fighting."

After hanging up, Collins summoned his secretary.

"Marion, cancel everyone I'm supposed to see today, the rest of the week, and the weeks after."

He saw her raised eyebrows.

"I'll explain later. Just tell everyone I'll be away. And book me and Mrs. Collins on the latest flight to Sacramento tonight."

"But, Mr. Collins, you were going to Chicago tonight. Have you forgotten? You're scheduled to address the Society of Former Special Agents of the FBI tomorrow at their convention. You're the main luncheon speaker. Following the speech, you have a meeting with Tony Pierce."

He had forgotten completely. Long ago he had agreed to this address, and more recently, after privately resolving to oppose the 35th, he had also decided to meet with Pierce, his onetime antagonist on television and the head lobbyist of the Defenders of the Bill of Rights.

"I'll have to cancel that appearance in Chicago. As for Tony Pierce, call his DBR headquarters in Sacramento and ask him to stay put. Tell him I'll see him in Sacramento tomorrow morning."

After Marion had left, Collins settled down to compose his letter of resignation. He had just begun when Marion hurried in. "Mr. Collins," she said breathlessly, "Director Tynan is here to see you. He's in the conference room."

Collins was confounded. Not once during Collins' short tenure of office had Tynan called on the Attorney General. He speculated on what this was all about. One thing for sure: Tynan was the last person he wanted to see today. With distaste, he went to the conference-room door.

Tynan came striding toward him. "Sorry to break in on you like this, but I'm afraid it's important." He patted the briefcase under his arm. "Something I have to discuss with you now."

"All right," said Collins. "Let's go into my office."

Tynan did not budge. "I think not," he said evenly. He glanced around the conference room. "I think it might be better here. I wouldn't want anyone to overhear what we discuss. I don't think you would, either."

"Vernon, I don't have my office hooked up. I don't believe in taping my visitors."

Tynan merely grunted. "You miss a lot, then. Let's sit down. What I have to say won't take long."

Annoyed, Collins took the red leather chair at the head of the table and sat a few feet from the FBI director. "Well, to what do I owe the honor of this visit?"

Tynan placed his hands flat on the table. "Let's get right down to it. I heard from the President a little while ago that you intended to resign—and I heard the reasons. Trying to get Vernon T. Tynan fired was a very dumb thing to do. I figured you were smarter than that."

Collins tried to control himself. "I did what I had to do."

"Well. So did I." With maddening deliberation, Tynan began to unlock and open his briefcase. "And since you've been looking into my affairs, I thought it only fair to look into yours."

"I'm perfectly aware you've been investigating me again," said Collins. "I have nothing to hide."

"You're sure of that?" Tynan removed a manila folder from his briefcase. "Well, you'll be flattered to know we've looked into you with very great care."

"Surprise me. What did you find?"

"I found something you've deliberately hidden from the public—or, possibly, something that's been hidden from you." Tynan opened the folder, briefly studied what was inside, then met Collins' eyes. "You happen to be married to a woman with a very suspect recent past."

Collins felt a flare of anger. "Vernon," he said, "I don't know what you are implying, but I won't have my wife dragged into our differences."

Tynan heaved his shoulders. "Up to you, Chris. Either you listen to me, or your wife will have to tell it to a judge and jury again." He paused. "Now, can I go on?"

Collins could feel his heart thump. He remained silent.

Tynan glanced at his papers. "Your wife was a widow when you met her. Her name was Karen Grant. Her husband's name was Thomas Grant. Is that right?"

"You know it's right, so why—"

"It's wrong, and I know it's wrong. Her maiden name was Karen Grant. Her husband's name was Thomas Rowley. Her married name was Karen Rowley."

Collins had not known that, but he was quick to defend her. "So what? There's nothing unusual about a widow's using her maiden name."

"Maybe not," said Tynan. "Or maybe there is. Let me see. . . . You met her in Los Angeles, where she was working as a model. Before that, she lived with her husband in—"

"Madison, Wisconsin."

"She told you that? She misinformed you. She lived with her husband in Fort Worth, Texas. Her husband died in Fort Worth."

Collins pushed back his chair to rise and terminate this inquisition. "Vernon, I don't give a damn."

"You'd better," said Tynan coldly. "Do you know how your wife became a widow?"

"Her husband was killed in an accident."

"Really? What kind of accident?"

"I believe he was hit by a car. Does that satisfy you, Vernon?"

"No, it does not satisfy me. According to the FBI records from Fort Worth, he was not hit by a car. He was hit by a bullet—at close range. He was murdered."

Prepared as Collins was for some disturbing information, this was an unexpected blow. His poise dissolved.

The FBI director continued relentlessly. "All evidence pointed to your wife as the murderer. She was arrested and tried. After four days of deliberation, she got a hung jury. Possibly because of her father's influence—he was a political bigwig in the area, he's dead now—the authorities decided not to initiate a second trial. She was released."

"I don't believe it," Collins protested.

"If you have any doubts," said Tynan coolly, "this will resolve them." He lifted some papers from his folder and placed them neatly in front of Collins. "A summary of the case, condensed from court records, identified with the appropriate case number. And photostats of three newspaper clippings. You will recognize Karen Rowley in them. Now we get to the crux of the matter. . . ."

Collins ignored the papers in front of him.

Tynan went on. "The jury did not find your wife guilty. On the other hand, they did not acquit. As you know better than I, that leaves the case wide open and casts a shadow of doubt on your wife's behavior. This is the part that interested me. I suggested to our agents that they pursue their investigations further. They did, and came up with a valuable new lead. How the local authorities could have overlooked it, I can't imagine. But sometimes they can be slipshod. As you know, the FBI is never slipshod."

Collins waited.

"We have a new witness, one previously overlooked, a woman who claims to have seen Karen Rowley—or Karen Grant or Karen Collins, whichever you prefer—an eyewitness who claims to have heard an altercation, heard Karen tell Rowley she'd like to kill him. The witness decided to leave the Rowleys' house, and as she did so, she heard a gunshot and had a glimpse of Karen with the weapon in her hand, standing over her husband's body."

Collins felt the constriction in his chest. He continued to remain silent.

Tynan resumed, picking his words slowly. "Now, this witness won't come forward of her own free will. She doesn't want to be involved in such an affair. But if forced to testify under oath, she will do so. It would mean a second trial. This time it is unlikely there would be a hung jury. However, I did not permit my people to submit their new evidence to the district attorney in Fort Worth. I thought that would be improper without consulting you first. Furthermore, I have a certain amount of sympathy for Mrs. Collins. Her husband was an unsavory character—and he used her shamefully. Certainly that was a consideration in my mind when I ordered the evidence withheld. Finally, perhaps most important, I would prefer not to embarrass a member of the Administration at a crucial time like this. I think everyone connected with the case has suffered enough, and there is no need to make it a public matter again. Under the proper circumstances, it could all be easily forgotten."

Collins was sickened—not only by the information about Karen but by Tynan's undisguised blackmail. The revulsion he felt toward the man burned inside him. He sat very still, trembling inside. At last he was able to speak. "What do you want from me?"

"Only your cooperation, Chris," said Tynan blandly. "Your pledge that you'll stay on the team with the President and myself and support the 35th Amendment to the very end. That's the price. Very reasonable, I think."

"I see." Collins watched as Tynan closed his folder and carefully returned it to his briefcase. "Aren't you going to let me see the rest of the evidence?"

"I'd better hold on to it for safekeeping. You have enough to go by. You also have your wife. She'll fill you in on anything you haven't heard."

"The name of the new witness. I'd like to have that, at least."

Tynan smiled. "I think not, Chris. If you want to see the witness, you'll have to see her in court." He locked the briefcase. "I guess I've said about all there is to say. What happens next is up to you."

Collins stared at him with loathing. Finally he slumped back in his chair.

"Okay," he said wearily, "you win."

After Tynan left, he stayed on late in the Justice Department, torn by conflicting emotions. There was shock at what he had learned of Karen's background, disappointment in her for having withheld the events of her past from him, confusion about her guilt or innocence in her husband's death, fear that harm would befall her now that Tynan was ready to have the case reopened.

He had no idea what stance to take toward her, how to handle her. These attitudes were still unresolved as he entered his home. He wanted to put off the confrontation, avoid her.

"Chris?" she called out from the dining room.

"I'm here," he called back, and headed into the bedroom.

He had pulled off his necktie when she appeared.

"I've been on tenterhooks all day," Karen said. "I started to pack. We are going to California, aren't we?"

"No."

She had been walking toward him, to kiss him. She stopped and searched his face. "You did resign, didn't you?"

"No. I started to write the letter of resignation. After Tynan came to see me, I tore it up. I had to."

"You—had to," she repeated. "You tore it up because of"—she looked stricken—"because of me?"

"How did you know?"

"The other night when that writer said Tynan knows everything about a person's life, I knew he might go after you—and find me.

470

I was scared, Chris. That night I decided for the hundredth time to tell you, but you'd already fallen asleep. Then in the morning everything else happened, got in the way. I should have told you. Oh, heaven help me, what a fool I've been. Such a poor secret. One you should have heard from me."

"I should have known, Karen, if only to be able to protect you."

"You're right. But not to protect me. To protect yourself. I don't know what Tynan's told you—but you'd better hear the story from me."

"I don't want to hear it now, Karen. I've got to go to Chicago."

"No, listen." She came up close to him. "Tynan told you—what? That my husband was killed by a gunshot wound in Fort Worth, in our bedroom? That I'd been overheard more than once saying I wished he was dead? The truth is, we'd had another terrible fight. One of a million fights. I ran out, went to my father's. Then I decided to return home. Try one last time. There was Tom on the floor. Dead. I had no idea who had killed him. I still don't know. But several people had heard us fight, had heard me say I wished he was dead. Naturally I was accused. The evidence was flimsy, circumstantial, but we had a new DA, trying to make a name for himself. I was indicted, tried. Is that what Tynan told you?"

"Most of it. He said you got a hung jury."

"That hung jury," she said contemptuously. "Eleven of them were for my acquittal from the first. One man, the twelfth, held out for guilty for four days before the jury gave up. That one holdout was finding my father guilty, not me. He'd once been fired by my father, I learned afterward. The DA's office knew it was useless to try me again, because the evidence and jury had been so overwhelmingly in my favor. They freed me, and dropped it. To escape the notoriety, I stopped using my married name and went to work in Los Angeles, where I met you a year later. That's all of it, Chris. I never told you, because it was behind me—I knew I was innocent—and after I fell in love with you, I didn't want anything to spoil our relationship or put doubts in your mind. I wanted a new start. It was a mistake not to have told you." She caught her breath. "I'm glad it's out at last. That's the whole story."

"Not quite the whole story, according to Tynan," Collins said.

"He found a new witness, a woman who says she saw you standing over Rowley with the gun. The witness saw or heard you do it."

"That's a lie! I didn't do it. I came in and found Tom dead. Who is this witness?"

"Tynan wouldn't tell me. That's what he's holding over our heads. He threatened to open up the case again unless I played ball. So I decided to remain on the team."

"Oh, Chris, no." She went into his arms, fiercely holding on to him. "What have I done to you?"

He tried to soothe her. "It's not important, darling. All that's important is you. I believe you. Let's forget Tynan—"

"No, Chris, you've got to fight him. I'm innocent. Let him re-open the case. In the long run, it won't hurt us. You can't let him blackmail you into silence."

He started to move away, but she followed him. "Chris, if you're afraid to fight him over this, you must believe his version of the story, not mine."

"That's not true! I just won't subject you to another ordeal."

"You're going to keep silent, while the California assembly passes the 35th tomorrow and the senate ratifies it three days later? Oh, Chris, please don't let it happen."

"Karen, I've got twenty minutes to pack and call Tony Pierce in Sacramento before the driver comes to take me to the airport. I'm addressing a convention of ex-FBI agents in Chicago tomorrow. I've got to hurry." He took her in his arms and kissed her. "I love you. We'll talk tomorrow night."

"Yes," she said almost to herself. "If there is a tomorrow night."

9

STANDING at the podium before the six hundred guests crowded into the ballroom of Chicago's Ambassador East Hotel, Chris Collins turned another page of the speech he had been reading to the Society of Former Special Agents of the FBI.

His delivery had been lifeless and the reception lukewarm. His mind was on his native California, where in less than an hour the assembly would vote on the 35th Amendment.

He had been deeply discouraged since last night, and his mood had pervaded his entire speech. Above all, to the detriment of his delivery, he'd been afraid. The members of the society—many of whom had gone on to successful business careers after retirement —were preponderantly Tynan men. He knew, of course, that there was also a small coterie of listeners who were anti-Tynan and anti-35th, led by Anthony Pierce. Collins had been cautious about contacting Pierce late last night. He had arranged to meet with Pierce in an unoccupied single room of the Ambassador East Hotel—reserved under another name—after he had finished speaking, to watch the live television report on the California assembly vote. If necessary, he would risk revealing to Pierce his defection from the 35th and help the lobbyist in any strategy possible to defeat it in the senate three days from now.

Finally, Collins reached the last page of his speech. Applause was light. He returned to his seat and shook a few limp hands.

Half an hour later he left the ballroom and was joined by Hogan, his bodyguard, who saw him up to his suite on the seventeenth floor. At the door, Collins told him that he would be in his suite the rest of the afternoon and suggested Hogan grab a bite to eat.

Collins waited a brief interval, then opened his door and glanced into the corridor. It was empty. Hastily he slipped out, found the stairs, descended to the fifteenth floor, and located room 1531. Making certain he had not been followed, he entered it, leaving the door ajar.

He considered the wisdom of using the telephone to call Karen in Washington and reassure her again, but before he could decide, he heard a short knock on the door. He spun about prepared to greet Tony Pierce alone, but to his surprise two other men entered the room with Pierce.

Collins had not seen Pierce since they were adversaries on the television debate. The freckled, frank face was as good-natured and enthusiastic as ever. "We meet again," he said, shaking hands with Collins.

"I wasn't sure you would come," said Collins.

"I welcomed the chance. I also wanted you to meet two of my colleagues. This is Mr. Van Allen. And this is Mr. Ingstrup. We were all together in the FBI, and we resigned within a year of one another."

Collins shook hands with each. Van Allen was blond, with a prominent jaw and restless eyes. Ingstrup had a shock of chestnut hair and a weather-beaten visage that sported an untidy brown mustache.

As the others took places on the bed and two chairs, Collins remained on his feet. "You must wonder why I asked you to meet with me," Collins said to Pierce.

"Not at all." Pierce fished for his pipe. "We've been keeping an eye on you, even up to early yesterday afternoon when you were planning to go to California to testify against the 35th Amendment. We know where you're at today."

Collins was startled. "How could you possibly know that?"

"Since we can trust you now, we can tell you," said Pierce, enjoying this. He tamped tobacco into the bowl of his pipe. "After the three of us left the FBI, we went our own ways. I formed a law firm. Van Allen has a private detective agency. Ingstrup is a writer, with two exposés of the FBI under his belt. We all shared a single belief. That Vernon T. Tynan, for whom we'd worked so long, was a dangerous man for the country. We saw him becoming more threatening every year. We found other former FBI agents around the United States who felt precisely as we felt. All of us still possessed the skills we had practiced in the FBI. So, at my suggestion, we set up a loosely knit, unpublicized organization of ex-agents who would be investigators—to counter Big Brother. We don't have an official name, but we like to call ourselves the IFBI— the Investigators of the Federal Bureau of Investigation. We have sympathetic informers everywhere. We have six in your Department of Justice, including two in Tynan's J. Edgar Hoover Building. We gradually learned of your defection to our side. Yesterday we learned you were planning to fly to Sacramento. From our previous dossier on you, we deduced that you were making the trip to break from the President and Tynan and to denounce the 35th publicly."

"That's correct," admitted Collins.

"Yet you are not in Sacramento," said Pierce. "When I found

474

the message from you last night, I worried that your change of travel plans might mean your political plans had changed again also. But then I decided that this could not be, or you would not have wanted to see me."

"Once more, correct," said Collins. "My politics remain the same. I'm wholeheartedly against the 35th. I wanted to go to Sacramento to fight it. At the last minute, something came up—"

"Tynan came up," said Pierce simply.

Collins wrinkled his forehead. "How did you know?"

"I didn't," said Pierce, "but I was sure."

Van Allen spoke for the first time. "Tynan is everywhere. Never underestimate him. He's all-knowing and he's vindictive. When he assigned me to investigate the personal lives of the Senate and House majority leaders—that was some time before the 35th was presented to Congress, he wanted something on them to be sure it passed—I told him I'd prefer another assignment. The next thing I knew, I had been exiled to Montana, Tynan's Siberia. I got the message. I resigned."

Collins studied these men in the room with him who had opposed the director of the FBI and his mammoth apparatus, and he suddenly felt close to them. They had gained his confidence completely. "I'll tell you why I can't side with you in public. I went to see President Wadsworth yesterday. I told him that I had information that Tynan had been responsible for the murder of Chief Justice Maynard—"

"Wow!" Pierce exclaimed. "We hadn't heard that. Do you know it to be a fact?"

"I believe it to be a fact. I have it from a person who was involved. But I can't prove it. Nevertheless, I laid out a good case against Tynan before the President and demanded he fire Tynan. He refused. I told him that I had no choice but to resign and go to California and take a public stand against the 35th Amendment. The next thing I knew, there Tynan was, in my office."

"To blackmail you into silence," said Ingstrup.

"Yes." Haltingly, Collins related every detail of the evidence Tynan had collected against his wife, the new eyewitness being held in the wings, and the terms of his own surrender.

"But she told you she was innocent," said Van Allen.

"She *is* innocent. I believe her. Still, I couldn't let her be put on the rack again."

He saw Pierce glance at Van Allen, who gave a nod, then saw Pierce look at Ingstrup, who also nodded. Pierce's gaze rested on Collins once more. "Maybe we can help you, Chris—if I may call you Chris—by getting into this with our little counterforce, our IFBI. We have one of our best men in Texas—a rancher, Jim Shack. He was an FBI agent for ten years, but he became fed up after Tynan became director. We have two others down there, still members of the FBI, who hate Tynan. They could check out your wife's old case, find out what it was really all about. Then they might poke around, try to find out if Tynan actually has a new witness, as he claims, or if he's rigging a blackmail scheme on evidence that doesn't exist."

Collins frowned. "I don't know. If Tynan found out . . . Let me think about it."

"There isn't much time," Pierce reminded him. "The California assembly votes today." He jumped to his feet and turned on the television set. "Let's see if all our lobbying did any good. If the assemblymen should vote against it, our work is done. But if they pass it—"

"What are the odds?" asked Collins, sitting down.

"At last count, the assembly was leaning toward passage. It's the senate that's a flip of the coin. Yet you never can tell. Let's see."

All four gave the television set their undivided attention. The camera had pulled back to reveal the eighty assemblymen at their desks and the standing microphones in the aisles. The hushed voice of the network newsman said, "The critical vote is about to begin. Keep your eye on the electric scoreboard, where the votes are automatically totaled. A mere majority—forty-one votes—will pass or reject this constitutional amendment. If it is passed, that would put the final decision as to its ratification into the state senate three days from now." He paused. "The vote is beginning."

Collins sat glued to his chair, watching the tallies, as the minutes ticked by. The yes votes dominated the scoreboard. The count moved to thirty-nine, forty, forty-one. A roar of delight could be heard from the visitors' gallery, intermingled with groans. The voice of the newsman interrupted:

"It's over in the California assembly. The 35th Amendment has gained its majority vote, forty-one votes out of eighty."

Pierce turned off the set. "Looks like our work is cut out for us." He stepped toward Collins. "Chris, we need all the help we can get from you. Let us try to help you, so that you can be free to help us. Let me get our men working in Fort Worth."

The discouraging event on the television screen had already made up Collins' mind. "Okay," he said, "go ahead." His last hope lay with these three men. "There's something else you might help me with, too, if you can. Have any of you ever heard about a paper, possibly a memorandum, called the R Document?"

"The R Document?" Pierce shook his head. "It doesn't ring a bell." Van Allen and Ingstrup also had not heard of it.

"Let me tell you about it, then," said Collins. "It all began the night Colonel Noah Baxter died. . . ."

For an hour Collins talked as the others listened, rapt. The R Document ("dangerous—must be exposed . . . I saw—trick—go see"), Tule Lake, Argo City, Radenbaugh, Escobar—everything was laid out before them.

When he was done, his voice hoarse, Collins expected to find incredulity in their faces. Instead, they seemed unmoved. "You're not shocked?" Collins said.

"No," replied Pierce. "We know Tynan has the capability to do anything to satisfy his own ends. He's utterly ruthless, and he's going to win, unless we take advantage of our own capability. If you give us your full cooperation, Chris, we'll set our entire counterforce of ex-FBI agents and informers into motion within hours. I want you to stay here tonight. I'll send Van Allen out for some food and drinks. Let's hole up here until midnight and work out our plan. Then we'll separate, hit the pay phones, get the lines buzzing to our counterforce members. By morning they should all be on their assignments. How does that sound?"

"I'm ready," said Collins.

"Great. The most important contacts we'll reserve for ourselves. Fast as possible, we'll have to go over the ground you've already covered. I know you did a thorough job, but investigation is our life. We might be able to elicit information you couldn't. I'll interrogate Radenbaugh again myself. Van Allen will case Argo City once more. Ingstrup will sit down with Father Dubinski. But you, I think, should see Hannah Baxter again, Chris."

"I'll see her," Collins agreed. "What about Ishmael Young?"

Pierce shook his head. "I'm sure he's on our side, but he's too close to Tynan. He might let something slip accidentally; then all our heads would roll." He paused. "Is there anyone else?"

Collins had a thought. "Ishmael Young mentioned, the last time I saw him, that Vernon Tynan has a mother. She's in the Washington area. Tynan sees her every Saturday."

"No kidding? Tynan with a mother? It's hard to believe. Well, obviously, we wouldn't dare interview her. But still—who can tell? Let me sleep on it. Meanwhile, we have more than enough to keep us occupied in the seventy hours we have left. Now, let's take off our coats and ties and settle down to some real planning about our field force. I'll contact Jim Shack to get into Fort Worth tomorrow to tackle your wife's case. We have more than fifty other men and women almost Shack's equal. They're going to be looking at every rock Tynan ever lived under. No stone will be unturned."

Early the next morning Collins arrived back in Washington. His limousine was waiting outside National Airport. He ordered Pagano to take him directly to his house. Opening his front door, he let himself in quietly, assuming that Karen might still be asleep. He went through the house, entered the bedroom, and saw that the bed was made. He backtracked, expecting to find her in the kitchen. She was not there.

Collins returned to the bedroom. Then he entered the bathroom and saw the note taped to the mirror. He pulled it free, and from the time scrawled on it realized that Karen had written it the night before. With apprehension he began to read:

My darling,
I'm really doing this for our sake. I'm leaving for Texas on a late plane. I feel miserable about what I've done to you. I should never have withheld anything at all about myself from you. I should have

known that as a public figure you were vulnerable, and someone like Tynan would ferret out the information about me and misuse it. I swear to you that I am innocent.

I'm afraid, however, I have not fully convinced you. The fact that you were afraid of a second trial tells me you don't know how it might end. Since you would not defy Tynan (because of me), I've decided to defy him myself. I'm going to find his so-called new witness, and wring the truth out of her. I did not want to wait till you came home. I did not want you to talk me out of this. I want to prove my absolute innocence to everyone—no matter how long it takes.

I'll be staying with friends in Fort Worth. I won't be in touch with you until I've solved our problem. Don't worry. The important thing is—I love you. I want you to love me—and trust me.

Karen

Collins dropped the note on the sink, dazed. The thought of his pregnant wife out of reach and deeply troubled was almost more than he could handle. He was planning to take the first flight to Fort Worth and try to find her, when he heard the telephone ringing. With a silent prayer that it might be Karen, he hurriedly picked up the receiver. It was Tony Pierce's voice. "Good morning, Chris. I'm in Washington. I came in right after you."

"Oh, hi . . ." He almost addressed Pierce by name, but caught himself, remembering the ground rules worked out in Chicago last night. No mention of Pierce and his friends on the telephone.

"One thing to report," said Pierce. "We just got information that Tynan is flying to New York on business tomorrow night, and then going on to Sacramento. He's scheduled to make a personal appearance Friday before the state senate judiciary committee to give the 35th a strong pitch. He'll be the last witness before the bill goes to the senate floor."

Collins was too distraught to react to news about Tynan. He said, "I just came home and found a note from my wife. She's—"

"Hold on," Pierce interrupted. "I can guess. But don't discuss it on your phone. Go to a public phone booth in your neighborhood and call me back at the number I gave you last night. I'll be waiting."

Collins snatched up Karen's note and hastened out of the house. A few minutes later he walked into a filling station, closed himself in the telephone booth, and dialed Tony Pierce. Pierce answered immediately. "You can talk now. It's safe."

"My wife left for Texas. She wants to clear herself for me, but defying Tynan is foolhardy. Karen doesn't realize how dangerous that can be."

"You mentioned she left you a note," said Pierce calmly. "Do you mind reading it to me?"

Collins pulled it out of his pocket and began to read. When he had finished, Pierce said, "You stay put. We'll find her for you. I'll get our man Jim Shack on her trail. It would save time if we had some leads. Her note says she's staying with friends in Fort Worth. Do you have her address book at home?"

"I think so."

"Good. The minute you get back to the house, dig it up, if she left it behind. Use another pay phone on the way to the office—then read me all the names and addresses in the Fort Worth–Dallas area. I'll pass them on to Shack. He'll find Mrs. Collins as well as finding Tynan's star witness."

"Thanks, Tony. Only—how can you find Tynan's witness?"

"No problem. I told you we have two informers in the FBI building. One is a night man. He'll get a peek at the dossier on Mrs. Collins after Tynan and Adcock have gone home. He'll relay the name of the witness to me and I'll pass it on to Shack. Trust us to handle this. Your wife and her case are in good hands."

"I can't tell you how grateful I am, Tony."

"Never mind," said Pierce, "we're all in this together. I'd like to spring you in time to get to California and counteract Tynan's testimony. If he's the only government witness, he'll stampede the senators into passing the amendment. My other hope is that we can nail down the missing part of the R Document by tomorrow. We're seeing Father Dubinski and Donald Radenbaugh for follow-up interviews in the next few hours. Are you seeing Hannah Baxter today?"

"She couldn't make it today, but she agreed to see me tomorrow morning. I have an appointment at her place at ten."

480

"Okay. If there's anything new, I'll call you at your office. Is your phone clean for incoming calls?"

"It will be by the time you call. I'm having it debugged every morning now."

"Good. I'll be in touch."

FOR the first time in many years, Vernon T. Tynan was on his way to see his mother on a day that was not Saturday. What had inspired this precedent-shattering trip on a Wednesday afternoon was a telephone call Tynan had had from his mother no more than ten minutes ago. "I'm just calling to thank you," she had said. "The television set works perfectly now."

He had not known what she was talking about. "What do you mean?" he had asked.

"I want to thank you for having my television reception improved. The repairman came this morning. He said you'd sent him. It is very nice of you, Vern, to think of your mother and her problems when you are so busy."

He had been silent as he tried to assemble his thoughts.

"Vern? Are you there, Vern?"

"I'm here, Mom. Uh—I may see you in a little while. I have some business in Alexandria. I'll put my head in for a minute."

After he had hung up, Tynan had tilted back in his chair, trying to sort it out. One thing for sure: he had not sent any television repairman to fix his mother's set. Immediately he had heaved himself out of his chair to find his driver and car and get himself over to Alexandria as fast as possible.

Now, having arrived at his mother's apartment in the Golden Years Senior Citizens Village, he tested her security-alarm button to be sure it was working, and let himself into the apartment.

Rose Tynan was in her chair before the television set, watching an afternoon variety show. Tynan absently brushed her cheek with a kiss.

"I'm so glad you could come," she said. "Can I get you a bite?"

"Never mind, Mom. I stopped by for only a minute." He indicated the set. "So it's better now. I can't remember—what did you say was wrong?"

481

"Sometimes the picture jumped around."

"So the repairman came this morning? Tell me, was he wearing a uniform?"

"Of course."

"Do you remember what he looked like, Mom?"

"What a silly question," said Rose Tynan. "He looked like a repairman. Why?"

"I wanted to be sure they sent their best man. How long was he here?"

"A half an hour, maybe."

He wanted to pursue this without worrying her. "By the way, Mom," he said casually, "did you watch him fix it, to see he was doing his job? Were you in the room with him all the time?"

"We talked a little while. But he was very busy. Finally, I went to do the dishes."

Tynan walked over to the sofa and looked at the telephone on the stand beside it. "Mom, where can I find a screwdriver?"

She struggled out of her chair. "I'll get it. What do you need with a screwdriver?"

"I thought I'd check your telephone while I'm here. I couldn't hear you very well when you called. Maybe I can adjust it."

His mother returned with the screwdriver, and Tynan removed the base of the telephone and the casing. The inner mechanism lay bare. He began to examine it minutely. After an interval he exhaled softly. "Ahh—"

He had located the monitor—a transmitting bug smaller than a thimble encased in adhesive and resin. The eavesdropping device was the very one the FBI used. Tynan pocketed the monitor and restored the casing and base to the telephone.

"Was something wrong, then?" Rose Tynan asked.

"Yes, Mom. It's okay now." The important thing was what they—whoever they were—had picked up on the telephone since this morning.

"Mom, have you used the telephone today? Anybody call you, or did you call anyone?"

"I talked to you."

"That's all?"

"Yes. Except—wait—was it today? It was today—I had a long talk with Hannah Baxter."

"Can you remember what you two talked about?"

Rose Tynan began to recite the matters she and Hannah Baxter had discussed. It was all trivial. "She tries to keep busy," Rose Tynan was concluding. "She misses her husband so much. Having her grandson, Rick, in the house means she's not alone. Of course, she will have the new Attorney General there tomorrow—"

Tynan perked up. "Christopher Collins?"

"Yes. He's coming to see her tomorrow morning."

"Did she say why?"

"I don't know. She didn't say."

"Collins going to see Mrs. Baxter," he said more to himself than to his mother. "Well, now. What time did you talk to Hannah Baxter on the phone? After the repairman came?"

"On the phone? I didn't say that. I talked with her in person. She dropped by to have coffee with me this morning."

"In person," Tynan said with relief. "Good. Well, I've got to run, Mom. Got a lot to do before going to California tomorrow. One thing. Don't let in any more repairmen without checking with me first."

"If that is what the director wants."

"That's what I want." He kissed his mother and departed.

It RAINED the next morning, and the sky over Washington was dark as Collins rode to the Baxter residence in Georgetown.

Throughout the drive his mood had matched the weather. Since yesterday there had been no calls from Pierce or Van Allen or Ingstrup. Apparently their investigations had produced no clues that might lead to the R Document or Karen. Tomorrow afternoon, in the California state capitol, the 35th Amendment would be put to its final vote before the senate. A majority vote—twenty-one senators—was needed to ratify. According to a story in the Washington *Post* this morning, the latest poll count revealed that thirty were in favor. By tomorrow night the 35th Amendment would be a part of the Constitution of the United States. The future had never looked so bleak to Collins.

Going up the stairway of the old white brick house, Collins was too disheartened to have any expectations about this visit. He had seen Hannah Baxter at the outset of his hunt for the R Document, and she had been able to offer very little. True, she had led him to Radenbaugh, but it had not been enough. He doubted if she would have more to offer the second time around. He rang the doorbell. Hannah Baxter opened the door.

Her plump countenance was as hospitable as ever. "Christopher, how good to see you again." She accepted his kiss.

"You're looking better than last time, Hannah. How are you getting along?"

"Managing, Christopher, just managing. Thank heavens I have little Rick around. His parents are coming back from Africa next week. But I think they'll let him stay with me until the semester's done. Maybe all summer, too."

They had reached the living room. Hannah pointed to the sliding glass doors visible through the partially drawn heavy maroon draperies. "Too bad I couldn't arrange sunny weather for you. We could have sat on the patio. No matter, let's make ourselves comfortable here."

Hannah settled on the couch, and Collins sat down in the high-backed armchair across from her. "Is there anything I can get for you, Christopher? Coffee or tea?"

"Not a thing, Hannah. I'm perfectly content. I want to talk a little business. As a matter of fact, it has to do with the same business I came to see you about last time, shortly after Noah's death. Do you remember?"

Her brow furrowed. "Not exactly. So much has happened. . . . Wasn't it about some papers of Noah's you were trying to find?"

"Yes. It was about one missing paper connected with the 35th Amendment, a supplementary paper. Noah had wanted me to dig it out and review it. He said it was called the R Document. But I've never been able to find it. I must. I was hoping, if we tried again, you might remember some occasion when he—"

"No, Christopher. If I'd heard him mention it, I'd remember."

Collins decided to attempt another approach. "Did you ever hear Noah mention a place called Argo City?"

"No, never."

Disappointed, he determined to go back over some old ground once more. "Last time I was here, I asked if Noah had any friends he might have confided in, someone who might help me find the R Document. You suggested I see Donald Radenbaugh in Lewisburg penitentiary, which I appreciated."

"Did you see Donald Radenbaugh?"

"No. He had died before I could meet with him."

"Poor man. That was a tragedy. What about Vernon Tynan? Did you ask him about the R Document?"

"Right after I saw you. But he was of no help."

Hannah Baxter shrugged. "Then I'm afraid you're out of luck with that R Document, Christopher. If Vernon Tynan couldn't help you, I'm sure there is no one else who can. As you know, Vernon and Noah worked closely on the 35th Amendment. In fact, Vernon and Harry Adcock were right here in this room conferring with Noah when he had his stroke. It happened in the middle of their conversation that night. Noah suddenly had a seizure, pitched over, and fell to the floor. It was terrible."

Collins had not heard this before. "I never knew Noah was with Tynan and Adcock when he was stricken. Are you sure?"

"I'm not apt to forget," Hannah said sorrowfully. "It was an unusual meeting. Noah made it a point—for my sake, I think—rarely to meet with people at night. I remember Vernon was insistent upon seeing him, and he came right after dinner."

"And Harry Adcock was with him?"

She hesitated. "I'm almost certain. I'm sure about Vernon, of course. But—it was a confusing evening—I could be mixed up. Noah's appointment book might tell us. It's in his study. I'll find it."

She left the room. Collins sank back in the armchair, more discouraged than ever, realizing he had learned nothing useful from Hannah Baxter. There wasn't anyplace else to turn now. He felt utterly lost.

He thought he heard a sound behind his chair—a kind of rubbing or shuffling. He snapped his head to the left in time to see the maroon drapery mysteriously swaying. He looked down, and the bottom of the drapery was rising, and from beneath it crawled Rick Baxter, Hannah's grandson, his ever-present portable tape recorder in his hand.

"Hey, Rick," Collins called, "what were you doing there behind the drape—eavesdropping on us?"

"The best hideout in the place," said Rick, flashing a grin.

"How's your tape recorder been working?" Collins asked.

The boy stood up, pushing his shaggy brown hair away from his eyes. "It's been working perfectly since you fixed it, Mr. Collins. Want to hear it?" Rick pressed the REWIND button, stopped the machine, then pressed down the FORWARD button. "I just recorded you and Grandma."

Collins listened. There was Hannah's unmistakable voice, and the fidelity of the taping, even done from behind the drapery, was remarkable. "As you know, Vernon and Noah worked closely on the 35th Amendment. In fact, Vernon and Harry Adcock were right here in this room conferring with Noah when he had his stroke. It happened in the middle of their conversation—"

"Remarkable, Rick," interrupted Collins. "I've heard enough. I'm going to be careful when I come here next time."

The boy stopped the machine and sat down cross-legged on the floor beside him. "I'll bet you I've made a hundred recordings from behind that drape. Nobody ever knows I'm there. Except once, when Grandpa caught me doing it."

"Your grandpa caught you?" said Collins.

"He saw part of my shoe sticking out under the drape."

"Did he mind?"

"Oh, he was sore, all right. He told me never to play a trick like that again."

Unaccountably, Collins stirred in his chair. "I'm sorry, Rick. I didn't get what you were just saying. What did your grandpa tell you when he caught you behind the drape?"

"To never do it again, that if he ever saw me play a trick like that again he'd punish me."

Colonel Baxter's dying words flooded back: *The R Document— it's—I saw—trick—go see.*

Rick Baxter's last words, just now: *If he ever saw me play a trick like that again he'd punish me.*

486

Had the colonel, with his last feeble words, been trying to direct Collins to Rick—or Rick's trick? His behind-the-draperies eavesdropping?

I saw—trick—go see.

Had the colonel in his last conversation with Tynan, minutes or seconds before his stroke, seen the flutter of the drapery, the toe of the boy's shoe protruding beneath the drapery, and known the boy had taped their secret—and remembered it after recovering briefly from his coma?

Had he tried to tell Collins: *I saw trick,* meaning Rick? Or meaning *I saw* Rick's *trick* and now you *go see* him?

See what? See if Rick had taped that last confidential conversation—because it held a clue to the secret of the R Document?

Could this be? Could it possibly be?

Collins cleared his throat, then tried to keep his voice natural. "Uh, Rick, I meant to ask you . . ." He hesitated.

The boy looked up. "Yes, Mr. Collins?"

"Just between us, of course, but despite your grandfather's warning never to try that trick again—hide behind the drape to record someone—did you ever do it again?"

"Oh, sure. Lots of times."

"Weren't you afraid your grandfather would catch you?"

"No," said Rick with assurance. "I was careful. Besides, that made it more fun, taking the risk."

"Well, you were pretty brave," said Collins. "Did you make any tapes of your grandfather himself?"

"Of course. Mostly him. He was the one always in here talking. You should hear some of the tapes I made of him."

Collins stared at Rick. Go carefully, his inner voice told him. Don't frighten him. "So you kept taping your grandfather. Even up to the last night when he was with Director Tynan and he suffered his stroke?"

Collins held his breath.

"Yeah," the boy said. "Though it was pretty scary hiding there after everybody started running around."

"You mean after your grandfather had his stroke?"

"Yeah. But I got every word before that."

"No kidding, Rick. You actually got Noah—your grandfather—his last conversation with Director Tynan—on a tape?"

"It was easy. Like I got you a few minutes ago. Director Tynan was sitting where you're sitting now. Grandpa was sitting where Grandma just sat. Mr. Adcock was in that chair over there. They talked about the R Document the way you and Grandma were talking about it just now."

Slowly, Collins sat upright, feeling the goose pimples rising on his arms. He fought to keep his tone calm. "You say Director Tynan and your grandfather talked about the R Document?"

"Grandpa didn't talk about it. Only Director Tynan did. He was talking to Grandpa when Grandpa suddenly got sick."

"And you heard every word Director Tynan was saying?"

"Sure. I was behind the drape with my recorder on. I taped them the way I taped you."

"Did the tape come out okay? Could you hear them clearly?"

"You heard this machine, it's perfect," said Rick proudly. "I played back the tape the next morning when Grandma was at the hospital. It didn't miss a thing. It was all there."

Collins clucked his tongue. "That's quite a machine you've got. I'll have to get one just like it." He paused. "Uh, what about that tape? Did you erase it? Or do you still have it around?"

His heart stood still as he waited for the boy's reply. "Naw, I never erase tapes," Rick said.

"Then you have it here?"

"Not anymore. I didn't keep any with Grandpa on them. When he got sick, I took the last tape—I wrote on it AGG, which means Attorney General Grandpa, and when it was made, January—I took it and all the others and I put them in the top drawer of Grandpa's special file cabinet along with his own tapes he made, so they would be safe."

"And Grandpa's file cabinet was moved out of here, wasn't it?"

"Yeah. It's supposed to be just for a while."

"Rick, on that last tape you made of Grandpa and Director Tynan, do you remember what was said about the R Document?"

The boy screwed up his face. "I didn't listen very hard—I just wanted to make my tape."

"But you must remember something. You said you heard Director Tynan speak of the R Document."

"I did," Rick insisted. "But I don't remember any more. Director Tynan kept talking. Then Grandpa got sick suddenly—and there was all kinds of running around, and Grandma crying—and I got real scared and shut off the tape and stayed hidden until the ambulance came. When everyone was by the door, I got out from under the drape and ran up to my bedroom. That's all I remember, Mr. Collins. I'm sorry."

Collins clapped the boy on the arm. "It's enough."

Hannah Baxter was returning to the living room. "Is that boy being a pest again and bothering you with his tape recorder, Christopher?"

"Not at all. We've been having a good talk. Rick has been very helpful to me."

"About Harry Adcock," Hannah said. "I checked Noah's appointment book. He had both Vernon and Harry marked down for a visit that night."

"I thought so," said Collins. He winked at Rick. "I'd better get going. Thank you for your time, Hannah. And thank you, Rick. If you're ever looking for a job at the Justice Department, call me."

As he went out the door, Collins was sure it could not still be raining or cloudy. But it was. The sunshine was in Collins' head. There was only one dark spot. Noah Baxter's personal file cabinet, with Rick's telltale tape, was secure in the private office of the director of the FBI.

"Pagano," Collins said as he entered his limousine, "let me off at the first pay phone you see."

10

It was late afternoon when Chris Collins approached the classic Roman façade of Washington's Union Station, passed the fountain and statues in the station's plaza, and went inside. The huge grotto was almost empty. He sauntered toward the magazine stand to his left, peered in as he bought a copy of the Washington *Star,* and decided that he had arrived first at the rendezvous point. He found a seat facing the station's entrance, opened his newspaper wide, and over the top of it kept his eyes on the door. In minutes a man with sandy hair came in jauntily, looked in Collins' direction, gave the briefest nod, and walked on toward the magazine stand. He browsed among the racks briefly, bought a paperback, and crossed the station toward Collins.

Tony Pierce settled down on a seat a few feet from Collins. "I can't get over it," Pierce said in an undertone. "It's fantastic. The kid, Rick, really got it all on his Mickey Mouse recorder? He heard Tynan speak of the R Document?"

"So he says. It's a very good machine. Rick left no doubt that the fidelity of the recording was perfect."

"How do we recognize the tape?"

"It's a Memorex cassette labeled AGG, and it's dated January in Rick's hand. It would be easy to find among Noah's tapes. Noah used miniature Norelco cassettes for his home dictation. The question is how do we get to it. I told you. It's in Noah's file cabinet in Tynan's office."

"Tynan will be in his office until eight forty-five tonight," said Pierce. "He will then leave to fly to New York. Later, at Kennedy, he'll catch the eleven-o'clock flight to San Francisco, and from there drive to Sacramento. His office will be empty. We'll be nearby. The moment we're notified the coast is clear, you and I will enter the Hoover Building by a Tenth Street door. I told you we have an informer on the night shift. He'll let us in. He'll see that the door to the director's office is unlocked."

"But Noah's file cabinet may be locked."

"Oh, it will be," Pierce promised. "It's an old-fashioned Victor Firemaster cabinet with a combination lock. I'll unlock it. We've done our homework."

"Great," said Collins with admiration.

"Now, about your wife. Jim Shack knows where she is in Fort Worth. He didn't say where, but she's all right. More important, we had a peek at Tynan's dossier on Mrs. Collins' case. We have the name and location of his witness. An Adele Zurek. She now lives in Dallas. She was a part-time housekeeper. On the days your wife's regular housekeeper was off, Mrs. Zurek filled in. Jim

Shack was going to see her this afternoon. If he has anything to report, he'll call you tonight after ten. Van Allen is making an electronic sweep of your house to be sure it's safe for calls and talk. Now, tonight. E Street and Twelfth—two blocks from the FBI building. There's a hamburger joint with a neon sign, FILL-UP CAFE. Be there at eight thirty sharp."

"I'll be there," Collins assured him. "I just hope we can pull this off."

"Don't worry about that," said Pierce. "Just hope what's on that tape is worth the effort. All our chips are riding on it." He glanced around. "Okay, I'll go first. See you tonight."

At eight thirty that evening Collins, tense with trepidation, threaded his way through the white Formica tables of the Fill-Up Cafe and sat down beside Pierce, who was coolly finishing his hamburger.

"I'm nervous," Collins admitted.

"What's there to be nervous about?" asked Pierce, wiping his mouth with a napkin. "You're only going to visit the FBI director's office. You've been there before. What are you going to do after you get your hands on the goodies?"

"If the tape is as damning as Noah indicated, I'll call Sacramento immediately and request an appearance before the judiciary committee in the morning, right after Tynan makes his pitch. That should swing it."

"Perfect," said Pierce. "Tomorrow night at this time we should be celebrating in a classier restaurant."

"It's a long way to tomorrow night," said Collins.

Pierce nodded toward the door. "Here he comes."

Van Allen was approaching between the tables and the counter. He reached their table, bent low. "All clear," he whispered. "Tynan left for the airport ten minutes ago."

Pierce pushed back his chair. "Let's move."

They emerged into E Street and walked swiftly, silently, to the corner of Tenth, where the massive colonnaded FBI structure loomed up before them across the way.

"I'll part with you here," Van Allen said. "I'll station myself across from the parking ramp. If something goes wrong and Tynan happens to return, I'll get to you before he does. Good luck."

They crossed the street and hastened along the Tenth Street side of the J. Edgar Hoover Building. Pierce went up the steep stretch of steps two at a time, with Collins following close behind. At the locked glass doors above, a figure materialized out of the inner shadows, unlocked a door, and held it ajar.

Pierce pushed Collins ahead of him into the building's public walkabout, then slipped in after him. Collins had only the briefest glimpse of the agent who had let them in. A youngish man with a thin face, wearing a dark suit. He whispered to Pierce, who nodded.

Pierce said under his breath to Collins, "We're to take the fire staircase to the seventh floor."

They attained the seventh floor without encountering a soul. Except for their footsteps as they circled the central well, there was a tomblike silence. They reached a door with the legend DIRECTOR OF THE FEDERAL BUREAU OF INVESTIGATION.

Pierce beckoned Collins past it to a second, unmarked door. He tried the knob. The door opened. Pierce went in, with Collins right behind him. They had entered directly into Tynan's private office, the room dimly illuminated by a small lamp beside the sofa.

Collins stood unsteadily, taking in the office. There was no file to be seen. "It's in his dressing room," Pierce whispered, pointing to an open doorway.

They went into the narrow dressing room. They were standing in front of Noah Baxter's green Victor Firemaster filing cabinet. The combination lock was on the third drawer down. Pierce tried each drawer. Each was securely shut. He rubbed the fingers of his right hand along his thigh. "Okay," he whispered, "let me work on it. Should be easy."

Deft as a safecracker, Pierce twirled the knob of the combination lock. Collins looked on, aware of the passing minutes. Only three had passed, but they seemed like hours. He heard Pierce utter a happy sigh, saw him try the third drawer, saw it partially pull out. Pierce straightened up, yanked open the top drawer, and stepped back.

"All yours, Chris."

492

Heart pounding, Collins came forward. He looked down into the drawer, which was neatly stacked with miniature Norelco cassettes encased in small plastic boxes, and beside them were a half dozen larger cassettes of the type that Rick had been using.

He had raised his hand to reach into the drawer when suddenly a shaft of light entered the dressing room and the sound of a grating voice behind them paralyzed him.

"Good evening, Mr. Collins. Don't bother."

Collins spun around, as Pierce beside him had already done.

The bathroom door was wide open now, and filling it was the compact form of Harry Adcock. His countenance was scarred by an ugly smile. He held out the palm of one hamlike hand. In it lay a Memorex cassette tape. The plastic casing had already been pried open.

"Is this what you're looking for, gentlemen?" he asked. "The R Document? Well, here it is. Let me give you a better look at it." He pulled the plastic casing apart. Then, his gaze never leaving them, he looped a finger under the tape inside, loosened it, and slowly unwound it. Tossing the casing on the carpet, he dangled the thin brown tape before them.

From the corner of his eye, Collins saw Pierce's hand dip to his coat pocket, but then he saw that Harry Adcock's free hand had moved even faster to his shoulder holster and already held a snub-nosed revolver, which he pointed at them.

"Don't try, Pierce," he said. "Here, Mr. Collins, hold this tape for me a moment." He dropped the tape into Collins' hand, frisked Pierce, and pocketed Pierce's .38 police special. He smiled at them. "A shoot-out between the deputy director of the FBI and a man cooperating with the U.S. Attorney General wouldn't read well in the press, would it?"

He reached out and recovered the tangled strand of tape. "That's the nearest you'll get to the R Document, Mr. Collins."

Holding the tape in one hand, the gun in his other hand still trained on them, he backed into the bathroom. "Have your last look," he said. "It was never a document, you know. Never on paper. It wasn't supposed to be on tape, either. The most important things on earth are usually in people's heads."

Adcock's leg had bumped up against the toilet bowl. He dangled the loose tape over it.

"Wait a minute," Collins implored him. "Just listen to me—"

"First, you listen to this." Adcock dropped the tape into the bowl, pressed down on the handle, and flushed. There was the rushing, receding sound of water. He grinned. "Down the drain, like your hopes, Mr. Collins." He emerged from the bathroom. "Now, what did you want to say?"

Collins bit his lip and said nothing.

"Very well, gentlemen. I'll see you out." He waved his revolver toward Tynan's office. Adcock remained at their heels until they reached the center of the office. Then he moved crabwise away from them to the director's desk, where he put his free hand on Tynan's large, silver-colored tape recorder.

Adcock addressed himself to Collins. "I don't know what kind of Attorney General you are, Mr. Collins, but you sure wouldn't make an FBI agent. You and your boys debugged most of the city to conceal your visit here tonight, but you overlooked something."

He pressed the PLAY button on Tynan's machine. The voices through the speaker were loud and clear and identifiable.

Rick's voice, telling about the tape he made the night his grandpa got sick; Collins' voice, asking the location of the tape.

Adcock had been enjoying himself. But now his finger pressed down, shutting the machine off. "The one thing you overlooked was Vernon Tynan's mother. She heard you were going to be at Hannah Baxter's house and she repeated it. You can underestimate the FBI, Mr. Collins, but never underestimate a mother's love of gossip with her son—and her friends."

He waved his revolver at them once more. "Two agents will be in the hall to escort you downstairs. Good night, gentlemen."

CHRIS Collins slumped in the front seat of Pierce's rented car as Pierce, also a picture of dejection, drove. In the rear seat, Van Allen was equally miserable. Hardly a word was exchanged until they drew up in front of the Collins residence in McLean. As the car stopped, Pierce said, "Well, you can't win them all, but this wasn't the one to lose."

"We were so close," said Collins. "The R Document—I had the thing in my hand."

"They outsmarted us. For the life of me, I don't know how. What was all that about Tynan's mother?"

"She must have found out from Hannah Baxter that I was going to be seeing Hannah. Mrs. Tynan must have mentioned it to Vernon, so they covered the Baxter house. They took no chances of missing anything."

Collins unlocked the front door and let them in. They had just reached the living room when the telephone started ringing. Collins looked at Pierce. "Is it safe? Can I take calls on my phone?"

"The entire house has been swept," Pierce assured him.

Collins snatched up the receiver. "Hello?"

"Mr. Collins? This is Jim Shack in Fort Worth. Some good news for you. I spent the entire afternoon in Dallas with Mrs. Adele Zurek, the witness Tynan claimed had seen your wife commit murder. It was an outright lie."

Collins sighed with relief. "Thank God."

"Mrs. Zurek confessed that Tynan had blackmailed her— threatened her with an episode in her past, and she was too scared not to agree. But when I promised her you'd see she wasn't harmed, she spilled out the truth. The truth was, she'd heard the Rowleys fight. It was nothing unusual. She'd left to go home—after Mrs. Collins had already gone—and she'd got across the street, out of sight, when she saw a car drive up. A man got out, went to the front door, monkeyed with it, and let himself in. She was wondering about his entry and what to do, when she heard a shot from inside the house. She was frightened, and she ran off. The next day, when she heard Thomas Rowley was dead, she didn't go to the authorities, because she didn't want to get involved. About the man who probably killed Rowley—there seems to be some evidence Rowley was having an affair with this man's wife. We could pursue it further, if you like."

"I don't give a damn about that right now. What matters is that you got to the bottom of this. You don't know how grateful I am. As long as Karen is all right."

"She's shipshape—here with me now, waiting to speak to you."

When he heard her voice, he loved her more than ever. She was weeping, and she was happy. "Oh, Chris," she said, "it was such a nightmare."

"It's over, darling. Let's forget it."

"But the important thing is now you don't have to worry about me—about Tynan. You can resign and go to California and speak out while there is still time. You will, won't you?"

"It's too late, darling," he said dispiritedly. "Tynan's won. He outwitted me completely in the end."

Wearily he recounted the events of the long day, with its highs and final low. "And now the tape of the R Document is gone forever," he concluded. "The only piece of evidence that might have saved us all."

There was silence at the other end of the phone. Then her voice burst upon him, alive with excitement. "Chris, listen. Rick's tape—that wasn't the only piece of evidence! There could be a copy of that tape—"

"A copy? What are you talking about?"

"Yes, listen. Remember the night we dined with Tynan's ghost-writer at the Jockey Club? He told us—I can recall almost his exact words—'I got my hands on a whole new cache of material for the book. I got papers and tapes that Tynan gave me to copy. Lots of the late Attorney General's papers. I've been copying the research at my place in Fredericksburg so I can return the originals to Tynan.' Do you understand, Chris? He told us he'd just made copies of things from Colonel Baxter's private file—that would have been before Tynan knew that one of the tapes was the one made by Rick. If Ishmael Young made a copy of that, along with everything else—then the tape you need, the R Document, still exists—and Ishmael Young has it."

"He must have!" Collins exploded. "You're a genius. Karen! I love you—I've got to run now—I'll see you here!"

At five minutes to one the three drove up to Ishmael Young's small bungalow in Fredericksburg.

Collins rang the bell. The door opened and Young made out Pierce and Van Allen standing beside Collins. "Hey, what's going on at this hour of the morning?"

"I'll explain," said Collins. Hastily he introduced his two friends. "We're here because maybe you can help us. I can't tell you how important this is."

"Come on in," said Young.

In the living room, Young eyed them inquisitively as Collins asked, "You do want to see the 35th Amendment killed?"

"I'd do anything in the world to kill it. But there's no chance."

"There is a chance. It depends on you. Where do you keep your research for Tynan's book?"

"In the dining room. I converted it into a study."

He led them into a small room with an old rolltop desk piled high with papers. Beside it, on a stand, rested an electric typewriter. Against one wall stood the dining-room table, also strewn with papers, with a large Wollensak tape recorder at one end. Two more tape recorders—a seven-inch Norelco and a portable Sony—sat on a chair beside the table.

"It's a mess," Young apologized, "but it's the way I work. What do you want, Mr. Collins?"

"Remember when we had dinner at the Jockey Club? You mentioned that Tynan had loaned you part or all of Colonel Baxter's private file to copy for your book. Did you actually make copies of everything in Baxter's file?"

Ishmael Young nodded. "Practically everything. Certainly everything that pertained to Tynan. Except for the tapes"—Collins' heart fell—"everything is done," Young went on. "I duplicated the tapes, too—that's why you see two machines over there—but I haven't finished actually transcribing the tapes. That's a tedious job. I have to do it all myself, because Tynan doesn't want me to have any outside help. I started typing up what's on the tapes just three days ago."

Collins' heart lifted. "But you did duplicate all the tapes taken from Baxter's file?"

"Whatever Tynan gave me, and I think he gave me everything."

"How did you copy them?" Collins asked quickly.

"Well, there were two sizes, so I had to use two different machines to play them into my larger Wollensak recorder."

"That's right," said Collins, "two sizes. Norelco miniature cassettes and Memorex normal cassettes. Did you hear them when you were recording?"

"No—I'd lose too much time. There's a jack, and they record from one machine to another silently."

"Where are the Memorex cassettes?"

"I returned the originals to Tynan some days ago. I rerecorded maybe six of the cassettes on larger reels I had."

"Do you know what's on those spools of yours?"

"Not until I transcribe them. But I identified each one and noted its place on the larger spool. Every cassette had some kind of identification or date. I kept a sort of index." He stepped to his desk and found several sheets of paper clipped together.

"I'm looking for one special Memorex cassette," Collins said. "It's marked AGG and January, on the outside. Would that help?"

Young began to scan and flip the pages of his tape index. In a state of feverishness, Collins watched.

"Sure, it's here," Young announced. "That tape is the first recording on my second spool."

"You have it? You're sure?"

"Positive."

"Man, oh man!" Collins exclaimed jubilantly. He gave the writer a bear hug. "Ishmael, you don't know what you've done. You've turned up the R Document!"

"The what?"

"Never mind," said Collins excitedly. "Play it."

The three huddled around the Wollensak as Young found the reel of tape, threaded it through the machine, and attached it to the pickup reel. He said, "I don't know what this is all about, but I'm ready if you are."

A moment later the voice of Vernon T. Tynan filled the room.

11

SEATED restlessly in the back seat of the limousine that had brought him from San Francisco to the suburbs of Sacramento, Chris Collins leaned forward once more to speak to his driver. "Can't you go a little faster?" he implored.

"I'm doing the best I can in this traffic, sir." He wheeled the car into the right lane, picking up state highway 275, which would soon lead them up before the Capitol Mall.

Soon, Collins knew, but perhaps not soon enough. It was ironic, he thought, that the success of his long quest might be thwarted at its climax by a conspiracy of nature. The fog was lifting now, but the Sacramento airport was probably still socked in.

He had been due to arrive in Sacramento by air at twelve twenty-five. His date to meet with Assemblyman Olin Keefe, Lieutenant Governor Edward Duffield, president of the state senate, and Senator Abe Glass, president pro tempore, was for one o'clock in the Derby Club of Posey's Cottage, the restaurant where legislators gathered for lunch. Collins might yet have time to reveal the R Document to the senate leaders before they convened at two o'clock.

The final vote would take place minutes after two. Once under way, it could not be stopped. Once tabulated, it could not be reversed or voted again.

His wristwatch told him it was nineteen minutes to two.

He dragged steadily on a cigarette, reliving the events of the night, the dawn. Leaving Ishmael Young's with the crucial tape, they had driven to Collins' office in the Department of Justice. There was much to be done, and only a short time to do it in.

Pierce accepted the task of authenticating the tape through voiceprints. There must be absolute proof that it was Tynan's voice. Van Allen set about acquiring a portable tape machine. Once the voiceprint was made, he would transfer the portion of Young's tape that carried the R Document to a cassette for Collins' trip to California.

All had gone smoothly. Collins called the head of a major network in New York, invoked his authority as Attorney General, and asked the executive to arrange for the network's manager in Washington, D.C., to cooperate. Pierce roused an old acquaintance, Dr. Lenart of Georgetown University, from his bed. The criminologist agreed to scan the spoken sounds in his laboratory.

Pierce then hastened off to the local network offices to pick up the film and sound track of an interview Vernon T. Tynan had recently given, as well as a videotape unit on which to play it. These, along with Young's tape, Pierce carted off to Dr. Lenart's laboratory. There, the renowned consultant in voice identification applied his sound spectrograph equipment to selected words Tynan had spoken in his network interview and to those same words when he had uttered them on the Ishmael Young tape. When Dr. Lenart had finished, it was clear that the voice heard on the tape of the R Document was Tynan's. Dr. Lenart wrote a certificate of authentication and packed Pierce off with his proof.

Meanwhile, Van Allen, after locating a portable tape machine for Collins to take with him, obtained a plane reservation for him on a flight to arrive in Sacramento at twenty-five minutes after twelve California time. The schedule was perfect, and Collins was pleased.

Collins then put through a call to Assemblyman Olin Keefe and got him immediately. "I'm going to be in Sacramento by one o'clock this afternoon," he told Keefe. "I have momentous evidence against the 35th that must be heard before the vote. Can you round up Lieutenant Governor Duffield and Senator Glass for me? I must see them."

"They'll be lunching in the Derby Club—it's in the rear of Posey's Cottage—at that time. They're sure to be there until a quarter to two. I'll tell them to wait for you. In fact, I'll stay with them."

"Tell them it's positively urgent," said Collins.

"I'll do my part. Just be on time. Once they go back to the chamber and begin the vote, you won't be able to reach them."

"I'll be there," Collins promised.

It was settled, and he felt easier. He stretched out on his office sofa and slept fitfully for two hours, until it was time to head for National Airport.

Everything went on schedule, up to an hour out of Sacramento. The captain of the 727 jetliner announced that heavy fog at the Sacramento airport was diverting their flight to San Francisco. They would deplane in San Francisco at twelve thirty. A special bus would take them the eighty miles to Sacramento.

For the first time on the journey, Collins was worried. This would add an extra hour and a half to his trip. Even by hiring a private car, he could not reach Posey's Cottage much before Duffield and Glass would be leaving.

All of this he now relived as his limousine entered the center of Sacramento, with the golden dome of the state capitol within sight. "Here we are," the driver said, stopping in front of Posey's Cottage, a block south of the Capitol Mall. Collins had the car door open, and picking up his attaché case, he hopped out. It was nine minutes to two. He was fifty-one minutes late. He wondered if Keefe had managed to hold Duffield and Glass for him.

Collins hurried into the Derby Club and was directed to a back room of the restaurant. Dismayed, he saw that the room was empty except for a lone melancholy figure at the bar.

Olin Keefe slipped off his stool. "I'd just about given up on you," he said. "What happened?"

"Fog. We had to land in San Francisco. I've been driving the last hour and a half. Duffield and Glass . . . ?"

"I couldn't hold them any longer. They went back to the senate. There's still seven minutes before the final reading and vote. We can try to pull them out of the chamber."

"We have to," insisted Collins in desperation.

Half walking, half running, dodging pedestrians, they headed toward the capitol building. Keefe said, "The senate chamber is at the south end of the second floor. We may barely make it before they close the doors."

Hastening up a short flight of stone steps, they crossed the Great Seal of California inlaid at the entrance of the capitol. "The staircase over there," Keefe directed Collins. Going up the stairs, Keefe added, "You knew Director Tynan was here this morning?"

"I knew. How did he do?"

"Too well, I'm afraid. The judiciary committee voted overwhelmingly for ratification of the 35th. It'll go that way in the senate, unless you can do better than Tynan."

"I can do better—if I get the chance." He held up his attaché case. "In here I've got the only witness who can destroy Tynan."

"Who?"

"Tynan himself," Collins said cryptically.

They had arrived at the senate entrance. While most of the forty

502

senators were in their chairs, a few still stood in the aisles. Lieutenant Governor Duffield was on his feet behind the raised desk at the head of the chamber.

"Hell," said Keefe, "the sergeant at arms is closing the doors."

"Can't you get to Duffield?"

"I'll try," said Keefe. He hurried into the chamber, explained something to a guard, continued on to the front, and from beneath the podium called up to the president of the senate.

Anxiously, Collins watched the action across the chamber. Duffield leaned sideways to catch what Keefe was saying. Then he threw up his hands and made a gesture toward the filled chamber. Keefe was talking again. At last, Duffield, shaking his head, stepped down to join him. Keefe kept on talking, pointing to where Collins stood. For a hanging moment in time, Duffield seemed undecided. Finally, obviously with reluctance, he followed Keefe to where Collins waited.

They met just inside the chamber entrance, and Keefe introduced the senate president to Collins.

"Out of deference to you, Mr. Attorney General, I consented to leave the podium. Congressman Keefe says you have new evidence related to our vote on the 35th Amendment—"

"Evidence that it is vital for you and the members to hear."

"That's quite impossible to arrange, Mr. Attorney General. It's simply too late. The hearings wound up this morning with Director Tynan. We're about to come to order, hear a reading of the 35th Amendment, and put it to a vote. I see no way to interrupt the process."

"There is one way," said Collins. "Hear my evidence outside the chamber. Delay the session until you listen to my evidence."

"That would be without precedent. Highly unusual."

"What I have to present to you and the members is also without precedent and more than unusual. I assure you, if I'd had this evidence earlier, I would have been before you with it. I was able to obtain it just last night. I immediately flew to California with it. The evidence is of the greatest import to you, to the senate, to the people of California, to the entire United States. You cannot vote without hearing what I have in this attaché case."

The intensity of Collins' speech made Duffield weaken slightly. "Even if what you have is of such importance—well, I don't know how I can prevent an immediate vote."

"You can't vote if you don't have a quorum, can you?"

"You want to ask a majority of the members to absent themselves from the chamber? It wouldn't work. There'd be a motion for a call of the house. The sergeant at arms would be instructed to bring in the absentees—"

"But I'd be finished with my evidence before the sergeant at arms could do that."

"How much time would you need?"

"Ten minutes, no more."

"And how are the members of the senate supposed to hear the evidence?"

"You'll summon them informally—in two groups of twenty at a time—and you'll advise them to hear what you've already heard. By then, you'll *want* them to hear it."

Duffield still hesitated. "Mr. Attorney General, this is an extraordinary thing you are requesting. If you had evidence to prove the joint resolution about to be voted upon was fraudulent or harbored elements of conspiracy—if you could prove that—"

"I can! I have evidence of a national conspiracy. The life or death of our Republic depends on your hearing this evidence, and keeping what you've heard in mind when you vote. If you fail to hear the evidence, you'll carry the burden of your mistake to the grave."

Impressed, the lieutenant governor gave Collins a long, hard look. "Very well," he said suddenly. "Let me arrange for Senator Glass to see that we have no quorum for ten minutes. You go up to the fourth floor, the first committee room off the elevator. It's vacant. Assemblyman Keefe will show you the way. Senator Glass and I will join you shortly." He paused. "Mr. Attorney General, this better be something."

"It's something, all right," Collins said grimly.

Moments later the four of them were seated about the table in the committee room. Collins had just finished explaining to Duffield and Glass the circumstances under which he had learned

504

about the R Document, a supplement to the 35th Amendment, which Colonel Noah Baxter had warned on his deathbed must be exposed.

"I won't bother you with the details of my long quest for the R Document," said Collins. "Suffice it to say, I located it early this morning. It proved to be not a document but a verbalized plan, which was caught on tape accidentally by Colonel Baxter's twelve-year-old grandson. There were three persons present when the tape was made last January. One was FBI Director Vernon T. Tynan. Another was Deputy Director Harry Adcock. The third was Attorney General Noah Baxter. Only the voices of Tynan and Baxter will be heard on this tape, which the boy made as a lark, unaware of its importance. To be certain beyond question that Director Tynan's own voice had been captured on this tape, we had a voice-print made of Tynan's speech on the tape and Tynan's speech during a recent network interview. You will see that they are one and the same."

Collins took the sheaf of voiceprints and Dr. Lenart's certificate of authentication from his attaché case and handed them to Duffield. The lieutenant governor gravely examined the materials, then passed them to Senator Glass.

"Are you both satisfied you will be hearing the voice of Director Tynan?" Collins asked.

Both senate leaders nodded.

Collins brought his portable tape machine out of the attaché case. He adjusted the volume to HIGH. With deliberation he set the machine down in the middle of the table.

"We can proceed, then," he said. "You will hear Tynan's voice first, then Baxter's. Listen closely. This is the secret known as the R Document."

Collins reached out, pressed down the PLAY button, and fixed his eyes on the president and the president pro tempore of the California senate.

The cassette in the machine was rolling. The speaker came to life.

Tynan's voice: "We're alone, aren't we, Noah?"

Baxter's voice: "You wanted to see me in private, Vernon. Well,

I guess my living room here is about as safe a place as there is in town."

Tynan's voice: "It should be. We've spent thousands of dollars having your house debugged. I'm sure it's safe enough for what we have to discuss."

Baxter's voice: "What do we have to discuss, Vernon? What's on your mind?"

Tynan's voice: "Okay, it's this. I think I have the last element of the R Document figured out. Harry and I think it's foolproof. Just one thing, Noah. Don't go squeamish on me at the last minute. Remember, we agreed we must sacrifice anything—and, might I add, anyone—if we are to save this nation. Now, you've been with us all along, Noah. You've agreed the amendment is the only real hope, no matter what obstacles had to be overcome to get it through. Well, there's only one more step. Remember, you've been in it with us up to now. You're in too far to back out. You couldn't back out if you wanted to."

Baxter's voice: "Back out of what? What are you talking about, Vernon?"

Tynan's voice: "It simply amounts to doing something for the people that they can't do for themselves. Bringing security to their lives. As soon as the 35th Amendment becomes part of the Constitution, we put the R Document into effect—the reconstruction of the country. We put into motion all our legal prerogatives under the 35th—"

Baxter's voice: "But you can't, Vernon—you can't invoke the 35th. Under the Constitution, with the 35th, there will have to be an actual, legitimate crisis—emergency—conspiracy—before we can move. If there is none, you can't—"

Tynan's voice: "But we can, Noah. Because we *will* have our emergency, our crisis. That's been arranged. I've taken care of it myself. Often one person has to be sacrificed for the survival of the rest. One of us—you or me—probably you—will invoke the emergency in a television speech. You will address the nation. That's the essence of the R Document. I've got the essentials of the speech worked out. You'll begin something like this: 'Fellow Americans, I have come to speak to you in this hour of mourning.

We are all equally bereaved, all suffering the deepest grief together, over the shocking assassination of our beloved President Wadsworth yesterday. His terrible death by an assassin's hand—a hand directed by a conspiracy to overturn the nation—has cost us the person of our greatest leader. But perhaps his death will serve us all in life, and will serve the life of the nation. By uniting together, we must see that such violence is never repeated inside our borders. To this end, by the order of our new President, I am taking direct steps to curb the reign of lawlessness and terror that now exists. I am now proclaiming suspension of the Bill of Rights, as provided for in the 35th Amendment, and announcing that hereafter the Committee on National Safety—"

Baxter's voice: "My God, Vernon! Did I hear you right? President Wadsworth assassinated—by *your* orders?"

Tynan's voice: "Don't be a sentimental slob, Noah. There's no time for that. We sacrifice one two-bit politician to save an entire nation. Do you understand, Noah? We'll save—"

Baxter's voice: "Oh, God, God, God—ohhh—"

Tynan's voice: "Noah, we— Noah—Noah! What is it? What's wrong with you? Harry, is he having some kind of stroke? Try to hold him up. Let me get Hannah. . . ."

End of tape.

Collins studied the faces of Duffield, Glass, and Keefe. They all sat frozen in shock.

"Well, gentlemen," said Collins, "does justice have its day in court?"

Duffield came heavily to his feet. "Justice has its day," he said quietly. "I'll go summon the senators."

IT WAS night in Washington, D.C., when the sleek Boeing jet dipped earthward, floating lower and lower toward the landing strip of National Airport. From his window seat, Chris Collins watched the lights dance toward him, rise swiftly, and then the plane touched down and he braced himself for the jolt of homecoming.

Minutes later he followed the line of passengers into the air terminal. It was Hogan he saw first, and his bodyguard was wearing an uncharacteristic broad smile. "Congratulations, Mr. Attorney General," Hogan said, taking over Collins' attaché case. "I was upset when you got away without me. But I'd say it was worth the risk."

"It was worth anything," said Collins. "I have no luggage. The attaché case was all I needed."

Tony Pierce was also on hand to greet him. A smiling Pierce pumped his hand as they moved toward the escalator, then pulled a newspaper out of his pocket and unfolded it before him. The big black headline read:

PLOT AGAINST PRESIDENT, NATION EXPOSED
Tynan Implicated
The 35th Amendment Defeated

"Chris, you pulled it off," Pierce exulted. "Did you see it? The California senate vote was on television. Forty to zero, the 35th turned down. Unanimous."

"I saw it," said Collins. "I was in the gallery."

"Then the news conference. All the major networks broke in on their programming to show it. Duffield and Glass told how the turnabout happened. Told what was in the R Document. Well, Chris, you really did it."

Collins shook his head. "No, Tony. We all did it—including Colonel Baxter, Father Dubinski, my son, Josh, Olin Keefe, Donald Radenbaugh, John Maynard, Rick Baxter, Ishmael Young, and you yourself. It was everyone."

They had reached the car, which was not the one Collins used but the President's own bulletproof limousine. The President's chauffeur, at the open rear door, offered him a proud salute.

Collins looked at Pierce questioningly.

"The President asked to see you the minute you came in."

"Very well."

Collins had started into the car when Tony Pierce's hand on his shoulder restrained him. "Chris, do you know Vernon Tynan is dead?"

"I didn't know."

508

"Two hours ago. He committed suicide. He shot himself. And Adcock disappeared."

They got into the car and sped toward the White House. When they arrived at the South Portico, McKnight, the President's chief aide, was waiting to welcome them heartily. Collins and Pierce were led through the Diplomatic Reception Room to the elevator. They took it to the second floor, and followed McKnight to the Yellow Oval Room.

Collins had not expected a party, but one was in progress. He could make out Vice-President Loomis, Senator Hilliard and his wife, the President's secretary, Miss Ledger, and Appointments Secretary Nichols. Then, next to the Louis XVI chairs flanking the fireplace, he saw Karen chatting with President Wadsworth.

That instant, Karen became aware of him, and she broke away from the President and came running across the room. She fell into his arms, and he kissed away her tears. "I love you, I love you," she whispered. "Oh, Chris . . ."

Over her shoulder he saw that the President was coming toward him. He released Karen and went to meet him. There was an odd expression on the President's face. Collins decided he looked as Lazarus must have looked.

"Chris," President Wadsworth said solemnly, clasping his hand with genuine warmth, "I don't have words to thank you enough— for preserving my life, and that of the country as well." The President wagged his head. "I was an awful fool. I can say it now. Forgive me. I'd lost my sense of direction." He searched Collins' face. "You heard about Vernon Tynan?"

"I did. I'm sorry he brought himself. to such a pass."

"He must have been unhinged to have hatched anything like that. Thank God you persisted. My debt to you can never fully be paid. But if there's anything at all I can do for you—"

"There are two things," Collins said bluntly.

"Tell me."

"There's a man who, like yourself, must be resurrected from the dead. He played a major role in helping you. I want you to help him. I want you to give him a full presidential pardon and restore his name."

"Just prepare the papers. I'll sign them. And the other thing?"

"The worst is over," said Collins, "but we still face the problem that gave rise to this insane plot. The problem of crime. Repression won't solve it. As a wise man once remarked, burning stakes do not lighten the darkness. There has to be a better solution—"

"There will be," interrupted the President. "We're going to do it right this time. Instead of tampering with the Bill of Rights to solve our problems, we're going to use the Bill of Rights and use it properly. Tomorrow, early, I'm going to appoint a special blue-ribbon commission—you and Pierce will be on it—to investigate the FBI, clean out all Tynan influence, make recommendations toward overhauling the bureau, and setting up new guidelines for it. And then, Chris, I want to sit down with you and discuss a new program of economic and social legislation that will bring an end to the lawlessness and crime in our cities. We're going to do something about it at last. We had a dangerous moment. But now we're going to hold on to our democracy."

Collins nodded. "Thank you, Mr. President." He hesitated. "You know, I was thinking all the way home—in Argo City, an esteemed friend of mine said that if fascism ever comes to the United States, it'll be because the people voted it in. Well, the people almost did this time. Now that they know what they know, maybe they'll never come that close again. And maybe we can help them remember this lesson."

"We will. That I promise. We're going to solve what is humanly possible to solve." He took Collins by the arm. "But not tonight." He beckoned Karen to join them. "Tonight we're going to have a drink to the future. Let's relax an hour or so—we can afford to, at last—before we begin again."

510

Irving Wallace

When Irving Wallace's parents presented him with a rebuilt Underwood typewriter, his career was under way; he sold his first article at fifteen and has been a free-lance writer ever since. Today he is the immensely popular author of eight nonfiction books and ten best-selling novels. All have been written on that same ancient Underwood and all, as a concession to superstition, have titles that begin with the word "The". His secrecy about works in progress is legendary, and he will not discuss a current manuscript with anybody.

Wallace and his wife for the last thirty-five years, Sylvia, now make their home in Los Angeles, California. However, for three months of every year they travel abroad, researching backgrounds for his novels. In recent times, writing has turned into something of a family tradition. Sylvia Wallace, a former editor, published her first book, *The Fountain*, to warm critical reception; and Irving joined their son, David, in the compilation of a big nonfiction bestseller, *The Book of Lists*. Clearly, talent runs in the Wallace household.